The
MX Book
of
New
Sherlock
Holmes
Stories

Part XV – 2019 Annual
(1898-1917)

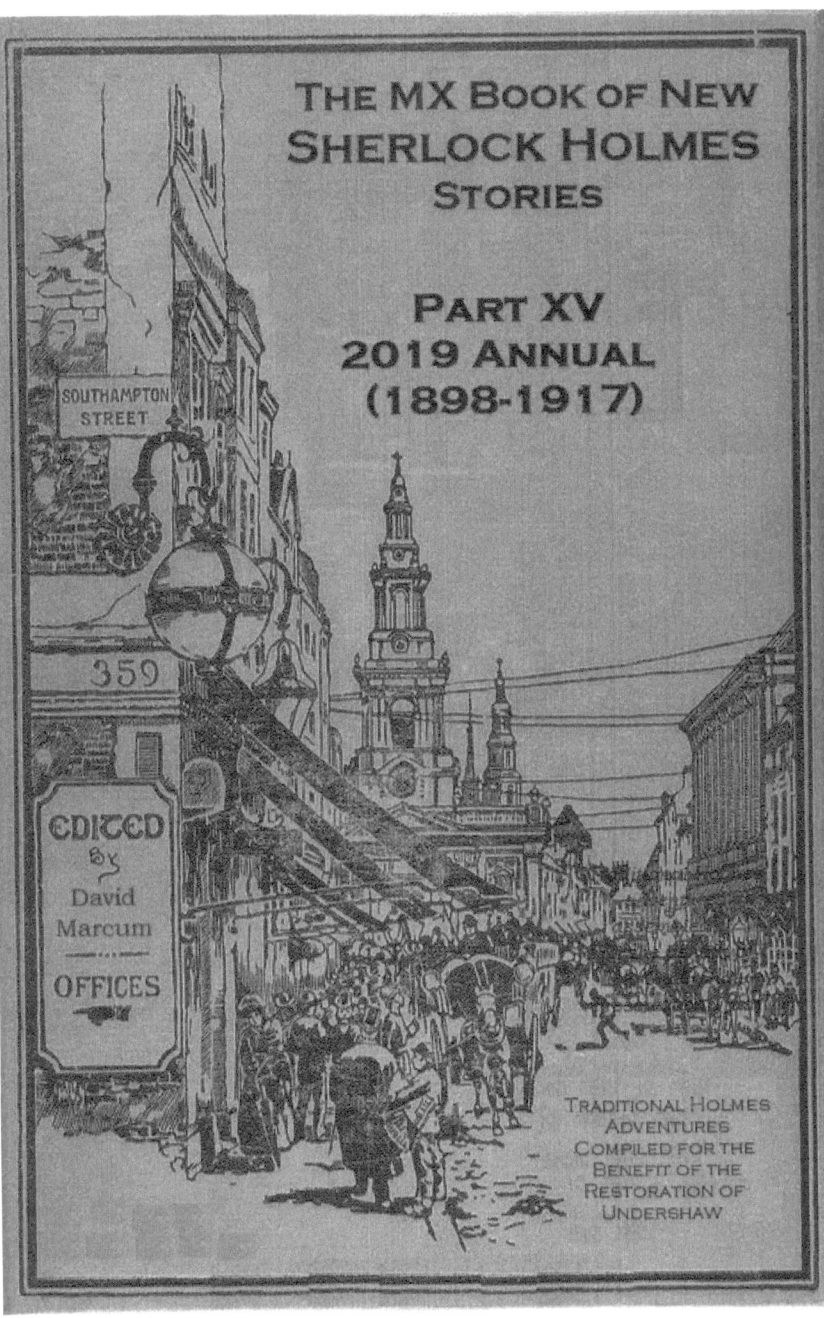

THE MX BOOK OF NEW
SHERLOCK HOLMES
STORIES

PART XV
2019 ANNUAL
(1898-1917)

SOUTHAMPTON
STREET

359

EDITED
By
David
Marcum

OFFICES

TRADITIONAL HOLMES
ADVENTURES
COMPILED FOR THE
BENEFIT OF THE
RESTORATION OF
UNDERSHAW

ISBN Hardcover   978-1-78705-450-9
ISBN Paperback   978-1-78705-451-6
ISBN AUK ePub   978-1-78705-452-3
ISBN AUK PDF   978-1-78705-453-0

Published in the UK by
MX Publishing
335 Princess Park Manor, Royal Drive,
London, N11 3GX
www.mxpublishing.co.uk

David Marcum can be reached at:
thepapersofsherlockholmes@gmail.com

Cover design by Brian Belanger
www.belangerbooks.com and *www.redbubble.com/people/zhahadun*

CONTENTS

Foreword

Adventures

(Continued on the next page . . . .)

(Continued on the next page . . . .)

The following can be found in the companion volumes
The MX Book of New Sherlock Holmes Stories
Part XIII – 2019 Annual (1881-1890)
and
Part XIV – 2019 Annual (1891-1897)

(Continued on the next page . . . .)

These additional Sherlock Holmes adventures
can be found in the previous volumes of
The MX Book of New Sherlock Holmes Stories

(Continued on the next page . . . .)

PART III: 1896-1929

PART IV – 2016 Annual

(Continued on the next page . . . .)

PART V – Christmas Adventures

(Continued on the next page . . . .)

PART VI – 2017 Annual

(Continued on the next page . . . .)

The Tempest of Lyme – David Ruffle
The Problem of the Holy Oil – David Marcum
A Scandal in Serbia – Thomas A. Turley
The Curious Case of Mr. Marconi – Jan Edwards
Mr. Holmes and Dr. Watson Learn to Fly – C. Edward Davis
Die Weisse Frau – Tim Symonds
A Case of Mistaken Identity – Daniel D. Victor

PART VII – Eliminate the Impossible: 1880-1891

Foreword – Lee Child
Foreword – Rand B. Lee
Foreword – Michael Cox
Foreword – Roger Johnson
Foreword – Melissa Farnham
No Ghosts Need Apply (A Poem) – Jacquelynn Morris
The Melancholy Methodist – Mark Mower
The Curious Case of the Sweated Horse – Jan Edwards
The Adventure of the Second William Wilson – Daniel D. Victor
The Adventure of the Marchindale Stiletto – James Lovegrove
The Case of the Cursed Clock – Gayle Lange Puhl
The Tranquility of the Morning – Mike Hogan
A Ghost from Christmas Past – Thomas A. Turley
The Blank Photograph – James Moffett
The Adventure of A Rat. – Adrian Middleton
The Adventure of Vanaprastha – Hugh Ashton
The Ghost of Lincoln – Geri Schear
The Manor House Ghost – S. Subramanian
The Case of the Unquiet Grave – John Hall
The Adventure of the Mortal Combat – Jayantika Ganguly
The Last Encore of Quentin Carol – S.F. Bennett
The Case of the Petty Curses – Steven Philip Jones
The Tuttman Gallery – Jim French
The Second Life of Jabez Salt – John Linwood Grant
The Mystery of the Scarab Earrings – Thomas Fortenberry
The Adventure of the Haunted Room – Mike Chinn
The Pharaoh's Curse – Robert V. Stapleton
The Vampire of the Lyceum – Charles Veley and Anna Elliott
The Adventure of the Mind's Eye – Shane Simmons

PART VIII – Eliminate the Impossible: 1892-1905

Foreword – Lee Child
Foreword – Rand B. Lee
Foreword – Michael Cox
Foreword – Roger Johnson
Foreword – Melissa Farnham
Sherlock Holmes in the Lavender field (A Poem) – Christopher James

(Continued on the next page . . . .)

Part IX – 2018 Annual (1879-1895)

(Continued on the next page . . . .)

(Continued on the next page . . . .)

Part XII: Some Untold Cases (1894-1902)

The following contributions appear in
Part XIV – 2019 Annual (1891-1897)

The 2019 Annual, Parts XIII, XIV, and XV of
The MX Book of New Sherlock Holmes Stories,
are dedicated to

Joel Senter

Joel passed away in July 2018.
He was a wonderful and very supportive
Sherlockian, and
he will be missed.

Editor's Introduction:
The Great Holmes Tapestry
by David Marcum

Way back in early 2015, when the world was a much simpler place, I woke up early one morning from a very vivid dream where I had edited a Sherlock Holmes anthology. Instead of going back to sleep, I arose and started thinking about it. What a wild hansom cab ride it's been since then!

Who would have then suspected the future of *The MX Book of New Sherlock Holmes Stories*? Since that time, we've had over 330 new Sherlock Holmes adventures, plus poems and forewords, from over 150 contributors, and along the way, through the very generous efforts of the participants, we've raised over $40,000 for the Stepping Stones School for special needs students at Undershaw, one of Sir Arthur Conan Doyle's former homes. Additionally, the books have raised awareness of the school around the world.

Back in 2015, when the initial hope for a single book of possibly a dozen new Holmes tales had grown and grown to three massive simultaneous volumes of 63 new stories, I sat down to write a foreword. In it, I referred to a phenomenon that I had observed during my previous four decades of collecting, reading, and chronologicizing literally thousands of traditional Holmes stories: All of these different narratives – the pitifully few original sixty of The Canon and all the rest from so many other later literary agents – fit together remarkably well as one wonderful whole. To describe it, I coined the term *The Great Holmes Tapestry*, and I've been proud since then to see it mentioned that way in other places when describing *The Big Picture* of all these stories, and not just Watson's initial sixty tales that crossed the *First* Literary Agent's desk.

As I've explained in other locations, this Tapestry consists of the overall and complete lives of Holmes and Watson from birth to death, filling in all those pieces of the picture that the original Canon does not. The Canon indisputably makes up the main fibers of the illustration, but there are so many other pieces to examine. Another way to look at this is to think of all the days in a life. I'm sure that someone somewhere has calculated the amount of time in Holmes and Watson's lives that are actually represented in The Canon. (There are always people who are carrying out these various scholarly tasks – counting the exact number of times a gasogene is used, for instance, or the total number of words uttered by Inspector Lestrade during all of his combined appearances. This information is undoubtedly out there – *somewhere* – if one just knows where to look.)

The actual amount of on-stage time chronicled in The Canon adds up to just a limited number of days. In Holmes and Watson's full lifetimes – and as a deadly serious player of The Game, I emphatically declare that Holmes and Watson *had very full lifetimes!* – there were far more moments that have not been "officially" described than the little bit that is related within The Canon. Some would be satisfied with only ever knowing what's related in The Official Sixty Adventures, endlessly examining and re-examining these cases and preferring to think of Holmes spending the rest of his time between cases moping about the Baker Street sitting room in a brown study limbo for weeks on end. And that isn't correct at all. There is more to the complete lives of Holmes and Watson than the little time recorded in The Canon.

Even during those years when the First Literary Agent was still alive, before he had a chance to examine and evaluate first-hand his spiritualistic assertions, new stories from other directions were appearing to start filling in the missing pieces of these complete lives. Consider Vincent Starrett's "The Adventure of the Unique Hamlet", which was published in 1920. There are people who know much more about Starrett than I do, and they can probably relate what the First Literary Agent's reaction was to someone bringing forth one of Watson's manuscripts from a different source. What interests me is that someone so revered in the legendary Sherlockian Halls of Fame as Mr. Starrett chose to make public an extra-Canonical adventure – and such a well-regarded one to boot! – more than a decade before he produced his scholarly work, *The Private Life of Sherlock Holmes* (1933). In this regard, I like Starrett's priorities, and commend them to those who favor the more scholarly side of Holmesian Studies.

Some people – too many, actually – are satisfied only with The Canon, and go no further – either through ignorance or stubbornness. I'll admit that there is a certain completeness to the solid and wonderful Canon. I well remember the first time that I finished my reading of all sixty of the "official" adventures. I can only imagine how sad it must be for someone to reach that final story and mistakenly believe that there are no more. I was quite fortunate that I knew better from nearly my first encounter with Mr. Holmes. I discovered him in 1975, when I was ten years old, reading the abridged Whitman edition of *The Adventures* that only had eight of the twelve stories. I next found a tattered paperback copy of *The Return* – and I still have both of those very books on the shelves holding my collection. After obtaining *The Return*, I plunged into "The

Empty House" – thus learning how Holmes survived his encounter with Professor Moriarty at the Reichenbach Falls before I even knew that he was believed to have died – an incredibly valuable lesson in reading things in chronological order! And very soon after that, I discovered pastiches, and it became apparent that there was no need to feel sad when finishing The Canon, because it was simply a gateway to a much larger world, and not simply a closed and finite sixty-sided dead-end room.

Not long after my first introduction to Holmes, I received a copy of Nicholas Meyer's *The Seven-Per-Cent Solution* (1974). I recognized, even then, that some parts just didn't fit with the True Canon, and I was much more thrilled from beginning-to-end with Meyer's next book, *The West End Horror* (1976). In those early days, still before I'd even read all of The Canon, I was electrified by William S. Baring-Gould's biography *Sherlock Holmes of Baker Street* (1962 – and it's hard now to get my head around the fact that when I read Baring-Gould's incredibly influential masterpiece in the mid-1970's, it was only thirteen years old to my ten years.) And over the next few years, I occasionally found other Holmes books that thrilled me as well, including *Enter the Lion* by Sean M. Wright and Michael P. Hodel (1979) – which showed that a Holmes adventure doesn't have to come by way of Watson's pen to give a true account – and various books by the prolific and fun (and sadly deceased) Frank Thomas, such as *Sherlock Holmes and the Golden Bird* (1979) and *Sherlock Holmes and the Sacred Sword* (1980).

Through the years, I've been very fortunate to have the opportunity to track down and acquire literally thousands of traditional pastiches – as well as to read and study and chronologicize them. In the mid-1990's, I began to make notes as I re-read my favorites and also caught up on all those stories that I had acquired at that point but hadn't yet explored. In the years since, I've been constantly expanding and revising those original notes while acquiring many more pastiches, and now I have a massive Sherlockian Chronology of both Canon and pastiche, well over 800 dense pages, stretching from 1844 – with a story relating the meeting, courtship, and marriage of Holmes's parents – to January 1957, and Holmes's death, as shared by Baring-Gould. (I'm a staunch Baring-Gouldist, although I'll admit he didn't get everything right.) Through this entire Chronology, I've broken down traditional adventures in my collection – novels, short stories, radio and television episodes, movies and scripts, comics, fan-fiction, and unpublished manuscripts – by book, story, chapter, or paragraph into year, month, day, and even hour. And it never ceases to amaze me how well it all fits together.

As I've related elsewhere, all of the traditional Canonically-based Sherlock Holmes stories are linked together to that spark of imagination that sets these narratives in motion, *The Great Watsonian Oversoul*. Although there are contradictions and incorrect statements at times – and usually the blame can be placed upon modern editors who foist their own agendas or unverified assumptions onto Watson's original notes – the overall consistency of this myriad of adventures is astonishing. For example, an obscure story brought forth by one later literary agent in the 1940's will fit perfectly – chronology-wise – with another written in the last year or so, and I'm almost certain that the more recent literary agent didn't have any clue about the earlier one when tapping into *The Oversoul* to bring forth the narrative. Somehow, as each of these little sparks from *The Oversoul* are revealed, their connection to the whole becomes apparent. And while editing these current three simultaneous volumes, *Parts XIII*, *XIV*, and *XV*, I saw this same thing happening yet again.

When I solicit and receive stories for these books, I only set out a very few requirements: The stories must be absolutely traditional. They have to be set in the correct time period, of equivalent Canonical length, and with no aspects of parody, anachronisms, or actual supernatural encounters. Sometimes participants will want to float an idea by me before beginning, or even send a draft of a story to get my input along the way, but I refuse to read it. I want the first version of a submission that I read to be the final version. But by doing it this way, I cannot say ahead of time if someone is going to submit something that has a relationship or connection to another entry. I'll leave it to perceptive readers to have fun spotting the overlaps in this new collection.

A few times through this amazing journey of over 330 stories (so far), there have some overlaps. In one volume, two of the contributors submitted stories that were both set within days of each other, and in one Holmes fools Watson with a false investigation, while in the next Watson fools Holmes (or tries to) in the same way. Rather than tell one of the contributors, "No," I happily used both of their stories, side-by-side, as to my mind they strengthened rather than diminished each other. On another occasion, one author was worried to discover that his story about a jewel theft had been placed chronologically in that particular book next to another story that was also about a jewel theft. However, the two narratives were so different, and diverged immediately into such varying directions, that I don't believe that anyone noticed or was bothered by it.

That's one of the thrills of reading a Holmes story – one never knows which way it will go. It may be a straight-forward narrative or convoluted, with international consequences, or of huge importance only to one person. It might be comedy or tragedy, or a procedural investigation, or gothic horror. It might have a London setting or take us to the countryside, or to the Continent or North America, Asia or Africa. It could cover just hours, or be spaced to relate connected incidents that occur years apart. We might find ourselves early or late in Holmes career. Holmes or Watson – or neither! – might not even appear at all. There may be a comfortable trope, such as Holmes and Watson hiding in a supposedly empty location waiting to trap the criminal, or something brand new.

Mysteries may range all the way from murder down to nothing more than a simple misunderstanding with a crime-free solution. The tale may involve great historical events or the tiniest of mysteries that only affect the lives of a few people. It might be Victorian or Edwardian, or possibly a little bit later. The story could be narrated by Watson or Holmes, or someone else. There may be a treasure hunt or a series of mysterious warnings, brought to Holmes from high-born clients or low. The majority of the story might consist of the client's strange tale, narrated while sitting in front of the fire in the Baker Street sitting room, or we may find Our Heroes in the foreground from start to finish.

To paraphrase Bilbo Baggins, who warned his nephew about the dangers of stepping onto the road: "*It's a [fascinating] business, [Watson]. You [start a new adventure], and . . . there's no knowing where you might be swept off to.*"

It never gets old, and there are never enough.

I mentioned my requirements for a story to be included in these books, but I neglected to list perhaps the most important one of all: Holmes and Watson have to be *heroes*.

When I first dreamed of editing a Holmes back – specifically on January 22nd, 2015, as evidenced by the email that I still have proposing it to publisher Steve Emecz – the reason that I wanted to do so was simple: People were forgetting that Sherlock Holmes is a hero. More than just forgetting, actually – they were desperately going out of their way to actively destroy him. It has become fashionable to use the names of Holmes and his associates in ever-more lurid and demeaning and insulting representations – as if each iteration has to outdo the one before it in terms of just how outrageous and broken Holmes can be. He has to be absolutely hopeless and irredeemable, or a sociopath, or a murderer. He can only function if Watson serves as a caretaker at best, and Watson is given his own set of defects as well. A push-back was needed.

I'm so fortunate to have been able to find like-minded individuals who also want to support Holmes the Hero, and who write stories about the True Sherlock Holmes. In the four years since the idea first occurred to me, these 330-plus adventures have served as an alternative against those who would erase and replace the heroic Holmes of the Victorian and Edwardian years, instead trying to make him some sort of damaged goods, or Van Helsing, where "Ghosts can apply after all", or a Dr. Who-like character who regenerates in a multitude of decades or formats, or worst of all, as a morally defective creep. Playing The Game means that Holmes is not a Magic Man who lives forever, or someone whose spirit dances into different realities or even completely different personalities with the same name. There are still bulwarks that stand to defend the True Holmes – these books and others like them – and I cannot thank those enough who contribute to and support them for all that they have done and continue to do.

Luckily, the True Holmes has continued to burn like a beacon through all of the greasy fog that still threatens to obscure him. There are still legitimate adventures appearing – *almost daily, it sometimes seems, and thank God for that!* – that tell us more – *but never enough!* – about Mr. Sherlock Holmes of Baker Street.

As these anthologies continue – and there's no end in sight, as at this writing, as I'm already receiving stories for the next two collections! – what will *not* change is that Holmes and Watson will continue to be represented as *heroes*. You won't find a story where Holmes or Watson turn out to be murderers, or Holmes deduces that he's been created by a writer. (I regularly turn these down, along with many other stories with objectionable premises.) One thing that has changed, however, is an informal rule that I had for a long time with the earlier books – only one story per author per collection.

This seemed to make sense for a long time, as I didn't want to be appearing to favor someone over another, and also because initially space was limited. After all, the first collection had humble ambitions, although it grew over time. At first, Steve Emecz and I had many discussions about what to do as more stories arrived and the initial single book grew fatter. Keep making the font size smaller as more stories arrived? The contributors kept contributing, and I didn't want to keep any new Holmes adventures away from the public. Just when I thought that things were about to get locked into place in that spring of 2015, I had a sudden surge of new submissions. What to do? Why, expand to two volumes. And as that year progressed, what was two books then became three, containing 63 new Holmes adventures.

When we decided to continue beyond the initial record-breaking three-volume set as an ongoing series, the plan was to have modest one-volume editions. That worked for *Parts IV* and *V*, when we we had ended up having enough contributions to issue new collections in both the spring and the fall. Then came *Part VI: 2017 Annual*, which was huge and really should have been split into two books. After that, when the number of contributions pushed the boundaries, we decided to expand into multiple simultaneous volumes, as needed. (We were happy to discover that these multiple volumes were more popular anyway.) So the next sets have appeared in twos: *Parts VII* and *VIII, IX* and *X, XI* and *XII*. And now, with this new collection, I've again received so many stories that they can only be contained in three large books, and this time with more stories than the initial record-breaking 63 from *Parts I, II*, and *III* in 2015.

And part of this is due to allowing multiple contributions from authors. In *Parts XI* and *XII: Some Untold Cases*, I had two different stories from the great Mike Hogan that fit the collection's parameters, and I couldn't pick one or the other. Then I saw that one would go in the *Part XI* and the other *Part XII*. Problem solved. It wasn't my intention to make this a new accepted policy – it just worked out that way. Then, when I first began assembling and editing another anthology, *The New Adventures of Solar Pons* (2018), I was worried that I wouldn't have enough stories, so I also said that authors could contribute more than one. We ended up with a really great collection of 20 stories with some from multiple participants, so I needn't have worried. By then, my mind was open to additional contributions.

I was in the early days of preparing this set in mid-2018 when I received an email from reader Ed Enstrom. I'd never heard from him before, but he reached out through the email address shown at the end of this foreword to discuss errors that had slipped through and into the previous book. (I'm always mortified when this happens, but I have to point out – as I did to Ed – that sadly I can't devote a professional amount of effort to these books, as professionally I'm a licensed civil engineer, and my editorship is as an unpaid amateur who does this in his spare time. I look upon this work as that of a missionary of The Church of Holmes. I don't have any true publishing software, just the common version of Microsoft Word in which to assemble the book files.) I replied to Ed's email and, as a diligent amateur editor, I concluded – as I often do – by asking if he'd like to write a story.

He'd never considered such a thing, but he went away and, eight days later, he sent me his first-ever pastiche. I read it and saw that it was exactly what I'm always looking for, and promptly confirmed that I could use it. And then, soon after, Ed sent me a second story. And then a third. He had the fever.

Of course, just like in the case of Mike Hogan's two stories in the previous set, I hated to pick one over another when I could bring *all* of them to the public's attention. I was happy when this ended up being three volumes, because that way I could put one of Ed's stories in each book.

By then, some of the other much-treasured regular participants – Tracy Revels, Mark Mower, Roger Riccard, Arthur Hall, Dick Gillman, and Peter Coe Verbica – had sent more than one story as well, and I was very pleased to include all of them. And then, having written my own initial contribution, I decided to have a go at another, and then another – thus making me a multiple contributor to the books too. And that's how we reached *66* stories this time, beating the record of *63* set with *Parts I, II,* and *III* in 2015, way back at the beginning . . . .

"Of course, I could only stammer out my thanks."
– *The unhappy John Hector McFarlane,* "The Norwood Builder"

These last few years have been an amazing. I've been able to meet some incredible people, both in person and in the modern electronic way, and also I've been able to read several hundred new Holmes adventures, all to the benefit of the Stepping Stones School at Undershaw, one of Sir Arthur Conan Doyle's homes. The contributors to these MX anthologies donate their royalties to the school, and so far we've raised over $40,000 – maybe $50,000 by the time you read this! More importantly, thousands of people have been made aware of the Stepping Stones School, and this has been a wonderful and unexpected added benefit.

There are many people to thank. First and foremost, as with every one of these projects that I attempt, my amazing and incredibly wonderful wife (of thirty-one years by the time you read this!) Rebecca, and our truly awesome son and my friend, Dan. I love you both, and you are everything to me!

I have all the gratitude in the world for the contributors who have used their time, energy, and creativity to be part of this project. I'm so glad to have gotten to know all of you through the process. It's an undeniable fact that Sherlock Holmes authors are the *best* people!

I also must thank the people who buy these books and support them in so many ways. And don't forget – if you like reading them, considering joining the party and *writing* a story too! One of the things that makes me most proud of these books are the first-time authors who sent a story, and sometimes another for the next book, and so on, and now some of them have had enough for their own books to be published, and along the way they've learned about writing and publishing.

Next, I'd like to thank those who offer support, encouragement, and friendship, sometimes patiently waiting on me to reply as my time is pulled in so many other directions. We often go great amounts of time between communications, but I always enjoy our discussions. Many many thanks

8

to (in alphabetical order): Bob Byrne, Mark Mower, Denis Smith, Tom Turley, Dan Victor, and Marcia Wilson.

Additionally, I'd also like to especially thank:

- Steve Emecz – From idea to book, and then repeating the process, I've had a wonderful time ever since I first emailed Steve back in December 2012. Everything that has happened since then is amazing for me personally, and I owe so much of it to Steve, a great guy in every respect. Thank you for each opportunity!

- Will Thomas: I first heard of Will when I bought and read his first Barker and Llewelyn book, *Some Danger Involved* (2004) when it was initially published. I was thrilled. There are several authors who have taken Canonical characters and made them their own, filling in the details beyond the cursory Canonical descriptions – Marcia Wilson and the Scotland Yarders (especially Lestrade) for instance, Michael Kurland's Professor Moriarty, Carole Nelson Douglas and Irene Adler, Sean Wright and Michael Hodel's Mycroft Holmes, and Gerard Williams's Dr. Mortimer – and now we know the truth about Barker, Holmes's *"hated rival upon the Surrey shore"*. Others have written about Barker – he's been in one of my stories, and he appears in another by someone else in this very volume – but Will told us his first name ("Cyrus") and provided his background and a circle of friends and has given us so many amazing adventures.

  I've been able to make three Holmes Pilgrimages to London (so far), and while nearly everywhere that I went related to Holmes, I did work in a few other stops, such as the former homes of Solar Pons, Hercule Poirot, and James Bond. And several times I've stopped into Craig's Court in Whitehall – both because it was one of the locations of Watson's old bank, Cox and Company, and also because it was where Cyrus Barker's office was located. (As is the case with Mr. Holmes and several others, I also play *The Game* in regard to Barker and Llewelyn.) I'm only on one certain social media succubus to connect with other Sherlockians, and it was amazing fun to photograph myself and my ever-present deerstalker in front of Barker's office on several occasions and post the photo, letting Will know in real time that I was right there right then, and then to see him immediately respond.

I'm very thankful that he both wrote a Holmes story for the first three-volume MX collection back in 2015 ("The Adventure of Urquhart Manse") and now that he's a part of this set too. Long may he continue to chronicle the adventures of Barker and Llewelyn!

- Roger Johnson – To one of the most knowledgeable Sherlockians and one of the most gracious and supportive people that I know! I'm incredibly grateful that Roger reviewed my first book, and then others after that. He and his wife Jean Upton have done so much to help promote these books, and they wonderfully hosted me for a few days during my Holmes Pilgrimage No. 2 in 2015, when the first MX anthologies were published. Since then, there have been many other projects – these books, and others – where Roger has stepped up and written scholarly forewords, no questions asked. I can't imagine these books without him.

- Derrick Belanger – Derrick and I started emailing in late 2014, and haven't stopped since. Soon after, I had the idea for the MX anthologies, and he was one of the initial group that I asked to join the party. (He recently reminded me that my invitation led him to write his first traditional pastiche.) Since then, he and his brother Brian have gone on to create Belanger Books, home of many successful projects – several of which I've been fortunate enough to edit – and Derrick has also written a great deal more new Holmesian material. Derrick: Thanks very much for your friendship, and for all of the additional Sherlockian opportunities.

- Brian Belanger – Although we've yet to meet in person, I've really enjoyed getting to know Brian over the last few years, both in connection to these projects, as well as those with Belanger Books. He's an incredibly talented graphic artist who continues to amaze me even more with each new project – and all of the people who have book

10

covers designed by him will certainly agree. Brian: Thank you so much for all that you do – it's appreciated by many people besides me!

- Sean M. Wright – Finding pastiches in my hometown was difficult when I was a kid, just starting out as a Sherlockian. As mentioned above, one of the first pastiches that I ever encountered was the Mycroft Holmes-narrated *Enter the Lion* (1979) by Sean M. Wright and Michael P. Hodel. It's still an amazing book forty years later, and it showed me that others besides Watson could provide narratives within The World of Sherlock Holmes. Others have written about Mycroft since then – Glen Petrie, Kareem Abdul-Jabbar and Anna Waterhouse – but for me the best and most definitive will always be *Enter the Lion* by Wright and Hodel. I was thrilled a few months ago to be put in touch with Mr. Wright and, as your diligent amateur author, be able to ask him for a new Mycroft Holmes story. Amazingly, he has several which he hopes to publish in the future, and more amazingly, he allowed me to use one of them here first. The boy Sherlockian in me, who back then had a Holmes collection on his shelf only about one-foot wide – including *Enter the Lion* – is thrilled, and so is the adult Sherlockian, and I cannot thank Mr. Wright enough!

- Ian Dickerson – In a couple of contributions to previous MX anthology volumes – "The Strange Adventure of the Doomed Sextette" in *Part IX (1879-1895)* and "The Giant Rat of Sumatra" in *Part XI: Some Untold Cases (1880-1891)*, Ian explained how he came to be responsible for a number of long-lost scripts from the 1944 season of the Holmes radio show, starring Basil Rathbone and Nigel Bruce, and written by Denis Green and Leslie Charteris (under the name Bruce Taylor).

  Since then, he's published two sets of the scripts – *Sherlock Holmes: The Lost Radio Scripts* (2017) and *Sherlock Holmes: More Lost Radio Scripts* (2018). There are still a few more of them that remain unpublished, and I'm very grateful to Ian for allowing "The Haunted Chateau" to appear here. When I first discovered Holmes as a boy, I quickly found a number of Rathbone and

11

Bruce broadcasts on records at the public library, and that was where I first "heard" Holmes. I can't express the thrill of getting to read these rediscovered lost treasures, having been tantalized by their titles for so long. Many thanks to Ian for making these available.

- *The Nashville Scholars of the Three Pipe Problem* – The area where I live in eastern Tennessee is not noted for Sherlockian activity, or even awareness of the great man. I've worn a deerstalker as my only hat year-round since I was nineteen in 1984, and no one ever seems to recognize who I'm honouring. The closest Sherlockian Scion is in Nashville, a nearly-four-hour drive each way. Understandably, I don't get there as often as I'd like, but I'm very grateful to be a member of The Nashville Scholars, now in its fortieth year, and to visit when I can. In particular, I'd like to thank four of the Scholars:

  o *Jim Hawkins*, who works tirelessly to promote the group, and with whom I was very glad to spend some time at the 2018 *From Gillette to Brett V* Conference in Bloomington, IN;
  o *Shannon Carlisle, BSI*: I met Shannon, an award-winning teacher, at my first Scholars meeting. She is noted for using Holmes as the basis for much in her classroom, and her students were particularly interested in Stepping Stones and Undershaw. I was able to provide some information, including descriptions of my visit there in 2016. I'm grateful for her friendship;
  o *Bill Mason, BSI*: I met Bill at *From Gillette to Brett III* in 2011, when someone mentioned that we were both from Tennessee. We exchanged copies of our first books and have stayed in touch ever since. He's very supportive, and I've enjoyed hearing much of his insight since then;
  o *Marino Alvarez, BSI*: I became aware of Marino when he published A Professor Reflects on Sherlock Holmes (2012 MX Publishing.) I met him at *A Gathering of Southern Sherlockians* in 2012, but I doubt if he remembers it. I next met him at my first Nashville Scholars meeting. And

then, to my great surprise and enjoyment, he unexpectedly submitted a Holmes story for this collection. I'm very happy and thankful that he's a part of this!

- Ray Betzner, noted Sherlockian and especially noted Vincent Starrett Scholar: Thanks for taking time to answer a Starrett question!

- Melissa Grigsby – Thank you for the incredible work that you do at the Stepping Stones School at Undershaw in Hindhead. I was both amazed and thrilled to visit the school on opening day in 2016, and I hope to get back there again some time. You are doing amazing things, and it's my honor, as well that of all the contributors to this project, to be able to help.

- Joel Senter and his wife Carolyn have been legends in the Sherlockian community. I personally got to know Joel through telephone conversations, starting in the late 1980's, when I would order items from their amazing *Classic Specialties*. Later, I would call Joel with product ideas or questions. When my first book was published by a publisher who didn't actually intend to sell it, Joel gave me great advice, and furthermore, he sold the book for me through *Classic Specialties.* I only met him and Carolyn once in person, at *A Gathering of Southern Sherlockians* in 2012, and they arranged for me to sell books at a vendor's table (shared with Tracy Revels, whom I also met there for the first time,) and at that same event, Joel made a point of presenting me with a check in front of everyone for the profits my books that had sold through their business. When I first thought of the MX anthology, Joel was an incredible supporter, and he and Carolyn wrote an amazing story, "The Adventure of the Avaricious Bookkeeper", which closed out the final of the first three volumes with a case set just before Watson's death. It was an amazing way to conclude those books. Joel and I continued to communicate by email until shortly before his death in July 2018, and I – like so many Sherlockians – was devastated to learn that he had passed. He helped so many people with his enthusiasm

13

and support, and this set of MX volumes is dedicated to him.

In addition those mentioned above, I'd also like to especially thank (in alphabetical order): Larry Albert, Hugh Ashton, Deanna Baran, Jayantika Ganguly, Paul Gilbert, Dick Gillman, Arthur Hall, Mike Hogan, Craig Janacek, Tracy Revels, Roger Riccard, Geri Schear, and Tim Symonds. From the very beginning, these special contributors have stepped up and supported this and other projects over and over again with their contributions. They are the best and I can't explain how valued they are.

Finally, last but certainly *not* least, **Sir Arthur Conan Doyle**: Author, doctor, adventurer, and the Founder of the Sherlockian Feast. Present in spirit, and honored by all of us here.

As always, this collection, like those before it, has been a labor of love by both the participants and myself. As I've explained before, once again everyone did their sincerest best to produce an anthology that truly represents why Holmes and Watson have been so popular for so long. These are just more tiny threads woven into the ongoing Great Holmes Tapestry, continuing to grow and grow, for there can *never* be enough stories about the man whom Watson described as *"the best and wisest . . . whom I have ever known."*

David Marcum
March 20th, 2019
The 122nd Anniversary of the
Radix pedis diabolic *experiment*

Questions, comments, and story submissions
may be addressed to David Marcum at
thepapersofsherlockholmes@gmail.com

14

"Take up and read!"
by Will Thomas

I cut my teeth on Sherlock Holmes. I still recall being enthralled by Basil Rathbone at ten, and reading *The Boy's Sherlock Holmes* a year later. When I was seventeen I joined a Holmes scion, The Afghanistan Perceivers, in which the average age was fifty. What does one do with a rambunctious seventeen-year-old? One makes him the book reviewer for the club journal, something that doesn't require attending actual meetings. I didn't mind – I was studying The Canon, the history of Victorian London, and the other great fiction of that golden age. I was giving myself an education of sorts. Then Nicholas Meyer came along with his *The Seven Per-Cent Solution* and rocked my world.

There is an itch many writers have to pen a Sherlock Holmes story. Twain had it. What is *Pygmalion* but an homage by George Bernard Shaw? It is an itch that begs to be scratched. Picture a bear upright against an old oak tree. I've never thought to myself, "You need to write a Hemingway story," or "A sequel to *The Catcher in the Rye*! Brilliant!" Yet countless times I have put pen to paper and scribbled "It was in the year 1894 that I first . . . ."

What is the fascination? I cannot explain it, but I feel it keenly. Many Sherlockians do as well. We want to create our own tale, or to read others' in the hope that for twenty minutes or so we can be transported back to when we read our very first Sherlock Holmes story.

Some cannot visualize a time when The Canon was so sacred one wrote a pastiche with trepidation. It would be like walking on Doyle's grave. Luckily, we live in more enlightened times now. The book in front of you, featuring stories from a slew of modern masters, is proof of that. The world of Holmes has become less stodgy, and a lot more fun, if such a thing is even possible.

I never wrote that Sherlockian novel I was planning. Another pair of fictional detectives . . . sorry, make that private enquiry agents . . . came along and demanded my time and attention. Yet I admire the attempts others have made to try on Doyle's slippers, if only for a brief while. Holmes fans are the better for it.

Rather than quote from Doyle, let me turn to St. Augustine, who said:

"Take up and read!"

The book lays in front of you, open and insistent. Shall you heed its siren call? Oh come, what are you waiting for? The game's afoot!
Oh, look. I quoted Doyle after all.

Will Thomas
February 2019

"When I Glance Over My Notes and Records . . ." *
by Roger Johnson

. . . I realise, with a certain surprise, that this remarkable series of books began only four years ago. And here we are in 2019, celebrating the 160th anniversary of the birth of Arthur Conan Doyle in an entirely appropriate manner by helping to maintain the house that he helped create for himself and his family.

But there are other anniversaries this year. On the 30th August 1889, for instance, J.M. Stoddart, who had come from Philadelphia to commission material from British authors for *Lippincott's Monthly Magazine*, gave a small dinner party at the Langham Hotel. His guests were Thomas Patrick Gill, Oscar Wilde (whose 165th birthday falls on the 16th October) and Arthur Conan Doyle. Gill may have been invited on the strength of his own editorial experience. If so, he can share the credit for the magazine's publication the following year of *The Picture of Dorian Gray* and *The Sign of the Four*.

Conan Doyle published no new Holmes stories in 1919. The masterly "His Last Bow" had appeared two years before in both *The Strand Magazine* and *Collier's*. "The Mazarin Stone", rather less inspiring, was published in 1921, adapted from Conan Doyle's one-act play *The Crown Diamond*, which had enjoyed a brief and unsuccessful run earlier in the year.

But if we look two decades further back, we see that *Sherlock Holmes: A Drama in Four Acts*, credited to Arthur Conan Doyle and William Gillette, had its copyright performance at The Duke of York's Theatre in London on the 12th June 1899, with Herbert Waring as Holmes. Gillette himself was the star, of course, when the play opened on the 23rd October in Buffalo, transferring to the Garrick Theatre in New York the following month. Its success, which owed much to Gillette's performance, certainly helped stimulate public demand for more adventures of the great detective – a demand that was shortly to be satisfied in part by the publication of *The Hound of the Baskervilles*. (Gillette's play was triumphantly revived by the Royal Shakespeare Company forty-five years ago, with John Wood magnificent as Holmes.)

1929 saw both the last silent Holmes film, *Der Hund von Baskerville* (now restored and made available *this year* for home viewing) and the first talkie, *The Return of Sherlock Holmes*, with Clive Brook in the lead. A

17

print of the latter is held at the Library of Congress, but is apparently inaccessible to the public.

In 1939, however, there was a true cinematic landmark. Fox's lavish production of *The Hound of the Baskervilles* paired Basil Rathbone and Nigel Bruce for the first time as the detective and the doctor. Moreover, it was the first Holmes film to be set in the correct period. Late Victorian London was superbly re-created in Hollywood – and the sets were used again that same year for a similarly excellent production, *The Adventures of Sherlock Holmes*.

Twenty years later, Hammer's flawed but entertaining version of *The Hound of the Baskervilles* presented Sherlock Holmes in colour for the first time, and showed that a British studio could match Hollywood for action and suspense. In its sixtieth anniversary year, critical appreciation of this good-looking film, with its fine performances from a cast headed by Peter Cushing and Andre Morell, has grown. (I remember when the *Radio Times* critics gave it a rather harsh two-star ranking. Now it merits the full five stars. *Tempora mutantur . . . .*)

In 1954, while Carleton Hobbs and Norman Shelley were playing Holmes and Watson in a series for children on the BBC Home Service, the Light Programme transmitted twelve new dramatisations from the Canon, starring John Gielgud and Ralph Richardson. Unusually, these were produced by an independent company, and for some reason the BBC declined to broadcast the remaining four plays, though the whole series was eagerly taken up by stations in America and elsewhere. (Hobbs and Shelley remained British radio's definitive pairing for another fifteen years. 2019 marks the fiftieth anniversary of their final series as Holmes and Watson, which concluded, most appropriately, with *His Last Bow*.)

That same year, American audiences could see the great detective on television, in a light but very enjoyable series of short films with Ronald Howard and Howard Marion Crawford in the leading rôles. On this side of the Atlantic, we had to wait until video recordings were released some fifty years later, but meanwhile we had something rather better to look at. Fifty-five years ago, in an anthology series called *Detective*, BBC TV presented a superb, authentic Holmes and Watson. The actors were Douglas Wilmer and Nigel Stock, and the story was *The Speckled Band*. Its success led to a fondly remembered series the following year.

2019 also marks the thirty-fifth anniversary of Jeremy Brett's first appearance as Holmes, with David Burke as his Watson, in Michael Cox's series for Granada TV, *The Adventures of Sherlock Holmes*. It was the start of an extraordinary decade-long world-wide phenomenon, which at its best was unbeatable. In Burke we saw the true Watson, brave, intelligent, loyal and down-to-earth. Brett, for many, remains the ideal Holmes.

What else? Well, eighty-five years ago, The Baker Street Irregulars, which, in terms of its combined age and influence ranks as the world's senior Holmesian fellowship, was founded. Moreover, The Sherlock Holmes Society held its inaugural meeting in London at the same time as the BSI's first meeting in New York. Indeed, the two groups exchanged congratulatory telegrams! But while the Irregulars' sodality persisted through the hard times of the thirties and forties, the very differently constituted British society survived only until 1938, lying dormant until its revival as The Sherlock Holmes Society of London in 1951.

I can't conclude without mentioning the twentieth anniversary of two remarkable achievements. In 1999, thanks to the imagination and hard work of certain members of the SHSL – notably, of course, the sculptor John Doubleday – and the financial support of Abbey National plc, an imposing statue of the Great Detective was at last erected in London. Its unveiling on the 23rd September was the focal point of a week-long festival, which included an evening at the Cockpit Theatre to see *Sherlock Holmes: The Last Act!* written by David Stuart Davies for Roger Llewellyn, who had first staged it earlier in the year at the Salisbury Playhouse.

I doubt that even the author seriously believed that it would become an international success, but that's exactly what has happened. The play itself is first-rate, and even then Roger Llewellyn's interpretation was revelatory. Roger died last year, but his performance in *The Last Act* and its successor *Sherlock Holmes: The Death and Life* can still be enjoyed, as he recorded the two plays for Big Finish in 2010. (And as I write, we're less than a month away from the premiere of David's new play, *Sherlock Holmes: The Final Reckoning*, in which Michael Daviot and Mark Kydd play the detective and the doctor.)

I remember the explosion of interest in 1987, stimulated by the centenary of the first Holmes story, *A Study in Scarlet*. 2019 is another year peculiarly rich in significant anniversaries – *and opportunities*. David Marcum, MX Publishing, and the many contributors to this volume have created one of those opportunities. Let's make the most of it!

Roger Johnson, BSI, ASH
31st January, 2019

---

* "The Five Orange Pips"

An Ongoing Legacy
for Sherlock Holmes
by Steve Emecz

Undershaw
Circa 1900

As we enter the fourth year of *The MX Book of New Sherlock Holmes Stories*, we reach a staggering fifteen volumes – by far the largest collection of new Sherlock Holmes stories in the world. Through authors donating royalties and licensing, the series has raised over $40,000 for Stepping Stones School. With this money, the school has been able to fund projects that would be very difficult to organise otherwise – especially those to preserve the legacy of Sir Arthur Conan Doyle at Undershaw.

There are now over three-hundred-thirty stories and well over a hundred-fifty authors taking part – many MX authors, but many others including bestselling authors like Lee Child, Jonathan Kellerman, Lyndsay Faye, and Bonnie MacBird.

Volumes XI and XII continued the tradition of getting starred reviews from *Publishers Weekly*:

MX Publishing is a social enterprise – all the staff, including me, are volunteers with day jobs. The collection would not be possible without the creator and editor, David Marcum, who is rightly cited multiple times by *Publishers Weekly* and others as probably the most accomplished Sherlockian editor thus far. In addition to Stepping Stones School, our main program that we support is the Happy Life Children's Home in Kenya. My wife Sharon and I have recently returned from our 6th Christmas in a row at Happy Life and can report back that huge progress has been made and the lives of over 600 babies saved. You can read all about the project in the 2nd edition of the book *The Happy Life Story.*

Our support of both of these projects is possible through the publishing of Sherlock Holmes books, which we have now been doing for a decade.

You can find out more information about the Stepping Stones School at: *www.steppingstones.org.uk*

and Happy Life at: *www.happylifechildrenshomes.com.*

You can obtain more books from MX, both fiction and non-fiction, at: *www.sherlockholmesbooks.com.*

If you would like to become involved with these projects or help out in any way, please reach out to me via *LinkedIn.*

Steve Emecz
February 2019
Twitter: *@steveemecz*
LinkedIn: *https://www.linkedin.com/in/emecz/*

The Doyle Room at Stepping Stones, Undershaw
Partially funded through royalties from
The MX Book of New Sherlock Holmes Stories

A Word From the
Head Teacher of Stepping Stones
by Melissa Grigsby

Undershaw
September 9, 2016
Grand Opening of the Stepping Stones School
(Photograph courtesy of Roger Johnson)

"The world is full of obvious things
which nobody by any chance ever observes."
– Arthur Conan Doyle, *The Hound of the Baskervilles*

As we travel into the next journey of Stepping Stones School, the words of Arthur Conan Doyle ring so very true. Our developing outreach and employment support programs based at Undershaw focus on social mobility for young people with Special Educational Needs. Our work sits with Business and Companies that so often miss the obvious things and get caught up in practical barriers, rather than seeing the potential of the young people on our watch.

The funds gifted to us have allowed us to start developing a more sophisticated communication systems, which in turn will open doors to allow the world to observe the obvious things and look deeper at the skills and opportunities the young people of Undershaw bring to the community.

23

Dr. Mortimer looked strangely at us for an instant, and his voice sank almost to a whisper as he answered:

"Mr. Holmes, they were the footprints of a gigantic hound!"

The royalties we receive are the footprints in a gigantic story for Undershaw and the young people that learn under its roof.

Melissa Grigsby
Executive Head Teacher,
Stepping Stones, Undershaw
January 2019

Sherlock Holmes (1854-1957) was born in Yorkshire, England, on 6 January, 1854. In the mid-1870's, he moved to 24 Montague Street, London, where he established himself as the world's first Consulting Detective. After meeting Dr. John H. Watson in early 1881, he and Watson moved to rooms at 221b Baker Street, where his reputation as the world's greatest detective grew for several decades. He was presumed to have died battling noted criminal Professor James Moriarty on 4 May, 1891, but he returned to London on 5 April, 1894, resuming his consulting practice in Baker Street. Retiring to the Sussex coast near Beachy Head in October 1903, he continued to be associated in various private and government investigations while giving the impression of being a reclusive apiarist. He was very involved in the events encompassing World War I, and to a lesser degree those of World War II. He passed away peacefully upon the cliffs above his Sussex home on his 103rd birthday, 6 January, 1957.

Dr. John Hamish Watson (1852-1929) was born in Stranraer, Scotland on 7 August, 1852. In 1878, he took his Doctor of Medicine Degree from the University of London, and later joined the army as a surgeon. Wounded at the Battle of Maiwand in Afghanistan (27 July, 1880), he returned to London late that same year. On New Year's Day, 1881, he was introduced to Sherlock Holmes in the chemical laboratory at Barts. Agreeing to share rooms with Holmes in Baker Street, Watson became invaluable to Holmes's consulting detective practice. Watson was married and widowed three times, and from the late 1880's onward, in addition to his participation in Holmes's investigations and his medical practice, he chronicled Holmes's adventures, with the assistance of his literary agent, Sir Arthur Conan Doyle, in a series of popular narratives, most of which were first published in *The Strand* magazine. Watson's later years were spent preparing a vast number of his notes of Holmes's cases for future publication. Following a final important investigation with Holmes, Watson contracted pneumonia and passed away on 24 July, 1929.

Photos of Sherlock Holmes and Dr. John H. Watson courtesy of Roger Johnson

The MX Book
of
New Sherlock Holmes Stories
Part XV:
2019 Annual
(1898-1917)

Two Poems
by Christopher James

The First Floor Ghost

He's the dropped book at midnight,
the empty pipe bowl still warm in the morning;
a shiver at your neck as you retire to bed.
In the small hours he has the run of the place,
lounging in your favourite chair, thumbing
through Shakespeare and sipping your sherry.
He plays violin and lets you think it's birdsong.
Some nights, he is not beyond a few light chores:
a little graphology or reading of the ashes.
He has been known to hang his gown on the door.
Leave him a glass of good Bordeaux
and a note to say: If you must read my books,
try The Hive and the Honey Bee but please
do not leave your tobacco in my slippers.

Sherlock of Aleppo

Two boys, Victor and Sayid, crawl like bees
through the ruined honeycomb of Aleppo.
Dust clings like pollen to their skin. Victor
has a copy of *The Memoirs of Sherlock Holmes*
dropped by an aid worker, committed to memory.
"Now I am Holmes," he says, "and you are Watson."
and smears a mud moustache on Sayid's lip.

Their home is 221b Al Khandaq Street, a bombed out
paint shop. Victor plays a violin with no strings;
his friend has fashioned a bowler from a tin of emulsion.
Mrs. Hudson is an old woman called Rasha
they found living alone with her cat.
Each morning, they visit Mycroft, once Akram,
three weeks after he caught the barrel bomb.

They wear bottle-top monocles and smoke Alhamras.
"We must eliminate the impossible," says Victor,
"and find the man who murdered our brother. I have seen
his face in the ashes." They find a soldier obeying orders.
"We have the evidence," Victor tells him,

The Whitechapel Butcher
by Mark Mower

One chilly evening in the March of 1898, Holmes and I returned from the theatre to find the upstairs study of our Baker Street apartment occupied by a burly fellow of the roughest hue. I was about to challenge the rogue when my colleague stepped forward and placed his hand ahead of me to halt my advance.

"My dear Watson – let me introduce you to Mr. Henworth Paterson, diligent tradesman, purveyor of fine meats, and a genuine *knight of the cleaver*."

Our visitor rose quickly from his chair, removed his ill-fitting cloth cap, and extended a huge hand towards Holmes. "Thank you, sir. I hope you don't mind me waiting like this, but my business is somewhat urgent."

The tone of his voice was low and refined, belying his coarse appearance. He stood close to seven feet in height, his enormous upper body covered in a faded blue tunic, over the top of which was tied a brown leather duck apron. His muscular lower limbs were clad in grey worsted leggings, and on his feet were the largest pair of ankle boots I had ever seen. A mop of unkempt brown hair and whiskery sideburns framed the chiselled features of his long face.

"Not at all," replied Holmes, gesturing towards the chair.

Our guest resumed his seat and looked up quizzically. "How did you know who I was?"

"When I note that Mrs. Hudson has allowed an evening caller to enter her home and ascend the stairs, and has then offered him a cup of tea while he awaits the return of her lodgers, I anticipate that this is no ordinary visitor." He nodded towards the empty teacup on the small side table. "That you wear the livery so beloved of the *Whitechapel butcher* tells me your obvious profession. And knowing that Mrs. Hudson has purchased her meat from the same supplier for over ten years and refuses to shop anywhere else, it is but a small matter to conclude that you are the Henworth Paterson of whom she speaks so highly."

I fancied that I saw Mr. Paterson blush on hearing this and he smiled momentarily – a smile that was quickly replaced by a look of some concern. "Gentlemen, I will come straight to the point, for I am at my wit's end. I know something of your work from talking to Mrs. Hudson and thought that if anyone could help, it would be you. So I called this evening, explaining that I was desperate to seek your advice. And yet I could not tell that dear lady the nature of my anxiety – for I fear that tonight I shall murder a man!"

Holmes responded with no more surprise than if Paterson had announced that he had mislaid a favourite watch. "On that basis, I will ask Dr. Watson to pour each of us a large glass of whisky and must ask you to set before me the full details of how you have arrived at this most remarkable conclusion."

I busied myself doing as Holmes had requested and also offered Paterson a cigarette from a box on the mantelpiece. He readily accepted the scotch but declined to smoke. I lit one myself and settled back into the sofa. Holmes sat in an armchair facing the man and brought his fingertips together under his chin. Paterson took this as his cue to begin.

"I am now thirty-four years of age and have been a master butcher for some twelve of those years. I learnt the trade from my father, who passed away two years ago, leaving me the business. The shop has continued to provide me with a reasonable living, but I supplement the income with the rent I receive from two lodgers who live in the small rooms above the butchery. My wife, Louise, and I have our own living quarters downstairs at the back of the shop. Am I devoted to her, and we share everything. When we married, she put all of her savings into the business to allow us to take on other staff.

"We took in the first of our lodgers just after my father passed away. His name is Henry Rawlings, a middle-aged bookkeeper for the Great Eastern Railway – a quiet and meticulous man, who pays his rent promptly each week and sits down with us most evenings to enjoy a meal. Louise also takes in his laundry, and it has been Henry's custom since he arrived to pay a little bit extra for this and the meals he receives.

"Our second lodger, Ronald Moody, has been with us for just three months. He is five or six years younger than I and something of a gadabout. He works at a theatre in the West End and fancies himself as something of a stage performer. As well as a job in the booking office, he takes to the stage once or twice each week as 'The Great Ronaldo', entertaining audiences with his magic tricks and mind-reading shows. Unlike Henry, he has proved to be unreliable in paying his rent, and were it not for my wife's intervention on two or three occasions, I would gladly have shown him the door."

Holmes interjected at this point. "I know of 'The Great Ronaldo'. In fact, Watson and I attended one of his shows three or four weeks back."

I remembered the evening well. It had not been the most edifying of experiences.

Paterson continued. "About a month ago, I felt an enormous change come over me. I began to find it hard to get to sleep and to wake in the mornings, and have felt continuously lethargic and anxious. Louise is convinced that I'm working too hard, as I routinely open the shop at five-thirty each morning and rarely close before seven in the evening. But other aspects of my behaviour have been more troubling. For it seems I have been sleepwalking into Henry Rawlings's room and trying to attack him."

"And you're convinced that this has something to do with the general change in your demeanour?" I asked.

"Yes," replied Paterson. "Prior to this, I have never experienced any ill-health and have always been able to sleep soundly."

Holmes seemed tetchy at the interruption. "Mr. Paterson, I would be grateful if you could explain specifically what has occurred, omitting no detail, however small it may seem."

Paterson nodded. "Each evening we sit down to eat at seven-thirty. Henry joins us for the meal most nights, while Ronald departs for the theatre. After the meal, Henry stays talking to Louise and reading his newspaper while I generally complete some of the paperwork and orders for the following day. My wife turns in at nine o'clock, by which time Henry has also headed upstairs to bed. But it has long been a habit of mine to leave the house at that time and to walk for a couple of hours before returning home. It helps me to clear my head and relax after a long day. I then take a large glass of strong Madeira wine before undressing, washing, and getting into bed.

"On Monday the fifth of March, having followed exactly that routine, I woke in the early hours to find myself in Rawlings's room with a large steak knife in my hand. I was stood beside his bed as he cowered under the covers. Ronald had apparently come to Henry's aid and was trying to persuade me to hand over the knife. I can't begin to tell you how embarrassed and concerned I was. I was relieved of the knife and began to apologise to Henry, admitting that I had not been feeling well. But to make matters worse, he then showed me a note which he said had been pushed under his door the previous evening. It read, '*I will kill you*'."

Holmes sat forward in his chair and pointed towards Paterson. "A-ha! A note which he believed *you* had written?"

Paterson nodded slowly. "There was no denying it. It looked to be in my hand and had been written on a sheet of headed paper torn from one of the butchery's order books – a book which I keep locked in a bureau at the back of the shop."

I had begun to scrutinise Paterson a little more closely with this revelation. The symptoms he had described and the reference to the death threat seemed to me to be strongly suggestive of his deteriorating mental state. Coupled with the obvious paranoia he was now demonstrating, I was inclined to believe that he might be suffering from the debilitating effects of mania, brought on by the long hours of work and his increasingly erratic sleep patterns. I had seen many such cases in both military and civilian life.

"That is most suggestive," said Holmes, reaching for his churchwarden and matches, "but how had Rawlings reacted to this earlier message?"

"He admitted that he had been most confused by it and had shown it to my wife. Louise had apparently reassured him that I had been feeling unwell and had been making mistakes and acting in ways that were out of character for me. On that basis, he had thought no more of it until he awoke that night to find me coming towards him with the knife. He had cried out in order to get Ronald's help. After I had been escorted back to bed, Louise and Ronald had convinced Henry that this was likely to be an isolated incident which would not occur again."

"I see. And have there been other incidents since that time?"

"Sadly, yes. A few days later I took the decision to close the shop and let my three cutters go home early. It was probably around five o'clock that afternoon. Having locked the doors, I made my way through to our living quarters and was surprised to find Louise sitting beside Ronald and whispering something which I could not catch. Both looked up in surprise and I saw Louise flush. Fearing that I had walked in on some infidelity on my wife's part, I was about to grab Ronald when he said that things were not as they looked. He then held up and passed to me a folded note which he said had been posted beneath Henry's door the previous evening. It read the same as the earlier message."

"And you were convinced once more that you had written it?"

"Yes, Mr. Holmes. I could think of no alternative explanation. And later, when Louise and I sat alone to discuss the matter, she herself had to admit that the notes looked to be in my hand. She said that she had not wished to talk to Ronald behind my back, but was growing increasingly concerned about my health."

Hearing this, I was now even more convinced about my diagnosis and wondered if Holmes might be reaching the same conclusion. But he allowed Paterson to carry on and outline what had then occurred. In short, only two days after the appearance of the second note, Paterson had once more come around to find himself in Rawlings's room in the early hours, this time armed with a heavy cleaver. Ronald Moody had remonstrated with him to drop the weapon and order had then been restored. Unfortunately, Rawlings had not been inclined to let the matter rest and had approached the police that night, explaining what had occurred and presenting them with one of the notes that had been pushed under his door. The police had viewed the matter seriously, but hadn't taken any further action because Rawlings had announced later that he did not wish to press charges. Holmes seized upon this disclosure with some relish.

"What did you make of that, Mr. Paterson?"

"I was very relieved and grateful for the intervention of Ronald, who had accompanied Henry to the police station. He told me later that he had persuaded Henry to drop the charges, arguing that this was a medical concern rather than a criminal matter. Henry was unhappy with the situation and made it clear that he would go to the police again if any further incidents should occur. That was two days ago. For my part, I agreed to seek medical help and have arranged an appointment with a doctor for tomorrow afternoon."

"And yet you fear that the consultation may come too late. I take it that another of these mysterious notes has appeared?"

Paterson looked surprised. "Yes, but how did you know?"

My colleague responded somewhat wearily. "Something has clearly precipitated your fear that you are to commit murder this very night. It seemed most likely that this would be a third note."

Paterson fidgeted uncomfortably and then reached into the front of his apron, from which he withdrew a small, somewhat crumpled, piece of paper which he passed across to Holmes. My colleague regarded it keenly. Looking across from the sofa, I could see a message scrawled in large black letters on the headed paper. It read simply, '*I will kill you tonight*'.

"When did Mr. Rawlings give you this?" Holmes asked, placing his churchwarden down on the hearth.

Paterson looked confused. "He didn't. It was an odd thing. Some time back, Ronald had mentioned to me that the ceiling above his bed appeared to be getting damper and he wondered whether there might be a leak in the roof. I agreed to investigate, but with all of the events I have described, had quite forgotten about it until this afternoon. Business was slow in the shop and when the matter came to mind I decided to leave one of my assistants in charge and to venture into the loft to see if I could see the source of the dampness. The entrance to the loft is in Henry's room. Had he not been at work, I would have been reluctant to approach it. But with a small ladder to hand, decided that this would be the best time to act, particularly as Ronald and my wife were also absent at that time. Having gone up into the roof space, I could see no discernible leak, so climbed back down through the hatch. As I was about to leave the room, I swung the ladder and knocked over a wicker basket beside Henry's desk. The contents were scattered across the floor so I had to tidy up the mess. I found *that* screwed up amongst the other bits of discarded paper."

Holmes beamed at our guest. "Indeed. And you can confirm that this headed sheet has also been torn from your order book?"

41

Paterson answered in the affirmative. Holmes then asked, "What do you make of it?"

Our visitor looked dejected. "I don't know what to make of it, sir. I am consumed with fear. I cannot recollect writing such a terrible thing, and yet cannot deny that it looks to be in my hand and set out on my own stationery."

I then asked, "What did the others say when you told them about finding the note?"

He shook his head. "I'll be honest, Doctor, I didn't raise the matter. I took the note and went back to work. Louise returned late in the afternoon and began to prepare the evening meal. Henry and Ronald both arrived back at about six o'clock. Nothing was said by any of them and, at Louise's invitation, both men agreed to join us later for the meal. Despite the circumstances, Henry seemed relaxed in my company and we talked amiably enough. But I could not help but think this was some play-acting on his part, with him knowing full well of the third note, yet choosing not to raise the matter with me."

Holmes rose from his seat and took a few steps over to the table near the window. He picked up a sheet of paper and an ink pen and handed them to Paterson. "Could you write, '*I will kill you*' on this sheet?"

It took him but a few seconds to comply. When the sheet was passed back, the detective began to compare both messages, poring over each character with a magnifying glass. At the end of this examination he uttered just two words: "Most enlightening".

I sensed then that Paterson was beginning to get a little impatient. Holmes had clearly noticed this too, for he announced suddenly that he had just two final questions. Firstly, he asked if our client had told anyone back at the house of his planned visit to Baker Street. When Paterson confirmed that he had not, Holmes then asked a most extraordinary final question: "While at your house, has Mr. Moody ever asked you to take part in one of his stage acts?"

Paterson seemed puzzled by the inquiry. "I'm not sure I understand what you mean, Mr. Holmes. Are you asking whether he has ever invited me to the theatre to assist him?"

Holmes clarified his line of enquiry. "No. I realise that I should not have talked so obliquely. What I need to know specifically, is whether Moody has ever offered to hypnotise you while at your house?"

Paterson looked at him incredulously. "It is odd that you should ask such a question, for I did at one stage wonder if my sleepwalking could be explained by that. Like you, I am well aware that Ronald occasionally uses elements of hypnosis in his stage act. When he first came to lodge with us, he told me as much, explaining that he is occasionally called upon to assist people outside of the theatre, for hypnosis can be used to treat certain conditions."

I could not help but interject. "Yes, it was the Scottish surgeon James Braid who first coined the term *hypnotism* in the 1840's. Like many others, he had discovered that a mesmeric trance could be induced in some patients by the use of a protracted ocular fixation. He believed that this left certain parts of the brain fatigued and in a state of 'neuro-hypnosis', and suggested that in this condition some individuals can be susceptible to influence and might be persuaded to alter their normal patterns of behaviour. This could be useful in the treatment of addictive or destructive behaviours."

Holmes seemed bemused by my interruption and asked the question again. "Did Mr. Moody offer to hypnotise you?"

Our visitor responded most definitively. "He did ask, explaining that hypnosis might help me to cope better with the demands of my work, without the need to rely on long evening walks and strong Madeira wine. But I told him I would never agree to such a request, however beneficial it might prove to be. I have no time for such quack remedies. I hope that does not offend you, Doctor?"

I laughed. "No, I take no offence. In fact, I share your concern. I believe it to be a pseudo-science at best, which could be misused by the unscrupulous."

"Then we are all agreed," concurred Holmes. "But in this case, it would appear that hypnosis was not the cause of Mr. Paterson's erratic behaviour. It seems we have some further work to do. I suggest that the three of us take a carriage to Whitechapel to continue our investigations. I believe it will be to our advantage that no one knows of our impending arrival."

As Paterson and I made our way through the door of the sitting room and out on to the landing, I glanced back and saw that Holmes had paused to retrieve a magazine from his extensive archives. Smiling at me with a sly wink, he slipped the thin pamphlet in an inside pocket of his jacket and began to make his way towards the door. I had little doubt that the magazine would reappear later as our adventure unfolded.

It took us some time to travel across to Paterson's shop in Whitechapel. Even at that late hour the streets were awash with life and I noticed that a few shops and street vendors were still doing a brisk trade. As we bumped along in the four-wheeler, Paterson explained that many of his more unscrupulous competitors used the hours of darkness to sell off any meat which had gone past its prime. The aromas which had begun to fill my nostrils provided strong confirmation of this.

Holmes had spent much of the journey leafing through his magazine. When he eventually returned the document to his pocket, Paterson asked him directly, "Do you believe that I wrote those notes, Mr. Holmes?"

My colleague shook his head. "Not a bit of it. When I compared the note you had written for me to the writing on the sheet retrieved from Rawlings's basket, it was clear that the two did not match. The forgery was well executed, but I am convinced that another hand has been at work. Beyond that, I cannot say more until I have further data."

Paterson seemed greatly relieved to hear this and turned back to me. I knew not what to make of the revelation, still believing that the butcher's mental state had some bearing on the case. A few minutes later we pulled up outside a baker's shop a short distance from the Paterson butchery and then continued on foot. Paterson led the way, holding a small lantern he had brought with him to Baker Street. By means of a narrow side passage, we were able to approach the back of the shop quietly and discreetly. As Paterson unlocked the thick oak door to enable us to gain entry, I could see only one dim light in the middle of the three upstairs windows.

We followed our client into the property, where he lit a couple of candles and then coaxed a gas lamp on a wall bracket into operation. I could see then that we were in a spacious kitchen and storage area containing two large sinks, a free-standing chopping block, some cupboards and shelves, and a large oak refectory table. Ahead of us ran a long passageway which I envisaged led to the butchery at the front of the property. On the left, some way along this, was a small staircase bathed in an orange glow. Paterson pointed to this and whispered that it led to a landing and the bedrooms of Rawlings and Moody. He then gestured towards a second stairwell in the corner to our right which provided alternative access to all of the upper rooms. A door beside this led to Paterson's living quarters.

There was not a sound in the property beyond the gentle ticking of a wall-mounted clock in the passageway. In a hushed tone, Holmes asked if he could first see the butchery's order book. Paterson tip-toed off down the passageway and returned a couple of minutes later clutching a blue-and-red-bound book. Holmes placed it down on the chopping block and began to leaf through the stubs of the sheets that had been torn from the book. He then looked up and asked Paterson how the bureau was secured. Our client explained that the bureau was housed in a small office at the back of the shop and there were only two keys to its lock. One was kept in a secure cash till, while the other was attached to a key chain on Paterson's tunic.

Holmes then asked if Rawlings or Moody ever had reason to go into the shop. "No," he replied. "It is a condition of their tenancy that the shop space is off limits to them. Both men come and go using the stairs in the passageway, and enter and leave the building using the door behind us. We take our meals in this main room and the lodgers have a small shared washroom just off the landing. They have no need to venture into the shop at all."

Seemingly satisfied with this new piece of information, Holmes then outlined his plan. Paterson was to rouse his wife from her slumbers and request that she go upstairs to bring both Rawlings and Moody down into the kitchen. If required, he was to explain that he wanted to apologise to both men for his recent behaviour. I was to stay hidden behind one of the larger cupboards until both men appeared and, after revealing myself, would then ensure that no one left the room. With no further elaboration, Holmes slipped away towards the second staircase in the corner of the kitchen and disappeared from view.

It took a good five minutes before Louise Paterson came through into the kitchen. Tucked into my hiding place, I could hear her remonstrating with her husband about the unexpected interruption to her sleep. She seemed markedly reluctant to comply with his request to wake the lodgers, but eventually headed upstairs. Hearing her light footfall on the wooden stairs, I stepped out into the kitchen and took up a new position just out of sight of the passageway. Paterson took a seat at the table and waited for the drama to unfold.

The first to come down the stairs and into the kitchen was Henry Rawlings, who entered wearing a red dressing gown and black carpet slippers. Ronald Moody followed, dressed only in a thick cotton nightshirt, while Mrs. Paterson was clothed in a full-length night gown and wrap-around shawl. She too was wearing slippers, and her long brunette hair was tied back with a blue ribbon. All three looked first towards Paterson and then, seeing me, recognised that he was not alone in the kitchen. While the men continued to stand, Mrs. Paterson took a seat at the refectory table.

Rawlings seemed the most surprised. He was fair-haired, of slender build and approaching six feet in height. A thick moustache ran along his thin lip line, and I could see that he had some considerable bruising around his left eye. He held my gaze. "Who is this, Henworth?" he asked quickly. The tone was accusatory. Paterson said nothing.

Moody then stepped forward, looking nervously between the two of us, before settling on the butcher. "Yes, who is this man?" He was also of slender build, clean shaven and boyishly youthful in his appearance. He looked very different to the man I had seen some weeks before on the stage. On that occasion, he had worn thick theatrical make up.

Mrs. Paterson then intervened. "Henworth, please! What is the meaning of this? Have you finally lost your mind?"

To this point, none of the three had heard or observed the tall figure of Holmes, who now entered the kitchen behind them and stood commandingly by the doorframe, a piece of paper visible in his hand. "Perhaps I can answer some of your questions," he announced, startling Mrs. Paterson and Moody. "We have been called here to investigate the alleged threats to you, Mr. Rawlings. '*I will kill you*' says this note. It was lying on the desk in your room. Is it evidence of Mr. Paterson's deteriorating mental state?"

"Are you the police?" asked Rawlings.

"I am a private detective, sir." He waved his free hand towards me. "And this is my colleague, Dr. Watson. Now, what am I to make of this message?" He waved the note once more and then placed it in the left pocket of his jacket.

Rawlings's jaw was set hard as he answered. "I know not what trickery you are attempting to perform here this evening, but I will tell you that it is not the first time Henworth has threatened me with violence. On two previous occasions he has entered my bedroom during the night, intent on assaulting me. And earlier this evening he once more accosted me in my room armed with a meat cleaver. The bruising on my face provides clear evidence of the attack. Had it not been for the timely intervention of Mr. Moody here, I would not have escaped with my life."

"Ah, then you witnessed this episode, Mr. Moody?"

The younger man looked at Holmes somewhat timidly. "Yes, I did. I heard the commotion in Henry's room, and when I reached the landing could see Henworth brandishing the cleaver. Twice I saw him lunge at Henry. If you have taken that note from the room, you cannot have failed to notice the damage that has been done to the dressing table."

"Indeed, there is a most remarkable gash in the furniture. And I have no doubt that it was made by a meat cleaver. But what time did this incident occur?"

"It was close to eight-thirty this evening."

Henworth Paterson rounded on Moody and was about to rise from his chair, his fists clenched and his face crimson. Holmes intervened swiftly and placed a firm hand on the butcher's shoulder. "Please stay seated, Mr. Paterson. I believe we are getting to the nub of this matter, so would ask you to remain silent for the moment." Despite the man's anger it was clear that he trusted Holmes's judgement, for he resumed his seat and remained silent.

Holmes now turned to Louise Paterson. "Were you aware of this attempted assault, Mrs. Paterson?"

She flushed and spoke quietly, "I did hear some commotion upstairs just before Henworth left the house for his evening walk. I was in my

46

bedroom at the time, so did not get a chance to speak to him about it. To be fair, Henworth has not been himself recently, so anything is possible."

Her husband's head dropped at this point and he looked meekly towards the tiled floor of the kitchen. I still retained some doubts about his mental state.

"And nothing was said by your two lodgers?"

It was Moody who answered as the tears began to well in Mrs. Paterson's eyes. "We didn't feel it was the right time to tell Louise. But Henry has now determined that he must refer the matter to the police. The situation has got out of hand. Something has to be done."

Holmes regarded him for a few moments and then replied. "And yet you have not gone to the authorities. Why is that?"

Rawlings seemed agitated by the query. "We were waiting for Henworth to return home. We then planned to tell Louise about the assault and go to the police."

Holmes began to shake his head slowly from side to side. "This will not do! You tell me that you are planning to report an assault, and yet the two of you were tucked up in your beds. This is all lies. So let me set the record straight. When Mr. Paterson left the house this evening, he came to seek my assistance. He was concerned to know whether he had been sleepwalking and writing the threatening notes."

The bookkeeper stood his ground. "Good. And I'm telling you that his threats and attacks have been real enough."

Holmes took a couple of steps towards Rawlings and stared deep into his eyes. "You are lying, sir, as I will prove shortly. Now, I want you and Mr. Moody to take a seat at the table beside Mrs. Paterson."

There was no resistance from either man and no further words exchanged as both moved to take their seats. Holmes then addressed our client. "Mr. Paterson. You mentioned earlier that you like to take a large glass of Madeira before retiring to bed each evening. I would be grateful if you could retrieve the bottle from your living quarters and bring it to me."

Paterson looked up in surprise. For a brief moment he seemed bewildered by the request but then nodded and rose from his chair. A couple of minutes later he was once again seated at the table and Holmes held within his hand a large bottle of the fortified wine. To the bemusement of us all, he removed the cork and began to sniff at the contents. He then took a small sip and appeared to be savouring the taste, before resealing the bottle and placing it on the chopping block beside the order book he had scrutinised earlier. From the passageway came the melodic chiming of the clock announcing the arrival of midnight. Holmes then began to speak.

"Mr. Paterson is a master butcher with an enviable reputation. He works hard and, like his father before him, does his utmost to serve his ever-loyal customers. And yet his diligence is not enough, for he is forced to take in lodgers to provide the additional income he and his wife require to live a decent life in this busy metropolis. Now, what if one of these lodgers had designs on the business and the income it affords? How might he go about removing our industrious butcher?"

Henry Rawlings pushed back in his chair and rose from the table. I braced myself, fearing that he might launch himself at Holmes, but he just stood, red-faced and angry. "How dare you! What right have you to come in here and start flinging these wild accusations about in our home?"

Moody clearly felt that he too should offer up some challenge. "That is absurd, Mr. Holmes. If anything happened to Henworth, it would be Louise that would take over the business. On what basis would Henry or I have any interest in the affair?"

Holmes raised his eyebrows and pointed at Mrs. Paterson. "For exactly that reason. Your phraseology is unfortunate, yet revealing – after all, one of you has been *conducting an affair with Mrs. Paterson.*"

There was an explosion of activity in the room. Henworth Paterson flung himself across the table towards Moody, clawing viciously at the front of the lodger's nightshirt. Rawlings began to use both fists to pummel the outstretched body of the butcher, while Mrs. Paterson jumped up, screaming wildly and tearing at her hair with both hands. Holmes took it upon himself to wade in and break up the skirmish between the three men. I went to Mrs. Paterson's aid, calming her down and preventing her from harming herself further.

It was a good five minutes before order was restored. Mrs. Paterson continued to sob gently at one end of the refectory table. Her husband was seated beside the chopping block, while the two lodgers were slumped, somewhat dishevelled, in their original seats. I had taken a chair beside Mrs. Paterson, which left only Holmes standing and facing the two lodgers.

"Yes, I'm afraid that your wife is very much in the thick of this plot, Mr. Paterson. I suspected as much when you revealed who had access to the bureau where the order book is kept. Neither lodger could have routinely used the key from the locked cash till. And it would have been no easy matter to steal your key chain without the help of your wife."

The butcher cast Holmes a sideways glance and murmured, "I always suspected that Ronald was a little too close to Louise. He'll have put her up to this."

"On the contrary, it is Mr. Rawlings who is sweet on your wife. That much is obvious from the concerned looks they have been exchanging since we first arrived."

Paterson was clearly dumbfounded by the declaration, but did not move. His wife continued to weep. Rawlings laughed derisorily and then said, "Perhaps if you'd shown more interest in your wife and less in your precious business, she might not have fallen into my arms. I had no intention of taking her from you, but the closeness grew as we sat talking each evening, while you went back to your orders. And the long walks before bedtime gave us further time together . . . ."

Holmes cut him off. "This *closeness* has been going on for some time, hasn't it? Certainly before Mr. Moody arrived."

"I'm not ashamed to admit it. And in that time Louise has grown to despise Henworth, with his penny-pinching ways."

I was as stunned as Paterson to hear this, and then asked a question of my own. "Was it Mrs. Paterson's idea to convince her husband that he was slowly losing his mind?"

Rawlings sneered at me contemptuously. "I'm saying nothing more. If you drag the police into this, I can provide plenty of evidence that Henworth has been threatening to kill me and finally attacked me this evening. There are the written death threats, the damage to the furniture upstairs, and the bruises around my eye. Mr. Moody will confirm everything I say."

My colleague snorted. "Of course he will. I would expect nothing less from your *younger brother*." He reached inside his jacket and withdrew the magazine he had been reading earlier in the four-wheeler. Flicking through the pages, he added, "I like to keep back copies of *The Stage*, and have a keen interest in theatrical performers. Watson and I attended a less than impressive show given by 'The Great Ronaldo' some weeks back. I remembered reading something about the man in the magazine prior to that. Before coming here this evening, I located the article and looked back over it. Very instructive it was too. While he may operate professionally under the name 'Ronald Moody', the man beside you was born 'Richard Rawlings'. When I look at you together, there is no mistaking the familial similarities."

It was Moody's turn to look shocked. "It's no use, Henry. This gentleman clearly has the better of us. How he has fathomed it is beyond me, but I suspect he knows the full story. Am I right, Mr. Holmes?"

"I have a working hypothesis which I shall share with you. You may wish to correct any errors or omissions I make."

"We're all ears," retorted Rawlings with heavy sarcasm.

"The romance between Mr. Rawlings and Mrs. Paterson develops to the point where both feel they cannot continue to live under the same roof as Henworth Paterson. But having no particular money of their own, conclude that they cannot afford to move out and set up home elsewhere. Mrs. Paterson, in particular, has too much to lose, having invested all of her savings in the business. They cannot countenance the idea of murder, so set about devising a more cunning plan in which the butcher is cast in the role of villain. In short, they aim to convince the authorities that Mr. Paterson is in a fragile mental state, threatening – and actively trying to kill – Mr. Rawlings. Their objective is to see him imprisoned or removed to a criminal lunatic asylum.

"Mr. Rawlings hits upon a novel idea. His younger brother is a stage performer who routinely uses hypnotherapy as part of his act. He persuades Mrs. Paterson to convince her husband that they have a need for a second lodger. Knowing that Richard Rawlings uses the stage name 'Ronald Moody', they are convinced that Mr. Paterson will not realise the two lodgers are in fact brothers. And with 'The Great Ronaldo' on board with their scheme, they set out to persuade the busy butcher that a course of hypnotherapy will benefit his health.

"Of course their biggest setback is that fact that Mr. Paterson absolutely refuses to go along with the planned treatment, so an alternative strategy has to be devised. Knowing that he likes to partake of a large glass of Madeira each night, a strong sedative is added to Mr. Paterson's wine. It has a soporific and mesmerising effect on him, such that Mrs. Paterson and the two lodgers are able to rouse him from his bed in the early hours, walk him upstairs and place him in Mr. Rawlings's room armed with a weapon of their choice. They then bring him around and act out the charade that he has entered the room intent on harming the unfortunate lodger. To add further credence to their claim, Mr. Rawlings then begins to produce the forged death threats on headed pages torn from the butchery's order book.

"With everyone playing their part, they begin to achieve some success. And with the second of the faked incursions into Mr. Rawlings's bedroom, the plan is moved on. In short, the police are informed about Mr. Paterson's alleged threats and shown one of the forged notes, with Mr. Rawlings artfully deciding *not* to press charges at that time. It was a clever move, alerting the authorities to the fact that *something* was going on in the household, and providing early evidence that Mr. Paterson was in the thick of it."

Rawlings cleared his throat, causing my colleague to pause. "This is fanciful speculation, Mr. Holmes. Do you have proof for any of this?"

Holmes turned and pointed towards the chopping block. "Indeed. The Madeira wine has a faintly bitter taste. I will need to test it, of course, but feel certain that it contains a small quantity of laudanum. The opium alkaloids of the drug – the morphine and codeine in particular – would help to create the hypnotic effect experienced by Mr. Paterson and leave him increasingly lethargic and anxious during daylight hours. And as a reddish-brown liquid, it is easily disguised in red wine."

The bookkeeper appeared to have no response to this, so Holmes continued. "I am something of an artist myself when it comes to disguise, so recognise how illusion and deception can be achieved by altering one's appearance. While it is well done, the bruising around your eye is nothing more than stage make up, applied – I imagine – by your brother, the theatrical performer.

"But it is the order book which contains the most crucial evidence against you. I have already suggested that Mrs. Paterson must have been involved in giving you access to it. You yourself forged the notes. I am something of an expert on handwriting and will be more than willing to present to a jury a compelling case as to why I believe the note taken from your desk and the earlier death threats are forged – particularly now that I have a comparable note written in Mr. Paterson's own hand."

He withdrew from his inside pocket the note which Paterson had replicated at 221b and explained how he had obtained it. He then retrieved the note which Paterson had brought with him to Baker Street and held it up alongside the first. "You will see that the hand in each case is remarkably similar, but to the trained eye there are at least six points of distinction between the two, leading me to conclude that they have been written by two different people. This second note, which is written on one of the sheets taken from the order book, was removed from the wicker basket in your room earlier this afternoon. Of course, you would not have known that, as Mr. Paterson did not discuss the matter with you and you did not raise the issue during your evening meal. The wording differs slightly from the earlier missives as it reads '*I will kill you tonight*'. It is a subtle, yet significant, difference, because it proves that you made a mistake and sought to correct the error. Had you later presented the note to the police, it would have cast doubt on your assertion that Mr. Paterson had slipped it under your door the previous night, as you maintained he had done on each previous occasion. Realising your error, you screwed up the note and discarded it in the basket, most likely planning to empty the contents later. You then wrote out another note, this time with the correct wording."

Moody interrupted. "How do you know that?"

Holmes walked across to where Mr. Paterson sat and placed the two notes down on the chopping block. "A good question, yet one which is easily answered. You see the order sheets are numbered sequentially. The discarded note was numbered '*2571*'. I have the note which followed it." He withdrew a third sheet from the left hand pocket of his jacket and held it up for all to see. "This is the note which I took from the desk in Mr. Rawlings's room only a short while ago. If you look closely at the small number printed along the top of the sheet you will see that it reads '*2572*'."

Moody looked unconvinced and threw out a further challenge. "I still don't see the relevance. It could be suggested that Henworth wrote both notes, particularly as you have now confirmed that he was in Henry's room earlier this afternoon."

This time it was Rawlings who responded, with some agitation. "Be quiet, Richard! The whole point of the notes was to suggest that Henworth was on the verge of lunacy and writing in a confused and sleep-like state. A man in such a condition is hardly likely to start rationalising how his notes might be interpreted and correcting his wording. There's no point denying what we've done."

It was an unexpected capitulation, after which Holmes sought to conclude the synopsis. "So having set the scene, you expected to conclude your plan this evening?"

"Yes," admitted Rawlings. "Henworth was to be led to my room once he had succumbed to the sedative. We'd already used the meat cleaver to damage the furniture and I asked my brother to create the bruising on my face using his theatrical make up. The note was to provide further evidence of Henworth's intent. With the police notified and all three of us sticking to our stories, I felt certain that we couldn't fail. Until you arrived, that is."

"Then there is nothing more I need to say. This will now become a police matter."

Henworth Paterson rose from his chair and glanced across to his wife, who continued to gaze down at the table. "I feel completely betrayed, Louise, but cannot see you languish in a prison cell for what you have done. You can dress, pack your bags and leave this house tonight, alongside these two." He pointed a thick finger at the lodgers, who also refused to look up. "I will not go to the police if you do as I say, but be clear about this – I never wish to see you again."

There was no doubting the resolve of the man. Mrs. Paterson made no attempt to remonstrate with her husband. Without a word, she rose from the table and headed towards her living quarters. The two lodgers also slipped away quietly to gather their belongings. Holmes took a few steps across to the butcher and placed a comforting hand on his shoulder.

"Thank you, Mr. Holmes. And you too, Doctor. I would not have wished for any of this, but thank you for getting to the bottom of it. There is a small thread of comfort knowing that I am not going insane. Beyond that, I have little to cheer."

We continued to stay with him for the time it took Mrs. Paterson and the two lodgers to pack their bags. There were no further words at their departure as the three left unobtrusively by the back door and slipped away into the night. We followed shortly afterwards, making it back to Baker Street as the first pale streaks of the new day emerged through the dawn.

We were later to learn from Mrs. Hudson that the Whitechapel butcher had opened the shop early the next day and had continued to serve customers in his usual meticulous fashion. And as Holmes had steadfastly refused to take any fee for his involvement in the case, Mr. Paterson insisted on filling Mrs. Hudson's basket each week with only the very best steaks, chops, and sausages, all free of charge. As Holmes had stated earlier, Mr. Paterson was a genuine *knight of the cleaver*.

The Incomparable
Miss Incognita
by Thomas Fortenberry

There are some cases that I'm reluctant to ever publish – not because of official pressure, but rather due to personal feelings. Some revealed a little too much about Sherlock Holmes's private life or inner struggles. This case seemed to do all of the above. The government, Holmes, and I were all exposed to enormous trauma. I thus refused to complete these notes for many years. But the truth must out, as Holmes would chastise me, so here I report on a sordid crime that also happened to include my first meeting with a most incomparable lady.

Chapter I

A startling thunder of noise awoke me early one February morning. Shocked, I struggled upright in bed. It was a fierce knocking on the door of 221 that continued frantically. I heard movement from Holmes on the stairs and a muffled, "Oh, dear!" from poor Mrs. Hudson, as well. Gathering my wits, I rose from bed, lit a lamp, and put on my robe. It was still extremely dark outside the window and momentarily, when I lit a clock face, I was informed it was not even four-thirty in the morning.

"Good Lord!" I swore, and headed downstairs.

I heard voices from below and was met by Holmes and a young lady swathed in a royal-blue hooded cape dusted with snow coming up the stairs.

"I have taken care of it, Mrs. Hudson," Holmes shouted to our landlady, escorting our unexpected visitor into the sitting room. "It is nothing. Return to bed!"

I followed, curious to discover the nature of this emergency.

"Won't you join us, Watson?" Holmes said. "Ah, and stoke the fire and knock off the chill."

I was crossing the room when she threw back her hood and a wealth of red curls sprang forth, framing a breathtakingly beautiful young face with eyes so green they almost glowed in the twilight. I dare say I stumbled before recovering my step. She opened the front of the fur-lined cape and unclasped the top. Her dress was of very fine cut and fabric, with lines of exquisitely sewn flowers running down either side. She took her offered seat.

Holmes handed me the kettle and I placed it above the Bunsen burner on his chemical bench. He informed her, "We shall have a cup of tea to warm you, and, hopefully, calm your nerves, as I see you are very upset."

She drew a ragged breath and said, "Thank you, Mr. Holmes."

I darted a glance at Holmes, and then turned back to study her face more intently. I could see now by the growing light that she had been crying.

"I – I'm sorry," I began with a slight cough, so common this time of year, "I see to be at a loss. Your name is, Miss . . . ?"

She looked at me and then turned her gleaming emerald eyes down towards her lap. She twisted her hands, which were shaking, though I knew not whether from the cold or from something else. "Perhaps he should go – "

"No. Watson is my friend, of whom you have heard. He is safe to share this conversation."

"Thank you," I said. "So that I might understand, with whom am I speaking?"

There was a long moment of silence, and then Holmes clapped his hands. "This is . . . 'Miss Incognita'. An old friend," he added. She looked up at him, smiling in a rather grateful way.

I said, "Let me get the cups. Milk and sugar with your tea – " I hesitated, unsure – " Mademoiselle?"

She shared her luminous gaze with me and actually smiled with her eyes. "Yes, please. And it is Madame." She spoke with a bit of a Continental accent, as if she were British but had been abroad for some time and had the inflections of French and Italian, perhaps.

"Ah," I nodded. I went downstairs for milk and sugar and soon returned, setting about preparing three cups of tea, all the while furiously wracking my brains to remember if I had ever seen the young lady before or heard mention of her from Holmes. Without a doubt I had never seen her face, because it was so strikingly beautiful that one would not be able to forget it. Perhaps he had discussed her in the past? Or had she somehow been connected to one of his cases? I drew a blank, but he obviously knew her and wasn't sharing at the moment.

"Actually, though, no. No!" She suddenly stood up, her hands fluttering. "What am I doing? I must be in shock." She ran across to Holmes and grasped his hands, as if trying to pull him up from his seat. "We must leave! We must go now! We don't have time for tea and conversations!"

"Now, now – " he began.

"No!" she cried. "I know it is the middle of the night – I mean morning. But, we must go, now! She is *lying there*!"

My friend's eyes grew dark. "She is lying where? What has happened? To whom?"

This mysterious lady was growing more frantic. "I – I left her. My friend. She's in an alley. Oh, please, you said you would always help me!"

Holmes nodded. "I did, indeed. You said she is lying in an alley. In this cold? Bah. We can dispense with alcohol and even drugs, given your frantic state and having abandoned her to flee here. You would not have left her in a simple stupor after a party or at the end of a frivolous night. She is obviously unconscious and injured. However, then you could have summoned a doctor or simple help from a passerby. No, beyond injured. Perhaps . . . dead?"

The beautiful red-haired young lady stopped moving. She was still holding his hands but looked frozen, like a deer. Her eyes glazed. She even stopped breathing.

Holmes's brows furrowed and his countenance grew grim. "Then she is dead. What happened? Is this one of your . . . *employees*?"

For several minutes she seemed to hang there, frozen before him, and then she began to collapse. Her legs went out and she folded slowly towards the floor.

Holmes shot up and caught her form on the way down. He carried her over and returned her to her chair.

Crossing over to render aid, I was stunned as Holmes briskly slapped her face.

She came out of her daze with a gasp and sat up. She raised her left hand to her reddening cheek.

"You fainted, Charity," Holmes said sternly. I noted the name, but said nothing. He shook her none too gently by the shoulders. "It's going to be all right. You came to me for help. But you have to tell me what happened. I can't help you or your friend if you don't tell me. You implied time is of the essence. However, your friend is already deceased. Time no longer applies to the dead. You cannot help save her now. Do you understand? She will wait until I arrive. But I can help *you*. Now, tell me what happened in that alley!"

She nodded. "Yes. I will."

Holmes smiled again and walked over to the mantel and packed his pipe.

Seeing that she was fully back to her senses. I hurried back to the tea cups and brought her one. "Here, dear," I said. "Sip this to regain your strength. It sounds like it has been an awful night."

"Yes," she whispered. "It has." However, she only took two sips of tea before she put the cup aside on the side table. She was already steady enough that the cup and saucer didn't rattle. Whomever she truly was, I could see that this young woman had nerve.

Holmes blew a cloud of smoke up into the air and said, "Good. Fully recovered, are we? Begin. Who is the lady?"

"Ava. Ava Bowen."

"Is Ava one of yours? Was she working?"

"Yes. Well, no. She . . . ."

"She is one of yours, but wasn't working tonight?"

"Yes." The young lady took a very deep breath and held her mouth with both hands steepled.

"Then where does she work?" I interjected. "What is her occupation?"

Glad to see her speedy recovery, I still thought it best to engage in a conversation in order to give her time to fully regain her footing and have a moment to clear her head. I had been around Holmes long enough to know that he could glean a fantastic amount of details out of a casual conversation. He often used me as a foil to the guests to elicit such exchanges.

They both turned to stare at me. Then she looked at Holmes with a pained expression. "Mr. Holmes . . . ." she began.

He held up a hand. He said to me, in a rather dry voice, "Ava is a prostitute, Watson. Her Madame – her *employer* – would be this young lady seated before you. Miss Incognita, may I formally introduce you to my inquisitive companion, Dr. John Watson. Dr. Watson, Miss Incognita."

I had been in the company of Holmes long enough to be somewhat inured to his life's strange surprises. I mumbled an apology and stepped forward to shake her hand. Her grasp was surprisingly strong, yet I could still feel the coldness of the night in her fingers. "Nice to meet you, Miss Charity Incognita," I said, emphasizing her name for the benefit of Holmes.

Her eyebrows jumped and she gave me a tense smile.

He did not acknowledge what I had said. "Very well. Introductions out of the way, we can continue. Please describe Ava Bowen."

"She is eighteen. Brown hair, brown eyes. She is originally from Warwick. Been through some very difficult times with family in the past, and hence has been on her own in London for nine or so years. All in all, she is a very nice, reasonable young lady."

Holmes rubbed a finger alongside his nose. "Is Ava Bowen her real name?"

"Yes. Well, I believe so. It is the one by which I have always known her. She's been with me for almost three years now."

"Very good. Did she insist on going out tonight?"

She rubbed her hands. "Yes. Well, *he* insisted. I told her not to go out. She isn't supposed to. I – I removed her from rotation. She doesn't have to work any longer. You know my rules. I don't allow girls to work once they're – "

"Of course not," he acknowledged. "You've always been overly compassionate. But you said that he 'insisted'. To whom do you refer? Not a relative or friend, since you said she no longer has to work. But rather, one of her, to put it colloquially, *clients*?"

"Yes. He is . . . oh, I don't know! He is – he . . . ." She looked at me again.

"You can say anything in front of the doctor," Holmes said. "He has my highest confidence."

She nodded and looked pleadingly at Holmes. "I . . . don't know his name. But he's older. An older gentleman. He is . . . he is – " Her voice dropped to barely a whisper. " – an aristocrat. He has a seat in the House of Lords. I believe he is a Baron. Mr. Holmes, he's very, very rich and powerful! But, he is also exceedingly wicked!"

"Licentious."

"And cruel. I have talked to her after their encounters. I always discuss . . . matters with my girls. She told me things he . . . did. Horrible. Disgusting. I have also seen her afterwards . . . her bruises."

"Similar to the one from before? That drunkard, Randall?"

"In a way, yes. Mean like him. But, this Lord's tastes are . . . more perverse. Not just . . . mean. You can easily see how I felt. I did not approve of her continuing to see him, but he paid immense sums and she enjoyed the money. I always give them the freedom of choice and she chose to keep seeing him, despite my warnings."

Holmes steepled his hands and leaned back. We were all quiet for a while. Then he resumed. "So she continued seeing him, despite your misgivings. And thus, last night, or in your sleepless view, tonight?"

"He called on her again. I told her not to go. Ava has a certain way about her. She is stubborn, but also overly naive and kind. I told her she owed him nothing, did not have to talk with him or explain anything, since they had already ended their relationship when . . . . Well, it had been over two months since we heard from him and I hoped he was gone for good. But, he contacted her again out of the blue and asked to meet tonight, and she went with him anyway, to discuss . . . the . . . the delicate matters."

"I see. It now becomes quite clear," Holmes said. "How did you come to find her in the alley?"

"I . . . I usually don't do this, but this time I decided to follow her. They always work on their own and then meet with me at the beginning or end of their . . . *assignment* to make a report and settle the payment. No, this was different. She wasn't working. He simply sent a message that they must meet. Urgently. Something just felt . . . wrong. Do you understand what I am saying? That he came to her and wanted to discuss things now, after all these months? And that he wanted to see her again, despite the way she was, and with him being – as he was? Do you understand?"

"Yes."

"She was to meet him as they always did, in a park. I took her and then, instead of simply leaving, I waited to see the meeting."

"Did you tell her? Did she know your intentions?"

"No, not about following her. That was simply a sudden idea. I had told her several times before that she should not meet him, but she went anyway. I believe that she thought he might actually make something of their relationship."

Holmes made an exasperated sound and smoke stuttered out of his mouth almost like a chuckle.

"I know, I know. How many times have these girls heard that foolish line? Some man is going to leave his wife, or home, or job, and run away with one of these poor girls – take her off the streets and make her a respected Lady."

"The same sad line always."

"Only a few of them ever truly learn not to feel. It is hard not to start believing in someone who is giving you beautiful things and saying lovely platitudes all the time. Sometimes they are quite wonderful and the men are actually well-intentioned."

"Fools."

"Perhaps. But, it goes both ways. Occasionally the men accidentally fall in love with these girls as well. It happens."

"But, in the cold logical light of day, as with a blade at a blacksmith's forge plunged into the cooling pool, all this dross falls away."

"Usually," she agreed. She let out a sigh. "Maybe she truly believed he was going to offer something. But, a man that cruel . . . . She should have known better."

He nodded. "I couldn't have said it better."

The lady Holmes called Incognita took another drink of her tea. I saw her hand tremble, but in the firelight I couldn't tell if she were crying. "She should have known better, but it's my fault. I should have stopped her! I should have absolutely forbade her leaving tonight!"

"No, It isn't your fault. She made the choice. You aren't a slave master. You cannot lock an adult up. If she chose to leave, it is on her. She could have accidentally walked off the curb in front a wagon and been run down. You cannot blame yourself for what happened. You did warn her. Repeatedly. Plus, though she is a fool for going, the only fault lies with

59

whomever planned and committed this act. Speaking of which . . . we must return to the park. Let us focus. Why meet so late and in a park?"

"He always met her very late. Usually after midnight. Some blokes are like that. It's usually the ones who have jobs and family that keep them busy all the evening long until late at night when they can sneak away. He was one of the late-night men."

"Was he in a cabriolet or a private coach?"

"It was a right nice-sized coach. Rather fancy. Not a chaise, though. It certainly wasn't one of the small cabs we usually use to get about. I studied it as much as possible. There was some kind of crest on the door. A cloth over hung most of it, but I could see blue on the sides, with crosses, I believe."

"Excellent. Did you see him with her?"

"No. No, I didn't really see him at all, other than his arm and edge of his top hat, when she got into the carriage."

"But there was a driver?"

"Yes. Of course."

"Good. So then you followed them?"

"I – yes, eventually. They stayed there for a quite a long while, and then drove about for an hour more. Before . . . ."

"Did you ever get the impression that they knew you were following them? Or that they were trying to lose you in the city?"

"No. I followed as best I could, and I am pretty good, as you know. I can follow someone right through the entire city and they'll never know. Plus, the fog helped immensely. It's very thick tonight and they had a difficult time noticing me as I did following them."

"Good. So they stayed in the park and then on the road about for an hour and then . . . Then I presume they reached the alley that you mentioned upon arrival."

The beautiful young lady looked down. She seemed to age before my very eyes. A deep sadness fell over her. "Yes."

"They left her. But did they do anything? Was there an argument? Did they fight? Was there anything you heard or saw?"

"No. It was deadly quiet. They were actually there only a brief moment. I believe they threw her body out or dragged it into the alley. But they had stopped for a very a few minutes and then raced away. I saw them moving something in the fog, so I went in to see. I found her there. She was – "

Her voice broke and she sobbed.

I rose and handed her my handkerchief.

"She was . . . ?" Holmes prompted.

"She was already dead. She had been stabbed. I tried to see if there were any way to revive her, but, oh! Too late! It was horrible! He cut her up in terrible ways! It reminded me . . . it was like the time before, in Whitechapel. Oh, please! You must go! I can't bear the thought of her lying out on the ground in that alley any longer! In the snow! Oh, God!"

"You are quite correct. We will go as soon as Dr. Watson and I dress. But first, what of you, my dear? Are you willing to accompany us?"

She sat in silence for so long I thought that perhaps she had fainted again. I stepped over beside her chair and knelt down.

She passed my handkerchief back to me. "Thank you, Doctor."

"You are most welcome."

"I cannot. I must not be seen there . . . or identified. If I accompany you, the police will see me and want to question me. If they question me, then I'll be in for it. I would be interrogated about everything. I cannot. I'm sorry. It's why I raced here for your help. You can help without involving me."

"Quite so. You are absolutely correct. We shall leave you out of it. Hmm, Watson, please look upstairs and find the Venetian masks – the ones that I obtained from the carnival. Bring them and get dressed. We must go immediately to the scene of this poor girl's murder."

I did as I was instructed. One may wonder, as do I sometimes, why I put up with such abrupt demands. Holmes is eccentric, more so than anyone I've ever met. However, he is possessed of such a sharp intellect that often I have found myself utterly confused by his actions at first, only to later be shown the shortcomings of my failings in the full light of his explanation. He always has a reason, and I have grown to trust his instincts without question.

When I returned, fully dressed and carrying four masks from *Carneval de Venexia*, I found Holmes also ready and in conversation with our visitor.

Holmes stood and clapped his hands. "Ah! Here we are. Excelsior, Watson! These are just what I need." He took the four masks and shuffled through them. Withholding one, he handed the other three back to me. "Those stay."

He turned back to our guest on the settee and handed her the elaborately painted mask he held. "I want you to wear this when you leave. It's just a precaution. No one will know who was here, or that it was you. Your identity will be protected. Actually, from now on, you should wear it when you conduct business with such evil men as the cruel, murdering man we now hunt. They will never know with whom they are doing business and you will be safe. You will be a Madame X to these men."

She nodded and held up the mask to her face. The effect was quite dramatic. It was surreal and ethereal to behold the transformation of the lady before me. She was truly faceless now, but in an even more coldly beautiful way granted by the artistic mask. After a moment of gazing at Holmes, she turned her back to him. He tied the mask in place.

"Incognita," I blurted, somewhat in awe. She looked my way, and I was somewhat embarrassed as I realized I had spoken aloud, but I cannot say if she smiled. Attempting to cover myself, I stepped over and took her hand. "Miss Incognita, indeed. A pleasure to have met you, ma'am."

"Doctor," she said demurely, her voice somewhat muffled by the mask.

Holmes stood. "If you need anything, contact me in the usual way. If for some reason you are in danger, come immediately as you did tonight."

"I will. And again, thank you! Ava did not deserve this."

"No one deserves to have their life taken, except those criminals which have eternal justice coming to them."

She rose and Holmes helped her don the blue cape. She drew up her hood and proceeded to leave our apartments.

A mere breath afterwards, he said, "Not now, Watson. Are you ready? I have the address. Let us make haste. We have a murderer to catch."

Chapter II

This was a terrible, brutal morning. I had bundled myself appropriately, but it was still bitterly cold. Snowy and fog-bound, the situation was compounded by a bilious yellow fog due to the city burning coal to keep houses and businesses warm. I had to keep my scarf around my nose and mouth to keep from coughing. I wished I were back in the cab – or better yet, at home and settled by the fire with a warm cup, rather than in that cruel alley.

The police were already on the scene by the time we arrived. A passerby had discovered the body during Miss Incognita's absence and alerted them. They knew Holmes and let us inspect the corpse. The police were quite happy that I was a medical doctor, because there was a lot of damage to the young lady.

One of the more crude patrolmen said, "Welcome to Hell, Doctor. Looks like another terrible night we've had."

Ava Bowen was as Miss Incognita had described her. She had been stabbed repeatedly and had several slashing cuts as well across her throat and face. I made an examination of her cold, white body. She had been stabbed in the heart, which had probably been the killing blow, as well as into the lungs. Most disturbing of all, she had been stabbed in the belly numerous times.

Holmes crouched beside me, his face more grim and severe than any time I had seen it. "This poor creature. So what do you estimate, Watson? Four months along?"

"Over five. You can see the skin darkening in this line. The stretching of the skin, these scars on her sides. The size of the bulge."

"I see. And these stabs wounds, all angled inward, almost in a circle around the stomach. They seem intentionally aimed at the baby."

"My surmise as well – trying to make sure it would not accidentally survive. But notice the cuts. The blood."

"Or lack thereof."

"Exactly. They all occurred after death. The heart blow was catastrophic, from the amount of blood on her clothes. But not these – look inside the lacerations. Organs all intact. Little blood loss. And even wounds upon the face and neck were all made after death." I reached up and showed him her neck. "For instance, this cut to the throat – I believe that she was strangled first."

"Very well. So we have someone who kills and then hacks. The body blows are largely cosmetic. Perhaps to look like the savagery of the Ripper, but it obviously is not. Everything is wrong, including the lack of finesse and intact organs. The stabbing into the belly, however, was intentional. It was specifically to kill that baby."

"Yes."

He stood up and stared down at the body a while. I began covering up her corpse once more. "Watson."

"Yes?"

"Look at the surrounding snow and cobblestones as well, and the lack of bloodstains."

"Yes, I saw."

"The body was dumped here. Everything points to that coach as the murder scene. She was long dead, perhaps as far back as the park. I presume that she was killed soon after she joined the murderer, and then he went about staging the rest to try to throw off the trail. Perhaps the final hour was merely the cosmetic savagery and searching for a suitable dumping ground – a nightmare drive through the city."

I nodded. "As implied by our mystery lady's story. But you don't question her involvement – "

He shook his head and turned away and walked briskly over to the inspector in charge of the scene. They spoke for some time, and then they both spoke to the small man who had discovered the girl.

I watched the yellow wisps curling like smoke over and around the body. This fog lent a hellish and unnerving aspect to the scene, probably due to the color more than anything else, I kept imagining that I could smell sulfur. I was reminded of Milton's descriptions of hell, with the cold heat of hellish fires that gave off darkness instead of light. It was more that the cold that was giving me goosebumps.

It was such a waste – a young life snuffed out. I had grown somewhat hardened, being used to viewing murder victims, but this one was rather harder to take. The utter savagery, plus the fact that she was so young and with child. It was an utterly godless act, and so heartbreaking to see a young mother to be treated this way, lying in a dirty alley, her brutalized body as cold as the winter night.

When Holmes returned and motioned for us to leave, I was more than ready.

Once inside our hansom, I lay my head back and squeezed my eyes tightly shut. I didn't want to talk or even think. Thankfully, Holmes held his tongue and we made our way home in silence.

But I found myself growing nauseous during the swaying ride. All I could see was her body, and I kept thinking of the silent coach ride, of the vicious beast who stabbed her over and over, even after death.

Chapter III

I awoke in the middle of the afternoon. I hardly remembered arriving home after that hellish night. Mrs. Hudson put on some tea and informed me that Holmes had been gone since shortly after we arrived back home at t dawn.

"Who was the visitor in the middle of the night? Mr. Holmes refused to answer me this morning. I assume it is about this case. Why else would you race out in the middle of the night?"

"Yes. It was just that.. Unfortunately, a young woman was murdered. It was . . . most ghastly. That, and the lack of sleep, put me off, I suppose. I appreciate Holmes helping me to bed."

Mrs. Hudson gasped and held her hand to her throat. Unconscious on her part, it was an unpleasant reminder of the young victim. "Oh, dear. I would imagine so. Let me make you a bite to eat."

I drank tea and read for the remainder of the afternoon. It was almost dinner time when Holmes finally returned.

"Ah, Watson, you have arisen! Feeling better, I presume?"

"Yes, quite. Thank you."

He rubbed his hands together and went over to his desk. Picking up his pipe, he lit it as he sat down. He then wrote out letter.

Curious, I finally inquired, "So, how did you spend the day, Holmes? Was it looking into the tragedy of last night?"

"Indeed." He puffed and continued writing.

"Did you make any headway?"

He whirled about in his chair. "I did. I first made sure that the dead girl's rooms were searched – dreadful dump that they are. As you know, it is vital to be first on the scene. The undisturbed tableau provides the clearest picture. I had hoped that Miss Incognita would arrive before anyone else might search the place or, worse, if news spread and neighbors decided to loot it for trinkets."

"Oh, dear Lord!" I cried. "You told her to do that? Are you mad? That was exceedingly foolhardy."

"Perhaps. But worth the risk."

"The risk to her life?"

"Yes. When we went to the murder alley, she went to the victim's apartment. We arranged it while you were upstairs retrieving the masks. She is an amazingly capable young lady and knows how to take a risk. She did so willingly. Miss Incognita has remarkable talents. She is a polymath. Multilingual. A skilled dancer, singer, actor, and artist – actually a gifted architect if you will. I have known her for years, as have many in government. She often worked for the state itself. Even my brother has made use of her services. In fact, she even enjoys the favor or the Queen herself."

"Good Lord!" I said. I raised my cup and then put it back down without drinking. I wasn't sure what to think, but it did make more sense to me. Pieces were clicking together. "No wonder you already knew her and deferred to her. You mention the government and your brother. Is she . . . a *spy*?"

"Something of the sort. She is, in fact, her own unique self. A free agent, you might say. No one is quite like her."

"But she is so young."

Holmes laughed. "Well, to be rude, she is older than you think. However, to your point: Yes, she is still young, and has simply lived twice as much in her few years as most people have in a lifetime."

"Yet you said she is a madame of prostitutes."

"Indeed. She is that as well. A lady with her own empire – yet one built of the lowest sort of ladies."

"And still you cannot reveal her true name to me. We must use that infernal sobriquet, *Miss Incognita*?"

"Indeed. I could not tell you, even if I actually knew." His eyes twinkled. "Alas, she was interrupted before she could complete her search."

"Did she find anything of value?"

"Yes, she discovered two things of great import."

"They are?"

"Ava Bowen's diary and a locket."

"Then we have them! Perhaps some clues – "

"No, not quite."

"I don't follow."

"The first is now missing. Her diary. It's gone."

"How? If Miss Incognita found it – "

"She did, but not long after her own arrival and discovery of the diary, the man that she recognized as the father of Ava's baby arrived to search the apartments as well. Apparently he was seeking to ensure no clues of his presence remained. Miss Incognita barely managed to find escape via the window. The poor thing crouched outside in the frozen darkness. She had to abandon the book in the drawer even as she had barely discovered it. Unfortunately, the man and his driver ransacked the place thoroughly. They removed the diary, along with other articles of clothing and what-not – presumably all gifts he had given."

"This is a tragic blow! They have removed all evidence. Ah, well, you say she at least went undiscovered and escaped, since she told you this tale?"

"Exactly! Plus, all of evidence was not lost. She still clutched the locket that she had secured from the room. I daresay, if not for the blessed arrival of civil twilight, we might have lost everything this morning. In their frantic haste to escape the dawn, the man and his man failed to search as thoroughly as they might, and hence did not catch Miss Incognita outside the window. Furthermore, she was able to see them clearly and – much more to our interest – follow them!"

"Follow them? Is she mad? The man had just butchered that poor girl!"

"Indeed. Which is why it was imperative that she learn who they were. I had told Miss Incognita to follow them if the chance presented itself. We had to establish his identity. We couldn't allow such a vicious beast to escape justice."

"Then we know?"

"Yes. We now know."

"Who?"

"Ah!" He clucked his tongue and wagged a finger at me. "You will have to be patient. We must not disparage a Right Honourable Lord of the House of the Lords Spiritual and Temporal of the United Kingdom, without proper evidence and a confession."

66

I sat for some time digesting things. He finished his letter.

Eventually I looked at Holmes sourly. "But we know who he is. She followed him. Why are we waiting?"

"Sadly, for my brother."

"Why sadly, Sherlock?" a voice came from the door. "In dire times, one needs the mighty hand of government to weigh upon the scales."

I turned to observe the massive figure of Mycroft Holmes filling the doorway.

"Perfectly timed, dear brother," Sherlock Holmes said. He held up the note that he had written and from his hands dangled a glittering chain ending in a golden locket. "Here is the missive and the locket."

Chapter IV

Though caught literally red-handed, the sordid affair was not over so easily. The power of nobility goes a long way.

Apparently, when confronted by the police and Mycroft Holmes at his manor, Lord ----- was in the presence of his dead driver. The man was found hanging from the rafters above the coaches. Lord ----- explained that yes, he had indeed learned of an adulterous affair with a prostitute, who had unfortunately become pregnant, and that the embarrassed, disturbed, and fearful driver who had been conducting the illicit affair acted unconscionably when pressured to leave his wife and marry said prostitute. He had apparently gone out that night, using the coach without permission, and killed the girl. Then, unable to bear his grief, he had confessed his guilt to the Lord upon his return. The Lord had naturally been horrified by the revelation, had terminated the man's employment on the spot, and had told him to gather his things while he notified the police. Then, before any other action could be taken by the Lord, the man had committed suicide.

Upon searching, the police found that the seats in the coach had been removed and that original blood-stained seat fabrics had been apparently burned behind the stables. The fire was mostly ashes, but still smoldering when the police discovered it. Lord ----- explained that this fire was what had prompted his encounter with the driver, leading to the driver's confession. The girl's diary was never recovered, and Lord ----- said he had no knowledge of it, or the girl, or the details of the affair.

Holmes had anticipated something like this. He surmised Lord ----- had burned the diary along with the fabrics and killed the only eyewitness to his crimes, the driver. Or so the Lord thought. There was in fact one last eyewitness: Miss Incognita.

In order to protect her identity and involvement, Holmes simply took her place. The letter he had handed Mycroft outlined a fictitious account of how Miss Ava Bowen, the prostitute victim, had originally approached Holmes with the account of her affair with a powerful politician and the resulting pregnancy. She had feared the worst and conceived that he might in fact view her baby as a potential threat and thus attempt to kill her. So, as proof, she gave to Holmes a locket that had a picture of the Lord in it and was engraved, "*To my love.*" She told him the full story was recounted in her private diary.

Holmes claimed to have taken to shadowing the girl had seen him rendezvous with the Lord. On the final, fateful meeting in the park, he had simply been unable to prevent the killing, but had followed the Lord afterward, first to the dumping of the body in the alleyway – which is how he knew where it was later – and then back to the apartment, where she had watched from the window and had seen the Lord and driver take the property of Miss Ava Bowen, including both clothing and the diary.

When confronted with this letter of revelation, after several arguments of denial, the Lord had eventually admitted his guilt. Then, asking for a moment to gather his thoughts, he had entered his study and committed suicide by shooting himself in the head with a gun from his collection.

The government, being the government, stepped in and, with the sturdy broom of Mycroft Holmes, swept up the mess.

As one might surmise from the newspaper accounts of the time, the story became this: The honorable Lord, bravely confronting his driver who had been involved in a duplicitous illicit affair, was unfortunately shot by his employee, a madman who then hung himself in the stable.

Weeks later, late one night, there was a knock upon the door. I answered it, as Mrs. Hudson was asleep and Holmes was out prowling the city, as was his wont at various times.

A cloaked Miss Incognita, complete with her elaborately painted Venetian Carnival mask, was at the door. She asked for Holmes, and I explained his absence. When offered, she refused entry. She then passed me a copy of a book. I turned the spine into the light. It was a copy of *The Letters of Abelard and Heloise*.

"This is a gift for Mr. Holmes," she explained. "Please give it to him."

I assured her that I would.

She turned to leave. Looking back at me, she added, "Thank you both again for everything. I truly appreciate what you did. I did not want poor Ava to have died in vain . . . or that beast to get away with it."

"He didn't. But thank you as well. Without you . . . I fear he would have escaped justice," I said honestly.

She nodded. "Thank you, Dr. Watson. We all did what was needed to help her."

I agreed. "Miss Incognita?"

"Yes, Doctor?"

"I apologize for being forward. However, I must know your name. I dislike using this Latin substitution. Whatever shall I call you?"

She laughed and it was one of the most delightful sounds I've ever heard. It was spontaneous and bubbling, cascading with merry excitement, like a waterfall in Scotland. "Oh, Dr. Watson! You know I cannot do that. Just . . . ." She reached out and took my hand. "Call me whatever you wish. Any name you desire. That is my name."

That night was not the last time I saw Miss Incognita, but it was the first time I actually knew who she was.

The Adventure of the Twofold Purpose
by Robert Perret

Criminals don't keep regular hours, and neither do patients, so I was long accustomed to being roused from my repose at all hours. Yet that insistent knocking upon the door of 221b Baker Street, just as I had lost myself in one of Stevenson's novels, was nonetheless vexing. Holmes, of course, took no notice of it, so absorbed was he in pinning some rare specimens of African beetle to his felt entomological board. They were splendid beasts, and yet it was impossible that my friend was truly oblivious to the racket down below.

"It seems someone wishes to speak with you, Holmes."

"Mrs. Hudson will soon greet our caller."

"If she is forced to rise from bed and dress simply to open the door, there will be an earful for each of us tomorrow."

"I am in the midst of a delicate maneuver," Holmes sighed. "You are certainly welcome to make the trip down the stairs and back again."

"It's just that I've had a tipple of brandy, you see," I began just as the debate became moot. Mrs. Hudson's door slammed open at the bottom of the stairs, and an icy reception was offered to the poor soul outdoors. A few moments later Inspector Gregson shuffled up the steps, stooping like a chastised pup.

"Sorry to bother you at this hour, gentlemen," Greson began.

"Think nothing of it," Holmes replied, turning away from his workbench with a jeweler's loupe still resting in his eye. "We do not keep the same hours as dear old Mrs. Hudson."

"Or rather, Holmes, she does not keep the same hours as you," I replied.

"What brings you here on this fine autumn evening, Inspector?" Holmes asked.

"A bit of an unusual case, as you might expect," Gregson said, sitting heavily upon the sofa. "A bit sensational. We'd like to get a handle on it before the newspapers muddy it all up."

"The press has already caught wind of it?" Holmes asked.

"Not that I know of, but this kind of thing always finds its way onto newsprint."

"If the opportunity yet remains, I should prefer to see the scene before any journalists have arrived," Holmes said. "They always insist on making

70

such tawdry sketches of me as I conduct my investigations. Of course, the newspaper artists are well-practiced in creating scenes from whole cloth, but at least I shan't be distracted by serving as a live model. I take it you have a carriage waiting?"

"Why, yes, Mr. Holmes," Gregson said with palpable relief.

"Bundle up, Watson," Holmes said. "A cold wind blows this evening."

"You have the inspector with you, and I'm rather in for the night already," I said.

"Tut, you've had your feet up all day, Watson. A little sport will be good for your constitution."

I cast a longing glance upon my novel as I placed it on the side table and retired to my room to bundle up. It was a night when I felt a gentleman would be well served by a muffler around his collar and a Webley in his pocket. When I returned, Holmes was already at the front door calling for me to hurry along. It was a short ride to Bushy Park and a good thing too, for Gregson refused to comment on the case along the way. As we entered the park, I noticed policemen standing just off the road at regular interviews.

"Is the road blocked off?" I asked.

"Not as such," Gregson said. "We don't want to draw attention to the situation. And besides, they're more on foot in here than in a carriage, so a barricade wouldn't do much. We decided to cast a net rather than build a wall. Anyone who wanders by is being redirected out of the area. We're telling them there are convicts on litter brigade further along."

"What is actually further along?" I asked.

"See for yourself," Gregson said as the carriage came to a halt.

We alit. The surrounding park was lost in the deep dusk. Directly ahead, three lanterns were placed facing inwards, giving the patch of land in between a shadowless, otherworldly feel. Gregson gestured and Holmes moved forward, examining the ground.

"Judging by the battalion-worth of footprints, this is clearly the mushroom that elicited so much interest," Holmes said.

"That is the one that started it all, yes," Gregson said.

On tiptoes, Holmes stalked closer. "Ah, yes, I see."

"There was a group of boys with snares and sticks. You can take a couple of rabbits easy and a pheasant or two with a little luck. It's not precisely legal, but nobody is spending any time enforcing poaching laws out here. Plenty for all."

"They didn't take it with them?" Holmes asked. "I would have when I was a boy."

"Of course not! Although I understand they did pick it up before they knew what it was."

"That is unfortunate," Holmes murmured.

"The others are intact," Gregson said.

"The others!" Holmes said, practically skipping to the next mushroom. "Ah!" With the toe of his boot he gently nudged each fungus he came across before letting out a sound of satisfaction.

"What is all of this?" I asked.

"A fairy ring," Gregson said.

"I can see that it is a fairy ring," I replied. "Common cloud funnels. I don't see what all the fuss is about."

"Walk directly to this one," Holmes instructed, indicating the first mushroom he had examined. "You can't do any more damage to the ground there than has already been done."

Somewhat irrationally I paused at the edge for a moment, fearing the curse that would fall upon anyone who broke the sanctity of a fairy circle – nursery rhyme knowledge well known to every child in Britain. I could hear Holmes snort, but I noted that Gregson made no move to cross the circle. Chiding myself, I stepped in and knelt by the fungus. On the far side lay a delicate skeletonized hand, the radius and ulna terminating sharply, as if the hand had been severed with a blade. More bones lay all around.

"There is a piece of this mortal puzzle under every large growth," Holmes said.

"Someone scattered a dismembered skeleton around a fairy ring?" I asked.

"Perhaps," Holmes said. "Or perhaps the fungus colony grew up through a buried body. Was this ever a cemetery?"

"We won't have access to that kind of record until the morning," Gregson says. "But the bones look fresh. Too fresh for an ancient burial anyway."

"Watson, do you concur?"

"It is difficult to date exposed bones precisely, but I would tentatively agree that these are modern remains, and I don't think they were ever properly buried."

"I'd like to take a few samples if you don't mind, Gregson. I suspect the place will soon be picked clean by morbid gawkers if you don't move the remains. I'd take the mushrooms as well, just in case they contributed to this death. They should be edible, but a corpse is always a cause for caution." With that, Holmes gathered a morbid curio sack of phalanges, teeth, and hair. He topped it off with a couple of mushrooms and a vial of dirt.

"Clean it all up, then?" Gregson asked.

"Document it twice, then gather it all together and lock it up," Holmes advised. "And send the policemen home so that no one can be sure exactly where the ring was. I'll contact you with my findings soon."

"Very good," Gregson said. "The carriage can take you back to Baker Street."

When we settled inside, Holmes turned to me. "This may be more in your line than mine, Watson." Then he called up to the driver, "To St. Barts!"

"Surely it was a gruesome flight of fancy to imagine that the body was torn asunder by villainous fungi," I said.

"I find it remarkable that such things don't happen more often," Holmes replied. "A decaying body is such rich fertilizer. In the ancient caliphates surrounding the Egyptian kingdoms, legend says that squatters would sometime be shackled to saplings and then fed and nurtured until being disjointed as the tree grew. A gruesome form of execution that would sometimes take years."

"Surely not," I objected.

"Don't give Mrs. Hudson any ideas, just in case," Holmes laughed.

We soon arrived at my old hospital and Holmes led the way to the pathology lab, as sure as if he were the superintendent. The place was empty this time of night but, of course, my friend had his own keys. With his help, we made quick work of examining the specimens Holmes had collected. "A lady it would seem," I concluded, "with a diet high in sugars and acids. She drank purified water. Her flesh did not rot away – these bones were cleaned. A body snatcher perhaps?"

"It is not beyond the realm of possibility," Holmes said. "There is yet a macabre trade in human remains for the amateur physiologist."

"Or worse," I spat.

"See what you make of the mushrooms," Holmes said.

"As an accomplished naturalist, you have me there."

"Just look," Holmes said, indicating a slide he had prepared resting under a microscope.

"It is pitted," I observed.

"Only in this cross-section. Hold one up to the light and you will find it is perforated with tiny passages."

Indeed tiny pinpricks of light shown through all over the fungus.

"Bacterial mycophagy," Holmes pronounced.

"Which developed intro *necrotizing fasciitis*?" I scoffed. "I've never heard of such a thing."

"Rather the other way round, I imagine. The bacteria ran out of flesh and made a go of it with the meat of the mushroom." Holmes said.

"Have we been exposed then?" I didn't fancy the chemical bath that awaited me.

"We will keep an eye on this sample, but it looks to me as if the bacteria were starved to death."

"Simple misadventure then?"

"I don't see that she wore any clothes, or indeed had any belongings. Unlikely in someone with such healthy teeth, and certainly unusual in a public park, so I expect there is another party involved in some capacity. Of course, the severed hand is also suggestive."

"Where can we even begin? Our only witness is an infested mushroom."

"Perhaps," said Holmes. "Perhaps not. I know of an *outré* art gallery where we can find what we need to know."

"At this time of night?"

"My dear Watson, the dead of night is the only time this gallery is open."

It didn't make much sense to me, but the clock had already struck that dreadful predawn hour when I knew the night's slumber had escaped me, and so I followed my friend back out onto the street. I had expected that we would take a carriage to the East End and so was surprised when Holmes started threading the alleys leading north. We quickly found ourselves in unfamiliar and unseemly territory, with the footfalls of unseen persons seeming to dog us and a disconcerting racket coming from every darkened door. I was just about to pull at Holmes's sleeve and demand that we return to the streets of *our* London when he suddenly sprinted up some steps and threw open the door of what smelled like an opium den. Only my rational desire not to be left alone on these forbidding streets compelled me to enter, my hand resting on the grip of my Webley.

Inside was something like a sitting room but with black lace hanging down from the ceiling over each piece of furniture like mosquito netting. Within each cocoon lulled some dope fiend nodding his or her head to the strange music being picked out on a stringed instrument I didn't recognize. Around the room were paintings with images akin to tarot cards, but as if designed by the Grimm Brothers, all cragged trees and blood red moons. Squires slaughtering strange beasts or sometimes the opposite and, of course, there were pale maidens cavorting in the moonlight. I am a worldly man, but it was all a bit too French for my tastes. I wondered exactly why Holmes might be so familiar with this so-called gallery. My friend was at the stairs in a heated debate with a woman who appeared to be the madame of this establishment.

"Absolutely no," she declared, her arm barring Holmes's way.

"I must insist," Holmes said. "Show him my card. Monsieur DeValet will see me."

"It is impossible," the woman said. "He is working and not to be disturbed."

"Mademoiselle, DeValet can speak to me now or speak to the Yard in the morning."

"You have no right," she protested.

"Perhaps we should come back later, Holmes," I intervened.

Holmes sighed. "Perhaps you are right, Watson. *Bon Nuit*," he tipped his hat to the woman.

"Now you see sense," she said, taking each of us by the elbow and moving us to the door. It seemed we weren't the first visitors she had put back out on the streets.

"Perhaps we might make an appointment," I offered, and as the lady considered this Holmes spun away from her, flying up the stairs before she could yelp. It was my turn now to take her elbow while Holmes quickly raked the lock and flung the door open. The madam had pushed me away and I found myself taking two stairs at a time to try and catch her. Together we burst into the room at the top of the flight and found a man sprawled on the floor with a nearly empty bottle of absinthe in his grasp.

"Oh, Henri, no!" the woman cried, rushing to cradle the man's head in her hands.

"He should vomit before that vile liqueur does him in," Holmes observed.

I fetched a chipped washing bowl from the bureau and handed it to the woman. "Why, Henri, why?" She pulled him forward so he was slumped over the bowl which she placed in his lap. DeValet was unresponsive to her entreaties.

Holmes stepped forward and tossed a snippet of the victim's hair into the bowl. DeValet tossed the bowl away as if it had scalded him and curled up in a ball.

"Give me a name, DeValet," Holmes whispered.

"Mug Ruith," DeValet wheezed.

"The lady's name was Mug Ruith?" I asked.

"Mug Ruith was a powerful druid," the madame interjected. "DeValet has been painting the *roth rámach*."

"Irish folktales," Holmes interjected. "Mythological nonsense."

"I wish that were so, Mr. Holmes," DeValet said, seemingly recovering from his momentary terror. "I am afraid that I have angered the ancient masters with my foolishness."

"How so?" Holmes asked.

"I have painted all the great mythologies, Norse, Egyptian, Mycenaean, Roman, Greek," De Valet said.

"I am familiar with your previous handiwork," Holmes said.

"Until recently I would have agreed with you that it is all nonsense. The Pythagorean Mysteries become a fad one season, and are replaced by the fire dances of the Zoroastrians and so on and so forth, and as my patrons chase the latest philosophy, I provide the paintings that give the whole affair a certain dignity."

Holmes made a non-committal sound.

"But there is something to this Cycle of Kings, Mr. Holmes. Something like I have never experienced before. It is real – the visions are not just hallucinations. You hold the proof in your hands."

"I hold the remains of a woman who died playing your parlor games," Holmes said. "Supply me with a name, or I have the Yard turning this place over by breakfast."

"We were told her name was Bella," the madame interjected.

"She was not a regular of this establishment?" Holmes asked.

"She was just a model," the madame said. "Most of the young ladies are. This hocus pocus is mostly the domain of wool-headed old men and a few silly ladies. It's an excuse, you know, to obtain these boudoir images, to spend a little time with ladies dressed up like fairies or what have you. Play-acting is what it is."

"Pardon me, Madame . . . ?"

"Vivienne Corbeau," she replied. "Yes, it is a horribly false name. Unlike Henri, I have a regular life to live during the day."

"Yes, well, there are any number of establishments in London that provide, ahem, 'play-acting'. I don't quite understand this arrangement."

"That's just it, Mr. . . . ?"

"Er, Watson," I stammer. "Dr. Watson."

"Of course, who else would be at Mr. Holmes's side. I quite enjoy your stories."

I felt a flush escape my collar.

"The salon, the companionship, all of that is part of an experience that ultimately surrounds the art, and Henri's art is quite splendid. Someday he will be considered a major painter of our age, but for the moment he must toil among the throngs of grasping London artists. We have created an environment that has an element of the salacious without ever being scandalous. None of our patrons need fear being caught out here, but at the same time it is just indecorous enough that there is a thrill to it."

"May we see the paintings for which she modeled?" Holmes asked.

"There was only one, and the patron was quick to pick it up. He was gone before Bella came back, even."

"Bella came back after she was painted but before her death?" I asked.

DeValet sobbed. "Cursed she was!"

"She'd taken ill all of a sudden," Corbeau said. "Deadly ill as it turns out. She'd wanted the costume she had worn."

"Costume?" Holmes asked.

"She dressed up as Tlachtga, the daughter of Mug Ruith. Wore a bull skin robe and feathers, the traditional ceremonial dress for the festival of the Hill of Ward."

"She thought the costume was the cause of her illness?" Holmes suggested. "Did you give it to her?"

"Would that I could have, the poor thing," Corbeau said. "The outfit had been provided by the patron, and he had taken it with him again."

"None of this matters," DeValet spat. "The whole thing was brand new. A more perfect bull skin I have never seen."

"And the feathers?" I asked.

"Pristine, straight from the peacock, I'd imagine. It was Mug Ruith punishing us for our sacrilege!"

"That's as may be," Holmes continued, "but I will need to speak to this patron."

DeValet and Corbeau shared a quick look.

"We don't know who he is precisely," Corbeau said. "Part of what our patrons pay for is discretion, and that takes care of itself if we don't ask too many questions. We do recognize some of them of course, but not in this case."

"DeValet, you will provide a sketch of the man," Holmes commanded.

"I never saw his true face," DeValet said.

"I can do it," Corbeau said. "I am nothing compared to DeValet, but I had some tutelage in the arts as a girl." She set about making a charcoal sketch.

"Fine, then. DeValet, you shall provide a sketch of your painting, with every detail accounted for."

"I had the ghoulish things destroyed after Bella's horrible end. Oh the agony. It was a terrible thing to see."

"I can provide the sketches as well," Corbeau interrupted. "I keep the ones DeValet discards. As I say, he will be a great name someday, and someday I will be in want of a comfortable retirement."

"Most accommodating, Madame Corbeau," Holmes said.

"Meet me down in the parlor," she replied.

"And you will be here if I have further questions, DeValet?" Holmes asked pointedly.

"If there is any mercy, death will have taken me first," the artist spat back.

A few moments later Corbeau joined us in the parlor and presented us with a couple of loose sketches. The first few were rough figures crudely blocked in.

"Not much to go on, I'm afraid," she said.

"So long as he laid out all of the essential details, these shall suffice," Holmes said.

Last in the bunch was a striking charcoal portrait, so remarkable that there was a spark of life to it.

"Why, Madame Corbeau, is this your work?" I asked. "If you ask me, this is the superior of DeValet."

"Henri is a genius," she replied. "I am but a dilettante."

"You should be making your own fortune, if you ask me," I added.

"Good evening, gentlemen," she ushered us back out.

"Was I mistaken, Holmes, or did that drunken boor just admit to being present at this young woman's death. I'd have put bracelets on him right then."

"Madame Corbeau was being so helpful, and I didn't want to interfere with her. We shall visit Gregson on the way home and advise DeValet's arrest. That will serve the twofold purpose of giving the artist a place to sober up and keep the good inspector out of our way for a while longer."

As always, behind a thin veneer of bullishness, Gregson was quite happy to receive any intelligence that Holmes could provide. Because the street addresses in the warren we had just left were casual, to say the least, Holmes put a pin in the station's map to demonstrate DeValet's location.

"You are certain he killed the girl?" Gregson asked.

"I am certain he was present at the event, and he clearly feels much remorse," Holmes said. "DeValet is easily a party to the lady's death, but exactly what part he played I leave to you to discover."

"You've done well on this one, Mr. Holmes. If this pans out, I'll stand a round tonight, gents. Even you are invited, Lestrade," he called over his shoulder to his rival and our sometimes collaborator. Lestrade responded with a knowing smirk. Each of the policemen could see Holmes's games when they were being played upon the other. I tipped my hat to the other inspector as we left.

I fell straight into bed when we, at last, surmounted the stairs of Baker Street, without so much as removing my shoes. When I awoke, the white tendrils of dawn had been replaced by the red cheeriness of afternoon. I entered the parlor to find Holmes barricaded behind stacks of books – dream analysis and pagan rituals and all sorts of things that Holmes didn't usually go in for. I idly looked about on the shelves to discover what dusty corner of his collection these tomes might hail from, without success.

"Ah, Doctor Watson," came Mrs. Hudson's chiding voice. "I was a bit disappointed that you left it to me to open the door to every strangler and masher in London last night. Then again, you look as if you have joined their ranks."

Unthinkingly, I felt the stubble at my jawline and looked sheepishly down at the clothes in which I had slept.

"I was just getting up to answer the knock when you beat me to it," I replied. "In a contest of the spriest, I do not fancy my chances against you."

She clucked but lay the tray she was carrying down upon the table. Removing the cloiche revealed a desultory meat sandwich and some cold tea.

"Ta," I sighed.

"The first time I brought this tray up it was a feast. You slept through that and the next two as well. I may provide a light board but I'm not your cook." With that, she spun on her heel and exited.

"Back at it already, Holmes?" I asked as I poked at the rainbow sheen on the meat.

"Steady on since last night," he replied.

"You need to sleep."

"In this case, a little deprivation may serve us well," Holmes said. "What little we know about the patron is encoded in these sketches. Symbols and archetypes, that sort of thing."

"And the excellent portrait Madame Corbeau rendered."

"The lady is a true talent, but this city is home to millions. Even our friends at the Yard don't just wander around with a sketch in hand hoping someone recognizes it."

"Attempting to identify someone with a few token scraps from their memories seems just as hopeless."

"Perhaps. The subject of Tlachtga itself is suggestive. She was ill-used by the three sons of Simon Magus and died from grief after giving birth to three boys, one by each of her assailants."

"Ghastly!" I cried.

"The followers of Simon Magus held a different, distinctly unmodern ethos. So, was the patron perhaps casting Miss Bella in the role of mother, perhaps even unwilling mother?"

"Why go through the rigmarole of DeValet's studio?"

"Because the mythology is important to him. He wants to embody that archetype. For the moment I am also presuming he is Irish."

"Pre-Celtic religion just happens to be DeValet's current subject. That may not mean anything."

"The patron came ready with his own costume – with his own costumes, if I don't miss my guess. An immaculate bull skin as described is likely a specialty item. That is one place to begin. All the better if one could purchase a peacock mask at the same establishment."

"I'm surprised you didn't leave that plodding work for Gregson," I said.

"Normally I would, but in this instance, I think a little more diplomacy is required than the inspector finds natural."

"What of the other symbols?" I asked.

"The orientation of this wagon wheel indicates a particular time in association with the equinoxes and solstices. It is difficult to know how precise this sketch is, but based upon the ancient constellations depicted above, it suggests a mid-century date. The white flowers wound through it suggest a wedding."

"A wedding sometime in the last fifty years?"

"Or about four-thousand years ago, or four-thousand years in the future. Within the last few decades seems most likely. It reinforces the theme if nothing else."

"That makes the bull skin look more appealing," I said.

"The rest is worse – crows and hearts within trees, triskele – all treacle that could mean anything. We can only hope the combination proves telling as we proceed."

Alongside his more esoteric researches, Holmes had also drafted a list of fine leathercrafters around town. We paid a call on them one by one, beginning with those who might also supply the peacock mask. At each Holmes posed as a customer, asking after an authentic buffalo robe so as not to tip his hand. By the end of the day we had three of the things to cart around, and a bearskin that had been presented to us under false pretense besides. None who produced anything of quality dealt in whole bull skins, and none who dealt in bull skins showed signs of artistic quality.

"We are going about this business the wrong way," Holmes sighed. "We need a proprietor who can do top-flight work but we must also account for the parasites."

"Perhaps he works in the theater?" I offered. "That would be in keeping with the patron's apparent affinity for high culture in low places."

"He certainly seems to have a flair for the dramatic," Holmes conceded. "Let us consider for a moment the idea that the patron brought the parasite to the robe, rather than vice versa."

"It is also strange that this well-bred woman has yet to be reported as missing," I mused.

"There are thousands of governesses and lady's maids and other genteel servants in London who might be little missed by the outside world

80

in such a short time. No, let's follow the line of the parasite for a moment. Strange illness, exotic interests, money to spend on garishly eccentric pursuits. Let us exchange our bull skins for dinner jackets," Holmes said.

"What do you have in mind, Holmes?"

"I have long had a standing invitation at the Royal Geographical Society. I'd say it is past time to accept it."

We returned to Baker Street where I am afraid I met a wardrobe of slim choices. I would never pass for one of the peerage but at last, I cobbled together a suit which I felt was presentable. When I returned to the sitting room I found Holmes gazing idly out of the window in an exquisite suit of deep emerald wool woven so fine and smooth I had initially mistaken it for velvet.

"Holmes, where did you ever get such a thing?"

"Dreadful, isn't it? After that Savile Row business, Morton sent it over. You know how our more illustrious clients like their little mementos."

"What Savile Row business?" I asked. "Who is Morton?"

"Last Boxing Day, don't you remember?"

"I remember waiting outside the opera half the evening for you to arrive with the tickets and nearly catching my death of pneumonia."

"Yes, that's right. I was briefly delayed by the Morton case. I'm sure you wrote about it. 'The Adventure of the Double-Breasted Double-Cross', or somesuch."

"This is the first I've heard of any of this. You told me your carriage threw an axle."

"It did," Holmes says. "In any event, Morton sized the suit from memory. Even I would be hard pressed to do better. Shall we?"

The Society met in Lowther Lodge, a whimsical red brick building of gable pitches and ornate chimneys. Legend had it there were vaults below filled with literal treasure troves of arcane artifacts from around the globe. As we approached, the man at the entrance stiffened for a moment before bowing and sweeping the door open for Holmes. In contrast, I found a white glove pressing against my midriff.

"Is this, er, gentleman with you, Mr. Holmes?" the doorman asked.

"I'm afraid so," Holmes said. "He is most indispensable to me."

"The invitation was really just for you, Mr. Holmes. If we allowed our guests to invite guests and so on and so forth, you can see how things would quickly get out of hand."

"Perhaps we should ask Lord Markham?" Holmes pressed. "I am sure he won't object."

"Just let the man in, Stilson!" came a boisterous voice from inside.

Stilson sighed heavily. "Very good."

Inside, the Society looked much like any other posh social club in which I'd ever been, which was a bit of a disappointment. That feeling only lasted a moment, however, when we came face to face with the very figure Madame Corbeau had sketched – although decidedly more disfigured.

"Mr. Sherlock Holmes, the famous detective!" the man bellowed. "What brings you here? If you take it into your head to start exploring the empty spots on the map, there will be naught for the rest of us to do, and London will be the worse for it besides."

"Worry not, Professor Flynn, I am here in my traditional capacity."

"You know my name, do you? You are a clever sort."

"I must admit I did not immediately place you, but now that I see the *Ordú a Cláirseach órga* around your neck, along with your accent and the characteristic discoloration of your fingernails, ears, and nose . . . ."

"Occupational hazard of the professional mycologist, I'm afraid," Flynn said.

"Indeed, I endure a few occupational hazards myself," Holmes said. "Your treatise on the trans-Pacific diaspora of the *amanita muscaria* was most insightful."

"Ha! Men in my line of work have very few admirers," Flynn said. "Let me get you a drink." He whistled through his fingers and a tray of whisky glasses soon appeared. "Only the finest *uisce beatha*, of course."

We toasted to good health and then I unadvisedly downed the amber liquid. It tasted of wood polish and felt worse as it slowly trickled down my esophagus. I noticed too late that Holmes left his dram swirling in his glass.

Flynn pounded me on the back. "There's a good man. It's my family's private reserve. Comes from sacred peat that was trodden by St. Patrick himself."

I could only wheeze in response. Thankfully Holmes intervened.

"Where have your travels taken you recently?" my friend asked.

"I'm on expedition right here in London if you can believe it," Flynn said. He leaned in close. "I caught wind of an ancient Celtic cairn that has recently been upturned right here in the city. The fool who discovered it thinks it is cursed, so he relinquished his claim to me in exchange for the promise that I would exorcise the place." Flynn laughed cruelly.

"Why did he turn to a mycologist for an exorcism?" I asked.

"I actually went to him. Recognized some unusual specimens in some sketches he had done for me in advance of a painting I had commissioned. Investigating the site, I discovered the cairn underneath. A cache of pre-Celtic treasures, and a colony of unknown fungi worth more than the rest.

My findings are already in press and the colony removed to a secure location. My fortune is made, gentlemen."

"Might I see the cairn?" Holmes asked. "I have a professional interest in how bodies might be hidden and rediscovered."

"I don't know," Flynn said. "I think it might be wiser to keep my secrets until my findings are published."

"I suppose you are right," Holmes sighed. "I'm afraid the cut-throats of the West End have nothing on those in academia." With that, he raised his glass to Flynn and downed it. "I can never hope for a whisky this fine again. Might I have another taste?"

"That's the spirit, Mr. Holmes!"

To my surprise, Holmes spent the next hour going drink for drink against a man three stone his superior, keeping up a patter of jokes and off-color stories to distract Flynn. Finally, the boisterous scientist was unable to even lift a glass, so Holmes offered to see him home. My friend's eyes were glassy and there was an unusual sway to his step, but he seemed to have held the liquor much better than his rival. When he called for our coats, he also slipped a note to the waiter, who returned with a concoction that looked and smelled of the liquid refuse of a fish cannery. Holmes downed the loathsome mixture in one gulp and by the time we were on the street he seemed much recovered, apart from the fact that he had donned Flynn's coat and put the somnambulant man in his own.

"I wonder where we shall hail a carriage at this hour, old chums?" he declared loudly to no one in particular. It was only then I realized that Flynn likely had a valet waiting for him and Holmes was trying to throw the man off their scent. It must have worked, for no one intervened as we hoisted Flynn to the corner and loaded him into a passing hack.

"Take him to Bushy Park and wait for me, Watson," Holmes said.

"What am I to do if he awakens?" I asked.

"I doubt that will be an issue, but should he rouse, do your best to keep him in the park. Lead him towards the fairy circle if you can."

With that, Holmes slapped the side of the carriage and it clattered away with myself and Flynn on board. I just had time to see Holmes hail a dogcart before we were around the corner and gone. When we arrived at the locked gates of Bushy Park, the cabman took little notice of me dragging an unconscious man out of the vehicle and depositing him on the ground. I supposed those who drive in the lonely hours of the night must be used to all manner of things. Just in case, I pressed a few more coins into his palm before he departed. I waited next to the snoring Irishman for what seemed like an eternity, but which my watch only read as slightly less than an hour. Holmes then came stalking down the road with a buffalo skin over one shoulder and a lantern dangling from the opposite hand. He simply nodded to me as he let his burdens settle to the ground and made quick work of the lock on the gate. We spread the buffalo skin out and used it as a litter to carry Flynn to the fairy circle at the heart of the park. The man slept on, oblivious to the whole affair.

When we at last arrived, Holmes began stomping around the fairy circle until he found a soft spot in the dirt. We turned the lantern upon it and dug with small hand spades Holmes had secreted in his pockets. The freshly turned dirt soon gave way to a large stone. When Holmes had pried that away, there was a black hollow beneath us. Holmes took the lantern and revealed a small chamber within. He slid inside and I watched the light dance around as he made his inspection.

"All right, let's lower him in," Holmes said from below.

"You mean to bury him alive?" I protested.

"Only symbolically," Holmes assured me.

"But we are putting him in a hole in the ground?"

Holmes gestured impatiently, so I dragged Flynn by his heels and fed him through the opening to a waiting Holmes, who laid him out as if for his final repose.

"Now, the buffalo skin," Holmes said.

I passed that through as well. Holmes wrapped himself in it and produced a feathered mask from the inside of his coat. Then he knelt down and wafted smelling salts beneath Flynn's nostrils. The repugnant mycologist shot bolt upright and regarded the strange figure above him for a moment before screaming.

"Please, Tlachtga, I didn't know this was real," Flynn begged. "I thought it was all a laugh."

Holmes stepped forward and lifted Flynn by his lapels, pressing him into the crumbling dirt above.

"We were modeling for DeValet when the girl lost her breath. Just the spoors, I thought, so we left. She was better once we were away. I paid her the full fee and that was the end of it as far as I was concerned. Then a few days later, I hear she is looking for me because she has developed a sickness and she blames me for it. Well, as you can plainly see, I developed a sickness too and I blame *her* for it. These artistic types, beautiful on the outside, rotten on the inside."

Holmes tossed the man to the ground. "You never meant the girl any harm?" he asked in an eerie falsetto.

"I swear to you, Tlachtga, I don't know a thing about her, save that she said her name was Bella and she wanted me to pay her directly. I had already paid the fee to DeValet's woman, but Bella demanded it all over again. I paid her just to be done with it. Had I known whatever foul taint she carried would eat away at my face like this, I can assure you I would have handled the situation much differently. Thank providence I had just had that portrait made. I've had it photographed to be used for publicity. As it is, I can only give lectures to darkened halls. I can blame it on the mushrooms, but I shan't see a tenth of the revenue that I might have garnered had not she blighted me."

"That is why you struck her down?" Holmes asked.

"I never saw her again after she demanded her ransom."

"And the robe?"

"Yes, she went on about the robe, but I only had it the day of the portrait sitting."

"From where did you get it?"

"DeValet's woman gave it to me. I understand that the costumes come as part of the service."

Holmes shrugged off the buffalo skin and mask. "Well, this is a merry chase we have been led upon, Watson."

"Holmes?" Flynn gasped. "What is this?"

"My apologies, sir," Holmes said. "We had been led to believe that you had murdered the woman who modeled for your pictures. I'm afraid my predilection for the sensational led me down the wrong path. What we have here is a very trite domestic issue dressed up as a mythological tragedy. Help Lord Flynn up, Watson."

I reached down into the hole and pulled the man out. He yet smelled like a bar rag, and I suspected most of this would be but a hazy impression in the morning. Holmes sprung out behind and let out a sharp whistle. Gregson and his men appeared from the trees.

"I heard it all, Mr. Holmes, but I don't know what it means," Gregson said. "Is this our man or isn't he?"

"Well, he has stolen a bit of Britain's history from the heath of this Royal Park, an ancient trespass punishable by death," Holmes said. "However, should those artifacts find their way to the Royal Museum as a donation, I don't think there is any need to be draconian about it."

"And my fungal colony?" Flynn asked.

"I think it would be an unconscionable waste to leave that in the hands of anyone other than the top mycologist in Europe. I look forward to reading your paper, sir. Good evening."

An understandably befuddled Professor Flynn wandered off into the Park.

"I say, Mr. Holmes, it will mean my job if I come back empty handed."

"Let us pray we are not yet too late," Holmes said. "We need to get to DeValet's studio as quickly as we can."

"We still have the man in custody."

"I'm afraid it is Madame Corbeau we need to account for now."

As we galloped across London in the lumbering paddy wagon Holmes explained.

"I must say, it seems like a lot of pomp and tomfoolery to me," Gregson replied.

"That is precisely why I maintain that there is hope for you yet," Holmes said.

The patrolmen quickly turned the studio over, but it was Corbeau had absconded.

"If only I were as clever as your stories make me out to be," Holmes said. "She has a day's jump on us and could be anywhere. What are the nearest banks? Cander and Son? No, she'd be conspicuous there. Scottish Widows? Perhaps. Blount's? Yes, part of the *Societe Generale*, a consortium of banks centered in France. Gregson, see if Madame Corbeau, or any woman of her description, has a vault lease there. I must send a telegram to our friends at the *Sûreté*."

A sober DeValet was able to fill in many of the gaps for us. It seemed that he had been most beguiled by Bella, falling in love with her instantly, as only a gin-soaked artist can. Madame Corbeau called the girl an unnecessary distraction who caused the painter's work to suffer when she was the subject. In fact, DeValet felt he did his best work when Bella was around.

"So she was not unknown to you," I asked.

"Not at all. I had known her for two blissful years, though I hardly think she took notice of me. Many of these models hope to catch the fancy of a rich husband. The artist is invisible to them. I saw her only infrequently because Madame Corbeau refused to book her. It was only on those rare occasions when she was out and I made the arrangements myself that I could bring my beautiful Bella in on a job."

"Why did you not tell us this before?" Holmes said. "We might have saved some time."

"I was not in my right mind, for one. The most recent crate of absinthe which Madame Corbeau brought back from France seems unusually potent. Besides, I do not believe Bella's family are aware of her exertions. They have lost their daughter once already. To find out she lived a secret life of scandal would be too much to bear, I should think."

"Has it ever occurred to you that Madame Corbeau herself might be the villain in all of this?" I asked.

"To what end?" LeValet asked.

"It is my surmise that she loved you," Holmes said. "In her own villainous way. At the same time, she hated you, jealous of the attention you received when she was the superior artist."

"Madame Corbeau an artist?" DeValet said. "I think not."

"And that oversight cost Bella her life," I said. "Unable to disentangle you from the girl, Madame Corbeau decided to murder her and ruin you in one swoop."

"Impossible!" DeValet said.

"We have caught her in a number of lies already, including framing an innocent man. Worse, she has long been stockpiling your art as a nest egg, and the moment we arrived she put her plan to escape into action."

"But for a murder, it was so poorly done," DeValet said.

"Poisons are a tricky business, and *outré* poisons even more so. Had Miss Bella might have died on the spot, which was part of the plan, along with Professor Flynn and perhaps even yourself. As the wearer of the tainted bull skin, Bella was intentionally exposed to certain parasites to an extent that eventually proved lethal. Professor Flynn received only an incidental exposure, and I believe even that was mitigated by the fungal colony that he saw fit to steal from the underground chamber. The parasites introduced into the robe seem to be as attracted to that as to human flesh. Nonetheless, he will be scarred for life."

"As will we all."

"When Miss Bella returned demanding satisfaction, Madame Corbeau took the opportunity to finish the job, taking the stricken girl to the location of the Professor's discovery, which she had likely discovered by following him, and creating her own morbid tableau. Little did she realize the symbiotic relationship between her toxin and the mushrooms that would quickly create a more gruesome scene than she could have ever dreamt of. Have you any paintings of a dismembered woman lying within a circle? Or worse, sketches of a design yet unpainted?"

"That could describe dozens of paintings I have made," DeValet said. "The general composition is reminiscent of '*The World*' card in the Tarot, but women represent fertility, the cycles of nature, motherhood, and more. And circles are just as multifaceted."

"Did Bella ever pose for such a painting previous to this?" Holmes asked.

DeValet's face fell.

"Where is that painting?"

"Madame Corbeau manages the practicalities," DeValet said.

"It will soon be discovered," Holmes said. "It is the smoking gun meant to convict you if her frame-up of Professor Flynn did not take."

"This is beyond belief, Mr. Holmes!" Gregson objected.

"And yet, listen to the newsboy," Holmes replied.

Indeed, through the window we heard the whelp's pitch. "Madman artist paints his murders before committing them! Every shocking detail for two-pence!"

Gregson yelled out the window for the boy to hand a newspaper over. He was refused until he had coughed up the two-pence.

"Well, I'll be, the blaggards!" Gregson said, crumpling the paper and throwing it at the floor.

I picked it up and smoothed it out. "'The Globe *has made a breakthrough in the faltering investigation of the Bushy Park Witch Slaying,*" [I read.] "*A salacious painting had been delivered to our offices proving that eccentric artist Henri DeValet has long held murderous designs upon the woman, known only as Bella, found in Bushy Park. It is impossible to ignore the occult aspects of the bloody murder and we can only lament that the poor girl had lost her soul to Satan afore she lost her life to DeValet.*' It goes on like that. They have all but strung DeValet by his neck, and the depiction of the Yard is . . . unflattering."

"I'll show them who is a wooly-headed plodder!" Gregson bellowed.

"I'm certain you will, Inspector," Holmes said. "Nonetheless, you must now protect Monsieur DeValet until this furor has died down."

"It would be no small help if we could put the cuffs on this Madame Corbeau," Gregson puffed.

"I regret that I allowed her to slip away," Holmes said. "That pleasure will be had by our Gallic friends across the Channel."

Suffice it to say, Gregson was not well pleased. When the notice of Madame Corbeau's arrest came across the wire, Holmes tasked half-a-dozen patrolmen with peddling copies to all the major news desks of London.

"The morning editions were DeValet's execution order. The afternoon editions shall be his reprieve," Holmes said.

"This says they arrested her in the remote hamlet of Bois d'Coeur," I observed. "How did you know to look for her there?"

"Upon further examination, I realized the elements in DeValet's sketches which we were unable to place came from another hand. As you rightly observed, there was another artist involved. Madame Corbeau seems to have assisted DeValet in his compositions as well as his receipts. While the crow and the triskele and the heart within a tree were so much noise within Celtic iconography, they were much easier to place within ancient Galli culture. Corbeau was signing her work, such as it was. I imagine she even expected to be the subject of this portrait."

"And when DeValet put Bella in her place – " I offered.

"It was an insult Corbeau no doubt felt on both a practical and emotional level. It drove her to murder."

"Where did she get the flesh-eating bacteria?" Gregson wondered.

"Bois d'Coeur is in the dairy-rich grassland that flows onwards to Switzerland. Each family there has their own secret for making the rich, pungent cheeses for which the region is known. The French police will have no trouble identifying the family that risks death in pursuit of *belle fromage*. The locals surely know already. Gourmands take a perverse pride in conflating danger and luxury."

A month later a crate of soft cheese wheels arrived from France.

"Ah, Watson! You've spoiled your Christmas present," Holmes lamented.

"Surely this is not the poisoned cheese from the DeValet affair," I protested.

"Don't be foolish," Holmes replied. "The cheese isn't poisoned. It never was. The bacteria used in the fermentation simply happen to devour human flesh." Holmes had pried the crate open and sliced a sliver of cheese with his penknife. "It is perfectly safe, and delicious."

"Get this dreadful stuff out of here!" I demanded.

"Just a few weeks in the larder and then I'll have Wiggins set about delivering them."

"Don't draw a helpless child into this!" I said. "If so much as one person dies, we'll all hang."

"By this stage, all the bacteria have perished, Watson. You know this better than I. This is nothing more than a piquant *amuse bouche* with a compelling anecdote behind it."

"How did you get all of this anyway? It must have cost a fortune."

"Monsieur DeValet meant to dispose of this like any other perishable evidence. I offered to accept it *in lieu* of a monetary award. He seemed to be as eager to be rid of it as you."

The Adventure of the Green Gifts

by Tracy J. Revels

"It is driving me mad, Mr. Holmes. I do not wish to suspect my wife of an impropriety – what decent man would agreeably believe that his spouse is unfaithful? And yet the gifts arrive, and she dotes on them. If you knew my Elizabeth, you would know she would never betray me. She is both spiritually and physically incapable of being untrue. But still, the presents arrive, almost daily now, and I can make no sense of them. The green – all that green! – it torments me! I must have relief!"

My friend Sherlock Holmes regarded his visitor with a cool, appraising eye. Attempting to follow Holmes's methods, I likewise studied our guest, trying to deduce what I could from his appearance and actions. His card told us he was Mr. Joseph Sterling of the firm Sterling and Scot, manufacturers of agricultural equipment. Mr. Sterling was approximately forty years of age, tall and broad-chested, clearly a vigorous and active fellow. His hair was black, thick, and curly, and his face was square, with high cheekbones and a look of almost romantic savagery. There was something of the peacock in his attire: Top hat, diamond stickpin, ruby cufflinks, and a golden silk handkerchief in his lapel. Overall, he bordered on the *gauche*, but his size and handsome face no doubt garnered numerous admirers of the gentle sex. At this moment, however, he seemed completely unmanned, his deep voice trembling and tears coursing down to drip from his chiseled jaw.

"Mr. Sterling," Holmes said, with some asperity, "this is not an agency that deals in domestic intrigues. If you suspect your wife has committed adultery, or is receptive to the advances of another man, then I can recommend other professionals who may be able to assist you."

"But that is just the problem!" Mr. Sterling growled, "I *know* she is not unfaithful! She has not betrayed me. It is neither in her nature nor, to be perfectly frank, physically possible for her to love another."

Holmes frowned as he leaned back in his chair and made a steeple of his fingers. "Indeed? Then perhaps your problem is one that *is* appropriate to our talents. Pray, compose yourself and tell your story from its beginning."

The client nodded, brushed away his tears, and took a few steadying breaths. "I must, I suppose, tell you a few things about myself. I was born in a Devonshire village, to a milkmaid mother who never put a name to

90

my father. She died when I was only a month old, and the village squire gave me to his gamekeeper. I grew up wild, unschooled, and unchurched, knowing little except guns and dogs. Fortunately, I had been blessed with good looks, and in my lustful youth I exploited this to my fullest advantage. At sixteen, I feel deeply in love with a girl named Ellen, the daughter of the local cobbler, and many a night I scaled the ivy that grew over the old stones of the family home and slipped into her bedroom window. We had an understanding, and would have married, if my life had not been dramatically altered on the morning of my seventeenth birthday.

"That day, a gentleman arrived from London. His name was Mr. Michael Scot, and he was the executor for the estate of his business associate, Mr. Allen Sterling, who had recently passed away and bequeathed his fortune, amounting to some five-thousand pounds, to his natural son – myself! I was to inherit it all when I reached the age of twenty. It was like something out of one of Charles Dickens's novels, and I will not burden you with the details – only to say that the news went immediately to my foolish head. Fortunately, Mr. Scot was a wise and kind gentleman, and he offered me a chance to come to London, where I might be prepared to make better use of my bounty. His only condition was that I cut all ties to my past, so that I would be reborn as a new creature. Needless to say, I was glad to leave that dirty place behind. I came to London with Mr. Scot, received an education, and in a short time I was transformed from a ribald youth into a proper gentleman. I learned, about a year after my departure, that my former sweetheart had drowned herself in the millpond, but this sad news only confirmed the wisdom of Mr. Scot's insistence that I put my past behind me.

"Upon coming into my inheritance, I joined Mr. Scot in his manufacturing ventures. For over a decade we prospered. I had a natural turn of mind toward mechanics, and we purchased several factories in the North, expanding our company with an eye to the future. But five years ago, two tragedies came together: Mr. Scot died in a carriage accident, and there was a dreadful downturn turn in the market. My benefactor had unwisely left most of his assets to a pair of wastrel nephews, and suddenly I found myself in danger of losing everything that we had built together. I needed money desperately, and knew where it could be found – In the dowry of Miss Elizabeth Winchell, whom I had met while engaged in business with her late father."

Holmes, who had given the appearance of being rather bored by this biographical recital, paused in the act of lighting his pipe. "The heiress? Her father's foundries were, at one time, among the greatest suppliers of iron to Her Majesty's Navy."

Mr. Sterling nodded, his eyes on the floor. "Yes. Though the money is divided between a number of cousins, Elizabeth's share saved my business and has provided a comfortable life for us. Without it, I would no doubt be back in that wretched village, fixing ploughs."

"You are not the first man to have married for money," I said, thinking even as I did of my beloved Mary Mortsan, and how, if the Great Agra Treasure had been retrieved, I would never have proposed to her, for fear she would have taken me as just such a malignant creature. Holmes, meanwhile, had snatched his Index from the shelf and quickly consulted it. His nod suggested that he had received confirmation of a memory.

"Tell me," Holmes asked, "has marriage transformed your bride from a wheelchair-bound invalid into a hale-and-hearty matron?"

"No . . . and I hear the judgment in your voice, Mr. Holmes. God knows I deserve it, for when I stood beside her on our wedding day, I saw nothing except the funds that would soon be mine. But in my defense, I have been a gentle, kind, and indulgent husband to her, even if our marriage is hardly conventional. I have installed her in a lovely home in Hampstead, provided a fine staff to meet her needs, and I tolerate all of her whims and fears, which are legion. She is afraid of all types of animals, of trains, and of lightning. She is terrified of the dark, but equally of gas, so that our home is lit only with lamps and candles, as if we reside in the past century. Another man would enforce sanity on her, but I give way to every strange obsession."

"Are you as faithful as you are indulgent?" Holmes asked. Again, the man's cheeks turned crimson.

"No. We are men of the world, so you understand that I can hardly confine myself that way. However, I limit my connections to women of a professional class. No other woman but Elizabeth shall have my heart and soul. In the five years we have been wed, she has made me a better man, and it would kill me to lose her to another."

"Yet someone has come between you?" Holmes said.

"Yes – that is why I seek your aid, sir. Exactly six months ago, I arrived at home to find Elizabeth in a playful and affectionate mood. At dinner, she thanked me for the gift I had sent her."

"'Gift?'

"'This,' she said, holding out her arm. On her wrist was a bracelet of bright green beads, a cheap and gaudy thing like one might purchase from a peddler. 'Didn't you send it? Mrs. Brown found it on the doorstep. The card on it read '*For E.S.*'

"'It was not from me.'

"'Oh. Very well.' I could sense her disappointment. 'But I shall keep it.'

92

"'Why,' I challenged. 'If I chose, I could give you something much finer than this trinket!'

"'But you never do!' she answered. I immediately understood my error – it was the surprise she had enjoyed, not the gift itself. But I brushed the matter aside – after all, she was indulged enough without adding foolish presents to the list. Then, a week later, when I returned from a trip to Plymouth, I learned that my wife had received another mysterious gift.

"I would not call it an offering to inspire passion. It was a large roll of wallpaper, in the most garish green tone I had ever seen, an affront to the eyes in its painful hue. It also had arrived with a note saying '*For E.S.*', and, despite my objections, Elizabeth brought in decorators to hang the monstrosity in her bedroom. No amount of criticism, from myself or the staff, could deter her.

"Shortly after this, there was a crisis at a factory, and I was required to be away for two weeks. On my return, I was greeted by a startling sight. Elizabeth was swathed from head to toe in green finery – a green gown, green shawl, and an atrocious headpiece of false vines and leaves, modeled on a Grecian wreath.

"'What the devil is all this?' I demanded. She was cool in her answer.

"'Presents from my mysterious admirer. He, at least, knows the shade that brings out the colour of my eyes.'

"God forgive me, Mr. Holmes, but I was incensed at this display and her attitude toward me. I ripped the shawl from her shoulders, tore the headpiece from her hair, and would stripped off the dress had not Alice, her maid, come running into the room, frightened by her mistress's screams. I fled the house and spent the night in a hotel, drinking myself into a stupor. The next morning, I returned and begged forgiveness, which Elizabeth reluctantly granted. I spent the day interviewing the servants, peppering them with questions, but they had no explanation for the gifts. Each present had been found on the doorstep, at many different times of day, with no messenger or deliveryman in sight."

"Was any of the wrapping paper or packaging preserved?" Holmes asked.

"No, but some of the cards were saved. I have them here. It occurred to me that one of the servants might be lying, be in on the game, and so I acquired samples of their handwriting as well, when they were unaware of my purpose. I see no similarities – but I do not have your expertise."

Holmes took the cards, along with an assortment of foolscap, from Mr. Sterling's hand. He spread them out across the table, motioning for me to join him.

"Do you have any reason to suspect devilry among your staff?" Holmes held up one of the cards to the light. "Describe them, if you will."

"They are all good people – I have no prejudice or suspicion. Jonas and Sarah Brown – our butler and housekeeper – are husband and wife. I inherited them from Mr. Scot upon his demise. Alice Smith has been with my wife for over a year now, and is more of a lady's companion than a true maid, though she is essential to helping my wife dress and fix her hair. There is another girl, Maryanne Edwards, who assists Mrs. Brown with the cooking and cleaning, and Rupert, a half-wit boy – some relation of the Browns – who runs errands and does odd chores. All of our people live with us, as our home is substantial."

"Does your wife go out at all?"

"Never. She has been confined to her wheelchair since childhood, and suffers from a painful deformity of the spine. She is also extremely sensitive to sunlight. The least exposure causes horrible rashes. No, she does not even go out to church, or to concerts, or to pay calls, but is confined to our dwelling."

Holmes turned from studying the cards, indicating that he had found no clue within them. Even I could see that the writing on the card was strong and firm, clearly a man's hand, and different in every way to all the scripts that our client had collected.

"Does your wife receive visitors or have correspondents?"

"Her two female cousins have come down from Scotland to visit, but not in the last year. She corresponds with them, but no others. Her parents are dead, and I handle any necessary business papers."

"What pleasures does she have?" Holmes asked.

"She reads incessantly, all the London newspapers and the ladies' magazines, as well as romantic and sensational novels. When she wants some new book she tells me of it, and I purchase it in the city. There is no regular correspondence from within the house."

Holmes looked away, towards the pictures over the mantel. "And have there been more gifts since your unfortunate show of temper?"

"I believe so. I have not seen them arrive, nor has she spoken of them, but the house seems to be filling with green things: Hair combs, brushes, picture frames, lace gloves, and even a strange doll dressed almost to mimic Elizabeth, seated in a miniature rolling chair. I had told myself that if I did not speak of it, then it would cease . . . yet it grows, and I can bear it no longer."

"You know of no rivals for your wife's affections? An admirer from her past, who might resent your marriage?"

"None. She was as cloistered as a nun until I began to woo her. I was her only sweetheart. No man could possibly have a claim on her!"

"This is truly an interesting case, and yet – I do not see how I can aid you," Holmes said. "You could, of course, seek a divorce, for she is clearly alienating your affections."

"Sir! How can you say that?"

"Then my only other suggestion would be for you to spend more time with your wife, and so overwhelm her with your love that she casts aside both the gifts and the unknown giver. Watson, you have been a married man. Is my bachelor advice sound?"

Mr. Sterling shook his head. "I am not hopelessly naïve, Mr. Holmes. I know what you are suggesting – that my wife somehow, perhaps in league with the servants, is sending these gifts to herself in order to provoke me. I know full well that green is the color of jealously, and it would not be beyond the fanciful female mind to conjure such a trick. But if you knew her, you would grasp the error. She is as innocent as an unspoiled child, without guile, completely devoid of any talent for conspiracy. She would never do such a thing. I would stake my life on it."

Holmes considered this impassioned statement for some moments. At last, he spoke.

"Could I spend the day at your house, on some pretext?"

"In disguise, you mean? Well, we are having a terrible problem with the drains, so if you know anything about plumbing – "

"As it so happens, I do. I shall arrive at nine."

"Should I be there?"

"It would be better if you were away."

"Very well. Who should I tell my butler to expect?"

Holmes smiled. "His name is Escott."

Holmes returned to Baker Street late the next evening, looking and smelling remarkably authentic for his role. Once he had washed away the grime and dirt, he sauntered into our sitting room with a smoldering pipe between his teeth.

"Did you learn anything?" I asked.

"I learned a great many things. For example, I learned that the pious butler, Mr. Brown, has an impressive collection of risqué stereoscopic pictures and Mrs. Brown, despite being a good temperance woman, drinks more sherry than she applies to the cooking. Maryanne, the maid-of-all-work, plans to abandon the household without notice as soon as her handsome sailor returns with the fleet. Rupert, the 'half-wit' boy, is no more disabled than you or I, but is a malingerer of exceptional skill. Alice, the wife's companion and personal maid, is quiet and bookish like her mistress, which makes her heartily disliked among the downstairs staff, who find her pretentious. None of them have any idea where the gifts come from, but they all hope the strange offerings continue to appear, because they have added an air of mystery to their otherwise humdrum existence and boring household routine."

"And the lady?" I asked.

Holmes settled into his chair. A scowl pulled his brows together. "A true puzzle, Watson. I am now inclined to agree with the husband's assessment, for Mrs. Sterling would have to be an actress of international acclaim to be anything other than a very sweet, innocent, helpless, and somewhat nervous little creature. She has an open expression and manner, and was very eager to have her people see to my comfort, even though I was nothing more than a plumber. Her rooms are all on the third floor of the house – hardly a convenient arrangement for a lady confined to a wheelchair, but she insisted that the air was purer away from the street, and I could hardly dispute that assertion. As her husband mentioned, she has a fear of almost all modern conveniences, and her rooms resembled the boudoir of some fairy-tale princess, lit only by candlelight at mid-day."

"Is she a homely woman?" I asked.

"She is not handsome in her face, for time and illness have taken their toll, but her hands are exceptionally delicate and her hair is quite remarkable. Even a professional beauty of the stage would be envious of its thickness and blonde tint. During my visit, Mrs. Sterling had this hair fixed in the most elaborate coiffure I have ever seen on a female head, layers of braids and chignons, all held together with ornate green combs." Holmes chuckled. "The green wallpaper, by the way, is most atrocious. It was more offensive on the eyes than the odors of the drains were to the nose."

"Did another package arrive today?" I asked.

"Not while I was working. But just now, as I walked down Baker Street, I was greeted by a messenger. He is a former Irregular, and the rascal recognized me at once, even in my Escott persona. He carried a message from Mr. Sterling, who must have arrived at the house only minutes after my departure. It seems that yet another gift – this time a very ugly green pendant – had followed in my wake."

"I hope he does not now suspect you of being his wife's secret admirer!"

Holmes chuckled. "Considering his rustic roots and sturdy physique, he is not a man I would wish to run afoul of!" My friend rose and knocked the ashes of his pipe into the grate. He paused, a thoughtful look stealing over his features. "Despite her sad status as an invalid, Mrs. Sterling is not without her charms, and were the marriage between the Sterlings to be dissolved, she would not lack financial resources to bestow upon another lover."

This statement shocked me. "Holmes, do you really think the lady is unfaithful?"

"No. I see a method to this madness, but not a motive. There is something missing, some link that is as of yet invisible in the chain. I think I must search for it beyond London, and I shall begin in the morning. In the meantime, I should send a note of reassurance to Mr. Sterling. Let me see if the messenger is where I left him in the kitchen, devouring one of Mrs. Hudson's excellent pies."

The youngster returned in Holmes's wake. For the next hour he regaled us with stories about his adventures with the agency he served. I had often suspected that Holmes assisted his Irregulars as they aged beyond the ability to serve as his eyes and ears, helping them to find good jobs or acquire the rudiments of an education. Someday the world will learn of the adventures of Wiggins, who most resembled his master in drive and intellect. This youth, whose name was Sullivan, was finally coaxed into ending his narration and taking Holmes's note to Mr. Sterling's residence. Yet less than an hour later, the lad was back in our rooms, breathless and red-faced.

"Fire, Mr. Holmes! The place is on fire!"

Holmes and I exchanged one startled look, then we were both out of our chairs and grabbing for our coats. A blast of Holmes's whistle brought a cab around, and soon we were flying across London toward Hampstead, where the Sterlings resided. We saw the glow of the blaze and the ugly smoke swirling up into the sky many streets before we reached the inferno. Several engines had responded to the call, and neighbors in a variety of dressing gowns and cloaks were huddled around, watching in horror as the large and stately home seemed on the verge of collapse. Holmes consulted with the commander of the fire-fighters, learning that Mrs. Sterling was dead and her husband had been rushed to the hospital, though there was little chance that he would survive his ordeal. The servants were all accounted for, gathered in a small knot on the corner, weeping copiously.

"I will speak to them," Holmes said. "Hurry, Watson, and see if by any chance our client is able to shed light on this tragedy."

Another bone-jarring dash took me to the hospital, and it was my good fortune to have been a classmate of the doctor in charge of the ward where Mr. Sterling was being attended. I walked inside the room, repelled by the smell of charred flesh. A quick glance at the unspeakably damaged body told me our client would soon be beyond our assistance and free of all pain. His eyes were glazed from the strong drugs he had been given, but he somehow noted me. He screamed, clawing in my direction with the ruined stubs of his fingers.

"Her hair – fire – the green is on fire!"

Even as physicians and the nurses rushed to try to calm the agitated man, his body went rigid and his gaze became fixed. I walked backward, expressed my sympathies to my brother medical man, and quietly departed from the ward. It seemed most reasonable to return to Baker Street, and when I arrived I found Holmes pacing our sitting room. He read the news from my sad and downcast expression.

"A tragedy," he said, "though mercifully the servants were spared. They were all away from the house – Alice was visiting a friend and the others were attending a performance at a music hall. From the firemen I learned that Mr. Sterling staggered down the stairs with his dead wife in his arms, then collapsed immediately from his own wounds." Holmes sighed and settled into his chair. "I assume you arrived too late to take a statement of any sort?"

"He spoke a few words, though what he said was likely delusional, as he was in agony." I repeated the dying man's frenzied statement. I had expected Holmes to dismiss the words, but he sat up straighter.

"Green fire? In her hair?"

"That was my interpretation."

Holmes rose, his hands clasped behind his back. For a moment he was as still and silent as some ancient statue upon the banks of the Nile. Then, with an oath, he spun around and stomped to his room, slamming the door.

"Watson, I have failed to provide justice, therefore I must settle for clarity."

It had been nearly a month since the tragic fire at the Sterling residence. I had said no more of it to Holmes, for his manner was dark and feverish, indicating that he was furious with himself, and in such a humor he was not a man to be engaged. He had disappeared for over a week, and a few brusque telegrams informed me that he was looking into some peripheral matters in Devonshire. Meanwhile, I had learned through the papers the results of the firemen's investigations. The blaze had begun in the upper floor of the Sterling house, probably from a candle that had been knocked over. The extreme damage to both bodies indicated that Mrs. Sterling's clothes has been ignited, and while trying to beat out the flames, her husband had only succeeded in spreading the conflagration. As the Sterlings lacked children, the couple's fortune had passed to the wife's cousins and to several charitable societies. Their servants had been comfortably provided for as well, though not to such a degree as to attract suspicion.

"Holmes," I said, as gently as I could, "it was clearly an accident. You must not blame yourself for not foreseeing it."

"No, Watson, it was cold-blooded murder, and if I had possessed the brain you credit me with having, I would have raised an alarm that could have saved two lives and perhaps a soul." I had never seen such self-loathing mar my friend's face. "Unfortunately, I have no way to prove it was a murder."

"Could you trick the villain into a confession?"

"Perhaps, but such an unlikely revelation would not stand up in court. No, it must be enough for me to know, beyond any shadow of a doubt." He nodded toward our clock. "The murderer will be here momentarily."

This last statement startled me. "Should I get my pistol?"

"That will be unnecessary. Ah, there is the bell, Mrs. Hudson's stately tread, and now the opening of the door. Sit down, Watson, and calm yourself. We must both project an air of serenity."

Such was easier said than done. One would think after so many years with Holmes I would lack the ability to be surprised, but learning that a murderer capable of incinerating two people was even now ascending our stairs did, I confess, set my pulse to pounding. A moment later, as I struggled to draw an even breath, Mrs. Hudson appeared.

"A Miss Alice Smith to see you, sir."

The young woman who presented herself was dressed in a smart grey tweed walking suit, with a neat felt hat on her head. Her hair was dark and lustrous, and her skin was like milk, but the strange heaviness of her brows and the square cut of her jaw kept her from ascending to true beauty. Still, she was a striking personage, a slender yet formidable presence in our rooms. She settled onto the divan with the air of a woman accustomed to handling her own business.

"Your message was very strange, Mr. Holmes. I do not see how it could be to my advantage to hear any story from you. As you are no doubt aware, my late employers – may God rest their souls – were generous to me, and I am now living a retired life."

"Ah, but my story is a very interesting one. It does not begin in London, but in a Devonshire village, many years ago. A handsome youth fell in love with a sweet maiden. He was bold and she was overwhelmed with his passion, so they soon had an understanding, as country folk often do. Then, quite unexpectedly, the young man came into an inheritance and was whisked away to London. At the insistence of his new guardian, the youth cut all ties to his former life and threw the girl over, dismissing her from his future. He did this without ever learning that she had conceived and had given birth to his daughter."

Miss Smith jumped to her feet. "What are you implying? I will not stay here and listen to such insults!"

Holmes raised his hand. The lady stared at him, but did not move. Holmes continued to speak, and perhaps it was the even, almost songlike quality of his voice that caused the lady to slowly crumple back into her seat. "It was a cruel and cowardly act on the boy's part, for it broke the poor girl's heart and disordered her mind. So terribly wronged by the person who should have loved, protected, and provided for her, she lost her senses. No one could blame her for the act of self-destruction, when she drowned herself in a pond."

Miss Smith said nothing, but her face was rigid and her eyes were locked to Holmes's.

"The babe was sent to an orphanage where she was raised, then to a charity school, where she was trained for domestic work. But the girl proved clever. Being far more intelligent than those around her, she refused to accept the life of a common household drudge. By her drive and savvy, she rose within the servant caste, and acquired enough education to be placed as a lady's companion, rather than a scullery or parlor maid. But in her heart a flame of vengeance began to burn. The mother she had never known lived in her imagination, and she conceived a hatred for the man who had abandoned them both. In time, she learned her father's name and tracked him to London. She might have revealed herself and demanded her patrimony, but instead she decided to take revenge for her mother's mistreatment.

"But how best to do this? She first won a place in her father's household as the maid and confidante to his invalid wife. She watched the couple carefully, studying the dynamics of their relationship. She knew that Mrs. Sterling felt ignored and neglected by her husband. She used this to her advantage."

"You can prove nothing," Miss Smith hissed. Holmes ignored her interruption.

"At first I made the mistake of assuming that this lady's sole intention was to cause disharmony in her father's marriage. It would be easy enough, living under their roof, to plant suspicions on both sides. Even Mr. Sterling – a crass man, certainly no deep thinker – noted the symbolism of the strange gifts that appeared at his wife's door, and which she accepted with such delight. Green for bile, green for bitterness, green for jealously."

Holmes paused. Miss Smith's lips had twisted into an arch, smug smile.

"And green for arsenic."

The lady gasped. Immediately, she brought one gloved hand to her mouth, as if to hold back any further responses.

"Green dyes are often toxic, yet the villain virtually wrapped her mistress in gowns and shawls of this deadly colour, brought in wallpaper

100

and headdresses and beads that dripped with poison. It was slow and steady, and over time the invalid would have shown symptoms, especially with her delicate, easily irritated skin. Therefore, the avenger needed something that would work faster. Then she came upon a masterful stroke, a way to commit a perfect murder. She would cause her mistress to kill herself by accident.

"I will never forgive myself for not recognizing this plan in time to prevent the tragedy. While I was in the house, in the guise of the plumber, I saw Mrs. Sterling's ornate coiffure, her hair dressed in a fanciful style with almost a dozen green celluloid combs holding up her tresses. Celluloid is highly flammable, and the lady lived in a room filled with candles. The villain knew her fellow servants would be away from home that evening – and to her small credit, she bore them no enmity – so she arranged her mistress' hair in a way that would be most difficult to unravel. She made some excuse to leave before the lady retired, knowing that it was unlikely her mistress would seek aid when it came time to undo her hair for the evening. Mrs. Sterling, despite her infirmity, was a proud woman, and the recent unpleasantness between the spouses virtually guaranteed she would not ask for her husband's assistance. It is easy to imagine what happened next . . . the tugging at an un-cooperative lock, the rough pulling at a tangle, the need for more light . . . and then the sudden, fatal combustion."

I had though Miss Smith a stone, but as I watched, a single tear ran down her cheek. She made no move to wipe it away.

"You have no proof of this," she whispered.

"Indeed I do not. But you will go to your grave knowing that someday, when all are called to answer for their sins, you will be judged by a higher authority, and held to account for what you have done." Holmes pulled out one of the cards from his pocket, revealing the inscription '*For E.S.*'

"It never occurred to anyone that you mean *Ellen Smith*, not *Elizabeth Sterling*."

Miss Smith rose with a sudden burst of resolution. Her face, which for just a few moments had softened, suddenly turned hard. "Are we quite done here? I have learned nothing to my advantage, and do not wish to waste my time further."

"Only one question, if I may. You required an accomplice to deliver the gifts and pen the notes. Is the gentleman who wrote this card your lover?"

The lady tossed her head. "I have no idea what you are talking about. Perhaps you, the famous detective, have missed some details in your research. Good day, Mr. Holmes."

She stomped past me, slamming the door as she exited. Holmes moved to the window, then motioned me to his side.

"Your conclusion, Watson?"

I followed his gesture. There was a young man lounging across the street, and I gave a gasp of shock, for it seemed as if Mr. Sterling had returned from the grave. The youth bore such a strong resemblance to Holmes's late client that I had to rub my eyes. This man was younger, but of the same build and coloring as Mr. Sterling, and dressed in a remarkably similar style. As I watched, Miss Smith emerged from our building and crossed the street to the fellow. They spoke, and she inclined her head. When he looked up toward our window, all was clear.

"Twins!"

"Yes – a double dose of vengeance." Holmes gave a rueful snort. "And indeed, I was told of only one child of the union. I found only the evidence of an unwanted girl in the records of the orphanage and the school. Clearly the boy was given to someone else, passed off as a legitimate scion of a barren home. She snared him and made him feel wronged as well, so that he became her accomplice in murder. How twisted is the world we live in, my dear friend?"

Miss Smith took the man's arm and, with a final, defiant tilt of her chin, turned away. We watched them disappear into the throngs on Baker Street.

"A sad conclusion to our story," Holmes sighed. "You will not write this up as one of my successes, Watson, but perhaps it might serve you well should you be in need of a morality tale. Now hand me my violin, and I shall turn my poor talents toward composing a requiem."

The Turk's Head
by Robert Stapleton

The investigative powers of my friend Sherlock Holmes were matched only by his skill with the violin. Both these areas of his life were the subject of constant and focused development during the many years of our acquaintance.

My notes from those days remind me that it was on a sunny September morning in 1899, as I returned to our rooms in Baker Street bearing the morning mail, that I discovered Holmes, standing at the open window, striving to master a particular stanza from a Bach concerto.

"No! No! No!" he yelled as he turned from the window, with frustration evident in his voice. "This will not do, Watson. I fear old Johann has the better of me today."

I sorted through the correspondence, placing a handful unopened upon the table, but retaining another letter for closer inspection.

"Is that for me?" asked Holmes, returning his instrument to its case.

"That is indeed how it is addressed," said I, turning the sealed envelope over in my hands. "But what attracted my specific attention was the postmark: Penzance, Cornwall."

"An area of the world we visited on a previous occasion," he observed.

"I recall it well," I replied coldly. The incident known as the Cornish Horror was still too recent in my memory to allow me much ease at the prospect of revisiting that area of the country.

"Then kindly read the letter for me, my dear fellow."

I took hold of my letter-opener, a souvenir I had purchased a few years previously on a visit to the Crystal Palace, and slit open the envelope. I began to read.

Dear Mr. Holmes,

We are in a desperate plight down here. One innocent man is dead, and another is due to stand trial for his murder. We urgently need your assistance, and hope you will be willing to visit this corner of the realm before it is too late.

"Succinct," observed Holmes.

"The letter is from a Miss Merryn Penrose, who gives her address as the village of Port Caer."

I handed the letter to Holmes and took down from our book shelving an atlas of Great Britain. This I placed upon the table, and found it readily fell open at the section dealing with the Cornish Peninsula. "Here it is. With a name like that, it had to be on the coast."

Holmes proceeded to examine the letter.

"An educated lady, I see," he said, "judging by the fastidious copperplate handwriting. Also, a lady with passion in her heart. See how strongly she forms her letters. Especially that last line. All in thick black ink, which had hardly dried before she sealed it."

I could see from his expression that Holmes was already intrigued.

He looked up at me. "What think you, Watson?"

"Although I have no wish to visit that area again in a hurry, I feel we must definitely respond to the lady's *Cri de Coeur*, even though she tells us absolutely nothing about the matter."

"On the contrary," said he. "This letter tells us a great deal. We know a murder has been committed there, and we know that the local police are involved, having possibly made one of their customary errors of judgement. We also know that the accused is a man for whom the lady holds strong feelings."

Having made further study of our atlas, Holmes turned his attention to our dog-eared Bradshaw.

"Watson," he cried, "would you be kind enough to arrange for two berths on the overnight train from Paddington Station to Penzance? From there, a carriage should bring us Port Caer soon after midday tomorrow."

For the final few miles of our rail journey, I looked out at the rugged coastal scenery passing by our carriage window. The sight of the ocean, which likely thrills the heart of every Englishman, had a sinister look about it that day.

Holmes stepped down onto the platform at Penzance, rested by his night in the sleeper carriage. He drew a deep breath. "Is that sea air not refreshing, Watson?"

"It certainly blows away the cobwebs," I replied, not having enjoyed the same soundness of slumber.

We found a horse and trap which took us along a dusty coastal road towards our destination. We rolled through open moorland, strewn with russet bracken and decaying foliage lying beneath a cold and oppressive sky.

"Port Caer," announced the driver as we swayed into the main street at the top of the village. "The very last place on Earth the Good Lord made. And that's a fact."

"Why do you say that?" I enquired.

"Begging your pardons, gentlemen, but not many people come to this place. And them as do will just as soon make a speedy return to civilization."

After we had paid him off, the driver left with greater alacrity than that with which he had arrived.

Holmes and I stood at the top of the main street, with our luggage on the ground around us. The smell of the sea wafted towards us on the breeze, with the mewing and squawking of gulls filling the air around us.

"What now?" I asked.

Holmes brightened. "I see the village inn, beneath the sign of the Seven Stars. Come, Watson, we must make our reservations for the night."

The landlord, who introduced himself as Henry Rowe, appeared not the least bit surprised to see us. "Good afternoon, gentlemen," said he. "How may I help you?"

"We need two rooms for the night," I told him.

"With views overlooking the sea," added Holmes.

We signed the visitors book beneath the landlord's careful scrutiny. "You gentlemen up from London?"

"Indeed we are," I told him.

"Then Mr. Holmes here must be the detective Miss Penrose wrote to."

"You know about that business?"

The landlord chuckled. "There are very few secrets in a place as small as this, Dr. Watson. But I would counsel you both to conclude your business here quickly, and then leave as soon as you can."

"That sounds like a threat."

"Oh, my goodness me, no. Merely a word of friendly advice."

"Then we must begin at once by visiting Miss Penrose," announced Holmes. "She gives her address as 20 High Street."

I glanced at Rowe. "Where is that?"

"You go out of the door here," said Rowe, "turn right, and follow the road downhill. You'll find her house along the terrace towards the bottom of the hill."

We thanked him, deposited our bags up to our rooms, and immediately set off in search of the lady who had summoned us to Cornwall.

The village looked to be a typical workaday Cornish fishing community. A small harbour lay between protective stone jetties, with precipitous cliffs rising on both sides. Behind the village, two roads led across wild moorland – one leading back the way we had come, and the other trailing away towards the north.

The sight made me shiver. "This is a bleak place, Holmes."

"Bleak in many ways, Watson," he replied. "These small communities can often hold great darkness. The hearts of the men and women in such places are liable to harbour as much evil as you will find in the darkest backstreets of London."

Miss Penrose answered our knock and we found ourselves facing a proud lady in her thirties, with sharp facial features and dark hair tied back in a severe bun.

"Mr. Holmes?"

"Indeed," he replied. "And this is my colleague, Dr. Watson."

"Please step inside, gentlemen," said Miss Penrose. "I am glad you felt able to come all this way at such short notice. And thank you for your telegram, Mr. Holmes. It made me quite a celebrity in the village. Not many people receive such things around here."

She led us into the parlour and invited us to sit on either side of the fireplace.

"I imagine you will be tired after your long journey," said Miss Penrose. "May I offer you a cup of tea?"

I readily accepted the offer. Holmes declined, and sat with his attention riveted upon our hostess who, a few minutes later, took an upright chair facing Holmes.

"Let me begin by repeating what I told you in my letter. One man is dead, and the other is to stand trial for his murder."

"Dear me! And both innocent men, you say."

"That is the tragedy of the matter."

"And what exactly do you wish me to do?"

Miss Penrose looked down at her hands, now folded in her lap. "I had been entertaining hopes that you might rescue the one accused of murder."

"Who exactly is he?"

"A local man, by the name of Jowan Marrack. The accusation is that he pushed the victim from the top of the high cliff just to the east of here. A place called the Turk's Head."

"Marrack is a man for whom you hold some affection."

She blushed. "Is it so obvious?"

"He certainly has a place in your heart."

"He is a married man, Mr. Holmes."

"Nevertheless, you have feelings for him."

"I have known Jowan ever since I came to this village, some ten years ago, and I am certain he would never kill anybody. I came to work as a teacher at the school here in Port Caer. I still teach the little ones – the infants. Jowan was the first person to show me any kindness when I came here as a stranger – which is more than can be said for his wife. A nasty piece of work she is. Why Jowan married her, I really cannot imagine. And I don't think he could tell you either. Their relationship has been difficult for many years now, but divorce, even if they could afford it, would cause a scandal in the village. So they stay together out of convenience. They have no children, which is perhaps the greatest blessing."

"And the man who was killed?"

"His name was Michael Warrington. It seems he was a police detective, on assignment from Truro. Although nothing official was told us, everyone in the village imagined he was here to investigate allegations of smuggling."

"Are there grounds for such an investigation?"

"Smuggling is nowhere near as bad as it was a century ago."

"But smuggling does go on here."

"That is beside the point, Mr. Holmes." She looked up at us, glancing from one to the other. "Whatever my personal feelings, the point is that an injustice is being perpetrated here, and somebody needs to put an end to such a terrible state of affairs."

Holmes leaned forward. "Miss Penrose, I need to know all the facts if I am to make any progress with this matter."

"I have told you everything that I know."

"Perhaps."

"Then I suggest you pay a visit to our local policeman, Constable Evans. He understands the situation better than I. The Police House is on the waterfront down beside the harbour. Between the chapel and the village Post Office. You will recognize it by the public notices exhibited in the window."

"Then let us waste no time in calling upon the man." Holmes stood up, turned, and strode from the house.

I thanked Miss Penrose for her hospitality and followed in his wake.

We found Police Constable Evans at home when we knocked upon his front door and introduced ourselves.

"Do please come inside, gentlemen," said the upholder of the law. "I've been expecting you."

As Evans led us into the front room, his attitude felt cold and formal. He glared towards Holmes. "I imagine you are here to investigate the murder of Michael Warrington."

"Merely at the request of one of the locals," replied Holmes.

"Miss Penrose, no doubt."

"We have just this minute come away from visiting the lady."

107

"This is all highly irregular," said Evans, "but how may I help you?"

"I should like to examine the scene of the crime," said Holmes. "Miss Penrose tells us the victim fell from a place known locally as the Turk's Head."

"He was pushed, Mr. Holmes. The Turk's Head lies on the highest point of the east cliff. The locals keep it whitewashed, resembling an Arab turban, to act as a landmark warning shipping of the dangerous rocks along that stretch of the coastline."

"Then please lead on."

The policeman pulled on his coat and led us along a footpath which took up to where stood the great white rock, a position which commanded a wide view of the ocean and the jagged rocks which projected from its surface.

Holmes stood looking out at the scene, his cloak billowing in the breeze. "Is this the place?"

"The exact spot, Mr. Holmes. Warrington died from injuries sustained by falling from this cliff onto the small beach more than a hundred feet below."

Holmes knelt down to examine the earth closest to the clifftop edge. "Too many people have visited this spot to leave much in the way of evidence," said he. "Hello, what's this?"

"What is it, Holmes?"

"The prints of a man's boots, scraping the turf on the very edge of the cliff. Perhaps the last trace of a man losing his footing. And the footprints are facing out to sea. I commend that to you for further consideration."

Evans shook his head. "Purely incidental. We know he fell from here."

Holmes stood up again. "And what motive might there have been for the murder?"

"The motive is clear as day," said Evans. "Michael Warrington came here from our Police Headquarters in Truro to investigate rumours of smuggling."

"Accusations which focused on the accused?"

"Jowan Marrack. Indeed."

"And were the rumours well founded?"

"The issue of smuggling became a secondary matter when Warrington was killed."

"And suspicion of both fell upon Marrack."

"It seems he had been involved in some recent smuggling. So he had a motive."

"Really?"

"I am sure Miss Penrose would have you believe the man to be innocent. But Jowan Marrack is a fisherman, Mr. Holmes – a member of the crew of a local fishing boat. The skipper, a man called Jago Stark, has given evidence in the Magistrates' Court that he heard Marrack whisper dark threats against Warrington. He even threatened to kill him if he began to make trouble."

"The suggestion being that he then carried out those threats."

"More than a suggestion, Mr. Holmes. Considering the circumstances, I can see no other reasonable explanation."

"And can you place Marrack at the scene?"

"A button, identified by his wife as belonging to her husband's jacket, was found here, beside the Turk's Head rock. Marrack must have invited Warrington up here to discuss the problem of smuggling. They had an altercation, during which Warrington ripped the button from his killer's jacket before plunging to his death."

"A neat story," said Holmes doubtfully. "But you cannot prove the matter beyond all shadow of doubt, can you?"

"I placed the facts before the local Magistrate, who decided there was sufficient evidence to send the accused for trial at the Assizes in Truro."

"Who is the local Magistrate?"

"Major Ebenezer Rosdew. He has a large house along the road to Truro, with magnificent views of the harbour and the village."

"Does he live alone?"

"He has never married, but he does have a faithful housekeeper."

"Then it seems we must call upon the major."

"You are welcome to try, Mr. Holmes, but he is unshakable in his judgement."

"I am sure of it," said Holmes. "So, the death of Warrington benefitted Marrack. Hence the accusation."

"Correct."

"But who stands to benefit from the execution of Marrack?"

Constable Evans rubbed his chin thoughtfully. "Justice will benefit, Mr. Holmes."

"No other person?"

"There is, of course, his wife."

"Indeed?"

"Talwyn."

"I have heard that their marriage is not a happy one, but how might she benefit by the death of her husband?"

Evans took a deep breath. "I suppose you are bound to find out sooner or later, Mr. Holmes. It's an open secret here in the village that Talwyn

Marrack and Major Rosdew are friends, and frequently enjoy each other's company."

"And if Marrack is hanged for the murder of Warrington, she would be free to marry the major."

"I suppose that is true."

"Do you not think that suspicious?"

"If you are suggesting that Major Rosdew is unjustly accusing Marrack of Warrington's murder simply so he can marry the man's widow, then you are venturing onto dangerous territory, Mr. Holmes."

"It is too early to make such an accusation," said Holmes. "I merely commend the idea to you for consideration."

On our return to the Police House, Sherlock Holmes asked to see a sample of the major's handwriting. Puzzled, Evans handed him a sheet of paper. "Here is a letter, in the major's own hand, informing me of the date set for Marrack's trial at the next Assizes."

Holmes took the letter. "May I retain this document for the moment?"

"You will have to sign for it," said Evans.

Holmes and I repaired to the bar of the Seven Stars and ordered food and drinks. "I see you are a musical man," Holmes told the landlord.

Rowe looked surprised.

"The way you draw the ale suggests you play the violin."

"In a very amateurish way, Mr. Holmes," said Rowe. "The instrument has remained untouched in my living room for several months now."

We took our seats in the inglenook and looked around. A group of men stood at the far end of the room, casting furtive glances in our direction.

"I see we have attracted the attention of the locals," observed Holmes.

One of the men detached himself from the gathering and sauntered across the room to stand directly in front of us. His face displayed defiance.

"You must be Jago Stark," said Holmes.

"And you must be Sherlock Holmes," replied the man, with a sneer. "As unwelcome in this village as the plague."

"And you are the skipper of the fishing boat, *The Merry Maid*."

Stark raised his eyebrows in surprise. "How do you know so much about me?"

"I observe, and I listen," replied Holmes. "Tell me, Mr. Stark, is it true that your crewman, Jowan Marrack, stands accused of murder almost entirely upon your own evidence?"

The man leaned his knuckles upon the table, and brought his face to within a few inches of my colleague's withering gaze. "What are you saying, Mr. Holmes?"

"Merely that any man in the village might be guilty of killing that policeman."

Stark stood upright. "Are you accusing me of lying?"

"I am accusing nobody of anything. But, remember this: If it is discovered that you gave false evidence in a court of law, then you will find yourself in serious trouble."

"I don't like what you're saying," growled Stark. "And I don't like you being here in this village. Asking questions. Go back to where you came from, or you might find yourself in deep trouble."

Holmes stood up, removed his hat and cloak, and stepped forward to confront Stark.

In his turn, Stark stood back, the more carefully to survey his opponent.

"I need your cooperation, Stark," said Holmes.

"Well, I'm not going to help the likes of you."

Stark threw a punch towards Sherlock Holmes, who dodged to one side and easily avoided contact with the fisherman's fist.

After being caught momentarily off balance, Stark recovered himself and threw another punch. Again, it missed the mark.

Holmes stepped forward and landed a solid blow in the centre of the other man's face.

Stark staggered backward, creating chaos among his friends, and collapsed onto the floor. The man's fellow drinkers picked him up, dusted him down, and led him out of the public bar.

Holmes collected his garments, and returned to his seat.

From somewhere in the shadows, I heard somebody chuckling. I looked around, and found an elderly man sitting a few feet away. So well was he hidden in the shadows that I had failed to notice him at first. His gnarled hands and weather-beaten face gave every impression that he had worked for most of his life as a fisherman.

"He's always ready from a scrap, is that one," the septuagenarian told us.

"Then he needs to learn to take less drink before he picks a fight," said Holmes.

The old man beckoned us into conspiratorial closeness. "My name is Enoch," he told us. "I spend so much time in this place that most people forget I'm here at all. Believe me, I know what's going on, both in this inn, and in the community as a whole. Like you, I keep my ears alert and my eyes open."

"And what do you have to tell us?" Holmes asked him.

"You need to be careful of Stark," said Enoch. He took another deep gulp of his ale. "He is Major Rosdew's man."

111

"How do you mean?"

"With the major being the principal person in authority, both in this village and for several miles around, and with him living outside the village, he needs somebody to represent him within the local community. Stark is the man who provides him with that information. There's nobody who knows the community better than Stark – except, through his communication, the major himself."

Holmes called for another drink for the old man. "Then the major will be aware that we are in the village."

"Undoubtedly. Especially after what just happened here in the bar."

"In what else is Stark involved?"

"Anything that's doubtful. He organizes some small-scale smuggling. And, with his influence over the major, he can make life very difficult for anyone in the village and surrounding area whom Stark imagines threatens his interests."

"And the accused man's wife?"

Enoch lit up his pipe and began to blow clouds of tobacco smoke across the table. "Talwyn Marrack. Yes, she knows what's going on here as well. She's a good friend of the major. Has been for several years now. She'll be glad when they put her husband's neck in that noose. Can't come soon enough for her. And the major."

Holmes took out his own pipe, lit a bowl of shag tobacco, and sat deep in thought. For several minutes, the two men sat side by side, enveloped in a cloud of smoke. They reminded me of a pair of Toby jugs, steaming with hot punch.

Eventually, Holmes broke the silence. "I cannot understand why a detective from the county force should come here merely to investigate a minor case of smuggling."

Enoch nodded. "Curious."

"Something else is going on here," continued Holmes. "Some matter dark enough to justify the killing of a policeman, and the execution of an innocent man."

Enoch removed his pipe. "You will find this a law-abiding community, Mr. Holmes. Anyone who causes trouble here is removed from the village. And they never return."

"Removed? By whom?"

"By the magistrate, of course."

"A good friend of Talwyn Marrack."

The old man nodded.

Holmes stood up. "In that case, we need to call upon the lady. Come along, Watson."

I followed my companion outside, conscious that all eyes were trained upon us, not least those of our new friend, Enoch.

Mrs. Marrack lived at a fisherman's cottage down beside the harbour, at the very heart of village life. To Holmes's knock, Mrs. Marrack answered by opening the door and glaring out at us.

"Mrs. Marrack?" said Holmes pleasantly. "My name is Sherlock Holmes, and this is my associate, Dr. John Watson."

"You'll be the man who attacked poor Mr. Stark." It was a statement of fact. "I do not approve of men brawling in public, Mr. Holmes."

Holmes bristled. "We have plenty of witnesses who will testify that he threw the first punch. And the second. Striking him was the only way I could bring him to his senses."

"I'll admit he can be a hot-head at times."

"May we come inside?"

Mrs. Marrack stood aside, and allowed us to enter the parlour. I detected the scent of lavender in the air.

Seated in a chair in the middle of the room, we found Jago Stark.

"Come to gloat, have you?" he asked.

"Not at all," returned Holmes. "I am merely in search of a few honest answers."

Stark and the lady of the house looked at each other, seemingly uncertain as to how to respond.

Holmes turned his attention to the whitewashed wall on the far side of the parlour. His eyes fixed upon a pair of black wooden objects resting on a series of metal brackets fastened to the wall.

"Those look like Polynesian war-clubs," said Holmes.

"That's right," said Mrs. Marrack. "My father was a sea captain for many years. He sailed the world, saw plenty of places, and met a great many people. He brought those back to this country maybe fifty years ago. They have remained in the family ever since, and have been in this house since my husband and I moved in here."

"Very interesting."

"May I get you gentlemen a cup of tea?" asked Mrs. Marrack, evidently trying to distract our attention from the war-clubs.

"That would be a good idea," replied Holmes. "Meanwhile, my companion here will give Mr. Stark a thorough medical examination."

So, as Mrs. Marrack left the room, while casting a suspicious glance towards Holmes, I bent to my task of examining my patient. "The swelling around the eyes appears to be coming out already." I announced. "You'll have a real shiner by the morning."

Stark chuckled. "It won't be the first time."

"Your nose has been bleeding, but I'm fairly sure it hasn't been broken."

"Nor should it be," replied Holmes. "When I strike a man, it is with the precision of a surgeon."

With Stark facing me, and with Mrs. Marrack busy in the kitchen, I watched Holmes take out his magnifying glass and study the two war clubs. By the time I had reassured my patient that he would survive to see another day, Holmes appeared satisfied and sat down beside us.

Mrs. Marrack returned to the parlour and handed us each a cup of tea. "Now, how may I help you, Mr. Holmes?" she asked as she sat down beside Stark.

"I am interested in Major Rosdew," said Holmes. "Can you tell me anything about him, Mrs. Marrack?"

"You have no doubt heard that he and I are friends."

"That in itself is no crime."

"Then allow me to tell you, Mr. Holmes, that the major is a wonderful man. He is kind-hearted and generous."

"He is also the local magistrate."

"Indeed he is. Many in this village, and for miles around, will tell you that he is a good and thoughtful man. Young men have a tendency to get themselves into trouble. Often they are either misguided, or struggling to find their feet in the world. Most are not bad people, Mr. Holmes, and the major recognizes the fact. But he has to be hard on anyone who commits a crime. So whenever one of these young men appears before him to answer for his misdemeanour, rather than sending him for trial and possible imprisonment, the major will impose a fine. The amount will be high enough to deter any other would-be criminals, but far too high for any of the young men to pay. The major gives them an alternative: To pay off their fines by instalments by leaving the village and taking on various labouring jobs."

Holmes turned to the man sitting beside Mrs. Marrack. "Do you know about this, Stark?"

He shrugged. "I know it happens."

"You know more than that. Now tell me."

"I see no reason why I should wash somebody else's laundry in your presence, Mr. Holmes."

"Are you afraid of what the major might do to you?"

"He is a powerful and influential man, Mr. Holmes."

"I also have influence," said Holmes. "And let me tell you, Stark, that unless you give me every assistance in this matter, I shall make sure you face the full weight of legal wrath."

Stark returned a dark look. "What do you want to know?"

114

"Those young men – the ones the major sends away from the village. Where do they go?"

Stark took a deep breath and looked down at his hands, as though embarrassed by what he was about to tell us. "Major Rosdew has a number of places across the county that house these men. They stay overnight at some farm or outbuilding far from civilization, and travel each day to undertake labouring work."

"Such as?"

"Some work on the land, or care for animals. Others are set to work in factories."

"And the money they earn?"

"It pays for their accommodation, and the employment of those who organize this work."

"And the rest of the money?"

"Any remaining is returned to the major."

"To pay off their fines?"

"I'm not privy to the details, Mr. Holmes."

I could see Holmes's expression growing ever darker. "May we conjecture then that, however hard and long these young men work, they will never pay off the entire fine they owe?"

Stark remained silent. He obviously felt he had spoken too hastily.

"Let us call this business exactly as it appears," said Holmes. "Men working for the enrichment of others. We are talking about slavery."

"That's not how it is." Mrs. Marrack's voice rose to a crescendo. "You cannot say that about such a good man. This is not slavery, Mr. Holmes. How dare you even suggest it!"

She turned to Stark. "Tell him, Jago. Tell him he's got it all wrong."

Stark shrugged. "It depends how you look at the matter."

Holmes leaned closer. "Take me to see one of these farms, Stark. Show me. And allow me to judge for myself."

"When?"

"Now."

"But the hour is late, Mr. Holmes. It will be midnight before we can reach even the nearest one."

"Then let us delay no further." Holmes stood up. "Arrange a carriage to collect us outside the Seven Stars, and take us to this farmstead. As soon as possible."

The carriage driver, a local man, let us know by a torrent of colloquial invective that he objected to being called out so late in the evening. Holmes placated the man by promising him a handsome fee when he brought us safely back again at whatever hour our business was concluded.

Holmes and I sat opposite Stark in the enclosed carriage as the driver whipped up the horses and we drove briskly away.

With night already creeping across the Cornish countryside, I looked out at the shadowy fields as they moved by our window at a steady pace. We passed the occasional windswept tree, and lights shining from the windows of dwellings out across the moor. I had no idea where we were heading, but Holmes looked to be taking the entire business in his stride. He plied Stark with questions about village life and the Cornish language.

Almost an hour after leaving Port Caer, I saw the cold light of the moon casting its rays across the buildings of a lonely farmstead, set in a landscape devoid of interesting features.

A low, barn-like structure lay to one side of the farmyard.

Somewhere, a dog was barking.

"Did you bring your revolver with you, Watson?" asked Holmes.

"I have it here," I replied, checking that the weapon was loaded and ready in the pocket of my coat.

Holmes looked around. "There's no knowing what dangers might lie out there in the night."

Immediately the carriage drew to a halt, Holmes opened the door and jumped down onto the ground. "Keep them talking for as long as you can, Watson," he told me, as he disappeared into the darkness.

I followed Jago Stark out into the cool night air. A door in the farmhouse opened and a man appeared. In one hand he carried a lantern, and in the other he held a leash attached to a ferocious looking dog which appeared determined to sink its teeth into us given the chance.

We stepped closer.

The farmer, a thickset, squat fellow, demanded to know who we were. He looked at Stark. "I recognize you, but I don't know the other man."

"My name is Dr. John Watson," I explained.

"And your business here, Dr. Watson?"

"I have come from Port Caer to check on the physical health of the young men labourers you have living here."

"Have you, indeed?" he replied, doubtfully.

"The major is concerned about their welfare."

"Then this is the first time he's ever shown it."

"May I have your permission to examine them?"

"Certainly not," he thundered. "If any of them need medical care, then it's my job to provide it. I send a fair slice of their wages back to Major Rosdew every month, so he ought to be satisfied with that."

"He merely wanted me to check on their condition."

"If you failed to understand my meaning the first time," said the farmer, "then allow me to repeat myself. You are not going to see those

116

men. They need their sleep if they're to put in a proper day's work tomorrow. You should leave now."

When we hesitated, four more men emerged from the house. All large and bulky, with a couple of them carrying pick-axe handles.

"It really is time for us to leave, Dr. Watson," came Stark's voice from close beside me.

The moment we climbed back into the carriage, I found myself sitting opposite a dark figure.

"Ah, there you are, Holmes," said I. "I kept them talking for as long as I felt it safe."

"You did an admirable job, my dear fellow," said Holmes. "It allowed me time to interview a couple of the men inside that building." He nodded toward the barn.

"How did you gain entrance?"

"That will remain my secret," he replied.

"And what did you discover?"

"It merely confirms what we already knew. Those men are sent to provide casual labour wherever they are needed. Some in fields, others in factories or warehouses. They believe they are here to pay off their fines, but they are being held under threat of harsh treatment if they step out of line."

On our return to the Seven Stars, Holmes paid off the driver, asking him to collect us again first thing the following morning.

"Where to now?" I asked Holmes, as we sat together at breakfast.

"This matter is rapidly coming to a head," replied Holmes.

"Well, I'm dashed if I can see it," I admitted.

"I have sent a note to Constable Evans, asking him to accompany us this morning. I think it is time to involve the County Constabulary."

At the sound of horses' hooves and carriage wheels outside, we emerged into the open air to find our transport awaiting us – and Constable Evans standing beside the same carriage we had employed on the previous evening. We all climbed on board.

"I hope this will be worth the loss of an entire morning," said Constable Evans. "I have work to do here."

"As do I," said Holmes. "First, it is time for us to interview the magistrate, Major Rosdew. I think it would be wise to have you with us."

"In your note, you mentioned visiting Truro."

"Indeed," said Holmes. "Once we reach Truro, I hope you will arrange matters so that I can view both the body and the accused."

Evans drew a deep breath. "Very well, Mr. Holmes."

"But let us deal with one matter at a time, shall we?"

The house occupied by Major Rosdew stood at the end of a long drive, leading up from the main road to Truro.

The housekeeper opened the door and invited us to step inside. Our reception was made easier by the presence of the policeman, and we were asked to wait in the library for the major to complete his morning ablutions.

The moment the major entered the room, I could see why people held him in such high respect. He stood over six feet in height, with a mop of black hair topping a face with a firm nose and thick lips.

"We are sorry to arrive so early," said the policeman effusively. "Mr. Sherlock Holmes here is trying to tie up a few loose ends regarding the recent murder."

Major Rosdew smiled and held out his hand to each of us in turn.

"Please tell me, Major," Holmes began. "Why do you consider the evidence against Jowan Marrack sufficient to send him to stand trial for murder?"

Rosdew's face broke into the sort of smile normally reserved for small children or recalcitrant domestic animals. "You are a stranger here, Mr. Holmes," said he. "You need to have lived in this community a long time to understand both domestic and community life here. I consider the evidence against Marrack to be complete."

"Even though circumstantial."

"His button was discovered at the scene of the crime."

"Perhaps planted."

"There is also his expressed antipathy towards the detective who was killed."

"In haste, we all say things that might incriminate us in the eyes of others."

"And then there is his personal confession."

"His confession?"

"You didn't know about that, did you? Yes, his freely made a written and signed admission of guilt. You see, Mr. Holmes, I am not the unjust and uncaring man that some in the village would have you believe."

"Like the families of the young men you send to pay off their fines by the sweat of their brows?"

"They would find life in the army or navy a great deal more brutal, Mr. Holmes. They are well-fed, and comfortably provided for. So, as you can see, there is no reason for you to remain here any longer."

"Are you trying to be rid of me, Major?"

"Merely preventing you from wasting any more of your valuable time, Mr. Holmes."

118

Once more in our carriage, and on our way down the long driveway, Constable Evans glared at Holmes. "Does that satisfy your curiosity, Mr. Holmes?"

"Not in the least," replied my companion. "And that man knows it."

"Do you still wish to visit Truro?"

"Oh, most certainly."

We arrived at the cathedral city of Truro within a couple of hours. All that time, Holmes had remained quiet, lost in gloomy speculation.

As we drew to a halt outside the Police Headquarters, Holmes announced, "First, I wish to see the body. Then, I should like to interview Jowan Marrack. I think, given the developing intelligence surrounding this case, that would be the most important business of the morning."

"Very well," said Evans, as he climbed out of the vehicle. "I shall make the necessary arrangements."

Detective Chief Inspector Branwell emerged to greet us at the door. "Good morning, gentlemen," said he. "I understand you are investigating the murder of Sergeant Warrington."

"That is correct," replied Holmes.

"Frankly, I don't see any reason for your being here, Mr. Holmes. We have a man due to stand trial for that murder."

"We can deal with that matter later," said Holmes. "But first, I should like to examine the body."

"As you wish. But I don't see what you can gain other than confirming our own conclusions."

"Nevertheless."

"You are fortunate that we still have the body. It has been released to the family, and they are due to remove his remains later today."

The stench of death always reminds me of my time in Afghanistan. Even now, after many years, those memories continue to haunt me.

In the mortuary, the police surgeon led us to where Warrington's body lay on a slab of cold marble, covered by a white shroud. The surgeon removed the covering.

Now, several days after the murder, the corpse showed signs of decomposition.

Holmes stepped forward. "Would you please help me turn him over, Doctor?"

Together, the two men turned the corpse onto its front, giving a clear view of the back of the head.

Holmes took out his magnifying glass and examined the skull.

"How did he die?"

"That is a matter for the coroner, sir," replied the medical man.

119

"Come, come," said Holmes petulantly. "Just tell me."

"The evidence suggests he died of multiple injuries consistent with having fallen from a great height, and having collided with rocks on the way down. His broken neck suggests he landed on solid ground with considerable force."

Holmes stood back. "What is your professional opinion, Watson?"

I stepped forward, and examined the corpse. "I concur," I told him. "But I would suggest that the man was dead before he fell. That heavy blow to the back of the head must surely have been the fatal injury."

"Those are my own conclusions," said Holmes. "I have seen all I need to see."

As the surgeon covered the corpse, Holmes looked at those gathered around him. "Thank you, gentlemen, for your time and patience. Now, we need not prolong our visit, but I must speak with the man accused of this crime. Jowan Marrack."

As we followed the Chief Inspector towards the cells, Holmes sighed. "Things look dark for our friend Marrack. Don't you think so, Watson?"

"How much darker can they possibly become?"

"That blow to the head."

"Clearly inflicted by some heavy blunt object."

"Such as a Polynesian war-club?"

"Exactly so."

"I examined those clubs when we visited Marrack's home. On one of them I discovered a minute spot of blood, and traces of skin."

"Then his guilt appears more certain by the minute," said I.

"Indeed. We have the accused, in possession of the murder weapon, together with incriminating evidence and a possible motive. And, if the major is to be believed, a confession of guilt."

We found Jowan Marrack sitting in his cell, his blanched face displaying the horror he now faced: Trial for murder.

"I didn't kill him, Mr. Holmes," the accused man insisted. "I have no idea who did it, but it certainly wasn't me."

Holmes stood over him. "Despite your denial, Marrack, things look bad for you."

"I blame that Jago Stark," said Marrack. "We've been friends all our lives, and I've helped crew his boat for the past fifteen years, but those things he told the magistrate were pure fantasy. Lies."

"Tell me about those war-clubs hanging in your house."

"What about them? I never touch them. Horrible things. I don't know why you want to talk about them. That detective died after being pushed from the Turk's Head, didn't he?"

"Allow me to put one question to you, Marrack," said Holmes. "Did you ever sign a statement of confession?"

"A confession? Certainly not, Mr. Holmes. I never signed any such thing. If such a document exists at all, then it has to be a forgery. Yes, Major Rosdew did try to pressure me into admitting guilt. But I would never do such a thing."

"That is all I needed to know," said Holmes. "Rest assured, Mr. Marrack, I shall do everything in my power to have you released at soon as ever possible."

Outside the cell, I gasped. "Then it must have been Stark. Or even the major."

"We shall see."

As we took our leave of the Police Headquarters, Holmes paused and turned to face Branwell. "What about the other matter, Chief Inspector?"

"You mean the business concerning Major Rosdew?"

"Indeed."

"A delicate matter. But we have no solid evidence to warrant further investigation."

"Then, perhaps I can provide some for you."

The moment we alighted from our carriage, and again entered the Seven Stars, we were met by the landlord.

"I'm glad I've found you, Mr. Holmes," said he, handing over a folded sheet of paper. "I have a message for you."

Holmes read the note. "It appears to be a request by Major Rosdew that we meet him at the place where the body was discovered."

"The beach directly below the Turk's Head?"

"The note makes that clear."

"At what time?"

"At four o'clock this afternoon, according to the note."

"Less than an hour from now."

Holmes had a sparkle in his eye. "Watson, come with me to the laundry room at the rear of this building. And bring a bowl of water with you."

I found Holmes standing beside a draining board, and placed the bowl of water in front of him.

"Excellent," he declared. "I have here three pieces of correspondence: The initial invitation letter that we received from Miss Penrose, the note we have just been handed, and the letter written by Major Rosdew to Constable Evans." He laid out the documents side by side.

"Now, watch as I allow a drop of water to soak a small portion of each sample of script."

121

I watched as he dropped a small amount of water onto the final word of the first document, and saw the ink dissolve. Holmes held the paper at an angle so that the drop of dissolved ink ran down the page. After setting this aside to dry, Holmes did the same with the other two items of correspondence. Finally, we had three pieces of paper, with ink stains trailing from the script.

Holmes took out his magnifying lens, and closely studied the three items. "See, Watson," he told me. "In each case, the water has separated out the constituent elements of the ink."

He picked up the first letter. "This clearly shows that Miss Penrose used one kind of ink, almost certainly a commercially used brand. The second letter, the invitation we received this afternoon to meet at the beach, is written with the same ink used by Miss Penrose."

"Did she write that one as well?"

"I think not. I would hazard a guess that the ink used for both letters is available at the local Post Office for anyone in the village to use. Also, although the note has been written in upper case characters, no doubt to obscure the writer's identity, the hand is different. See how Miss Penrose forms her capital letters."

"A woman's hand, then."

"Undoubtedly. The merest hint of lavender still clings to the paper. But the writing on the invitation matches Mrs. Marrack's hand. I studied a sample of her writing whilst you were caring for Stark."

"And the third letter?"

"The letter Evans received from the major – the ink is distinctly different. Possibly made to his own recipe."

"What do you conclude then, Holmes?"

"That this afternoon's invitation came not from the major, but from Mrs. Marrack."

"To what intent?"

"We shall soon find out."

Our descent to the small patch of sand at the foot of the cliff was by way of a rough and steep pathway. Sea pinks and other hardy flowering plants clung to the rocks as though for dear life.

"The tide is rising," I told Holmes. "What do you suppose Mrs. Marrack has to show us down here?"

"Nothing at all, Watson. In fact, I very much doubt that either she or the major will make a personal appearance on the beach."

"So, why did we come?"

"There are important facts yet to be revealed in this case, Watson. If Mrs. Marrack has asked us to come here, then we need to at least accede to her request."

As we stood on the rapidly reducing stretch of sand, I felt something fall upon my head. A pebble bounced from my hat, and landed in the water. I looked up in time to notice a rock descending toward us.

"Holmes!" I cried, pushing my companion aside. "Watch out!"

The grey rock landed at our feet, and buried itself in the sand.

I looked up, and saw a figure, standing at the top of the cliff, silhouetted against the sky.

By the time I had brushed myself down and looked up again, the figure had gone.

"Somebody tried to kill us."

"So it would seem, Watson."

"And our way back is now cut off by the rising tide."

"And the sea is too rough for us to swim to safety."

At that moment, we both heard the sound of a maroon rocket exploding above the village.

"I think we shall not die today, though, Watson," said Holmes as the local lifeboat approach us from the direction of the harbour. The boat, powered by a dozen oarsmen, rounded the promontory of hard granite rock, and drew towards us from the sea. A man stood in the prow.

"There you are, Mr. Holmes and Dr. Watson!"

I recognized the voice. "Enoch!" I shouted back against the growing wind. "What a surprise. It is extremely good to see you."

"We got your note, Mr. Holmes," came the old man's voice. "It seems you were expecting to become trapped down here."

When the men had brought the lifeboat to within a few yards of the beach, one of their number threw a life-line in our direction.

Within a couple of minutes, soaked to the skin by flying spray and momentary immersion in the sea, we were safely on board the boat.

As we drove through the waves, on our way back to the harbour, I looked back at the cliff, and at the Turk's Head high above. If anybody had been there, they were long gone now.

I noticed Holmes's face light up. "Now I have all the evidence I need," said he. "My case is complete."

After changing into dry clothing, and having paid for drinks for the entire crew of the lifeboat, Holmes and I made our way once more to the house of Miss Penrose. The lady was keen to hear of our progress in the case. Night was falling, and the wind was blowing in from a dark and brooding ocean. We were both glad to be in the warmth of her parlour.

"Are you now convinced that Jowan is innocent, Mr. Holmes?" asked Miss Penrose.

"The evidence forces me to conclude that he is indeed innocent of the murder of the police detective," said Holmes. "And, following our adventure down on the beach this afternoon, the identity of the murderer is now clear to me."

"Can you tell me who it is, Mr. Holmes?"

"Not yet. Let us just say that there is more going on here than merely the one murder."

"What more?"

Our discussion was interrupted by a heavy knock at the front door. Miss Penrose answered, and found Constable Evans standing in the entrance.

"I'm sorry to disturb you, Miss Penrose," said the policeman. "But I'm looking for Mr. Holmes."

"Well, he is here," she replied. "Please step inside."

The policeman made his way into the parlour. "Mr. Holmes. Come quickly. Major Rosdew has climbed up to the Turk's Head. And the people of the village are following after him. Somehow, they heard that he is to be investigated for corruption and malpractice. They are all extremely angry."

I gasped as I followed Holmes to the doorway, and we both looked out towards the cliff, and to the Turk's Head rock, standing prominently against the darkening skyline. In the darkness, we could see lights moving – a procession of burning torches, indicating the presence of a great many people, all converging upon the rock itself.

"Come, Watson," said Holmes. "I believe this is a crucial moment for our investigation. And far more so for Jowan Marrack."

We made our way as fast as we could to the highest point of the cliff, and found almost the entire village gathered beneath the white rock of the Turk's Head. The people were shouting a variety of taunts towards a man on the very brink of the cliff – a man standing lonely but defiant, challenging the entire world by his stance: Major Rosdew.

Holmes and I pushed our way through the throng, until we stood facing the major.

His face lit up as he recognized us. "Well, Mr. Holmes, what conclusions have you come to following your investigations? Have you identified the murderer?"

"I believe that I have," called Holmes. "I've heard the tales people have told me, and I've spoken with the police at Truro. I've interviewed the suspected man himself, and I've seen, in his own house, the murder implement – the Polynesian war-club hanging on the wall above his fireplace. I examined the head of both clubs, and discovered that one of them carried traces of skin and blood."

124

"And your conclusion, Mr. Holmes?"

"From my initial examination of the facts, I concluded that Mr. Marrack was indeed the murderer. But I held that opinion for only a short time. This afternoon, Dr. Watson and I were asked to meet you down at the foot of this cliff. The result was that we very nearly lost our lives. Not once, but twice. A rock fell from up here, and narrowly missed us both. On looking up, I noticed a figure. Then we were left at the mercy of the tide, with no way of escaping from that beach. Having examined the letter inviting us there, the truth became undeniable when I noticed that the figure on the clifftop was a woman."

He turned to face the person standing closest to the major. "It was you, Mrs. Marrack. You tried to kill us earlier today. It was when I saw you, standing high above us, that everything finally fell into place. When I examined the body of the dead man, I noticed that the back of his head had been struck with a blunt instrument, the dimensions of which matched the war-club in your house. He died, not from landing upon the shoreline, nor from striking the rocks on the way down. The man died from a heavy blow to the back of his head. A war-club was indeed the murder weapon, but the hand that wielded it was *yours*, Mrs. Marrack."

"But Holmes," I exclaimed, very much puzzled, "whoever delivered that blow did so with considerable force."

"That is indeed true," replied Holmes, his gaze still fixed upon Mrs. Marrack. "But fishermen's wives are a tough and hardy breed. Sturdy of arm and strong of will. Such a woman, with passion in her heart, could easily have delivered that killer blow."

"But how would she have carried the club all the way up here without it being seen?"

"It takes but a moment's thought to imagine that she hid it beneath a voluptuous coat, like the one I saw hanging in the entrance to her house."

With all eyes now fasten upon her, Mrs. Marrack clutched the major's arm, her eyes showing terror. "You seem to know everything, Mr. Holmes."

"I believe I know enough to have you tried for the murder of that policeman, rather than your husband."

She looked up into the face of the major, as they stood together, swaying against the strengthening wind.

"It was the motive for the killing that had me baffled," said Sherlock Holmes. "Why would the police send a detective to investigate a minor incident of smuggling? Then again, why would anyone choose to lure the man up here and then push him to his death? There had to be more to this business."

125

Holmes turned once more to the major. "The detective from Truro was not interested in smuggling, was he, Major? He was sent here to investigate *you*, and your disgusting arrangement of selling young men into slavery."

"You don't know what you're talking about!" spluttered the major.

"Why would the detective from Truro come all the way up here, to the Turk's Head rock, unless he had been lured by the promise of incriminating information about you, Major? From the person who knew you best of all – Mrs. Marrack."

"So," he growled, "you intend to have me broken, and Talwyn hanged for murder. Is that your game?"

"That would be a matter for the law."

"I am still the magistrate in Port Caer, Mr. Holmes!" roared Major Rosdew. "I shall deal with this matter in my own way."

"Then permit the truth to prevail. Admit that you forged the confession that now threatens to convict Jowan Marrack of murder."

Rosdew nodded. "It is as you say."

The major then turned to face the open sea.

Standing beside him, Talwyn Marrack also turned.

Without saying anything further, the two grasped each other by the hand, and launched themselves into the abyss, together tumbling into the darkness below. No sound came up to us other than the howling of the wind, and the crashing of relentless waves against ageless rocks. Nothing more was ever heard of the two who jumped, and no trace of their bodies was ever found.

After a moment of stunned silence, Constable Evans turned to face the crowd. "I shall take steps immediately to have Jowan Marrack released from prison, and all those young men returned to their families."

The crowd gave a cheer, and gathered around their local policeman.

"Let him receive their plaudits," said Holmes, as we turned away. "People need their local heroes."

The following morning, as the villagers set about their daily work, Sherlock Holmes stood in the open window of his room at the Seven Stars, picked up the violin he had borrowed from the landlord, and began to play. Across the rooftops of the village, and the boats in the crowded little harbour, the sounds of Bach's violin concert spread as a healing balm, bringing sweetness and harmony to this stunned but now liberated community.

When he had finished playing, he looked round at me. "Watson, this instrument may not be up to the standard of my Stradivarius, but at least I have finally matched the master himself."

126

It seemed to me that Holmes had accomplished something even more amazing: He had exorcized from our minds something of the horror of our previous visit to Cornwall.

A few weeks later, back in Baker Street, we received an invitation to attend the marriage of Miss Merryn Penrose and Mr. Jowan Marrack. Of course, Holmes would never have accepted the invitation, but he did consent to write a letter of congratulations to the happy couple – which, for him, was a substantial demonstration of his esteem.

A Ghost in the Mirror
by Peter Coe Verbica

Chapter I – A Green Dress

Scientific study to Sherlock Holmes was akin to a religion which he practiced as zealously as an Anglican missionary in the bush. Unlike a religious proselytizer, however, he sought to attract few converts to his way of thinking or belief. Holmes believed that truth was self-evident, and, as Cicero advised, *res ipsa loquitur* – namely, facts would eventually speak for themselves. He would be the first to admit that at times, like quarry, they needed to be flushed into the open. Hidden apples were bound to drop when a tree's branches were probed with a fruit pole. In the quietude of my mind, I wondered, had their lifespans overlapped, what conversations might have transpired between Holmes and men such as Newton, Galileo, daVinci, or Copernicus? To me, the men were kindred spirits. The difference wasn't that Holmes was somehow the lesser because of the scale of problems he sought to tackle. He preferred to focus his keen mind on the applicable rather than the theoretical. The conundrums he solved meant that a man, wrongly accused, would avert the hangman's noose, a damsel would be spared of some nefarious distress and compromise, a government could avoid damage to its reputation due to diplomat's indiscretion. I am convinced that for Holmes, saving a single life was no less noble than determining the trajectories of the planets.

"Watson, did I ever tell you about how the color of a woman's dress helped me absolve her husband of attempted murder?" Holmes asked, seated comfortably in his favorite chair. It broke my reverie of listening to the persistent patter of autumn rain as it tapped on the window panes like a frenetic telegraph operator. He leaned forward and retrieved his well-oiled pipe from the bowl of a hammered-brass ashtray.

"Attempted murder?" I responded, retrieving my notebook and pencil from inside my coat pocket. "I don't believe so, Holmes. I don't believe so."

Holmes held a lit match with his slender fingers, held it steady, and drew its fire onto a fresh mound of shag tobacco. A blue cloud of smoke began to animate above him. He extinguished the match and continued.

"She was an heiress from one of England's wealthiest families. Her husband inherited a minor title and, due to a series of economic misadventures by besotted forbearers, stewarded a much-reduced estate.

128

In contrast, his bejeweled wife owned stake-holds in profitable companies chartered by Her Majesty, including the ubiquitous purveyor of the shoeshine which you apply to your boots and saddle soap that stable hands use to clean bridles. Her farms dotted the landscape from Surrey to Hereford."

"Not an uncommon occurrence for a family in economic decline to go hunting for a dowry," I replied, awaiting more detail. "What sort of malice befell her?"

"Her husband was accused of attempting to poison her for pecuniary gain, summarily imprisoned, and vilified as a coward."

"I gather you identified the real culprit. But, how did the color of her dress save him from the gallows?"

"It was a deep, shimmering green, Watson," he explained, his grey eyes holding steady upon me.

"Green?" I responded. "I'm still trying to follow."

"I immediately realized the dressmaker was to blame," Holmes said, waving his outstretched hand as if to parry my ignorance.

"Please continue," I encouraged. My pencil nub dulled as I continued to scribble.

"Arsenic, Watson. Once I learned the color of the garment, I realized that the tailor, though renowned, was a poor student of chemistry. In order to get the green shimmer, the dress had been drenched in an arsenic-based pigment. Perhaps fine for a painting one hangs on a wall, but a poor choice for fabric worn against a woman's delicate skin. My indulgent storytelling, though, is now at a close. I hear Inspector Lestrade's galoshes traipsing up our steps."

As Holmes had predicted, a rain-soaked figure opened the door without knocking. A wet hat was pulled off of a head of matted dark hair, and I could see the inspector squinting like a disoriented rodent. He pawed at the buttons of his overcoat.

"Better leave your boots and wet coat at the hall tree, Lestrade. Mrs. Hudson will give you forty lashes if you don't," Holmes advised.

The detective grunted in response.

"Would you care for tea, Inspector?" I asked while putting away my notebook.

"Usually I would decline," he huffed, "but I'll take a spot. This rain has been torrential."

Once seated with his beverage, the inspector fidgeted in his chair, appearing more irritable than usual. We sat in silence for some moments and I noticed that the sound of the rain had subsided.

He held his china cup the way a man might a draught of beer and took several slurps before setting it into its saucer.

"The Five Foxes pub fire and murder from a week ago, I presume? I've been expecting you," Holmes began. He reached over to an end table and picked up a copy of *The Times* between his index finger and thumb, adroitly unfolding it to the front page with a quick shake. The result was a display of the article and headline on the very topic.

Lestrade's tight lips loosened, exposing his angular teeth. "Correct, Mr. Holmes. Ceagan, the owner, appears to have been killed in the wee hours after closing. Shot in the back at relatively close range. We found his body in front of an open safe. He had a fowling gun nearby, but it appears to have been undisturbed. A cash box was sprung open and emptied. There were no witnesses. The annex, a bit of a lean-to really, burned to the ground, but the pub proper is still standing and is largely untouched. We found a gold pocket watch in the man's pocket.

"The pub is a remote midpoint," the inspector continued. "The main building didn't burn, despite being fueled by scotch whisky and brandy, because none were stored in the annex. This past week's rains and the stone exterior probably helped as well."

"I suppose by now gawkers and neighbors have managed to trample over much of the grounds," Holmes said tersely. "Do you have a list of patrons which you could share with me?"

"I've compiled one and I'll get it to you, but it won't help much," Lestrade replied, wrinkling his forehead. "It's a baker's dozen of unsavory individuals – any of whom is capable of this sort of thing. So far, I've interrogated a blacksmith, a tenant farmer, a part-time cook, a millworker, and a milkmaid. They're being dutifully cooperative, out of fear, I presume, that I could jail any one of them. One has a record of theft, but we searched a room that he rents and found nothing but old socks and bottles. The culprit we're after could well have been a random vagabond or transient."

"Any evidence of any of them spending like one of the Royal Navy's finest?" Holmes asked.

"Not to my knowledge, but you seem to have a knack for discovering that sort of thing," Lestrade replied, getting up.

"Inspector, would you be able get me a report of Ceagan's land title and that of the neighboring owners?"

"I'm not a barrister or a clerk, Holmes. I have criminals to catch, not papers to sort," the man replied, abruptly opening the door.

"Understood. We'll be in touch, Inspector."

Chapter III – A Primer on Foxes

The following morning after a light breakfast of tea, hard-boiled eggs, plum jam, and toast, Holmes asked, "Watson, are you ready for a trip to the countryside? It's time to visit the Five Foxes, a pub unimaginatively christened in honor of those preeminent and much-maligned chicken thieves."

"Country pubs relish the animal references, don't they?" I responded, handing Mrs. Hudson my cleaned plate and half-folded napkin.

"While many public houses are named after a place – heraldry, or even an abandoned boot – It is true that the images of animals abound. Stags, lions, boar, eagles, swans, goats, horses, and even unicorns are just some of the iconography. Though I do find the reference to foxes an interesting one," he said, pushing back his chair. "Most men associate foxes with their canine lineage, and rightly so, but their behavior at times is more akin to that of a cat," Holmes expounded. "I wonder if the resplendent Reverend William Heathcote or his peerage, so well-articulated by the painter Daniel Gardner – or, for that matter, others portrayed in hunting scenes in our gentlemen's clubs – understand the characteristics of this intriguing animal.

"If you study the paws of certain foxes, such as greys in the Americas, you will notice that they have claws which partially retract. I've observed them climb straight up a tree trunk of a Norway Maple when spooked. And like felines, foxes are more nocturnal, walk on their toes when stalking, and pounce on their prey. Some even will sleep in trees. Unlike dogs, they don't hunt in packs – they're loners, so seeing 'five' foxes together would be unusual – unless they were pups. But who am I to criticize a proprietor's whimsy, especially one who's deceased, when it comes to the naming of his establishment?"

"Who, indeed," I responded.

"I could lecture on foxes for hours – they are creative collectors. I knew a golfer from Perth who would complain about the shrewd creatures collecting lost golf balls. Additionally, foxes have a remarkable vocal range – barking, clucking, and even shrieking. Watson, I fear that in this instance, we may be after a human fox who has shown his victim an absence of any mercy."

While I knew Holmes to be a polymath, his range of knowledge on variety of subjects appeared boundless. I suspect it was his intense

131

curiosity, along with his near supernatural ability to master and memorize the nuances of different subjects, which allowed him to draw together disparate strands – to come upon conclusions which forever astound me. Taking a respite from my medical duties would have its rewards, for our day, undoubtedly, would be filled with more surprises.

Outside, I detected a slight change in color in Holmes's face, evidence that he was warming to the challenge which Lestrade had laid in front of him. We climbed into a hansom and headed south toward Melcombe Street. Turning in the direction of Paddington Station. From there, our route would eventually take us through Hayes, Slough, and Maidenhead, and on to the more rural parts of Woodcote, including nature's bowers of elms laden full of lush leaves.

The air was still damp, but without any dreariness. The tops of posts and fence edges were still dappled with water drops. For some reason, perhaps because of brief journey ahead of us, even the dreariest of London's buildings seemed to be painted fresh with my expectations.

Chapter IV – Pub Brawl

Soon after arriving in Woodcote, we stepped down from the small carriage that we had hired at the station. As I stamped the blood back into my feet, Holmes negotiated with the driver to return at a later hour. From the angle of our arrival, we could see that the deceased owner's home was behind the pub's main structure. The smell of damp charcoal was still detectable, though nine days had passed since the arson, murder, and robbery. We walked the perimeter of the building, slowly, as if measuring distances with our strides. I could see ivy climbing up the north-facing shadier side – it reached up to the dark slate roof and around a small gabled window. Holmes had yet to remove his magnifying glass from his coat pocket, and instead walked up to the barricaded threshold. He tested it with a stout pull on one of the handles.

"Watson, give me a hand with this door, won't you?"

"Should we wait for the current proprietor?"

"He was a widower, with no next of kin."

The small porch had a low, stone overhang jutting above the entrance. We stooped and put both our shoulders towards the door and lurched forward. I looked at Holmes briefly and he had one eye shut. At first it held fast, but with a renewed and second effort, the vintage hasp gave way with a loud crack. Its bolts dislodged from the weathered frame and hung from the open door. Once inside, the interior was quite dim, lit feebly by light from a side window's small panes.

"Hullo! You rascal!" I heard Holmes blurt, and the sound of feet scuffling. He was in a vigorous engagement with dark hulk which appeared more bear than a human. I felt helpless, trying to discern what was occurring, when I saw Holmes employ some sort of Oriental wrestling technique, hurling the large figure off of him and flattening him onto the floor. Since I was without my Webley, I took a boxer's stance, projecting my elbows forward, along with my clenched fists. In the alarm of the moment, my eyes began to perceive opaque objects: Framed paintings on a stone wall, tables askew, upturned chairs, and rounded bar stools.

"Careful, Watson, he has a knife!" Holmes shouted, as the large man lunged for me. Somehow Holmes deftly struck the assailant just below the shin with a foot, and the brute fell towards me with both hands outstretched. Reflexively, I connected squarely with the top of the attacker's head, snapping it back, and he landed like a toppling of stones in front of me. To my relief, the bully remained inert.

Holmes found a small kerosene lantern, half-full of fuel, and got it to glow brightly. I rubbed my knuckles, grateful that none had been broken in the altercation – despite the opponent's hard skull. To lose my ability to perform surgery due to such an incident would be a high price for a country outing. This was a calculus which I rarely, if ever, performed – such was my addiction to participating in the great detective's undertakings.

I took stock of our opponent's features as he began to stir. I guessed him to be twenty stone and at least six-feet in height. He was muscular in build, with a square jaw and *Brachycephalic*-type cranium. My strike, which had brought him down, was more luck than skill, and my uneasiness increased as he glared at us with glistening, coal-black eyes.

"Watson, may I introduce you to the village farrier, Mr. Seth Lans. He was in the process of liberating Ceagan's pub of its spirits when we decided to enter the premises."

"How do you know my name," he grunted in reply, rising to his feet and squaring his shoulders with a wince.

"I have a list from Scotland Yard of all the locals. Allow us to introduce ourselves. My name is Sherlock Holmes and this is my trusted companion, Dr. Watson. We have been asked by Inspector Lestrade to assist in solving Ceagan's untimely demise. Though you aren't wearing your leather apron, I note your trade from the scars on your hands from horseshoe nails, the crushed middle phalanx of your middle finger, the dots on your skin caused by sparks, and evidence on your left cheekbone that you were once kicked by a stubborn horse. Your carriage also shows the strains of your profession on your lower vertebrae, as you spend much of your time stooped over the fetlocks of a horse or mule."

"I had nothing to do with the old man's death!" the blacksmith replied. "Nothing at all."

"Really?" answered Holmes in a quiet voice. "Were you present the night Ceagan was murdered?"

"I already answered the detective's questions. I was, but I wasn't the last one out. Willie, the stableman, was. And, he's the one with a record of stealin' things, not me!"

"Anyone besides you two present that evening?" Holmes demurred.

"Claude, who works down at the mill had a pint or two. Marguerite, who helps Seldridge's dairy cows on the farm next door. Thomas, the pub cook."

"Did Ceagan speak in a loud voice?" Holmes asked.

"Yes, I suppose he did. He was always yelling about something."

"Mr. Lans, you have been very helpful to this investigation. Now, may I suggest that you gather the rack of whisky that you've collected for yourself and leave. And, Mr. Lans . . . ."

"Yes, Mr. Holmes?"

"May I also encourage you stop greeting strangers with knives."

"I wasn't going to use it," the blacksmith replied. "I was just going to threaten you."

"You were very effective in your objective," Holmes responded.

The man lifted a large wooden box covered with a gunny sack – we could hear the bottles underneath clank against each other as he walked. As the distance between us grew, the sound became quieter and quieter.

I turned to Holmes. "I realized you used the pirate's tactic earlier when we first breached the entrance. You kept one eye shielded from the light to make sure that the other could adjust quickly once you were inside the dark pub."

"You're a quick study, Watson. An eye patch would have made today's task a bit easier, but I've been told that I'm off-putting enough as it is . . . ."

Picking up the kerosene lamp, Holmes stepped towards at the rear of the main room. While not ordinarily superstitious, the light gave our pathway an otherworldly feeling, as if we were descending like Virgil and Dante or Christian mystics of old to some lower, dreaded place. Holmes, absent any of my delusory misgivings, intoned, "Come! Let us review the scene of the crime and see what further insights are to be gleaned."

Chapter V – Holmes Cracks a Safe

Together, we stepped past overturned bar stools and heard the sound of glass crackling under our soles. The door to the back room was ajar – it

134

measured approximately fifteen-by-twenty feet. An oblong window with undamaged panes near the ceiling allowed additional light into the room. A small, stone hearth adorned the west end of the room and harbored a pile of burnt ashes. A bronze rack held a fire-poker, sweep, and ash shovel alongside. Above the mantel, a burlwood-framed mirror spanned about two-and-a-half feet in length – it was angled slightly from the wall, capturing our reflections as we migrated about the room. Drawers had been pulled from a dilapidated partner's desk which faced the wall and were stacked next to it. A squat, dark-green cast-iron safe was tucked in the room's corner. Its door was closed. It had a brass locking level and handle, and in the middle of the door, the blackened shape of an oval was located about three-quarters up from the floor. On a walls over his desk, a landscape painting approximately sixteen-inches-by-twenty in size displayed rugged terrain. When I examined the painting's corner, the signature had what looked to be the figure of a crown. On each side of the figure were two numbers: "*18*" and "*63*".

"Well, I see that Lestrade's men have outdone themselves yet again. I can see evidence of their arrival – the canvas stretcher to remove the body was first set down here. There are the remnants of the inspector's cigar ash." He knelt and rubbed the tobacco between his fingers. "Since they've closed the safe, I suppose we might as well have some fun. Though the front plaque is missing, I can see that was made in West Bromwich by Thomas Witmere and Sons. Since it uses a key, I brought along a few handy items."

From his breast pocket, Holmes pulled out a small leather folio and opened it. The inside was padded and he extracted a ring of odd-looking keys. Many of their ends had miniature rakes. Others had their points bent at odd angles. Holmes deftly began working a number of the picks into the safe's master lock.

"While the French may be renowned for their perfume and soaps, this set of picks is courtesy of a very talented Parisian whom I befriended a number of years ago."

In moments, Holmes had cracked the safe and swung open its thick door – as Lestrade reported, the main container area was empty. "Watson, shine the lamp over here, won't you?" Two small interior drawers also had locks, which Holmes dispatched even more quickly.

After a moment, he closed the safe and stood. He then walked over and unlocked the small den's exit door, surveyed the hardware and frame, and then closed and re-secured it. He reviewed some of the inexpensive etchings on the walls. One was a Herbert Dicksee of two tigers leaning over a watering hole. Another, less formal and more humorous, was entitled, "*The Enraged Musician*". A couple of short candles held in pewter candlesticks had served their usefulness and were in need of replacing. One of the walls was papered in deep burgundy and imprinted with a recurring flourish.

"Watson, I have decided to abscond with the mirror over the hearth."

"Holmes – " I questioned, for he was certainly not a looter.

He read my thoughts stating, "I have a general idea, and I believe that I can make use of it during the investigation. Given its weight, I would like to enlist your help – if in doing so, you won't aggravate your old war injury."

"That Jezail bullet only distresses one of my limbs, Holmes – if there's trouble, I have the others to pick up the slack."

With a bit of zest, we dislodged the corded strand of wire from the wall hangers and negotiated the mirror through the pub. Holmes managed to keep the kerosene lamp in tow as well. Once out the main door, he went back in to extinguish it. Upon his exiting, I pulled the door fast and affixed the broken hinge in a way so that it appeared intact.

"That ruse won't keep the mice out of this barn for long, I imagine," he said.

The carriage driver helped us strap the mirror to the top of the cab.

"Watson, we have one more stop to make. I'd like to pay a visit to the neighboring farm owner by the name of Robert Coo."

"Do you think Coo will know of additional suspects?"

"A truism. Farm owners are always being approached by wayfarers for work."

Chapter VI – The Coo Farm

We proceeded up a country lane, demarked by well-lined fences and verdant hedgerows to protect crops. A light wind moved the tree branches with synchronicity. The setting was one which might have inspired Ponchielli's *Dance of the Hours*. For some reason, the flight of redwing blackbirds reminded me of a classical pianist's spirited run up and down the keyboard. A group of red-and-white Herefords were gathered in a meadow by a well-constructed barn. The estate struck me as one that was overseen with disciplined care.

A woman wearing a black dress, contrasted by a white coif and apron, could be seen carrying a wicker basket into the main farm cottage. She gave us a brief look before disappearing into the dwelling. A blue belton English setter loped towards us, barking enthusiastically. A woolly fur emanated from his undercarriage, along the underside of his wagging tail. A black, upturned outline along his muzzle made the dog seem as if he was looking at us with a slight smile. A man, dressed somberly and wearing an outdated felt hat, rode towards us on a bay gelding. He checked the reins and the horse responded promptly, stopping in front of our carriage.

Holmes exited with alacrity and walked up to the rider. I did my best to follow suit, following a few steps behind.

"Gentlemen," the farmer announced, his voice resonating a deep bass, "how may I help you?"

"Mr. Coo, I am Sherlock Holmes and this is my colleague, Dr. Watson."

"We have no need of a doctor, here. You must have the wrong address."

"We are investigating the murder of your neighbor, Mr. Ceagan, at the behest of Inspector Lestrade."

"My wife and I are simple folk, Mr. Holmes. We have little interaction with the likes of a pub owner."

"Understood, Mr. Ceagan. I see that you have a game bag on your saddle."

"Rabbits. They are the nuisance of any farmer. But, when prepared correctly, make a decent stew."

"A skittish quarry," Holmes observed.

I thought of hare soup, Florendine, and other dishes. It was obvious to me that I hadn't eaten enough breakfast for the journey. Nor had we time for lunch. To distract myself from my mild hunger pangs, I tendered a question:

"Any laborers or wanderers who were here and now departed since the incident, Mr. Coo?" I asked.

"I haven't seen Cyrus Johnson in the lane over the past week, Doctor. He hires himself out to some of the farms in the area. His perpetual poverty keeps him indentured to others."

"What does he look like?" I asked.

"He's not hard to miss. You can spot his red beard from a mile away."

"Well, Mr. Coo, I appreciate getting to meet you." Holmes turned to the driver. "Make sure that mirror is strapped on properly. I don't want it to break on our return to the station."

"Superstitious, Mr. Holmes?" the farmer asked with a resonating chuckle.

"Mirrors may or may not capture our souls, Mr. Coo, but I do sympathize with the caution," Holmes replied. "If nothing else, but for the hazard of the shards. Good day and, dare I say, 'Good luck to you'."

With those well-wishes, we climbed back into the carriage and started to make our way toward the familiar surroundings of 221b Baker Street.

Three days after our trip to the country, I found myself in our sitting room. Subconsciously, I inventoried the bullet holes in the wall, the lab microscope, Holmes's violin, the Persian slipper replete with tobacco, and the bachelor's sense of decorating. I looked on the table in front of the divan and noticed an array of postcards depicting headless torsos. They stood erect and most cradled a severed head in their arms. With a free hand, a number of the characters held a large knife or scythe. The effect suspended my disbelief briefly.

"I see that you are examining the popular work of C.W. Allen of Canterbury, Watson. Sensationalism, melodrama, eroticism, and shock all move along postcard sales, especially among the most gullible. Surgery performed by the photographer. All doctored to provide macabre titillation and get tourists to part with their pocket change."

"Some convince me more than others," I said, perusing the images.

"I suppose, Watson, that at some point, with the aid of such trickery, spiritualists will have us believing in fairies . . . ."

"Surely the English aren't that naïve!" I scoffed.

138

"You have a sturdy appreciation of the British intellect, Watson. After all, just in this century, Her Majesty's subjects have invented Macadam to construct efficient roads, Portland cement to construct buildings more quickly, the Analytical Engine, the incandescent light bulb, Boolean Algebra, the hypodermic syringe, and more. If you will turn your attention to this newspaper headline, Watson, I think that your presentiment will be confirmed yet again."

Holmes unfolded his long legs and extended a folded *Times* toward me. As I secured the periodical, I caught the headline which honored Holmes – no small irony as he was one of its chief critics. The private detective often derided the press for its rumor-mongering and spurious proclamations. In this instance, he was being heralded with breaking news:

Irrefutable Proof that Our Souls
Are Captured in Mirrors!
by Wm. S. Furten, Reporter
London, England

Eccentric Amateur Detective and Investigative Scientist, Sherlock Holmes, demonstrates that mirrors, under certain circumstances, capture images, similar to the science of photographic processing. The spectacle included the ignition of a substantial pan of phosphorus in front of a mirror. With an application of a secret process, to the amazement of all, Mr. Holmes was able to unveil a crisp and permanent image in the mirror of those present during the controlled explosion. The astounding unveiling occurred before a bevy of preeminent scientists at the Royal Academy and a standing room only gallery of onlookers. The location and academic qualifications of witnesses underscored the veracity of the remarkable process.

Holmes explains, "Even schoolchildren understand that mirrors are made by applying a reflective coating to a suitable substratum surface, usually glass. The coatings can be an amalgam of tin, silver, or mercury. Our modern mirrors are coated with silver nitrate, allowing for a more cost-effective coverage of a larger surface. Now, we understand that certain substances are affected by exposure to light. Most in this room are familiar with the daguerreotype process. Talbot perfected and expedited this process by using paper coated with silver iodide. Gentlemen, my breakthrough was discovering that

139

applying certain chemicals to the reflective coating of a mirror allows us to see images which have been captured under a unique set of circumstances, such as intense light – one instance I can envision is when an electrical discharge, such as a lightning bolt, occurs. Another instance, more pertinent to my profession, is the capturing of images when there is the discharge of a weapon in a darkened room. This has opened up a new repository of evidence helpful to one's methodical investigation of a crime. The mirror, ever-present, silent and watchful, can serve as a valuable witness."

Beyond science, spiritualists, including the famed Madame d'Esperance, *are abuzz and believe that this phenomenon offers a gateway into the supernatural. Inspector Lestrade, also present, admits, "Holmes presents us with a new, more science-based approach to the investigation of crime. While I am not a fan of private detectives, I admit that Mr. Holmes has taught this old dog a new trick."*

"Quite a concession by Lestrade, Holmes. Once again, your methods of investigation extend beyond my imagination."

"I invite you to look at the date of the article, Watson."

"Two days from today, I note. You were able to get an advanced copy?"

"Yes, I was able to secure twenty advanced copies. Because I had them printed myself. The article is pure fabrication, but it is my hope that it will allow us to shuck guilt out of a particular oyster."

"Gracious, Holmes! You are not playing by the Queensberry Rules, I see."

"Neither is our murderer, Watson . . . ." Holmes ruminated, placing his fingertips together as he studied the ceiling.

Chapter VIII – Closing the Net

The sun peeked through the bluster of the late morning. I found Holmes studying a sheaf of legal documents. A fire in the hearth warmed the room and the haze of tobacco smoke colored the air. A full ashtray next to Holmes provided evidence that the intricate wheels of his contemplative mind had been ratcheting their centrifugal turns throughout the night.

Rubbing his hands in a self-satisfied manner, Holmes began. "Watson, we will be closing our net soon on this heinous culprit. Before we continue, let us review the pertinent facts" And he proceeded to list them:

1. The Ceagan murder, arson, and robbery occurred in the early morning hours.

2. Only money and other unknown contents of the safe were taken.

3. The victim was shot in the back.

4. There were no witnesses to the crime.

5. Heavy rains and a plethora foot traffic by constables and the curious eliminated any helpful evidence we might have found outside the pub's grounds.

6. Only the lean-to of the main building was damaged in the fire, despite flammable contents inside the pub.

7. Ceagan had no heirs.

8. No known enemies have been identified.

9. He had a gold pocket watch in his pocket after the robbery.

10. A landscape painting of modest size hung on the wall over his desk.

11. Ceagan was known to shout rather than speak.

12. The money, if taken by a local, has so far remained unspent, requiring an unusual amount of discipline.

"What do these things tell us, Watson?"

"I am of the opinion that a gypsy or laborer of some rough sort waylaid the poor man, absconded with his money, and is long gone. "

"That is a possibility, and in alignment with the police's theory. Let us center on motive. Since Ceagan has no heirs, who would stand the most to gain from his death?"

"It confirms my theory that it was a crime of opportunity."

141

"That's always within the realm of likelihoods. What was Ceagan's most valuable asset?"

"His pub and home, I suppose . . . ." I replied.

"Precisely! And, in the absence of heirs, who would have the most to gain?"

"I'm at a loss there."

"A *creditor*, Watson! And, we know that a going concern is much more valuable than one which is not. For a business to lose its operator will, under most circumstances, ensure that if there was any outstanding debt, even a modest amount, would be unpaid, allowing for the mortgagee to foreclose on the mortgagor."

"So you had a sense of your quarry all along, I take it . . . ."

"My bloodhound instincts were set upon the correct course. Now, there are other interesting elements at play here – the fire on the property damaged an inherently worthless appurtenance, while the main building is constructed primarily of stone. If a murderer wanted to cover his tracks more thoroughly, he could have scorched the interior and roof. The pub was stocked full of flammables, so I determined that the fire was a diversion. In addition, Ceagan's watch had not been stolen, nor any of the pub's stock of spirits, nor the landscape painting, which is extremely valuable."

"Valuable? I'm not an art critic, but it seemed rather doleful and bleak . . . ."

"The stylized signature of the crown and date tipped me off immediately, Watson. It's a painting by Sir John Everett Millais. Perhaps you are familiar with his more famous painting, *Ophelia*, inspired by Shakespeare's *Hamlet,* Act IV?"

"The haunting image of a grieving woman floating in a river, her hands, in despair, turned upward?"

"One and the same. Yet this Millais painting remained in the pub, rather than stolen. All a thief would have to do is cut it from its frame and roll it up. He and his family would be set for a generation."

Holmes poured himself a cup of tepid tea and quickly drained the contents. He was undistracted by the temperature of the beverage, such was his single-mindedness.

"Now, we can also infer that Ceagan was hard of hearing, as he talked loudly. This allowed his murderer the opportunity to stalk and shoot him while he was bent over his safe. We can surmise that the victim never heard his attacker approaching. My suspicions turned to someone who could afford to lend Ceagan money – someone successful, who had prowess with a revolver. Someone who elected to leave behind a gold pocket watch and valuable painting, who perhaps doesn't revere such

142

things, and might even find them gaudy. Someone who could be a teetotaller."

"A Puritan farmer!" I exclaimed.

"Indeed, Watson. From our encounter, I could deduce something else: He was an expert with a revolver. For, though he had a game bag with rabbits, there was no hunting rifle across his lap or affixed to his saddle. In addition, the revolver he had on his person was concealed, probably inside his long coat. Also, from his manner of speaking, we can also infer that he had a comprehension of legal issues, as evidenced by his use of the word 'indentured.' But, without any witness, how was I to get him to confess to the murder? Here was a man with good standing in his community. Who shielded his true self behind respectability."

"Thus the ruse of the mirror and the newspaper article!"

"Yes, you are comprehending my logic. I have set a trap to catch this hunter of rabbits."

Chapter IX – The Bluff

"With a pecuniary encouragement of the newspaper deliverer, we have peppered the countryside near the Five Foxes Country Pub with our own newspaper. We're about to play a game of poker rather than chess. Let us hope that the ruse works."

At Holmes's request, Inspector Lestrade and a burly, sullen constable arrived at 221b Baker Street. Lestrade appeared wary and in ill-spirits, like a half-breed bulldog which had been dodging the hooves of carriage horses.

"This had better be good, Mr. Holmes. Your message said that you were having a visitor who's prepared to confess to the pub fire murder. I don't know how you're going to pull this off, as we still haven't had any decent leads to speak of . . . ."

Holmes put an index finger to his lips as one might an impetuous child and Lestrade's head seemed to recoil imperceptibly at the slight. Then, Holmes pointed to the door with the same digit.

Mrs. Hudson appeared, her hands clasped together, not so much in piety, but more as a way to restrain her exasperation – seemingly off-put by the number of residents and guests, she announced the arrival of Robert Coo, whom we learned had summoned at Holmes's request.

The farmer was still dressed in dark colors. When not atop his horse and in the city proper, the man appeared less cocksure. He held his hat in his hand. The official detective walked up and stood nearly toe-to-toe with him. Coo's lips formed a frown and his face looked more weathered than

143

when we had seen him last. There was perspiration on his forehead, unwarranted by the temperature.

"No need to check for his revolver, Lestrade," Holmes said. "I would have spotted his subtle but tell-tale disorder of his coat."

"You're a clever one, Mr. Holmes, I'll grant you that. Your novel brand of alchemy is most assuredly the surely devil's work."

Holmes stood next to a large easel which was covered with a black velvet shroud. It looked to be the same dimensions of the burl wood frame mirror which we had retrieved from Ceagan's pub office.

"You've been reading about me in the papers, I take it. You received my accusations and my method of confirming your culpability. Shall I unveil our findings, Mr. Coo? It will be my first opportunity to share it with the public, and I confess to an embarrassing affinity for the theatric – and the notoriety helps bring in new clientele."

This statements puzzled me, as they were in direct contravention of the habits and practices I had come to observe in the private detective. I realized that he was baiting as a means to get a rise out of his opponent.

"No need, you sorcerer! Does not the article in *The Times* which speaks to your abominable invention suffice? Such lust for flattery evidences your sin of pride! It was the bane of Lucifer himself."

"I don't have to show the crisp and irrefutable image of you firing at the hapless Ceagan with your revolver? I've resurrected your sly criminality in his mirror, through my ingenious use of certain photographic solvents and other uncommon chemicals. I am ready to unveil this silent witness."

"I appreciate you giving me the dignity to be arrested here, of my own volition, rather than being seized like a common criminal in front of my wife." Coo looked at his coal-black shoes and then over to the cloaked easel.

"You attest to your murdering of Mr. Ceagan, then?" Holmes asked casually.

"On the condition that you destroy this damnable evidence you hold against me if I do, Holmes," he boomed, gesturing towards the covered mirror.

"You have my word."

"Very well. I confess." The farmer seemed to be like a bellow which had fully dispensed of its air.

Lestrade turned to his colleague, "Secure this murderer and take him downstairs. I will follow you shortly."

After a minute had passed, Lestrade turned to Holmes, who was scooping up a fresh bowl of tobacco shag. The private detective procured a match and lit his briar pipe.

144

"How have you hypnotized this man, Holmes? What nonsense are you spouting about photographs in mirrors?"

"Guilt oppresses the mind in inexplicable ways, Inspector. Your question would be better directed to a man of medicine, such as Dr. Watson here."

"Let me look at the mirror, Holmes." Lestrade bent his head to the side slightly, revealing his curiosity.

"Inspector, allow a bluffer to mix his cards into the deck and not reveal his hand, won't you?"

"Very well, Mr. Holmes. You are an unorthodox gambler, but I dare say that I wouldn't want to play against you."

"I'll take that as a compliment."

"It wasn't meant as one," the inspector replied as he exited the flat. I could hear his hurried descent and the lower door close.

"A magician never reveals his tricks to his audience, Holmes, and thereby spoiling the suspense?" I asked.

Holmes clenched the pipe between his teeth and pulled a green-covered book from his shelf, entitled *The Secrets of Conjuring and Magic*.

"A translation of *Les Secrets de la Prestidigitation et de la Magie* by Robert-Houdin. The author describes how his conjuring would have those from a by-gone era suspecting him of '*supernatural powers*'. The illusionist goes on to explain, '*These mysterious arrangements are, in truth, simply ingenious applications of science to domestic purposes*'."

"I would say that your purpose in avenging Ceagan's death is more than 'domestic'."

"True. Add enough real science along with the fabrication, and the hot air balloon of one's hoax will traverse an entire continent. Edgar Allen Poe himself would have been quite proud."

Holmes drew on his pipe and exhaled a blue ring of smoke towards the ceiling. "Watson, would you be so kind as to remove the cover which obscures the easel?"

"Certainly." I lifted the cloth off of what I was expecting to be the pub mirror. In violation of my expectations, I was looking at the Millais landscape which had been in the victim's office – it was reframed with stunningly ornate gold leaf. The effect was as if a plain and severe woman had been brought to life with an elegant gown and radiant smile.

"I purchased it from the court-appointed handler of Ceagan's estate. I believe that the man's interest in art begins and ends with *Uncle Toby* by Uncle Toby. I plan, on my passing, to bestow it to the Royal Academy of Arts' permanent collection, in honor of their distinguished student."

"With more light on the piece, I could come to appreciate it," I offered in consolation.

145

With the slightest smile, Holmes replied, "Don't pander to me, Watson! Now, for the day's final mystery, let us wager what Mrs. Hudson plans to serve for dinner . . . ."

"Uncle Toby"

The Mysterious Mr. Rim
by Maurice Barkley

Several times over the years, I have taken pen in hand to document a very strange case, but until now I've set the pen aside unused. I'm not a man who believes in magic. I concede that the world abounds with mysteries that defy logical explanations and, when presented to me, I approach them as an agnostic with an open mind. I could not count the times when Holmes has made remarkable revelations that seem to have been impossible without the imposition of some mystical power. Then there are his exposés of the deductions and observations that led him to these miraculous destinations. I must admit that revealing the process at times diminishes the wonder of the solution, but Holmes had little interest in what he referred to as theatrics – he left that to me.

In the case of the mysterious Mr. Rim, I was completely taken in. I was there the whole time. I saw everything from start to the astounding finish, and although I pride myself on not being given to moods and fancies, I could not dispute the revelations as I witnessed them.

At the end, Sherlock Holmes and his brother, Mycroft, had explanations and reasons for keeping me in the dark. I had to agree there was logic to everything – but to be there and see what I saw . . . . Well, I still wonder.

His name was not Mr. Rim. I don't know his real name, although Sherlock and Mycroft Holmes do – or at least they *say* they do, but they told me that my knowing would not be wise. Although curious, I left it at that. The truth is that although I hold no grudge or defined fear, I hope never to see the man again. No human should have such power – if indeed he possesses it. Holmes said that his power was part illusion, but I know what I saw and what it did to the sorry victim.

It was a time of suspicion and intrigue. Secrets flourished around every corner, especially those many corners in the Foreign Office. Frequently Holmes was called upon to lend his special talents, which he did without hesitation. Just as frequently I was at his side, so I wasn't at all surprised when he asked me to assist him with one of his problems.

"There you are, Watson," said Holmes from the breakfast table as I came down from my room, having overslept a bit. "The food is still warm. I've finished, but I will wait, so do take your time."

"Oh," I said, "you have news?"

He waved a small paper. "A message from Mycroft. It is something in which he and I have been involved for several days. It has come to fruition."

"Is that so?" I said. "Several days you say? This is the first time you have mentioned it."

Holmes poured some coffee. "Until this moment, my involvement was limited to advice on particular procedures that involved following a subject unobserved – " He paused to sip the brew. " – which was well received and successful, up to a point."

I became so attentive that I over-buttered my toast. "Drat," I said, discarding the ruined slice. "So, are we – am *I* involved?"

"By all means," said Holmes, "Now is the time for action, and you have a part to play."

I bit into my newly buttered toast. "Excellent. What do I need to know?"

"We are going to a room in the Foreign Office. Mr. Rory Hogan, a man who is under suspicion, and his solicitor, Mr. Alfred Alcott, will be on one side of a table. You, Mycroft, one other person, and I and will be on the other. Mycroft and I will be the only persons who speak. Your task is to simply sit in view of the subject and observe. It's important that you not react overtly to what you may see or hear."

"Sounds rather strange," I said, "but I can do that. In fact, you have made me quite curious. Do I need any other information?"

"No," he said, "it is imperative that you know nothing. I need uncomplicated reactions to what you will witness. The man doesn't know what I may know. I hope to play on that fear."

This seemed most interesting. I lay my toast aside and we left without delay. On my infrequent trips to the Foreign Office, I usually visited the office of Holmes's brother, Mycroft. On that day, we descended to a rather dismal area in the basement and entered an equally dismal room. The weak winter sun pushed through a squat, grilled window high on the wall to cast a barred image on the surface of a plain wooden table. If it was meant to intimidate, it was more than adequate. The room held only six chairs and the one ugly table. Wall sconces shed adequate but uncertain light. Two occupied chairs were on the far side of the table. Holmes told me earlier that they would hold the man under suspicion and his solicitor, whom I noted, looked his part – elegant with a well-groomed beard. He was almost prim. The man under the cloud looked the part of an average office clerk, displaying a combination of resolve and uncertainty. His frock was somewhat threadbare as was his scalp, slicked down with an oily substance. *He is holding up well under the circumstances*, I thought.

148

The four chairs on our side stood empty, but just as I finished observing what lay before us, the door behind us opened and Mycroft entered. Nothing was said. Mycroft went to the end chair on the right and Holmes took the end one on the left while nodding me into the one next to him. The silence continued until it became a bit uncomfortable. The solicitor twisted in his chair, trying to decide whether or not to speak. I even became a bit uneasy for no rational reason. We just sat in a profound silence.

"Mister Hogan." Mycroft's voice boomed in the small chamber. I jumped a bit, as did the two opposite me. "You displayed surprise and indignation when I accused you of treasonous behavior and demanded you reveal the identity of the man to whom you report. You must think that we possess nothing but suspicion, but you are very wrong. There are things we do know – enough to send you to the gallows." Mr. Hogan's resolve began to wither, but the solicitor reached to lay his hand on the man's arm and place his index finger over his mouth – a warning to keep silent. Mycroft slammed his fist on the table top. "Yes, Mr. Hogan, do keep silent. In fact, you are to say nothing at all. Simply sit there and listen. Statements will be made, but you are not to answer, nor should you react at all. If at some point you decide to cooperate by naming the man we want, just raise your hands." Mycroft then stood and leaned over the table, towering over both the subject and his solicitor. "What you must do is keep you face turned to the man who will soon be occupying this empty chair next to me. Heed my words, Mr. Hogan – when we finish here, you will leave this room for a modest punishment, or you will soon see your executioner. It all depends on your cooperation." Mycroft sat. "Those are my final words. From this moment, the only one who will speak is the gentleman in the gray suit."

My suit was brown.

Sherlock Holmes, in a gray suit, stood and opened the door. "Come in, Mr. Rim," he said while indicating the second chair. "Make yourself comfortable."

I turned in my chair and saw a remarkable sight. Stooped and hesitant, an ancient creature shuffled through the door, leaning heavily on a gnarled cane almost big enough to be a staff. Bursts of grey hair shot out from under an overlarge round hat. What little of his small face I could see was as withered as a winter windfall apple – almost elfin. Halfway to his seat, he paused to look momentarily at each of us in turn. When he looked at me I couldn't look away. The thick lenses of his heavy glasses magnified glittering dark eyes that stared at me with fierce intensity.

Remarkable, I thought. *So this storybook creature is Mr. Rim, but what is he to do? His gaze is ferocious and disturbing, but if he speaks not, I do not see his value.*

While Mr. Rim was taking his seat, Holmes picked up his chair and sat it directly in back of the strange old man. Instead of sitting, he stood, his back to the subject. This I think was to force Mr. Hogan to constantly see those intimidating eyes. I could see him in profile and so did not react when he removed his hat, but the two across from him had an exceptional response. They both awkwardly jumped back even though seated, their faces contorted with astonishment. I was very curious, but I could not move to see what had caused such a reaction.

Holmes spoke to them. "Return to the table and do not look away. If you must, look at his hat or his beard, but do not look away."

Once again all was quiet and the effect became more dramatic. Both he and his solicitor were the picture of confusion and worry. Holmes struck a match over his pipe but decided against it and blew it out. Finally he broke the silence. "Mr. Hogan, my task is to make you reveal the name of the man you secretly meet every Friday evening. We have followed your path for some weeks, but you seemed to have gone directly home. This afternoon we shall learn the truth. Each statement I make you will know to be true or false – but again I warn you to keep silent and do not turn away." After a short pause, Holmes said, "Your true name is, Rory Hogan."

Thump. The old man brought his staff down on the floor.

"You have nothing to conceal."

Thump, thump.

The sound seemed to vibrate through the floor. The atmosphere was becoming bizarre. I began to see puzzlement and a degree of alarm on the faces of Mr. Hogan and his solicitor. It seemed obvious to me that one thump indicated true and two indicated false. Were we to believe that Mr. Rim was a mind reader? Was this a parlor game? I did not know what to think.

"I see," said Holmes, quietly. "Immediately you attempt to conceal, but you do so at your own peril." He continued asking half of a dozen simple obvious questions, and then he turned to face the table and sat down.

I was watching the subject intently and his face revealed quite a bit. As Holmes neared the end of his first series of questions, I could see the man's confidence return. He could not hide his smug superiority. Surely this was indeed a parlor trick, easily overcome. It was time for him to relax and enjoy thwarting the foolish efforts of the inquisitors. Holmes saw what

150

I saw and smiled slightly. He lit another match and this time set the flame to his pipe. Mycroft remained still as a Buddha.

"Mr. Hogan," Holmes began, "At the end of each day, you want us to believe that you leave the Foreign Office and go directly home."

Thump.

The subject could not quite conceal his smile. The solicitor's face became blank as his confidence returned.

"When you leave this building, you exit by the main entrance."

Thump.

"You turn left, walk to Whitehall where you hail a cab."

Thump.

"The cab proceeds to the Strand, then across Waterloo Bridge, and straight on to your apartment in Newington."

Thump.

The amusement in Hogan's face was changing to contempt. The solicitor's face remained blank.

"You are not fearful of being followed."

Thump, thump.

"Oh, you are," said Holmes. "I presume you know what will happen next Sunday." This time Mr. Rim's staff made a scraping sound as he drew it across the floor. "Ah, you are confused. Again, I thought as much. Now we can begin."

Hogan's face and countenance again shifted, this time to display concern. He leaned slightly to his right in an attempt to see his inquisitor's face, but Holmes moved to thwart his attempt. All he could see were the eyes of Mr. Rim.

"Now we must talk specifically about each Friday in the more recent past. You board the cab as usual and it arrives at your dwelling by the same route and manner."

Thump.

"Once there, you depart the cab and enter your apartment."

Thump, thump.

Now Hogan, and surprisingly the solicitor, struggled to hide the alarm they felt. The atmosphere of the room closed in and became thick. One of the wall sconces flickered and died, leaving just two others to create wavering shadows. *Was it by design?* I began to tense and found my hands gripping the seat of the hard wooden chair. Although I wanted to shake my head to clear it, my job was to observe and not react.

From the corner of my eye, I saw Mr. Rim momentarily remove his glasses. The two men opposite reacted as though they had seen something hideous. I glanced at the little man, but I was too late to see what they saw.

151

"Ah," Holmes spoke softly and both men unconsciously leaned forward, "When you left this building there was a cab waiting for you – not a random vehicle."

Thump.

"And it contained an associate dressed in a manner similar to your attire."

Thump.

Hogan coloured up and beads of moisture appeared on his forehead. Again his solicitor reached to touch his arm, but his client pulled away. His look of alarm turned to one of panic.

Holmes turned to Mycroft, whose face was in deep shadow. "Your people followed Mr. Hogan home every day for three weeks and I am sure you have each cab number." Mycroft nodded. "And was it the same cab each Friday?" Another nod. "Was the cab followed after leaving him at his destination?" This time Mycroft shook his head. "Regrettable," Holmes murmured, "but not critical. And now, Mr. Hogan, do you see where this is going? It will be a simple matter to talk to the cab driver. The net closes ever closer around you, and once it closes, you will be lost."

Hogan's eyes jerked back and forth as he searched our faces in a desperate effort to evade the eyes of Mr. Rim who simply sat motionless, leaning forward on his crooked staff. Holmes sat silent for several long minutes. The silence was as menacing as his voice. I began to wonder about the solicitor. *Is he involved in the crime? His behavior does not match the actions of one who is simply defending a client.*

Holmes relighting his pipe was a release from the terrible strain. I was so absorbed in the drama that I felt a degree of gratitude for this simple action, ending the episode. I chided myself for sinking so far into the spell. My attention was now focused intently on Mr. Hogan and his solicitor. Both were in a bad way. Their faces distorted as they tried to hide their fear. I didn't enjoy seeing this, though I knew Holmes was doing the right thing. The room seemed to shrink and become more menacing. Try as I might, I couldn't keep their terror from impacting my emotions. I began to perspire despite the cold clammy air.

"I see," said Holmes. "You're determined to hang onto that slender thread of hope. Very well, but if you cling to it much longer, that thread will grow into a gallows rope."

Tap, tap, tap.

I flinched as did the two across the table. *What the devil is that new sound and what does it mean?*

Tap, tap.

This time I noticed the movement and saw that it was Holmes knocking the ashes from his pipe on the side of a chair. I am sure he noticed their reactions, but no apologies were forthcoming and he resumed his statements.

"Once the cab leaves your dwelling, it reverses course and returns this way over the Waterloo Bridge."

Thump.

"Then back down the Strand."

Thump.

"Perhaps it is returning to the Foreign Office."

Thump, thump.

"It proceeds north along Charing Cross Road."

Thump.

"On to Tottenham Court Road."

Thump.

"And then Hampstead Road.

Thump. Thump.

"It turns right toward King's Cross."

Thump, thump.

"Left then, toward Regent's Park."

Thump.

The pressure was becoming unbearable. I could see Hogan struggling to breath – his chest constricted – his mouth dry. *Surely he must break soon.* The solicitor kept his eyes locked on his client. His behavior was abnormal for one who was merely an advocate.

Holmes stood. "Last chance, Mr. Hogan." While uttering his name, the door behind us opened and three burly officers entered and walked around the table to stand behind the two. "Regent's Park is an excellent place for a clandestine meeting. I will now explore that possibility." Holmes moved to stand beside Mr. Rim. He leaned forward and placed both hands on the table, much as Mycroft had done. "The carriage entered the park."

Thump.

"There you were to meet a . . . ."

"Stop!" Hogan tried to shout, but his breathing was ragged and it turned into a shriek. He looked at the solicitor, but at the same time shrank back from him. "You said it was foolproof! That we were dealing with idiots." He turned to look at Mycroft and with a false hysterical laugh. "He said you and the others are idiots."

The man collapsed back in his chair – mentally and physically exhausted. The solicitor all the while gave up all pretense of separation and sat with his hands covering his face.

"You are not finished, Mr. Hogan," Holmes's voice was hard and cold. "Name the man to whom you have given state secrets." Beyond speech, he could only point to the solicitor, who did not move to object.

"Take them," Holmes said to the guards and in moments we four were alone in the room. "Thank you, Mr. Rim. You have done well."

The small man stood, nodded, put on his glasses, and shuffled from the chamber, having yet to say a single word.

Back in Mycroft's office, we relaxed around his conference table with cigars and a generous amount of sherry.

Mycroft lifted his glass to us. "Highly satisfactory I would say. It was a stellar performance, dear brother. And you, Dr. Watson – your behavior was exceptional. I understand you were to witness without knowing what we were about, and you did it splendidly."

"My head is still spinning," I said. "What I witnessed was, on the face of it, beyond belief. Are you at liberty to enlighten me?"

"Most certainly, Doctor," Mycroft reached to refill my glass. "What I am about to reveal must be held in confidence, as long as Mr. Rim is alive." I nodded. "First I must tell you that there are only three people who know the extent of his talent – you will be the fourth. Although he is an extremely valuable asset, I would prefer he never existed." Mycroft rubbed his hands together, but not in satisfaction. He starred thoughtfully at his sherry for a few moments. "It is best that you know the entire story. Once you hear what I have to say, you will understand why Mr. Rim must be kept in secret and protected by us as long as he lives. If word of his abilities should be made public, I imagine the man would fall to an assassin's bullet in short order.

"It all began several years ago at the Diogenes Club. After having been served an exceptional vintage, I went in search of the wine steward. I found him in the kitchen, where conversation is not restricted. While talking to the fellow, I noticed a rather remarkable looking individual, hard at work in the scullery. His dress was shabby, but it was his large hat hiding most of his head and the extravagant beard that was most unusual. The wine steward told me what little he knew. He said that the man had frightening eyes. None of the staff liked him. Their irrational fear had turned to hostility, although he had never acted in a manner that would justify their enmity. I was curious and so had the wine steward arrange a meeting in one of the private rooms." Mycroft paused to sip his sherry. "I was there waiting for the man when he entered. He looked much the same as when you first saw him today. His large hat hid his eyes. I invited him to sit. He did, but did not remove his hat. I asked him to do so and with great reluctance he did, and I learned why his fellow workers feared him.

154

"Doctor, you know me. I am not a man who shrinks from danger, but this was not simply danger – I was looking at the unknown. Even now, I am reluctant to look directly at the man when I am talking to him. It is his eyes."

I nodded in agreement. "Indeed. He looked at me for just a moment, but it was a dreadful sight."

"Not the half of it, Doctor," he continued. "You saw his thick glasses that seemed to enlarge his eyes, but that was not their function."

"No?" I exclaimed. "What else could they be?"

"They are very special. We had them manufactured especially for him, along with dark glasses to use when out in public." Even though we were in Mycroft's private office, he leaned forward and spoke softly. "The glasses do not have convex lenses that *enlarge* how we view his eyes. They have concave lenses that *reduce* the image we see. The man is virtually blind when he uses them. That is why he shuffles along with a cane."

"But why," I asked, "reduce the apparent size of his eyes? It seemed more effective to let those two see them full size."

Mycroft bared his teeth and drew in his breath. "My friend, I have seen his unshielded eyes just once, and I hope to never see them again. You can attest to the fact that his glass-shielded eyes are fearsome, but he only displays them openly at my request."

I was still doubtful. "Is that it then – the man has frightful eyes? That does not account for what I saw in that room."

Mycroft filled his glass for a third time, leaned back, and nodded toward Holmes. "I will leave the revelation to my brother. I will listen along with you and struggle to believe."

I turned to Holmes. "Please tell me Mr. Rim is not some sort of mystic – a reader of minds or things of that sort."

"Watson," said Holmes, "I can assure you that I have a rational, although quite astounding, explanation. It is simply this: Mr. Rim reads *faces*." I'm sure my jaw dropped and I opened my hands wide in appeal. "Indeed, he reads faces much as you would read a book."

I shrugged in disbelief, "I am listening."

"Consider the average dog. Although we humans have greater intelligence and are masters of that creature, it has some capabilities far better than yours and mine. It detects an entire world of odors that are hidden from us. It detects a realm of sound that exists below and above our perception. Now – if you are a dog owner, perhaps you have observed your pet's ability to sense your mood by simply looking at you. We humans have that ability to a degree, but we can only recognize the more obvious facial contortions. Even a slightly raised eyebrow or a minimal elongation of one's mouth are like shouting to a dog. In that fashion, the dog often knows the intent of its master. It seems that we humans have the advantage solely in cranial capacity.

"Now, we normal people read faces constantly. There are the more gross signals, such as smiles, frowns, eyebrow movement, and so on. Then there are the more subtle signals created by minute muscle movements – a narrowing of the lips, a slight rising of the lower eyelid, an intensity of focus that can be difficult to describe. Even a blank look can be meaningful to a situation. Faces can flush from embarrassment, anger, effort, or excitement. Most of these topographies are presented automatically, but can often be suppressed or displayed artificially by one who is intent on deception. Are we in agreement thus far?"

"Quite clear," I said. "Is it that Mr. Rim is able to see more in a frown than the average person?"

"No, he sees what we cannot see or control – those things of which we are unaware. The average person gives little thought to the fact that there are over forty muscles in one's face and many react, creating very small facial signals beyond one's conscious control – minute muscle contractions and the movement of blood near the surface. All of these things can be detected by Mr. Rim and his frightful eyes."

I turned to Mycroft. "Have his eyes been examined? Have you determined how they function?"

"Our doctors have scrutinized him repeatedly," said Mycroft. "They think that somehow he is able to alter the shape of his lenses or eyeballs in the manner of powerful binoculars." He shrugged. "But then, it is merely an educated guess." He stood and glanced at the large clock on the fireplace mantle. "Our task is complete, my friends, and my chair at the Diogenes Club awaits."

We shook hands and departed. It was late in the day. A thin cold wind followed us to our cab, but I welcomed the change from that dismal room. The streets were darkened and slick – few people were about. Our cab was not air-tight, but the owner had provided heavy blankets.

"Watson," said Holmes, "my only fear was that at the conclusion of our session, you might have felt a bit slighted, having been left out in the cold as it were. I hope you do realize that your presence and reactions were vital to our success."

"Not at all, Holmes. It was a unique experience – somewhat disturbing, but utterly fascinating. I must say that I do not envy Mr. Rim his talent. In fact, I feel sorry for the man. His life must be most difficult."

"True," said Holmes. "The man is one of a kind – a human oddity. He has no children, which is a good thing. None of us would tolerate associating with one who could detect one's lies. Had Mycroft not discovered him, there is a good chance that he would have met a violent

156

end. As it is, he is provided for and protected by the government. When he dies, that will be the end of another experiment by nature."

"Now I feel a bit sorry for the poor fellow with that singular strange name." I said. "I cannot recall ever hearing Rim used for a person's name."

Holmes chuckled. "To further protect the man, Mycroft gave him that name after his lengthy interview when first they employed his talents. Picture if you will a wagon wheel, and apply it to the structure of our society. The axel would be the royal family and the hub the various forms of government. Then we have the spokes traveling outward. Near the hub you will find the nobility, leaders of industry and generally the upper class. Next are the middle class – sort them as you will, followed by the lower class and finally the rim, containing criminals and ne'er-do-*well*s – all persons who have no place in society. There you will find Mr. Rim."

As we turned onto Baker Street, I set aside the strange afternoon and my thoughts turned to the warm fire that was waiting for us.

The Adventure of the
Fatal Jewel-Box
by Edwin A. Enstrom

In all the world there is no weather as unpredictable as that of this great wen of London. All through the previous night, the wind had shrieked and moaned in the chimney and dashed great gouts of water against the windowpanes. One had to speak very loudly to be heard above the racket. This next afternoon, the sky was a cloudless, brilliant blue and the sun was drying the puddles in the street. Holmes and I were sitting in the front room at 221b Baker Street, enjoying the serenity of the day.

I was in my usual armchair, feeling very content. I had been out in last night's storm, attending at a difficult confinement, which eventuated in the appearance of a healthy baby boy, much to the joy of the new mother and father. I was now leafing through the latest issue of *The Lancet* in a somewhat desultory manner.

Holmes was sitting cross-legged on the floor in front of the fireplace, surrounded by half-a-dozen scrapbooks, a box of press clippings, and a pot of glue. He would take a clipping from the box, scan it quickly, and then paste it into one of the scrapbooks. I had been living with Holmes for a quite a few years by now, but I had never divined the arcane logic of his indexing system.

This happy scene was interrupted by the ring of the doorbell, followed by voices at the door. We heard steps on the stairs to our lodgings and then a knock at the door.

"Come in!" shouted Holmes.

Mrs. Hudson entered, followed by a man of medium height who had his bowler hat in one hand and a cardboard box under the other arm. I recognized him as an inspector from Scotland Yard, but one that I hadn't seen in some time and couldn't remember his name.

"Inspector Morton to see you, sir," said Mrs. Hudson, who withdrew, shutting the door behind her.

"If I am interrupting you, sir, I came come back later," said Morton diffidently.

"Not at all, Morton. Sit down and make yourself comfortable and tell us what brings you here after such a long time."

Morton stepped gingerly around the scrapbooks and glue, set his box down very carefully on the side table, and seated himself in the basket chair.

"Mr. Holmes, I have just come from a new case that I have been assigned. A curious feature of it reminded me of a case in which you and I were involved, and I thought you might be interested in hearing about it. Do you remember the affair of Culverton Smith?"

Holmes shot me a quick glance and then back to Morton. "Remember it? Hah! I think that was one of my best theatrical performances. I must admit that I regret having had to act so beastly to my stalwart Watson."

The memories of that sordid affair came flooding back to me. (I have written it up elsewhere under the title "The Dying Detective".) Holmes had pretended to be dying in order to lure the murderer into a trap. Morton had made the arrest. At the time I had been very angry at Holmes because he wouldn't let me near him to minister to him. I was later rather pleased when he confessed that he did this because he had enough knowledge of my medical talents to know that I wouldn't believe he was dying.

"So what reminded you of that case?" asked Holmes.

In reply, Morton very carefully reached into his cardboard box and took out a small jewel-box. He placed it gingerly on the table, facing it so it opened towards Holmes and me. Holding it with his left hand, he opened the lid with his right. Immediately a small window opened on the side and a sharp needle jutted out. He closed the lid and the needle retracted and the window closed. He opened it again and once more we saw the window and needle in operation.

"Tell us the whole story," said Holmes.

"I will, sir. First let me say that I have it second-hand from Jameson, the butler. I will have to go back tomorrow to speak to the housekeeper, who was in hysterics and had to be sedated. Yesterday, Andrew Pettigrew was found dead in his study. Do you know the man?"

"I have not personally met him, but I believe he is a rich industrialist, with steel mills in Birmingham. Is that him?"

"Yes, sir, you are correct. He has a large house in London and an extensive estate in Hertfordshire, as well as an interest in the mills you mentioned. Anyway, the housekeeper was bringing him his tea yesterday afternoon when she found him lying on the floor in his study, halfway between his desk and the door. She ran for the butler Jameson, who immediately called the doctor. The doctor pronounced him dead, but was quite bewildered as to the cause of death. Pettigrew was nearing fifty, but he was in excellent health. There were no marks on the body, and he had not eaten or drank anything since lunch, so far as is known. The doctor spoke to Pettigrew's wife and convinced her to allow an autopsy to be done. The body is in the morgue at St. Barts right now.

"So much for yesterday," continued Morton. "This morning, the housekeeper and a maid went to the study to straighten it up. The

159

housekeeper was adjusting the curtains when the maid cried out behind her. She turned around and saw the maid holding up a finger, which was bleeding from a pin-prick. The maid said that the jewel-box had stabbed her. The maid said she felt a little weak and wanted to sit for a bit. After a minute or so, she was able to gasp out that she couldn't breathe. Her face was contorted with fear. In another minute or two, she was dead. The housekeeper became hysterical and started screaming, which brought Jameson running. He rang for the doctor again and tried to calm the housekeeper. He was able to get this outline of what happened before she became incoherent. The doctor gave her a heavy sedative and she has been asleep since. That is all I know."

"Watson, please get me the fifth book from the left in the third row."

I retrieved the requested volume and saw that was titled *Poisons of the World*, by M. C. Jeffers, F.R.C.S. I handed it to Holmes, who quickly found what he wanted.

"A-ha! Listen to this," cried Holmes. "'*The poison dart frog exudes on its skin a poisonous alkaloid liquid called* batrachotoxin. *The poison causes paralysis and death when it enters the bloodstream, even in minuscule amounts. Death results in three to five minutes. The poison will remain potent for a year or more*'. I think this is what we are dealing with here."

Holmes got out his magnifying glass and scrutinized the jewel-box very closely. The initials "*AJP*" were inscribed on its lid. Turning it over, we saw a mark that looked like the capital letter "*H*" with wings, surrounded by a circle. I supposed it was some kind of maker's mark. Holmes copied it out on to a piece of notepaper. He then studied the inside of the object and said that it appeared to be a standard jewel-box that had been modified to add the window and needle. It must have been done by a real craftsman.

"We will report to you later, Morton," said Holmes. "In the meantime, Watson, let us be off."

"Where are you going?" asked Morton. "The Pettigrew house?"

"No, the morgue at Barts." replied Holmes.

We secured a hansom and drove the short distance to the hospital. Both Holmes and I are well-known there, so we had no problem gaining access to the morgue. We were introduced to the doctor who was going to perform the autopsy. He brought us to Pettigrew's body and removed the covering sheet. Holmes immediately inspected the left hand.

"As I suspected, there is a pin-prick on his index finger. Doctor, please wait a bit before doing the autopsy. I believe this man died from poison introduced through this wound. I will be able to tell you more soon. While we are here, may we examine his clothing?"

"Certainly, sir" said the doctor, opening a drawer in the wall. Holmes took out the clothing and examined it closely. When he came to the shoes, he gave out a little grunt and said "Watson, come look at this." He handed me his glass and I studied the shoes carefully.

"The shoes are well-maintained, with a high polish," I said. "There seems to be some kind of fluffy dust between the soles and the uppers."

"Exactly, Watson, exactly. Let us go now to Pettigrew's house to see if we can discover anything there," said Holmes.

Hailing another hansom, we made our way to Pettigrew's house, making a slight detour on the way to pick up the jewel-box from Baker Street, which Holmes carried in its cardboard box. Arriving at the house, Holmes asked to see Jameson the butler, who corroborated all the facts that Morton had given us earlier.

"Why were the housekeeper and the maid in the study this morning?" asked Holmes.

"That is a daily chore," said Jameson. "They tidy up the study every morning while the master is at breakfast. I suppose they did it this morning from force of habit."

"Most likely," said Holmes. "Have you ever seen this?" asked Holmes, showing Jameson the jewel-box.

Jameson looked at it for some seconds and then said, "No sir. I see it has the master's initials on the lid, but it doesn't belong to the master, if that is what you are thinking. I've been here nearly twenty years and have never seen such a thing."

"Thank you, Jameson. Now, did your master have any enemies? Arguments with anyone?" asked Holmes.

Jameson's face went white. It was plain to see that he was torn between loyalty to this master and the need to tell the truth. He did not meet Holmes's stern gaze. After some time, he final spoke. "Well, sir, last week the master had a blazing argument with his nephew, Gerald."

"Do you know what they were arguing about?"

"Not really, sir. It is not my place to listen, but they were shouting so loudly that I couldn't help but hear. I didn't hear everything, but I did hear the master threaten to disinherit his nephew."

"Thank you, Jameson. Will you take us to your master's wife?"

We were ushered into a sitting room that had the shades drawn. Pettigrew's wife, dressed in black, was sitting in a high-backed chair. Her eyes were red from weeping, but she seemed to have herself under control. Holmes expressed our condolences and she nodded mutely.

"I would like to ask you a few questions and then I will leave you be," said Holmes. "Did your husband have any enemies?"

Mrs. Pettigrew answered in a very soft voice, almost a whisper "He was in business for many years and undoubtedly there were some hard feelings among his business rivals, but I am sure that he had no personal enemies."

"I see," said Holmes. "Does this belong to your husband?" showing her the jewel-box.

"No, it does not. My husband's jewel-box is upstairs on his dressing table."

"Thank you. One more question. Does your husband have a will," asked Holmes, "and if so, where is it located?"

"Yes. It is kept at his solicitor, Marshall and Marshall, in the Strand."

Apologizing once more for our intrusion, we left the house and made our way to the Strand. Arriving at the solicitor's office, we were shown in to Mr. Marshall's room and introduced ourselves.

"And what may I do for you gentlemen?" asked Marshall.

Holmes replied that we would like to know the contents of Pettigrew's will.

Marshall screwed up is face. "Well, I'm aware that Mr. Pettigrew passed away yesterday, but I don't see that you have any right to pry into his affairs."

"Mr. Marshall, Pettigrew did not die a natural death. He was murdered. Any information that you can give us that will help us find the murderer will be most appreciated."

The look of astonishment on Marshall's face was almost comical. He pushed some papers around on his desk and fiddled with a pencil for some few moments before replying.

"In that case, I see no reason not to tell you what you ask. It will be public knowledge soon anyway when the will is probated. The London house and a very generous annuity to maintain it are left to his wife. A smaller annuity goes to his sister-in-law. The Hertfordshire estate and his interest in the mills are left to his nephew now."

"Why do you say 'now'?" asked Holmes.

"Originally, the estate and mills interest were left to his brother James Pettigrew, Gerald's father. Unfortunately, James was killed in a boating accident nearly a year ago, so James was replaced by Gerald."

"You mentioned Pettigrew's sister-in-law. Would that be James' widow?"

"Yes, sir. James' widow and Gerald's mother."

"Thank you," said Holmes. "Would you happen to have their addresses?"

Marshall opened a desk drawer and took out a largish notebook. He thumbed through it for a bit and wrote down the two addresses on a piece of paper before handing it to Holmes.

"That is all I need from you right now," said Holmes. "If I might be so bold as to suggest that you hold off from submitting the will to probate until you hear further from me."

Marshall gave us a questioning look, but Holmes would add nothing further and he agreed to wait.

We next found ourselves rattling off to Wapping to speak to Pettigrew's sister-in-law. When we arrived and explained the reason for our call, she invited us into the sitting room of her flat. Holmes started by expressing our condolences for the loss of her brother-in-law.

"Save your condolences," she said. "While I cannot say that I am glad that he is dead, I am not sorry that the old skinflint is gone."

I thought that this was an unseemly attitude, and Holmes begged her to explain her feelings.

She turned to me and asked, 'Dr. Watson, do you know the history of digitalis?"

I confessed that I knew digitalis to have been in use for nearly one-hundred years for heart conditions, but didn't know anything further.

"I thought so, very few people do," she replied. "A doctor named Withering had a patient with a very bad heart. None of Withering's treatments were able to help him. In desperation, the man turned to a gypsy woman, who gave him an extract of plants. The man immediately got much better. Withering tracked down the gypsy woman and eventually was able to get from her the ingredients used in her potion. After much experimenting, Withering identified the active ingredient as purple foxglove. Up to this time, that had been considered a dangerous poison and had even been used in trial by ordeal in the Middle Ages. No one had ever researched it."

"Excuse me," said Holmes, "but what does this have to do with your brother-in-law?"

"Very much, Mr. Holmes. My husband was a chemist, a very talented one with advanced ideas. He speculated that if one life-saving drug could be found in a poisonous substance, there very well could be others as well. One room of our house was set up as a laboratory where he did his research into this. He also spent much time in the British Museum, the Zoological Gardens, and the Botanical Gardens. Unfortunately, ours means did not allow him to get very far. He went to his brother and put forward the idea of setting up a company to pursue further research and then manufacture whatever new drugs might be discovered."

She stopped for a moment and tears filled her eyes. She didn't speak for a minute or two and then recovered herself.

"You see, Mr. Holmes, this was not a plea for charity but an authentic business proposition. My brother-in-law laughed in my husband's face. He belittled my husband's talent and said his ideas were pie-in-the-sky tomfoolery. He refused to put any money into it. My husband was mortified and angry. It was soon after this that he died in an accident. Now do you see why I have no love for Mr. Andrew Pettigrew?"

"Yes, ma'am, I see. I did not know. I'm sorry to have reminded you of the subject. Thank you for speaking to us."

Once again on the street, I remarked to Holmes "There could be a revenge motive here."

"Perhaps, Watson. I have no theories as yet. Let us speak to the nephew."

So off we went to Chelsea, where Gerald Pettigrew had a watchmaker's shop, with his living quarters on the floor above. The shop looked prosperous enough, with clean windows and fresh paint on the jambs. Holmes spoke to Gerald and explained that we were looking into his uncle's death. He called to his assistant to take over the shop and motioned us to follow him into a back room. The room was obviously where he performed his watchmaking craft. A bench on the far wall held a tiny lathe and an even tinier vise. The screwdrivers and saws were of a similar minuscule scale. I had seem many mechanic's shops before, but this one appeared to have come from Lilliput. I could not help smiling at the thought.

"How may I help you, sirs?"

"Can you tell us something of your relationship with your uncle?" asked Holmes.

Gerald's face clouded over in a frown. He looked all around the room before replying, "I suppose you could say that it was more or less a typical uncle-nephew relationship. It was not close, but we got along. Of course, we had differences of opinion."

"Such as loud arguments?" put in Holmes.

"I see you have spoken to the servants. Yes, we had a bad argument a week or so ago. They have been ongoing for some time, but it all came to a head last week. My uncle wanted me to take over his interest in the mills and I did not want to. I love my work here and have no interest in being enmeshed in business. My grandfather started this shop more than forty years ago and my father lived here until he went away to college. As a boy, I used to sit with my grandfather and he showed me all about watchmaking. I was fascinated by the intricacy and precision of the work.

I still am. My grandfather left the shop to me when he died a few years ago. I will never give it up."

Once again in the street, I asked Holmes, "Do you believe him? He would certainly be able to modify the box. And his uncle's money would be a strong attraction."

"I do not know, Watson. Either he is telling the truth or he is a superb actor. We must find some more facts. We've had a busy day, but I need to make one more stop before we return to Baker Street."

We hailed a hansom and drove to a jeweler's shop not far from the shop we had just left. Holmes introduced me to Julius Rosenberg, saying he was one of the most knowledgeable jewelers in London, at which Mr. Rosenberg blushed to the roots of his hair.

"Now, Julius," said Holmes, "can you tell me who this mark belongs to and where they can be found?" showing him the copy of the maker's mark found on the jewel-box.

"Why, yes I can. That is the mark of Harcourt and Brothers. Unfortunately, they are not to be found. They went out of business six months or so ago."

"Well, that is a surprise, but it may be an important piece of information. Thank you, Julius. Give my best to your wife and daughter."

We went back to our rooms in Baker Street, where we partook of a hearty meal prepared by Mrs. Hudson, and then on to a concert of German music. Holmes appeared enraptured, gently waving his fingers in tempo. One would never guess that he was investigating a most puzzling crime. Meanwhile, I was cudgeling my brain to try to make some sense of it. There seemed to be only three suspects: The wife, the sister-in-law, and the nephew. Neither the wife nor the sister-in-law seemed to have the skill to have contrived the jewel-box mechanism. The nephew had the skill and was the heir to a quite sizable fortune, but for some reason I had my doubts about his guilt.

The next day we went back to the Pettigrew house and spoke to the housekeeper. She was still somewhat shaken, but she was able to answer our questions. Her story tallied exactly with what we knew from the butler.

"Do you know your master's movements on the day he died?" asked Holmes.

"Yes, sir. He had his breakfast and then went to his study to read his mail and look at the newspaper. Then for some reason he went to the attic for a while. He came down and went to his study again and that is where I found him."

"Why do you say 'for some reason'?"

165

"He has not gone to the attic in over five years. There is nothing up there but Mr. James' furniture. I can't imagine why he went there. Maybe Mrs. James may know."

"Thank you very much. You have been a great help. Come Watson, let us speak to Mrs. James again."

Back we went to Wapping, where Mrs. James Pettigrew received us with some surprise.

"Mrs. Pettigrew, we have just learned that your brother-in-law spent some time in the attic on the day that he died. We also learned that there is only some of your furniture there. Do you have any idea what he may have been doing?" asked Holmes.

"I think I can guess. When my husband died, I didn't have enough money to maintain the house, so I sold it and moved to this flat. It has only three rooms, and I furnished them with furniture from the house. I had no room for the excess furniture, so I asked my brother-in-law if I could store it in his attic, which was empty. He kindly allowed me to do so. There is more than furniture stored there. There are also paintings, my husband's jewelry, some ceramic pieces, and assorted knick-knacks, all packed away in boxes. When I moved out, several of my friends helped me to pack. I must confess that everything was arranged in a rather haphazard manner. A few days ago, I was looking for a cameo that had belonged to my grandmother but I couldn't find it. I hadn't worn it since before the house was sold. I suspected that it had been inadvertently packed away in the boxes that went into the attic. I wrote to my brother-in-law, explaining the situation, and asked him if I could come by and look through the boxes. I suspect that he was taking a look for himself."

Thanking Mrs. Pettigrew, we left the house and stopped on the pavement for a bit.

"Watson," said Holmes, "the chain is almost complete. I need just one more link."

We hailed a hansom and drove to the nearest post office, where Holmes sent off a telegram. When he returned, I asked him if he had really solved the puzzle.

"If the answer to my telegram is what I expect it to be, all will be revealed tomorrow. Are you free at eleven o'clock?"

"Absolutely, Holmes. I wouldn't miss it for the world."

I had several appointments to fulfill that afternoon, so I didn't speak to Holmes until the next morning at Pettigrew's house. I could see that he had been busy setting up this meeting for his dramatic *dénouement*. In addition to Holmes and myself, in attendance were Inspector Morton, Mrs. Andrew Pettigrew, Mrs. James Pettigrew, Gerald Pettigrew, Jameson the butler, and the housekeeper. Also, there was a middle-aged gentleman who Holmes introduced as Alastair Carrington, of the Zoological Gardens.

Holmes started right in. "I won't keep you long. I've asked you here to hear me name the murderer of Andrew Pettigrew and the maid. The murderer is . . . James Pettigrew."

Several people gasped. Most looked astonished, including myself. Morton frowned.

Gerald Pettigrew jumped up angrily. "This is outrageous! My father died a year ago. This is no time for foolishness."

"Pray calm yourself, Mr. Pettigrew. I am sorry to have to bring this affair to light, but I believe that knowing the truth is always the best. I don't have definite evidence of my theory, but there is enough circumstantial evidence to back up my deductions. I might also say that, although I believe that your father at one time planned to kill your uncle, I also believe that he changed his mind and didn't carry it through. His better nature won out, so to speak."

Somewhat mollified, Gerald sat back down.

"Mr. Pettigrew," asked Holmes, "did your father have watchmaking skills?"

"Yes, he did. My grandfather taught him quite a lot and he would help out in the shop before he went away to college."

"Thank you. Mr. Carrington, did you know James Pettigrew?"

"Yes I did. He came to the Zoological Gardens many times. He was interested in investigating various kinds of poisons to see if new drugs could be derived from them. He looked into snake venom, spiders, poison toads, stinging insects, and the like. I and several other members of the Zoological thought that it was a very promising line of research and we let him take several samples."

"Thank you, sir. Now here is the chain of events as I see it: James had made some progress in his investigations but he couldn't go much further without more monetary resources. He approached his brother, who turned him down flat, and ridiculed him to boot. Remember that James was his brother's heir at the time. James decided to kill his brother to gain the estate. I think that he might have been declared to be temporarily insane at that time. He purchased the jewel-box from Harcourt, which was still in business a year ago, and modified it with the needle mechanism, using some of the poison toad alkaloid from his sample. He must have come to his right mind because he never carried out his plan. He hid the box away someplace. A short time later he was killed in a boating accident. When Mrs. James had to sell the house, the box was found and thought to belong to James and was packed away in this house's attic. And there it has sat all this time. Mrs. James sent Andrew a letter saying that she was missing a cameo that she thought might be packed away in a box in the attic. Andrew decided to have a look for himself. While rummaging through the boxes, he came across a jewel-box with this own initials on it. He must have been intrigued and brought the box down to his study. He opened it and was jabbed with poisoned needle. He closed the box, which explains why nobody took any interest in it. Then he died. The next day, the maid saw the box on the desk and opened it out of curiosity. Fortunately, the housekeeper was present and was able to tell us what actually happened. Sadly, the two deaths were only tragic accidents."

No one said a word. I think that all of us were trying to digest the fantastic tale we had just heard. Finally, Inspector Morton asked, "Mr. Holmes, will you come down to the station and make a statement reporting all that you have said here?"

"Why certainly, Morton. I was fully expecting to do so."

One by one, everyone left the room. Gerald Pettigrew was the last to leave. Before he left he came up to Homes. "I don't know whether to shake your hand or punch you in the face."

Holmes just nodded in understanding.

Mass Murder
by William Todd

It was a year bookended by loss. In 1901, country lost its queen in the beginning weeks of the year, and Holmes and I lost a dear friend on the last day of December. We were, however, lucky enough to have had the pleasure of spending some time with him before his death. Yet life does not sit idle as you have your last moments together. It goes on in all its glory and all its indignity. It is these indignities of life with which my friend Sherlock Holmes so competently deals, and he must deal with them regardless the circumstance or time in which they arise. So, it should not surprise the reader which path Holmes took when presented with such a dilemma during a time he would rather have spent with a sick friend.

As I stood waiting for the slowing train to stop, I could not help but feel a sense of relief that Holmes had finally found time to pull away from his investigations for a break. I had convinced him to come over to Woodford-Upon-Lea in Essex for some sunshine and cool, fresh air, which had been the climate at the time of the telegram. Now, unfortunately, the blue skies of early October had been replaced by grey, windswept clouds which constantly dropped their burden with enthusiastic abandon.

I myself had gone two weeks earlier to help a long-time mutual friend, Phineas Whympenny, convalesce as he recuperated from some serious hypertensive issues. It was those issues from which he, unfortunately, never fully recovered.

Holmes had said he would pay a visit once his current affair wrapped up, and I received a telegram the day before that he would be on the morning train.

Shaking hands once he arrived, I said, "I am glad that you could finally get away."

"Once I was sure the broker was stealing his own diamonds, I set Lestrade on that trail to do the work for which he is best suited. It took some time to prove my deductions correct, but alas, here I am. Better late than never. So, is the good Mr. Whympenny recovering sufficiently? I hope he has not taken a similar turn as that of the wonderful weather you promised."

"The conditions that I communicated were from a week ago," I replied as we retrieved his baggage. "You cannot expect our finicky British weather to keep its good humour for any great length of time. And as far as our friend Phin is concerned, he is feeling better now, but he is

169

not yet out of the woods. I fear for the man, but he refuses to change his diet. As you know, he is nearing sixty-five, and was never what one would call *fit*."

"I dare say, Watson, that for a man whose height and circumference are practically interchangeable, 'fit' has *never* been a useful adjective to describe old Phin. It may be that his taste for food has finally taken its toll."

"Yes, but he is as jolly as ever," said I. "A smile never seems far from his face, and he is anxious to see his favourite customer."

"Is he well enough for some oysters and a brace of grouse?" Holmes asked when we climbed into the cab.

"He is out of bed for short spells a few times a day. I am sure, with some help on our part, he would be willing to boil, bake, *sauté*, smoke, or pickle just about anything you ask."

Phineas Whympenny's home was the last amongst an assemblage of large, well-kept cottages on Old Oak Lane at the edge of the village. And here, the separation was abrupt between civilization and an expanse of low-rolling farmland and wood. I was pointing out Phin's cottage as we slowed, but Holmes was more interested in the happenings across the street. A constabulary wagon was situated in front of a small sandstone church. Four officers were at its entrance – one talking, the others listening intently.

"It seems the Church has need of a little law and order," said Holmes as I disembarked with the bags and he paid the driver.

"I wonder if Phin caught a glimpse of anything," I added. "Maybe he could fill us in on what we missed."

"Or better yet . . . ." Holmes replied as he walked briskly across the street.

I looked at Holmes then to the cottage. I noticed Phin's bulk framed by the parlour window. His massive shoulders bounced as he chuckled, and he waved me off, as if to say, *Go join Holmes*.

I smiled at him and shrugged sheepishly. I then put the overnight bags down on the small front porch and joined Holmes on the other side of the street, as he was reading the signage on the front lawn which read *Saint Anne's Catholic Church*.

We were met on the walkway by a young, clean-shaven constable whose forlorn features betrayed a tragedy. "I'm sorry, gentlemen, but Saint Anne's is closed."

"May we inquire as to the reason for its shuttering?" asked Holmes.

"It is the scene of a crime," said the constable laconically.

With aplomb, my friend replied, "Well, I am Sherlock Holmes, and this is my colleague, Dr. Watson."

"Ah, the famous consulting detective from London," he said in a revelatory tone. "Here on holiday? You missed some nice walking weather by a few days, but I'm sure the sun will return if you are patient enough. Or could it be that your deductive powers are more impressive than what the Good Doctor chronicles, and you were brought here by mere instinct."

Looking over the constable's shoulder at the church, ignoring the thin smile of amusement that creased the officer's face, Holmes replied with a bit of veiled sarcasm, "No holiday and no super-human feats of intellect. I apologize if that revelation lessens your impression of my ability to deduce or my colleague's ability to write. Yet, my arrival was not a fortuitous one. We are here visiting an old friend across the street." He engaged the constable with a cold, direct stare, "and since we're here, would the local authorities have any need of my assistance?"

The constable's smile disappeared at the subtle reproof. He cleared his throat. "Of course, of course." Shaking our hands, the man went on, "I am Constable Milks, Benny Milks. And please, come, let me show you what we have. It's not the usual fare in a village this size, and probably a bit dull for the likes of you, Mr. Holmes, but having the great detective on board will all but ensure the proper outcome."

"What about poor old Phin?" I asked Holmes. "He has been anxiously awaiting your arrival."

"My plan is for a week's stay, Watson. A few stray moments here and there will not hurt the quality of our company."

"Gentlemen," Constable Milks said as he opened the left side of the double doors. "Please come through this door, as the right is part of the scene which I will explain momentarily."

It was when the constable moved to open the door for us that I noticed briefly detritus of some sort, possibly stomach contents, upon the entranceway just in front of the right-side door.

We followed Milks into the narthex of the small church. From there we looked out into the nave, consisting of a central aisle and fifteen rows of pews on either side. Each row could accommodate roughly ten people. In front of us, five rows back, a body lay awkwardly, half in the center aisle and half hidden by a pew. Three more bodies lay at slumped angles, all in the same pew. Between the communion railing and the front of the altar table, a priest knelt, head bent in prayer, with an officer standing over him.

"Instead of simply relaying what was said to us, I shall let the priest explain things," Milks said. "I will just say that sometime before the benediction, all the attendants became quite ill. A fifth attendant, Miss

Mary Holowczak, a housemaid and cook, became ill as well, but managed to crawl to the door and was halfway through before she retched and collapsed. A neighbor walking his dog saw her there and notified us."

"And she is still alive?" I asked.

"At the moment, but she is in a bad way."

Looking on at the scene like an anxious terrier being held back by a leash, Holmes responded, "I should like to see the bodies, if I may."

Acquiescing with a sweep of his arm, Constable Milks said, "After you, gentlemen."

As we approached the first, lying half in the aisle, Milks offered, "This is Ramsey Montfort. He is Sir Gordon Montfort's eldest child and only son. Sir Montfort is the local squire, whose noble name can be traced all the way back to the Battle of Hastings."

At this, Holmes knelt and examined the figure, which was crumpled in a heap upon the floor. The Montfort boy, no more than in his early twenties, was on his stomach, head cocked to the side, arms and hands at awkward angles. Holmes sniffed around the young man's mouth and examined his clothing.

"The three others here," Milks continued, pointing to the other bodies, "are John Wallace, Harold Harker, and Oliver Warleggan." They were each slumped over in various positions. There was no visible frothing or vomiting, and I, using my own olfactory senses, smelled no scent of bitter almonds or garlic, so my personal opinion was that – whatever the poison – it was not arsenic or cyanide.

Somehow knowing my inner thoughts – or more likely seeing me sniff the air – Holmes spoke up, "I don't think it is strychnine, either, Watson. My guess is hemlock. It mixes well with wine and other liquids. Depending on the dosage, it could have been administered anytime from breakfast to the blood of Christ."

"I don't see how they could drink and die," said I, "and yet the priest seems to have suffered no ill consequences."

Milks spoke up, eyeing the praying priest intently. "He might have put his lips to the chalice, but that does not mean he drank. And his back is turned to the congregants. He could have easily concealed the fact that he actually did not drink from the cup."

"You think that he did it?" I asked

"As you say," Milks responded, "the priest is alive while all else are dead."

"Not quite everyone," Holmes added sagely.

"If the girl survives, it will be by luck alone."

As he eyed the priest at the altar, kneeling in prayer while a constable stood over him, Holmes asked in a low voice, almost to himself, "Why would a man in charge of another man's spiritual life so callously take his physical one?" Turning back to Milks, Holmes then asked, "Where was the girl sitting?"

"According to Father Harrison, she was in the next pew behind the men."

"I would like to speak to the priest now, if I may," said my friend.

Milks relieved the constable guarding Father Harrison of his duties, and the priest finally stood, regarding the three of us with worry deepening the wrinkles around his weathered yet handsome features.

"This is Sherlock Holmes from London. He would like to talk to you," Milks offered. "I shall be nearby if you need me, gentlemen."

"I – I do not know what to tell you," he said, regarding us. "They were all fine one moment, and the next . . . ." his voice trailed off.

"Come, sit with us at in this first pew, here," Holmes suggested with forbearance, "and relay to me the events of the morning."

The three of us sat in the front pew while the officers set about investigating around us.

Holmes took a languid position in the pew, fingers interlaced introspectively, eyes closed, and began. "So, is it the habit of these gentlemen to attend morning Mass?"

Taking out a handkerchief and wiping the copious perspiration from his forehead with a shaking hand, the priest said, "If it weren't for them, there would be no morning Mass when I have it. They only come after hunting."

"I am not sure I understand. Please elaborate, and start from the beginning."

"All the land around, including the property on which the church sits, is owned by Sir Gordon Montfort. He gave the land on which the church is built for his son, Ramsey, who converted to Catholicism three years ago. They often come over for meals, and breakfasting before a hunt has become their habit."

"They breakfasted with you this morning?" Holmes asked.

"Oh yes. Miss Holowczak makes a big breakfast before every hunt. They and Miss Mary are often my only company." With an earnest smile he then added, "We are a small congregation at the moment, but we are slowly growing. Most Sundays it is only Ramsey and his four friends and Miss Mary, with but a few others, but on holidays and some holy days of obligation, we are able to get upwards of thirty people for Mass, much to the chagrin of Sir Gordon."

I wrinkled my brow. "I don't think I follow. You just said that Gordon Montfort gave the land on which the church was built. Why then would he not wish for the church to grow?"

"Sir Gordon is a staunch Anglican, and saying he wasn't fond of Catholics would be a severe understatement. He was heartbroken when Ramsey told him he was converting. But Ramsey is his only son, so he usually gets what he wants. I have tried to accentuate what we have in common when we have a chance to converse, but our short dialogues never blossom into any sort of constructive conversation."

"Getting back to this morning," Holmes said with no slight irritation, "did anything unusual happen at breakfast?"

"No, nothing. It was as it has been every other day. Miss Mary came in this morning around five. I know this because I myself arise early and pray in the church, so I was there when I heard her come in through the rectory."

"Does she live nearby?"

"She rents a room five cottages down from the church. She doesn't normally come in that early. Ramsey tells us when the spirit moves him for a hunt, and she arrives accordingly to start on breakfast."

"Of what does your breakfast typically consist?"

"Mary usually has sausage, kidneys, eggs, toast, and marmalade set out for us, along with both coffee and tea. Oh, yes, she also sets out a bowl of czarnina soup for herself and me, as the others do not think it appetizing. We all eat together, and all was heartily consumed before they set off."

"Czarnina soup – Mary is Galician?"

"That is correct."

"It is your habit to let the help eat meals with you?"

The priest frowned. "I do not consider Miss Mary *help*. This might be her situation, but she is God's creature all the same. She is always welcome at table, especially when it's her meals that are being consumed."

Holmes finally opened his eyes and engaged the priest directly. "The men had no problem with this arrangement?"

"No, sir, they did not. All seemed to enjoy her company. And if allowed this one discretion, Miss Mary is a quite handsome young lady and wonderful at conversation with a good sense of humour. And I believe her accent adds to her allure. I doubt many men, regardless of their difference in class, would find fault in letting her sit at their table."

"I see. Did anyone leave the room for any reason during the meal?"

"Mary was always in and out, serving and taking plates. She would sit and eat and converse a bit then be up doing it all over again. I believe Ramsey got up and helped her once to bring in some dishes. That was it. The rest of the time we were all together. Mary cleared the table while we said our goodbyes, and off they went to hunt."

"What time was that?"

174

He thought for a moment. "About close on seven this morning, I suspect. They came back from hunting empty-handed, and I set up for Mass shortly after they arrived at half-past nine, as was our custom."

"What of the others?" Holmes asked. "What do you know of them?"

"They are all very close friends. Ramsey, John, Harold, Oliver, and William have grown up together. Their families are all close, and I believe distantly related. Through governesses, school, and university, they have been inseparable."

Holmes stopped the priest. "You have mentioned four friends of Ramsey, yet only three bodies are here. Who is the William that seems to be the one friend missing?"

With his trembling hand wiping his flushed and sweaty cheeks, Father Harrison said, "That is the only anomaly on the entire morning. Ramsey said that William – Waverly – has been away, it seems. They were all to go to London for some function given by Ramsey's father. He is there now. The assumption of the others is that William went early, and he would meet up with them when they arrived on Thursday morning. He tends to be a free spirit in that way."

"How long has he been absent?" Holmes asked.

"Only a few days, I believe."

"Please be honest with me when I ask this next question," my friend then said with much solemnity. "It will do you no good to lie."

"Of course," the priest replied weakly.

"Did you partake of the wine?"

Harrison seemed offended at the question. "Of course, I did. It is the Blood of Christ! Why would I not partake?"

"And everyone else did, as well?" pressed Holmes.

He was silent for a moment, and then sighed and went on. "I believe so. At their age, Mr. Holmes, it can be hard sometimes to completely get the boy out of the man. You see, there are times when they will completely consume the contents of the chalice before it gets to Miss Mary. They do it in jest, but it is a cruel thing to do, and I admonish them when it happens."

"Did it happen today?" Holmes asked.

He nodded as he wiped his flushed cheeks once again. "But you consume the Whole Christ in the Eucharist, so it would not matter if you didn't partake of the wine. I do believe, however, that there were a few drops left when she drank."

It was at this point that we were interrupted by Constable Milks. "I am sorry, Mr. Holmes, but we will have to cut this interview short." He held up a small, clear, glass vial with a small amount of a milky fluid still within. "This was found in the pocket of your coat, Reverend, which was

175

hanging on a hook in the entranceway of the rectory. Now, I'm sure I don't know my poisons as well as Mr. Holmes, here, but the smell to me says he was right when he guessed hemlock." He pulled the priest up from the pew by the arm. "You are coming with us, Mr. Harrison, on suspicion of murder."

"I did not do this," the priest implored. "As God is my witness."

"Well, unless the Almighty comes down here in person to vouch for you, our evidence says otherwise." Milks then turned to us. "I apologize, Mr. Holmes, that this wasn't much of a puzzle to solve. I guess you shall have all your time back to visit your friend."

Milks and another constable led the priest down the center aisle.

"So that is that?" I asked.

Holmes ascended the altar. "You know me, Watson. *That* is never that."

On the left side of the altar was a small table with a gold chalice and crystal decanter of wine. "They took the vial but were derelict in leaving the chalice and wine." He sniffed the decanter and frowned. "Hemlock, indeed. It has a bit of a mousey smell. But why poison the whole decanter? Why not just the chalice of wine. He certainly had the opportunity with his back to the congregation the whole time."

"And it is obvious that he is having ill-effects from drinking, with his sunken, grey features and profuse sweating," I added. "Why would he poison himself?"

"And why would this murderous letch," he said with sarcasm, "be so foolish as to leave the poison in his coat, sure to be found by the curious constabulary? Come, Watson. Let us examine where the poison was found."

At the west end of the building, just beyond the first set of pews, we were shown through a small hallway that opened into the rectory. The front entrance was the first door past the hallway with the hook which held the coat next to the door. Next to that was a large secretary desk. Other rooms opened up off that small greeting area.

Holmes noticed something on the marble floor in front of the door. "Ah, a partial footprint. A left, I believe."

The constable with us said, "The priest's, no doubt. The yard around is rather muddy from all the rain the past few days."

Holmes said nothing.

He next wanted to inspect the secretary desk next to the door, but the constable cautioned him, "You may look only, sir. Nothing is to be touched or handled in any way."

"Yes, that does seem to be how investigations are handled here," Holmes mumbled to me, as he looked over the desk.

After a cursory glance, he turned and walked quickly back through the hallway into the church with me at his heel.

"Did you see anything of note?" I asked.

"You know me, Watson. My eyes tend toward that which is ignored. The shoe print was not Harrison's. His shoes are soft-soled with tread and a rounded toe. The print on the floor had no tread and a pointed toe."

"A dress shoe," I finished.

As we turned and went back up the center aisle, he added, "In lieu of a miraculous Providential appearance, I think Father Harrison will have to make do with us. Come, we shall look in on good old Whympenny for a bit, then let us see what we can do about these murders."

Phineas met us at the door with a smile and a sweep of his giant arm bidding us enter. "Come, come, gentlemen. You must sit and tell me of the mischief happening on my doorstep. Sherlock, it is so nice to see you again!"

Holmes chuckled, "Phin – as robust as ever, I see."

"Yes, the clean, country air has not, unfortunately, deterred my love of cuisine. If I have my way, when I go to that Great Beyond it shall be with a pastry stuffed between my cheeks!"

A bit breathless, he forced himself into a rose-carved, balloon-back chair. "We have plenty of time to talk food. For now, though," he added with anticipation, "indulge this fat, old man and tell me what is what across the way."

Holmes succinctly relayed what we had learned, and afterward Phineas said, "There has been something brewing over there for some time now. That it ended like this is not surprising to me."

"Why so?" asked Holmes, interest peaked, brow askew.

"If you don't already know – but I suspect you do – Miss Mary, as she is wont to be called, is a very pretty young lady. If I were forty years younger and possessed a bit less girth – "

"You would cook her a dinner then eat it all yourself," I finished.

He nodded his head and laughed. "*Touché*, John. Let us then stick to fact and not fantasy. As you know, I have a perfect view of the church through my front window here."

"And you have seen things," Holmes anticipated.

"Some things. Not much. But enough to know that something like this was coming."

Holmes was going to interject something, but Phin cut him off with a sausage-sized finger, "Such as the Montfort boy showing some affection to that lovely Miss Mary right out in front of the church. It was dusk, and they thought it too dark for anyone to see. But I was blessed with the eyes

177

of an owl. They embraced and kissed. The whole affair was over in a second, maybe two. Anyone else would not have noticed."

I asked, "How do you go from a brief moment of intimacy to murder?"

Phin smiled wide on that full-moon face of his. "Because he wasn't the only admirer she cozied up to, that's how."

I gasped. "Which of the other young men was she playing?"

"The barrister's son, Will Waverly."

"Who has been absent from the group for a few days now," Holmes added somberly. "That is a dangerous game to play between friends, the effects with which she is now dealing. Was there one that she hoisted her affections upon more than the other?"

"I only witnessed a little slice of the pie – if I may use that turn-of-phrase because I am famished – but from the goings-on that I could see over this summer past in that little alcove, away from prying eyes, I would say that it was the Montfort boy who finally won her over. She spent more time in intimate conversation with him, touching him on the arm innocently, but not so innocently. They were close-in conversations, almost nose-to-nose. I could tell that she brightened considerably in his company. With that recessed entranceway and those two large rhododendrons on either side of the steps, no one would have been a witness to any of it but me. Nonetheless, as I have previously stated, I am sure I have seen but a small part of a larger and much darker picture."

"You have managed to see a lot just the same," I replied.

"As you can observe, my cottage is almost directly across the way. With my property and the church's property, all other homes are too far away at angles to see what goes on at the front of the church. And I believe the empty land on the other side gave them a false sense of security, so much tended to happen in that cozy little nook. Since I rarely go outside, they forget that I'm here – a man of my size, if you can believe that. So I get a front row seat to these little goings-on. Without friends with which to pass the time," he went on, feigning melancholy, "that was my only bit of theater."

I laughed, "It seems you kept company just fine, my dear fellow, and their names were Pumpernickel and Bechamel!"

Holmes's features darkened. "Jesting aside, if you could see her delight being in Mr. Montfort's company, then it isn't a far reach to think Waverly may have seen it, as well," Holmes said.

"And I also believe the priest must have known something," Phin added, "probably through their confessions, if they are good Catholics. I saw him one afternoon imploring her about something, hands upon both shoulders. She had just come through the front doors, but he was right on

178

her heels. She gave him a curt response, shook herself loose, then walked away. That was about two months ago."

"Did you see anything untoward today?" Holmes asked.

Phin replied, "I only saw them as they returned from their hunt."

"Did you happen to see anyone at the rectory door at any point today?"

"I didn't," was the reply.

"How does it all fit together?" I finally implored. "Did William Waverly find out he was being duped and in a jealous rage poison his friends and his would-be love? Why everyone and not just Montfort? And why was the poison found in Father Harrison's coat pocket?"

"Maybe this Waverly boy is casting dispersions elsewhere by setting up the priest," Phin offered with delight, rubbing his meaty hands together.

Holmes gazed out the window at the grey day outside and was silent for a long moment. Rising, he said finally, "You relish the game too much, my dear Phin, but forget that four are dead and possibly a fifth before the day is through. Come, Watson, the tangled mess in which we find ourselves has become more raveled. It is now time to attempt its unraveling."

"And in the meantime, how does pressed duck sound for dinner?" asked our portly friend. "A special press I had ordered from Paris just arrived, and I am dying to try it out."

"Salad and a few cold meats should be sufficient for all of us," said I in my doctorly voice.

Holmes and Phin both groaned at the statement.

Phin gave us the use of his dog-cart, and since I had already spent two weeks in Woodford-Upon-Lea, I knew my way around the place well enough. Phin knew where the Waverly place was due to their prominence as the area's largest law firm. He gave us the directions, and we proceeded there.

The village shared resources with the bigger Crofton Barrow a few miles away. The Waverly family occupied a large corner building in the middle of town. When we knocked, a dowdy, rosy-cheeked lady answered the door.

Holmes bowed slightly. "Good afternoon, Madame. I am Sherlock Holmes, and this is my associate, Dr. Watson. We are here on a matter of police business and are hoping to speak to Mr. William Waverly, if he is in."

Her cheeks flushed impossibly more. "Oh, I do hope everything is alright, sir. But Mr. William isn't in at present. Is he in trouble?"

"Is *trouble* routinely the sort of thing Mr. Waverly would be in?"

"Oh no, sir," she said rather unconvincingly. "It's just that, well . . . on a few occasions, his temper has gotten the best of him, as has happened with all of us I'm sure. On the whole, he is a good lad."

"An angel, no doubt," Holmes quipped politely, "No, madam, he is in no trouble, but we have some questions to ask that involve his friends and the new church in Woodford."

"St. Anne's. Yes I know the church. They all go there regularly. Is everything all right?"

"As I said, Madame," Holmes reiterated, trying to hide his irritation, "he is in no trouble at all, or it would not be me at your door. It would be Constable Milks, no doubt."

Relief slackened the features on the woman's face. "Well, Mr. William, I assume, is in London. He and his friends were supposed to attend an event for some function of Sir Montfort."

"You *assume*?"

"Well, the event wasn't supposed to be for two more days, this Thursday, and I know I have seen Mr. Ramsey with the other lads he goes about with. It is very unlike any of them to go anywhere without the others – thick as thieves, they are – but this Saturday past, I heard him tell his father at dinner that he was going to London with his friends for the Sir Montfort event on Thursday, but the next day he was gone. Why he left before the rest of them is beyond me."

"Did he pack an overnight bag?" Holmes asked.

"I never thought to check. Mr. William has a tendency to come and go as he pleases and is rather self-reliant. We had a loss to the staff recently, and I have been picking up the extra work till we hire more help."

"Would it be possible for us to take a look in his room?"

"I'm not permitted to let anyone in when the house is empty of its owner, which it presently is, but if you're willing to wait, I shall go up to his room and look. I shan't be but a minute."

A few minutes later she returned with a worried look upon her face. "His valise is still in his room."

Holmes asked, "Was any of it out as though he were about to use it and was perhaps called away before getting a chance to pack?"

"No, sir," she shook her head vigorously. "It was still put away. It's as though he left without even thinking about packing – and I think it was because of this: I found it on his writing desk." She handed him a card which smelled faintly of roses. On it was one word: *Come.*

"Do you know when this was delivered?" Holmes asked, slipping the card into his pocket.

"I do not. I have never seen this card." Her face deepened its rosy hue once more. "Oh dear. What does this all mean?"

180

My friend gave her a reassuring smile. "I'm sure there is a logical explanation to it, and he will soon be at home once more. Please tell him to get in touch with the constabulary should he return."

He said nothing regarding the card or missing young man as we next drove over to see how Miss Mary was faring in hospital. It was at the nearer end of Crofton Barrow on the road to Woodford-Upon-Lea. When we passed it on our way to the Waverly place, I wondered why we didn't stop then, but my friend has a certain order of things that others find hard to follow. I've learned to leave him to his circuitous methodologies.

We found Mary Holowczak lying in bed with pillows propping up her head. She was grey and saturated with perspiration. Her breathing was a bit laboured, and her eyes were drearily open.

When we told the head matron that we were there in an official capacity, she acquiesced. However, we were not to stay long.

"Miss Holowczak, I am Sherlock Holmes, and I am helping the constabulary with the unfortunate deaths of your friends and the attempt on your life. Do you feel well enough to answer just a few questions? If not, we shall go."

She nodded her head. "I look dreadful," she struggled out in a soft accent, "but I feel much better than I did a few hours ago. I am hoping worst is over. I think something was in wine. It smelled funny when I drank."

"Yes, we believe you were all poisoned. However, my inquiry at present involves your rather intimate relationships with William Waverly and Ramsey Montfort."

Her half-closed eyes opened in surprise. "How do you know this?"

"It is my job to know," replied Holmes.

After a moment, she nodded in acquiescence with tears in her eyes. "It is lonely not being from here and having no more family. People look at you. They . . . say things. I am all alone now, except church. They both showed interest and did not seem to care I am foreigner. I was . . . how you say – hedging my bets. But Ramsey won my heart and soul. It was wrong what I did and made act of contrition for my sins."

Holmes then asked, "Did you send a note to William that simply said 'Come'?"

She wrinkled her brow. "No. No note."

Holmes produced the card and handed it to her. "Is this your writing upon this card?"

A look of recognition washed over her. "Oh, yes, this my card. I am teaching everyone my language. It is much fun. I make cards at home with words, English on one side and Polish on the other. I show card in English, and they say word I teach them in Polish. I show them word in Polish, and they say it in English if they remember. This one, I write '*come*', but must forget to put Polish word on back – '*chodz*'. Did you get this from Father's desk drawer in rectory? There are many cards in there. He pulls them out when everyone wants lesson."

"It was found in Mr. Waverly's room on his writing desk," Holmes replied somberly.

"But why would he want card?" the young girl asked and began to cough.

"I don't believe that he took the card, Miss Holowczak. I believe it was sent to him. How did the perfume come to be on it?"

Wiping her mouth with a kerchief and breathing a bit of color back into her face, she replied, "I have small room and have more on my writing desk than I should. I spilled perfume on some cards. There are many that Father has that don't smell like roses. You will see if you look in his desk."

"The large one next to the rectory entrance?"

"Yes, there. He keeps them in one of the drawers."

"Turning to the relationship: Did Waverly know about you and Ramsey Montfort?"

Her face grew dark, and she replied, "Yes, Ramsey told Will just recently, but he seemed already to know. He was not happy, but he is best friend of Ramsey, and they reconciled quickly. But Will grew quiet, and I could see the hate in his eyes when Ramsey was not looking."

She began to sob, and the color drained from her face. "I believe it is my fault this tragedy happen. How could I be so cruel to a person? Now all my friends are dead!" Her face suddenly went slack, and the poor girl fainted.

"It is time for you to go, gentlemen," the head matron demanded. "You've pushed her too far. She needs rest if she is to recover sufficiently from her near-fatal poisoning."

As we were leaving, I asked, "Why did we not inquire about her poison. It was obvious to me at the church that she wasn't given the same type. She was the only one who vomited and didn't die where she sat."

Holmes patted me on the back. "Bravo, Watson. You do yourself an injustice by saying that you cannot learn my methods. You're right. Mary was poisoned by arsenic. The garlic smell was quite noticeable on her breath. But she ingested only a small amount – just enough to make her sick. Another strike against the local force, which did not catch that *de minimis*. I'm glad that I came down to see old Phin, for had I not, the wrong person might hang for this."

We arrived back on Phin's street after a short drive. I stopped the dog-cart in front of the fifth cottage down from the church. Holmes knocked on the door, and a thin, pale, grey-haired woman answered.

"Hello, Madame, I am Sherlock Holmes, and this is my colleague, Dr. Watson. We are here on police business."

"Yes, the news makes its way down the street rather quickly here," she replied. "Poor Mary. I do hope she pulls through. She is a good tenant – " She leaned in close – "despite being, well . . . you know."

Irritated, Holmes replied, "No, Madame, I don't. Are you referring to her Slavic heritage or her Catholicism?"

Her eyes widened. "Both!"

"And yet you found it in your heart to rent a room to the girl."

Sensing Holmes's sarcasm, she only replied, "As I said, she seemed a good girl. Pleasant. Has some trouble grasping English, but she is understandable enough. She keeps a small garden in the back for her cooking, keeps to herself, and pays on time. What more could a landlady want."

"Indeed," Holmes retorted dryly. "As I said, we are helping Constable Milks in this matter, and I was hoping to press upon your sense of civic duty and let us inspect her room."

"Let no one say that I was an obstacle to the Crown." She pulled out a ring of keys and picked one out from the six. "If you go around to the right side of the cottage, her door is the last one down. The rooms in the back have their own entrances. You can leave the key ring on her bed when finished, and I'll retrieve it later."

As Holmes unlocked the door, I gave a cursory glance over at Miss Mary's garden, which was about thirty feet away at the back of the property against a fence. The dirt was soggy and bare, with bricks and stakes and a shovel thrown over top of it. With the growing season all but over, all the vegetables had already been picked, the last of which having probably been used in that morning's breakfast.

Once inside, the room was just as Mary said it would be – cluttered but not dirty. She had books in English, some in Polish, pictures of her homeland and what I assumed was family and, true to her word, her writing desk was awash in blank cards, paper, and a half-used bottle of perfume.

"It looks like she enjoyed the theater, Watson," Holmes said as he looked through the contents on her dressing table. "She has been to the Queen's Theater in Crofton Barrow a few times, but most of these playbills are from her homeland, the last being – five years ago if I am reading the dates correctly." He looked through a few of them. "And it seems our Miss Mary not only liked the theater but was part of it. I do not claim an extensive Polish vocabulary, but I am somewhat familiar with it. I'm quite certain this particular scribble on at least three of these playbills show Mary Holowczak in the cast."

"I wonder why she didn't try her hand at theater here?" said I.

At that, there was a knock at the door that led to the interior of the home. Suddenly, the owner poked her head through the door. Rather sheepishly she said, "I couldn't help but overhear your conversation from the other side of the door, and she has actually tried out for a few parts at the Queens. She and her sister both did. I overheard them preparing their auditions – "

Holmes put up his hand to stop her. "Her sister? No one mentioned a sister."

"Her sister, Anna, poor thing, has been dead for two years, now. They both shared this room. She was accosted walking home one night from Crofton Barrow. No one knows who did it. She was found dead by Mary and the priest who went to look for her when she didn't come home that night. Mary was in a bad way for some time, but eventually got over it, deciding that life had to go on for the living."

Angry, Holmes lamented, "Why oh why, Watson, would we not be made aware of this vital information by the constabulary? Instead, we find out from the landlady!"

He handed the woman her key ring. "Thank you, Madame. You've been most helpful," Turning on his heels, he rushed for the door and exclaimed, "Come, Watson! We need to make haste before it's too late!"

"Where are we off to?" I asked as we mounted the dog-cart.

"We have one stop, and then we need to get back to the hospital as quickly as we can make this old horse gallop!"

When we returned to see Mary Holowczak, she seemed to have fully recovered from not only her faint, but also the poisoning as well. Her colour was back, and she was out of bed and back into her clothes, looking alert. She was speaking to Constable Milks when we arrived.

"Ah, gentlemen, come to pay your respects? It looks like the lady will not only make a full recovery, but leave hospital in record time. We're still trying to tie up loose ends, but I think we have this in the bag. The priest admitted that there was another friend who had been absent this morning, William Waverly, and I was just talking to Mary as to any suggestions where we might look for him. It seems odd that, on the day all his friends are murdered, he is absent. I believe the priest is the culprit, and Waverly might be a co-conspirator, though I admit a motive still eludes me."

"I believe I may know where William Waverly is," offered Holmes.

"Well spit it out, man. We need to speak to him."

"Since he is dead and buried in Miss Mary's garden, I doubt that you'll get much from him."

Mary gasped, and Milks looked wide-eyed at Holmes. "What on earth are you talking about, sir?"

"I shall put forth what I know, and Mary will have to fill in some gaps – if she is willing to oblige. I shall go first."

Mary said nothing, only glowered at Holmes.

Holmes began his dissertation of the crime. "Over the course of the last two years, you have been scheming to murder these five men, and what a patient schemer you are – one who could rival that of any in London, save a few unique specimens."

"But why?" asked Milks.

"The why we shall get to, momentarily, with Mary's help. Let us stick with the *how* for a moment. She poisoned the decanter with hemlock."

"That much is known already, but the *who* in your deductions are a bit flawed, Mr. Holmes," said Milks. "Don't forget why we are having this conversation in a hospital. Mary was poisoned, as well. Why would she poison herself? That is preposterous."

"And you completely missed the fact that Mary was affected by a completely different poison. She had to poison herself with arsenic instead of the hemlock in the wine, and one small grain of arsenic, easily concealed, was all she needed. Much can be gleaned by asking the right questions, Constable. Father Harrison relayed that the men would often, as a puerile prank, drink all the wine in the chalice before she had a chance to partake. She knew if by chance they played that little game today, there would be no more poisoned wine left to drink, so she would need a backup poison to throw authorities off her trail. For, as you say, why would anyone poison themselves, knowing the outcome would be their own demise?

"Indeed, Mr. Holmes. Doing that would be tantamount to suicide. You have yet show how it can be done – and why."

"Mithridatism, is the how" my friend replied.

Milks *harrumph*-ed at the statement, but not before throwing an unflattering glance at the young woman who had sat back down on the bed wearing a look of distress and anger. "What in the world is that?" he asked.

"Mithridates was an ancient king who constantly worried of being poisoned," Holmes stated. "He conquered this burden by slowly ingesting small amounts of different poisons until his body built up an immunity to them. He did this with many poisons and so was impervious to their effects. Yet, when the Romans over-ran his kingdom, and he feared being paraded through the streets in humiliation, he tried to poison himself, but the attempt was fruitless. The legend has it that a friend finally ran him through with a sword."

"And you are saying that she did this – made herself invulnerable to the poison hemlock?"

"Not just her," Holmes responded with a wagging finger. "Father Harrison, as well."

"They are in this together?" Milks asked in disbelief.

"No," Holmes replied, "But she did not want the death of the priest on her conscience. He was innocent of the crime for which she was dispensing her justice. So she made him resistant, as well."

Milks interrupted, "Then he would be an accessory to the murders, if he knew what she was planning and went along with it."

"That would indeed be true, Constable, if only he knew what Miss Holowczak was doing. I believe that she was secretly doing it through the czarnina soup that she was serving at breakfast. It was the only thing that they alone ate."

"What on earth is that?" he asked.

"It is duck's blood soup. As part of the legend, it is said the way in which Mithridates accomplished becoming immune was to feed each particular poison to ducks in increasing amounts, and whichever ducks did not die, he would kill and drink their blood. Miss Mary's method was a bit more tasteful than was the king's."

He looked upon the young woman. "Have I been correct thus far?"

She said nothing, only stared blankly at the floor.

The constable shook his head, still in unbelief, but I could tell the reasons for not believing Holmes were quickly fading. "But she almost died. You saw how sick she was. I was told that she fainted while in your company earlier. Poisoning yourself is an awful heady risk to take, knowing it might not work out the way you think it should."

Holmes smiled in that confidently smug way he has when in possession of all the facts. "Poison is in the dose, Constable. One grain of arsenic is enough to make one visibly sick – and she was. She was genuinely ill the way a bad piece of beef makes one ill. But one grain of arsenic will not kill you. Some of what you saw was authentic, and the rest was acting. As Watson and I found, she and her sister were quite fond of it. All this evidence was at your fingertips, had you not stopped your investigation once the poison was found in Harrison's coat pocket."

"So you are saying she planted the poison on the priest? Why?"

Holmes sighed. Even in the face of critical elucidations, the facts were not presenting themselves as clearly to the authorities as they were to him. With exasperation he said, "This was her grand plan – please stop me, Miss, if I stray from facts: She would elicit the affections of both Montfort and Waverly and play off of them. She needed two men to make her plan work. She would eventually pick Montfort over Waverly as her

186

beau, and Waverly would then become the scapegoat for everything else that happened. He seemed a bit of a free spirit, I believe it was put, and comes and goes as he wishes, so he would be the least likely of the friends to evoke worry for being absent. With Waverly, whose affections were eventually spurned by Mary for Montfort's, gone from the group during the poisonings, you would now have a second viable suspect. With an alternative explanation of the facts, and with no obvious motive, she knew you would eventually have no choice but to let the priest go. It would have just been a waiting game. And to that end, she even gave you Waverly's footprint in the entranceway. A cursory examination of the priest's footwear would have shown the print wasn't his – more proof that the man you would never find was setting up the priest for the fall. I do not think she had much time to hide it, so with a careful search of the grounds, I would wager the finding of that shoe."

"All very elaborate," Milks finally agreed, "but what was the game here? That piece of information is still eluding me."

"It is because Mary thinks that her sister died at the hands of these five young men."

The young woman finally looked up, face reddened in anger. "They *did* kill her. I hear them. I hear their confessions to Father Harrison. I hear Will tell Father they pushed her out of wagon and left her to die. I wanted *zemsta* – revenge. I am patient woman. Two years it took, but I got revenge for my dear Anna."

It was at this time that Father Harrison entered the room in the company of a constable.

Milks was on the verge of objecting that a suspect in four murders was out of his cell, but Holmes put up a hand to stop his protestations.

The priest said, "Dear girl, whatever you heard, you only heard part of the confession. What happened was an accident."

Milks interjected somewhat perturbed, "We investigated that for weeks, and the whole time you knew what happened?"

"I cannot break the seal of the confessional. I will not divulge anything any of them told me of each person's particular culpability, but I think I can say, without asking for guidance from the bishop, this much: Anna was walking home from Crofton Barrow. The boys, on their way back to the village themselves after a social gathering, offered her a ride, and she agreed. At some point, she became . . . uncomfortable sitting next to one of them and stood to change seats. At that point, the wheel hit a divot in the road. She lost her balance and fell from the wagon, landing awkwardly on her head. They stopped to render aid, but it was too late. She had broken her neck and died instantly in the fall. At the vehement request of one, they decided that it would be better for them to keep quiet.

They all had a bit too much to drink, and one was worried that authorities might not believe their story. There was nothing they could do to save her, and there was no need for anyone to know of their involvement – even though, as I said, it was an accident."

"And how do we know they were telling you the truth?" Milks asked.

"Point proven," replied Holmes laconically.

Harrison said, "In confession there is no reason to lie. Your confession is to God, not to me. God already knows the truth."

"You are telling this now. Why did you not tell me this then?" Mary asked with tears in her eyes, anger in her voice.

"They did not come to me until a month after it happened. By then, you seemed to have been on your way in recovering from the ordeal, and I didn't want to reopen such a fresh wound. I had no idea you overheard any of the confessions."

"And now you find out that your revenge was for what – an accident?" Milks interjected.

Wiping away her tears, Mary said, "Their silence alone was deserving of the noose."

"Well, this didn't end the way I thought it would," said Milks. With a note of acquiescence, he then asked, "And where again did you say Waverly was?"

"Buried in the garden behind the cottage where she rents a room. His will be the corpse with the missing shoe."

I would have laughed at the remark had the situation not been so grim.

Holmes pulled out the card and handed it to Milks. "I believe she enticed Waverly to her room with this note. It is one of many you will find in Harrison's desk in the rectory. She made the cards to teach them all her native language. When Waverly saw the one word, he knew its author and where to go. When he arrived, it was probably nightfall. When she saw him coming down the walkway to her door, she called him back to the garden where she struck him with a brick or a shovel and quickly buried the body in a grave she had no doubt already dug for him in the fresh, loose soil while she awaited his arrival."

As Milks led Mary away, she stopped momentarily in front of Father Harrison. She looked so sorrowful. "If you knew I hear some of confession, would you have broken the seal and told me truth about my Anna then?"

The priest thought for a moment then said, "No."

Milks led her away and said over his shoulder, "You're free to go, Reverend."

When we were alone, Holmes engaged Father Harrison. "You lied to her. You would have told everything had she asked."

"You're right, Mr. Holmes, but why let her know that her fate could have been changed. She would spend her remaining days wondering *what if* instead of *what now*. For her, the *what now* is more important, and that is what she needs to focus upon." He sighed a deep, sorrowful sigh. "If I had known this was to be the ending, I would have forsaken my vows altogether to save those six souls. I can't help but feel that I have let them all down."

"Yet, on at least one occasion you were seen in a heated discussion with the girl in the front alcove. My guess is you saw how she was playing both men and warned her of the possible consequences."

"You are correct once again, Mr. Holmes. It wasn't fair to her or either man doing what she was doing. One or all would have ended up hurt in the end. Now, I must live my life having seen just how hurt all would end up being. I shall end my days on my knees in prayer over this ordeal."

"Then you are a better shepherd than you give yourself credit for," replied my friend earnestly.

Holmes was unusually quiet as we rode back to Phin's cottage. I felt – and I knew Holmes felt – that sometimes justice seemed incomplete. An innocent man was almost incarcerated for a crime that he didn't commit, and a young woman, grieving the death of her sister, would hang for five deaths that didn't have to happen. Too many crimes went unpunished or the wrong people punished due to powerful influences, or mere folly, or both. He had many times mentioned writing a volume on his methods of deduction once he retired to his bee-keeping in Sussex. It was at times like this that I wondered why he waited. The world would be without the great detective someday, yet it was now – and would always be – in dire need of his services.

To break him from this silence, I spoke up, for there were questions I needed answered. "When did you begin to suspect Mary in all of this?"

"Poison is a woman's preferred method of murder, Watson, so I tended towards Mary from the beginning. And when I learned of Waverly's temperament, I knew he couldn't be the murderer. He would have bludgeoned a man before resorting to poison. Once I was provided a motive, all the pieces of the puzzle fit perfectly into their rightful places."

"And how on earth did you know Waverly was buried in Mary's garden?"

"Two things, Watson," said he. "It was a convenient place in which the earth was already disturbed – it wouldn't cause suspicion. And the middle of the garden was a full five inches higher than at the edges. That is precisely the amount of displacement for a body."

After a brief silence, he added, "Thank you, Watson. I prefer fact over feelings and was at a precipice. Those perfectly timed questions have brought me back."

When we walked through the door into Phin's cottage, wonderful aromas filled the air, which seemed to reconstitute my friend.

Phin emerged from the kitchen, apron affixed, sweat beading on his forehead, a bit out of breath. "I am sorry, John, but salad and cold meat just will not do for us old friends. I took the liberty to use my new press on a duck, and these exquisite fragrances are the result. My mouth is watering at the thought. Please sit at the table. I have a first course that we can enjoy, and you can tell me how your investigation went. It will be like old times."

We sat at the table, and Phin brought us each a bowl of hearty, hot soup. The three of us ate a wonderful meal and talked of the good old days in London.

The Notable Musician
by Roger Riccard

Chapter I

As the fame of my friend, Sherlock Holmes, the consulting detective, spread throughout the English-speaking world in the late nineteenth and early twentieth centuries, it became a frequent occurrence that visiting Americans would seek him out during their London excursions. Of course, his dealings with foreigners were well documented. Both the famous and infamous crossed his path, from Buffalo Bill Cody and Samuel Clemens to the Ku Klux Klan of "The Five Orange Pips". [1]

On a late November morning in 1901, I was awakened by the blaring of a marching band which seemed to have invaded our sitting room. I threw on my dressing gown. Groggily, I made my way down to my friend, sitting by the gramophone with his eyes closed and hand waving in abbreviated motion to the beat of the music.

I crossed the room to the dining table to pour myself a cup of tea from the hot pot. As I sank into a chair, Holmes removed the needle from the cylinder and greeted me.

"Ho, Watson! Do you not appreciate the stirring tones of 'The March King'?

I set down my cup after taking a sip and put my head back with eyes closed as I faced the ceiling. "Not when I've been up until three in the morning delivering Mrs. Otterberry's baby girl. I didn't get to bed until almost four."

I paused and then looked across the room at him, asking, "Who's 'The March King'?"

Holmes *tsk-tsk*'d me as he handed over a telegram while he stood and poured more tea for himself. "The famous American composer and band leader, John Phillip Sousa, of course."

I attempted to read the form through my sleepy, unfocused eyes but failed miserably and merely tossed it on the table and took another sip of tea, hoping to stir my consciousness into being.

"I'm in no condition for mysterious missives, Holmes," I grumbled, as I rested my jaw on my palm, closing my eyes again. "What does he want?"

"He is deplorably lacking in specifics, but does mention a theft of some sort. I replied that he may come 'round at ten o'clock this morning to discuss it further."

"What time is it now?" I mumbled.

"It's just after nine, dear fellow. Surely you must have had five hours sleep by now. Time to break your fast and prepare to meet our potential client."

I glared at him, "Five hours may have been enough twenty years ago when I was a callow youth, but now it is intolerable."

In answer, he *harrumph*-ed and started up the gramophone again.

I gave an abrupt shake of my head, "What is that infernal tune anyway?"

He gave one of his mischievous grins and replied, "Something that could easily be dedicated to you, dear Watson. *Semper Fidelis*. Always Faithful."

Somehow I managed to make myself presentable and returned to consume some morning pastries and a cup of the now-lukewarm tea prior to our client's arrival. At precisely five minutes before the hour, Mrs. Hudson brought the gentleman's card up the steps and asked if we were ready to receive him. Holmes answered in the affirmative. Soon we were sitting across from a well-dressed man in his late forties wearing eyeglasses and sporting a short, neat beard with a moustache that curled up at the tips, in the fashion of the day. His brown hair was closely cropped and parted down the middle. His bearing was exceedingly military. Even sitting down, he seemed to be at attention. So much did this perception exude from him that, during our introductions, Holmes enquired if there was a rank by which we should address him.

He flashed a brief smile and responded, "I'm afraid my Marine training has become ingrained in me, having been immersed in it since I was apprenticed to the Marine Corp Band at the age of thirteen. But to answer your question, Mr. Holmes, I am a retired Sergeant Major, so 'Mr. Sousa' will do just fine."

"Very well, Mr. Sousa," replied the detective. "Now, your message was rather cryptic. I gather that something of value has been stolen, but you did not wish even the telegrapher to know what it was. May I suggest that perhaps it was one or more of your band's Sousaphones? Or was it something of a more personal nature?"

His military training allowed our guest to remain impassive at this declaration, unlike so many of our clients, who are flabbergasted at Holmes's deductive reasoning. He merely nodded his head and said, "Your reputation is well-earned, sir. Both of our Sousaphones were missing when our instruments were delivered from the ship to the hotel. Why did you suspect that to be the case? Is there a gang of brass thieves plaguing London these days?"

Holmes gave a shake of his head, "Hardly a lucrative profession. However, unless it were some personal item of yours, the Sousaphones would seem the most likely target to cause you concern, as they would be the most difficult to replace. Their absence could affect your upcoming performances, so naturally you wish to avoid publicity by coming to me instead of the official police."

"Indeed, Mr. Holmes. That is my precise concern. We are scheduled for a Command Performance for His Majesty on December first, in honor of Queen Alexandra's birthday. While my marches are unique and have made my band famous throughout the States and much of Europe, the Sousaphone is also an integral part in distinguishing our signature sound. I should hate to disappoint King Edward or his guests by their absence."

"When was the last time anyone observed the presence of these instruments?" enquired the detective.

"I, myself, checked on the storage of all our instruments when the coast of England came into view. I wished to verify that they were all packed together in the ship's hold so that their separation during transport would be unlikely. Unfortunately, ship's cargo seems to be stored by size and weight, and everything wasn't together, but it was all accounted for."

"Don't you have a traveling secretary for that sort of thing?" I asked.

He nodded in reply, "Indeed I do, Dr. Watson. Mr. Lytle performs those sorts of tasks for us and he was with me at the time."

"Has he been with you long?" asked Holmes.

"Oh, yes. Since before the War. [2] He was a member of the band – a Sousaphone player, in fact. But he was severely wounded in Cuba and lost a leg, so he can no longer march with us. He still sits in on occasional concerts, but his primary duties now are making our travel arrangements and working with my agent on bookings."

"So he is above suspicion?" prodded my flat mate.

Sousa sat up even straighter, if that were possible, and raised his voice. "Absolutely, sir. The boy is like a son to me. He would never betray my trust."

"No offense, Mr. Sousa," Holmes nodded. "I just need to be aware of all possible players in this game of intrigue. Are you equally passionate about the loyalty of all your band members?"

"Indeed. They've all been with me for years. Even the most recent additions have performed with us for over a year and none have given any indication of dissatisfaction or acted in any suspicious manner."

"Very well. We will act on that premise for now and assume that the perpetrator is someone outside your organization. You've checked with the shipping office, of course?"

"My first line of inquiry. They verified that all instruments were unloaded."

"I'm sure they did. Could you write down the ship's name as well as the name of the freight officer with whom you spoke at the docks?"

A brief nod of his head indicated that Holmes wanted me to give Mr. Sousa my pencil and paper for this task and I complied. Having completed this effort, Holmes addressed our client one last time. "At what hotel are you staying, sir?"

"We are at the Langham, about a mile from here."

Holmes smiled, "Yes, we are quite familiar with the Langham. A number of our clients have stayed there. We shall begin our investigations immediately and contact you there when we have news."

We all rose and Mr. Sousa shook our hands, expressing his confidence in our quest as he left us. I turned to my companion and asked, "Where to first, Holmes – the shipping office?"

"Yes, Doctor, but I need to send out some telegrams first. Be a good fellow and ring for Billy."

Our pageboy was quick to respond and arrived up the stairs while Holmes was writing out his messages. He said, "Take this to the telegraph office, then run this over to Wiggins. Here's something for his trouble and cab fare for you." He placed the letter and some coins in the boy's hand and Billy bounded down the stairs, much to Mrs. Hudson's consternation.

"You suspect the thieves will pawn the goods, then?" I asked. Wiggins was now a married man and working at the pawn shop of Jabez Wilson, a former client whose case I had published some ten years earlier as "The Red-Headed League".

"A possibility, Watson. Though unlikely, we should cover all avenues. Wiggins can put the word out to all the other pawn shops from London to Southampton. The telegram was to our old associate, Shinwell Johnson [3], who can check out the freight company for us."

We bundled up against the cold November weather and caught a late morning train to the port of Southampton. Having had some time to consider his statement, I queried Holmes during the ride. "You said it was unlikely that the Sousaphones will be pawned. Wouldn't that be the logical pattern behind thefts at the docks?"

"Usually, yes. However, I believe that, if the thieves realise what they have, they will take advantage of their unique acquisitions and either ransom them or advertise them for sale to the highest bidder on the black market. In any event, we must move quickly, for instruments of that size are not likely to remain hidden for long and our thieves will wish to divest themselves of their ill-gotten gains and cash in as soon as possible."

Upon our arrival on England's southern coast, we made our way to the offices of the White Star Line to determine the processing of the cargo from the *RMS Oceanic,* which had conveyed Sousa and his troupe from New York.

Chapter II

As we approached the building, I noted in the distance the skeletal framework of a new vessel under construction. A single stacker, she couldn't have been more than two hundred feet in length. Certainly not one meant for transatlantic crossings, I thought.

Just as we were about to enter the White Star offices, a gentleman emerged. He was a lean, clean-shaven, grey-haired man, though I would have put his age at less than forty. He wore a knee-length overcoat against the chill of the sea breezes, but was hatless. Nearly bumping into us, he apologized.

"Excuse me gentlemen, I was just running out to deliver a message. Would you be Mr. Holmes and Dr. Watson by chance?"

My companion answered in the affirmative and the man replied, "Splendid! You're a bit earlier than I expected, but most welcome I assure you. I am Mr. Utley, one of the directors for the White Star Line. Would you mind walking along with me? I believe you'll wish to examine the area where I am going."

This was agreeable to Holmes, and we walked in step with our host. On the way I questioned him about the new ship.

"You're quite right, Dr. Watson. That's the *Phoenix.* At least for now. Her formal naming will take place when we get closer to completion, since current events can affect how ships are christened. She'll be assigned to channel crossings, river cruises into Belgium and the Netherlands, and various ports in the Mediterranean."

My curiosity satisfied, Holmes spoke up, "Can you tell us what steps have been taken to determine how Mr. Sousa's instruments disappeared?"

Utley shook his head and we entered a large warehouse. "It's impossible, Mr. Holmes! Oh, I do not doubt that Mr. Sousa is totally honest when he claims they are missing. It's just that a container of that size could not be removed from our docks without being recorded. I'm sure you noted the guards at the gate when you came in. They inspect every freight wagon that leaves and check the cargo against the manifest."

"What about cabs and carriages?" asked the detective.

"Every departing passenger must show identification and have their baggage claim ticket compared to the actual luggage and trunks they are leaving with."

"I mean no disrespect, Mr. Utley," I enquired. "But is it possible a guard could have been bribed to look the other way?"

"I understand you must look at every possibility, gentlemen," he said with a slight irritation. "but our guards are thoroughly vetted. Most of them are former military men and there are always two of them on duty checking the cargo together. One dishonest guard would be extremely rare. Two would defy all odds."

Holmes chimed in with a more melodious timbre in his voice, "Just so, Mr. Utley. We will proceed with that as a given for now. Is this the warehouse where Mr. Sousa's cargo was stored upon unloading?"

Mollified by Holmes's tone, Utley replied, "Yes, and there is Mr. Turner, whom I wanted to see and who you will wish to interview, I am sure."

Utley led the way to where a stocky young fellow was barking out orders to his crew. Turner was most notable for his long hair and bushy beard, both the color of a summer carrot. I could not help thinking that, if Father Christmas were Irish, this would be what he'd look like.

After relaying his message, Utley introduced us and instructed Turner to give his complete cooperation. "You'll be in good hands here, gentlemen. Feel free to come back to my office when you're finished."

"Well, gentlemen," asked the young supervisor. "Where would you like to start?"

"First of all," replied Holmes, "when a ship is unloaded, is the cargo kept in the same order as it was while on board?"

"As a general rule we'd unload in the reverse order as freight and baggage were placed in the hold – but that doesn't mean one's belongings all stay together. For instance, the crew that loaded the *Oceanic* in New York would have separated larger pieces of freight and spread the weight as evenly as possible throughout the hold, so as to maintain the proper ballast, you see."

Holmes nodded in understanding and asked, "The crate we are seeking is roughly six foot long and three-by-three. Do you recall anything of that size?"

"Ah, Mr. Holmes, there would have been several crates fittin' that description. It's a common size for freight companies to use."

"I thought as much, but it doesn't hurt to ask. Do you know where the luggage and freight for the Sousa troupe were stored after unloading?"

"That I can help you with. With so much for one party, we sectioned off this area down here." He pointed and began leading the way toward a space near the far end of the warehouse. When we arrived, we found that the only cargo separating Sousa's space from the warehouse opposite-end doors was that designated for the construction of the *Phoenix*. The area we looked at was now empty, of course, all cargo and luggage having been delivered to Sousa's troupe at the Langham hotel.

Still, my friend walked the perimeter, noting footprints and tracks of carts. At one point he stooped with one hand on the edge of a crate filled with parts bound for the shipbuilding dock and picked up a small piece of paper from the ground. He handed it to me, merely stating. "Well, we know Sousa's equipment *was* here."

The paper was actually thin card stock and had the New York dock and ship information in the upper left corner. The destination address for the Langham Hotel in London with J.P. Sousa as the recipient was in the middle. In the lower right there was a '*Contents*' box. It was through this box where the paper had been sliced free of its container. The only word left intact was '*Sousa*'.

Showing the paper to Turner, he asked, "If this is still here, how would the dockworkers know where to send the crate?"

Turner tilted his head to one side, his beard brushing the front of his coat and some few hairs catching on a button. "Likely it got torn as it was unloaded with the rest of Sousa's equipment," he answered. "It was already in the designated space, so it should have stayed with that batch as it was bundled up for delivery to the Langham. Obviously, it's not here now."

Holmes spent a few more minutes in his investigation and then asked Turner if we could board the *Oceanic* and examine the hold. The supervisor led us to the ship and turned us over to Petty Officer Pedersen, who led us down through the maze of passages and into the depths of the dark and damp cargo hold.

This deep into the bowels of the ship there was little sway and it almost felt as if we were still in the warehouse, save for the dampness and lack of windows. Nearly all the cargo had been unloaded and what was left was quickly reviewed and determined not to include the missing instruments.

I asked the fellow, "Are the holds guarded during the voyage, or are passengers free to come down and get things from their luggage?"

"There's a watch posted at all times, Doctor," he replied. "Anyone who does come down is escorted to their luggage by one of my men. That's not just for security. It's unlikely they could find their luggage without a guide to show them where to look."

Holmes spoke up, "So the guards have some sort of diagram indicating where everything is stored?"

"Yes, Mr. Holmes. I can get you a copy if you like."

"That should prove most efficient. Thank you, Petty Officer."

With the diagram as a guide, we were quickly able to discern the location where the Sousaphones would have been kept. They were far from any exit, and packed as they were for the voyage, impossible to remove without being seen.

"The crate would not have been moved after it was loaded for any reason?" asked Holmes.

"Not moved, Mr. Holmes. But it was opened at one point."

"How's that?" exclaimed Holmes in surprise.

Pedersen tilted his cap back on his head and tucked his thumbs into his belt. "Well, sir, on our third night out, the captain prevailed upon Mr. Sousa's band to perform for the passengers. It was a lively time that night. Yes sir!"

Holmes took in that information with a tilt of his head and a nod, then responded, "Thank you, Petty Officer. I understand the ship has been thoroughly searched, in case the instruments were merely misplaced."

"Aye, aye, Mr. Holmes. Every cabin, closet, and storeroom. I'll guarantee those instruments are not on this vessel."

Holmes bid the sailor to take us topside. Darkness was beginning to fall, and we made our way back to Mr. Utley's office. Upon our entrance he enquired, "Any progress, gentlemen?"

Holmes replied, "Only that we know where they are not, Mr. Utley. However, I have a fair picture of the sequence of events and that should prove useful. We need to check into our hotel and I must send out some telegrams. I should like to return first thing tomorrow morning and continue my investigation in daylight."

"Certainly, Mr. Holmes, but I doubt there's anything to find. Have you considered the freight carrier?"

"I have an associate looking into that possibility."

"I think that's your best bet, but I'll let the dock guards know that the two of you have permission to look around tomorrow."

"Thank you, sir. Good evening."

We left the director's office and caught a cab for a nearby hotel. Holmes sent out three telegrams after we checked in. From there, we went on to a nearby restaurant for dinner.

As we awaited our food I queried him. "What are your thoughts? Could Utley be correct in presuming the freight company to be responsible?"

"I'll need answers to my telegrams before I can hypothesize any further. For now let us enjoy our meal, for tomorrow may be a very busy day."

198

Chapter III

The next day, we arose with the dawn and bundled ourselves against the morning chill to make our way to the docks. The early fog all but obscured the great ships in port. The *Phoenix* was completely enshrouded, and the *Oceanic* only became visible when we were within one-hundred feet.

We found Mr. Turner, but he was quite busy, as the *Oceanic* was loading cargo for her next trip to New York. He apologetically but firmly turned us over to a subordinate.

"Sammy!" he called out to a young man passing by. The fellow came over and Turner instructed him to help us with whatever we wanted. Then he left us to tend to the rest of his crew.

Sammy must have been a year or two shy of twenty, judging by his manner and vestiges of baby fat around his face, which seemed unable to sprout either beard or moustache. His size however, indicated a recent growth spurt. He stood at least six-feet-four, and must have weighed in excess of two-hundred-and-fifty pounds – a fine specimen for a dockworker. He also reminded me of my university days when I would have gladly welcomed him to my old rugby team.

His sleeves didn't quite cover his wrists and his barrel chest threatened to pop the buttons off his faded blue chambray shirt. Like his clothes, his voice did not quite seem to fit, as he spoke in a high cockney tenor rather than the *basso profundo* I would have expected.

"'Ow can I helps you gentlemen?"

Holmes explained our mission to find the missing crate and enlisted the young man to walk us through exactly the steps that would have been taken – from the unloading and storage of the cargo, to the shipment of all the Sousa troupe's luggage to the Langham Hotel.

This re-enactment took us from the docks to the warehouse, where goods were sorted by passenger or destination instead of size. Again, we came to the space where Sousa's band instruments and luggage would have been gathered.

Holmes asked Sammy what the procedure was for loading cargo and luggage bound for the Langham.

"We trys to keep things bundled by passenger. Most times we can get several folks' luggage onto one wagon. But there was so much for that 'Sousa' group (he pronounced it "*Sow-sa*"), that it took up a whole wagon, just by itself."

"How is it stacked?" asked the detective. "Is it tied down, or could something have fallen off?"

"Oh no, Mr. 'Olmes. Once we gets a wagon loaded, it's covered by a tarp to protect it against the weather, y'see. Then we crisscrosses ropes back 'n forth and ties her up good and tight. I'd bet a wagon could tips right over and not lose a single case."

We then had the young fellow walk us through the loading area and trace the route to the gate where Holmes questioned the guards thoroughly as to their procedures. We proceeded on to the train station and interviewed the personnel there as well.

By now midday was upon us. The fog had lifted and Holmes suggested we return to the hotel to check on any answers to his telegrams. I was in favor of that idea, as it was approaching lunchtime. Upon arrival, we found several messages waiting for Holmes at the desk.

He perused them quickly, tossing some aside and placing others into his pocket, but he didn't enlighten me as to their contents. Instead, he suggested I take advantage of the hotel cuisine. He was going to "go for a walk and smoke a pipe or two". After so many years in his company, I knew this meant his mind was reeling with possibilities and he needed to bring them into coalescence.

I retired to the dining room for a savory meal of fish and chips, finished off with an excellent ale. Afterward, I obtained an afternoon newspaper and caught up on the news of the day in the comfort of the hotel lobby. Its nautical theme included paintings of sailing ships, with fishing nets and life preservers hanging on the wall. A large stuffed swordfish mounted over the fireplace completed the scene.

My companion returned some two hours later. From my seat near the window I could see him bound up the entrance stairs two at a time. Upon his appearance, I caught his attention. He strode over, smartly sat down, and lit his pipe with a satisfied look upon his face.

"You seem to be in a good mood," I observed "You've solved Mr. Sousa's dilemma, I take it?"

"Indeed, Watson," he replied. "We shall be on the six o'clock train to London tonight."

"Marvelous!" I cried. "How did you do it?"

He gave me one of those enigmatic smiles that I know all too well and answered. "In your medical journals, have you read of the condition '*wortblindheit*', identified by Dr. Adolph Kussmaul some twenty years ago?"

"The term rings a bell, Holmes, but not very loudly, I'm afraid."

"You may be more familiar with the word coined by the ophthalmologist, Rudolph Berlin: '*Dyslexia*'."

Chapter IV

True to his word, Holmes and I were back in London late that evening and a telegram brought Mr. Sousa to our flat early the next morning.

The famous conductor was flush with excitement as he entered our flat and I took his overcoat and homburg. His countenance was likened unto a schoolboy on Christmas morning as he sat on the edge of the chair indicated by the detective.

"You found them, Mr. Holmes? Where are they?"

Holmes sat opposite him while I took up space on the other end of the settee and offered a cigarette, which Souza politely declined. Holmes, already smoking, stubbed out his own cigarette and folded his hands on the knee crossed over his leg.

"I've engaged a most trustworthy cohort of mine, Mr. Shinwell Johnson, to deliver them to your hotel at ten o'clock this morning. Your concert shall be with full complement, I assure you."

"Marvelous! Where were they? Did you rescue them from some scoundrel attempting to sell them? Tell me all, sir!"

Holmes shook his head, "Nothing so nefarious, Mr. Souza. Merely an unfortunate and accidental misdirection. Once I received your telegram yesterday that no ransom had yet been demanded, and my other sources turned up no evidence of attempted sales to pawn shops, music stores, or scrap yards, I determined that they had never left the dockyards. However, a search of the ship and the warehouse had proven fruitless. The only physical evidence I had discovered was this."

He handed Souza the torn shipping label. Our client scrutinized it and asked, "If this was torn off the crate, it might never have gotten to our hotel. Where did they send it?"

"By process of elimination and observation, I was able to determine it could only have gone one place."

Souza shuddered as a thought occurred to him, "Overboard?" he asked, with trepidation at the damage seawater would have caused.

"The White Star Line is much too efficient for that," answered Holmes. "While it is as yet undetermined how this label was torn, it was undoubtedly done so in the warehouse, after your goods were unloaded and set aside for the freight wagon. Unfortunately, this particular box was on a side next to the storage area for material bound for a ship under construction."

"I don't understand."

"Your instruments would have been found eventually by the construction crew. My investigation merely sped up the process by a few days. Watson, dear fellow, I believe your story-telling skills need refreshing. Perhaps you would care to explain?"

I hadn't published any of my friend's cases since his return to London in 1894, except for a single narrative regarding an affair in Dartmoor, though I had several sheaves of notes. I was not prepared for this and I hesitated briefly, gathering my thoughts as to how best to relay our actions of the previous afternoon. Souza leaned back and looked to me for his answers. At last I shifted myself to better face him. I put my arm upon the back of the settee and began gesticulating with my other hand, as if to punctuate my speech.

At three-thirty the previous afternoon, Holmes and I had called upon Mr. Utley and prevailed upon him to accompany us. With Utley, Turner, and young Sammy in tow, Holmes led us to the dry-dock where the *Phoenix* was under construction. We entered the building where materials were stored, awaiting their turn for installation. The construction chief, Mr. Roberts, was waiting for us by a crate, which already had its top pried loose and laying unfastened upon the wooden box.

"Gentlemen, please observe," said the detective as he grabbed one end and Roberts the other. Together they flipped the lid off the crate. Inside were quilted rugs, acting as padding. When Holmes threw back the top layer, two brass funnels were revealed.

Sammy looked inside and said, "Aye, those were them fancy chimney funnels what I sent over for the *Phoenix* t' other day."

Holmes removed the torn tag from his pocket, which he had picked off the floor of the cargo warehouse previously. The half still attached to the crate said '*PHONE*'. The *S*'s at the end of the word had a hole punched through it for the string which tied it to the crate, and was thus unreadable. Holding the two halves together, it now spelled out "*SOUSAPHONES*".

Sammy whistled and shifted his cap back on his head. "What kind o' word is that, Mr. 'Olmes? With the tag torn, I opened it up to see what they was and figured this was a construction crate what just got shifted over too close to the Sousa cargo. Besides, even with the hole in it, the tag looked like '*Phoenix*', though I can't for the life of me figure out why it's spelt like that."

I should interject at this point that there is a condition called *dyslexia*, in which some people's eyes mix up the order of letters in the word they are reading. They are so accustomed to it that they can still usually read. But to an undereducated fellow like Sammy, errors are inevitable. He confused the letters in *PHONE* with the name *PHOENIX*, which he saw on the ship every day.

The group of us, except Holmes, stood dumbfounded for a moment. Utley raised a hand to his forehead in embarrassment over this mix-up. Sammy just looked around, wondering what was going on. Chief Roberts stifled a laugh. Turner, his face beginning to resemble the crimson of his beard, looked about to explode, but Holmes held up his hand to the Supervisor to forestall any display of temper.

"No harm done, Mr. Turner," observed Holmes calmly. "Just a couple of days' rehearsal lost for two band members. Sammy showed initiative based on the information he had. I suggest a new procedure of checks and balances be enacted to prevent this type of incident in the future." He placed a hand upon the young dockworker's shoulder, "I would further recommend some sort of tutor be brought in for your workers lacking in formal education. Communication skills are just as important as strong backs."

Utley and Turner appeared to take Holmes's suggestion under consideration. We personally watched the crate re-labeled and loaded onto a wagon, which delivered it to the train station where it accompanied us back to London.

Having finished my narrative, Souza slapped his hands upon his knees and chuckled merrily. He then stood and we arose to shake his hand.

"That's one for the books, all right. Thank you, Mr. Holmes. Doctor. I shall return to the hotel and await my delivery. Please send the bill for your fee, and I'll see that it is promptly paid."

Still smiling, he donned his hat and coat, descended the stairs, and strode off into the wintry day, all the while whistling, what seemed to me, a marching tune.

Holmes and I returned to our seats by the fire. He took up the morning paper and I took up paper and pencil and began making notes. Observing this, my companion asked, "Thinking of writing up this case, Watson?"

I replied with a bit of a grin, "Just recording the facts for future recollection, Holmes. Someday I may publish it as your most *instrumental* case ever."

NOTES

John Philip Souza would receive the Royal Victorian Medal from King Edward VII of the United Kingdom in December 1901 for conducting a private birthday concert for Queen Alexandra.

1.   Submitted by Arthur Conan Doyle in 1891

2.   Sousa is undoubtedly referring to the Spanish American War of 1898

3.   See "The Illustrious Client" for more detail about the reformed convict, Shinwell Johnson.

The Devil's Painting
by Kelvin I. Jones

I have good reason to recall the winter of late 1901, for not only was it one of the coldest of the decade, but it also marked what might be called the zenith of the career of my friend, Sherlock Holmes. It was in the November of that year that he was unexpectedly called upon by the monarch to look into the little matter of the Russian monk, an affair which was to have significant consequences in Britain's relationships with that mighty empire. Hard upon its heels came the business of Scorley Rectory, a large rambling building set in the wilds of Suffolk and, according to its owner, possessed of a presence so destructive that it took all the energies of my companion to reveal its true and fraudulent nature.

These and other notable occurrences I see before me, set out in the familiar blue-bound chapbooks on my desk. There are others, perhaps more remarkable, which one day I hope to lay before the discerning public, but for the moment their details must remain a secret, for they contain the names of several notable families to whom I owe a certain discretion.

However, there is one case in particular which catches my fancy as I turn the pages of the chapbook for the December of that memorable year. It was perhaps one of the most bizarre episodes of our long association and it involved no famous names save one, which remained hidden until the last chapter could be told. Indeed, had we known the identity of the man in question early on, we should both have been more able to comprehend the peculiar and terrifying experiences my companion and I were forced to suffer. As it was, what appeared to be the ravings of a madman led us into a downward spiral so that, for a short while, it seemed as if our own reason had given way to insanity. And, in the end, insanity was the key to the mystery.

It was on the Saturday of the 28th of December that Chief Inspector Jarvis of Scotland Yard arrived at our lodgings in Baker Street. He had come unannounced and unnoticed. The former was no more a surprise than the latter, for he was a familiar enough figure to our rooms. A tall, lean man with a pronounced stoop and thin, round spectacles perched on the end of a decidedly Roman nose, he possessed a quietness of manner which set him apart from his colleagues.

The reason that Roger Jarvis arrived unnoticed was that a thick layer of fresh snow had fallen upon the street – had fallen indeed upon the face of the capital – so that the familiar sounds of footsteps and the rattle of hansoms was done away with. The quiet that followed the festivities of Christmas was therefore matched by the silence of the street.

Holmes and I had fallen into a post-prandial snooze following one of Mrs. Hudson's gigantic roasts, the consumption of which in itself vied with The Labours of Hercules. Holmes had been smoking his old clay pipe, which was balanced precariously between his parted lips. He had been attempting to catch up on some research regarding the Utrecht murders. At last, overtaken by stupor and the effects of a strong vintage brandy, he had, like myself, entered the still waters of Lethe.

It was the doorbell which finally summoned us from our sleep, a new, costly and jangling affair which Mrs. Hudson had installed at great expense and which had earned her some sarcasm from my acerbic friend.

"Drat the woman," Holmes exclaimed, as the pipe, still smouldering, dropped from his nether lip and the glowing embers began to scorch the velveteen of his waistcoat. "Who on earth can that be at this hour?" as the door opened to reveal the inspector.

"An unofficial call, you said?" asked Holmes after various pleasantries had been observed. "Why, pray?"

"Partly to wish you the compliments of the season – and you, Doctor, naturally. But no, I must confess that there is another reason for my visit."

"Come then, my dear Jarvis. Let us have no more ado," said Holmes, offering him a cheroot. The inspector took it and, biting off the end, lit it with a spill from the fireplace. Soon a rich aroma began to pervade the room, banishing the stale cooking smells that had earlier persisted.

"I must tell you that my being here today would not go down well with some of my colleagues at the Yard, since they regard the affair as an open-and-shut case of natural causes – nothing more."

"But you disagree?"

"Profoundly."

"Then perhaps you had better begin at the beginning, for the Good Doctor and I had nothing planned for this evening."

Roger Jarvis drew upon his cigar and leaned back in the basket chair whilst I made notes in the notebook to which I now refer. "Very well then. On the 23rd of December, I received a call requesting me to attend the body of a man found in lodgings in the Paddington area of London. You are probably familiar with that neck of the woods, gentlemen – a dingy area consisting of boarding houses and cheap rented accommodation.

"The place in question was a large Georgian property comprising three floors, the top two of which constituted the flat of the deceased, a man in his middle-forties called George Pinder. This fellow followed a rather unusual trade, in that he was both an artist and a restorer of pictures for the National Gallery at Charing Cross. It appears that his own work was not sufficient to earn him a decent living, so he supplemented it with restoration.

"When I got to the flat and climbed the stairs, I found a police constable and the Detective Inspector – a man called Brigson – waiting for me. The room in which they sat was a large, soulless studio with a miserable coal fire burning in the grate and two tall, grimy windows facing the street. There was an easel in the centre of the room, and on it what I can only describe as an oil painting the like of which I have never before seen. On the floor, some three feet away from the picture, lay the body of the deceased, one arm across his chest and a look upon his face of sheer, unadulterated terror."

"How long had the body been there?" asked Holmes laconically, making a note on his shirt cuff.

"The police surgeon reckoned for at least six hours."

"So it might have been *rigor mortis*?"

"Possibly. However, there was something about the attitude of the body that convinces me otherwise," Jarvis replied. "It was – how shall I put it? – contorted in a way which suggested that the victim had died in extreme agony."

"Cause of death?"

"Oh, that's simple enough. Heart failure. The *post mortem* confirmed that."

"A severe heart attack might have caused that effect," I observed.

Jarvis looked unconvinced.

"Proceed, Chief Inspector," remarked Holmes, leaning towards the fire to relight the pipe which had caused him so much grief. "We must not quibble at such an early stage of the narrative, Doctor."

"I questioned the detective present. It appears that Pinder was something of a recluse. The rooms in this particular house are rented by an agent and there is no landlord present. However, one of the neighbours did recall something rather odd which coincided with the time of Pinder's death. Apparently at about midnight during the previous evening, she had heard someone – she could not decide whether it was Pinder or not – talking excitedly. Then there was another voice – this time a high pitched voice like that of a child, which came and went, as if in argument. The voices got louder and louder. Then there was the sound of Pinder's voice, as she put it, imploring, pleading, followed by a short scream, and then silence. One thing which struck me about the woman's testimony was that she referred to the voice of the child as menacing in the extreme."

"You believe what this woman says?" asked Holmes.

"I have no reason to disbelieve her," Jarvis replied, knocking the ash off the end of his cigar. "In fact, her testimony was corroborated by her husband, a commissionaire and a man known to us in the force as a former witness in a burglary case."

"Were there any other witnesses? What about the occupant of the flat below, for example?"

"It belongs to an elderly widow who is rather deaf, it seems. However, one curious feature did emerge when we questioned her. It seems that her sitting room (which also doubles as a bedroom) has a large window at the side looking onto the porch. Being something of an insomniac, the lady in question says that she had sat reading by the window from about 11:30 p.m. until the early hours of the following morning. During that time, she did not once see the front door open or a visitor enter or depart. It was of course this neighbour who alerted the police when she noticed that Pinder had not taken in his milk from the doorstep or emerged from the house to take his usual constitutional – a regular event, so it appears. What I should like to know is what happened to the child visitor, and why did no one see the person in question arrive or leave?"

Holmes nodded, recharging his pipe in a thoughtful manner. "Forgive me, Jarvis, but I fail to see why this case should be of especial interest to me."

Jarvis leaned forward towards the fire and eyed him intently. "Call it an instinct if you wish – an intuition. I can't explain it precisely. There was something about the room – an atmosphere which I have encountered before. You remember the case of the Wickham Poltergeist, for example?"

Holmes nodded and smiled. "I recall it. A preposterous and most fraudulent affair."

"Well, the room had the same coldness – and that feeling of someone watching."

Holmes looked skeptical, and I asked, "Did you share this feeling with Brigson?''

Jarvis shook his head. "You should know me better than that, Doctor. As you are no doubt aware, my consultations with you haven't gone down well at the Yard, despite the undoubted success of our joint investigations."

"Well, then, my dear fellow," said Holmes, "I shall be more than happy to assist you in whatever way I can. Tell me, what have you discovered regarding the painter's employers? You say that he worked in a part-time capacity for the National Gallery?"

"That's right. Unfortunately the galleries have been closed since Christmas Eve, so as you can appreciate, my investigations have been somewhat impeded by the festivities."

Holmes pulled on his pipe, sending spirals of blue smoke to the ceiling. "No matter. I shall be happy to make a few inquiries on your behalf. Also, of course, I will need to see the room and the oil painting. I take it you have left everything intact?"

"Except for the removal of the body."

"Very well, then. When may we see the premises?"

Jarvis held up a mortice key. "Presumptive of me I know, but I thought . . . ."

Holmes stood up and tapped the bowl of his pipe against the flat of his hand. "And why not? Watson and I have nothing better to do and it will be a good opportunity to walk off the excesses of the Yuletide indulgence. Are you game, Doctor?"

I glanced at the blazing hearth with some reluctance, murmuring my assent.

"There will be few cabs about at this hour, so I suggest we don our galoshes. Perhaps you will be so good as to summon Mrs. Hudson, Watson.''

Outside, the chill of the winter evening gripped our faces and throats. Holmes, wrapped in a thick ulster, his head protected by the fore-and-aft cap that he favored, walked ahead, the untrodden snow crunching under his feet. By his side walked Jarvis, his bowed form looking even more ungainly than when he was recumbent, his lean face pinched by the cold, his hands gripping the lapels of his coat.

As we made our way across the deserted city, I was struck by the awful melancholy of the place.

Holmes had taken a complicated path, winding through back streets with which I, for my part, was unfamiliar. Here and there we passed a squalid pub, its inhabitants glimpsed through the translucent windows. And once, at the end of a row of decaying terraced houses, we came across a group of three children, dressed in rags. The eldest of these rushed towards us as we approached and demanded money. I noted that the youngest, a girl of no more than five, lay in a comatose state, her legs drawn up under her, her mouth hung open, so that she resembled a cadaver. Holmes placed a shilling in the palm of the girl's trembling hand.

After taking time to find shelter, warmth, and food for the children, and making sure that the girl's condition was much improved, we continued, emerging into the Edgware Road, turning left into Praed Street, a bitter wind hurling gusts of snow into our faces. By the cab stand alongside Paddington Station, we turned left into a narrow opening bearing the nameplate "*Worth Street*", and thence to Cleveland Gardens, our destination.

Halfway round the square we spotted the agitated form of a police constable, stamping his way to-and-fro at the bottom of a series of steep steps, fronting a dingy-looking Georgian property with a somewhat incongruous Palladian frontage. Jarvis kicked the snow from his shoes and greeted the officer.

"Brigson?"

"Left about an hour ago, sir," replied the constable, saluting him smartly.

"Any other visitors?"

"Not a soul sir, apart from the milkman."

"All right, Jones, you are excused for half-an-hour. I understand that there's a working-man's *café* round the corner."

The man beamed at Jarvis and bade us farewell as the Chief Inspector opened the front door and ushered us inside.

If the exterior of the premises had appeared dingy and dilapidated, then the interior confirmed Jarvis's fleeting description. A wide oak staircase stood in the centre of the lobby, and many of the bannister rails were missing. What once had been a fine private mansion had long since given way to the worm and the attentions of its destructive tenants. A threadbare, filthy carpet occupied the main concourse, and the only light present came from a single low-watt bulb dangling from a cracked and cobwebbed ceiling. We climbed the creaking staircase and soon came to the landing which marked the living quarters of the late George Pinder.

"This is the studio," Jarvis explained, as he reached into his pocket for the key. "Pinder's living room and bedroom occupy the top floor."

After some persuasion the door opened, admitting us into a large room, bare save for a moth-eaten chaise-lounge, a single wicker chair, a stool, and an easel. There was nothing else of importance in the room save a few personal items spread across the mantelpiece, comprising some battered books, a well-used briar, a box of matches, and an empty bottle of scotch.

There was a smell of disuse and damp about the place, but also an intense cold, in spite of the low fire burning in the grate. I noticed that Holmes had stopped by the fireplace and was staring intently at the painting on the easel. My immediate reaction, on entering the room, I must confess, was one of dread and terror. To all appearances, the place presented a sterile, blank aspect, and yet to a person of sensitivity there was something loathsome about the room, and the longer I stood taking in my surroundings, the more it seemed that the dimensions of the place appeared uncertain and blurred. It was like one of those dreams one experiences on waking where the perspective shifts and moves with the eye of the beholder. This surreal reverie was interrupted by a comment from Holmes, who had now advanced to inspect the canvas more closely.

"Quite a remarkable painting, isn't it?" Jarvis remarked, moving forward to join him.

"Indeed. The technique is vaguely familiar, and yet . . . ."

From his pocket he had drawn out a small magnifying lens which he now used to inspect the canvas more closely. Jarvis was correct in his observation. The canvas was indeed unusual both for the boldness of its execution, and also for the nature of its composition. Measuring approximately two-feet-by-three and painted in brilliant blues, greens, and crimsons, it depicted the execution of a young woman. When I say that the picture was terrifying in its depiction of this act of barbarism, I refer to two aspects in particular: The young woman's face and that of her executioner.

The victim of this atrocity appeared to be a person of nobility judging by her dress, a gown of scarlet silk edged in gold brocade and let out at the shoulders. The young woman's hands, soft and delicate, were clearly those of a person unused to manual work. Her hair, long and golden, hung down her back almost to the ground, and on the crown of her head was a circle of woven gold thread, reminiscent of the Pre-Raphaelite headgear depicted by Rossetti in his painting, "*Guinevere*". On her face was an expression of consternation, fear, and horror such as I have rarely seen depicted in a painting. Her mouth lay open and her eyes were wide as if she had just cried for mercy. Her hands grasped the gown of her attacker so hard that one could see the veins standing out beneath the skin. The sharpness and realism of the figure was truly remarkable.

But this was nothing compared to the visage of the woman's attacker, who stood framed against a party of curious onlookers. A man of immense strength and size, he towered over the distraught woman, his legs astride, his right arm raised, his sword poised for the downward stroke. With his left hand he grasped the woman's head, thrusting it backwards so that the neck lay bared, ready for the cut of the gleaming blade. On his face was a look of determination and cruelty. His sharp blue eyes shone in the sunlight, his mouth drawn into a hard line and his dark hair and beard serving to emphasise the brutality of the act.

Holmes lowered his lens and stood back from the painting. "No sign of an artist's signature," he commented.

"No, nor on the back," agreed Jarvis.

"As I say, the style is somewhat familiar. It is not one of the Pre-Raphaelites, yet there are distinct similarities. A later painter, perhaps. Would you not agree, Watson?"

My reply was not forthcoming. For some while I had been staring at the painting and been aware of Holmes's commentary, and during this period something most odd and disconcerting had taken place. Whether the diffused light pouring in through the grimy windows gave rise to what I saw or whether my eyes had played a trick upon me I cannot rightly say. All I can be sure of is that the figures were moving. I saw the glint of the sun on the blade and the slight movement of the man's eyebrows and mouth. And when I glanced at the woman, I saw that her eyes were filled with tears. Both figures had the roundness and solidity of the living. And there was something else besides: A distinct smell, a smell I remember from my childhood when, on the road from Faversham to Canterbury, the great dray horses would sweat and heave their way along, depositing their ordure behind them. Leather, sweat, and dung – an acrid smell all of its own – and it was here, now, in this dingy room, coming at me from out of the picture with such intensity that I almost coughed.

At last I tore my eyes from the painting and found Holmes and Jarvis staring at me oddly. "My dear fellow, what on earth is wrong?"

Holmes had stretched out his hand and guided me to an armchair. Afterwards he told me how deathly pale I had turned. From his hip pocket Jarvis produced a small silver flask and applied it to my lips. When I had told my companions of the sensations I had experienced on viewing the painting, Holmes got up and stood studying the canvas in silence. Then he pressed his nose to the surface and sniffed hard.

"Now, let's see," he murmured. From the pocket of his coat he drew out a white linen handkerchief and began to rub the oil paint gently. Then he folded it in four and returned it to his pocket.

"Hmm. I should like to take this painting away for further analysis, if you've no particular objection," he said.

"I see no reason why you shouldn't. At present I've no idea who the owner is," Jarvis replied.

"Of course, you may have it back when required. These artist's materials and the paints – I should like those too."

"I'll have them packaged up and sent round to you," said Jarvis obligingly.

"And now I think we shall take a look at the other rooms."

I was glad to hear this, for it still remained intensely cold in the room, and despite my being wrapped in a thick ulster and scarf, there was a dankness which I found oppressive.

As we made our way onto the landing, I glanced down through the stairwell and became aware of a dark figure hovering there in the gloom. I touched Jarvis's arm lightly and he stopped abruptly, following my gaze. "Ah, the widow," he explained. "And our only witness."

Holmes turned at the door to the flat.

"Might I speak to her?" he asked.

Jarvis nodded.

"I shall join you in a few minutes." And so doing, he tripped down the stairs and hailed the old woman in his usual vigorous fashion.

It did not take us long to examine Pinder's apartment, for there were few possessions on display and the room had all the appearance of a place that was merely an extension of a man's work. A bookcase, a rickety bed, a small cane bedside table on which a yellow backed novel had been carelessly flung, occupied one end of the bedroom, while at the other end lay a collection of about twenty to thirty canvases. I knelt down and began to examine these while Jarvis lit a cigarette and watched from the doorway.

The paintings appeared to comprise a number of widely differing styles. Some were evidently of great antiquity, as the dark layers of varnish testified. Then there were others of more recent date, landscapes and portraits in both oil and watercolour. It was clear that some of these were awaiting cleaning and restoration, whilst others were by the painter himself. It was the latter to which I now turned my attention.

They were executed in what I can only describe as an impressionistic style and were reminiscent of the work of William Turner, yet lacking that artist's delicacy of brush work and visionary content. All three seemed to deal with the same subject, but the third of these employed a more violent use of colours and contrasts and was somewhat disturbing.

The composition of each of the paintings showed a long cart track winding its way beneath two lines of beech trees. In the distance, to the right, could be seen the crenellated towers of a large Elizabethan mansion, just peeping from beneath the slope of the hill. To the left lay another dip which ended in a sharp drop. This appeared to be a chalk pit, but because of the technique employed, it was difficult to be precise about this.

The scene might have represented a number of estates adjoining a place of antiquity. There was nothing particularly unusual or worthy of comment about the background. It was the foreground and middle ground which commanded my interest.

In the middle ground, half-shrouded in mist, stood the figure of a man in his middle to late years. Judging by his posture, he appeared to be in the act of running, yet his head was turned and his face contorted. In his right hand was a silver topped cane which he held aloft as if protecting himself against an assailant. There was something about the man's demeanour which struck me as pitiful and suggested that he might be the victim of an imminent assault.

This leads me to the foreground of the first painting, which showed only the back of a figure, dressed in a large black cloak and felt hat. The pursuer – for so it appeared he was – had his left arm crooked at an angle as if he were in the act of drawing something from his belt.

In the second painting the pursuer had advanced and now the left hand was raised and I could discern the silver pommel of a dagger protruding through the thumb and forefinger. The older man had sunk to the ground, one hand across his face, only the terrified eyes being visible. In the top left of the picture was an intense centre of light from which two demonic eyes appeared, though what relevance this piece of fantasy had to the composition I cannot think.

The third painting was unbearable for, although it was not so explicit as the first two, it left one in no doubt as to the fate of the older man. The figure in the cloak had now advanced to the middle ground and had lost his felt hat, revealing a fine head of hair, falling to the shoulders and swept to one side by a gust of wind. He was crouched over the older man, his cloak enveloping him. One hand gripped the older man's shoulder, whilst the other was half raised. A thin trickle of crimson stained the green turf at the older man's feet, leaving one in no doubt as to his gruesome fate.

"Strange stuff," commented Jarvis, who had moved forward to gain a better view of the canvases.

"From the imagination I would hope," I said, rising to stretch my legs.

The door opened and Holmes appeared. He moved into the room with the alacrity and agility to which I had grown accustomed during our association, then stood before the paintings in company with Jarvis. At last he turned. "How minutely has the room been examined?" he asked.

"This is not a murder enquiry. A minute examination would not be conducted in the case of death by natural causes."

"Yet you found the circumstances suspicious. The neighbour seemed certain about hearing a child's voice. Is there anything here that would corroborate that suggestion?"

"I examined the room myself but found nothing of importance."

"Then I suggest that you did not look closely enough." He made a quick search, and then, from under the mattress, he drew a small cloth-bound volume measuring approximately six-inches-by-five. Jarvis flushed. "Pinder's diary, by all accounts," he observed. "This might provide some illumination."

And so it did, though with that illumination we seemed to descend ever deeper into the spiral of dreams and madness which formed the distinguishing characteristics of the case of the late George Pinder.

NOV 2 – It seems that my connections with the gallery are worth cultivating after all! Received a letter from C. today, telling me of a dealer in Chatham who is interested in having several paintings cleaned. Had heard of my work through J. V. of Bond Street, he of the military moustache and foul-smelling cigars. Three oils in particular, but I must collect them myself, as they are too fragile and valuable to send down by mail and he is somewhat infirm. Offered to pay my train fare down and a handsome fee for the task of restoration, so I suppose I must go down and do my duty. The cost of heating this place is downright scandalous and since I haven't sold a single canvas for several months now, the money will come in handy.

NOV 4 – Late. Got back around 11 p.m. last night after a long and tiring journey. The trains give one appalling backache and are freezing cold if one cannot afford the luxury of first class. A cab's ride through squalid back streets to the shop in question. My client is a dark-skinned Jew of suspicious mien, probably not to be entirely trusted. Had a fine selection of canvases on display, including a Turner watercolour, a Whistler (miniature) showing the fog-bound Thames, and an etching by Rossetti which was truly exceptional. It seems that this fellow has some very wealthy clients and that he might be able to put a deal of business my way. We shall see.

The canvases I am to clean are all signed save one – one by Holman Hunt, a smaller piece – a portrait by Morris, and the third I cannot say by whom since it is not signed. It is a curious piece, approximately two-by-three, and done in the most vivid crimsons, blues, and greens. I have it propped up on the easel as I write. There is something positively hypnotic about it – some quality which I find it almost impossible to put into words.

The scene depicted is an unpleasant one: The execution of a young woman – in fact, I should say a girl of probably no more than twenty years old, and with such a fresh bloom to her cheeks that it makes her predicament seem all the more tragic. She kneels before her attacker, pleading for mercy. Yet there is on his face such a look – such cruel intent – that the gazer knows instinctively there is no hope of remission. The

215

candle has burned low whilst I have been writing this and it seems that the figures have become sharper and more lifelike – although I know that that is mere fancy on my part. Yet there is such a lustre to the woman's face and her arms are surely those of a living person. If I close my eyes for an instant, I am almost able to smell the sweet musk of her body and the rank sweat of her executioner. It is late and I appear to be somewhat overwrought. To bed then.

NOV 6 – Slept late yesterday and rose feeling distinctly unwell. How should I describe it? A feeling of nervousness. I slept badly and remember only snatches of my dreams. Something involving two men walking past a long row of trees. One was young, the other middle-aged. Both wore heavy black cloaks, the elder held a walking stick, but neither was contemporary. There was something rather odd about the younger man's movements. He appeared to be extremely agitated and every now and then would stop and converse with himself. At one point he threw his hands to the sky and I detected in his left fist the gleam of a blade. I feared that he would do some mischief to the older man. This fragment seemed to repeat itself each time I drifted into consciousness, and the effect was somewhat unnerving. There was another episode, but of this I recall little. It was dusk. I was in a hollow, surrounded by high chalk banks. This time I was not the onlooker but a participant. I recall that I was stooping and peering down at my hands. Some feet away lay a large black bundle. I remember that my hands were wet and sticky and that my trousers were wet through. There was about me a sickly sweet smell that had drawn innumerable flies to me in the warm summer air, and an overwhelming fear possessed me that I had been witness to some tragedy.

NOV 10 – I have neglected my diary of late. Small wonder, for I have been feeling distinctly odd since my return from Chatham. This room has become irksome to me. Have I been here too long, become too solitary in my ways? It's true that I have chosen not to seek out company in the past, yet there are times when I have regrets on that score, especially since my parents' death.

For some reason (perhaps none at all) I began by cleaning the work by Hunt – an Arthurian piece which

216

appears to be a rather sentimental portrait of the Lady Guinevere. Not one of his best, I fear, and the technique not up to his usual standard. Still, it is done now and without the grime. The Morris was also a portrait, this time of a young girl, beautifully executed, and with a pastoral background. The third canvas I left to last. And here I must admit to a confession that seems too absurd for words as I write it down in the cold light of day. It seems ridiculous that it should be so, yet I own up to it nevertheless.

It is that I desire only to clean the canvas during daylight.
Let me explain, for it is myself I must satisfy.

There is about the painting a luminosity which is readily apparent in darkness. Two nights, ago, I had occasion to get up and walk into the studio where I had left a book. As I passed into the room – and I am certain of this – I saw the canvas on the easel as if it had been lit from beneath by several candles. Naturally I stopped in amazement, wondering from whence came the source of light. As I stood pondering, I became certain that the figures in the painting actually moved. When I awoke the following day, it seemed plainly ridiculous that such a thing might have happened, yet there was such a glow from that young woman's face and such a look of ferocity on the face of her attacker that I must believe it to be true. Besides, there is something not quite right about the piece – something in the composition of the oils that perplexes me. When I apply the cleaning fluid on the soft cotton rag, there is a curious odour which arises. It is somewhat reminiscent of cloves, yet more acrid. I would open the window but it is so intensely cold outside that I dare not.

NOV 15 – I have been examining the painting most closely. Some of the grime has been persistent but I have persevered. Around the edges, I discovered what I would imagine to be traces of blood – whether animal or human I do not know, nor dare to conjecture. Elsewhere the dirt appears to be intermingled with decayed vegetable matter. It would appear – though how can it be? – that someone has deliberately smeared these substances onto the surface of the canvas, though for what reason I cannot imagine!

The discovery of this fact certainly has not encouraged my endeavours. The studio appears to be getting colder. I took a walk down to the high street late yesterday and discovered

217

to my surprise that it had turned somewhat milder. Why then is it so cold in my flat?

NOV 30 – Have not had the heart to write in my diary lately since I have been most unwell and quite out of sorts. I would visit a doctor if I thought I had an idea of what was wrong with me. Yet I know instinctively what the matter is. The point is how to explain it without becoming irrational or incoherent?

After I removed most of the surface grime of the unsigned painting, I applied a little solution of weak alcohol mixed with amyl nitrite – something passed onto me from my friend Roberts of the Academy. The solution is remarkably effective and usually brings the canvas up beautifully, restoring the deeper tones and colours.

I had started this last stage of my cleaning operation around three o'clock in the afternoon. I suppose that I had not noted the time, so absorbed was I in my task, and it was only the striking of the town clock which drew my attention to the fact that dusk had turned swiftly to darkness outside my studio windows.

The jarring note of the clock sent a tremor through me. I do not know how to explain it, but I felt a sudden fear of the canvas before me. There was little light in the room now, and behind the canvas there lay a deep well of blackness so that the picture before me seemed to gleam with life.

I suddenly realised that I had been staring at the canvas for at least three hours and that now every contour and speck of colour was known to me. It was almost as if by now I had become a part of the picture, as if I had entered into the scene. A realization dawned on me that I no longer regarded it as a picture, a construct of reality, but as a window through which I had become the reluctant voyeur of this most unpleasant of scenes. My instinct at this point was to stand up, move to the mantelpiece, and light the lamp that stood there. Yet I remained seated and found myself staring at the canvas. There was something about the piece which continued to fascinate me, some dark secret trapped in the arrangement of the figures which compelled me to stay and act as a witness.

It was by now utterly black in the room. I knew that my suspicions about the work's luminous qualities were confirmed, for I could see every detail of the canvas.

218

Moreover, the brush strokes had receded, leaving the outlines of the figures a photographic brilliance which no painter could achieve.

It was then that I dropped the rag I had been holding and cried out aloud.

The figures before me were moving. The effect was like that of a carousel lantern of the type that amuse children, or like those hand-turned cinematographs that often appear on seaside piers. As I watched, so the face of the young woman sprang into life. I could see – one frame at a time, for thus it seemed – the beautiful eyes glistening, the mouth trembling with fear, and the hands which clutched the robe of the executioner shaking with fear. My eyes moved upwards to behold the face of her attacker and I could see distinctly enough the coarse, swarthy features of the man and his mouth, twisted into a sadistic smile. His left hand gripped the girl's hair so tightly that I could see the strands rising up out of the skin, so that she must have experienced considerable pain.

At this point I could sit no longer, such was the fear and anguish on that young woman's face. Acting on impulse, I leant forward and stretching out my hand, plunged it into the canvas.

Then a most remarkable thing happened. Instead of my hand making impact with the surface of the canvas, it simply went clean through, as if I had dipped it beneath the surface of a pool!

The sensation that accompanied this act was a most peculiar one. At once I felt an intense cold shoot up my wrist into my arm. Simultaneously, the figures' movements became rapid. The executioner turned and fixed me with a look of demonic intent such as I hope never to see again, while the young woman released her left arm from the folds of his robe and, turning her head as far as she might, uttered a long, drawn out wail of fear and pain.

Then I withdrew my hand and the vision had passed.

What shall I make of this? Can it be that I am hallucinating? I begin to fear for my sanity. Immediately after this event, I ran from the room into my bedroom where I sat shaking with trepidation. The following morning, I went back into the studio and, rather reluctantly, placed my hand against the canvas. The event did not repeat itself, yet I felt there a warmth and vibrancy which denoted living things. Could it be *that a painter might, through his imagination, bring such figures to life and bestow on them corporeal substance? I cannot bear to think of such a thing.*

DEC 7 – I have taken to locking the studio room. There is nothing else for it, for I cannot sacrifice my sanity for the sake of that painting. I have become convinced that the painting is in some way possessed. Let me set out a few facts.

Before acquiring the piece for restoration purposes, I was, I believe, of a cheerful disposition and not subject to fancies and morbid feelings and suspicions. Yet now I find myself in the grip of all manner of inexplicable fears, and I begin to think that I am losing my mind.

After I had finished the cleaning of the canvas, I retired to bed, where I slept unevenly. Let me say more about this business of sleeping, for it requires elucidation – possibly by someone more expert than I in matters of the psyche.

I think I mentioned earlier in this diary my dream of the two men, one the older and the other the younger. At the time the dream meant little to me and to tell the truth, I had forgotten all about it until the night following the business with the painting.

Sometime around three o'clock in the morning, I awoke in a great sweat so that at first I believed I had contracted a fever. Then, as I entered into full consciousness, the substance of the dream unfolded. So terrifying were the events it contained that I lit the lamp on my bedside and found myself shaking with stark fear, unable to convince myself that this was merely a dream, but a terrible reality.

The dream began in exactly the same way as before. I beheld a long row of trees – beeches I think they were – these skirting a narrow track, on the other side of which lay a column of ashes and silver birches. To my right a green meadow dropped down to a winding lane which, it seemed, led up to the gates of an Elizabethan mansion of great dimensions. It seemed to me that this was a real and not an imagined place, for it had about it the clarity which one does not normally associate with dreamscapes.

As I stood looking, there appeared into view the two men of whom I spoke, one young with long, flowing hair to his shoulders and a full, bushy black beard. I remember most distinctly his large, rather melancholy eyes. It struck me most forcibly that they were the eyes of someone troubled in the extreme – one might almost say mad.

When I first set eyes upon them, the two were walking arm in arm. Then, about midway along the path, the younger man stopped and, flinging his arms up to the sky, called out a name which sounded to me like "Syrius". The older man, whom I now perceived to be grey-haired, and not unlike the younger, save that the eyes were smaller and more calculating, looked at the younger and I heard him mutter something to the effect of "Come, come," or words similar, as if he were attempting to quieten him. There followed a sharp interchange. Then the younger struck the older with his fist, causing him to stagger back and almost lose his balance. Then the older man walked on, glancing back once or twice with an expression of consternation on his face.

Now, as I watched, the younger man stopped and, drawing back the folds of his black cloak, pulled out what looked like a rigger's knife from his belt. Then, from his left pocket he withdrew a small black object which proved to be a cut-throat razor. With these weapons in either hand, he pursued the older man, stopping every now and then to converse with himself. The substance of this monologue was so clear that I retained a vivid memory of it afterwards. I shall attempt to reproduce it here:

"So . . . now it must be . . . regrettable, yet necessary . . . the spirit has spoken and the divine force carries with it an onerous task . . . Lucifer, your machinations have been discovered. I had thought him alive, but now I see that he is already dead, and the thing that talks and walks and smiles at me is a mere shell, a piece of carrion fit only for the crows. How dare they hide in his body, sullying him with their excrement? . . . I shall do the deed now before they depart. Look, even his step is different . . . Quick now, before the demons gain the upper hand . . . The razor and the knife be my companions . . . ."

Still carrying on this conversation, the younger man broke into a run, his arms flailing wildly above his head, uttering shriek upon shriek, so that the older of the two stopped in mid-stride, his mouth open in amazement. Thus paralysed, he received the full force of the younger man's blow as with his left hand he thrust the rigger's knife into his companion's stomach. For a moment there was silence as the *attacker twisted the blade twice, then pulled it out, blood splashing his hand and face. The older man staggered back, a look of immense bewilderment on his face. Then his legs crumpled beneath him and he sat on his knees, holding his stomach.*

I stared in horror, for I could see that his attacker was not content to deliver just the one blow. He was relentless and merciless in his attack. Gripping the older man by the throat, he drove the knife into the abdomen of his companion again and again until his hands and cloak were saturated with blood. Then all of a sudden he turned and, casting the knife aside, he called out the name I had heard previously and turned to face his victim, this time drawing the cut throat razor across his throat. Sickened by what I had witnessed, I began to cry out, but I found myself locked in the dream, unable to close my eyes or shut out the terrible moaning of the dying man as he lay on the green sward in a pool of crimson with that hideous ululation of his attacker the only accompaniment.

For several days afterwards, I could not rid myself of the memory of that nightmare. So repugnant were the images of the dream that I found myself unable even to use the cut-throat razor that lay in the bathroom, and I have since confined it to the kitchen drawer.

What troubles me most, I think, is the terrible resemblance between the painting and the dream itself. Consider: In both an execution is depicted. In both the attacker shows no remorse for his actions, and in both the suffering of the victim is unbearable to behold. Can there be some connection between the two, or is the dream merely a piece of phantasmagoria inspired by the painting? I need to discover the truth about the painting and am certain that I shall gain no rest until I have done so.

DEC 15 – I have tried. God knows I have tried, but it is no use. I had thought – mistakenly – that if I tried to exorcise the whole thing from my mind I would begin to feel better again, but if anything I feel much worse. I have even attempted to depict the events on canvas but to no real effect. It is as if locking the door to that room has made the images grow stronger, more terrifying in their intensity.

Two days ago I had occasion to enter the studio. I had need of several brushes and an unfinished canvas. Besides, it was absurd, I kept telling myself, to avoid looking at the canvas. It was an inanimate object, nothing more, and the dreams – what were they but the product of an over-excited imagination? Perhaps I was truly unwell and, if so, then I would see a doctor and get the matter sorted out.

Quite resolved, I opened the door and entered. It struck me straight away that the room was intensely cold, so much so that I shuddered. The windows of the studio were dank. I advanced into the room and stood for a few minutes, staring at the canvas. In the cold light of day it seemed quite unremarkable – Much less vivid and lifelike than when I had first begun to work on it. How ridiculous, I told myself that I had allowed my imagination to run riot in such a fashion.

I stooped down to examine the detail of the painting. It was clearly the work of an extremely talented artist and one with great technical expertise. In fact, the technique was faintly familiar. Picking up the canvas, I turned it over to examine the back. It had been crudely stretched onto a cheap frame, which looked as if it had seen better days, for at one corner there was a split in the deal where someone had, perhaps, dropped it. There was also a curious odour to the thing, a smell of disinfectant or carbolic – I could not tell which.

By now I had grown confident that the canvas was thoroughly innocuous and was on the point of replacing it on the easel when I heard the door click shut behind me.

I turned, thinking that a draught had pulled the door to, but there was no draught and the door had shut with a definite movement, as if someone had pushed it from outside. I put down the painting and walked over to the door. I turned the handle. It was locked. For a moment I stood by the mantelpiece, considering what I might do next. Perhaps the lock had broken and the door had locked shut. The mechanism was old and probably faulty. Yes, that would be the most likely explanation.

I walked over to the door and was in the process of jiggling the handle when I became aware of what sounded like a low chuckle coming from the far corner of the room. I turned swiftly and caught – at least I thought I caught – something small and dark moving rapidly across the boards towards the back of the canvas. Suddenly I felt terribly afraid.

For now, as I stood with my back to the door, staring intently across the room in the direction of the canvas, I could see the room growing steadily darker, and with the darkness came that low, dry chuckle again, and with it came other voices, whisperings, echoes of voices from all around me, voices much like the first, sinister in intent. And as I stood, unable to speak or act, so the voices grew in strength until they became a chorus of demonic utterances, vying in strength. There were voices raised in cruel chastisement, voices that screamed abuse, and others which I dare not recall now, older voices urging me to unspeakable actions, nameless obscene desires. I put my hands against my ears – yet still the voices came and went.

I opened my eyes and I could see now that the dimensions of the room had appeared to shrink. A terrible darkness engulfed everything and from the darkness there emerged tiny pinpoints of light that seemed like eyes, watching me remorselessly. Then, from the centre of the blackness, came the thing I had most dreaded: Two voices, one a man's, the other that of a young girl. Both cried out and I knew by those cries that they were being murdered even as I stood there, inside this very room, trapped there for an eternity within the frame of the canvas. The man's voice was worse I think in some ways, for his physical torment was greater – long, drawn out cries, each louder and more harrowing than the last and, as the cries came and went, I could see in my mind's eye his attacker, the blade swinging back and forth without hesitation, butchering with slow deliberation. Then the girl's, thin, fearful cry, followed by a few words, pleading mercy, then a sobbing and a final brief shriek of pain.

I could stand it no longer. I beat against the door in such a frenzy that my knuckles and fingers were rendered black and blue. Eventually the mechanism of the door splintered and snapped and I was thrown forward into the passage, weeping uncontrollably. Since that moment I have not dared venture forth from the confines of this bedroom.

DEC 20 – It is no good. I shall have to resolve matters. Since that awful moment in the room, I have sat here trying to convince myself that I need only walk into the studio, pick up the canvas, and return it whence it came. It is quite straightforward really, yet I know that I cannot do it, for there

224

is some force trapped within that picture, a memory of some foul deed, which has somehow latched onto me, a succubus which I need to exorcise from my memory.

At night I lie awake and hear her trying to open the door to the studio. It is not locked, yet he has kept it locked – he the abuser who eternally re-enacts her death. It is the same man who I saw in the dream, the young man in the cloak. They are one and the same person, there is no doubting it. I have taken the razor from the kitchen cabinet and I keep it under my pillow, for I feel sure I shall have occasion to use it very soon. God knows she has suffered enough torment.

Last night I dreamt of her. It seemed that I awoke and she was standing by my bed. I called to her and she came to me. Her breath was sweet and there was that same sweet musk smell about her body as before. She bent over me and I reached out to touch her soft arms and her flesh was firm and supple under the thin cotton shift. I knew then that I must kiss her full upon the lips, those red lips that bore down upon me. Then the eyes turned and they were the hollow, watery eyes of him and the face was coarse and bearded and there was such a malicious and cunning smile set there beneath the lean cheekbones that I screamed aloud and found myself sitting up in bed, the bedclothes twisted into a knot inside my fist, my heart pounding, my chest tight with anxiety.

I have decided. Tomorrow I shall enter the studio, pick up the painting, and shred it into ribbons. It is not mine to shred, but there is little alternative.

God help me!

"Well, Jarvis, what do you make of it?" enquired Holmes, after he had concluded his reading of the narrative back in our lodgings in Baker Street.

"I should say that it was the work of a disordered mind, quite frankly, though as to what gave rise to the disorder – that is another matter."

"I would tend to agree with you, Chief Inspector," I replied. "The man's ramblings bear all the marks of monomania."

"Well, how do you think we should proceed in this matter?" asked Jarvis at last after Holmes had lit his pipe and enveloped us both in wreaths of acrid tobacco smoke.

"Simple. Identify the painter and we will unlock the mystery."

"That should not prove too difficult," I observed. "There cannot be too many art dealers in the town of Chatham. No doubt a visit to the local police will yield the result you require."

"I shall attend to it immediately," Jarvis replied, standing up in readiness to leave.

"A moment before you go," Holmes enquired. "As I think I requested earlier, would it be possible to bring the painting to Baker Street? I should like the opportunity of conducting a thorough examination."

"As I said, since you have been of some assistance to me in the past, I see no real objection."

"Considerable assistance . . . ." muttered Holmes. Jarvis smiled at me.

"I shall have it sent around within the hour."

In the interval that elapsed between Jarvis's departure and the arrival of the canvas at our lodgings, Holmes had summoned Mrs. Hudson and requested half-a-dozen toasted muffins and a pot of Earl Gray tea. When we had satisfied our hunger and Holmes had yet again poisoned the air with his reeking pipe, he leant back in his chair. However, it wasn't long before he sat forward again. "Do I not hear the bell?"

He was correct in his assumption. I rose and went to the window, where I observed two uniformed officers getting out of a police-wagon bearing four small rectangular objects, covered in brown paper and string.

In a short while, we heard the rather intrusive knock of Mrs. Hudson at our door. "Pray let them in," called Holmes

When the officers had departed, he took an ivory-handled penknife from his trouser pocket and began to cut the string, soon revealing the four canvases.

"I had thought Jarvis would send us just the one," he remarked.

In fact he had been kind enough to send us Pinder's own rough oil sketches illustrating the dream sequence. When Holmes had recharged his pipe, we began to lay out the oils executed by Pinder on the dining room table. He then lit the tall brass oil lamp, which customarily occupied the mantelpiece, and placed it in the centre of the table. The soft lamplight somehow bestowed upon the paintings a peculiar vividness and brilliance, despite the crudity of their execution. I have already described the content of these canvases to the reader, yet I have not remarked on the manner of their execution. I once had the misfortune to visit Broadmoor Hospital to see a former patient of mine who had murdered both his parents, disposing of their bodies in a vat of quick lime. The patient in question was officially diagnosed as suffering from *dementia praecox*, which several years later came to be known by the modern term of *schizophrenia*. He was, as are many in his unenviable condition, a highly intelligent man, extremely intuitive and creative, making the circumstances of his incarceration doubly tragic. Whilst in Broadmoor, he had produced a number of paintings, employing a somewhat impressionistic technique. His subjects were invariably the same: Versions of fantastic dreams he had experienced or people he had known, intimately set against gothic backgrounds. Always, however, these paintings would be superimposed with sets of gleaming eyes. Now the feeling of being watched and persecuted is common among those suffering his particular condition, and it confirmed my opinion of Pinder that he too had experienced a rapid lapse into this psychological malaise. I felt it my duty to point this out to Holmes, who stood pondering for a moment before replying.

"I have to say that they are an attempt at objective reporting," he observed, speaking slowly and thoughtfully, tamping the bowl of his pipe. "I have rarely seen such accuracy." He cleared his throat. "There is only one thing to do."

"And what is that?"

"Attempt to duplicate Pinder's experience with the painting."

"I trust that you are not suggesting anything so crude as a séance?" I asked derisively.

"Really, you do me a disservice. But it is entirely possible that we may at least reproduce some of Pinder's experiences, as well as your own in Pinder's rooms this morning, as suggested by this remarkable canvas – that is, of course, if you have no objections."

"None whatsoever," I replied, although in truth I had several.

"Then let us inform Mrs. Hudson that we are not to be disturbed."

While Holmes carried over and dimmed the lamp from the mantel and drew the heavy curtains, I rang the bell and informed our landlady of our intentions. Upon my return, I discovered Holmes behind the dining room table, his eyes fixed on the canvas that had caused Pinder to lose his reason. By the dimmed lamplight, it was far less terrifying than his narrative had suggested. True, the scene was an unpleasant one and the execution of it graphic in the extreme. Yet I felt no sense of empathy and I wondered if our experiment would yield positive results.

"Now then, Doctor, will you sit opposite me and record in your notebook anything of significance?"

I assented. Holmes extended his hands, rubbing his fingertips against the canvas. In a short while, his eyelids began to droop and the muscles of his face relaxed.

I had begun to fall into a trance-like state myself and had thought our experiment entirely without incident when I became aware of what seemed to be an imperceptible drop in temperature within the room. At first I imagined that the blazing fire provided by Mrs. Hudson was in need of replenishment, but when I glanced across to the hearth, I could see that I was mistaken.

I looked back at my companion. What transpired next I shall do my level best to convey, though I should point out that my recollection of the episode is quite confused, and I was unable to keep an accurate record of the sequence of events.

I have already remarked that there was what felt like a sudden sharp drop in room temperature. This was now followed after a short interval of perhaps four minutes by yet another seeming drop. The room now felt like an ice box and I shuddered involuntarily. I noted that Holmes's breathing had become markedly shallower, and the muscles of his face had relaxed to such an extent that his mouth had begun to fall open.

It was then that he began to stir.

At first I heard a long yawn, then a sob. Slowly it stopped and was replaced by a low chuckle which ceased as abruptly as it had begun. There was a long exhalation, then Holmes's fists banged the table, as if in anger.

I cannot describe what I too began to see, and the voices that I began to hear. Holmes continued to murmur, but his voice took on a high-pitched tone full of menace and cunning and anger – or so it seemed to me in my hallucinations. Even as I watched, my companion's customary aquiline features appeared to blur into the face of a demon. The head appeared to have been compressed, thrusting the forehead and jaw outwards and downwards. But it was not this which horrified me so much as the hideous eyes and mouth. I call them hideous, yet even that word cannot convey the feeling of revulsion and disgust I experienced on glimpsing that sight. The eyes were, I recall, like those I had seen in the second of Pinder's paintings: Small pupils, burning with fire, yet possessed of a green phosphorescence which hypnotised and held the onlooker. There was so such cunning and guile in those eyes.

I somehow realized what was happening – that something about the cursed painting was causing these terrible visions. I knew that that I must act quickly if there was any hope to rescue my companion and myself from certain madness, or even death.

I stood up and, pushing the chair from me, picked up the lamp, hurling it at the canvas – for surely, I reasoned, that must be the source of the emanation which I was seeing.

The bowl of the lamp hit the canvas and there was a sudden explosion as tongues of flame licked at the surface of the painting. An acrid stench filled the air, and I found myself gasping for breath, suddenly free. I staggered to the other side of the table and dragged at Holmes's chair, hoping to rescue him. He sat there like a stone, like a lifeless shell.

How long we both lay upon the floor before Holmes and I were discovered I do not rightly know. But discovered we were, and by no less a person than our attentive landlady. Thankfully the fire never spread, and we were neither of us greatly injured, the only real casualty being the green velour table cloth that had been Mrs. Hudson's pride and joy.

At first I had imagined that Holmes might have succumbed to apoplexy, so faint was his pulse and so intermittent his breathing. However, he finally came to, looking deathly pale and shivering violently. I pulled the rug from in front of the sideboard and wrapped it around him, and within a short while he revived a little, though he was far from his normal self. Then his eyelids fluttered a bit before finally regaining consciousness. After Mrs. Hudson had plied us with hot coffee, removed the cloth, and opened the window to air the room, he suddenly sat up and began to interrogate me closely. I told him exactly what had happened and he registered little surprise.

"To be honest with you, I had suspected something like this might arise," he commented, clasping the coffee cup in his hands and shivering a little. "In the early stages of the trance, I too felt the drop in temperature you described. Shortly afterwards, I realized that some substance in the painting, and our proximity to it, was causing the extreme hallucinations – mine to a greater degree. It had a prodigious strength. You did well to break the lamp against the canvas, for otherwise we might have been lost. I fear that this is what eventually killed Pinder."

"But what does it all mean?"

"Patience, my dear Doctor, patience. If we are prepared – as we must be – to wait until morning, we may yet be enlightened."

With that, he settled into a silent study of the paintings which occupied him for the rest of the day.

The following day – the 29th, as I find it recorded in my journal – dawned sunny and bright, despite the intense cold which had turned the snow-laden streets to sheets of glazed ice. Holmes and I had slept well, having been fortified by some hot coffee laced with whisky and one of those remarkable cooked English breakfasts at which the Continentals marvel.

Holmes was in a good mood that morning – an event that was not as regular as it might have been – and had even attempted a few minor jokes involving members of the police force.

Our sitting room clock had just sounded the hour of nine-thirty when there was the sound of heavy footsteps upon the stair, heralding the arrival of our friend Jarvis. Red-faced, he sprang into the room, a look of triumph upon his face.

"You have found the dealer?" Holmes enquired, looking up from his bacon.

"I have."

"And the artist?"

"As yet I do not have the name. However, I hope to obtain it by the end of the day."

Holmes put down his knife and fork and clasped his hands in exasperation.

"My dear Chief Inspector, what exactly is the problem?"

"The problem is that the dealer does not know the identity of the artist. He was given the painting by a client who prefers to remain anonymous."

"Then that anonymity cannot be allowed to continue," Holmes snapped. "It is paramount that we know the identity of the painter."

"As I say, matters are in hand. As a matter of fact, I intend to go down to Chatham this very morning and apply some pressure to the dealer."

Holmes stood up.

"Then you must of necessity take us with you, Chief Inspector. Come, come, my dear fellow. The bacon will surely wait."

How well I remember the journey down. There is nothing quite so unpredictable as a British winter, and that particular day proved no exception to the rule. By the time we had reached Victoria Station, the sky had become overcast with a promise of snow, and no sooner had we passed the cab ranks than the heavens opened. Inside the train, conditions were freezing and I was glad of the metal water bottles we had purchased at the rail terminus. Holmes sat on one side of the carriage and I on the other, deeply ensconced within our ulsters, conscious of the blizzard that beat against the compartment windows and blue haze rising from Holmes's oldest and most of oily of pipes.

Silence prevailed for much of the journey until at last the low flat marshes between Gravesend and the Medway towns loomed into view. The snow-bound level flatlands lay deserted, save for a few restless seagulls and curlews wheeling overhead.

"We are not far now," said Holmes.

As he spoke, we plunged into a deep cutting and were at once surrounded on all sides by a great entanglement of beeches, oaks, and ashes. Flashes of snow-laden branches were intermingled with patches of darkness, until at length we emerged onto a broad bank from which I was able to make out the spire of a cathedral and the ruins of a Norman castle. The train pulled into a drab and rather gloomy station some miles east of Rochester, which, upon examination, we discovered to be Chatham

Station. Outside, we hailed a cab and were driven a short distance through snow-laden streets whose only occupants were a number of ragged children and a knot of drunken seamen. The cab stopped at a crossroads and the cabbie tapped on the glass that divided our respective compartments. I leaned forward and peered out at a broad shop window, behind which I could glimpse a number of antique chairs and several large oil paintings. Holmes and Jarvis got out to pay the cabbie, asking him to wait, then I followed them inside.

Samuel Schumacher was a quiet, watchful man of middle years who clearly had suffered much, judging by the cautious way in which he approached us. No sooner had Jarvis announced himself than he began to shrink visibly and retreat to the back of the shop. When the Chief Inspector went to some pains to explain that his mission was not a punitive one, nor did he regard Schumacher as a potential malefactor, he began to relax a little and asked briskly what was the exact nature of our visit. At this point, Holmes produced the remains of the burned painting and began to unwrap the brown paper covering, saying very little, for he had persuaded Jarvis that this was the best approach. When he caught a glimpse of it, Schumacher turned as white as a sheet. "What does this mean?" he demanded.

"We had rather hoped you might furnish us with an explanation," Holmes replied softly.

"This painting I had wanted back two weeks since, and in a restored condition! Where has it been?"

Schumacher explained that he had been visited earlier in the day by two uniformed policemen who had enquired about the painting, but that they had told him little else of the affair. Holmes explained to him the circumstances of Pinder's death, and when he had finished, the little man clasped his forehead with his hand and let out an oath in Yiddish.

"Will you now tell me who the owner of this painting is?" Holmes asked.

"It is a confidence. This I cannot break."

"Come, this is a grave matter Mr. Schumacher. A man has died because of this painting, and yet you talk of confidences?"

"Very well then, though this will do not much for my reputation. The painting belongs to the Earl of Cobham."

"Of Cobham Manor?"

"Yes, the same."

"And do you know the artist?"

Schumacher shook his head. "No, I do not. I do know that I have tried to have it cleaned for the Earl three times, and each time I have had to change the restorer."

Holmes eyed his face closely. "Why, pray?"

He shrugged his shoulders. "This I don't understand. Both of the first restorers, they complain of headaches and seeing things. Then they return the canvases to me before the job is done. I tell them no money if the job is not done properly, but this doesn't concern them. Crazy people the English. The Earl, he was furious. He will be even angrier now."

"It cannot be helped," my companion remarked. "Come, Chief Inspector Jarvis, we shall return this canvas to its owner ourselves. It is the least we can do under the circumstances."

"I wish you would," said Schumacher ungraciously.

By now it was growing dark and we could see little of the streets of Chatham and Rochester until we passed over a narrow bridge spanning the River Medway from which we could see the lights of the barges below. A mist had risen up from the river and our journey through Strood into Cobham was made slower by the inclement weather and the impenetrable darkness that lay on either side of us.

At last we plunged down a tree-lined embankment which twisted and turned as the cab swayed from side to side. The horse champed, steam curling from its nostrils and mixing with the swathes of mist that surrounded us. Finally we turned a corner and found ourselves descending a steep driveway, lit on either side by Edison lamps. I looked out and caught a glimpse of two high towers and a series of lighted windows.

"Cobham Hall," called the driver.

It took some while before the Earl agreed to see us for, as his butler was at pains to explain, his master had not quite finished his dinner and was anxious not to spoil the port wine. We were ushered into a high-beamed room with heraldic designs and flags, and there we waited until a series of light footsteps marked the Earl's approach. A tall, rather feminine man with a high-domed head, the Earl stretched out a limp hand to each of us in turn before Carter explained the purpose of our mission.

"Will you be so good as to take a seat, gentlemen, and sorry this has caused you such a deal of trouble. Before I tell you the artist was, I should perhaps explain how I came to acquire this and other pieces. And I must emphasise that what I tell you I would prefer to remain a secret – at least for several years, at any rate – for the matter is a delicate one. I am sorry, however, that a man's death has been the consequence of a little restoration work."

We had seated ourselves either side of a wide stone fireplace whilst the Earl's butler plied us with whisky and soda.

"I was little more than a boy when the tragedy occurred. My father, David, knew more of the matter than I did, and was reluctant to divulge the details of the affair. It was only recently that I read up on the circumstances of the murder and learnt about the subsequent incarceration of the unfortunate artist concerned.

"One day in the August of 1843," explained the Earl, "a tradesman – a butcher from Cobham – called at the door of the manor house here. The fellow was in a very excited state, having just discovered a body in the road that runs along the edge of the estate known as Halfpence Lane. When some of the servants went to investigate, they discovered the mutilated body of a middle-aged man, respectably dressed, who was later recognised as a pharmacist from Chatham. After some investigation, it transpired that this poor fellow had been lodging at the Ship Inn in Cobham with his son, an artist of some renown, and that they had set off that morning for a walk."

"Anyway, they removed the body from the hollow where it had been discovered and placed it here in the chapel for the time being. The following day, two police officers arrived from Chatham with a relative of the murdered man's family and it was then revealed that the younger son, Richard, had disappeared, thus making him a murder suspect. He subsequently re-emerged in France, near Fontainebleau, where he had played with the collar of a man sitting opposite him for some fifteen minutes before producing a cut-throat razor and hacking at his throat. Fortunately the Frenchman overpowered his assailant and the young man spent the next year in a number of French asylums before being deported back to England. He was then incarcerated in Bethlem and subsequently in Broadmoor for the rest of his life."

"And the name of this unfortunate fellow?" Holmes enquired.

"Dadd. Richard Dadd. "

Holmes noted it on his cuff while Earl of Cobham observed him closely. "Thank you," he said. "Pray continue with your account. You have not yet told us, for example, how you came by the paintings."

"Indeed I have not. Well then, let me explain that the Dadd family was at that time resident in Chatham, and that my father was visited by the daughter shortly after Dadd was brought before the county magistrates at Rochester Court in the July of 1844 for committal at Maidstone. She said that she wished to express her gratitude, and that as a token of respect she wanted to donate some of the paintings executed by her brother. I suppose that she imagined we might sell them in due course, but my father, being something of a collector himself, ensured that they remained in the family. After father's death, I inherited them, but it was only recently that I actually discovered them, hidden under a great deal of debris in one of the attics of the house."

"Tell me," said Holmes, finishing his drink, "is there anything like a catalogue of the paintings? Any record as to the year of their completion?"

The Earl thought for a moment. "Yes, my father kept a catalogue. It is probably in the library, for I haven't consulted it for some while. Let me call Roberts, and if it is there we shall obtain it for you. I had the collection valued and indexed quite recently, so it should not take long."

In a few moments, the butler was called and returned forthwith with a small black-bound volume in copperplate writing. Holmes turned it over in his hands. "Hmm . . . . It bears the inscription of Broadmoor Prison and has been signed by Dr. William Charles Hood, evidently the steward of Broadmoor. Yes, indeed, this is seemingly a complete list of the artist's work. How very fortuitous. Ah, here we are, the very painting. Executed in 1851 and entitled "*Dymphna Martyr*". Curious. This mentions that it is inscribed in the bottom right hand corner and that it is a watercolour. It would appear then that the remains of the oil we see before us was a later version of the same. I wonder why he should make such an exact copy but in a different medium?"

"That is something I have observed myself," remarked the Earl. "There are at least five oils which we discovered, all of them being apparent copies of watercolours."

Holmes thought for a moment. Then he stood up and I could see a gleam in his eye, which was for me always a signal that he had made some intuitive leap which would provide a key to the mystery.

"Your Grace, would you mind if I borrowed one of the Dadd paintings for a day or so? I wish to try a small experiment which may well shed some light on the matter."

"What sort of an experiment?" inquired the Earl, rather suspiciously.

"Oh, a scientific experiment – a simple test, nothing more."

"I should prefer the paintings to remain here, if you don't mind," replied the Earl.

Holmes looked slightly dismayed. "Then I must ask you if I can do it here. Tell me, do you possess any wood alcohol?"

"I think we may have some. Roberts, will you check in the outbuildings for me? And have one of those paintings brought down as well." Roberts retired to do his duty, leaving Jarvis and me to speculate as to the nature of the promised "experiment". At length a maid delivered a painting from the attic, and the butler returned, bearing a small transparent bottle and a cloth. Holmes laid the canvas on a table and dipped the cloth into the solution.

234

"Now then," he said, his eyes gleaming avidly. "Let us apply a little of this solution to the oils. You stand here, Doctor, at this side, and you at this side, Your Grace, and you just so, Chief Inspector.''

As we bent over the picture, he began to smooth the alcohol onto the canvas with slow, deliberate strokes. All at once there arose a repulsive smell which I can only compare to rotting vegetable matter. My impulse was to withdraw, but I found myself being drawn inexorably into the canvas – hypnotised, as it were, by the figures that formed part of the tableau. The painting, which was entitled *"The Death of Richard II"*, showed Richard being set upon by one of his nobles and three armed servants. As I watched, the figure wielding the axe above Richard's head seemed to leap at me from the canvas and I was amazed to find that I could make out rapid muscular movements of his taut face and see the fingers moving about the haft of his axe. Then, in an instant, I realised that I was again seeing what Pinder had also seen – that the painting had for a moment in time literally come alive.

The next moment, Holmes had pushed the canvas away from him and cast aside the rag. We all stared at one another. Each looked pale and somewhat bewildered by what had happened.

"You also saw it, then?" cried Holmes, jubilantly, glancing across at the three of us. We each nodded before replying in the affirmative.

"You see, Watson," Holmes explained a day or so later, when he had completed more research into the story we had heard in Chatham. We were ensconced in our comfortable rooms on either side of a warm fire. "I had thought the paintings the product of a distorted mind and capable of triggering a psychological response. What I had come to suspect was that Dadd had actually imbued the oils with a chemical substance which caused an hallucinatory effect."

"But could Dadd have known that the chemical reaction would have been so pronounced? Surely that was purely a coincidence he could not have foreseen."

"Ah, you are forgetting that the substance would have been introduced to the surface of the canvas when the oils were wet. The idea, I think, was to work in the chemical reagent and in so doing heighten the artist's awareness. Dadd was obsessive about his work, and you must also remember that many of these paintings were executed amid scenes of incredible barbarity and violence – especially when he served his term at Bethlem. No doubt he found the effect of the reagent helped to shut out the madness and bestiality of the other prisoners."

"And what was the substance he used?"

"Of that I am not entirely sure, though I think it was almost certainly a form of the mould which he may have extracted from rotting vegetable matter. I have no doubt that he cultivated the stuff without much interference. It seems likely that, for the latter part of his life, he was left very much to his own devices. Certain types of mould form a very powerful hallucinogen, as no doubt you are aware, Doctor. However, I did not anticipate that this element would react so effectively as it did on the human nervous system when combined with a cleaning agent."

"What made you suspect that the canvases had been impregnated?"

"I should have seen it before when Schumacher mentioned to us that two other restorers had experienced hallucinations. Also, of course, there are the distinct references to similar experiences in Pinder's diary. All in all, I have been remarkably obtuse in this affair. It is a sure mark that my powers are on the wane."

"And the demonic visitations were nothing more than a hallucination," I concluded.

"Precisely" Holmes replied, drawing on his pipe so that the acrid shag glowed and emitted a thick curl of grey smoke. "The visitation seemed real enough in psychical terms, and I have no doubt that the painting itself acted as a catalyst. You recall the title of the piece, "*Dymphna Martyr*"?"

"Yes, I was going to ask you about that."

Holmes stood up and drew from the bookcase a volume entitled *A History of the Irish Kings*. "This book describes Dymphna – or Saint Dymphna, as she later became known, as the daughter of an Irish pagan king and a Christian mother. Her father wished to marry her after his wife's death, so she fled with her chaplain Gerebernus to Gheel in Belgium, where the king caught up with them and had Gerebernus killed. However, he himself executed his own daughter. Their relics were subsequently rediscovered in the thirteenth century, and an invocation to St. Dymphna was found to be efficacious in cases of insanity. Gheel itself rapidly became a centre for pilgrimage with a convent and a hospital. In fact, to this day a colony exists there for the care of the mentally disturbed."

"I begin to see the connection now. Dadd himself became insane – "

" – and executed his father. Precisely. The painting represents a reversal of the roles. In, 1842 Dadd left England with a patron, Sir Thomas Philips, on a drawing tour of Europe and the Middle East. It was on this trip that he first began showing signs of insanity. The trip was extremely arduous, and by the time the two men reached Egypt, Dadd was exhausted. After a trip to The City of The Dead, he began to believe that he was under the power of the Egyptian god Osiris and that he was being persecuted by

236

devils. When his studio was broken into by the police, incidentally, they found numerous portraits of his friends, each with their throats slit. And in his pocket he had a list of people – including the Emperor of Austria and the Pope – that the spirits had commanded him to kill in order to rid the world of evil. He thought he had killed the devil, and at no stage did he associate the crime with the death of his father. Apparently the irrational impulses all stemmed from the same source, the feeling of being controlled by Osiris and other spirits, and this belief remained with him all his remaining life."

"So there is no doubt that the murder was premeditated?"

"None whatsoever. As Dadd explained himself in a paper he wrote for Dr. Wood at Bethlem – yes, here it is in the introduction to the catalogue the Earl so kindly lent me: '*These and the like, coupled with the idea of a descent from the Egyptian god Osiris, induced me to put a period to the existence of his whom I had always regarded as a parent, but whom the secret admonishings had counselled me was the author of the ruin of my race. I inveigled him, by false pretences, into Cobham Park, and slew him with a knife, with which I stabbed him. after having vainly endeavoured to cut his throat.*'" Dadd saw himself as an envoy of the god Osiris and his role was to "'*exterminate the men most possessed with the demon*'."

"But Holmes," I asked. "How did Pinder know any of this? Surely he didn't have the benefit of the same research where you learned these details. How did he hallucinate the story, and thus paint the scenes of Dadd's father's murder?"

Holmes simply raised an eyebrow and continued to smoke.

There was silence for a while as I recalled my own realistic vision when first encountering the painting in that cold dank room.

"I think I read your thoughts, Watson," said Holmes, quietly replacing the catalogue. "You are, I think, wondering if Dadd was not mad after all."

"By your standards and mine, he might not have been."

"It very much depends on your definition of evil, and indeed of reality."

"Well, I have no doubt in my mind that evil resided within that painting," I observed.

"As the Bard once said, '*The evil that men do lives after them.*' I may not have got the quotation exactly right, but the idea is one that I find singularly unappealing. Come. We have had enough horrors for one week. What say you to a brisk walk now that the snow has begun to recede?"

I agreed, and within a few minutes we had donned our coats and hats and were striding forth into the sunshine of a bright December morning.

The Adventure of the Silent Sister

by Arthur Hall

It was as, I recall, a beautiful June morning when Sherlock Holmes appeared in high spirits. I had risen early and finished my breakfast, but offered immediately to call Mrs. Hudson in order to accommodate my friend.

"Thank you, Watson, but that will not be necessary, for I have no appetite this morning," he replied in an almost light-hearted tone. "However, I see that our good lady has supplied an extra cup and that the remaining coffee in the pot is still hot, since that which you have poured for yourself is steaming. That will suffice for me until lunch-time, I think."

"Your cases are progressing well then?" I asked as I poured the dark liquid for him. "You are rarely this cheerful in the morning."

He lowered himself into the chair opposite. "As it happens I have four current cases, all nearing successful conclusions."

"No wonder you are in such good spirits. Congratulations, old fellow."

I knew little about Holmes's recent activities, since a bout of influenza had prevented me from accompanying him for the past two weeks. A *locum* had maintained my practice, satisfactorily as far as I knew, and I was as yet unable to relieve him. Although past the contagion stage, I still felt quite weak, and tired easily.

"What do you say to a leisurely walk in St. James's Park?" he asked unexpectedly as he emptied his cup and got to his feet.

"That would be very much to my liking," was my puzzled reply, "but it is unusual for you to suggest such a thing."

He gestured towards the window. "It is a warm and windless day, and I expect no results from the enquiries I have made towards concluding my investigations until later in the week. What else would come to mind at such a time?"

"Your reasoning, as usual, is impeccable," I laughed, elevating my mood to match his. "We have but to pick up our hats and canes as we leave, and shout to Mrs. Hudson that she can now clear away our breakfast things, before strolling into the sunshine."

We left our lodgings behind and walked along Baker Street, I moving a little more slowly than usual. By contrast, Holmes was truly light-hearted today, seeming exhilarated by the very air he breathed.

"You know, Watson . . . ." he began as we neared a corner, then paused abruptly as a heavy-set man with a red beard suddenly accosted us.

"Sir," the stranger addressed me breathlessly and in a concerned manner, "are you Mr. Sherlock Holmes?"

We came to an immediate halt. "Not at all," I replied, "but *this* is Mr. Holmes."

His attention switched to my friend. "Mr. Holmes, thank God I caught you. I have urgent need of your services, if you will accept me as a client."

"To that I may agree," Holmes said, scrutinizing the man carefully, "but first you must tell us of your circumstances. Allow me to introduce my friend and colleague, Doctor John Watson."

The stranger identified himself. "My name is Septimus Todd," he began. "Inspector Lestrade of Scotland Yard recommended that I consult you."

"Most kind of him." Holmes suppressed a smile.

"I am desperately worried about my sister. She is a changed woman."

"Then are you certain that it is I who can be of assistance? If it is a question of altered behaviour, there is most often a medical explanation, in which case Doctor Watson would be far more useful to you than I. Or he may be able to recommend someone."

I felt immediate concern at the man's reaction to this. Tears came to his eyes and the depth of his emotion was apparent. "No sir, it is nothing like that. Since my dear wife passed away, some three years ago, Elinora has been all I have left in the world."

"She lives with you, I presume."

"That is correct. She has done so since soon after Margaret's passing, and looks after me completely. She dismissed the servants, saying that their services were an unnecessary expense, and so it has proved to be."

Holmes nodded. "Mr. Todd, you are clearly upset. Watson and I are about to walk to St. James's Park. You are welcome to join us. Please feel to tell us your story when you are able."

We progressed south for quite a while in silence, until Holmes finally spoke. "Mr. Todd, we are now entering The Mall, and will soon be approaching the park. I suggest you use the remaining time until we reach there to further calm yourself and to collect your thoughts. Then, after we arrive, you can relate your problem from its beginning in that peaceful setting so that we can decide your best course of action."

We entered the park a short while later and soon came upon a long bench near the lake, where pelicans, swans and other water-fowl swam freely in their perpetual hunt for food. We sat, with Mr. Todd still clearly distressed.

"Now," Holmes said to him, "if you would care to relate to us the nature of your sister's difficulties, we can arrive at a decision as to who can best help you. Pray be precise, leaving out not the smallest detail from the beginning."

Mr. Todd stared at the lake for a moment, as if wondering where to start. Then he turned to us, having apparently decided.

"Elinora has always been a quiet girl," he began, "but with a quick mind. A few years ago, she persuaded our father to pay for a course in mathematics at one of the minor universities. She was the only female in the class and endured some badgering from the others, but went on to silence her tormenters by obtaining the highest marks of them all. She would not speak of her objective in immersing herself in this knowledge, saying only that it was her insurance against poverty. Soon after the completion of her instruction, our father died.

"His estate, derived mostly from a Derbyshire coal mine which he sold during his final years, was divided equally between us. I invested heavily in gold stock, which has produced a reasonable living since, while my sister was persuaded by a friend to invest through several banks in a South African diamond mine which soon ceased to yield. Left almost penniless, she became my companion and housekeeper and ran things with an almost military precision. We lived together quite happily until she met a certain Mr. Arnold Trent, through a friend from her weekly sewing circle. He began to court her, and even though it seemed to me to be a rather cold relationship, I approved for her sake.

"Then a fellow I know from the Chamber of Commerce pointed him out to me in the street one day as a man of doubtful character. I decided to learn something of Trent's past, and discovered a history of petty theft and attempted embezzlement. At this, I acted at once to sever all connections with Mr. Trent, though this naturally was the cause of much friction between my sister and myself, until she came to realise his true nature."

"One moment," Holmes interrupted. "You have said that this man Trent has a dishonest reputation. What then, did you imagine was the reason for his courtship of your sister, as she was penniless and dependent on yourself for her living? Did you consider that his interest might have been genuine?"

"Not for an instant. From the description of his past activities that I received from various sources, I formed the opinion that he was most likely planning to use Elinora to somehow gain access to my finances. This would not have been the first time he had hatched such a plan."

"I understand. Pray continue."

"Elinora was always a girl to take things very much to heart, and has not been the same towards me since, despite the miserable life she would

240

have had without my intervention. She is now constantly morose, and we exist in silence for much of the time we are together."

"Not unusual surely," I commented, "in the circumstances you describe."

"There is more to it than that, Doctor. One day she returned from Hampstead – we live quite close to the village – where she had ordered groceries. There she had chanced to meet one of her tutors from her university days, an elderly lady by the name of Elizabeth Heald."

"Elinora told me then that she and this Miss Heald had arranged to meet regularly every month, and she would stay with her for several days. When she returned from such meetings, she was markedly evasive when I enquired about how they had spent their time. Usually she would continue the silence which had by now become normal between us, but on more than one occasion she conveniently claimed to have no memory of whatever transpired. I doubted the truth of this, but at the mention of such lapses I became seriously worried. I insisted, much against her protests, that she seek medical help. Several doctors have examined her and discovered nothing amiss, and her only comment was to shrug off my concern and make light of it, saying that no harm could come of her continuing to see Miss Heald."

"What did you do then?" I asked.

Our new acquaintance moved restlessly in his seat. "I convinced myself that Trent's hand was in this, somewhere. Remembering his past, I consulted Scotland Yard with my suspicions that my sister was being drawn into something of a criminal nature. Inspector Lestrade concluded that nothing could be done, since no crime had yet been committed, but suggested that I enlist your assistance for my own peace of mind."

"Hence your arrival at Baker Street," my friend surmised.

"That did not follow immediately. It occurred to me that you might dismiss me in the same manner, and so I sought something to give credence to my fears. In her absence, I searched for and found the key to Elinora's desk. I was unsure what to look for, but in one of the drawers were papers from her university days, including the whereabouts of Miss Elizabeth Heald. Armed with this knowledge, I journeyed to Watford to see her, only to discover that her house is derelict and the lady passed away more than a year ago."

"This situation begins to have some interesting features," Holmes remarked.

"I am very relieved that you think so."

"Have you, by any chance, recorded the dates of your sister's meetings with this woman?"

"As it happens, I have. I did this to support my case at Scotland Yard."

Holmes nodded. "When did these meetings begin?"

"The first was in February."

"So you have dates for February, March, April, and May – presuming that this month's meeting has not yet taken place?"

"Not until now." Mr. Todd drew a folded paper from his pocket. "The dates were, February 4th, 5th, and 6th, March 13th, 14th, and 15th, April 5th, 6th, and 7th, and May 18th, 19th, and 20th."

Holmes threw a quick glance in my direction, to ensure that I had noted these.

"Three consecutive days, on each occasion. I must impress upon you, Mr. Todd, the importance of informing me at once when the date of the next meeting becomes known to you. If you could do this in advance, it would be of immeasurable assistance."

"I undertake to communicate with you by telegraph at the first possible moment, Mr. Holmes. I cannot express adequately my relief that you have consented to come to my aid. You would have me continue as usual then, until the time of the next meeting becomes known to me?"

"Not at all." Holmes turned to our client wearing a mild expression. "I was about to suggest that Doctor Watson and myself accompany you to your home on some pretext, so that we can meet your sister this morning."

We left St. James's Park shortly afterwards. I flagged down a passing four-wheeler and we found ourselves in Hampstead well before mid-day.

Mr. Todd and his sister lived in a square, three-storey town house in a mews near the local parish church. Holmes had suggested that he introduce us as prospective investors in gold shares, in search of advice, and our client represented us as such to his sister. She was a tall slim woman who could have been attractive, but for her unvarying grim expression and her aura of sadness as she served us tea. Her dress was plain, almost funereal, and her black hair gleamed. I saw that her eyes were dull, presumably from the lasting pain of losing Mr. Trent.

The conversation during our short visit proved to be sparse. Mr. Todd spoke haltingly in the presence of his sister, but maintained the deception as to his connection with Holmes and myself.

I reflected, as we left, that she had hardly spoken a word to us.

"I have reminded Mr. Todd again of the necessity of informing us immediately the next time Miss Elinora prepares to attend such a meeting." Holmes hailed an approaching hansom. "I have also assured him that he will hear from us soon."

"But if she seeks to conceal her movements, how is he to distinguish between her usual short absences for household matters and her next meeting with whomever she is seeing?"

"I suggested that he accompany her on each excursion. When her intention is to meet her mysterious friend, she will do all in her power to ensure that she makes the journey alone."

The next few days were largely uneventful. Apart from a thorough examination of his index, my friend occupied himself mainly with his endless chemical experiments. I continued to recover my strength, and began to consider the prospect of returning to my practice soon.

It was during the early evening of the 27th, that two telegrams arrived for Holmes. He received them eagerly, obviously relieved at this end to a period of monotony.

"At last, Watson!" he cried as he read the contents of the first. "One of my pending cases has finally come to fruition. If I enlist the help of the Yard tomorrow, a child should be restored to its parents and an abductor should be behind bars not long after mid-day."

"Excellent. The second telegram is doubtlessly a satisfactory conclusion to another pending affair."

He tore open the envelope, and I saw his expression change. "This is from Mr. Todd. He is certain that his sister intends to embark on another meeting in the morning."

"That is of less importance than the other case, surely?"

"Not if my deductions are correct."

I cast my mind back. "When we returned from Mr. Todd's house, you spent much time consulting your index. Am I to assume that you learned something further?"

"You are indeed. If we are to prevent a serious crime, and possibly injuries to innocent people, it is essential that Miss Elinora Todd is observed when she ventures forth from their house tomorrow. Yet I am now bound to see this other matter through. I may be a detective of some standing, but I cannot be in two places at once."

"Barker has assisted you several times since the Josiah Amberley affair."

"Which I expect that you will dramatize out of all proportion for your future readers." His thin form paced the room restlessly, wrestling with indecision. "No, I have established that Barker is at present occupied in Newcastle, on a rather involved case of murder. I fear that I must search elsewhere."

Without thinking, I said quickly. "Time was when you would have used my services for such as this, Holmes. They are still available to you."

"My dear fellow!" he turned towards me at once. "I could not think of it. You are not yet recovered, and probably will lack the energy for some time. It is a pity though, your assistance here would have been invaluable."

I sat up straight in my chair. "I have felt stronger, Holmes, these past four or five days. In fact, I am at the point of deciding the date of my return to my practice. I would willingly delay this, if you think I can be useful."

"Are you sure that you could undertake such a task? Were it not for your indisposition, I would have thought of you at once, but I would not delay your recovery for the world."

"I am certain. Yet something has just come to mind that precludes such a course."

A quick smile passed over his hawk-like features. "I can imagine no such thing in the face of your enthusiasm."

"But the lady knows me from our visit to see her, with Mr. Todd. I have not your expertise at following people, and would quickly be noticed."

To my great surprise, Holmes threw back his head and laughed.

"Give that not a moment of consideration, my good friend. I assure you, that is the least of our worries."

I was to discover, after being roused from my bed early the next morning, why my friend was unconcerned. As soon as Mrs. Hudson had reclaimed the breakfast things, he revealed his strategy.

"Do me the kindness of sitting in that upright chair, Watson. I am about to make you invisible to anyone you might care to follow."

With that he hastily wound a towel around my neck and produced the case containing his theatrical make-up that I had seen him use often with great effect. I closed my eyes as he brushed my face lightly and applied some of the contents of several jars and bottles. Finally, he placed a grey wig on my head and stood back to admire his work. After a critical appraisal, he appeared satisfied and held a mirror in front of my face. The image I saw reflected was of an older man who did not resemble John Watson in the least.

"And so, old fellow, you will be able to pursue Miss Elinora Todd with impunity. I think that even your patients would not recognise you without difficulty."

"It does not surprise me that no disguise of yours has ever failed."

He nodded. "We have no way of knowing at what time Miss Elinora will set out. Therefore it would be as well to be waiting near the house early. I wish you well, Watson. As always, I know there is no one I can more safely depend upon. Goodbye, old fellow, until we meet here again later."

Moments later, I found myself in a hansom on my way to Hampstead. On arrival, I instructed the cabby to wait near some overhanging trees within sight of the house. At first he seemed suspicious of my motives, but

I implied, rather than stated, that I was connected to Scotland Yard. My vigil was not a long one, for less than half-an-hour had passed before Miss Elinora Todd emerged to board a brougham that had appeared, obviously by appointment.

We followed at a distance, just keeping the vehicle in sight. It approached a church then turned away, whereupon we were obliged to draw nearer. Crossing several side-roads full of houses with long and blossom-filled front gardens, we emerged into a main thoroughfare lined by shops, a few inns, and a livery stable. The brougham passed a warehouse building and began to lose speed. A few yards further on it came to a halt and Miss Elinora alighted. I handed the cabby his fee and stepped onto the pavement cautiously, anxious that Miss Elinora should be unaware of my presence.

I crossed the road with the intention of observing her reflection in a shop window as I had seen Holmes do on many occasions, but she did not walk far. Nearby was an Italian coffee shop called "Callino's", with some of its seating spilling onto the pavement in the Continental style. She approached a table where a man dressed in brown sat, and he immediately rose to seat her and order coffee for them both.

For I while, I observed their conversation, which appeared to be quite animated. Then, trusting in my disguise, I strolled with what I hoped was an unconcerned air back across the road. I saw to my relief that more of the tables were now occupied, and that one of those remaining was situated near where my quarry and her companion continued their discussion. I seated myself, and a waiter took my order of coffee and a slice of rich cake. I paid the bill immediately, since this would otherwise delay me should Miss Elinora leave suddenly.

This was, in fact, what happened some ten minutes later. The man in brown rose and paid the waiter who appeared, before holding the chair for Miss Elinora and leaving with her. They boarded a passing hansom, causing me some difficulty because I had no means to follow. I watched with my spirits sinking until they were almost out of sight. Then a four-wheeler came to rest and four men alighted outside a tailor's shop. There was something about their demeanour that suggested to me that they were about to be dressed for a wedding, but I dismissed this irrelevant thought as I boarded and ordered the driver to proceed at all speed. This instruction was apparently not unusual to him, for he whipped up the horses without a word and we sped away. We quickly caught up with the hansom and, at my direction, adopted a slower pace. This man had clearly followed other vehicles before, since he at no time appeared surprised and conducted the pursuit largely without my further instructions. We eventually reached Tottenham Court Road, where the hansom turned into a narrow side-street.

I ordered the cabby to stop a few yards past the junction and, after dismissing him, hurried back to the side-street. I was in time to see Miss Elinora and her companion enter a nearby house as the hansom left. There seemed to be no sign of life in this small and silent street and so, feeling rather foolish, I stationed myself in concealment behind a thick bush in an opposite front garden. After little more than an hour, she emerged alone. Immediately a hansom appeared from the direction of Tottenham Court Road, evidently by arrangement. She was then swept away, and this time I had no means to continue my pursuit. When she passed out of sight, I walked until another hansom presented itself and was thus conveyed back to Baker Street, already hearing in my mind Holmes's reproach at my failure to carry out the task that he had entrusted to me.

He laid aside his clay pipe as I entered. His expression told me that his day had gone well, and I was grateful.

"Ah, Watson," he beamed. "You have returned earlier than expected."

"I assume your case concluded satisfactorily?" I enquired, hoping to delay the inevitable.

He nodded, cheerfully. "The child is now safely at home and a cruel abductor is where he can do no more harm. But tell me, what of your day? I am anxious to hear your progress."

First I called for a pitcher of hot water and, ignoring Mrs. Hudson's horror at my appearance, restored my normal self.

Holmes watched impatiently as I settled myself in an armchair with a glass of brandy. I then related to him all that I had observed and heard since the interlude at Callino's, as he sat silently listening with his chin upon steepled fingers.

"Did you overhear any of the conversation between Miss Elinora and the man who wore brown?" he asked when I had finished.

"I did, and I am at a loss to understand what hold this man has over her."

"Pray elaborate on what was said."

"It was strange talk, much like the planning of a military campaign. I listened, but could make nothing of it."

I saw from his eyes that this was not unexpected, but a possibility occurred to me.

"Holmes! Could it be that Miss Elinora, with her precise nature and mathematical skill, has devised some strategy for the government, and the man is their representative?"

The faintest of smiles crossed his features, and was quickly gone. "I think not, old friend."

"Then I can think of nothing more."

"Was there anything of significance about the appearance of this fellow?" He asked after a moment's silence.

"I noticed that he had a squint, probably of nervous origin."

"Was there anything more? Think, Watson!"

Seeing his increased interest, I searched my memory. "He had a pronounced limp, favouring his right leg."

"Capital!" Holmes looked positively elated. "You have done well, old fellow."

"Holmes, I was unable to follow Miss Elinora when she left the house off Tottenham Court Road. I can hardly claim any success."

"Much to the contrary," he held up his hands and smiled with satisfaction. "You have virtually solved the case."

"I confess to being confounded."

Holmes stretched his long body and stood up. "In ten minutes, if she follows her usual custom, Mrs. Hudson will serve dinner. I recognise the aroma that has pervaded this room for some little while as that of curried chicken. Afterwards, we will repair as usual to our chairs around that unlit fire and read or talk over our past experiences. Tomorrow morning we will visit Lestrade at the Yard, and I will give him information which he will gratefully receive. But I perceive, Watson, that you are impatient to learn of the truth of this case and of my deductions. It was not a difficult problem, and I will tell you all when we hear of its successful conclusion, but for now I will ask you one question: What is situated opposite Callino's, where you sat near Miss Elinora and Erdwell Cornish?"

"Who is Erdwell Cornish?"

"That is the real name, and the one known to Scotland Yard, of the man who wore brown."

I tried to remember my surroundings, as they had been while sitting at the coffee shop. Finally, it came to me. "The Landworkers and Stonemasons Bank!"

"Precisely," said Holmes, and would be drawn no further.

Inspector Lestrade did not sit down with us. He paced his office with the air of a man with a great weight on his shoulders.

"I hope you are not here for information and advice, Mr. Holmes. I have little time to spare, since my investigation into this latest series of bank robberies is not going well. We have exhausted every line of enquiry, and discovered nothing."

"Which is why we are here," Holmes suppressed a grin. "If you would care to spare us a few moments, I am quite certain that I can provide you with the time and place of the gang's next appearance."

The inspector ceased his pacing at once. "How could you have learned of this?"

"Oh, it was something that arose from a trifling affair that I was asked to look into. It often happens that way."

"I admit to being desperate enough to listen to any theory. I am clutching at straws, and would welcome anything new."

I could see that Holmes was enjoying the situation. He let a few moments pass before answering. Apprehension filled Lestrade's face.

"I can tell you only this," my friend said. "You will successfully conclude your case if you station six armed constables inside The Landworkers and Stonemasons Bank, in the late afternoon but before closing time tomorrow. I suggest that they enter the premises in plain clothes, in case the gang are observing the place."

"How did you come by this information?" Lestrade asked in astonishment.

"As I said, Inspector, it was incidental. However, I do urge you to follow my instructions, and not to delay."

To my surprise, Inspector Lestrade appeared unconvinced.

"Have you any other advice, Mr. Holmes?" he said with a hint of sarcasm.

"I have, Lestrade. Do not be surprised if, in the course of this, you encounter Erdwell Cornish."

"I would very much like to do so."

"Act upon my instructions, and you will."

The following day proved uneventful. I felt much stronger than of late, and telegraphed my *locum* to announce my intended return to my practice soon. Holmes spent much of the time bringing his index up to date, but there was an air of expectancy about him at all times. I could tell that his finely-tuned senses were constantly alert for a ring of the doorbell or the arrival of the telegram boy.

It was just after dinner when a message finally arrived. Mrs. Hudson had no sooner cleared the plates away than she re-entered our room bearing a telegram.

Holmes thanked her and tore open the envelope. The door closed behind her as he cast his eyes hurriedly over its contents.

"Capital!" he cried. "Lestrade wishes to see us at the Yard in the morning."

"I fear that I cannot attend, Holmes. I have already made plans to relieve my *locum*."

He hesitated for a moment, I like to think because I was unable to accompany him. "No matter, old fellow. I will relate all to you after dinner tomorrow."

I slept uneasily that night, my thoughts divided between anticipation of what my practice might hold and the fate of Mr. Todd's sister. I hoped fervently that she had come to no harm at the hands of Erdwell Cornish and his gang. Try as I might, I could not form a clear picture of the part she had played in this affair, nor of what it was that Cornish apparently held over her head to gain from her some sort of complicity.

I breakfasted alone, Holmes having reverted to his usual habit of rising late. On arrival at my surgery, I noticed that my *locum* had an air of impatience about him, like that of a runner awaiting the firing of the starting pistol. I soon discovered the reason, as he explained that an unseasonable local epidemic of bronchitis had kept him far busier than he was accustomed. He left to return to his country practice with evident relief.

Throughout the morning I attended to a steady stream of patients. The time passed slowly, probably because I was anxious to hear from Holmes of Lestrade's account of the outcome of yesterday's events.

When at last I climbed the stairs to our rooms in Baker Street, it was to dark and mournful music. I recognised it as one of Holmes's own compositions, wrung from his Stradivarius with painstaking care.

"Watson!" Despite the tone of the music his mood appeared to be pleasant. I hung up my hat and coat as he put away his violin. "I have poured us both a glass of port."

Soon we were sitting opposite each other around the cold fireplace, having emptied our glasses.

"Mrs. Hudson has said to expect dinner in half-an-hour," he informed me, "after which I am sure you would like me to relate to you my interview with Lestrade."

"That has not been far from my mind all day, so I would appreciate a description now. There is much that puzzles me still, Holmes."

"Very well," he said with a tone that indicated his disapproval of my impatience. "I will begin at the beginning, which is always simplest."

He sat back in his chair and I leaned forward eagerly in mine. "You have my entire attention."

After a quick look in my direction, he closed his eyes and began. "When I arrived at Scotland Yard earlier, I knew instantly, from Lestrade's mood and the general atmosphere, that all had gone well the day before. He took great pride in explaining the strategy he employed, the result of which was the capture of the entire gang. There was but one casualty –

Erdwell Cornish was foolish enough to draw a weapon when several police guns were trained upon him."

"He is dead?"

"Of necessity."

"What of Elinora Todd?"

"Let me tell the tale, Watson."

"But is she unharmed?"

"She is."

"I apologise, Holmes. Please continue."

He straightened his posture, his eyes open now. "At my request, and in consideration of the assistance he obtained from us, Lestrade allowed me to interview Miss Todd, who is now in custody. As a result, I now have a full understanding of the part she played in all this. It may come as a shock to you, old fellow, when I say that I have seldom met such a scheming woman and hope never to do so again."

I felt my spirits plummet. "You astonish me."

"I first suspected that she was not all that she seemed, when Mr. Todd took us to meet her. The way she managed the house – the pictures in the exact centre of the wall, and everything in a clearly defined place – told of a precisely attuned mind, admirable in itself, but her eyes and expression, her entire attitude, told more. Mr. Todd attributed her ways to the loss of a suitor, and truly felt for her, when in fact they were symptoms of a burning jealousy of her brother's wealth and a strong hatred of the banks which, as she saw it, robbed her of her share of her father's estate.

"We will probably never have a true account of how she came to meet Trent, or Cornish as it turns out, for of that she would not speak. However, I consider it probable that she already had some sort of future plan in mind when she took up the study of mathematics before her father's death. Of course, when her brother later discovered her relationship with Trent and forbade her to continue, her jealous hatred was intensified."

"When we returned here, on the day we first met Mr. Todd, I consulted my index because this fellow Trent had stirred something in my memory. I discovered that the name had been used by Cornish previously for a variety of crimes, and asked myself what his objective could be now. The most prominent recent criminal activity was the series of bank robberies that Lestrade was so worried about, and so I reviewed such information that I had. I found that they had taken place on the 8th of February, the 17th of March, the 9th of April and the 22nd of May, whereupon I realised at once that each date was two days after Miss Elinora had returned home after her short stays with 'Miss Heald'. Further enquiries revealed that five banks were involved in the ill-fated consortium in which Miss Elinora had invested, and four of these were the subjects of the previous robberies. I am sure, Watson, that you have already deduced the name of the fifth bank."

"The Landworkers and Stonemasons Bank, of course."

"Precisely. The meetings were actually with Trent, or Cornish, and were never of a romantic nature. She grew weary of excusing herself to her brother – hence the 'memory losses' which absolved her from inventing anything more. Mr. Todd's insistence on medical help were a considerable inconvenience to her."

"But Holmes, what crime did she actually commit?"

He shook his head, with the air of someone explaining to a child. "Have you not realised yet? The study of mathematics, the precision upon which all her actions depended? She was the driving force, the planner of the whole series of crimes. Ample evidence of her guilt was found in Cornish's rooms, off the Tottenham Court Road where you concluded your observations yesterday. You heard as much yourself when you sat listening in Callino's."

"I would never have imagined it," I sighed. "Never."

"You see, Watson, that my mistrust of the fair sex is not so unreasonable, after all."

"She will doubtlessly share the fate of the rest of the gang."

"They were, without exception, men who have spent their lives drifting from one crime to another. Men who are for hire when someone of a superior mind and criminal inclination sees a dishonest opportunity. But yes, she will share their fate and, I fear, be considerably older when she is again a free woman."

We were silent for some time, before I remarked. "Sad as it will be, Holmes, we can now furnish an explanation to Mr. Septimus Todd."

He nodded slowly, and there was no cheer in his expression. "That is true, old friend, we will have given him an answer. But not, I am truly sorry to say, without breaking his heart in the process."

A Skeleton's Sorry Story
by Jack Grochot

Reminiscing, my friend Sherlock Holmes recounted the times his efforts at solving murders resulted in the hangings of the killers – yet only once in his illustrious career did the guilty party cheat death on the gallows due to a judge's sympathy for the accused.

Such was the case in mid-summer of 1902 with the demise of Aloysius McMonagal, whose life was brutally wrested from him at the age of twenty-three and whose skeletal remains posed a double mystery to Holmes: What was the identity of the victim, and who bashed in his skull, then buried him in a fallow field on a farm in Surrey?

Here, at length, is how this sordid conundrum unfolded:

We had traveled by train to the village of Guildford in Surrey on the investigation of the case involving the mortal terror of old Abrahams. Holmes wasn't anticipating another puzzle to present itself. Inspector Gregory of Scotland Yard accompanied us on the journey and introduced us to an up-and-coming deputy constable, Miles Stanley, who was preoccupied with a perplexing case of his own: The matter of the skeleton.

"Mr. Holmes, I have reached nothing but dead ends in my effort to identify the victim," Stanley complained. "Could you possibly see your way clear to assist me?"

"Perhaps I can, young man," Holmes informed him. "First let me wrap up what I came here to investigate, which will be today, I am certain, and then we shall sit down tomorrow to discuss what you have learned thus far. Take an early morning train to Charing Cross and then a cab to 221b Baker Street."

"Oh, Mr. Holmes, it will relieve me of the pressure I am receiving from my superiors," Stanley confided. "They want me to solve this confounded problem in the worst way, and I can't bear to tell them that my efforts have resulted in abysmal failure."

"You haven't failed yet, not if I can help it," Holmes assured him, then turned his attention to the more immediate matter. Young Stanley departed, humming a merry tune, convinced that Holmes would come to his rescue.

"A bright lad. He knows his limitations, and he isn't afraid to humble himself to seek assistance," Holmes was saying as we drank our second cup of coffee at breakfast the next morning while discussing Stanley's predicament. Just as we dropped the subject, we heard a hansom pull up to the curb in front of our rooms, followed by a ring of the doorbell.

Our landlady, Mrs. Hudson, answered the bell and climbed the stairs with Stanley to announce his arrival. Holmes had previously told her that he was expecting a visitor and asked her to show him to our flat and not delay him by probing for the reason he was there. Stanley crossed the threshold into the sitting room and gave Mrs. Hudson a polite smile. He appeared older than I recalled from the day before, apparently because his attire was more formal. He was wearing a pin-striped dark blue business suit with a bow tie and a starched white shirt with gold cufflinks, as well as highly polished black boots.

"Good morning, gentlemen," he intoned, "I trust I am here at a good time."

"Your timing is perfect, Constable," Holmes answered. "Do you care for some coffee?"

"No thank you, sir. I prefer to get down to business," Stanley said.

"Very well, then. Tell us the details of your grim discovery," Holmes directed, offering Stanley a seat on the sofa.

"It was actually a farmer, a Mr. Hubert Gall, who found it," Stanley began. "He was plowing in an area that hadn't been cultivated in more than twenty years when the digging blade caught on the rib cage of the deceased. Mr. Gall's two horses stopped pulling the plow because they were trained to stand in place if an obstacle interfered with their cadence. Thinking the obstacle was a root or a large rock, Mr. Gall went to the barn to fetch a shovel to unearth the obstruction. He dug and found human bones, then freed the plow. Not wanting to disturb the remains, he abandoned his project and hitched his team to a wagon to go to town to report his finding to the police.

"I was assigned the investigation and went immediately to the scene, where I deduced that it was a case of murder because of the condition of the skull. I brought the remains to the office of Dr. Robert Hull, the deputy coroner, who confirmed my deduction and took custody of the bones. He noted in his report that death had occurred approximately twenty years ago. The farmer, Mr. Gall, has lived on the farm for twelve years after buying the property from Augustus Hank, who owned it for four decades. My efforts to locate Mr. Hank have been unsuccessful. Old timers in the village told me he had gone to live with his daughter, Gwen, after selling out to Mr. Gall. He may have died by now, since he would be in his seventies today.

"That is where the inquiry stands, Mr. Holmes – at a dead end, no pun intended."

"Not so, Constable. There is much that can be done," Holmes countered. "If you wish, you may accompany Dr. Watson and me to learn how to turn a dead end into a solution of the crime."

"With your permission," Stanley beamed, "I shall be with you every step of the way."

"All right, we shall start at a place where you made your first mistake," Holmes stated. "It is at the makeshift grave, where you can take me after we have enlisted two or three volunteers to dig deeper than you did to extract the skeleton. There may be more that was buried there than the body –perhaps a wallet or some object that can provide a clue to the victim's identity."

Without further conversation, we left together for the train and arrived in Surrey by mid-morning. Stanley took us in a wagon to the local cemetery, where he persuaded a pair of grave diggers to meet us on the Gall farm to assist the police and the famous Sherlock Holmes in a homicide investigation. The grave diggers were impressed by the appearance of the detective about whom they had both read in the magazines. "Will you mention our names," one of them asked me, "when you write the story if Mr. Holmes solves the case?"

"What do you mean, *if*?" Holmes answered him. "Spell your names for Dr. Watson and I'm certain that he will give you both credit. Tell me, gentlemen – were each of you residents of this area when Mr. Hank owned the farm? I'm trying to determine his whereabouts."

"I remember him vaguely, although I was a lad when he sold out," said one of the men, Xavier Crenshaw. "Now Adam here, he would know more about that. He's older than me."

Adam Johansson, a quiet and shy sort, spoke up. "A maniac, was Mr. Hank. Took to fits and rages. Accused everyone of trying to steal from him. Threatened to send people to Hell."

"How came you to know so much about Mr. Hank?" Holmes wanted to determine.

"Used to work for him at harvest time," Johansson revealed. "Worked for him three years in a row until he said I cheated him on my hours. He didn't pay me for the extra work I did for him on Sundays, like splitting firewood. He said the Sunday dinner his daughter fed me was pay enough."

"What became of him after Mr. Gall bought the farm?" Holmes continued.

"He skedaddled – went to live with his daughter somewhere in the city. He said he was finished with country life," Johansson informed Holmes.

"Shall we be on our way to the farm to see what you gentlemen discover to help solve a murder?" Holmes inquired.

"Meet you there in half-an-hour," Johansson replied.

Stanley drove us to the spot where the skeleton had been unearthed and, in a matter of minutes, the two grave diggers arrived on horseback, toting shovels and rakes to sift through the dirt.

They began their task eagerly and in no time at all had uncovered a pocket watch on a gold chain. Holmes opened the timepiece, and on the inside was a discernable engraving: "*To A.M. with love G.H.*"

"We know the dead man's initials, *A.M.* The *G.H.* undoubtedly stands for *Gwen Hank*," Holmes purported. "Keep digging, men. We might find something that will tell us his full name."

They dug and sifted, dug and sifted, but found nothing more.

"Now back up two or three paces and start digging in the fresh ground," Holmes instructed, a request that perplexed the two workers and Stanley, too.

They began soon uncovered another skeleton, this one with a fatal head wound as well.

"I suspect there are even more graves," Holmes announced. "We are dealing with a killer who disposed of his victims in this fallow field. Dig over there, men!"

Altogether, seven more skeletons were revealed.

"How could you possibly have known?" inquired Stanley, shocked beyond description and breathless. Holmes responded, "Last night, in preparation for our visit here today, I consulted my Index, and under the heading 'Surrey', I found an old clipping from *The Times* detailing the disappearance of eight persons within a span of eighteen months. The article named the missing and stated that the police were at a loss to explain the phenomenon. One of those was Aloysius McMonagal – *A.M.* – a sailor who was presumed lost at sea. Now we know the truth."

"The awful truth, Mr. Holmes!" Stanley exclaimed. "My superiors will be grateful that the bones of the late Mr. McMonagal have been identified, but they will be horrified to learn that there are seven other victims of a crazed killer. Goodness, what do we do now?"

"Now we take up the challenge to find him," Holmes barked. "Come with us to London to locate Mr. Hank and his daughter."

"First, I must report our findings to my superiors, and then I can join you. Where shall we meet?" Stanley wondered.

"At the reference desk of the London Library in Saint James's Square," Holmes answered. "It is there that we shall take the next step toward solving the mystery of the whereabouts of the Hanks."

Stanley drove Holmes and me to the train platform, where we parted company. He then proceeded to the constabulary to make his report. He arrived as his superiors were preparing to leave for the day.

As he told us later, he began by addressing the captain in charge. "I have good news and bad news."

"Good grief, man, come out with it!" snapped the captain, Roger Stuart.

Stanley, with a dramatic flair, spelled out the developments as Stuart fell back into his chair. "I'm not sure you have enough experience to handle this," he surmised. "Better to let me reassign this case to a seasoned investigator."

"But, sir, I can manage it as long as Sherlock Holmes is involved and tolerates me," Stanley implored. "Please let me continue with it."

"I'll give you three days," Stuart promised. "If, at the end of that period, you don't make any progress, I shall transfer the duties to Mausteller."

"Agreed!" Stanley cried. "Now I must be off to meet Mr. Holmes in the city."

Stanley hustled afoot to the train and soon joined us at the London Library.

"Here, within these two volumes," Holmes explained to the young constable, "is the current address of the Hanks. *The Post Office Directory* never fails to enlighten."

"You make it seem easy, Mr. Holmes," Stanley sputtered.

Holmes went to the "*H*" in the alphabetical listings and pointed out an entry to the deputy constable: *Hank, Gwen and Augustus, 130 Elm Way, Streatham, Borough of Lambeth.*

"This *is* the easy part, Mr. Stanley," Holmes commented. "Once the tricks of the trade become second nature to you, finding someone in the city is no monumental task. Now that we know where to look, what say the three of us down a pint of ale along with some fish and chips at the tavern around the corner before we visit the Hanks?"

"You have my vote," Stanley beamed.

"I'll vote with the majority," I chimed in. "I'm famished."

At The Eagle's Perch Pub, Stanley quizzed Holmes about how he would start to investigate the killings, and Holmes suggested he wait until he heard what the Hanks would say. "There's no telling in what direction they might lead us," he offered.

After our refreshing meal, we climbed aboard a four-wheeler to take us to the Hanks' abode, where we encountered Gwen Hank standing outside, watering her flowers along the walk. Holmes handled the introductions and she invited us to sit in a small garden.

Miss Hank was a trim, attractive woman in her late forties with brown hair, which she wore in a bun. Understandably, she was puzzled by a visit from a policeman and a detective with a well-known reputation. "What brings you here, and why am I deserving of so much attention?" she began.

"We are investigating the disappearance of eight individuals in Surrey whose skeletons were recently plowed up in a field on the farm where you lived years ago," Holmes told her, a revelation that startled the lady. "Does the name Aloysius McMonagal ring a bell?"

"Good Lord, yes," she cried. "He was my one and only love. Please don't tell me his was one of the skeletons."

"I'm afraid it was," Holmes disclosed. With that, overcome by grief, Miss Hank sobbed.

"Oh, Lord, how did he die?" she cried.

"His skull was fractured by a blunt instrument," Holmes told her. "Do you have any idea who would have wanted to kill him?"

"Aloysius was a kind man, kind to everyone – he hadn't an enemy in the world," she replied.

"When did you last see him?" Holmes wanted to know.

"It was in the afternoon on the twenty-second of June, twenty-six years ago," Miss Hank recalled. "We were to elope that night and he never appeared at my window as we had planned. I presumed that he changed his mind and abandoned our life together, not ever to see me again. I was devastated for weeks and seldom left the house. Then other men came calling and I entertained them, but there was no one like Aloysius. The others reached a point where they didn't return to see me. It was as if I had the plague. I was an attractive young woman then, but I must have done something or said something that caused them to disappear like Aloysius."

"Tell me their names, Miss Hank. It is important that you remember," Holmes persisted.

Etched in her memory, she rattled off the names of the suitors, all of which matched the identities of the persons reported missing from Surrey.

"Do you know anyone who would want them killed?" Holmes probed.

"Are you saying they were *all* murdered?" Miss Hank, startled, asked breathlessly.

"It is they who were likely buried on the farm," he continued.

"Oh, my word!" she exclaimed. "Then his threat was genuine."

"Whose threat?" Holmes demanded.

"Adam Johansson's threat. He worked for my father briefly and asked me to marry him. I rejected him emphatically – a mere boy. I laughed at his proposal, and that made him angry. He boasted that if he couldn't have me, he would make sure no man could."

"It was Johansson, a grave digger, who helped us unearth the skeletons," Holmes disclosed. "I know just how to find him, and so does Deputy Constable Stanley. But before we go, allow us to speak with your father about this."

"My father will be of no help to you, Mr. Holmes. His memory is clouded with fantasy. He is demented and he thinks every man who calls on us is determined to take me away from him. You must not bother him – it is too risky. His health is deteriorating, and any disturbance to his routine will result in calamity."

"But I must insist, Miss Hank," Holmes persisted. "We are conducting a murder investigation, and no potential witness can be disregarded. You cannot protect him from the law."

"If you put it that way," she relented, "I'll coax him into the parlour, but don't say I didn't warn you."

Miss Hank made us comfortable inside and went to her father's room to fetch him. We heard them argue, but couldn't make out the words. She returned alone and apologized for her father's absence. "I told him the police were here to question him," she explained, "and he refused to cooperate. He said the police are evil and wished them to burn in Hell. He is in no frame of mind to talk to anyone."

Holmes and Stanley accepted her explanation reluctantly and we departed the household to start fresh in the morning. Holmes arranged for us to rendezvous with Stanley at the cemetery where Johansson was employed.

That night, Holmes slipped into his mouse-coloured dressing gown and slippers to pace the floor while drawing on his old and oily clay pipe. His hands were clasped behind his back or gesturing as if in conversation with someone. "I found Miss Hank's reaction to my news about the deaths to be peculiar, Watson," he remarked as I prepared to ascend the stairs to my bedroom.

"Peculiar? How so?" I responded.

"She was not shocked and she asked no questions about how her suitors met their end," he mumbled. "It gave me the impression she already knew everything there was to know."

"Now that you mention it, I suppose that it is peculiar," I added. "Here is something else to consider: She went to great lengths to protect her father from scrutiny."

"Yes, I found that troubling as well," Holmes contended. "I shall contemplate on these facts before I retire. Have a good night's rest, my friend, because our day tomorrow promises to be a full one.

The next day, at breakfast, Sherlock Holmes discussed his planned approach to the grave digger Johansson and the possibility that he might have pertinent information about Miss Hank.

"Did you come to any conclusions regarding Johansson's threat?" I queried.

"Only that it was an idle one, if one at all," he answered, without going into detail.

We hurried for the train to Surrey and our appointment with Deputy Constable Stanley.

At a shack where the cemetery workers wasted time, Johansson sat at a table playing euchre with three of his compatriots when we beckoned him outside for a chat.

"You're not very busy today," Stanley began the conversation.

"Nobody died yet," Johansson retorted.

"Let me be blunt, Mr. Johansson," Holmes interjected, before repeating the accusation Miss Hank made against him.

"Blimey! That's a serious charge considering the matter at hand," Johansson said. "It's bloomin' hogwash, though. She's makin' it up, I swear. Now why would she say such a thing?"

"Perhaps to lay suspicion somewhere else," Holmes conjectured, but changed the subject. "Tell me everything you know about her."

"I was too young to pay attention to talk then, but since then I've heard talk about Miss Hank that is none too kind – only talk, though, because I know nothing first hand," Johansson related.

"Rumors, you mean?" Holmes quizzed.

"Yes, rumors," Johansson went on.

"Let me hear them also," Holmes continued.

"Well . . . they said she was a harlot," Johansson confided. "That she enticed men to come home with her after spending the evening in a pub, watching for a man carrying a lot of money. Once she got him home, she entertained him and then robbed him. Her father knocked the fellow out with a club and carted him back to the pub in a wagon. He left him at the back door so patrons think he had passed out drunk."

"Where did all this talk originate. Who told you these things?" Holmes wanted to know.

"I heard it from customers at the pubs, and they heard it from the innkeepers, who were the only ones who would listen to the men who were robbed," Johansson averred. "The police were never interested."

"I believe you have solved the murders, Adam," Holmes postulated. "The dead men were the ones who did not survive the clubbing."

"Will I get the credit when Dr. Watson writes his story?" Johansson wondered.

"Your name will be prominently mentioned, I am certain," Holmes promised. "Thank you. You're free to return to your card game."

On our way out of the cemetery, the deputy constable turned to Holmes and inquired, "It's a good theory about the dead, Mr. Holmes, but how do we prove it true?"

"I have a plan, but we cannot execute it until well after nightfall," Holmes proclaimed.

The remainder of the day was consumed by the three of us, working separately, to locate and interview the surviving victims of the robberies, their identities provided by the innkeepers.

One of the victims, Nigel Culp, identified his attacker as Miss Hank's father and described his encounter with both of them. Mr. Culp said Miss Hank lured him to their home on the farm after he won a considerable sum of cash at a dice table in the Lion's Den Pub. He went on to say that Augustus Hank was introduced to him by the daughter and followed him up the stairs on the way to Miss Hank's room. Mr. Hank then hit him from behind when Gwen Hank, who was leading the way, turned to speak to him at the door. He said he lost consciousness briefly but regained it in the wagon when Mr. Hank was throwing him off at the rear entrance to the pub. When he came to his senses, Mr. Culp realised all his winnings were gone. His story was like all the rest – in those days it did not good to report something like this to the police, so the crimes continued unchecked. At the time, no one ever thought to connect the assaults to the missing men.

The interviews concluded in late evening as we met up again at the constabulary. Stanley was excited to be able to prove that Hank and his daughter were complicit in the assaults and thefts, but he was disappointed that proof of their involvement in the murders had yet to be established beyond a reasonable doubt.

"I am relying on your plan to bring about the impossible," Stanley moaned when the three of us sat at a dinner table in one of the inns that Holmes had visited during the afternoon.

"Not the impossible, but rather the probable," Holmes stated confidently. "Will a confession from Augustus Hank and his daughter satisfy your craving for evidence?" he queried to tantalise Stanley.

"That sounds more like the impossible to me," the deputy constable admitted. "How will you ever get them to cooperate?"

"With the element in this vial," Holmes boasted, holding up a glass object. "I formulated my plan last night at Baker Street, anticipating the outcome."

"What is in it?" Stanley demanded.

"A concoction containing white phosphorus," Holmes revealed.

"What are you going to do with it?" Stanley prodded.

"Wait until the stroke of midnight and see for yourself," Holmes answered coyly.

On the train, time passed quickly as Holmes regaled Stanley with stories of exploits that I, too, had never heard before. At eleven-thirty, we arrived at our destination and Holmes interrupted his story to announce that it was time to take a cab and make our way to the Hank's address.

"The sky is clear and the moon is full," Holmes proclaimed as the carriage came to a halt outside the dwelling. "Favorable conditions for our mission,"

Before he alighted from the vehicle, Holmes took the waxy phosphorus from the vial and rubbed it on his hair, his face, and his hands. To Stanley's amazement, Holmes glowed in the moonlight, giving himself a ghost-like appearance. "Now follow me into the house quietly, so as not to awaken the occupants," he ordered.

"This is highly irregular, Mr. Holmes," Stanley remarked, "but let us proceed."

Holmes picked the lock on the front door and led the way in the dark through the parlour in the direction of the old man's room. He stopped at the entrance and whispered instructions that once inside, we should find a dark corner in which to stand and not make any noise. He turned the doorknob and tip-toed inside, positioning himself at the foot of the bed. The moonlight through the window provided enough to illuminate his hair, his face, and his hands. Stanley and I crouched low in the corner so we wouldn't risk being seen when old Hank awakened at the sound of Holmes calling his name.

Hank stirred for a moment and opened his eyes to view a spirit from beyond the grave.

"W-w-who are you, and what do you want?" Hank, in a low voice, begged to know.

"I am a specter here to take you to Hell," Holmes replied in a deep voice.

"I won't go with you!" Hank protested. "I'm still alive!"

"I can change that," Holmes informed him.

"Don't kill me!" Hank pleaded. "Please don't kill me!"

"But you killed me!" Holmes seethed. "With your club . . . ."

"It was an accident, I swear. I only meant to knock you out," Hank contended.

"And what of the others? Were they accidents, too?" Holmes went on.

"Accidents, all of them," Hank insisted.

"Nonetheless, we are all dead before our time because of your greed," Holmes chided.

"Oh, please spare me your fate!" Hank quaked.

"I shall, on one condition," Holmes growled.

"Anything!" Hank pledged. "I'll do anything!"

"When the police come back, tell them the whole story and ask for mercy," Holmes proposed.

"All right," the killer agreed. "All right! Anything you say!"

"Now close your eyes and keep them shut until after you have recited *The Lord's Prayer* aloud, once for each of the eight men you murdered," Holmes directed.

Immediately we heard Hank praying, so we crept silently out of the room, through the parlour, and then through the front door.

We spoke not a word until after we had walked to the end of the block. Then Stanley was the first to express himself:

"You are a genius, Mr. Holmes! That was a magnificent performance. I shall return with stenographer and we shall have a signed confession by morning!"

"Don't neglect to pressure the daughter to admit to her role," Holmes cautioned. "I'm sure that she will cooperate, knowing that her father is prepared to face the music."

We left Stanley and continued on to Baker Street and went to sleep.

It was mid-morning when I arose from my slumber, my nostrils detecting the aroma of fresh-brewed coffee and bacon that Mrs. Hudson brought to our quarters with scrambled eggs and toast, topped by homemade grape jelly. "You deserve a reward for keeping the most inconvenient hours on the planet," she scoffed. "I'd wager that neither of you has had a decent breakfast since you've been trapesing off here and there the last few of days."

"Not nearly as decent as what you prepare," I complimented her.

"It goes without saying, my dear woman," Holmes chimed in, "that you take care of us as good as our mothers would."

"Oh, come now, gentlemen, don't make me blush," she warned.

We finished our meal and hired a hansom to take us to Charing Cross, where we boarded a train to Surrey, curious if Stanley accomplished his task. At the constabulary, he pointed to the lockup, where Gwen and Augustus Hank were pacing the floor. Here is how Stanley described the morning:

"Old man Hank owned up to the killings, just like he promised the ghost that he would, but the daughter was obstinate, until I let her read the statements of the robbery victims. Then she confessed, too. She claimed that she was a decent sort until the time her father murdered her lover out of fear that he would marry her and take her away. The brutal and senseless loss of her one true love turned her into a felon, she avowed in her sworn confession."

"Well done. A fine job that will hold up in court," Holmes congratulated.

"My captain thinks so as well, thanks to you, Mr. Holmes," Stanley crowed.

At the trial, the jury deliberated for only an hour before rendering a verdict of guilty upon charges of murder, robbery, and conspiracy. The judge, known for his leniency, spared Hank from the gallows, taking into consideration his age and deteriorating mental condition. Instead, he was to spend the rest of his life in prison.

The same fate befell his only child, Gwen, who, after three months of confinement, took her own life by drowning herself in bath water.

Holmes and I received word of Gwen's death from Stanley, who came to Baker Street with the news and to advise us of his promotion to constable as a result of his success in solving the case.

An Actor and a Rare One
by David Marcum

"**M**r. Holmes, my country is in your debt!"

Knowing that my friend was uncomfortable with public praise, the little Belgian policeman made no effort to embrace Holmes – or worse, kiss him upon both cheeks. Instead, he held out his hand, a gesture quite acceptable to all concerned. Holmes shook it gravely. Then the policeman turned toward me and did the same, while Holmes shook hands with Count von Und Zu Grafenstein, who was standing beside the Belgian. Then I shook hands with the German, who then pivoted toward the Belgian. As they gravely thanked one another, that only left Holmes and me. Keeping to the spirit of the occasion, we shook hands as well.

Meanwhile, watching from eight or ten paces away was the Nihilist, Klopman, firmly ensconced in a pair of manacles, and each arm gripped by one of a pair of stolid and expressionless constables. What they thought of all this *bonhomie* was their own secret.

The Count took a last contemptuous look at Klopman, who had just been prevented from killing him, and then turned without another glance, signaling for his gleaming *Aachener* motor car to pull forward. A liveried servant leapt out and held the rear door. He slid in smoothly, demonstrating his early fencing training, and within moments the vehicle had sped past the village church and was out of sight.

As the constables marched the prisoner to a waiting carriage for transport to Exeter, and so on to London, the Belgian touched his magnificent mustache, seemingly a compulsive trait, and said, his eyes twinkling, "Ah, *mon amies*, I believe that the Count will cause us trouble. Possibly what you accomplished here today, Mr. Holmes – saving his life, and more importantly, his honor – will count for something when our countries are one day at war."

"Surely you don't think it will come to that?" I said. It was hard to credit the idea, standing there in the only intersection of a remote village in the English West Country. Still, I knew that Holmes's brother, Mycroft, had been warning of such for years, and that Sherlock Holmes himself often assisted his brother in various matters designed to delay, if not actually prevent, just such a conflict. That was how we had become involved in this affair in the first place, beginning with a simple dinner in London, and ending here, with the trap sprung in the Grimpen Post Office, in the heart of Dartmoor.

"Ah, *Monsieur* P-----," said Holmes, "I have no crystal ball. We both know that the fates of nations can turn on a single breeze. For want of a nail, and all that rot. Who can say what twists may occur between tomorrow and tomorrow and tomorrow? Sufficient unto the day."

"Good Lord, Holmes," I said with a smile. "Can you use at least one more cliché?"

The little Belgian policeman laughed and indicated that he would visit us in London within the week, when the rest of Klopman's group had been rounded up. We had already told him of our plan to stay in Dartmoor for a further day or so. "To revisit old triumphs?" *Monsieur* P----- had asked with a smile.

Holmes winced. "Rather, to revisit a few old friends."

As we watched P-----'s carriage trundle away, the silence of our location became apparent. Perhaps silence is too strong of a description. The wind sighed through the tall trees and the grass in the nearby church cemetery. From a distance floated the sound of cattle. I knew from past experience that it wouldn't be unusual for them to make their way into the Grimpen street, wandering and grazing along the very walls of the church.

With unspoken agreement, Holmes and I walked up the hill from the post office. Old Carruthers, the Grimpen postmaster, had allowed us to remain in hiding there until Klopman could make his play against the Count. Klopman hadn't realized that Holmes had diffused his infernal device the previous night, when we had arrived in Dartmoor in secret. The poor radical had never had a chance, but we had needed to let him have the appearance of making his attack so that he could be stopped in the presence of the Count. This crucial act had to occur in order to provide legitimacy for the set of forged documents that had been cleverly prepared by Mycroft Holmes's agents and then stolen by the Count – with him thinking that he had done so without our knowledge. This had been done so that the Count would carry the false papers back to Germany, with the mistaken belief that he had accomplished something important for his own country while getting one over on the British. As usual, Mycroft Holmes had been seventeen steps ahead of him, leading the Count down a carefully devised trail that he would never observe or understand.

We made our way into the Grimpen teashop, a low white building across the street from the church of St. Pancras. I glanced at its tall four-spired tower and recalled with a smile the tales of the Devil's visit during a seventeenth century thunder storm. The Lord of Evil had certainly been active in those years of the mid-1600's, what with supposedly collecting the souls of sinners from a church service, and another occasion when he

265

arranged for his own pet hound to tear out the throat of black-hearted Hugo Baskerville.

As we ordered our tea and a plate of biscuits, served with a little pot of rich Devonshire cream, I considered raising the topic of the local legends with Holmes, but stopped myself. After his return to England in '94, following three years of absence and supposed death, I had refrained from publishing any of his adventures, upon his insistence. However, the previous year, he had reluctantly lifted the embargo, for reasons of his own, and I had, with my literary agent's assistance, written up our experiences here in Dartmoor, when Sir Henry Baskerville's life had been threatened by the supposed return of the Devil's hound. As Holmes had feared, the story's appearance in *The Strand* had led to all sorts of attention of the sort that he wished to avoid. The concluding chapters had been published the preceding spring, concurrent with the collected book edition, and since then, to Holmes's way of thinking, far too many of his current clients had made reference to it.

Our tea was just cool enough to drink when the shop door opened. In walked our old friend, Dr. Mortimer. "I had heard you were in the village!" he cried, approaching our table. Then, with a mock expression of stern accusation, he said, arms akimbo, "Is it possible that you would have visited without saying hello?"

We greeted him warmly. "I assure you, Doctor," said Holmes, urging the man to sit, "it was our intention to call as soon as we finished our refreshment. We have been up all night springing a trap – successfully, I might add – and we now plan to spend several relaxing days in the area. We already have rooms reserved at the Riverside Inn in Coombe Tracey."

"Nonsense!" cried Mortimer. "You shall certainly stay with me and my wife."

He refused to take no for an answer, and the upshot was that within the hour, we were sitting around the comfortable fire in the doctor's parlour while his wife fussed about, feeding us again, in spite of our insistence that we had just partaken.

I glanced around the room at Mrs. Mortimer's various spiritualistic appurtenances, standing on various shelves and tabletops. I recalled that she'd always had a turn for that sort of thing. It should have been no surprise when she finally finished bustling about and settled near her husband saying, "Have you told them?"

"No, my dear. They are here to rest."

She looked from her husband to Holmes. "I sensed that you would be arriving. The troubles have started again."

"My dear – " interrupted Mortimer, but Holmes raised a hand.

266

"Please, Mrs. Mortimer," he said. "Do go on."

She looked at her husband, who gave a patient nod. "At the Hall. Baskerville Hall. They say that there is something . . . unusual happening."

"Indeed?" said Holmes, raising an eyebrow. "Surely not a new set of footprints belonging to a giant hound? And certainly nothing worse – I would have seen it in the newspapers. In any case, after the last time, more than a dozen years ago, I would expect that the Devil's agents would refrain from resuming their activities. What has happened?"

"Writings," Mrs. Mortimer replied firmly. "That's what it is. Spirit writing at the manor house. On the outside walls."

"What does it say?"

Mrs. Mortimer started to speak, but her husband interrupted. "Rubbish. Someone is scribbling quotes from the old Baskerville manuscript." He looked at me, as if wary of offending me. "Since the publication of your chronicle, Doctor, there has been an increase in visitors to the moor, wanting a look at where the Hound supposedly roamed – the original of legend, and also the more corporeal version that was killed when it attacked Sir Henry." He pursed his lips. "Some of the local merchants are encouraging it."

"What does Sir Henry say?" I asked. "Surely he can get to the bottom of this."

Dr. Mortimer looked uncomfortable. "Sir Henry and his family rarely stay at the Hall anymore. They travel, a great deal. We . . . well, *I* had hoped that Sir Henry would use his influence to improve the lives of the poor folk upon the moor, but after the attack of the Hound, he was never quite the same. Right now, the Baskerville family is in Canada, leaving the manor in the care of the staff. I've agreed to exercise some responsibility as needed, but much of the day-to-day running of the place falls on the Greaves, a husband and wife who came after the Barrymores departed."

"And they are worried about these curious drawings?" asked Holmes.

"Not Mr. Greaves, I can assure you," answered the doctor. "But as for his wife . . . ."

"She is . . . unnerved," responded Mrs. Mortimer. She looked at Holmes with an earnest expression. "I had seen that help would come, Mr. Holmes. In the cards. The portents and signs were unmistakable. When you and Dr. Watson arrived with James this morning, I knew that it was true. Can you determine out what's happening?"

Dr. Mortimer tried to interrupt her several times, but she stubbornly finished her thought. Then, before the doctor could offer a counter-argument, Holmes said, "Yes, madam. I would be happy to look into it."

The next morning found us in Mortimer's carriage, making our way across the ancient dirt road through the moor, heading toward Baskerville Hall. The October sky reminded me of slate – when I could see it, as there was an intermittent bank of fog that trapped and then released us as we progressed steadily onward. I had nearly forgotten how difficult travel across such undulating landscape could be from a perch in a carriage, which swayed and pitched unexpectedly without cease. I recalled the day when I had first come down to Dartmoor with Dr. Mortimer and Sir Henry, when we were sometimes forced to climb down and help push the cart up particularly steep slopes.

That morning, Dr. Mortimer's route was much less rigorous. Occasionally we would encroach upon one or two of the wild moorland ponies, who had no fear of us, simply shifting out of our way and watching curiously as their brother in bondage pulled past with his head hung low. I wondered if they shared some secret communication, and which of them felt more blessed – the one who had to work, but was guaranteed shelter and care and regular sustenance, or the ponies, who faced the bitter weather with the fair in exchange for their freedom, but lived with feast or famine based upon the season, while listening for the occasional high whistle of terror when one of their fellows wandered into the Great Grimpen Mire –always hoping that the same fate wouldn't befall them.

I shook my head. This place inspired such thoughts. I couldn't blame Sir Henry too much for abandoning it.

As we rode, Holmes – who had refused to discuss the matter further on the previous day – questioned Dr. Mortimer about the scribblings. "As I said, they have been taken from the old manuscript, written to tell of the Curse of the Baskervilles, and the coming of the Hound. You recall it, Mr. Holmes. I read it to you in your rooms in Baker Street."

"And where is the manuscript kept now?"

"In one of the chest drawers in Sir Henry's study."

"Where have the quotes been found?"

"On the garden wall, just outside the moor-gate in the Yew Alley, which runs to the summer house."

"Yes. It was there that you first saw the footprints of a gigantic hound. Has there been any similar manifestation this time?"

"Not a thing, Mr. Holmes. I'm embarrassed to say that I checked. However, it is clearly a human hand at work."

"And you know this because . . . ?"

"A servant of the Devil would not use common white chalk to scrawl a message!"

"The Devil's servants take many forms," I said, somewhat teasingly, but with the knowledge that my statement was also true.

"There have been three instances of this *graffiti*? What did the first two say?"

"The first time, nearly two weeks ago, simply said, '*The same Justice which punishes sin may also most graciously forgive it*'."

"Hmm," I said. "One might think that was more likely written by some itinerant missionary than an agent of darkness."

"And the second?" asked Holmes.

"That was a bit more grim. '*Many of the family have been unhappy in their deaths, which have been sudden, bloody, and mysterious.*' I'll confess that I didn't recognize the first quote when I was initially told of it. But the second was very familiar, leading me to check the manuscript. That's when I realized that the first quote was from the same source."

"And now there is a third," said Holmes. "I take it that your wife had heard of its appearance, but not its content, through the typical country lines of communication?"

"Yes. She is friends with Mrs. Dobbs, the housekeeper at Sir Milton Frieze's home, who is in turn is friends with Mrs. Greaves at the Hall."

He fell silent, wrestling with the pony and the cart. Soon we passed over a small rise, giving a view into a cup-like depression. I could never understand why the original Baskervilles had built there – surrounded on all sides by land of a higher elevation, the place would have been nearly indefensible. Through a trick of the constant wind, the trees were stunted and bent, doing nothing to hide the high thin towers of the Hall.

Dr. Mortimer maneuvered the carriage down and through the massive wrought iron lodge gates, entwined with the boars' head crests of the Baskervilles.

We came to a stop and found our way to the ground. My legs were weak from wrestling to stay seated. I looked forward to getting inside, and perhaps obtaining something warm to drink, but Holmes set off around the building, obviously heading for the wall at the moor-gate. Dr. Mortimer and I shared rueful smiles – he had also clearly looked forward to entering the house – and then we followed after Holmes.

When we caught up to him, he was standing back from the wall, reading the latest quotation: "*Forbear from crossing the moor in those dark hours when the powers of evil are exalted.*" I recalled hearing Dr. Mortimer read those words in our Baker Street sitting room, and their chilling effect now was no less than then.

Holmes glanced at the ground, and then began a more thorough examination, peering closely at both the white chalk letters and the grass beneath them at the base of the wall. Finally satisfied, he indicated that we should proceed inside.

As we moved along the outside of the Yew Alley to circumnavigate the house and reach the main door, my distasteful look at the fine old yew trees didn't go unnoticed by Dr. Mortimer. The trees, so well-kept when I had stayed here with Sir Henry years before, were now shaggy and ragged. "I'm afraid that the work is a bit too much for just Mr. Greaves," he explained.

"If they aren't shaped up soon," I said, with a bit more of a critical tone than I should have liked, "it will be too late."

"I agree," said Dr. Mortimer ruefully. "They will be so overgrown that cutting them back to the proper shape might kill them. I suppose that I need to spend a bit more time checking on the place, as Sir Henry's agent. Perhaps I can hire a man in Grimpen or Coombe Tracey."

We walked silently the rest of the way to the front door, whereupon Dr. Mortimer rang the bell. "I have a key," he explained, "but there is no need to unduly upset the Greaves by simply barging in as if I own the place."

With that, the great door opened, and we were faced with a tall lugubrious man in his early forties. He was dressed in worn but clean work clothes, and not formally for house duties. Clearly he was not a butler.

"Mr. Greaves," said Mortimer, stepping past him. Holmes and I followed. "Good morning."

The man nodded. He had a careworn look upon his face, and vertical lines between his eyes and bracketing his mouth that gave a hint of dissatisfaction and opportunities long missed. "You'll have come about the latest writing, then."

"We have. My wife heard about it from Sir Milton's housekeeper. Why was I not notified?"

"It's harmless, I'm sure. We felt no need."

Dr. Mortimer appeared ready to make a rejoinder, but at that moment, an aproned woman came in from the back of the manor – clearly Mrs. Greaves. Approximately the same age as her husband, she had the same feeling of dissatisfaction, but hers was rather from having too many tasks for too short of a day. "Dr. Mortimer," she said, with the end of his name almost sounding like a question.

"These men," explained the doctor, "are my friends, Sherlock Holmes and Dr. Watson. They happen to be down here on other business, and I asked them to look into the matter of the chalk writing." I thought that a rather convenient adjustment, as it was his wife who had requested our help, and he had opposed it.

"Nothing to tell," said Mr. Greaves. "There are always gypsies upon the moor. Just a few weeks ago, a couple of them wandered in, looking for

270

work. It wasn't my place to hire them, so I sent them on their way. Not long after, the writing started. It's just their way of getting back at me."

"Do you then contend that the gypsies have read the story of the Hound in *The Strand* magazine, and that they are quoting from the Baskerville manuscript?"

"I couldn't say, sir. Their ways are mysterious."

At that moment, I noticed a movement in the darkness of a doorway leading to the rear of the building. Mrs. Greaves saw my change of focus and turned to look that way as well. A frown quickly crossed her face.

Of course it didn't escape Holmes's notice. "Ah, yes. The child. I planned to ask about that."

"Child?" exclaimed Dr. Mortimer. "What child?"

"Approximately ten years of age, I should think," said Holmes. "Probably male, although I'm not completely certain. Yours, Mrs. Greaves?"

"They have no children," said Dr. Mortimer, a frown across his face. "You have a child here?" he continued, directing his question to the housekeeper.

She twisted her apron in her hands. "My sister Anna's boy," she said. "He's down from London, staying with us for a couple of months. They are . . . things are a bit tight with them right now. Her husband's job . . . he's a mining engineer. He worked in South Africa, but had to come back seven or eight years ago because of the Boers. Since then, they've had their ups and downs. Right now Basil – he's the oldest, and just turned ten last June, as you say – well, it helps them to have him stay with us for a bit. Just temporary, sir."

"Might we speak to him?" asked Holmes.

"Oh, my," said Mrs. Greaves. "It's the writing! You think he wrote the sayings on the wall?"

Holmes nodded. "I believe so. But I don't think that he meant any harm. Can we speak to him?" he asked again.

She nodded, and Mr. Greaves turned toward the door. "You! Wart! Come here!"

But there was no response. The boy had apparently fled.

Mr. Greaves said, "I'll go find him."

"No matter," replied Holmes. "We can look. If you can tell us where his room is located, we'll start there, and let you continue about your regular duties."

Clearly Mr. Greaves wanted to join the hunt, but he simply nodded and explained the location of Basil's room – coincidentally, the same that I had occupied when I resided here while investigating the Hound.

Holmes led us upstairs while Mortimer muttered something about a breach of trust. In just a moment, we were in the room, which hadn't changed since my own sojourn here. A quick examination revealed nothing out of the ordinary. I don't know what Holmes expected to find, but he seemed a bit vexed. However, he pointed at some of the boy's clothing. "Notice the height, Watson. A bit tall for his age."

"And you knew there was a child, and his approximate age, from . . . how, exactly?"

"Clearly, the chalk marks were written at an eye level of a person around four-and-a-half feet in height. This was confirmed by the downward trend of the letters as they were written from left to right. A taller person leaning over to write at that level would have constructed the words at a different slant – as would an adult dropping to his knees to write the messages. Finally, the footprints in the grass, and the length of the stride, confirmed the height and likely age of the miscreant."

I started to reprimand this strong characterization of the boy, but I saw that he had a twinkle in his eye.

Holmes turned to Dr. Mortimer. "Before we continue our quest to find the boy, can I see the original Baskerville manuscript once more?"

"Hmm? Certainly, certainly. Follow me."

He led us to Sir Henry's study, now quite a bit different than when he had first taken possession of it. It reflected the current owner of the Hall, and I hoped that he had infused enough of himself here, and that the estate had done the same back to him, that he wouldn't stay away forever.

Dr. Mortimer opened a chest and pulled out the old document, which he handed to Holmes. Unfolding it carefully, my friend turned it this and that way in the light before calling us over. "There," he said. "On the edges." And we could easily see a set of boyish fingerprints, recorded in chalk. Dr. Mortimer harrumphed and brushed them off before refolding and replacing the manuscript in the drawer. "A breach of trust," he muttered once again.

"I think," said Holmes, "we must have an amnesty in that direction. After all, it isn't unreasonable for Mrs. Greaves to take in her nephew for a few months, and one cannot question a boy's high spirits – and there are worse things that he might have done! Why, if I were in his situation at that age, I would have likely behaved in exactly the same way."

"But the writing!" exclaimed Dr. Mortimer. "He could have panicked the countryside!"

"I think not. And I expect that aspect didn't enter his thinking. More likely, he was simply bored."

He led us through the house to the kitchen, where we found the Greaves conferring silently. When asked where next to look, Mr. Greaves confirmed that the boy seemed to spend a great deal of time in the barn. "Then that shall be our next stop," said Holmes with a nod.

A quick walk brought us to the ancient building. We spread out, looking for some sort of indication of young Basil. The hall's horse watched with patience as we prowled about his domain.

In a moment, Holmes called us over. There was some sort of closet near the back, and he had pulled open the door. Inside, we saw a small battered desk. We stepped inside, with just enough room for the three of us. I was amazed to see, on top of the desk, a scattering of *Strand* magazines. Beside them were hardbound copies of my narratives relating Holmes's investigations, including a copy of *The Hound of the Baskervilles*, published by Newnes just six months before.

There beside them was also a notepad and pen. Written on the pad was the line, "*The coming of the hound which is said to have plagued the family so sorely ever since*" – apparently the next quote to appear on the wall. Beside it was a magnifying glass. And centered on the desk in a place of honor was a deerstalker hat.

"He's watching us," Holmes said softly, and then louder. "Come out, Basil."

In a moment, we heard the lad climb down from the hayloft. He presented himself with an engaging mix of confidence and sheepishness – and I must say, a bit of awe.

"Mr. Holmes," he said, his voice already giving hints of deepening into maturity. "I . . . I thought that you were dead. 'The Final Problem' said – "

" – That was not the rest of the story. Dr. Watson hasn't yet published the tale of how I survived." Holmes leaned against the desk, crossing his arms. "You wrote on the wall." He said it as a matter of fact, and the boy nodded.

"When I found out that I would come here, to Dartmoor, and to the very house where *The Hound* took place, I was so excited! But then, when I arrived, Sir Henry was gone, and my aunt and uncle . . . well . . . they didn't really want me. There are no other children, and nothing to do. I was so bored. I . . . I started to play at being a detective, and would make my own clues about the case to act out." He lowered his eyes. "I'm sorry."

"Don't be," said Holmes, rising and then taking a step toward the boy, who tilted his head in order to face Holmes squarely. "It's completely understandable. But next time, consider how your actions might appear to others. This is an area with a long history of frightening legends. Part of being a detective is remaining aware of all aspects of a situation, and trying to see what will happen when this or that action is taken. And of course, behaving with honor at all times. In your continuing work as a detective, will you keep that in mind?"

The boy nodded, wide-eyed.

"Then I see no reason why you cannot continue to operate your agency here in Dartmoor. We shall be associates, and as such, I expect that you will communicate with me if you need assistance with any cases that you take on. Agreed?"

The boy swallowed. "Agreed." And they shook hands.

As we left, I pushed the closet door shut, and saw what had attracted Holmes's attention to the doorway. Scratched on it, at a ten-year-old's eye level, was something that looked like "*The* [Unintelligible] *Rathbone Detective Agency*".

We had a few words of explanation with the Greaves, who were given to understand that the boy should not be punished. Then, with a nod at the now-beaming and deerstalkered Basil, we climbed into Dr. Mortimer's cart for the return to his own residence.

He seemed to be a man with a new project. "Poor lonely boy! If only I had known. I shall find a way to get him involved in local activities while he is down here. Perhaps I can taking him upon around with me – he might end up being interested in medicine. Become a doctor! Or I can introduce him to the Vicar at St. Pancras. They are preparing their play for the fall festival. The boy can participate in that – get a taste of acting."

"Or," countered Holmes, "he might decide to continue his pursuit of a career as a detective."

I smiled. "He might even become known as the next Sherlock Holmes!"

My friend gave a barking laugh. "He's welcome to it!"

I stayed in touch with the lad, exchanging letters as he grew. When he reached adulthood, he neither became a doctor nor an actor nor a detective. Rather, in 1910, he became an insurance agent. However, he soon took to the stage after all, possibly pointed in that direction by his participation in the vicar's humble drama.

The Great War that Holmes, his brother Mycroft, and I had labored for so long to delay or prevent occurred anyway. Young Basil Rathbone's modest acting career came to a halt when he enlisted in 1916. He served with distinction, and used those acting skills – and dare I also say, detective skills as well – when carrying out many daring daytime missions behind-the-lines, literally disguised as *trees*, in order to obtain valuable information. For this, and for other brave actions as well, he was awarded the Military Cross for bravery on 9 September, 1918.

Just yesterday, I saw some mention of him in *The London Gazette*, and was moved to ask a friend in the Ministry about the details. The entire story is amazing, and not mine to tell. I don't know what's in store for young Basil Rathbone, but I believe that some of the skill and bravery that he exhibited upon the battlefield can be partially attributed to the continuing interest in his education that was shown by my friend, Sherlock Holmes, beginning on that long ago day in October 1902.

JHW
8 November, 1918

13166 SUPPLEMENT TO THE LONDON GAZETTE, 7 NOVEMBER 1918.

were all killed or taken prisoners. His example to his men was splendid throughout the operations.

———

Lt. (A./Capt.) John Armstrong Pratt, L'pool R., Spec. Res.
For conspicuous gallantry and devotion to duty during a raid. He showed great pluck and dash as a company commander, and set a splendid example to his men, being one of the first to enter the enemy line. For three nights previously he had reconnoitred the ground.

———

T./2nd Lt. Hector Lloyd Price, attd. S.W Bord.
For conspicuous gallantry and good leadership in charge of a patrol. He worked his way through enemy advanced posts, approaching the machine-gun posts in rear, and successfully locating four of them. Though heavily fired on from front and rear, he withdrew his patrol safely back to his lines, having attained his object.

———

Lt. Phillip St. John Basil Rathbone, L'pool R.
For conspicuous daring and resource on patrol. On one occasion, while inside the hostile wire, he came face to face with one of the enemy, whom he at once shot. This raised the alarm, and an intense fire was opened, but he crept through the entanglements with his three men and got safely back. The result of his patrolling was a thorough knowledge of the locality and strength of all enemy posts in the vicinity.

Capt. Thomas Purvis Reay, W. York. R.
For conspicuous gallantry and good leadership. He showed great initiative in an attack, and when the position had been captured he at once consolidated the position. He moved about under heavy fire, encouraging his men, and it was chiefly due to his skill and untiring efforts that the enemy counter-attack was defeated.

———

Lt. (A./Capt.) Sydney Ernest Redfern,

275

The Silver Bullet
by Dick Gillman

Chapter I – The Perfect Weapon?

It was towards the end of 1902, some little time after my departure from Baker Street, that the peculiar case of "The Silver Bullet" came to my attention.

I had ventured out from my home with the intention of visiting both Carlin's, the tobacconist's, and also, on my return, to call upon Holmes in Baker Street. Clutching my precious purchases, I had barely crossed the threshold at 221b when three shots rang out in swift succession, the sounds clearly emanating from our old rooms.

Having little regard for the limitations to my gait caused by my old war wounds, I bounded up the stairs and burst through the sitting room door. Holmes had his back to me and was walking calmly towards his armchair, his still smoking revolver hanging loosely by his side.

"Holmes! Are you injured?" I cried, between desperate gasps for air. Without turning, he continued towards his chair before deigning to raise his free hand and waving it, indicating his continued good health in a manner I thought to be most dismissive.

On reaching his armchair, he sat and scribbled something in his notebook before looking in my direction and then replying, in a most irritatingly crisp and obscure manner, "Hardly! You know, Watson, the work on kinetic energy undertaken by Leibnitz is really quite enlightening."

Holmes then appeared to look past me and I could only stand and gawp as he raised his revolver and fired once more. Instinctively, I dived to one side and several seconds passed before I felt able to stand upright once more. Looking towards Holmes, I sought to follow his gaze and was dumfounded to observe a bullet-riddled side of pork hanging from the hat-stand. This, in turn, was held upright by a coarse, sand-filled, Hessian sack.

"Great heavens, Holmes! Desist!" I shouted, as he cocked the revolver and took aim once more. Heeding my cry, he carefully lowered the hammer of his pistol and looked impassively towards me, barely raising an eyebrow at my obvious concern.

Placing his revolver to one side, he gestured for me to sit, before responding to my questioning look as I inclined my head towards the pig's carcass. "Ah! It is some personal research that I am undertaking regarding a somewhat novel method of murder that I have envisaged."

Feeling somewhat thankful that he had, for the moment, ceased his experimentation, I was now intrigued. "I take it that you are using the side of pork to represent the human torso?"

Holmes nodded slowly as he reached for his pipe. "Indeed so, for pork flesh closely resembles that of a human." Holmes smiled thinly and having filled his pipe, he lit it before then waving the stem in my direction, adding, "I am intrigued by the possibility of a new, and, perhaps, undetectable form of ammunition."

Holmes waved his pipe stem in the direction of the dining table and I noticed, for the first time, two small bowls of ice in which several cartridges were seen to be residing. Whilst this was indeed curious in itself, it was the nature of the bullet that fascinated me. Rising from my chair, I observed that in place of the usual snub-nosed, boxer round, there was what appeared to be a bullet fashioned from some florid, pink, frozen material. This, on closer inspection, I determined to be meat!

Frowning, I turned to Holmes, asking, "Might I ask whether this, err . . . 'meat' round, actually works, Holmes?" I stammered.

Holmes gave a brief nod, saying, "Somewhat, at close range. However, the friction between the frozen round and the barrel of the pistol, combined with the heat from the charge, does tend to thaw it." Holmes now paused, his eyes aglow. "But imagine, Watson, a bloody gunshot wound, but with no discernible bullet!" I pursed my lips and nodded slowly whilst I considered this. Accompanying Holmes, I moved to examine both the size and extent of the wounds on the pig carcass. These had been inflicted by Holmes from a variety of distances, each being marked by a chalk line upon the floorboards of the sitting room.

It was during our discussion as to whether the "pork round" could be identified as something other than the victim's own flesh, that the doorbell rang in the hallway below. On hearing this, Holmes paused, raising his hand as he listened intently, hoping to catch a snippet of the conversation between his visitor and Mrs. Hudson.

As I watched, a thin smile brightened Holmes's face as he clearly recognized the footsteps sounding upon the stairs to his sitting room. Even as the slightest of knocks was heard upon the door, Holmes called out, "It's all right, Mrs. Hudson. The good inspector need not be announced."

There now appeared to be a few moments of confusion upon the landing outside the closed door. Whilst this was happening, I murmured to myself, questioningly, "Lestrade?" to which Holmes smiled, wryly, in reply and gave a single nod.

The door finally opened and the head and shoulders of the familiar visitor peered round its edge, almost as though he were uncertain as to whether he was allowed to enter or not.

Holmes had returned to his leather armchair and, with a smile upon his lips, rose, and beckoned to the seemingly timid figure, "Come in, Lestrade. Pay no heed to my parlour games."

Lestrade entered the room and looked about him. On seeing the bullet-riddled side of pork and detecting the smell of spent ammunition, he asked, somewhat nervously, "Morning, Mr. Holmes . . . .Oh, and to you, Dr. Watson. I hope I'm not disturbing you?"

Holmes raised a hand, saying, "No, no, it's quite all right, Lestrade. Watson and I remain good friends. How might I be of service?"

Lestrade pressed his lips together and nodded to himself before turning and pointing towards the side of pork hanging from the coat-stand. "It seems as though my luck is in and I have, indeed, come to exactly the right place." Lestrade remained silent for a few seconds before continuing, seemingly in confirmation, "Yes, I have a very strange case that would benefit from your attention, Mr. Holmes."

Holmes reached again for his pipe and drew strongly upon it to encourage the tobacco within to ignite further. From his keen expression, it was clear that Holmes's curiosity was now piqued, asking, "How so, Lestrade?"

Lestrade moved to sit on our red velvet sofa and, once installed, he reached into his jacket pocket and took from it his official police notebook. "It's like this, Mr. Holmes. Two days ago, we were called to a house in a decent area of Westminster. On entering the premises, we found a lady shot dead." Holmes nodded slowly and then took his pipe from his mouth, waving the stem towards the inspector as a sign for him to continue.

Lestrade now licked his thumb and riffled through a few pages of his notebook before adding, "The lady in question was the wife of the occupier, a gentleman named Mr. Christopher Mallin. When he turned up, I found him a bit of an odd cove. He seemed surprisingly jolly, given that he had just been informed that we had found his wife shot dead on the sitting room floor." Lestrade looked more serious as he added, "He is not the kind of grieving husband what we usually comes across in these situations, Mr. Holmes."

I frowned and looked towards Lestrade, asking, "What do you mean?"

Lestrade pursed his lips before replying, "Well, he seemed a bit up and down, sort of mousy one minute and then a bit arrogant like, the next. Although, I have to say, he didn't strike me as the kind of bloke who would shoot his Missus – but what a mess that was!" Lestrade pointed a thin finger towards the pig carcass, saying, "Makes your pig look like a fine pin cushion, Mr. Holmes!"

Up until this point, Holmes had merely been courteous as he listened to Lestrade's tale but now his eyes burned as he asked, "The wounds – were they greatly dissimilar to those?"

Lestrade gave a dry laugh. "Yes, Mr. Holmes. There was just the one, but you could almost put your fist into it, and the exit wound was nearly the size of a tea plate!"

I considered this for a moment before asking, "Given the size of the wound, might it have come from the discharge of a shotgun at close range?"

Lestrade's lips were down turned as he shook his head. "No, Doctor. There were no powder burns on the victim's clothes and no pellets. Just a big hole." Lestrade paused before asking, hopefully, "The body is at Westminster Mortuary, if you care to take a look?"

Holmes moved further forward in his chair, now clearly intrigued as he asked, "Is this Christopher Mallin under arrest?"

Lestrade nodded his head. "Yes, Mr. Holmes. We took him in for questioning. He couldn't give us a clear explanation about where he had been that morning or what had gone on. So, at the moment, he's our guest, you might say, at Bow Street."

Turning to me, Holmes asked, "Would it greatly inconvenience you, Watson, if we were to spend some little time after luncheon at the mortuary in Westminster and then go on to Bow Street – if that is also agreeable to you, Lestrade?"

I nodded in agreement and we both then looked towards Lestrade for his answer. Lestrade rubbed his hands together, answering, "Indeed it is, Mr. Holmes! We would welcome any assistance that you might give."

Holmes rose, crying, "Splendid! I'll send word should we find something of significance." With that, Holmes almost leapt towards the sitting room door, opening it wide as a somewhat rather obvious invitation for Lestrade to leave.

Chapter II – Westminster Mortuary

With the door firmly closed behind Lestrade, Holmes now held his pipe aloft as he returned to his leather armchair, asking, "Intriguing, do you not think, Watson?"

I was somewhat thoughtful and placed my hand to my chin for a moment before replying, "Well, given your current interest in ballistics, it appears to be an ideal case for you to pursue."

Holmes slapped the arm of his chair loudly, shouting, "Us! Watson. Us! For I am, once more, in need of your support!"

As it was now nearing noon, Holmes reached out for the bell rope in order to summon Mrs. Hudson. After informing her that I was to be his guest for luncheon, it was barely some ten minutes later that we dined on a goodly selection of cold meats, cheese, pickles, and some satisfying, home-baked bread. This spread, I was gratified to find, was followed by a delightful slice of Victoria sponge cake which Mrs. Hudson had taken the trouble to halve and then fill with home-made damson jam.

I had barely retired to my armchair, replete after our feasting, when Holmes rose and patted my sleeve. As he made his way to collect his hat and cane, he called out, "Come along, Watson. There is a person of some interest awaiting us in Westminster Mortuary." For my part, I was content to remain in my chair and of the opinion that the lady in question was unlikely to be concerned by my lassitude.

Bounding down the stairs, Holmes raised his cane to an approaching hansom which then pulled sharply to a halt beside him. With a cry to the cabbie of "Westminster Mortuary!" and after tossing him a six-pence, we clambered aboard and were quickly on our way.

Whilst travelling to the mortuary, I began to consider the detail of the unusual gunshot wound described by Lestrade. During my service in Afghanistan, I'd had occasion to treat many gunshot wounds from a variety of weapons, but none seemed to match the one he had described. Holmes also seemed preoccupied, sitting back in the cab with his fingers steepled against his lips and eyes half closed. Having exhausted my own thoughts, I ventured to ask, "Have you an opinion regarding the nature of the victim's wound?"

Holmes's eyes slowly opened as he turned slightly towards me, saying somewhat distantly, "My initial thoughts are that it was inflicted by some form of soft-nosed bullet, but observation is the key."

I tried to press him further but he would say nothing more, returning to his own rumination. Soon we were drawing up in Horseferry Road before the imposing, detached building that was Westminster Mortuary. This recently completed, three-storey, redbrick and Portland stone, purpose-built edifice contained both the mortuary and Westminster Coroner's Court.

Architecturally, I observed that it was, in the majority, of the Georgian style, but with more than a hint of Jacobean influence. The wide, arched, Portland stone-edged carriage entrance, topped by a curious bow window was, indeed, most impressive. Once inside the grand atrium, we readily identified ourselves and were taken, without delay, to the mortuary proper.

Unlike many of the ages-old, parish "Dead Houses", this new building provided facilities to both store bodies and then to allow *post mortems* to be undertaken in ideal conditions. The room itself benefited from copious natural light and, from its odour of lye, was kept scrupulously clean. Looking about me, it appeared that the mortuary staff had been forewarned of our visit. Before us, a body had been laid out on a slab close by, ready for our examination.

With a nod, the attendant withdrew to one side. I looked on as Holmes circled the prostrate figure, her head and shoulders being the only part currently visible. After observing all that he could, he respectfully drew back the single mortuary sheet. Here lay the body of a woman who appeared to be in her middle years. In life, she had been quite striking but now, the savage wound to her body was the feature that immediately drew my attention.

Holmes took from his pocket his glass and began a thorough observation of the whole corpse, beginning at the head and finishing at the toes. On completion, it was only then that he returned to the gaping wound in her abdomen.

After a few moments of observation with his glass, Holmes called to the mortuary attendant, asking for a pair of forceps. Once supplied, he used them to probe deeper into the wound, opening it briefly before he suddenly stopped.

Standing upright and motionless, he remained so for perhaps half-a-minute before raising a forefinger to his lips and then calling again to the mortuary attendant. On this occasion, he asked for a small corked sample bottle and an eyedropper. At the time, I thought this second item to be a curious request.

I watched intently as he opened an area within the wound, inserting the eye dropper and then withdrawing a small sample of liquid. Beckoning me, he asked if I might assist him in turning the victim so that she lay on her side, giving Holmes access to the large exit wound.

On doing so, I observed that it was, indeed, as Lestrade had described. A ragged area, perhaps some four inches in diameter below her left shoulder blade, gaped horribly. Again, Holmes probed within the wound before once more using the eye dropper to withdraw a further small amount of liquid.

Seeming now satisfied with his examination, Holmes inclined his head and together we replaced the body in its original, supine position. Holmes placed the corked sample bottle into his jacket pocket and, on returning the forceps and dropper, he strode silently from the mortuary.

Walking out into Horseferry Road, he remained silent. Despite my querying looks, Holmes would say nothing until we were once more in a cab and on our way to Bow Street. I fear that my frustration boiled over as I demanded, "For pity's sake! Do not keep me in suspense! What have you discovered?"

Holmes sat hunched, clearly deep in thought. Frowning, he replied, cryptically, "I find it most curious, Watson. It is as I thought and yet, quite different."

At this reply I shook my head as it appeared to be something of a contradiction, causing me to plead further, "You cannot expect me to accept that as an answer. Tell me!"

Holmes sat forward slightly in the cab and then reached into his jacket pocket. From it he withdrew the small, corked bottle that he had obtained from the mortuary. He held it out towards me, but in truth, I could see nothing of interest within it except what appeared to be a small sample of blood and a little tissue from the wound.

I was aware that I was being observed and, perhaps, my expression may well have shown that I was, indeed, unimpressed by his offering. Holmes now sighed. "It is not the blood, nor the tissue, that is of interest, Watson. It is what is intermingled with it that is of supreme importance."

As I was about to enquire further, the cab shuddered to a halt outside Bow Street Police Station. As we passed up the steps and into the foyer, the desk Sergeant rose and saluted smartly when Holmes presented his card. Again, it was clear that our visit was expected and, within moments, we were invited to follow a burly constable along the dimly lit, granite-paved passageways towards the cells.

Stopping in front of a sturdy black iron door which displayed a white painted number "8", the constable peered through the "Judas", the peep hole in the cell door. Satisfied, he took a ring of keys from his broad, leather belt and unlocked the door. Pointing now towards a small chalk-board beside the door frame, he announced, "Here you are, sir. Christopher Mallin. Just give us a shout when you're done." Holmes raised his cane in thanks and then pulled mightily upon the heavy door, which seemed to open with something of a groan of resentment at being disturbed.

Holmes and I had visited Bow Street many times over the years and, on opening the cell door, it was noticeable that the furnishings within each cell had changed not a jot. To our left, an iron-framed bed was bolted securely to the wall and topped by a straw-filled, canvas mattress. Against the opposite wall stood a single chair and a small table upon which a stump of candle was fixed. Beneath the table lingered a pungent slop-bucket.

On entering the cell, a somewhat bedraggled figure rose and looked fearfully in our direction. The man before us was short in stature, a little rotund with a head of dark, straight hair. He peered at us through bespectacled eyes, as Holmes touched his hat and then reached into his waistcoat pocket for his card. "Mr. Mallin? I am Sherlock Holmes and this is my companion, Dr. John Watson."

The man's hand trembled as he took and then read Holmes's card. "A detective? Then you might care to find out why I am being held here!"

I was immediately uneasy, for his strident manner did not mirror his posture. His stance appeared fearful but his manner was bordering on belligerence. Concerned, I asked, "Are you not aware of the reason for your detention, Mr. Mallin?"

The man now sat and looked towards us, recalling sadly, "I am aware of my wife's death, but I swear that I have no knowledge as to how it happened."

I turned towards Holmes and inclined my head slightly as I gave him an enquiring look. Holmes now sat beside Mallin, who continued to tremble. The tremors, I noted, were indeed uncontrollable. I judged them to be not from fear, but from some other cause I had yet to determine.

Holmes's voice softened as he said, "Tell me of your work, Mr. Mallin and, if you can, what occurred on the day of your wife's death?"

The man again looked angry. It was most curious, as though his emotions soared to the heights of elation and then plunged to the depths of despair. Seeming now to be almost brazen, he began, "I am employed in the felting department of Messrs. Norris and Black, the hat makers, where I have worked these many years."

Holmes nodded thoughtfully and waited for Mallin to continue. "On the day in question I . . . yes, I had made my way, by omnibus, the two miles to my place of work, but then, on reaching the premises, I suddenly felt unwell and . . . and confused. Not knowing what else to do, I sought out the coffee house nearby where my wife was employed as manager. She had not yet arrived for work, but I thought I might rest a while and take a little refreshment." Mallin paused and began to wring his hands. "Feeling a little restored, although still unwell, I . . . I determined to make my way home, as best I could."

Pulling out the small chair, whilst taking the utmost care to avoid contact with the slop-bucket, I sat and then asked, "On your arrival home, did you observe anything out of the ordinary?"

Mallin slowly nodded, seeming now pained to recall this event. "Yes. A constable was standing beside our front door and . . . and he barred my way. I was asked my name and told to wait, which I found most curious, for it was my house! I enquired as to what had occurred and was informed that a passing constable had found our front door ajar. On entering, he had found Margaret dead upon the sitting room floor." Mallin now paused. Putting both his hands to his head, he began to rock slightly as he recalled,

"Little else do I remember, apart from being brought here and asked questions that I could not answer."

Holmes rose, touched his hat once more before shouting, "Constable!" Looking towards Mallin, he smiled, saying, "Thank you, Mr. Mallin. You have been most helpful." The cell door groaned again upon its hinges as the constable arrived to release us. Holmes nodded in thanks and we made our way swiftly from the cells to hail a hansom.

Holmes, I could see, was greatly troubled by our meeting. As we rode back to Baker Street, he sat back in the cab, his brows furrowed and fingers steepled against his lips. I turned to him, voicing my own concern. "I fear for this fellow, Mallin, Holmes. His state of mind is such that, if sufficient pressure were to be put upon him, I believe that he would agree to almost anything."

Holmes slowly nodded. "Yes, he is clearly disturbed. I believe I know the reason for his strange behaviour. The tremors, the varied emotions, and also his problems with memory."

I blinked on hearing this and turned slightly towards my friend, asking, "Do you believe that his state of mind renders him incapable of murder?"

Holmes shook his head firmly. "No, for we are all capable of murder, given the appropriate circumstances. His mannerisms and behaviour are, I believe, the result of a physiological condition brought about by his employment."

Frowning, I thought back to the very brief conversation we had had with Christopher Mallin. "Employment? He said . . . ." It was then that I had a sudden flash of inspiration, shouting out, "Felt! A hatter! Of course, the man has erethism – *Mercury poisoning*!"

Holmes nodded. "Indeed. As you have observed, he has classic symptoms . . . ." Holmes suddenly paused, his face clouded as he continued, "and, I fear, my analysis of the sample in my jacket pocket could well put a noose around his neck." I was stunned by this revelation, but Holmes would reveal no more.

Chapter III – Experimentation and Queen Anne's Gate

Once back in Baker Street, Holmes immediately set about gathering items from his vast array of chemical apparatus. Taking the small sample bottle from his jacket pocket, he decanted the contents and then proceeded to refine them by, it seemed, various stages of "digestion". This was followed by washing and then filtration until all that was left were a few grains of material which he carefully placed upon a watch glass.

I must confess that I was intrigued by his experiments and, indeed, keen to discover the fruits of his labours. I leaned forward to examine the contents of the watch glass before then exclaiming, "It appears to be minute fragments of metal, Holmes!"

Holmes by now had retired to his leather armchair and had lit his briar. He leant his head back as he blew out a thin stream of blue smoke towards the already almond-coloured ceiling, replying, cryptically, "Metal, yes . . . . Fragments? No."

I was confused by this, for I had clearly seen a glint of metal upon the watch glass. Holmes now reached into his jacket pocket and offered me his lens. Using it, I looked more closely at his findings and saw not fragments but a collection of tiny, silver balls that appeared to coalesce at my touch.

"Mercury!" I cried, and then halted in my tracks. At that moment, I struggled to understand why it might have been present in the wound but then suddenly realised its significance. "The bullet was not only soft-nosed, but filled with mercury!"

Holmes's face was without expression as he spoke. "It is, perhaps, the ultimate bullet. If you have ever closely observed the effect of a water droplet as it hits the floor, Watson, then likewise, when such a bullet deforms, it spreads its deadly contents over a wide area. Imagine the destructive power of such a dense, liquid metal against soft tissue."

I was appalled at what I had heard, asking, "Do you think that Christopher Mallin has the ability to produce such bullets?"

Holmes removed his pipe from his mouth and slowly shook his head. "It is indeed doubtful, Watson. However, he does have access to a supply of mercury." Holmes paused, deep in thought. "But if it is not he, then who, and for what purpose? I believe the answer may well lie in the actions of Margaret Mallin."

Holmes now rose and snatched up a telegram pad. "I think a request to Lestrade is in order." On dashing off two or three lines, he then reached for the bell rope to summon Mrs. Hudson. Having done so, he turned to me, asking, "Would you be agreeable to meeting me here again tomorrow morning? I would appreciate your company."

I rose from my chair, nodding as I did so. Holmes, I observed, had returned to his armchair and now seemed to be retreating from the worldly distractions around him, gazing fixedly at some point in the distance. I knew that it was futile to try to engage him further and I made my way homewards.

The following morning, I arrived in Baker Street at approximately nine a.m.. The disarray of Holmes's tray with its scattered cutlery and a part-eaten slice of toast showed that he had already breakfasted. He was now to be seen poring over the section of Charles Booth's 1889 Poverty Map which depicted Westminster. It was plain that his telegram to Lestrade had born fruit and I could see that he had marked the position of three points upon the map. I was immediately intrigued by them, asking, "What is the significance of these?"

He did not look up but simply pointed towards each with his pipe stem. "I was curious to see the location of the Mallin household in relation to their respective places of work. As you can see, it is as Mallin stated."

Tapping out his pipe upon the corner of the hearth, Holmes was suddenly animated, crying, "Come along, Watson, for we have a pressing appointment with Lestrade in Queen Anne's Gate." With that, Holmes made a dash towards his hat and cane, calling over his shoulder, "I believe it may be beneficial to take some small refreshment before luncheon!"

I followed the rapidly retreating figure down the stairs as swiftly as I could, whereupon he was to be seen waving his cane wildly at an approaching cab. The cabbie reigned in his horse sharply and pulled his cab to a halt beside Holmes. With an encouraging wave in my direction, he then shouted out our destination to the cabbie before hastening me to clamber inside.

Little was said throughout our ride but, on nearing the address in Westminster, I was intrigued to observe the differing types of housing that seemed to jostle each other, cheek-by-jowl. I found it quite strange that elegant town houses stood a mere stone's throw from some of the worst slums in London.

Our journey had lasted some fifteen minutes, but now the cab slowed and pulled in close to the kerb beside a most regal, Portland stone statue which was inscribed "*Anna Regina*". Holmes tossed the cabbie a shilling and, stepping back from the curb, took a moment to examine, in detail, his surroundings. As he did so, something of a wistful look appeared upon his face.

Holmes pursed his lips. "Let me ask you, Watson, for you have dealings with persons from the majority of classes. How much might a hat maker earn each week?"

Thinking of my patients and their occupations, I paused for a moment before replying. "Well, I would imagine, something in the order of £2."

Holmes nodded before asking further, "And the manager of, say, a coffee house?"

Again, I paused and considered his request. "I am unsure. However, one of my patients owns a small baker's shop. On grudgingly paying my fee, she informed me that she had other calls upon her income, one being the salary of the manager of her bakery to whom she paid the princely sum of £3 per week."

Holmes raised an eyebrow and then pointed, with his cane, towards a house a little further down Queen Anne's Gate. "Lord Haldane resides in that house and, I would imagine, that he might well require a weekly income in excess of £5 in order to maintain such a fine residence and household." I had to agree and this was something that I hadn't previously considered.

Walking past Queen Anne's statue, Her Majesty clad in her finery and holding the orb and sceptre of office, we proceeded towards a burly constable, standing guard before a fine, porticoed doorway.

At our approach, he saluted smartly and opened the front door to allow us entry. As we progressed along the hallway, a familiar lean figure leaned out from a doorway and beckoned us forward.

"In here, Mr. Holmes. This is where we found her, and what a mess that was, as you can see from the state of the carpet!"

Looking down, the pale, peacock-blue, Indian carpet placed before the fireplace was grossly disfigured by a large bloodstain spreading outwards from its centre. Holmes took out his glass and immediately fell to his knees to examine the stain.

Lestrade looked on, somewhat amused by Holmes's curiosity. "I don't think you will find much of interest there, Mr. Holmes. We blotted up most of the blood with some towels from the kitchen."

Holmes rose from the floor, his face showing no emotion as he replaced his glass. On seeing his lack of expression, Lestrade chuckled again, asking, "Find anything of interest, Mr. Holmes? I thought not!"

Holmes gave the inspector a thin smile, answering, "All that I needed, thank you, Lestrade. May we look around the room?" Lestrade shrugged and nodded in reply before disappearing further into the house.

"Mercury?" I asked, in a hushed tone. Holmes nodded briefly in reply before once more taking out his lens and began to quarter the room. At one point, he paused to examine an ugly, blood-spattered scar on the wall, a clear indication of where the bullet had come to rest. It soon became obvious that the bullet had already been removed by the police.

The sitting room was finely decorated for the most part, although it was not the room of someone with exquisite taste. It gave the impression, rather, that some of the contents of one class of housing had been mixed with those of another, as though the occupants were not at ease with their new circumstances.

It was as Holmes was examining an area beside a large, ornate, gilded clock on the mantelpiece that he suddenly stopped. Carefully, he placed the clock to one side before taking his penknife from his jacket pocket and then using it to tease an object from the gap between the fireplace and the wall. Moving closer, I saw that he had managed to draw up, with his blade, about a half-inch of paper from the gap which he was then able to grasp and draw free.

Holmes moved towards the window and examined his find. In his hands he held an envelope which I saw was addressed to Mrs. M. Mallin. Turning to me, he inclined his head and motioned me to stand by the door. I readily took on the role of "watchman" but, similarly, I was eager to see the envelope and, hopefully, its contents.

Now placing the envelope into his jacket pocket, Holmes strode to the front door and, before opening it, called out, "Thank you, Lestrade, you have been most helpful!"

Once more in the street, Holmes raised his cane to catch the attention of the driver of an approaching cab. As it drew up against the kerb, Holmes called out, "Tufton Street, cabbie," before we then hastily climbed aboard and were on our way.

I was, of course, most eager to learn the details of Holmes's discovery. Seeing my anticipation, Holmes leant forward saying, "I find that it is often the habit, Watson, of some classes, to rest their mail behind the clock or some similar object, upon the mantelpiece. Hence our good fortune!"

Without a further word, he drew the letter from his pocket and passed the envelope to me. The address, I noticed, was written in a bold, cursive hand which, I suspected, was male. The postmark was dated barely a week previous. Holding the envelope to my nose revealed nothing but the slight smell of soot, no doubt the result from residing in its niche in the fireplace. Having gleaned all that I could from the envelope, I peered inside and was pleased to find a single, folded sheet of quality writing paper.

The letter was in the same hand as the envelope, but it was the contents that stole my attention. These read thus. "*Mrs. Mallin, I am appalled by your immoral behaviour, as is my wife. You must cease this vile act or else the most severe consequences will follow.*" The letter was signed "*George Shipley*".

I sat back, perplexed. "What is this, Holmes? What has occurred to provoke such anger? Do you suspect blackmail, for that is what most readily springs to mind?"

Holmes was silent for a moment before replying, "I am unsure. Blackmail is one possibility, but there is a hint of something more." I returned the letter to him, as our journey to Mrs. Mallin's place of work was but a few minutes from her home.

Chapter IV – Coffee and Something More

Arriving in Tufton Street, we stepped down from the cab and were immediately greeted by the intense aroma of roasting coffee, emanating from a red brick and Portland stone doorway. Holmes looked up and down the street, seeming to register all with a single glance. Following our noses, we entered the somewhat gloomy, although still enticing, coffee house.

Once inside, I thought the seating arrangements of the coffee house to be somewhat peculiar. Tables and chairs were arranged, as one would expect, in front of the arched windows of the house. However, to one side, against the wall shared with the adjacent premises, were four small, private booths – three of which, I saw, were already occupied by gentlemen of varying ages. The booths were comfortably upholstered and benefited from heavy velvet curtains which could be drawn for the sake of privacy. On seeing this, I recalled that many coffee houses were used by city gentlemen to conduct their business and also as a place to exchange contracts.

As we stood, waiting, in the doorway, our presence was noted and we were quickly approached by a waitress. Bidding us welcome, she then proceeded to ask us where we would prefer to sit. I had no preference. However, Holmes pointed with his stick towards the empty booth, asking if we might sit there.

The waitress nodded, saying, "Of course, sir, but there is an extra charge: It's two shillings . . . each."

I spluttered and was about to object somewhat forcefully when Holmes touched my sleeve, replying, "Ah, excellent. We will sit there and take two coffees, thank you."

Holmes led the way to the unoccupied booth and settled himself into one corner. As I moved to sit in the opposite corner, I could contain myself no longer, exclaiming, "Two shillings, Holmes! That is extortionate! I can buy at least a dozen cups of coffee for that price."

Holmes face bore a grim smile as he replied, "Ah, but I believe that there may be additional 'benefits' for the gentlemen who opt to sit in these booths."

I looked questioningly at Holmes but he would say no more, having glimpsed the waitress approaching with our coffee on her tray. Nodding our thanks to the waitress, Holmes took a sip of his coffee, savouring it, before asking, "Would it be possible to speak to the manager? I find his blend of coffee is exceptionally fine."

The waitress' face clouded as she replied, "I'm sorry, sir, that would not be possible. Mrs. Mallin is no longer with us . . . ." With that she clutched her apron to her face and ran towards the rear of the coffee house.

Holmes now stood, held his finger aloft, and then drew the thick, velvet curtains of the booth, almost plunging us both into darkness. "What is this, Holmes? I can barely see anything!"

Holmes turned slightly, saying, "Ah, but I think that you will." He now examined the wall beside him before reaching out towards the corner of a small painting above his seat and then pulling upon it. Immediately, a slim ray of light shone into the booth from the wall. Illuminated slightly by this, Holmes now put his finger to his lips and motioned towards the small picture above my seat.

Feeling around the edge of the frame, I found that it was hinged and, on swinging it back, a similar ray of light now emerged from the wall. Attracted by this light source, I placed my eye to the small hole from whence it originated.

Immediately, I clapped my hand to my mouth to prevent myself from crying out. There, through the wall, was a clear view into what appeared to be a changing cubicle of a ladies dress shop. Before me was a young woman, dressed only in her undergarments, trying on a new dress. I swiftly, but silently, replaced the picture, noting that Holmes had done the same. Drawing back the heavy curtains, Holmes sat once more, his face grim.

Still shocked by these events, I hissed, "This is obscene, Holmes! It must be stopped!"

Holmes nodded, soberly, saying, "I agree. However, it must be done with the utmost sensitivity, Watson. The reputations of many fine ladies are at stake here. We cannot have Lestrade and his constables charging into this establishment." Holmes now became thoughtful, adding, "Yes, it will have to be done much more subtly, but our most pressing task is to find George Shipley and, I believe that might be achieved by a visit to the establishment next door!"

Paying our dues at the counter, Holmes led the way from the coffee house and then approached the door of the adjoining ladies dress shop. As we entered, a small brass bell attached to the door announced our arrival. Looking about me, it was immediately apparent that the shop had both an extensive and exclusive clientele. Several well-dressed ladies, some accompanied by their daughters, were choosing fabric or waiting to try on dresses.

Knowing that these ladies were now vulnerable to the voyeurs of the coffee house both angered and frustrated me in equal measure. I placed my hands behind my back as I felt them balling into fists of anger! Holmes put his hand upon my arm in restraint and then touched his hat as a matronly assistant greeted us. "Good afternoon, gentlemen. How might we be of service?"

Holmes smiled sweetly. "Good afternoon. A friend of mine, George Shipley, recommended your establishment and suggested that I might call. My wife is a great friend of the Shipley's, and I have often remarked to George that his wife wears some exquisite couture. I believe she purchases it from this very shop."

The assistant fairly beamed, replying, "Ah, a friend of Sir George and Lady Shipley. You are, indeed, welcome! Lady Alice often visits our establishment whilst her husband waits and takes coffee next door. Would you like me to make an appointment for your wife?"

Holmes smiled, saying, "I would not presume, but if you would be so kind as to give me your card, I will pass it on to my wife."

On hearing this, the assistant then reached into a concealed pocket in her gown and from it produced a silver card case. Taking a card from within, she proffered it, saying, "Here you are sir, Mr . . . ?"

"Holmes, Sherlock Holmes." Touching his hat once more, and with a smile, he swept from the shop, leaving me trailing in his wake.

By the time I caught up with Holmes, he already had a cab waiting to convey us back to Baker Street. The return journey was undertaken in almost complete silence. Indeed, I was still in turmoil from what I had observed and was eager to discuss with Holmes how he intended to proceed without the services of Lestrade.

Once more sitting at our ease and with a pipe of well-lit tobacco, we sat in silence again for perhaps five minutes. Only then did I feel calm enough to ask, "Have you heard of this fellow Shipley, Holmes?"

Holmes drew hard upon his pipe before answering, "No, but the turn of a page in *DeBrett's* will no doubt be of value." Rising from his chair, he made his way to the bookcase and then hefted the weighty tome onto the dining table. Thumbing through, it took less than a minute before a cry of triumph stirred me from my own thoughts. "Hah! We have him! George Hugo Shipley, son of Sir Edmond Frearson Shipley, married to Alice Elizabeth Broomfield, daughter of Colonel Alistair Fitzgerald Broomfield . . . ."

Holmes's voice trailed away as he stood motionless. It was as though he was now imagining a plethora of scenarios. Slamming closed the *DeBrett's*, he now plunged back into the bookcase to reappear with a gazetteer. "*Sir George Shipley, Dean's Yard, Westminster.*" With seemingly renewed vigour, Holmes now cried, "Come along, Watson! The game is afoot!"

Chapter V – Sir George and Lady Alice

Snatching up his hat and cane, Holmes now charged down the stairs once more and, within minutes, we were travelling at speed towards Dean's Yard.

After its publication in 1889, I had spent some little time studying Charles Booth's Poverty Map of London for the purpose of better understanding my own practice. From Holmes's copy, I recalled that the area around Westminster Abbey was coloured a golden yellow, indicating that the dwellings were those of the wealthy, upper classes. I had little doubt that Sir George was to be found amongst this class of person, and I was not to be disappointed.

As our cab slowed to a stop, I observed that Dean's Yard was a square of elegant houses of varied architectural styles from different periods that demonstrated how, over time, the square had come into being. The dwellings now enclosed a quadrangle of grass bordered by mature trees. Holmes stepped down from the cab and strode purposefully towards an impressive Georgian building. I stood at his side and as he regarded the brass nameplate beside the front door. Leaning forward, he pressed the bell on the plate that displayed the name, in fine gothic script, of Sir George Shipley.

Within perhaps half-a-minute, the front door opened and we were met by a footman in full livery. Holmes reached into his waistcoat pocket and withdrew from it one of his cards. This he handed to the servant who bowed, saying, "I would be grateful if you gentlemen were to wait a few moments. I will see if Sir George is available." With that, he closed the front door to us. A minute passed before he returned and, again bowing, he now led us into the building. Passing along a graceful, Italian marble-floored hallway, lit by an impressive crystal chandelier, he paused before a fine, mahogany door. Knocking briefly upon it before opening it, we were then ushered into a fine drawing room.

As we entered the room, I was immediately impressed by both its size and its grandeur. Oak panelling prevailed, together with large bookcases that extended the length of one wall. The opposite wall contained three ornate, stone-faced, mullioned windows. These, in turn, gave a fine view over the shady quadrangle.

To my surprise, I observed that, above the fireplace, the head of a large, male lion had been mounted. From its position, the lion appeared to glare down at us, its snarling mouth displaying a fearsome set of teeth. As I turned and looked in the opposite direction, the corresponding wall was bedecked with spears and hide shields, undoubtedly from the south of the continent of Africa. These were interspersed with a variety of animal head trophies, whilst the floor in front of the fireplace was covered by the hide of a zebra.

This collection of trophies seemed somewhat out of keeping with the elegance of the room and I had little doubt that Holmes had taken all this in with a single glance.

Before us stood an immaculately dressed be-whiskered gentleman of middle years, whose bearing clearly suggested that of a military man. This I took to be Sir George Shipley. Stepping forward, Holmes now took the initiative. "Good afternoon, Sir George. I am Sherlock Holmes and this is my companion, Dr. John Watson."

With a questioning expression, Sir George walked towards us, still holding Holmes's card, asking, "Gentlemen, I fear I am at a loss to know the reason for your visit."

Holmes bowed his head slightly before saying, "On the contrary, Sir George, I believe that you do." Holmes now reached into his jacket pocket and retrieved the letter he had found in the Mallin's sitting room, asking, "Would you, perhaps, like me to read it to you?"

I saw Sir George stiffen as he replied, "That will not be necessary, Mr. Holmes, for I know its contents."

Holmes put back the letter inside the envelope and replaced it in his jacket pocket. "You have not acted upon your threat then, Sir George?"

Sir George Shipley looked Holmes straight in the eye and replied, "No sir, I have not, although I understand from the newspaper that the matter may, perhaps, have been resolved by the actions of another person."

Holmes's face was without emotion as he asked, "Have you ever been to the coffee house in Tufton Street, Sir George. The one beside the dress shop?"

Sir George stroked his chin before replying, "Yes, on several occasions. I would sit and take coffee there whilst waiting for my wife to return from the premises next door."

"And where did you sit?" asked Holmes, his voice now steely.

A look of concern crossed Sir George's face. "I really don't understand . . . ."

Holmes pressed the point. "Please, Sir George. It is most important."

Sir George pursed his lips and thought. "Well, I would always sit by one of the windows. I pass the time reading my copy of *The Times* whilst I wait for Alice. It is so damnably dark elsewhere in the coffee house."

At this, Holmes raised an eyebrow and then pointed towards the lion head above the fireplace, asking, "He is a fine specimen, Sir George. A trophy of yours from a safari in Africa?"

Sir George smiled for the first time. "No, Mr. Holmes. These trophies are not mine. They are from my wife's late father. He became something of a big game hunter once he had retired from the army." Sir George swept his arm around the room, saying, "We inherited these and all his hunting paraphernalia, although where I might use an elephant gun, in Britain, is beyond me."

It was at this point that I suddenly recalled the name, exclaiming, "Colonel Broomfield! Ah, yes. He was something of a talking point in the mess during my service in Afghanistan. It was said that he would experiment with chain shot and all manner of projectiles for our canon, in an attempt to increase their lethal effect . . . ." My voice fell away as the import of what I had just said rang in my ears. I turned to Holmes, a querying look upon my face.

Holmes pursed his lips before asking, "Might I be able to see the Colonel's weapons that you inherited?"

Sir George nodded slowly and pointed towards a door, partly hidden by a large wall hanging. "Why yes. They are here, in the gun room."

Leading the way, Sir George opened the door to the gun room where a rack bearing rifles of varying calibres were on display. Holmes moved forward and examined each one in turn before then placing his nose next to the breach of each one. Turning to Sir George, he enquired, "Yes, a fine collection, Sir George. Might I ask if the Colonel ever carried a pistol whilst on safari?"

Again, Sir George smiled. "Indeed, and a mighty one at that." Opening a drawer, Sir George reached out his hand but then paused. A look of concern now crossed his face. "It's missing, Mr. Holmes. The Colonel's pistol was a .455 calibre Webley, Mark IV. He acquired it in 1900, almost a year before his death."

It was obvious that Sir George was genuinely concerned by the pistol's disappearance, as he then continued, "The Colonel took a great pride in his 'new toy', as he called it. He was forever tinkering with it to the point where, I believe, he even began to cast his own ammunition."

Holmes turned towards me briefly, raising an eyebrow, and then thanked Sir George as we returned to the drawing room. It was then that he asked, "How did you become aware of Mrs. Mallin's activities, Sir George?"

Sir George's face darkened as he recalled, "It was at my club in Mayfair, perhaps ten days ago. I happened to be in the presence of two of the members, who had drunk rather more whisky than they should, and began to brag of their experiences with the ladies. Of course, my ears pricked up when they mentioned both the coffee house in Tufton Street and the ability to observe the ladies next door."

Holmes nodded slowly and then asked, "Did you inform your wife of this?"

294

Shaking his head, Sir George replied, "No, not initially. I thought it might be all bravado, so I arranged to visit the coffee house once more. Only when I was sure of my facts did I have the courage to inform Alice of my discovery." He paused a moment, seeming to consider how best to continue. "Alice was incensed. In truth, Mr. Holmes, I have never seen a woman so angry, for she has inherited her father's fighting temperament. I almost had to restrain her, as she wanted to physically confront Mrs. Mallin."

Sir George paused. He pursed his lips and then continued, "After a good deal of effort, I was able to placate her, somewhat, by writing the letter that you have obtained. Although a most delicate matter, it was my intention to take some form of legal action against Mrs. Mallin should this vile practice continue."

At that moment, the door to the sitting room opened and a graceful lady of middle years entered. She was tall and elegant, her face oval, graced with sparkling emerald eyes and tresses of bright auburn hair. She was dressed in fine silks, and upon her arm she carried a rather commodious velvet opera bag, which, to my mind, seemed slightly out of place.

Sir George turned, exclaiming, "Ah! Alice. May I present Mr. Sherlock Holmes and his companion, Dr. John Watson? They have – "

Lady Alice held up a hand, saying. "It is quite all right George, I am aware of the reason. I have behaved in a most un-ladylike manner and have listened at the door for some time."

Turning to us, she continued, "I would have been content with the proposed actions of my husband, had it not been for a distraught visitor to our home last week." She paused, took a deep breath, and then continued, "A dear friend of mine had attended the dress shop in Tufton Street with her daughter, in readiness for the daughter's forthcoming wedding. After the visit, the mother received a note from Mrs. Mallin. This informed her that her daughter's reputation would be ruined if knowledge of her exposure was to be made known to her fiancé. In the note, she demanded fifty guineas to ensure her silence."

Sir George took a step back, clearly unaware of these events. Holmes now asked, "So you intervened on her behalf?"

Lady Alice nodded. "It was an intolerable situation. One's reputation is hard earned and easily lost . . . ruination follows. Margaret Mallin's address was easily found and I travelled to Queen Anne's Gate, where I sought to confront her." Lady Alice was momentarily tight lipped and then, with surprising vitriol, exclaimed, "She laughed in my face, Mr. Holmes! She knew very well that if these matters were to be made public, all would be lost."

Holmes asked quietly, "So you took your father's pistol . . . and the mercury bullets?"

Lady Alice nodded. "I am not the greatest shot, Mr. Holmes. I had witnessed the effectiveness of such ammunition during one of my father's expeditions in Africa and knew that but a single round would be sufficient."

Holmes now looked grave, saying, "I take it that you are aware of the grievous consequences of your actions, Lady Alice, even though you might judge them justified?"

With a toss of her head, Lady Alice replied, "Oh, yes, Mr. Holmes." Turning to her husband, she said, softly, "Have no fear, George. You will not have to suffer the indignity of a trial." With that, she plunged her hand into her bag, withdrew her father's pistol and with one swift movement, placed it against her temple and fired.

The pistol was still loaded with the mercury-laden bullets and the effect was almost indescribable. All three of us rushed forward, but there was nothing to be done. Lady Alice lay as a felled lioness. With a cry, Holmes and I lunged swiftly to support Sir George as he began to collapse before our eyes.

Chapter VI – The Hand of Mycroft

It was, perhaps, an hour later, after a cryptic telegram had been sent to Holmes's brother, Mycroft, that a discreet undertaker's carriage drew up in Dean's Yard. As for Sir George, we had summoned a cab with directions to take him directly to his club where he might stay the night. The involvement of Mycroft would, hopefully, ensure that the reputations of several ladies of quality and their respective husbands should remain intact.

With nothing more that could be done, we returned to Baker Street. Despite having missed luncheon, neither Holmes nor I could bring ourselves to eat dinner, managing only to consume a little bread and a noggin of cheese.

We sat together that evening, seeming to smoke incessantly. I recalled the events of the day in my mind and was now gravely concerned as to what might follow. Almost in answer to my unspoken questions, the steady, heavy footfall upon the stairs of 221b announced the arrival of Mycroft Holmes.

With the single acknowledgement of "Sherlock" to his brother and a nod in my direction, Mycroft settled down on the sofa. Reaching within his jacket, he took out his cigar case and proceeded to select from it a fine Havana. Having snipped off the end, toasted and lit the cigar with a Vesta, he drew upon it before speaking. "This is a bad business, Sherlock. After receiving your telegram, I immediately called for all the items retrieved by Lestrade from Queen Anne's Gate to be brought to me." Mycroft paused before announcing, "It was, indeed, enlightening to discover amongst them a record of Mrs. Mallin's dealings with the clients of the dress shop."

On saying this, Mycroft leant forward and passed a slim volume to his brother. I watched Holmes's face which displayed a variety of emotions as he digested its contents before exclaiming, "My word! She was, indeed, an industrious lady. There are certainly some names of interest amongst her 'clientele'."

Holmes paused, his forefinger now pressed firmly against his lips, before asking, "But what is to be done, Mycroft? This cannot become public knowledge. It is not only the reputations of the ladies who have been betrayed, but also the effect upon the careers of their husbands that is at stake." Holmes's voice took on a graver tone as he added, "In addition, we must not forget the events surrounding the demise of Lady Alice."

Mycroft nodded, slowly. "Indeed so. As to Lady Alice, I am to have supper with the Commissioner of the Metropolitan Police this evening. I am sure that he will be amenable to my proposal relating to the dreadful accident that occurred at Dean's Yard whilst cleaning a loaded pistol."

I looked towards Holmes as he tapped his forefinger meaningfully against Mrs. Mallin's ledger, saying, "Yes, given the circumstances, I am sure that the commissioner will agree."

"What of the coffee house itself? Surely it cannot be allowed to continue to trade, despite the demise of Mrs. Mallin?" I asked.

Mycroft Holmes leant towards me slightly, raising an eyebrow and inclining his head. In a barely audible voice, he replied, "It is, perhaps, better that you ask no further on this point, Doctor." I was unsure of the precise meaning of this but I thought it apposite to follow his advice.

We sat and smoked for a little while longer, saying little of any consequence. Mycroft finished his cigar and, on Holmes returning the ledger, went on to his supper appointment. Following suit, I too took my leave of Baker Street.

A further week passed before I called once more upon my friend. It was as we added to the wreath of blue smoke that hung around us that Holmes then tossed me his copy of *The Times*. "I have highlighted two items that you might find of interest, Watson. Perhaps you have a mind to read a little?"

Unfolding the broadsheet, I riffled through the pages until I found the items that he had circled. The first was a notice regarding the funeral of

Lady Alice Shipley. This having taken place "... *after the tragic accident at her home in Dean's Yard, Westminster.*"

The second item was something quite unexpected. It pertained to a small fire that had caused extensive damage to a coffee house in Tufton Street. The cause of the blaze had been ascribed to hot coals from the roasting process not having been quenched sufficiently at the end of the working day. No one, it appeared, was harmed by the fire and the adjoining premises were unaffected. I was gratified to then read that the coffee house would be closed for the foreseeable future.

Returning the paper to Holmes, I sat back and considered the closure of the coffee house, asking, "Is this not somewhat hard on the owner, Holmes?"

Holmes took his pipe from his mouth, waving the stem in contradiction. "I think not. It has since come to light that the owner was aware of the practices of Mrs. Mallin, allowing them to continue in return for a percentage of the profits."

I frowned, asking, "Do I detect Mycroft's hand in this charade?"

Holmes closed his eyes, settled further back into his armchair, and did not immediately reply. After perhaps a minute, he drew deeply on his pipe before uttering, '*Auctoritas non veritas facit legem*,' Watson!"

Whilst I admit that I was something of a dullard in my Latin class, I understood the chilling meaning of Holmes's words: "*Authority, not truth, makes law.*"

The Adventure of the
Throne of Gilt
by Will Murray

In all of my dealings with Mr. Sherlock Holmes, I never in my wildest imaginings conceived that one day I would have to turn to him, not as friend to friend, but as supplicant to consulting detective.

These events occurred not long after my marriage, and after I had again moved out of our shared flat. The year was 1903. It was spring. Edward had not been long on the throne. The world seemed to have been renewed, and only then settling into a new normalcy.

An envelope arrived at my Queen Anne Street home, bearing no return address, only a scribbled signature that appeared to say "*Mr. Thursday.*"

It was addressed to *Dr. John Watson, M. D.*

I thought immediately that this was the work of an ignorant fellow, inasmuch as the title would normally render the initials superfluous.

When I tore open the envelope, it contained only a single sheet of folded foolscap on which was written the following:

Dr. Watson:

You will one day be sat upon the throne of gilt.

The note was signed in the same crabbed hand, "*Mr. Thursday.*"

Normally, I might have thrown out such a bit of nonsense, but my long association with Sherlock Holmes inspired me to replace the note into its envelope and pocket it. While it might represent only a minor mystery, I thought it would be entertaining, if not instructive, to show it to my good friend.

Upon bidding my new bride *adieu*, I hied over to 221 Baker Street and paid Holmes a call. A hansom cab was loitering outside my door and the bewhiskered driver looked at me expectantly, but I did not care for the look of the fellow and his profusion of unkempt side-whiskers.

Ignoring the appeal of his glowering gaze, I walked on, for it was a pleasant day and the air was good to breathe.

Holmes greeted me with his usual diffidence as he lounged in his sitting room, wearing a pinched expression that I took to mean boredom. He was between consultations, and it showed upon his sharp countenance.

"What brings you here at the supper hour, Watson?" inquired he.

"That is a peculiar question coming from you, Holmes."

"Please be good enough to make yourself plain," grunted Holmes. He appeared to be in a foul mood. Not disagreeably so, but if I were a prescriber of remedies for moods, I would recommend direct and abundant sunlight.

"You may recall how many times have I or some other caller entered your presence and been subjected to a barrage of penetrating questions leading to definitive conclusions that possibly no other man in the world could arrive at from scant evidence."

My mild rebuke stirred Holmes partially out of his funk. He looked up, his penetrating eyes coming into focus.

They rested upon my shoes first, saw nothing of interest, and his gaze climbed to my throat and then shifted to my hands, making an inventory of details and, apparently, discarding most of them.

Something about the manner of which I held my right hand caused him to remark, "You bring me something, Watson. Something to read." He paused, then went on. "A letter perhaps?"

"Very good, Holmes. It is exactly that. But however did you know?"

"From the way you held your hand, close to your lower right coat pocket, you seemed poised to produce something of interest. It could not be a magazine or newspaper article, because I know you to present such articles whole, and not torn out or cut free. That meant that the article was not very large or thick, and this to me suggested a letter."

"Well done."

I produced the envelope without delay and handed it to my friend.

Holmes regarded the return address and the postmark, and then he lifted the torn flap, drawing out a coarse sheet of paper. He read this several times, despite its brevity. His expression did not alter.

"What do you make of it?" I asked impatiently.

"Well, there is very little to go on. I see that it was posted in Hackney this morning, which tells us precious little, for anyone can mail a letter from any convenient spot."

Before he could inquire further, I volunteered, "I do not know of any Mr. Thursday."

"What about a Mr. *Thorsday*? For that is the correct pronunciation of the signature, as I decipher it."

"It looked like Thursday to me. Are you certain?"

"The way the man shapes his letter *O*'s makes it absolutely conclusive. There is no doubt that the signature is *Thorsday*. And my question yet stands."

I said, "That name, too, is unfamiliar to me. But that is not as puzzling as the message itself. I can make nothing of it, other than my correspondent is a rough and untutored fellow."

"Nor can I, but I agree with your assessment. Furthermore, I imagine it to be a threat of some sort – veiled and obscure, but a threat nevertheless."

"Threat? I take nothing of the sort from the single sentence."

Holmes looked up. "Have you lost any patients in recent weeks?"

"None so far this year."

"But you have lost patients who have succumbed to their maladies, never to recover."

"There is hardly a medical man in all of London, never mind the world, who has not lost patients through no fault of his own. What of it?"

"I know you well enough, Watson, to understand that you are not a man who makes enemies, nor gives slights requiring an avenging rejoinder. Given your profession, I would judge that this letter was written by someone upset over your failure to preserve a life."

"Well, of course I have lost many patients over the years, but none of them named Thorsday *or* Thursday. But heavens, man, are you not making a great pile out of very little wool?"

"I think not," murmured Holmes. "If I were you, I would take precautions."

"Far be it from me to discount the soundness of your conclusions," I returned. "Would you be good enough to suggest how I may go about ascertaining the truth behind this veiled threat?"

Holmes seemed lost in thought, and his attention returned to the sheet of paper, which he examined on both sides.

"I do not think Thorsday is the name of your mysterious correspondent, Watson," he mused. "Nor Thursday. The first is not a name one could find in the London city directory, nor do I think in any city directory. It is entirely made up. Therefore, it must have significance, being the product of the writer's imagination."

"What do you make of the allusion to a 'gilt throne'?"

Holmes frowned reflectively. "Nothing at first blush. I believe this will require a pipe and some good tobacco. Why don't you run along, good fellow, and leave me to my ruminations? I will let you know when I have something of interest to tell you. In the meanwhile, please take all precautions. And kindly let me know if further communications are received from the mysterious Mr. Thorsday."

With that, Sherlock Holmes seemed to have dismissed me from all awareness, and I made a graceful exit, not as a reassured as I had expected to be.

Nothing transpired for exactly one week. Then the second letter came, posted from Hammersmith. I did not open it, but took it forthwith to my friend, of whom I had heard nothing in the intervening seven days.

After being ushered into his tobacco-fumed presence, I burst out, "I have received a second letter. I present it to you, Holmes, unopened."

"Give it here," said Holmes without outward expression of excitement. "And mark the day of the week."

"Thursday!" I exclaimed. "The same as previously. Do you think it significant?"

Holmes was employing a letter opener to slit the envelope.

"I do. But of what, I cannot yet say."

The letter fell out into Holmes's waiting palm. Unfolding it, he read in silence, then handed the sheet to me.

Taking it, I read it aloud.

My Dear Watson:

I intend to do away with you in a most novel manner, sir. Await my pleasure. The gilt throne also awaits. I promise you a hot tyme.

Looking up, I said, "I do not understand this business of a gilded throne, which is what this ignorant fellow evidently means."

"I disagree, Watson. Not about the fellow's ignorance, of course, but with his meaning."

"I will admit that this talk of a 'gilt throne' is obscure, but what could he otherwise possibly mean?"

"A throne cannot be fashioned of 'gilt', Watson. It is an impossibility, for gold leaf by definition is thin. Otherwise, the phrase would be 'throne of gold'. If it were 'gilded', Mr. Thorson would have written the words 'gilded throne'."

"An ignorant man might be unaware of this distinction," I countered. Then: "What did you say his name was?"

"Thorson."

"Are you psychic now, Holmes?"

"No, merely ordinarily observant. I have not divined his true name. Please look at the signature again."

I did so. And there I saw what I had carelessly overlooked before. The signature was *Mr. Thorson*, as was the one on the envelope proper. In my excitement, I had missed this.

I asked, "What do you make of it?"

"I prefer to hurl your question back at you, Watson. Tell me where your thoughts led you."

"Thorson. Thorsday. It appears clear that the latter name was not Thursday, as you surmised. Yet both letters were posted so as to arrive on a Thursday. Unless that it a coincidence."

"I think not," snapped Holmes. "Pray continue with your train of thought. The workings of a mind less rigorously scientific than mine are of interest to me."

"Thor was the Norse god of lightning and thunder," I mused. "A wielder of a magical hammer that produced earthly storms, according to legend. But I am not aware that he sat upon a throne. Odin, his father, may well have, but Thor was a warrior. Besides, he is entirely mythical. A superstition of a bygone age not our own."

"Yet, Watson, the legend survives into our time," prompted Holmes.

"Yes, in storybooks. But nowhere else. I seriously doubt that worship of Thor continues to the present day. Not in England, at any rate. Perhaps in some backwoods enclave in Norway, or elsewhere in Scandinavia. I must reject the notion that I have incurred the wrath of a modern-day Thor worshipper."

"You are overlooking the obvious, Watson," said Holmes pointedly.

"If I am, it is not obvious to me."

"You previously accused me of futile wool-gathering, as it were," continued Holmes. "Yet you overlook bright yarn lying in plain sight."

I stood there stupefied, thoroughly flummoxed. My brain refused to function. "I am at a loss," I confessed at last.

"I have not been idle these last seven days," remarked Holmes, apparently changing the subject and leaving me to stew in my mental confusion. "In reviewing the facts then at hand, I realized the significance of the day upon which you received the first communication. So I was not entirely surprised when the second arrived on this day. I half expected it, in truth."

No doubt my expression became extreme at that point. I was on the point of asking my astute friend to explain his reasoning, when the connection struck me forcefully.

"By Jove! Thursday is named after Thor!"

Holmes's tone turned dry. "You mix your mythologies, but you are correct, Watson. The present day of the week is a conflation of Thor's Day. From that weak thread, I began surmising that the fellow has a fixation on the mythological Thor. Although I cannot now rule out that his name is Thorson, of which many exist, but I think it unlikely. This trend of thought carried me through two pipefuls of tobacco without concrete result. But when I turned my attention to the connection with the day of the week, I found a measure of wool, as it were."

"I am under your spell, Holmes, as always."

"Searching my memory for unusual events that had taken place on Thursdays in recent memory, I found two, and they appeared to belong to the same strange skein. Three weeks ago, on a Thursday evening, a body was found in a field near Coddington. It was that of Mr. Ambrose Dexter."

"The retired tragedian?"

"The very same. He had apparently been out and about when a sudden electrical storm brewed up. The poor fellow was apparently felled by a lightning bolt."

"Surely not dispatched from Asgard by the red-haired thunder god himself!"

"Hardly. When the police discovered the body the next morning, the verdict was death by misadventure. The normally intelligent Dexter had been caught in a rainstorm and had the misfortune to attract a thunderbolt. There was no more to it than that, according to the coroner, who had seen such tragedies before."

"If this a coincidence, it is truly bizarre," I ventured.

"It was no coincidence," returned Holmes. "For on the following Thursday, now a fortnight ago, another body was discovered in another field, this one a cricket field in Shoreditch. Again, the victim was electrocuted. Once again, it was during a storm. But a *rainstorm*, Watson. Not a thunderstorm. No clap of thunder nor flash of lighting was reported by any inhabitant of the region. Yet such is the conventionality of the police and the local coroner that death was again attributed to an errant lightning bolt."

"A week apart, you say?"

Holmes nodded sagely. "And a week before the first letter was received by you."

"What do you make of this chain of Thursday happenstances?"

Pausing to puff on his pipe, Holmes replied diffidently, "I decided to visit Shoreditch and made inquiries of the locals. One witness claimed to have seen a hansom cab in the vicinity, and saw the cabman carry something onto the field hours before the body was discovered. "

"The body!"

"No doubt. So I made inquiries of the cab companies. No driver would admit to having been in the vicinity upon that night."

"Of course, the guilty man would offer no such confession," I pointed out.

"The peculiar thing is that the second dead man was himself a hansom cab driver," added Holmes. "Dunn was his name."

"A falling out among co-employees!" I cried.

"Yet accounts of no such argument could be unearthed. I think the truth lies in another direction. I think the man who deposited the body was not the cabman, but a thief. For Mr. Dunn's cab has not been recovered."

"So we are searching for a phantom cab and its gypsy driver."

"Almost certainly."

"But what would be the motive to steal the cab in question?"

"For a quick and unobtrusive escape, I would ordinarily conjecture. But not in this instance, for the cabriolet would have been found by now, abandoned. To store it somewhere would be the same as hanging a sign over a stable or barn, attesting that the owner is a murderer and thief."

"How do you imagine the dead cabman was killed, if the coroner believed him to have been electrocuted?"

"That answer to that, Watson, is so elementary that you should not have posed the question, but produced the answer on your own initiative."

"I cannot fathom it, Holmes. Therefore, I stand on my unanswered question."

"The unfortunate Mr. Dunn, Watson, was obviously and unquestionably electrocuted."

"But surely not by Thor incarnate!"

"Nor by Thorson, nor Thorsday. But by an unknown madman who may even now be prowling the byways of London in a stolen hansom cab in search of an unwary fare."

"I confess that I fail to perceive a recognizable garment amid all this gathered castoff wool."

"I suggest that we go for a promenade, Watson."

"To what end?"

"To see if we cannot entice your Mr. Thorson into offering you a ride to some unknown destination."

"Such as?"

"Possibly the grave," returned Holmes coolly. "Certainly towards eternity . . . ."

"You propose to use me to as bait in a murder snare!"

Holmes appeared unperturbed by my expostulation. "Why wait for your killer to come to you when you can draw him out on terms of our choosing, not his?"

I hesitated. "I had hoped to have supper before the hour grew too late."

Standing up, Holmes proclaimed, "And you will, Watson. It shall be my treat. Now, let us be in our way."

The old fire was back in my friend's eyes as he led me out the door of 221b Baker Street. I confess that I felt more like a lamb being led to slaughter than companion to the greatest sleuth hound in all of London, if not the world . . . .

Our promenade appeared to be aimless. First, we sauntered along Baker Street, and then turned into Paddington Street. From there, Holmes turned south and brought us to Weymouth Street. If he had a definite destination in mind, it escaped me, but we covered much of Marylebone.

After a long interval of silence, Holmes began speaking aloud.

"I would have liked to have examined the cadavers of the two electrocuted victims," he mused, "but of course they had been interred by the time the significance of their deaths had been discovered."

"Whatever would you expect to learn from them?"

"Persons stuck down by lighting often display certain types of burn marks and striation patterns on their epidermis. Often, these resemble lightning bolts, but with uncountable minute hairs or branches."

"I see."

"No two are alike, but many similar patterns recur," added Holmes. "I spoke at length with the coroners of the two towns where the bodies were found, and both reported localized burn marks that fit no pattern with which I am familiar. But I hasten to add that my study of such burn marks is limited, since murder by lightning is not a phenomenon that has presented itself for inspection up until now."

"How do you imagine such a weird thing might be engineered? By strapping a man down in an electrical storm and planting a lightning rod upon his helpless person?"

"An intriguing thought, Watson. I commend you for a rare flight of imagination. I daresay such a contrivance might succeed, if luck was on the side of the perpetrator and the intended victim was experiencing an utter absence of that metaphysical condition. But no, I believe the instrument of murder to be mechanical in nature."

"It is almost a relief to hear you state it so plainly, Holmes," I offered sincerely. "The thought of a blackguard such as Mr. Thorson being able to call down the elements upon his victims is intolerable to contemplate."

As we walked along, Holmes's sharp gaze went to every passing hansom cab. He studied the drivers' exposed faces in turn, paying no heed to the passengers safely ensconced within.

At one point on our perambulations, a hearty voice called out, "Holmes! I say, Good to see you fellow!"

A man waved from cab, and flashed his perfect teeth. I thought they were extraordinarily white.

I did not recognize the fellow, and inquired, "Who is that man?"

"That," my dear Watson, "is my esteemed dentist, Dr. Crawford. His passing is fortuitous. I must have a word with him."

Raising his right hand, Holmes attempted to flag down the cabman, but the driver instead gave his whip a sharp crack and the horse leaped ahead.

From the cab, Dr. Crawford began expostulating. The driver seemed not to hear, but instead turned a corner with alacrity, with Holmes following on his heels, as it were. The clink of horseshoes upon cobblestone became a rapid syncopation.

I rushed after my excited friend, panting, "Whatever is the matter, Holmes?"

"I merely wished to inquire for an appointment, but that cabman seems determined to prevent any conversation. It smacks of rank obstruction, Watson."

Reaching the cross street, we were in time to witness the cabriolet round the far corner. The rude driver cast a glowering glance backward before he disappeared. His face was dark with some emotion I could not decipher, his unkempt side-whiskers bristling like a startled hedgehog. I recognized him only then.

Realizing that he could never hope to catch up with the hurtling cab, Holmes pulled up short.

"Why would that cabman behave in such a disagreeable fashion?" I wondered aloud as I caught my breath.

Holmes pondered this question, or perhaps another that had occurred to him. For suddenly, he was pounding up a parallel street with renewed haste.

Following, I demanded, "What is the matter now? You cannot hope to catch up!"

"But I must! I must, if I am to preserve Dr. Crawford's life."

"What!"

Holmes soon outpaced me, and reached the distant corner, vanishing from my sight.

But the strenuous efforts of Sherlock Holmes were futile. No sign of the fleeing hansom cab could be found. It was lost in the choke of wagons, carriages, omnibuses and other wheeled flotsam of London.

In time, Holmes gave it up as a bad job of work.

I caught up with him as he was hailing a different cab. Motioning for me to join him, he clambered aboard. I did likewise.

Immediately we were off to join the endless stream of traffic.

As we rolled along, Holmes spoke bitingly. "Dr. Crawford must have been leaving his practice, for he was coming from the direction of his office on Devonshire Place. If he is bound for home, we might overhaul him *en route*."

Rapping out sharp orders to the driver through the trap, Holmes urged him to make all due haste in pursuit of the vanished cab.

"I say!" offered I. "That rude cabman wore a familiar face. He had been waiting outside my home the day I left to carry the first Thorson letter to you!"

"That, my dear Watson, was Thorson in the flesh," Holmes said bitingly. "The man works fast. He anticipated your impulse to carry the letter to me forthwith. He lay in wait, intending to abduct you upon the spot!"

"I did not like his glowering looks," I explained, "so I chose to walk instead."

"A choice that no doubt preserved your life."

We swiftly reached the Kensington home of Dr. Crawford, but no sign of him or his cab stood in view.

Dismounting, Holmes rushed to the door and pulled the doorbell. A maid answered.

"I am Sherlock Holmes, of whom you have no doubt heard. Has Dr. Crawford arrived in the last few minutes?"

"No, sir. But he is expected."

"Thank you," said Holmes briskly, leaping back into the waiting cab.

And once again we were off amid a clattering of hooves and the creaking and groaning of springs.

Our search ranged far and wide though the thoroughfares of London, but to no avail. We stopped at Shipley's Yard to inquire the cab-owner, but no bewhiskered driver such as we described worked for him. It was the same story at other hackney head offices. The man was unknown to all.

"A gypsy driver, I imagine," I suggested to Holmes.

"If that," was his succinct reply. "The man's crabbed handwriting suggested to me one unaccustomed to penning letters, and their brevity supports that assumption. I daresay a cab driver would be more literate, if only by a degree or two. Mark me, Watson. The man in question plies a manual trade of some sort."

The sun began going down when Holmes ordered the cab back to Dr. Crawford's domicile.

Again conversing with the distressed maid, we discovered that he had never reached home, and was in fact late for a prepared dinner. The maid was beside herself with worry.

Sherlock Holmes wasted no time in consoling the poor creature. He was back in the cab and soon we pulled up before Scotland Yard.

Inspector Lestrade listened intently as implored him to undertake a search for the missing dentist.

"You have good reason to suspect foul play?" Lestrade demanded.

"I have excellent reason. Put your men to work. The doctor's life hangs in the balance!"

"Very well, Mr. Holmes. You have never steered Scotland Yard wrong yet."

Nothing came of this expanded search. We were forced to our uneasy beds – or should I say, I did so. I cannot speak for Sherlock Holmes, who prowled the city like an errant wraith long after I left him.

But on the morn, a body was discovered in a field in Lower Brixton. It was quickly identified as the missing dentist.

Holmes was called to the scene. I accompanied him.

Examining the body, he noted scorch marks at the neck and temple. Lifting the inert wrists, Holmes brought two additional superficial burns to light.

"No natural lightning bolt did this!" he cried out, standing up. His voice shook as I have never before heard it shake.

"Why was Dr. Crawford killed in this horrible manner?" I wondered aloud.

Holmes shook a futile fist at nothing in particular. "Because he waved to me, Watson. Nothing more and scarcely less."

"And his motive?"

"That infernal cabman is our electrical murderer. Of that, I am resolutely certain. All masks have dropped. I now know his face and he knows that I know it. He will go underground now, like a human mole. At least for a time."

"None of this makes very much sense to me."

"I think, Watson, that you are safe for now. Small comfort in that realization. But mark me: Thorson will strike again. As the lighting strikes from the sky, leaving anything it touches smoking and riven."

As I pen these words, I confess that a shudder wracks my body even as it did when I first heard them from Sherlock Holmes's own lips. They left me shaken to my core, now as then.

A month passed, during which nothing more was heard from the murderous Mr. Thorson, whomever he might be. The Thursday letters ceased to be posted as well.

During this time, Sherlock Holmes retreated to his preserves, and I often found him reading electrical journals and, to my surprise, certain periodicals imported from the United States.

"Are you still pondering the matter of Mr. Thorson?"

"Among other things," said Holmes distractedly, laying a magazine aside. His chin was buried in his chest and his eyebrows were thrown together with such force us to suggest a collision of caterpillars.

"I am still at sea regarding the nature of the contrivance with which Dr. Crawford was so grievously slain," I observed. "I cannot imagine how so such a thing was engineered."

Holmes made a gesture as if to brush away my comment as if it were an annoying fly on the wing.

"I sometimes imagine," he stated, "that future generations will look back upon our musings with amusement, if not ridicule."

"Why, whatever do you mean by that?"

"Imagine a man of 1820 learning of the invention of the incandescent lightbulb or the telephone. If credulous, he would be astounded. If skeptical, he would be dismissive. The scientific marvels of our time verge upon being beyond his comprehension. Take, for example, the electric carriages appearing on the streets of this great city of ours. Within a generation, they promise to replace all horse-drawn coaches and carriages. No doubt greater marvels await us in this new century. We should welcome them, as we have embraced the taming of electricity and the harnessing of artificial light."

"I imagine that you are saying just because we cannot conceive of the means by which Dr. Crawford was so cruelly removed from this earth, does not mean that such means is beyond the fashioning of mortal men of our time."

Holmes staggered me with his snappish rejoinder.

"The means is known to me, Watson. I have satisfied myself up on that score. What I do not yet understand is the devil's motive, and where the diabolical contraption is kept."

"The so-called 'throne of gilt'?"

"I doubt that this makeshift throne is gilded in any way. It is clear to me that the man misspelled the word 'guilt'. His motive is revenge. But for what? If I have that, perhaps I can locate this demon who wields electricity the way a coachman wields his whip."

"Well, I cannot help you there. I have racked my tired brains for a motive for the man's evident enmity towards myself. I can think of none."

"Nor can I," admitted Holmes.

"It is baffling," I confessed.

"More maddening than baffling, I daresay. The criminal mind, however devious, spins its webs in discernible patterns. I am troubled by the absence of such patterns."

"Could it be the man is merely mad? Could his enmity be a product of imagination, or the poisonous influence on the brain of alcohol?"

"I would not rule it out," said Holmes flatly. "I am ruling nothing out."

"Well," said I, "it appears that your prediction that he has gone underground has proven correct. Nothing has been heard of him in nearly thirty days. We have seen his face and doubtless he is fearful of showing it again in London."

"Doubtless, doubtless."

My friend fell into a deep silence, punctuated by clouds of black tobacco smoke, for he was at his briar again.

Thursday the next was eventful.

I received a message from Mr. Thorson, this time signing himself Donner Thorson. It had been posted from Thundersley.

The envelope was addressed thusly:

The Honorable John A. Watson, M. D.

Did you think I had forgotten you? Well, I have not! I have been busy fashioning your hearse. Soon you will lie in it.

Yours sincerely,

Donner Thorson

I took this letter at once to Sherlock Holmes, forgetting in my haste my previous precaution of not opening it beforehand.

Holmes was unperturbed by this slight negligence. Without a word, he read the note and made a strange sound deep in his throat. I imagine it was a grunt that did not quite escape his larynx.

"My bedeviler is as careless as ever," I remarked. "Thorson is giving me the wrong middle initial and the honorific usually accorded to solicitors."

"He has an elevated if not inflated view of you," remarked Holmes. "Such as would a lesser man casting scorn upon his superior. This brands him as one occupying a lower berth among the classes. And I see that he is no longer fixated on setting you upon his fanciful throne of gilt. You are

311

to go directly to a hearse, no doubt by which means to be conveyed to the graveyard without delay."

"I had rather hoped that we had seen the last of Thorson."

"I hardly thought so," commented Holmes. "The poor devil is obsessed with you."

"But for what reason? It confounds me."

"I should like to ask him myself, if only I could lay hands upon the wretch."

I found myself pacing the floor. "Have you turned up nothing?"

"Not the fellow's name, not even a scratch of his identity. Donner is a German word, signifying thunder, so I imagine this name to be entirely fictitious. Note also that this communication was posted from Thundersley, in Essex, a hamlet which in pagan times was held sacred to *Thunor*, otherwise *Thor*. Taken all together, it smacks of concoction."

"You have nothing to go on then?"

"There is the matter of the dead horse."

"What dead horse is that?"

"According to the afternoon newspaper, a horse was discovered in a Hackney meadow without a mark on him, but he was deceased."

"What of it?" I asked in undisguised exasperation.

"The poor animal showed signs of having been struck by lightning, according to witnesses. Watson," said Holmes, coming to his feet abruptly. "Let us go to the animal rendering plant and examine the poor beast."

I saw no reason not to comply, but I confess that I was frustrated in the extreme.

Producing the soft sound that had inspired Londoners to dub the horseless vehicles "hummingbirds," a Bersey electric cab soon conveyed us to the unpleasant establishment. All but holding our noses against the horrid odors that assailed us, we were escorted to the corpse. It was a handsome bay horse, lying on its side covered with a coarse blanket.

Holmes examined it from nose to tail, and found no outward injuries.

Lifting one of the rear hooves, he saw that the horse's shoes had been removed. The underside of the hoof in question was very black and had split most grievously. If this happened when the horse was alive, the injury would no doubt have been very painful.

Turning to the plant manager, who was hovering nearby, Holmes inquired, "Where are the shoes of this poor creature?"

Cocking a greasy thumb finger over his shoulder, he grunted, "All shoes are disposed of in that big bin behind me."

Holmes hurried at once to the bin, and nosily picked through the horseshoes, finally lifting one into the light.

"Would you know if this was one of the shoes belonging to that animal?" he asked the plant manager.

The other shot back gruffly, "It was. I wondered why it was so black."

"Not black," mused Holmes. "Scorched. Fire did this. Fire also blackened the hoof and split it."

Dropping the shoe as if it was no longer of interest, Sherlock Holmes strode back and announced, "That horse was electrocuted, Watson."

"My word!" I cried. "Do you think this was an experiment gone awry?"

"No," replied Holmes thoughtfully. "I believe it to be an accident. But a very fortuitous one, as far as my investigation is concerned. I think I understand the significance of Mr. Thorson's most recent message. Watson, let us be off. The trail that was cold is now becoming warm. Soon it will be hot – I imagine quite hot. And we must step carefully if we are to avoid the fate of this unfortunate animal."

With that, we left the rendering plant and claimed a passing hansom cab, after first scrutinizing the features of the driver, which were non-descriptive and bland.

As we rattled along, Holmes remarked, "Our foe is attempting to keep one jump ahead of us. I reason that he has not abandoned his scheme to place you upon his 'throne of guilt'. But rather, he has modified this game. Knowing that we would be in search of the infernal throne, he has relocated it. And if my surmise is correct – and I believe it to be entirely correct – the fiendish plan has evolved in the most diabolical way."

After that pronouncement that smacked of doom, my friend Holmes fell into a deep silence, which he refused to break until we reached Baker Street.

There we parted company, but not before he asked me a question that took me aback.

"In your acquaintances in the medical profession, are you aware of another Dr. Watson? Specifically a John *A*. Watson?"

"Not in London, nor in any adjoining town. Why do you ask?"

"It may be that our careless antagonist is not always careless. Perhaps he has mistaken you for a colleague unknown to you."

"I can make inquiries, if you would like."

"Do so. At once. Ring me up if you discover such a namesake physician. He may prove to be the key that unlocks a most obdurate door."

My inquiries bore substantial fruit the next day. A Dr. John A. Watson, now retired, had formerly had a practice in distant Blackpool.

Obtaining his residence address, I rung up Holmes and we agreed to meet at Euston Station. Soon, we were rattling towards the seaside town, celebrated for its curative waters.

Dr. John A. Watson was a generation my senior and cordial in his easy way. Emphysema I judged to be the cause of his difficulties breathing. But he managed to answer our questions just the same in his thick Lancashire accent.

"This is a delicate matter," said Holmes after introductions. "And I pray that you take my questions in the spirit in which I pose them. That is, in the sense that this is an investigation into several mysterious deaths and not an inquiry into your medical competence."

Dr. Watson nodded faintly. "Well, please ask your questions. I am acquainted with your reputation, Mr. Holmes."

"Very good. Doubtless you have lost a patient or two in your many years of practice."

"I have lost several. What physician has not?"

Dr. Watson looked to me at that last, and I nodded in silent encouragement.

"Did you ever lose a female patient whose husband might have held a grudge against you?"

"It is conceivable, but I cannot call to mind any such specific case."

"How about a child?"

Dr. Watson hesitated only slightly before he spoke.

"There was a young boy. Rheumatic fever took him. I could do nothing. His mother was beside herself, for she was all alone, having divorced her husband, who was nowhere to be found."

"Do you recall the names involved?"

"The boy's name was Walter. Walter Smith. The mother was Anne Smith. The father's name I do not recall. I had no communication with him. It was said that he was a sailor, and his home port was Liverpool."

"Smith is a difficult name, of course," said Holmes. "But being a sailor from Liverpool does narrow the track. How long ago was this boy buried?"

"Seven, perhaps eight years ago."

"And where does the mother live?"

"I heard that she died in the interim. Broken heart and all of that. It was a double tragedy."

Rising from his chair, Holmes said, "I commend you for your earnest help, Dr. Watson. It may prove to be indispensable. Now let us bid you a good day, for we have much to do."

As we rode a trap back to the station, Holmes said, "This is clearly a case of mistaken identity. The sailor returning home from the sea learning that his wife and only son had perished, vowed vengeance against the physician who failed to save his only son. Through some subterfuge, perhaps on the part of neighbors, this Smith was told a lie to throw him off the track of the poor retired Dr. Watson. Perhaps he searched far and wide for him and, discovering another Dr. Watson, leapt to an erroneous conclusion. Hence, the letters you have received."

"As a theory, it appears sound," I remarked. "As to circumstances, I find it appalling. I have been marked for death by a person I do not know for an imagined crime I never committed."

"And it would do no good to communicate the truth to Seaman Smith, for he would only turn upon the actual Dr. John A. Watson. No, that would not do. I am afraid, Watson, we must once again bait the trap using your name and reputation. I'm sorry, but this must be done."

"I agree that I will know no rest until this man has been brought to justice, if not for my sake then for the sake of those he so callously slain."

Holmes suddenly made a noise in his throat. "Smith! I perceive the connection now. A blacksmith wields a hammer. The thunder god Thor possesses a hammer. His alias was a clue to his true name, but it was nothing that could have been arrived at by deduction, induction, or in the other rigorous means of reasoning. Yet it is good to know, along with his motive, for we may not be dealing with a demented soul, but a merely vengeful one. It is important to understand which one it is, if for no other reason then it will sharpen our wits for the struggle ahead."

"No doubt the fellow's habit of posting these taunts from places such as Hackney and Hammersmith are an equal part of his cruel game, I venture to say."

"Yes, yes. So oblique were these clues that I failed to perceive them as a species of sly mockery. Whatever we may think of Thorson, he is a man of details. For like the lowly spider, he spins his web exceedingly fine."

Holmes paused. I noted an almost imperceptible tightening of his aquiline features, and a decided inward turning of his gaze. Knowing my friend as well as I did, I understood that I should hold my tongue whilst his mental machinery toiled in silence.

At length, Holmes roused from his reflective posture. A fresh energy revitalized him. Turning to me with something like a wry grin, he said, "It may not be necessary after all to bait the hook with your irreplaceable life, Watson. Suddenly, pieces of the puzzle I did not suspect existed have fallen into place. All that is left is to investigate them. Come! We have a train to catch."

"Back to London?"

"To Hammersmith, to be precise. To the lair of the modern thunderer, whose lightning bolts are, in fact, as silent as they are insidious."

The train ride was swift, but passed slowly to my mind. From the station, a hummingbird cab whisked us directly to Hammersmith. Alighting there, Holmes went straight away to the first constable he could locate.

"Good afternoon, Constable. I am Sherlock Holmes, in the unlikely event that you do not recognize me."

"But I do recognize you, Mr. Holmes. It is good to make your acquaintance. Are you in need of official assistance?"

"I am, indeed. As a constable who patrols Hammersmith, you are no doubt acquainted with the various cabriolets who prowl these byways, are you not?"

"I am. Is there trouble?"

"There was always trouble. Trouble is a pestilence in greater London. But in this case, we are attempting to avert further trouble. I ask you to cast your memory back to the cabmen of your acquaintance. Is there one lately arrived to this area? One sporting side-whiskers, which may in fact have been recently shorn."

"I conjure up such a fellow," replied the officer. "But I do not know his name, nor where he hangs his hat and whip."

"No matter. When did you first notice him hereabouts?"

The constable rolled up his eyes as he searched his memory.

"No more than two months ago, and conceivably less."

"Ah. Good fellow! That narrows it down perfectly. Now if one were to purchase sulphuric acid in Hammersmith, who would be the likeliest purveyor?"

"Why, that would be old Burkholder, the chemist. He has a shop on the end of Black Lion Lane."

"Excellent, my man. When did you last notice the cabman?"

"Not two days ago."

"Was he driving his cab?"

"Not quite. He has traded up to a four-wheeled Clarence. A coachman, he is now."

"I see," mused Holmes. "Would you recall if either horse was the same?"

"They were not! The new ones are both dun mares."

"Was the former horse a bay?"

316

"You have it exactly right, Mr. Holmes. Exactly right. A handsome animal. I do not know what became of it, but I can make inquiries, if you wish."

"No need. I have it on good authority that the animal unexpectedly expired and was conveyed to a rendering plant. Thank you and good day, Constable. We must be on our way."

"If you need any further assistance," called the eager-voiced officer as we parted company, "I would only be too happy to pitch in, as it were."

"We may yet take you up on your kind offer," returned Holmes. Turning to me, he confided, "A four-wheeler coach, Watson. My suspicions are confirmed. Fearful of discovery, he has abandoned the stolen hansom cab and acquired an old growler. I think that this is a sinister development."

"How so?"

But Sherlock Holmes would not reply. Instead, he hurried to the chemist's shop and made swift inquiries, after first identifying himself.

"Sulphuric acid, you say? That could only be one man. Mr. Hammersmith."

Holmes frowned. "Hammersmith? Odd coincidence, that."

"No, not very odd at all. Common enough name around here."

"Is this Hammersmith clean-shaven, or does he sport whiskers?" pressed Holmes.

"The latter when he first called upon this shop, but more recently the fellow had removed all such facial adornment. Glowering gent, no matter how he presented himself."

"That fits him to a T," I remarked.

"Would you confide in me the address of the fellow?" pressed Holmes.

The chemist hesitated only briefly. "Normally, I would not reveal the address of a regular customer. But since you are Sherlock Holmes, I can hardly deny you this bit of data."

Consulting a ledger, the chemist swiftly wrote out an address and handed a slip of paper to Holmes, who read it.

"Hmm! Number five Hammersmith Mews. No doubt that is where he stables his horse and carriage."

"I beg your pardon?" grunted the chemist.

"Pay me no mind," murmured Holmes. "I was merely speaking aloud. Thank you for your time and trouble. We must be on our way."

Once we left the shop, Holmes resumed our conversation.

"When I remarked that our Mr. Hammersmith spun an exceedingly fine web, it occurred to me that he may have commenced his weaving immediately after leaving Liverpool. Hence, the selection of Hammersmith as his London headquarters."

"Is he Smith or Hammersmith?"

"The former, I would think. The latter alias relates to his fixation with the mythological Thor. It hardly matters, but he established his base of operations in Hammersmith for the same diabolical reason that have threaded through this affair. He saw himself as a righteous avenger of his shattered family."

I admitted, "I follow you only so far as this chameleon has laid his tracks. But what the devil does sulphuric acid have to do with the matter?"

Holmes was about to answer when he spied something up the way that brought him up short. Bringing up a sinewy arm, he forced me backwards. We withdrew into an alley, out of which Holmes peered carefully around the brick facade.

"What is it?" I whispered.

"It is Smith of the glowering countenance. And he is engaged in lively conversation with our friendly constable."

"A chance encounter?"

"A fortunate one, I fear," countered Holmes.

Distant voices escalated into a argument.

"I am placing you under arrest, pending further instructions from Sherlock Holmes himself!"

"I refuse!" raged the other. "I will hear no more about it!"

A moment later came a thud, followed by a sharp outcry.

Holmes sprang from the alley mouth like a hound after a fox. I pursued as best I could.

Holmes reached the constable first. The unfortunate one lay on the ground, blood seeping from his bare head, his helmet in the gutter. He groaned loudly. Of the elusive Smith, there was no sign – other than a braided blackjack of the type carried by sailors the world over lying athwart the cobbles.

"Watson! Attend to this man."

"Indeed! Will you pursue Smith?"

"Smith can await a kinder hour. Note that this man is grievously wounded. I must fetch medical help."

As I knelt down, tending to the insensate constable's head wound, Sherlock Holmes disappeared. In short order, an ambulance pulled up, no doubt summoned by my friend.

"This man has a concussion," I told the arriving medical man. "We must convey him to the nearest infirmary."

Together, we finished binding his head and set him on the stretcher, placing the dazed fellow in the back of the ambulance. I climbed aboard, and continued my ministrations.

In the back of my mind, my thoughts were of the missing Sherlock Holmes, and the peril into which he was no doubt plunging.

I remained in the infirmary for over an hour, attending to my duty. The constable would recover, but it would be some time before he was again fit.

Sherlock Holmes turned up in due course, looking both fatigued and pale, but nevertheless no more the worse for wear than that.

"Wherever have you been?" I inquired in relief.

Instead of responding directly, my friend said flatly, "Smith is dead. He will trouble us no more."

"Dead, you say? My dear Holmes, I am relieved for both of our sakes. But whatever happened?"

"The trail led to his flat in Hammermith Mews. Wrongly suspecting that the constable he had felled had betrayed his address, Smith resorted to the only recourse a marked killer could be expected to do in such damning circumstances. He did away with himself."

"Suicide?"

Holmes nodded somberly. "One might say that he executed himself, and in a most abnormal manner."

My medical duties discharged, we went out into the night. As we strolled along in the deepening dusk, Holmes recounted the events of the evening.

"I did not go directly to Hammersmith Mews," he explained. "Rather, I collected another constable and we approached the flat together. Inasmuch as it was situated over a stable, we assumed that the coach was sequestered within. As we approached, there came a flash of blue light from the horse barn, followed by an unpleasant odor that I took to be burning flesh. The constable and I forced open the stable door and discovered that the horrid smell was emanating from the open door of the four-wheeler.

"Opening the door, we beheld a beastly sight, Watson. Therein sat sprawled the late Mr. Smith, upon what he termed his 'throne of gilt', which he had lately installed into the capacious interior of the Clarence body. This coach was his means of concealing the diabolical device and transforming a commonplace growler into a murder machine. His scheme shattered and seeing no way out, Smith took his seat, attached a pair of electrodes to his head and ankle, then actuated an electrical switch. The blue flash resulted. He was quite deceased, as was evidenced by the fact

319

that his hair was ablaze when we discovered him – yet he took no notice of the fact."

"My word!"

I did not fully understand Holmes's explanation. But he soon enlightened me.

"Are you familiar with the so-called 'electric chair'?" he asked.

"Only vaguely," I admitted.

"It is an invention of American origin. The death-dealing contraption was devised for the purpose of executing criminals by what is considered a more humane means than shooting or hanging. A simple wooden chair is fitted with solid metal electrodes to receive a charge of alternating current from a prison generator. Once the condemned man or woman is strapped firmly into the seat, the connections are set up to electrocute him via the temple, ankles, and other points of his anatomy, leaving scorch marks, but no other signs of galvanic activity. I understand that the living brain is destroyed by the first jolt of voltage, and the heart shocked into lifelessness with a second application, thus insuring that the state's sentence has been carried out. Conceiving his plan to prosecute his grudge against the other Dr. Watson, Smith copied the idea, except that he devised accumulators for the storage of electricity which would then be discharged into the infernal throne, a generator being beyond his means."

"Hence the sulphuric acid purchases!" I cried.

Holmes nodded. "An essential ingredient to the required contrivance. The makeshift storage batteries were concealed inside the four wheeler. It was Smith's first idea to kidnap you via hansom cab, render you insensate with the braided blackjack he employed to such devastating effect upon our overeager constable friend, and convey you to the place where the so-called 'throne of gilt' lay waiting. But circumstances forced him to abandon that plan. He devised a variation in which the throne was installed into the carriage in place of the customary bench seat. He believed he could lure you into the cabin, and electrocute you at once before you realized that you sat upon no ordinary seat. This was the hearse referred in his last posted communication to you. No doubt Smith would have swiftly disposed of your body in the most convenient meadow, as he did the others."

"Ghastly thought! But Holmes, why was the poor guiltless horse electrocuted?"

"His original cabriolet and horse having been discovered, Smith thought it best to dispose of the inconvenient animal. Selling it was out of the question. Such a horse could have been traced back to its owner. But I suspect there was another reason."

"Oh?"

"Seaman Smith needed to test the newly installed electric chair to ascertain that it would do a proper job in its enclosed environment. By electrical means, he contrived to do away with the horse, no doubt by attaching an electrode to his shod foot, thus quietly eliminating the animal, which was known to us by sight. His previous victims were no doubt in the nature of experiments as well. Methodical man, Smith selected victims who happened to be abroad during electrical storms in order to test the makeshift apparatus and supply cover to his operations, counting than no one would question bodies discovered under such elemental circumstances to be the products of foul play."

"Remarkable! But where did this ordinary sailor acquire the knowledge to bring about his electrical murder scheme?"

"Elementary, Watson. Seaman Smith was rated an electrician. His Majesty's fleet of ships, having been systematically electrified, require continual maintenance, as you full well know. No doubt he was kept very busy. Until his desertion."

"Desertion?"

"I recently inquired of the Royal Navy, and learned of an Able Seaman Donald Smith, who had deserted his ship earlier in the year upon her return to home port."

"An electrician?"

"Need I confirm the obvious to you?" sniffed Holmes.

"There is nothing left for us to do then?"

"On the contrary. There exists one more item."

"And that is?"

"To seek out our evening meal, for we have richly earned it. The only question before us is whether we should eat in Hammersmith, or return to our familiar Marylebone and repair to a restaurant whose worth is known to us both."

"I am weary of the very sound of the name Smith," I replied truthfully. "As I recall, my dear Holmes, you once remarked that our next started repast would be your treat – a generous offer, upon which I have yet to collect."

"So I did, Watson. So I did. In that case, you may select the restaurant of your preference. Price is no object, for this has been a most intriguing case which brought a more than satisfactory conclusion. The truly-named throne of guilt has claimed its rightful ruler."

The Boy Who
Would Be King
by Dick Gillman

Chapter I – A Dash to the Diogenes Club

It was one evening in July 1903 when Holmes and I first became aware of the curious case that I have here recorded as that of "The Boy Who Would Be King".

I had spent the afternoon reading at Baker Street, enjoying a deserved break from my busy medical practice. Holmes had attended to business during the day and, on his return, we settled back to enjoy a quiet pipe after having consumed a fine dinner of roast pork, served with roasted potatoes and an exquisitely sharp apple sauce. As we sat, I noted that, within minutes, the sitting room had taken on that pleasant, pale blue haze, reminiscent of a gentleman's club.

Taking up my copy of *The Lancet*, I continued to read a most instructive article relating to public houses and the spread of tuberculosis. Holmes, I observed, was thumbing his way, somewhat testily, through his copy of *The Times*.

Tossing the broadsheet angrily to one side, he announced, "I can find nothing of interest here, Watson. The government continues to be inept in the majority of its dealings and the dalliances of the gentry are an impertinence best left unread!" Holmes's thin fingers now drummed in frustration upon the arm of his chair and I was indeed grateful when the ringing of the bell in the hallway below indicated that we had a visitor.

Holmes edged forward in his chair, eager to determine who was at the door. As I looked towards him, I could see by his frown that he didn't recognize the footfall upon the stairs. The quiet knock on the door, followed by the appearance of Mrs. Hudson, did little to enlighten us. Standing behind her were two gentlemen whom I did not recognize. Casting a swift eye over the pair, Holmes immediately became more business-like. Rising from his chairs, Holmes gave a nod of dismissal to his landlady, declaring, "Thank you, Mrs. Hudson. I will ring if I require anything."

With a smile and a brief nod towards us, Mrs. Hudson then left, closing the door behind her. The two gentlemen stood before us, one slightly behind and to the side of the other, almost in deference. Holmes, I observed, now looked particularly serious, asking, "I take it that my brother has instructed you to call upon me regarding some urgent matter, for you seem to have that formal, yet bland, look of Whitehall about you."

In truth, the two men did have something of the appearance of civil servants, but there was something more, a crispness that I had observed amongst many officers in my army days. Both men were well-groomed, dressed in the sombre, dark suits of the City, and wearing equally drab overcoats. The leading man was aged, I would say, around forty years, lean, with greying hair and sharp, chiselled features. From the way he held himself, it seemed to confirm my impression of a military man. The second, I observed, was much younger and clearly the junior partner. He was pale-faced with short cropped hair and stood shuffling nervously from one foot to the other. As I watched, his eyes darted from to his superior, standing before him.

With a brisk nod, the senior figure addressed us. "Mr. Holmes, I am Commander Thorn of the Naval Intelligence Department, and my colleague is Lieutenant Warren. I have been charged to arrest you and convey you to The Admiralty." On hearing this, my pipe almost fell from my mouth and I reached out towards my chair to support myself.

Holmes's face was without emotion. "I have little doubt that Mycroft has provided you with the necessary paperwork, Commander?"

Reaching into his overcoat, Thorn produced from it a slim document which he handed to Holmes. Opening it, Holmes's forefinger went to his lips as he scanned what I presumed to be the warrant. "It would appear, Watson, that I am to be held, for the moment, incommunicado. Is this correct?"

Commander Thorn nodded. "Those are my orders, Mr. Holmes. Now, if you please . . . ."

Thorn paused as Holmes swiftly moved forward to collect his coat and hat. As he did this, there was a metallic "clink" from an object that the junior officer had removed from his overcoat pocket.

I gasped and blurted out "No!" as I realized that Lieutenant Warren now held a pair of handcuffs in his grasp.

On hearing my outburst, Thorn turned to Warren, saying, icily, "Put those infernal things away, Warren! They will not be necessary." The embarrassed junior officer hurriedly obeyed and stood aside whilst Holmes disappeared towards the stairs.

To my shame, I could only stand, open-mouthed, unable to utter a single word. I was rooted to the spot, staring in disbelief as our visitors left the room before following Holmes down the stairs. It was several seconds before I was able to move and then run to the coat-stand, gathering my own coat before galloping headlong after them. I stood on the pavement, looking around me before wildly waving my arms to flag down a passing cab as I struggled to get one arm into my overcoat.

I found myself standing on tiptoe, frantically trying to catch a glimpse of my friend, but Thorn must have had a carriage waiting for, as I watched, a closed four-wheeler turned the corner of Baker Street. What help I could be to Holmes, I was not completely sure, and it was only as I clambered into the cab and called out "The Diogenes Club" to the driver that my task became clear.

After some minutes which, to me, seemed an eternity, the cab pulled to a standstill and I leapt from it, tossing the driver a shilling. Running up the steps, I barged my way past a startled, liveried doorman and into the atrium of the club.

Looking around wildly, I was quickly seized by a Sergeant-at-Arms as I shouted, "Mycroft Holmes! I must see him!" Startled members turned towards me, as an event such as this was unheard of. However, I would not be denied, shouting out once more, "Mycroft Holmes! Explain yourself!"

I now found myself pinioned by two burly footmen and being propelled, somewhat forcefully, towards the front door of the club. It was at this point that the familiar figure of Mycroft Holmes appeared and, with a single gesture from him, I was released. Mycroft walked towards me his face stern and angered. In a hushed, commanding voice, he exclaimed, "That will be enough, Watson! Come with me."

Mycroft Holmes led the way towards an unobtrusive, oak-panelled door into an anteroom at one side of the atrium. Opening it, he ushered me inside. With the door now firmly closed, he turned and addressed me, most sternly, saying, "This is disgraceful behaviour, Watson, what do you – ?"

My voice was glacial as I stood, barely inches away from Mycroft, with my finger pressed firmly into his chest. "If there is any disgrace, it is on *your* part, Mycroft. What is this charade with Thorn and your brother?" Mycroft Holmes instantly sensed the anger raging within me and took an unsteady pace backwards.

With brows furrowed, and in a calmer voice, he replied, "The Crown desperately needed the services of Sherlock, and I was uncertain as to whether he would accept the task if I were to ask him openly. There has been an . . . an 'occurrence' at his old school. It is imperative that Sherlock is, for the moment, isolated and has a completely open mind, with no preconceptions, when he meets the . . . ah . . . a person of great importance to the Crown."

I looked blankly at Mycroft for, from the time that I had first met Holmes, he had never spoken of his education other than a brief, passing mention of "university".

Mycroft pursed his lips before continuing, "Sherlock's school days were not the happiest for him. You are aware of his vast knowledge in certain areas and the gaping holes in his knowledge of subjects that hold no interest for him. This 'selective' nature of his learning caused him to be harshly dealt with during his time at the school. Although he keeps it hidden, it has left its mark upon him. I was concerned that if Sherlock were to meet the person in our care at the school, the very environment might cloud his judgement."

I considered this for a moment, now understanding Mycroft's actions and concern. However, this did not sit well with my knowledge of the emotionless logic employed by Holmes. "Could he not have met this person in a more 'neutral' environment?"

Mycroft slowly shook his head. "We could not guarantee this person's safety elsewhere."

I nodded, still not satisfied with Mycroft's answer and anger now once more tingeing my question. "Is your brother to be held prisoner for some time?"

Mycroft again shook his head. "I would imagine that he will be back in Baker Street within a day. In the meantime, Watson, you might wish to read an item of some relevance which you will find on page two of *The Times* tomorrow." With that, Mycroft turned on his heel, opened the oak door, and escorted me, somewhat hastily, from the club.

Finding myself once more in the street, I felt at least a little reassured by Mycroft's words. However, I was still unsettled by the evening's events as I hailed a cab to return home.

After spending a restless night, I washed and dressed quite early, leaving a little before eight o'clock to obtain a first edition of the day's *Times*. Finding a vendor on the corner, I handed over the few coppers to purchase the paper and quickly turned to page two of the broadsheet. What I read stopped me in my tracks. Across three columns was emblazoned the heading "*Mistaken Identity Saves Archduke From Assassination*". This was followed by the reporting of a young man being shot at one of our most prestigious schools.

Intending to peruse the piece more fully at my leisure, I quickly re-folded the paper and rushed to Baker Street. One can imagine my surprise upon entering the sitting room to find Holmes ensconced in his chair, drawing deeply on his pipe, hidden from view by the very same newspaper that I was holding. Lowering the broadsheet slightly, he enquired, "I take it that you have seen the item of singular importance on page two, Watson?"

I nodded before mumbling, "Err . . . yes, I've read the heading although I am not, as yet, fully aware of the content of the piece."

Holmes gave a single nod. "In that case, I will allow you to read it in its entirety before asking your opinion of it." With that, he raised his paper and was once more hidden from view.

Taking off my coat and hat, I made my way, with the newspaper, to my chair and settled down to digest the relevant item.

After, perhaps, two minutes, Holmes once more lowered his paper, asking rather bluntly, "Well?"

I had barely finished reading and was still running the import of it through my mind as I spluttered, "Ah . . . Well, from this, it seems that the Archduke, whilst playing football for the school, narrowly missed being assassinated because of his similarity in appearance to another boy. The other boy was shot and killed by mistake and there is, seemingly, no trace of the assassin."

Holmes sat back, eyes closed, drawing steadily upon his pipe. "There is a veneer of truth in what you have read, Watson – sufficient, perhaps, to appease the curiosity of the man in the street, but I am of the opinion that there is much more."

I gave my friend an enquiring look and waited expectantly for him to enlighten me. He took his pipe from his mouth and waved the stem in my direction as though he was, in some way, winding back time itself. "Allow me to recount the events that took place after I left Baker Street with Mycroft's lackeys. The journey was short, and on arrival at the Admiralty building, I was escorted not to some area of restraint, but to a rather grand, oak-panelled, corner office on the second floor with a fine view over St. James's Park." Holmes drew strongly upon his pipe before continuing. "Seated in the office was a young man of some thirteen or so years, well-proportioned, and whose most striking feature was his wreath of auburn hair."

I nodded before asking, "Was he able to give any further detail of the tragic events at the match?"

Holmes frowned. "Very little, as he appeared to be in something of a state of shock. The match, it seemed, was being played quite vigorously and a little way into the first half, a single shot rang out and a player of almost identical stature and hair colour to the person seated before me was killed instantly."

I frowned. "If they were so similar and it was a fast-moving game, how then would an assassin tell the two boys apart?"

Holmes leaned back and blew a thin stream of blue smoke towards our already almond-coloured ceiling. "Perhaps the assassin had observed the Archduke prior to the match . . . or . . . perhaps, from having familial knowledge." Holmes paused, adding thoughtfully, "It is something of a puzzle. Doubly so as the Archduke informed me that the two boys had colluded to play a practical joke on the staff by exchanging their team positions."

My eyes opened wide at his suggestion of familial involvement. "Surely a member of his own family would not stoop to . . . ."

The rest of my question went unfinished as it was interrupted by Holmes leaping from his chair, exclaiming, "Westminster Mortuary, Watson!" Rushing past me as he headed for the door, he cried out, "I need to examine the other young man." Gathering his coat and hat at the trot, Holmes thundered down the stairs.

My tired frame could not match his pace and by the time I had reached the pavement of Baker Street, Holmes was already aboard a cab and waving energetically for me to join him. Clambering aboard as best as I could, I was barely seated before Holmes hammered on the cab roof and we were off at a frantic pace.

Chapter II – A Mortuary and a Familial Visitor

Throughout our journey, I tried to press him further on his thoughts of family involvement, but he would say nothing more, returning to his own rumination as he sat back, eyes closed.

It was but a few minutes before we were drawing up in Horseferry Road before the imposing, red-brick building that contained both the mortuary and Westminster Coroner's Court.

From a previous visit the previous year, I remembered the Georgian style of the wide, arched carriage entrance edged with Portland stone and topped by the impressive, although curious, bow window. This purpose-built, new mortuary building provided facilities to both store bodies and then to allow *post mortems* to benefit from the copious natural light that it provided.

Once inside, it was clear that the figure of Holmes was known to the staff and we were taken, without delay, to the mortuary proper. Looking about me, it appeared that Mycroft had already anticipated his brother's actions. Before us, the body of a red-haired young man had been laid out on a slab close by, ready for our examination. Beside the body had been placed a small table, and upon it were the garments that the victim had been wearing at his death.

I leaned forward, asking, "What is this boy's name?"

Holmes's face looked grim as he replied, "Thomas Winslow. A young man who, unfortunately, had more than a passing resemblance to Archduke Wilhelm von Hallstatt . . . a resemblance that was to cost him his life. To have seen them side-by-side, Watson, you would have thought them cousins, if not brothers."

Holmes spent a minute or so examining the boy's mud-spattered clothing and then, with a nod from Holmes, the attendant withdrew to one side. I looked on as Holmes followed a familiar pattern, circling the prostrate figure like some wheeling bird-of-prey. The head and shoulders of the youth were the only parts currently visible. After observing all that he could, he respectfully drew back the mortuary sheet. He stood for, perhaps, thirty seconds before removing his lens from his overcoat pocket and moving forward to examine the neat entry wound in the very centre of the victim's chest.

Holmes stood, forefinger pressed to his lips. With the slight inclination of his head, he beckoned me forward and I too examined the body and the bullet wound. Quietly, he asked, "Does this wound look familiar, Watson? Help me turn him onto his side so that we might see the exit wound."

Grasping the young man's shoulders, we turned him through ninety degrees. Whilst in this position, Holmes again took his lens and examined the wound to Winslow's back. Satisfied, we replaced the body and, on completing our examination, we nodded our thanks to the mortuary attendant and then withdrew.

As we walked back towards Horseferry Road, I lingered slightly as I puzzled over Holmes's question. I had, during my career, seen gunshot wounds in a military context. In truth, the wound that I had seen was familiar to me. As I caught up with Holmes, I asked, "Do you believe that the weapon used was military in origin?"

Holmes paused at the kerb and waved towards an approaching cab. Turning to me, his face was grim. "It is a strong possibility . . . or even a small-bore hunting rifle."

Our ride back to Baker Street was uneventful except for the occasion when Holmes hammered on the roof of the cab to bring it to a halt. He then raced towards a nearby telegraph office before re-joining me some minutes later. I looked quizzically at my friend but he raised a finger and would say nothing as he once more returned to his own thoughts.

Within minutes of our arrival, the room took on that familiar blue haze as we enjoyed our pipes. Holmes seemed at ease and I ventured to ask him the question that had waited since his excursion to the telegraph office. "Might I ask for whom the telegram was intended?"

Holmes took his pipe from his mouth, saying, "It was to Mycroft. I wanted him to ask the young Archduke two specific questions."

I looked to him to say more and waited whilst he drew once more upon his pipe. Holmes took it and used the stem to count off the two items against his fingers. "First, I wanted to know what was the exact state of play when the fatal shot was fired. The second question was to ask when the boys made their decision to exchange their team positions."

I considered this information for a few moments, unsure as to the reason for asking such questions. I scratched my head before asking, "Holmes, I'm in something of a fog as to what possible benefit you might gain from knowing this."

He moved forward in his chair, his eyes now bright. "From my conversation with the Archduke, he had been given the position on the right wing for the team. I wanted to know if the fatal shot had been fired during play or, perhaps, when the team had been standing in their allotted position after a goal had been scored. If the latter, it would have been child's play for an assassin to identify a red-haired winger!"

I nodded, asking, "And for the second question, Holmes?"

Holmes sat back. "The reason for that I will keep until we have visited the school, for the timing may prove significant."

I gave a questioning look towards my friend but saw that he had now retreated from the world and was, once more, lost to me.

It was sometime after lunch that the bell in the hallway below almost rang off its mounting, such was the violence of its summons. Holmes was immediately alert and leaned forwards as a clipped conversation was heard from below. I noted that the familiar tread on the stairs of Mrs. Hudson was followed by the much heavier tread of another. Holmes stiffened, saying, "Our visitor may have family connections to the Archduke, Watson, for he has a crisp, military tread!"

Hardly had he spoken these words before the door to the sitting room burst open and in marched a commanding figure, with Mrs. Hudson hurrying at his heels. She tried to announce our visitor but was rudely interrupted.

The tall gentleman of military bearing stood stiffly to attention, demanding, "You are *Herr* Holmes? I want to talk to you . . . in private! I will not speak in the presence of your servants."

Holmes was granite-faced, snapping in reply, "Indeed you will not, sir, for this house is the property of Mrs. Hudson, the lady beside you, and I am her lodger." Pointing in my direction, he continued, "This gentleman is my trusted friend and associate, Dr John Watson, who is privy to all my affairs. You are a guest in Mrs. Hudson's house and I will receive you on those terms and no other."

Colour rose in the face of the man before us. I thought he might strike Holmes, but he showed considerable restraint and, with some distaste, turned to Mrs. Hudson and uttered, grudgingly, "I am in error, madame." At this he briskly nodded his head whilst clicking his heels together.

Holmes nodded and held out his hand towards a chair. I sat in my own chair and took stock of the man now seated before us. He was undoubtedly Germanic in his tone and manners and stood some six feet in height. His hair was iron grey but still held a hint of copper within it, and it crowned a somewhat angular, full-whiskered face. His suit was of quality and could have been bought at any tailors that served the aristocracy, although the cut clearly hinted at the Continent.

Now calmed, our guest began, "I am Count Ludwig von Hallstatt, the uncle of Archduke Wilhelm. I am here as it has been brought to my attention that my nephew was the victim of an assassination attempt and is in British protective custody. I am also informed that you have been to visit him, something that I have been denied. Is he safe and well?"

Holmes's face had softened slightly. "He is indeed, Count, and he is an extremely lucky fellow . . . which is more than can be said for his classmate."

I watched as the Count's face looked troubled. "Yes, our government has already sent its condolences to the family of the other boy. It is a bad business, Holmes. How are you involved with the investigation?"

Holmes pressed his lips together before replying. "I have been asked by His Majesty's government to look into this matter. You perhaps know my brother, Mycroft?"

A look of understanding crossed the Count's face as he replied, "Ah, yes. Mycroft. We know each other from my . . . my somewhat unofficial connection with the embassy."

Holmes nodded and then paused before asking, "The carriage accident that caused the death of the Archduke's parents must have been most grievous for him. I understand that he is now within a hairsbreadth of becoming king."

The Count's expression appeared to change slightly in a subtle way as he replied, "Yes, it was an event that could change history, for he is next in line. Do you believe this to be relevant? I had assumed that the attempt on his life to be the actions of anarchists, as London appears to be rife with such vermin."

I watched as Holmes replied, "It is one of several possibilities, Count. Your nephew is an accomplished sportsman, I believe. Does he follow in a family tradition?"

On hearing this the Count brightened. "Why yes, his father, Karl, and I were brothers. We often fished and hunted together on our family estates. Wilhelm is like the son I never had."

At this point, Holmes inexplicably turned to me, saying, "My colleague, Watson, is something of a fly fisherman. He has accompanied

330

me many times when we have ventured to Scotland for the salmon. And you hunt too, don't you, Watson?"

I was somewhat taken aback by this question, but managed to stammer, "Well, I wouldn't say I was particularly accomplished in either activity but, yes, I find it most enjoyable."

"Will you be travelling North for the 'Glorious Twelfth', Count?" Holmes smiled, asking innocently. "Watson has his rods and guns cleaned and ready, eh, Watson?"

I smiled and nodded and then looked towards the Count for his reply. "Yes," he said. "I have been invited by a Royal personage. I too have my guns, both fine examples from Johann Springer Erban of Vienna, of course!"

Holmes smiled, asking, "The 11-mm, bolt-action rifle with double triggers?"

At this, the Count raised an eyebrow. "You are very knowledgeable, Mr. Holmes. Yes, you are quite correct – the exact model."

Holmes rose and extended his hand. "I intend to visit the school tomorrow. If I discover anything further regarding your nephew, I will ensure that you are informed."

The Count rose, pursed his lips and grasped Holmes's hand. "Thank you, I am most grateful. Good afternoon, gentlemen." With a further nod and click of the heels, he was gone.

Chapter III – Unpleasant Memories

After the Count had left, Holmes slowly returned to his chair and took up his pipe, asking, "What do you make of that fellow?"

I sat and pondered for a moment. "Well, you mentioned the possibility of a suspect with a familial connection. He is, without doubt, an able marksman who has access to a suitable weapon. However, he does appear to have a genuine fondness for the boy."

Holmes nodded. "Yes, all that is true and, after meeting the man, there are now inconsistencies that gnaw at me. I must send a telegram to the school to inform them of our intended visit tomorrow."

After the telegram to the school had been duly despatched, we sat and smoked, reflecting upon our visitor. After ten minutes or so had passed, our thoughts were rudely interrupted by the ringing of the bell in the hallway below. The sound of Mrs. Hudson on our stairs made Holmes once more alert. Hardly had she knocked on the sitting room door and entered, a telegram in her hand, than Holmes leapt from his chair and almost snatched it from her grasp. I gave her an understanding look as she slowly retreated, shaking her head.

Holmes had, by now, ripped open the envelope and was devouring the contents of the telegram. "This is of some interest, Watson – a reply from Mycroft. As to the first question, the shot was fired as the teams stood in position after a goal had been scored by the home team." Holmes paused for a moment, gazing at some point in the far distance, before continuing, "As for the second, it would seem that the deception to change positions was only conceived on the morning of the match . . . ."

He retreated to his chair and was silent for, perhaps, some ten minutes. He sat, eyes closed and with his fingers steepled against his lips, almost as though in prayer. After this time, he began to slowly fill his pipe whilst he presented the facts as we knew them.

"Let us imagine, for a moment, that Count Ludwig is the assassin. He has, as you say, the weaponry, and is a skilled marksman. He would stand to gain in the event of Wilhelm's death . . . perhaps he might even inherit the crown!"

I was shocked by this, asking, "Surely not! The boy is like a son to him!"

Holmes took his pipe from his mouth and pointed the stem in my direction. "Our own history tells a different tale, Watson. Dare I remind you of the sad tale of the Princes in the Tower?"

I took his point and considered the matter further. Holmes allowed me to wallow before declaring, "I am almost certain that he is not our man. The calibre of his rifle is, I suspect, too large, and he has watched the boy grow from infant to almost adult. The Count knows Wilhelm's every mannerism and could easily identify him as the target, no matter where the boy might be on the playing field . . . ." Holmes paused before adding, "But not so a paid assassin."

Holmes's brow furrowed as he drew strongly upon his pipe before continuing. "No, there has to be more. I believe that we must wait for our visit to the school to gather more data. We must set off early tomorrow as I wish to scout the area around the football pitch before entering the school."

I found when I arrived the next morning that, true to his word, Holmes had risen a little after seven and had breakfasted by eight o'clock. Joining him, I was chastised as it took me until half-past to eat what I would describe as a meagre breakfast and ready myself for the journey ahead.

Holmes had decided to take the Metropolitan Railway's train from Baker Street out into the Middlesex countryside. From the station nearest the school, we were able to hire a pony-and-trap to convey us the short distance to the school's playing fields. Unbeknownst to me, Holmes had already received a copy of the police report of the incident and, as a result, we were soon making our way along a footpath into a copse that bordered the pitch.

Holmes was in his element, sighting angles and inspecting possible hides that might have been used by the assassin. It was as we came to a slight depression that Holmes froze. "Here, Watson! The man was here!" He fell to his knees, clutching his lens. After some minutes he rose and then picked up a small twig to use as a pointer.

"What do you notice about these depressions in the soft ground?" I peered as he pointed to some slight scuffs in the coarse grass but was unable to see any pattern.

"I fear that this piece of ground appears to me as any other in the vicinity."

Holmes frowned and gave me a hard look. "The feet, man, the feet! Can you not see how the legs have been splayed with the shoes lying sideways on the ground? You of all people should recognise this as the classic military prone-firing position . . . and here, the depressions from the elbows supporting the rifle."

I looked again and once Holmes had pointed out their relative positions, I could envisage the man lying as he described. Holmes swiftly delved into his overcoat pocket and from it he produced a small, waxed-fabric tape measure. This he used to take various measurements which he then jotted down in his notebook.

Holmes frowned. "The Count is definitely not our killer, for this man is barely five-feet two-inches tall, and has small feet to match his frame. Come along – The game is afoot!"

Returning to our trap, we made the journey along a circular country road towards the school. Arriving at the vast black-and-gold-tipped wrought-iron gates, we passed through and entered into a pebbled courtyard. Before us stood a magnificent red brick and Portland stone Tudor building. I goggled at its beauty whilst Holmes didn't give it a second look. He simply strode manfully up the angled steps towards the front door.

Trailing in his wake and trying my utmost to avoid the distractions of the building, I almost bumped into Holmes, who was now in conversation with a porter. In less than a minute, a commanding figure, in full academic robes, strode towards us.

Holding out his hand, he addressed Holmes. "Ah, good morning, Holmes. It has been some years and I have read that, surprisingly, you have made something of a name for yourself."

This I thought to be something of a barbed welcome and so I was not surprised by Holmes's response.

"Yes, so it appears, Headmaster . . . despite your instruction. This is my associate, Dr John Watson."

The headmaster's faced darkened slightly at Holmes's riposte, saying curtly, "If you would both follow me to my study."

In silence, I followed whilst Holmes walked beside the academic, which to me showed that Holmes was, indeed, familiar with the location of the Head's study and also that he was no longer subservient to the man at his side.

Walking through this Tudor wonder, I marvelled at the wooden carvings and decorated ceilings as we made our way into the building. Arriving before an oak door, blackened by age, the headmaster ushered us inside and invited us to sit before his desk. I noticed that, as he sat, he pressed a bell-push to one side of his magnificent mahogany desk.

The headmaster began thus: "Tell me, Holmes – how might the school be of service in this investigation?"

Holmes's face was without emotion as he replied, "It will be necessary for me to meet some of your staff and also some of the other boys who were close to both young Winslow and the Archduke."

The headmaster's voice now took on a superior tone. "As to the first, I can only ask if they are willing . . . but the second, I cannot allow – "

Holmes moved forward in his chair, his voice icy. "It is not a question of choice, Headmaster. Rest assured that I have the full authority of His Majesty's government in this matter." Holmes paused, his eyes as coals. "Should you attempt to obstruct my investigation, even in some small way, dire consequences will follow. There are already questions being asked as to whether the school took sufficient precautions to protect its pupils, and the term 'negligence' has been uttered."

Holmes paused for his words to be considered before continuing. "The hard-won reputation of the school is at stake, Headmaster. The Prime Minister is an 'old boy', and he has shown a keen interest in the case. I feel it only fair to inform you that I have his ear and he is most keen to avoid a scandal at any . . . *any* cost."

I looked towards the headmaster and, though his face was now pale, his expression was one of pure malice. "I will not be threatened by you, Holmes – "

Holmes interrupted, saying, "This is not a threat. You have the telephone, as does the Prime Minister. You are at liberty to speak to him, if you so please. I will wait for his answer before you allow me to proceed."

For a moment, the headmaster's hand began to reach out towards the telephone on his desk . . . but then it faltered and retreated. Any further response was cut short by a knock at the study door and a barked, "Come."

Entering the study was a slender man of some fifty or so years, with wavy, dark hair and a face that was delicately featured. He was dressed in the usual, black academic robe with a pale blue lined hood. Beneath this he wore a dark suit which, from the width of its lapels, appeared to have something of a Continental cut to it.

The headmaster introduced us coldly. "Gentlemen, this is Mr. George Hooper. It is not commonly known, but I am to retire at the end of the Christmas term. Upon my retirement, Mr. Hooper will become the new Headmaster. Until these tragic events, he was the House Master of both Archduke Wilhelm and Winslow." Pointing towards us, he declared, "George, this is Sherlock Holmes and his associate, Dr Watson. You are to answer their questions as fully as you feel able."

Holmes nodded to Hooper and invited him to sit. "I am grateful for the use of your study, Headmaster. Please do not let us detain you."

With eyes narrowed, the headmaster left, leaving us to question Mr. Hooper in something more of a relaxed manner.

Holmes smiled, asking, "Tell me, Mr. Hooper, what is your current role at the school?"

Hooper shuffled slightly. "I am the Head of French and have been for some years. As the Headmaster mentioned, I am Master of Wyvern House and I have a minor role in the provision of sports – athletics and football."

Holmes nodded. "So, you know both the victim and the intended victim quite well?"

Hooper looked pleased as he replied, "Indeed. They have been in Wyvern House from their very first day at the school, and therefore under my care."

I ventured to ask a question. "Were you officiating, in a sporting capacity, on the day of the incident, Mr. Hooper?"

He shook his head. "No, my only involvement was to pin up the team sheet on the 'Football' section of the school noticeboard. I unfortunately missed the match, having a verb test paper to mark for the lower fourth."

Holmes leant forward, asking, "Did you know that the Archduke and Winslow had planned a practical joke and had exchanged places on the field?"

Hooper again shook his head. "No, I only heard of this after the incident when I chanced to hear a conversation between one of the team and Simon Forrester, a friend of young Winslow."

My friend nodded and looked deep in thought. "Thank you, Mr. Hooper. I would like to speak to that young man after lunch, and also to examine Winslow's effects."

Hooper agreed. "I will ask him to meet you at the entrance at one o'clock. He can take you to the dormitory and show you Winslow's locker."

Holmes casually touched my forearm and rose from his chair. "Come along, Watson, it is almost twelve! As I recall, we passed a welcoming looking public house on the way here. Luncheon calls!"

Chapter IV – Misdirection at The Star and Garter

With a nod to Hooper, we left the headmaster's study and returned to our trap. I must confess that I relished the thought of some nourishment and a pint of best bitter. As we trotted along, Holmes turned to me, asking, "What do you make of Hooper, Watson?"

I thought for a moment. "Well, his physique is such that he may fit that of the killer . . . but, like the Count, he has known the boys for several years. He too could tell them apart quite easily."

Holmes stroked his chin. "Yes, your thoughts mirror my own.

Pulling the trap to a halt beside the pub, which proudly proclaimed itself to be "*The Star and Garter*", we tethered the horse and entered the public bar. The interior was that of many country inns, several small tables in the centre with some settles and trestle tables to the sides. At these sat local workmen and farmers, whilst others stood drinking at the bar.

Behind the bar, I noticed that there was a chalk board, and upon it was written, in a coarse hand, that luncheon today was pork pie with cheddar cheese, pickles, and home-baked bread. On seeing this, Holmes clapped his hands in delight. "A meal fit for any ploughman! A perfect foil for the straitjacket of academia!"

Within moments, we had placed our order and were enjoying half-a-pint of Walker and Stones. For some reason my mind turned to our reception by the headmaster. I could now clearly see why Mycroft had taken the action that he had, removing any taint that the school might have on my friend. The "wounds" inflicted by the school had not healed, despite the passing of many years.

The food arrived and, as the day was warm, I found that I had consumed my beer before finishing my meal. Holding up my glass, I was pleased when Holmes readily nodded at my unspoken suggestion.

Whilst I waited to be served, I noticed one or two of the locals watching a fellow who was performing some kind of magic trick with three walnut shells and a coloured, cork ball. Placing the ball under one of the walnut shells, he would then shuffle their position and ask the onlookers where the ball was now.

This seemed like child's play. Looking up, the fellow asked if I would like to place a wager on where the ball was. I nodded as it appeared obvious to me. The fellow shuffled the shells and I confidently placed a sixpence next to one of them. Needless to say, it was incorrect. I wisely decided not to continue!

Bringing back the ale to our table, I sat, looking downcast at my loss. Holmes noticed my long face, asking, "What is it, old fellow?"

I pointed towards the small knot of men, saying, "There is a trickster over there with three walnut shells and a ball. He is using some kind of mis-direction. I watched him move the shells around and the ball was not where I thought it should be. I lost sixpence!"

Holmes laughed but then suddenly stopped, his face frozen. It was if he had had a seizure! I panicked and moved swiftly towards my friend.

Wide eyed, he cried, "Watson! I have been so blind! Misdirection! There is no paid assassin! But why kill Winslow?"

Holmes hurtled towards the door as I hastened to the bar, placing half-a-crown upon it before rushing after my friend.

I barely had time to leap aboard the trap before Holmes slapped the reins against the horse's rump and we were off towards the school at breakneck speed. I clung onto the body of the trap with one hand whilst managing to consult my pocket watch with the other. It was a few minutes before one o'clock as Holmes pulled up the horse sharply and skidded to a halt on the gravel of the drive.

Holmes rushed up the steps and looked around wildly for young Simon Forrester. I tried to calm him and tugged at his sleeve. "Holmes, for pity's sake, man!"

Holmes stopped and faced me, his eyes aflame. "It is all an illusion, Watson! Seeds have been overtly sown to confirm our belief that the murder was an assassination attempt on the Archduke . . . when all the time, *Winslow* was to be the victim!"

I blinked and took a step back, almost unable to comprehend what I had just heard. "Winslow? Are you sure? But why? I doubt whether he is of any significance, except to his family."

Holmes pursed his lips and ground his fist into the palm of his hand whilst murmuring, "Why, indeed!"

Our thoughts were broken by the appearance of a blazered-and-capped young man who approached and addressed us. "Mr. Holmes? Dr Watson? I am Simon Forrester. Mr. Hooper has asked me to escort you to our dormitory. This way, sirs."

Turning on his heel, he led off into the building. I was still fascinated by the interior of this fine building, taking in the lists of honours, the large oil paintings of "old boys" which included knights of the realm, prime ministers, and other notables. It was as we stopped to allow a file of boys to descend a magnificent oak staircase that I chanced to idly look towards the large wooden plaque beside me. As I read the dated list of names, one leapt out at me.

I touched my companion's sleeve, asking, "What is the 'Ashburton Shield'?"

Holmes turned. "It is a vast, circular, embossed silver shield presented to The National Rifle Association by Baron Ashburton in, I believe, 1861. The shield is the major prize in a rifle shooting competition among several of the country's major public schools. Why do you ask?"

I pointed to the date 1866. Holmes's face clouded as he read, from the names of the members of the school's winning team, – "*G. Hooper*".

With the staircase now clear of the "crocodile" of boys, we ascended to the first floor. At the far end of the landing, Forrester opened the door to a room on the left, saying, "This is our dormitory, sir, and the door opposite is that of Mr. Hooper's room. Please come in."

We followed the boy into a large, airy room which contained a row of six beds along each long wall, each one neatly made. Beside each bed was a small locker which, no doubt, contained the clothes and items needed for daily life.

Forrester indicated the first bed inside the door. "This was Winslow's bed, sir, and that is mine." The lad pointed to the next bed in the row.

Holmes sat on Winslow's bed and encouraged Forrester to do likewise. "Was Thomas a good friend?"

Forrester nodded. "The best, sir. We helped each other with our prep. And I did my best to look after him when he sleepwalked."

I looked towards Holmes and then asked, "Were his eyes open when he did this?"

Forrester nodded. "Yes sir, always. But he didn't see anything. His eyes were glazed. He didn't walk far, either. Sometimes he would get up and open the dormitory door and just stand there for a moment and then return to his bed."

Holmes looked at the boy intently, asking, "Were the masters aware of this?"

The lad shook his head. "Oh, no, sir. I would guide him back to bed. I was afraid that, if they found out, they would send him away from the school."

Holmes softened his voice, asking, "On the night before the match, did he sleepwalk?"

Forrester seemed reluctant to answer. Holmes put his hand on the boy's shoulder, saying, "You won't get into any trouble, Simon. You have my word."

Nodding, he replied, "Yes, sir. I awoke as I heard the floorboard beside my bed creak. Thomas was walking towards the door and I could hear quiet voices on the landing. I couldn't reach him before he had opened the dormitory door and stood there gazing towards Mr. Hooper's room. I hid behind the door and could see . . . ."

The boy paused, in some distress. Holmes asked, quietly, "What could you see, Simon?"

The boy answered in hushed tones. "I . . . I saw Thomas standing, as if he was staring, wide-eyed, at Mr. Hooper and M. Le Fèvre who . . . who were kissing."

I sat down on Forrester's bed, asking, "Perhaps it was just a farewell. A brotherly gesture . . . as Continental men are sometimes prone to do?"

Simon Forester, shook his head. "No sir, it was more. It was as though it was a man kissing his wife."

Holmes's face was without emotion as he asked, "What happened when the two men saw Thomas?"

"They leapt apart, sir, and Mr. Hooper said 'Winslow!' Thomas must have wakened slightly as he then turned around and returned to the dormitory, closing the door behind him. I hurried to my own bed and feigned sleep as the door opened, and I think Mr. Hooper looked in."

Holmes sat silent for a moment. "On the day of the match, did you know that Thomas and Wilhelm were to change places?"

Simon Forrester nodded. "Wilhelm told me that Mr. Hooper had come to him that morning and suggested it to him as a jape. He had said that it would also be an excellent tactic as, in previous matches, Wilhelm's reputation as a fine footballer had become known and he had been closely marked from the very first whistle."

Holmes face was now as riven granite. He turned fully towards Simon Forrester, saying, "You are a loyal friend and if we are to obtain justice for Thomas and to save the reputation of the school, you must tell no one else of this. It is a matter of honour. Do you understand?"

The boy looked most serious and nodded. "Yes sir. Nothing will be said."

Holmes nodded. "Now, I would like you to convey a message to Mr. Hooper that I wish to speak to him in the Headmaster's study at five o'clock."

Young Forrester nodded and sped off down the landing.

I stood, anger burning within me. "This is a disgrace! A man takes a boy's life to save his reputation!"

Holmes was cold. "It is not just his reputation, Watson, for come Christmas time, he was to become the new Headmaster of this place of learning. Not so now, I think, but there is more to do to tie the noose."

Holmes stood and moved to the door of Hooper's room. Finding it locked, Holmes delved into his jacket pocket and removed the small leather case that contained a variety of metal lock picks. Within a minute, we were inside the small room that appeared to act as both study and bedroom.

A desk in front of the single window was piled with exercise books, and beside it stood a bookcase containing dictionaries and French texts. The walls were adorned with dingy green wallpaper and a print of Botticelli's *Venus* hung above the bed. Looking down, I noticed that on the floor, protruding from beneath the bedspread, were two pairs of slippers of different sizes.

After searching quickly beneath the bed, Holmes then moved to the large wardrobe with its carved motifs and central mirror. Opening both doors revealed only a selection of clothes as might be found in any gentleman's wardrobe.

It was as Holmes ran his hand along the top of the wardrobe that he stopped and then pulled forward the chair from in front of the desk. Standing upon it, he then passed down to me a heavy, cloth-wrapped bundle which I immediately recognised. Carefully replacing the chair, Holmes took the bundle from me and, unwrapping it, produced a Lee-Enfield long rifle. Holding the breach to his nose, he sniffed and raised an eyebrow before checking that the rifle was safe and devoid of cartridges.

After Holmes had used his lock picks to secure Hooper's room, we now faced the difficulty of concealing the weapon. Holmes's gait was indeed unusual as we made our way back to the headmaster's study. Knocking and finding the study empty, Holmes placed the rifle out of view behind a somewhat laden coat-stand.

Chapter V – The Noose Tightens

A little before five o'clock, the headmaster returned and once the door was secure, Holmes began to lay the foundation for confronting Hooper.

Holmes's face was without emotion as he began. "Headmaster, despite our differences, be assured that it is not my wish or intention that the school be harmed by the events of the past week. From my investigation, I have evidence that George Hooper shot and killed Thomas Winslow in order to silence him."

At this, the headmaster rose from behind his desk, exclaiming, "This is totally absurd and, no doubt, without foundation!"

Holmes continued. "Not so. George Hooper has been in a relationship with another member of staff, a M. Le Fèvre. Hooper believed that Winslow had observed him acting inappropriately with Le Fèvre and formed a plan to shoot the boy during the football match the following day."

The headmaster was speechless and reached forward to grasp his desk for support before whispering, "This cannot be so. There must be another explanation . . . ."

Holmes shook his head, saying, "There is none. Hooper used the boy's resemblance to the Archduke to make it appear that the killing was an assassination attempt. To cover his tracks, he persuaded the boys to change identities so that Winslow would play in the Archduke's position on the field. In doing so, it added weight to his innocence and also increased the probability that Winslow was killed, in error, by a paid assassin."

Looking towards the headmaster, I observed that he had slumped in his chair and now looked ashen. Holmes spoke more calmly, stating, "Hooper is to come here presently. I intend to prove to you his guilt, and would be grateful if you would not interrupt whilst I do so."

The headmaster simply nodded and within half-a-minute, a knock sounded upon the door. Holmes called, "Come!" and Hooper entered.

He looked towards the headmaster and his face clouded slightly. Once seated, he asked, "You wanted to see me, Mr. Holmes?"

Holmes smiled, saying, "Yes, Mr. Hooper. Our time here draws to a close. I was just remarking to the Headmaster that I had had a visit from Count Ludwig von Hallstatt, Wilhelm's uncle. He was grateful for my interest, and even invited Watson and me to Vienna. I travel so little in Europe these days but you, I expect, do so with your knowledge of languages."

Hooper had visibly relaxed and the colour had returned to the headmaster's face, although his expression was somewhat quizzical.

Hooper nodded. "Yes, I also speak German and have visited Vienna several times. It is a beautiful city and I have travelled extensively in France. I adore Paris."

Holmes nodded, asking, "Is that where you first met M. Le Fèvre?"

The colour rose in Hooper's cheeks. He paused before answering. "I met him at the Sorbonne. But why is this relevant?"

Holmes moved forward on his chair. "Because he became your lover and, no doubt, you sought to find him a position here at the school and provided a strong recommendation."

I looked towards the headmaster, who was now slowly nodding. Hooper's eyes flashed, crying out, "This is not true! Jean-Yves and I are simply friends and colleagues!"

Holmes was direct in his response. "Not so. You were observed behaving intimately with him on the evening before the fatal shooting.

Winslow appeared in the doorway of the dormitory, wide-eyed. You panicked and decided that the only way to preserve your reputation was to silence him. What you did not know was that Winslow suffered from somnambulism – sleepwalking – and though his eyes were wide open, he could see nothing!"

Hooper cried out, "No! It cannot be!"

"Unfortunately for you, Hooper, his friend, Forrester, was also present but hidden from view and observed you and M. Le Fèvre." Holmes paused and then continued, "Winslow was shot the following day after you engineered that he and the Archduke exchange positions on the pitch. The logical presumption now was that the shooting was an assassination attempt on the life of the Archduke . . . but it was simply a callous move on your part."

Hooper seemed to pull himself together and tossed his head. "You can prove none of this, Holmes. It is my word as a respected, senior master against that of a boy seeking to tarnish my good name."

Holmes nodded. "I agree that this could be argued in court, but there is more. I understand that you are something of a marksman, Hooper. You are named as a member of the school's winning team of 1866 for the Ashburton Shield."

Hooper gave a contemptuous laugh. "That was over thirty years ago, Holmes. I haven't touched a rifle since."

Holmes raised an eyebrow, saying, "You surprise me, Hooper. Allow me to jog your memory." Holmes rose and strode towards the coat stand. Pushing aside the coats, he removed the weapon and held it in full view. "This I retrieved from your room, concealed on the top of your wardrobe. It is a modern Lee-Enfield long rifle that has recently been fired and, I have little doubt, bears your finger marks."

I watched as Hooper stared incredulously at both the rifle and at Holmes. "You . . . you had no right . . . No warrant. It is inadmissible in any court!"

Shaking his head, Holmes replied, "Come, Hooper. Half of both the judiciary and His Majesty's government are former pupils of this school. They would provide me with a back-dated warrant in a heartbeat, in order to preserve the good name of the school."

Hooper now looked deflated but asked, "What will become of Jean-Yves? M. Le Fèvre?"

I was shocked as the headmaster rose from his chair, declaring, vehemently, "He will be dismissed immediately and leave the premises today!"

Hooper rose from his chair, defiant. "If this is so, I shall blacken the name of this school throughout my trial. You will be vilified and I will say you were complicit and turned a blind eye to my relationship with Jean-Yves!"

I thought the headmaster might explode as he stood and shook, uncontrollably. It was only Holmes's intervention that prevented violence between the two men.

Holmes raised his voice, crying, "Gentlemen, let us behave as such! Might I suggest a different path?" Holmes looked at both parties and waited until they had retaken their seats. "Mr. Hooper, there is no doubt as to your guilt and there is little doubt as to the outcome of your trial. However, it may be possible that M. Le Fèvre be spared a trial."

Turning to the headmaster, Holmes continued, "Would you consider allowing M. Le Fèvre to remain in his post until the end of the summer term, Headmaster? Perhaps, then, if I speak to my brother and you agree to allow M. Le Fèvre to resign at the end of term, then Mr. Hooper might then undertake not to involve the school in these private matters. Is that agreeable to both parties?"

I looked towards the headmaster. Though still angered, he gave a single brief nod. Turning my attention to Hooper, he had his lips pressed together before also nodding.

Holmes visibly sighed. "Thank you, gentlemen. Mr. Hooper, I will require you to accompany me and Dr Watson back to London. I will consult with my brother and discuss what is possible." Holmes paused, turning to Hooper and saying more quietly, "I will allow you ten minutes to gather what you need and to make your farewells. Please do not consider running away, for if that were to happen, I assure you that the full force of the law would be applied, most vigorously, to M. Le Fèvre."

Hooper nodded, saying, "Thank you, Holmes."

Holmes made a telephone call whilst I waited at the entrance to the school. After precisely ten minutes, Hooper appeared carrying a small attaché case and, on returning the pony-and-trap to the station, we boarded the train to take us directly back to Baker Street.

The journey was uneventful and undertaken in silence. We each appeared to be lost in our own thoughts. On arrival, I was not surprised when, as we passed through the ticket barrier, we were approached by two plainclothes police officers who escorted Hooper away to a waiting closed carriage.

Arriving at 221b, we sat and smoked until late into the evening. Finally, I plucked up the courage to ask what had been Mycroft's response to the tentative agreement made at the school.

Holmes sat back, drawing slowly on his favourite briar. "Mycroft is in general agreement, Watson, although the Home Secretary has added the *caveat* that M. Le Fèvre must leave the country once his tenure at the school ceases at the end of term."

I frowned. "You mean that he is to be deported."

"Exactly so. Sometimes I admire your aptitude for plain speaking."

Shrugging this rebuff, I asked, "And what of Hooper?"

Holmes took his pipe from his mouth and frowned. "It is my belief that there can be but one end for the man . . . one from which he will not return. The only blessing for the school is that the relationship between Hooper and Le Fèvre will not be the subject of prosecution."

I frowned, asking, "What motive, then, would Hooper have for shooting Winslow? Surely a reason will be demanded?"

Holmes nodded. "Mycroft implied that the prosecution will put it to Hooper that he was in need of money and that he became the paid assassin of persons unknown. Hooper is not stupid. He will readily agree, seeing this as a way of protecting Le Fèvre."

Drawing strongly upon his briar, he continued, "I have no pity for a man who takes the life of another, especially a child, in order to preserve his own reputation. However, perhaps we might learn from what drove him to this desperate act. Love is something that has barely been even a shadow in my life and yet, I have witnessed its tremendous power."

Holmes paused for perhaps half-a-minute, looking towards some far distant point. "Hooper was driven by the fear of prejudice and intolerance. How can the State, through law, decide what is 'natural' and lawful when, until seventy years ago, the state decreed that it was both natural and lawful to enslave another human being, simply because of the colour of their skin?"

I found myself unable to offer any kind of reasoned answer to this. Looking towards my friend, I observed that Holmes had now drawn up his knees, holding them tight against his chest and had withdrawn from the world.

The Seventeenth Monk
by Tim Symonds

To Télos

Chapter I – A Visitor Arrives at Dr. Watson's Clinic

The Whittington chimes of the grandfather clock flooded along the hallway. It was five o'clock. I was alone in the consulting room of my medical practice in London's fashionable Marylebone district. If no further patients came, I could soon stroll to the In and Out Naval and Military Club for Soup of the Day and Whitebait. I walked across to the window and stared out. A light drizzle put me into a contemplative mood. Some months had passed since, to the relief of the criminal underworld, my old friend Mr. Sherlock Holmes retired at the very height of his powers. The decision had taken me utterly by surprise. We were no longer lodgers together at 221b Baker Street. I thought I had become an institution around Holmes, like his Stradivarius, or the old, oily black clay pipe and his index books. Was it possible some of our more recent cases like "The Creeping Man" would be the last exploits in which we would work together? Would we never again be seated together in an agile hansom rattling towards Charing Cross Station, my service revolver tucked into a pocket?

The thread, I ruminated, that had united many of the cases was the manner in which they began life. Francis Bacon tells us, *"If the mountain will not come to Muhammad, then Muhammad must go to the mountain"*. Before Holmes retired to his bee-farm in Sussex, it could be said he was that proverbial mountain. The case I published as *A Study In Scarlet* established his credentials as England's premier unofficial Consulting Detective, praised by no less a pair of Scotland Yard inspectors than Gregson and Lestrade. From then on, there was no need for Holmes to advertise in *The Police Gazette*, nor ingratiate himself with the well-to-do to obtain custom. Holmes's new-found *droit d'entrée* extended even to the highest reaches of European Society. The stairs at our lodgings once took the weight of the giant Wilhelm Gottsreich Sigismond von Ormstein, Grand Duke of Cassel-Felstein and King of Bohemia. The King was desperate to regain possession of a photograph taken with a certain "well-known adventuress", Irene Adler. The curious case of "The Red-Headed League" commenced when a flame-haired pawnbroker by the name of Jabez Wilson climbed those same stairs.

345

Holmes's career had spawned as many want-to-be-Holmes-es as Scotland's turbulent geology spawned Munros. Portraits of him in watercolour, wood, and poker-work proliferated. Everywhere, men (and at least one woman) dressed in long grey travelling cloaks and deerstalker caps, old briar-root pipes *à la bouche*, expounding on the characteristics of different tobacco-ash (typically flakes of Latakia tobacco), poisons, stains, handwriting, and even the classification of mud and soil.

I returned to my desk. My eyes fixed themselves upon the framed picture of General "Chinese" Gordon. What had it been like, holding Khartoum against the overwhelming Mahdi forces for more than a year? My train of thought was broken at exactly five minutes to six o'clock by a tap of finger-nails on the mahogany door of the consulting room. It heralded the entry of the receptionist, Miss Campbell, to announce her departure for home. "No more patients, Doctor," she said, drawing on her winter coat, "but there's someone in the waiting room who would like a word. Seems to be acquainted with you."

It was Miss Campbell's habit to provide me with a brief description of my patients prior to bringing them into the room. Over the months these descriptions had grown more and more adventurous and even clinical. At the start of her engagement, she merely gave name and age. Now I might be given a fully-fledged diagnosis with a suggested remedy, as in a case the previous week involving the mistress of the illustrious Lord --------, who came complaining of faintness and indigestion: "You should tell her not to lace her corsets so tightly," I was advised, "and anyway, the small-corseted waist is falling out of fashion."

"He or she?" I asked, referring to the latest visitor.

"He."

"Did he give a name?" I asked.

"No," came the reply.

"Description?"

"Corpulent."

"Corpulent?" I repeated.

"Gargantuan, in fact."

"Gargantuan!" I parroted. I knew only one person for whom that description was invested with such meaning.

"Surely it can't be . . . ." I began.

"Indeed it is, Doctor," a voice interrupted from the corridor, "but I'd rather remain anonymous." He moved into the room. "Shall we say, 'Mr. Smith'?" he requested.

With a practiced move, his large hands took Miss Campbell by the shoulders and eased her out of the room, pushing the heavy door shut behind her.

346

I was quickly on my feet. "My Heavens, Mycroft, this is a surprise!" I exclaimed, extending my hand. I looked up at the steel-grey, deep-set eyes and masterful brow of Sherlock Holmes's brother, elder by some seven years. "And very welcome, of course!" I added. I pointed to the divan. "Please," I continued, "do have a seat."

I had last come across Mycroft Holmes a year or so ago on a brief visit to the Diogenes, the unusual club he co-founded specifically for the most unsociable and unclubbable men in town, where, save in the Stranger's Room, no talking is under any circumstances allowed. Mycroft operated in some indeterminate fashion at the very heart of Government. During the case I titled "The Bruce-Partington Plans", Sherlock Holmes said of his brother, "Occasionally he *is* the British government, the most indispensable man in the country . . . He has the tidiest and most orderly brain, with the greatest capacity for storing facts, of any man living . . . he is the central exchange, the clearinghouse, which makes out the balance. All other men are specialists, but his specialism is omniscience."

Holmes went on, "If the art of the detective began and ended in reasoning from an arm-chair, my brother would be the greatest criminal agent that ever lived. But he has no ambition and no energy. He will not even go out of his way to verify his own solution, and would rather be considered wrong than take the trouble to prove himself right."

I went to the door and called out loudly, "Miss Campbell, before you take your hat, please bring a fresh pot of tea."

I looked back at my guest.

"Any preference?" I asked.

"Gyokuro would be very welcome," he replied.

"Gyokuro," I relayed along the corridor. "And pastries and Devonshire cream, please!"

My visitor settled his vast bulk on the couch. He looked at me thoughtfully. A silence ensued. It's true, I thought. There *was* a suggestion of uncouth physical inertia about him.

Then, "Have you heard anything from Sherlock recently?" he asked.

"Not recently, no," I replied.

"Over the past month, say?"

I shook my head. "I rarely hear from him. Since your brother retired to his bee-farm, he hasn't made a habit of informing me of his every move."

Mycroft Holmes pointed at the telephone on my desk. "No telephone calls? Not even a telegram?"

I shook my head. "No contact from any quarter," I replied. "I assumed his wretched bees have been keeping him busy. But tell me, why of all people asking, if there's anyone in this world who would be *au fait* with his . . . ."

"Exactly," came the reply.

Conversation was suspended while the tray of tea and pastries was brought in and distributed. The door shut once more.

Mycroft Holmes resumed, "You see, two months ago my brother was temporarily persuaded to come out of retirement. At the express instance of the Foreign Secretary, the Most Honourable Marquess of Lansdowne. For a very important mission. We impressed on Sherlock that the fate of our Empire might be at stake."

"The fate of our Empire?" I exclaimed. "And you are here – in my surgery – because . . . ?"

". . . We need to find out what's happened."

"How do you mean, 'find out what's happened'?"

"For example, if he's still alive."

I stared at my visitor.

"Why would he not be alive?" I spluttered.

Mycroft Holmes pointed towards the day-book on my desk.

"The question is, can you take a few weeks off to go *incognito* and look for him? Your knowledge of his ways might be invaluable."

"I can always get a *locum* from St. Mary's to take over," I replied.

My guest set the cup down and pulled his great bulk up from the divan.

"I take it that's a yes?" he asked.

I nodded. Watching him rise, I asked, "Surely you're going to give me a few instructions?"

"Only that you must take your service revolver and a few pockets full of ammunition. As to how you'll get there, we'll arrange that. Best not to go with Thomas Cook's."

"Am I allowed to know just a little more precisely where I'm going and what I'm meant to do when I get there?"

"You'll be going to Sherlock's last-known location. There's a German we asked him to keep watch upon, someone whose movements have been reported to the Foreign Secretary. Our Defence Attaché in Berlin rates the man *facile princeps* among the secret agents of the Kaiser.

"And his name?" I asked.

"Otto Muller, though he won't be using his real name, any more than you'll be using yours. We've been aware of him for some time. As a young lieutenant, Muller was commissioned by the Kaiser to lead an expedition into uncharted territories of Central Asia, hand-picked for his unscrupulous nature. The group traversed vast plains and high, rugged mountains. They underwent the widest daily temperature ranges on Earth and suffered extraordinary privations. Muller was the only one to get back alive. We need to know what he's up to now. If he'd been born here, I would rate him the most dangerous man in England. Cross him and your life is not worth a pfennig, as Sherlock may have found out. If you come across him, under no circumstance – and I repeat – under *no circumstances* are you to directly approach him. Is that clear, Doctor? We simply want to know why he's there."

"Where are we talking about?" I asked.

"An impoverished island in the Mediterranean – two-thirds of it sterile rock."

"Why is the Kaiser taking such an interest in the place?"

"That's our question too."

"If it's so impoverished," I rejoined, "why would we care?"

"Because unlike other Empires – Russia, Germany, the Qing, the Ottoman – ours is a thalassocracy. We may rule vast areas of land and command further great stretches, but England's security lies in sovereignty of the seas. Britannia protects, manages, and controls oceans. Nothing must be allowed to threaten England's *Cordon Sanitaire* around our India possessions. The island in question is not isolated in a waste of waters. It straddles the sea lanes connecting England to our Empire in the East. Right now the island presents no danger, but if the Kaiser gains mastery over it and if war were to break out between Germany and Great Britain . . . ."

For a last moment Mycroft Holmes stood in the doorway, his frame completely filling it.

"I envy you the journey to the lands and seas of Perseus, Jason and the Argonauts, Heracles, and Theseus. You must visit ancient Itanos, the city famed in antiquity as the gift of Mark Anthony to Cleopatra. As to who *you* are," he continued, "don't adopt a *ruse de guerre* as a former riverboat captain on the Congo. There's always someone around likely to catch you out. Remain a medical man, but *not* by the name of Dr. John H. Watson. Were there other Assistant Surgeons with the 66th Foot at the Battle of Maiwand. For example, someone who attended you when you fell victim to an Afghan musket? You could use his name."

Any reminder of the heroism and incompetence of that fateful battle caused me to shudder even those many years later. It was a British trait to make legend out of abject military failure – the retreat to Corunna, the Charge of the Light Brigade, General Gordon's tragic death at Khartoum. At Maiwand, the 66th were not even aware of a ravine to our right. The Ghazi warriors used this cover to attack. We were exposed for three hours to the most horrific artillery fire an army ever had to stand, all concentrated from the front and flanks on a small surface not two-hundred yards long.

Finally the order came to up-and-run, or in my case to be hauled away bleeding by my brave orderly Murray.

"There was an Army Surgeon with me at Maiwand," I replied. "A British major by the name of John Pryor. He was killed by a direct hit from a shell."

"Even better. He won't be around to contradict your theft of his name – not in the flesh at least. For the rest, you can stay close to the truth. You were badly wounded and discharged with an Army pension, and you are developing an interest in archaeology."

"And the name of this poverty-stricken little place?" I asked.

"Not so little. It's some one-hundred-sixty miles from north to south and thirty-five miles at its broadest. The classic Land of Minôs – the Isle of Crete."

Holmes's brother chose to exit by the Tradesman's Entrance. Outside we shook hands. "Curious story, the Cretan Minotaur," he said. "Dante mentions him in the *Inferno*." In a warning tone he added, "Doctor, Crete is and has always been a land where death trumps life. It's possible my brother's bones lie there now. Take care yours don't get left there too."

He turned, climbed into a waiting Lanchester Tonneau, and was gone.

I went upstairs into an attic where I kept the battered old trunk from my military days. I knew little of Crete other than its location in the Eastern Mediterranean, its topography ribbed by bare, almost treeless mountains, a link between Asia, Africa, and Europe. I took out a map last used aboard the troopship *HMS Orontes*, sailing through the Mediterranean on my return to England, pensioned off with eleven-shillings-and-six-pence-a-day. I put my trusty service revolver on the side to oil up later. Moths had done their work on the tropical wear in the tin box. While uncertain that I would be in Crete long enough for the boiling summer to reach its apogee, I would nevertheless pay a visit to Marshall and Snelgrove's and order a suit of Sichuan paj.

Chapter II – Watson Prepares To Sail To The Aegean

Mycroft's visit left me in a state of considerable agitation. I'd assumed that his brother's silence was a consequence of absorption in a new life with his "little working gangs" of *Apis mellifera*, the European Honey Bee – or perhaps engrossed in writing his promised magnum opus, *The Whole Art of Detection*. Could it be that Sherlock Holmes was dead? If so, when word arrived in England, *The London Times* and *The Manchester Guardian* would come rushing to update their obituaries. I reflected how the announcements in the newspapers and journals at the time of his retirement had given the impression the great detective's soul had already departed for the Otherworld. Ruefully, I myself felt this was almost true, to forsake his convenient lodgings and a busy life at Baker Street – at the heart of the world's greatest metropolis – for the isolation of a villa on the Sussex Downs and harsh winter winds blasting in from the English Channel. *The Police Gazette* regretted his decision as premature, terming it "*disagreeable to all enemies of crime,*" and listing his accomplishments in the past tense – "*Born 1854, great-nephew of the French artist Émile Jean-Horace Vernet. Skilled violinist and learned in the Oriental art of baritsu. Interested in chemistry, he frequently dabbled with poisons and acids. According to his* amanuensis *Dr. John H. Watson, he was an excellent singlestick player, boxer, and swordsman.*"

There followed a list of some of Holmes's publications: "On Secret Writings", "Upon the Distinction between the Ashes of the Various Tobaccos", "On the Typewriter and Its Relation to Crime", "Upon the Tracing of Footsteps" and "Upon the Dating of Old Documents". Through his knowledge of the types of tobacco ashes, he could, *The Gazette* noted, "*identify the kinds of cigarettes found at a crime scene*" and "*distinguish different types of shoe prints, footprints, horseshoe prints, and hound-dog prints*".

The London Times noted Holmes was a master of disguises: "*With the ease of a great actor he became a bookseller, a groom, a clergyman, an old Italian priest, a seaman, a plumber, and even an old woma*n." *The Illustrated London News* remarked on Holmes's extraordinary facility with languages, "*as at ease with Middle Egyptian hieroglyphs as with Goethe's* Faust *or Hugo's* Les Misérables."

The next morning, the twelve-horsepower twin-cylinder Lanchester Tonneau returned to the surgery. The chauffeur's traditional four-in-hand knot in his tie gave a pleasant nod to the long history of the horse-carriage he was helping sweep away. Willingly he provided an inspection of the epicyclic gearbox and the ingenious balance of the horizontal engine, after which he handed over a package. It contained a *Laissez-Passer* in the name of Major John Pryor, M.D., plus a considerable sum in several currencies – English gold sovereigns, Ottoman gold *Kurush*, and Greek silver one- and two-*drachmae*. It would not be long before the whole of the Foreign Office knew of my involvement, The receipt called for my signature as John H. Watson and not Major Pryor. The oversight ensured only hours would pass before the whole of the Foreign Office learned of my involvement.

The delivery was followed an hour later by the arrival of a letter bearing the insignia of Manchester Ship Canal boatbuilders Abdela and Mitchell. The writing was distinguished by the ornamental style of the penmanship (the letter "*f*" upstroke twice the length of the downstroke, the upstroke for the shorter letter "*e*" two-thirds the vertical length of the downstroke). I opened the letter. It read:

Dear Major Pryor,

I understand you have accepted a position aboard a whaling ship and will be leaving for the Antarctic in four or five months' time. In the interim, I can offer you temporary employment. Our shipyard has completed trials of the Harouny, *a thirteen-ton launch destined for delivery via the French canals and Malta to a former Ottoman territory in the Eastern Mediterranean. Normally a surgeon would not be required, but there has been an outbreak of Mediterranean Fever along the route, occasioned by the* Micrococcus melitensis. *We therefore wonder if you might act as ship's Medical Officer at a fee of two guineas a day plus all expenses? If so, you would need to be packed and ready at Manchester Dock 9 in approximately two days' time.*

A response at your earliest convenience would be much appreciated.

I am,
Yrs very sincerely,

Isaac J. Abdela

I folded the letter and put it in my pocket. I would need supplies. I went to the telephone and placed an order with the Junior Navy Stores for a wicker luncheon basket to await my arrival at Dock 9. It would contain several packets of Fortnum's Royal Blend Tea ("*Notes of Flowery Pekoe from Ceylon uplifted with Maltier Assam*"), twenty-five tins of ox tongues, five of pressed beef, thirty of turkey and tongue pâtés, four of ham, fifteen plum puddings, twelve guava jelly, and twenty-five tins of sardines and a dozen jars of Burgess's Genuine Anchovy Paste. From John Bell and Croyden I ordered ten bottles of Enos's Fruit Salts and a supply of quinine pills. A visit would also be required to tobacconists Salmon and Gluckstein of Oxford Street to purchase a half-dozen tins of J. and H. Wilson No. 1 Top Mill Snuff and several boxes of Trichinopoly cigars, manufactured from tobacco grown near the town of Dindigul.

352

After that, to Foyle's Bookshop at Cecil Court for a copy of William Clark Russell's latest nautical yarn, *Overdue*. Its five-hundred-and-more adventurous pages would engage me aboard the *Harouny* through the roiling Bay of Biscay and the Alboran Sea and onward to my destination. By now a more optimistic mood had overtaken me. Would I once again, in distant Crete, be seated in a hansom next to Holmes, revolver at the ready and the thrill of adventure in my heart?

I reached into a drawer and took out the time-piece lying there, a scratched champlevé green, blue-and-black enamel pocket-watch by Boget and Olivet, Geneve, in eighteen-karat gold. I would take it with me. It had a double sentimental value. Along with the nine-tube grandfather clock, it was the only object I had inherited from my father via my dead brother. Once in Baker Street, it had been a test that I had given Holmes to gauge his deductive powers. Holmes had passed with almost magical powers.

The sea journey went without incident. I spent a nostalgic day at Malta's Grand Harbour, a port at which I had last stopped on my final journey back from Peshawar. At dusk, silver bugles brought the notes of "The Setting of the Sun" on the breeze from *HMS Revenge* at anchor, followed from the *Harouny*'s engine-room with a rousing chorus of "The Absent-Minded Beggar".

That evening I lay on my comfortable bunk. My eyelids drooped and I checked my pocket-watch. It was still early. I tried to postpone sleep by reading aloud from Clark Russell's nautical yarn at a gripping point – "S*tand by all three royal halliards – mizzen top-gallant halliards," rapped out Captain Mostyn, in the quick harsh note of the sea command. "Helm there, let her go off two points"* – but without success. I put the book aside and prepared to give way to the pleasant lassitude. Rather than dozing off, my mind leapt back to the most dramatic event in Sherlock Holmes's and my active years together: The fateful encounter at the Reichenbach Falls in the Swiss Alps between Holmes and the criminal mastermind Professor James Moriarty.

It had been in April and May of 1891 that Holmes had finally managed to outwit the Professor. The police had effected a series of arrests that cleaned up countless crimes and dismantled Moriarty's organization. As this occurred, Holmes and I had travelled to the Continent, while I was led to believe that it was because Holmes's live was in danger. It only later had I realized that my friend was using himself as bait in a trap to capture the Professor, who otherwise might have eluded the net.

Our journeys had led us by way of Meiringen and the Reichenbach Falls, where I was duped away from Holmes, allowing the Professor to confront him. The resulting clash of titans had ended in Moriarty's death and the assumption of Holmes's own demise, as it was believed that both had tumbled, locked together, into that dreadful cauldron. In fact, Holmes had survived, using his knowledge of Baritsu to defeat his opponent.

Many a criminal had underestimated Mr. Sherlock Holmes. I wondered if I would find that to be the case in Crete, or if this time Holmes might have met his match.

I reached out and turned off the small side light.

Chapter III – The *Harouny* Reaches Crete

We lay off Crete. The *Harouny* had dropped anchor in the moonlight. A short while later, dawn broke over the town of Candia and we edged forward. Coasters were already at work loading bags of caoba from lighters, as the horseshoe-shaped harbour able to take only the tiniest steamers and sailing vessels. We had sailed from Valetta into the seas and lands of Homer, the mountains and coastlines alive with legendary figures – Achilles, Agamemnon, Helen and Menelaus, Odysseus, Penelope and Telemachus. I stood on the deck staring out at the wondrous scene before me, "*a land . . . in the midst of the wine-dark sea; fair, rich and sea-girt is she . . . .*" Sea-girt, yes, but no longer rich, I thought. I gazed at the succession of tumbled-down, overgrown limestone walls of abandoned buildings. Ancient terraces ran wild with asphodels, marguerites, and rhododendrons. Beyond them rose a range of arid mountains. Was Holmes somewhere out there, lying dead, his fly-blown corpse awaiting the predation of *Gypaetus barbatus* – the Bearded Vulture? "How on Earth do I start the search?" I wondered out loud.

I received an answer the moment I stepped off the gang-plank. "Welcome to the land of King Minôs. My name," the man said with a bow, "is Stavraki Aristarchi." He wore white sheepskin boots and a costly alzarine silk sash about his waist. "I am a dragoman. I can be your guide." He turned his finger towards the *Harouny*'s jackstaff. "I speak excellent English, but if you wish I can switch to German or French or Greek or Turkish or . . . ."

"Hold on, Stavraki Aristarchi!" I chuckled, "English will be fine. First I need accommodation, and then we can discuss terms. I assume you'll be available for a fortnight or so?"

He would, he assured me, be available for the rest of my corporeal life, if needed, and wished me a long and happy one.

A second figure approached. "*Effendi*," he asked, looking furtively this way and that, "can I interest you in an amethyst scarab? Twenty of your English pounds. From the Egyptian Twelfth Dynasty." He pointed towards the island's interior. "My nephew found it over there. In the Kamares Cave, very high on Mount Ida."

I decided to take the bull by the horns. I replied, "I'm not here to buy antiquities. I'm here to join up with an old friend and go to the Acropolis of Polirinnia, but I am not sure of his whereabouts."

"Go to the Acropolis of Polirinnia, you say?" the man asked, eyeing me carefully. "Your name, *Effendi*?"

"Major Pryor," I replied. "I'm a Medical Doctor with an interest in archaeology."

"This friend, Major – is he a Cretan like this dragoman, or a foreigner like you?"

I replied. "*Anglos*. Like me, except he is this tall . . ." (I indicated about six feet) ". . . and thinner, with deep-set grey eyes."

The souvenir seller studied me as an archaeologist would study a terracotta shard. "We know every foreigner who arrives and every foreigner who departs," he continued. "We count them in and we count them out." He held up the amethyst scarab. "They are important to us. We like the money they leave behind. There is a man like that . . ." Again he pointed southward. ". . . except I cannot vouch for the colour of his eyes."

"And this man?" I asked. "How would I find him?"

"If you travel as I tell you, you cannot miss him. He's offering ten silver *drachmae* for any pieces of burnt clay or pots with ancient *grammata* – writing – on them. He must be a spy. Who else would wear a dark cloak with a crimson lining? Who else but a spy would dress like that? Also because he wears square blue sunglasses," the man continued, "and because we think every foreigner is a spy. My friend here, the dragoman – maybe he's also a spy. He worked for the Ottoman pashas until we kicked them out. Maybe we should shoot him down like a dog! Maybe you too are a spy." He pointed at the *Harouny*. "All spies arrive on boats like that."

As casually as possible I asked, "Why would a spy bother to come here?"

"Because Crete is now free. We had four-hundred years under Imperial Butchers like İkinci Abdülhamit, the Turkish Sultan. We worry we will become a pawn on some other chess-board. Even you British – wouldn't you like Crete to be another jewel in your King Edward's crown?"

I reached into my pocket for an over-generous gratuity.

"Finding this *Effendi* would be a good start," I replied.

The vendor spoke to the dragoman. Looking dismayed, the dragoman muttered back to me. "The place you want to go, '*Einai stou diaolou ti mana*', translating immediately as '*It's at the devil's mother*' – is somewhere very hard to get to.

I reached out with the handful of one- and two-*drachmae* silver coins. The souvenir seller took them with a nod and turned to point into the distance. "Go to the sacred cave of the nymph Eileithyia. I sold the *Anglos* an old pot there a week ago. This man Stavraki Aristarchi can take you. I have two good mounts you can hire." He pointed at the considerable pile of luggage and tinned goods waiting to be lifted off the deck. "And a good mule you can hire too."

We arranged to meet the mounts and mule in the town square early on the morrow. Pleased with our negotiations, the man departed with his scarab of dubious antiquity. I called after him, shouting above the harbour din, "And *your* name?"

"I was born on the island of the Aphrodite," he shouted back. "You can call me Milos!"

The sun was rising from behind a headland on our right as we left Candia's ramshackle agglomeration of dusty, friendly shops. I looked forward to the quiet of the countryside. It was "Little Easter" and snails were being brought in in pailfuls. The rattle of cart-wheels along the descending main street had kept me awake all night. Milos had supplied two strong-boned Anadolu Ponies, along with a mule for my baggage. In the cool of the morning, we clattered past a Venetian four-clog stone fountain before entering the long, dark tunnel of the Kainoriou Gate and crossing a narrow bridge over a Saracen moat. Two-wheeled one-mule carts, loose on their axles, rumbled past, the drivers asleep.

We overtook men on foot who seemed not at all to mind a load swinging between their legs like a bloated cow's udder. Bread, cheese, olives – anything needed along the way – went into and swayed about in the capacious slack of their trousers. A ragged assembly of lepers, let out for begging purposes from the nearby colony, blocked our way, exhibiting their deformities in the hope of evoking concern and a few coins. I had seen victims of this terrible disease in the squalid districts of Bombay and Calcutta, the bacterium remorselessly spread by contact with fluid from the nose of an infected person. My dragoman scattered a handful of five-*lepta* coins some yards to one side. The unfortunate creatures scrabbled in the dust for a share, opening up a passage for us.

Within the hour the roadside wine-shops died away. The dirt trail climbed through the remains of the sacred woods of Jupiter. Peasants astride wooden saddles on tiny donkeys passed us on their way to tend scattered patches of ancient olives whose fruit may once have been gathered by Minoan hands. At around seven o'clock, we passed within earshot of Knossos. A roar of blasting powder told us the archaeologists were already hard at work.

Onward we travelled through valleys scattered with bright red anemones and spurge and yellow sage, and then up through mountain passes overgrown with oregano and rosemary, a herbalist's pharmacopoeia. The mixed perfumes rose like a bewitchment from the strike of our conveyances' hooves. For several hot and stony miles, we followed on a track which rose and fell. At midday we tied our rides and mule to the trees at the route's edge and walked out across a ridge to a knoll brilliant with purple, white, and pinkish anemones and blue irises. We lunched on guava jelly and tins of pressed beef, warmed by a fire kindled from chunks of gnarled brushwood lying all around. "We shall stop there for tonight, at The Aphrodite," Stavraki Aristarchi informed me. He was pointing towards a lone limewashed building in the Cretan vernacular style on the far side of a small river. The inn was within shot of the bare limestone hillside in which the cave was sited. Two hours later we sat over our evening meal, set among ancient stirrup-jars at The Aphrodite's tables.

Chapter IV – The Party Arrives At Eileithyia's Cave,
Where Watson Gives Holmes a Talking-To

We set off early for Eileithyia's Cave. The day warmed up. Flies inflicted a bite like hornets on man and beast alike. The sun was almost directly overhead when the dragoman pointed to a dark patch on a hillside. "Our destination," he said. The crimson lining of a cloak flashed as the cave's occupant emerged. To my extreme relief I recognised my old comrade-in-arms. As I stared at him through my field glasses I wondered why he had struck so dramatic a pose. In private life, Holmes affected a certain quiet primness of dress – a tweed suit or frock-coat, the Norfolk coatee, occasionally an ulster. Heads would have turned at the square blue spectacles and a cloak with a scarlet lining even in London's busy West End with its litter of theatres. On reflection, I realised Holmes had always opted for boldness in disguise. Not for him the self-effacement of the nightjar with its plumage drawn from the autumnal colours and shapes of its woodland habitat – bark, dead leaves, dappled shadows, the tips of dry bracken fronds. Even when he chose to disguise himself in the sombre black of a Non-Conformist Clergyman, with stock or cravat, the image he projected was extraordinarily compelling.

We came up to him. Hurriedly I started to alert Holmes to my *nom de guerre*. He interrupted with the alarming words, "No need to continue with your subterfuge, Watson. I've informed every capital in Europe that you're

357

here in Crete." He strode towards me with hand outstretched warmly. "Welcome, old friend. Find a patch in the shade and sit yourself down. This landscape must remind you of your old Afghan days."

Almost before I could settle, he thrust forward a baked clay bar with script and what appeared to be numerals on it. "What do you make of that?" he asked.

I took the chisel-shaped object and examined it.

"I make nothing of it," I replied. "Perhaps you'll enlighten me?"

My comrade replied, "It's an unknown script used to write an unknown language. Whomever deciphers it will become famous in the annals of code-breaking. Men could read these tablets once. It should be possible even after forty centuries for Mankind to read them again."

"Holmes," I said, unable to prevent a smile crossing my face, "if anyone can decipher it, it must be you. No one alive is fonder of enigmas and conundrums and hieroglyphics."

"You may say that, Watson, but the cipher I solved in 'The Dancing Men' was infant's play by comparison with this."

I asked, "How will you start?"

"Somewhere on all these tablets must be a reference to the agriculture of the day – oxen, olive oil, figs, pistachio nuts – with pictographs for craftsmen – an armourer at Pylos, a purple dye worker at Knossos – but unless I can work out where words start and end, there's no way I can tell whether the system is logographic like Chinese, alphabetic like Persian, or, heaven help us all, syllabic like Akkadian. Not even what the language might be – or whether these strange symbols are writing at all."

"Now, Holmes," I interrupted, checking the dragoman was out of hearing range, "at least I've discovered you're alive. What of the *raison d'être* of your presence in the back of beyond? What of this Otto Muller?"

"What indeed?" came the rueful reply. "He's disappeared from the face of the Earth. No one has been reported charting the bays and inlets. It's possible he gained the information Berlin wanted and has been whisked away. Muller's not new to this game. The charts he made on his expedition to Waziristan are the epitome to geographers – and military planners. The ruthless part he played in Peking in drawing up the Boxer Protocol alongside Alfons Mumm von Schwarzenstein three years ago has yet to come to the eyes of the world."

Apologetically Holmes continued. "If Muller's still here, I may have put your life on the line too. I had to try to unnerve him in the hope of flushing him out. I needed to declare my presence. It was I who instructed Milos to meet you at the dock. I told him, 'Dr. Watson is my Boswell.' He said, 'Then all of Crete will know you must be Mr. Sherlock Holmes!' To which I replied, 'At your service!'"

I patted the pocket containing my service revolver. "I shall be ready, Holmes," I reassured him. "As to Muller, I'm informed on no less authority than this Milos that no one gets off the island unnoticed."

"If our German friend *is* here, it won't be for long," came the reply. "Two nights ago, a new type of Imperial German Navy submarine was spotted surfacing between the south of Crete and the island of Gavdos. A Type U-1. I take it as an indication of just how important the Kaiser rates his agent's mission."

Holmes stood up and tapped the tobacco from his briar on the cave wall. "We can continue this over dinner. Let's summon the dragoman and set off for a meal of jugged Cretan hare. I'll join you on your pony for the ride back to The Aphrodite. Even their beds ought to be softer than the floor of this cave."

Holmes and I met in the morning for a warm breakfast drink on The Aphrodite's small dust-strewn terrace. His words upon greeting me took me aback. "Well, Watson," he remarked, "it's time to start the journey home. I deliberately revealed our presence to force my quarry to break cover. He hasn't."

I looked at him quizzically. "Are you accepting your mission has failed?"

"Otto Muller arrived – that I know – and then he vanished."

Holmes gestured at the forbidding landscape around us. "If he's gone to ground, ready to emerge the moment we depart, certainly I have failed . . . ." He trailed off, looking hard over my shoulder. ". . . Unless . . . ." I turned to follow his gaze. A man on a sturdy Anadolu Pony was coming at an overly-fast canter up the steep incline. It was Stavraki Aristarchi. As he approached he called out, "There's been a murder. A young shepherd boy."

Chapter V – A Murder Delays Our Return to England

We dismounted from the ponies and walked the final rough stretch of ground to a stone hut reminiscent of the hovels left from the clearances in the Scottish Highlands, ruins considered so picturesque by Victorian artists and visitors. A line of ripening tobacco straddled the doorway. A badging-hook lay against the outside wall. We had come across a scene of extreme pathos. A man looking more desolate than anyone could adequately describe was seated at a wooden table. A home-made lyre lay on it. The moment he saw us, he seized an antique musket and waved us away, calling out in Greek in a thick accent. We stopped while our dragoman went cautiously forward, assuring him we were "good people".

"These *xenoi* have heard about your loss," he told him. "In fact," he added, pointing back at me, "this is a man of God, a Christian. He wishes to say a prayer over your son."

The dragoman relayed Holmes's first question. "No one," our host cried out in reply. "There was no one. Even with my old eyes I would notice a stranger at . . ." he pointed towards the hills, ". . . that distance."

He picked up a black-hilted dagger on the rickety table next to the lyre. The sturdy steel blade had only one edge which grew gradually thinner on approaching the tip, ending at a very sharp point. "My son Nikos never went anywhere without this dagger. He wore it in his belt to withstand evil spells, but it was this which cut his throat. Look at the blood on it. Perhaps a demon made him do it to himself. Nothing can withstand the magic powers of the invisible world."

"Why would demons cast a spell," I asked, "if all your son did was tend your sheep?"

"Because he dared to enter the old stone quarry."

Tears began to drip from eyes displaying advanced opacification. "Even then, Nikos may not have been harmed if he hadn't gone as far as that chamber."

"Chamber?" Holmes enquired.

The father spoke rapidly to our dragoman, hand gestures inviting him to translate sentence by sentence. "The boy came across it deep inside one of the abandoned stone quarries," Stavraki relayed. "The quarry consists of about two-and-a-half miles of interlocking tunnels with widened chambers and dead-end rooms. Two of the sheep went into the tunnel mouth for shade. Something spooked them and they ran down into the depths. Nikos lit his lantern. He had a ball of string which he let out just like Theseus so he could find his way back. Finally, he caught up with the sheep in a great rectangular *tholoi*, a vaulted chamber like a Royal tomb. Twice the size of this house and lined with masonry."

Filtered through our interpreter's imagination the words became lyrical.

"In the centre, among a ring of stone libation vessels," Stavraki translated, "the boy saw a beautiful bowl in the shape of a duck, made of what sounds like rock-crystal. In the bowl was a cornucopia of golden necklaces with jewels which sparkled like the night sky, probably amethysts and diamonds and pearls, and above all the boy described the jewel-seal of a magnificent gold ring. The bowl sat out of reach on a nine-legged ebony table inlaid with ivory and gold, under a fallen stone too heavy to move. The stone had unintelligible letters cut into it. On each side of the duck, this far apart . . ." Stavraki spread his hands a pace or two. ". . . there were small bronze hinges and pieces of limebark."

360

"The remains of the coffer the bowl must have been placed inside," Holmes remarked. "Stavraki," he continued, "he says his son made out the jewel-seal. Therefore, the ring was facing towards him?"

The father drew a piece of paper from a pocket and handed it to Holmes. Stavraki said, "That's the drawing the son made before the oil in his lamp began to run low and he drove his sheep back to the outside world."

I looked over Holmes's shoulder. Cut into the face of the ring was a tapering pillar. At its side stood a shrine-like building enclosing a tree. Holmes tapped the drawing. "This tree he's drawn, it's very like *Yggdrasil*, the sacred ash tree, the tree of life connecting the nine worlds in Norse and Teuton cosmology. The ash tree symbolizes the tree which joins the three worlds: The underworld, the middle earth, and the spiritual realm. I have no doubt," he continued gravely, "that the jewel-seal means his son found the famed Ring of Knossos. If so, Nikos was the first human to set eyes on the ring for two-and-a-half thousand years."

Holmes studied the drawing for a few moments more.

"I am certain of it," Holmes resumed. "Watson, see. Here's a god descending on a sacred obelisk which becomes his bethel. To the Ancients, the ring would bestow the power of Prometheus or Zeus on whoever wears it. They would also have believed it had the power of healing. To a German it would be the Ring of the Nibelung, fashioned by Rhinemaidens from divine light. The wearer would be assigned the power of Wotan or Alberich."

The old man rose abruptly to his feet. Our dragoman pointed to a patch of newly cleared earth some forty yards distant. "Come!" he beckoned. "We are being taken to where Nikos lies."

Stavraki, Holmes, and I knelt and cleared away the weightier stones placed to prevent excavation by wild animals, then scooped away the friable soil. We stared down at the thin torso. It had been a boy of about twelve years of age. His father had buried him in the son's treasured best clothes. A couple of inches of bare sunburned knees lay between the broken-down high boots and the skirt-trousers. I bent down over the child's head and recoiled in horror. "Holmes!" I cried back, "the boy's throat was slashed. Whoever did it made several cuts, one after the other. There can be only one reason to act like that."

In my time in the Army in India and Afghanistan, I had been called to many a corpse lying in the dust with its throat severed by a Pashtun blade. If the knife cut just the trachea below the larynx, the victim could no longer scream. Deeper, the carotid artery would be severed, preventing oxygenated blood from reaching the brain. Finally, unconsciousness and death would result from slicing through the jugular vein. Done slowly and with surgical precision, as had been the case with the shepherd boy, the person would be gargling blood and coughing for many minutes, the whole while taking giant gasping breaths through the severed wind pipe. A red haze filled my vision.

Holmes said quietly, "Watson, I'm to blame for this. I caused this boy's torture and death. My ruse in revealing our presence worked. It spooked Muller badly. It forced him to throw caution to the wind."

To maintain the fiction which had gained us access to the corpse, I performed gestures remembered from observing the Padre giving the last rites to so many fallen comrades in skirmishes on the North-West Frontier. Holmes beckoned to our dragoman to return to the graveside and replace the soil and heavy stones. Staying on one knee at the grave, as though the dead boy could hear and understand English, the dragoman said, "Milos is the cause of all this. You wouldn't be dead if Milos hadn't tried his tricks on your family."

"What sort of tricks?" I asked.

Stavraki got to his feet. "When Nikos came home and told the story, his father straight away wanted to make some money from it. He went to see Milos, hoping for a reward for giving him the information. Even a hundred *drachmae* would have been enough. Milos must have realised the story had the ring of truth, but said he'd only pay the father fifty *drachmae* and only after Nikos showed him the gallery. Everyone knows Milos is untrustworthy and the father refused. Milos said he'd give him time to think it over. Soon after, I saw Milos over at the Palace of Knossos talking to *Effendis* there. He was telling everyone he had discovered the location of the Ring of Knossos and would sell the information for a large sum of money. He came back and told Nikos's father a lie. He said the Englishman told him the real ring had been found many years earlier and had long since been spirited out of Crete. The one the son saw in the cave, Milos said, was therefore a fake. He would, however, do the father a favour. He would re-open negotiations with an offer of a hundred *drachmae*, saying he himself might get a hundred-and-fifty for the information by fooling one or other of the foreigners in *solar topees* at Knossos. Milos expected the father to capitulate."

Stavraki's hand gestured at the hovel. "You can see how impoverished this family is. Soon the hungry season arrives. But Milos didn't take into account the father's superstitious fears. What if it *was* the genuine Ring of Knossos? What if, disturbed from it long sleep, the ring had the power to do bad things as well as good? Out of sheer dread, he ordered his son to refuse to tell Milos anything further. Evidently it was too late," Stavraki speculated. By then rumour had got around that a shepherd boy had reported locating a treasure. "That must have been how the word got out to the one who did this."

Holmes addressed the dragoman. "Tell him we shall leave him in peace with his sorrows after one last question. Has he or anyone gone into those tunnels since . . ." he gestured towards the grave, ". . . since his son was there?"

The old man shook his head violently. "No," Stavraki translated. "Normally no Cretan would venture there. Tradition has it that in the quarry's depths, in a long sleep, live the Triametes, the strange three-eyed giants, both cunning and cruel. The third eye, on the nape of the neck, looks backwards. If anyone awakens them, he suffers a terrible fate. As his Nikos did."

We left the man to his grief, once again seated at his table. Holmes deliberately slowed my steps until we were out of anyone's earshot. With an anguished look he said, "Watson, incredible as it may seem, my brother Mycroft has made an ineffable blunder! And our War Office is the biggest fool in Europe! They believed Muller was here to prepare maps and organise fifth columns for when war breaks out between Germany and England. The true reason for his mission is completely different."

"What might that be, Holmes?" I asked, utterly confused.

"Erb's Palsy."

My jaw dropped. "Erb's Palsy?" I repeated, gaping at my companion. "What has that to do with Muller's presence on Crete?"

"You're the medical expert," came the reply. "Tell me – exactly what is Erb's Palsy?"

"It's a paralysis of the arm caused by injury – specifically the severing of two of the upper trunk nerves."

"And the most common cause?"

"*Dystocia.* An abnormal or difficult childbirth. An infant's head and neck are pulled toward the side at the same time as the shoulders pass through the birth canal."

"And the prognosis?"

"Poor. The paralysis sometimes resolves on its own over a period of months, but mostly it leaves the patient with stunted growth in the one arm with everything from the shoulder through to the fingertips smaller than the unaffected arm. The sufferer is unable to lift the arm above shoulder height unaided, as well as leaving many with an elbow contracture."

"And who is the most famous – infamous – ruler in the world suffering from Erb's Palsy?"

"Kaiser Wilhelm?" I ventured.

"Exactly, Watson," came Holmes's response. "Muller's mission here has nothing to do with menacing England's sea-lanes to British India. It has everything to do with a Kaiser's desperate search for a cure to his palsied arm. An *opera-bouffe* dictator of a Central European Power believing a ring may have a magical ability to cure his palsy may seem far-fetched, but when Wilhelm was six months old, his doctors slaughtered a live hare and tied the flesh of the dead animal, still warm, to the baby's left arm as a poultice, hoping the vitality of the animal would transfer to Wilhelm. This they did twice a week for years. He's already been blessed with enough Holy Water to fill the Kaiser Wilhelm Kanal twice over. The Ruler of Germany believes some inanimate objects have magical powers, such as sacred trees, belemnites, meteor stones – or the gold Ring of Knossos. The Kaiser would know an archaeologist by the name of Heinrich Schliemann who wrote about excavations in Crete – how he was searching for the ring. Schliemann believed it was buried around Mount Ida, a magnificent gold jewel-seal with representations of tree worship."

Holmes gestured back towards the broken-down cottage. "That's why Otto Muller was sent to Crete. The boy's murder proves he's still here. Even as we speak, he must be preparing to get his hands on the ring. The prospect of its return to the world has already brought death to an innocent child. Well-meaning men would try to use its powers for good, like the Ark of the Covenant, the Lance of Longinus, the Sword of Nuada, or even the Holy Grail, but clapped on the finger of a tyrant, it could become another Pandora's Box. The question is: Where is Muller?"

Holmes stared out across the desolate countryside. My eyes followed his. No matter in which direction we looked, other than the old man's hovel, there was nothing indicative of human activity.

With his brow more furrowed than I could ever recall, Holmes swung himself up into the saddle. Then his head turned abruptly. He pointed towards the mountains. I climbed onto my own horse and followed the direction of Holmes's finger. Rising from a plateau above the weathered ridges was the top of a tall tower.

"Toplou," Stavraki replied. "The Great Monastery. That's the belfry. Very high. It was also used as an observation tower. A lot of killings have taken place there over the centuries. Now it's a backwater. I visited them last week. Sixteen monks and the drunkard Abbot live there."

"And the name Toplou?" I queried.

"The monastery 'with the gun' – so-called by the Turks for the cannon and cannonballs the Christians assembled to fend off Muslim attacks."

"Stavraki," Holmes ordered, "go back to the old man. Press him again. When he went to discover why his son hadn't returned with the sheep, was he absolutely certain that he saw no one, no one at all?"

A few minutes later the dragoman returned, shrugging his shoulders. "No one," he said, "except what you might expect – just a *kalógeros*," he added.

"'*Kalógeros*'?" I queried.

Stavraki gestured up towards the plateau. "It's the name we use for the monks up there. It stands for '*beautiful ancient*'."

Both Holmes and I remained silent for much of dinner. Finally Holmes pushed back his dessert plate and said, "Nikos took a heavy risk in following those sheep. I doubt if any props are left holding up the tunnel roofs. Watson, what would happen if a rock-fall had trapped him inside with no one knowing he was there?"

"Potable water would be the main thing," I replied. "Presumably the boy would have a small container, probably just a pint or two. Even if he lay completely still, it wouldn't last long. If he tried to clear the rock-fall, he could sweat that off in a quarter-of-an-hour."

"And then?"

"Dehydration would set in."

"Which would mean?"

"A water loss of only five to six percent will make him groggy. He would experience headaches or nausea, and possibly *paresthesia* – tingling in the limbs. By the second day the lining of the stomach would dry out and he'd experience dry heaves and vomiting. His tongue would swell, the eyes would recede back into their orbits. The mucus membrane might crack and cause the nose to bleed."

"By day three?"

"The final stages. The urine becomes highly concentrated, leading to burning of the bladder. The brain cells dry out, causing convulsions. At that point, without immediate rehydration, other major organs, including the lungs and heart, cease to function."

"Therefore?"

"Delirium, unconsciousness, and death. In awfulness, I rate death from dehydration at the very top."

After a short pause Holmes said, "I must be away for a day or two. Meantime, there's something important I want you to do. Get the dragoman to take you to the monastery. Join the monks at their communal dinner and surreptitiously count all the bearded heads. Keep up your guard. I assume you've brought your service revolver with you?"

I carried out Holmes's orders. I was back at The Aphrodite from the Toplou Monastery when a note arrived from him. It was written in the Dancing Men cipher familiar to me, a continuous stream of stick figures, each representing one letter of the alphabet. The message translated as:

Time to return to England. Pack up our belongings and pay hotel. If convenient come to the quarry at once. If inconvenient come at once anyway. Keep our ponies. Discharge the dragoman. We go straight on to the harbour at Candia.

I packed quickly and settled with Stavraki and paid the hotel's modest charges before going to the stables. The lunch basket was now down to one tin of Pressed Beef and two jars of Burgess's Genuine Anchovy Paste.

I was a hundred yards from Holmes when his words carried to me on the slight breeze – "Matches" – followed by a more insistent, "Do you have a box of matches?" He was standing at the opening of what appeared to be an artificial cave. Rough-hewn steps led into the interior of the hill.

"I do," I called back, amused, assuming he wanted to light a pipe. He gestured behind him. "Dismount, Watson. There's something we need to do before we can leave." A bony finger pointed at the tunnel floor. "Note the light green and brown colour of the dust. Magnesium iron silicate hydroxide. Ideal for camouflaging the fuse wire. Now it's just a case of lighting it. I would have done it by now, but I found that I was without matches."

"Fuse for what?" I asked blankly.

"To set off the charges. I bought a considerable length of fuse wire and a good portion of gun-cotton from the archaeologists at Knossos. I told them I was on my way to dig at the cave-sanctuary of Psychro. I've explored the tunnels and found the cavern, exactly as Nikos described it. There are only two possible approaches to it. The explosions the fuse will set off will bring down so much rock no one, including Otto Muller, will ever find their way back inside to the treasure. The Ring of Knossos can be left in its slumber to the very End of Time. By the way," Holmes went on, "as a matter of interest, how many beards did you count at the monastery, in addition to the Abbott's?"

"Seventeen ordinary monks, Holmes," I replied, continuing with, "Perhaps you could explain why . . . ."

Before I could finish my sentence a look of alarm flashed across my comrade's face. "Seventeen *plus* the Abbott?" he queried. "Not sixteen? Are you certain?"

"Of course I'm certain," I replied.

366

"Quick, Watson – Do you hear it? Someone is coming. No time to light the fuse! Be as fleet as ever you were on the rugby pitch. We must get ourselves and the ponies into hiding. That clump of bushes up there. Mount and ride as though Lucifer himself was on your tail."

Chapter VI – The Seventeenth Monk

We crouched behind ancient olive trees at a distance above the tunnel entrance. My gluteal muscles pressed hard on the rock-strewn rise. The sun set. A half-moon came up over the hill behind us.

"Holmes," I asked cautiously, "isn't this a waste of time? I mean, surely the very fact the boy's throat was slit means he refused to give away the location of the ring? Why else . . . ?"

"We must assume the exact opposite, Watson," Holmes replied. "Nikos was given the *coup de grâce* precisely because his assailant had extracted the information he needed."

The sound of hooves came to us over the stony ground. Holmes and I rose in unison and slid fodder-filled nose-bags over the ponies' muzzles. An apparition came into view both absurd and sinister, a long-legged hooded monk on a donkey. He dismounted, hobbled the donkey at the quarry entrance, pushed back his cowl to reveal a mop of saffron-coloured hair, and consulted a scrap of paper. Crow-bar in hand and lamp above his head, he disappeared down the steps into the tunnel.

"The seventeenth monk," Holmes said, *sotto voce*. "Otto Muller."

I plunged my hand into a pocket and withdrew the service revolver. It had been within easy reach during countless moments in my years with Sherlock Holmes.

"I shall arrest him at once," I said.

"On what grounds, Watson?" my comrade asked.

Taken aback, I responded, "For the murder of the shepherd-boy, what else?"

"And you accuse him on what evidence?"

"Surely we can leave the investigation to the Crete authorities?" I exclaimed. "It's up to them to discover the evidence."

"From which witnesses? The father believes it was the work of three-eyed giants. You may take Muller at gun-point to the authorities, but once there he will claim diplomatic immunity. He would be on his way to Berlin in no time at all."

"What shall we do, Holmes?" I asked, deeply perturbed. "Surely we can't let him go free. You and I know he killed the boy."

"I have no doubt that he did," came the reply, "or he wouldn't be here at the quarry, but it's perfectly clear it's out of our hands. We can do nothing, nothing at all. He is inside. We have lost. At most, we can alert the Cretan authorities to our suspicions. After that, nothing remains but to carry on to the harbour and board ship for England."

"For heaven's sake, man!" I exploded. "He slashed the throat of an impoverished peasant's only child. Nikos died after half-an-hour of the most heinous torture imaginable."

"Watson, however egregious his crime, Muller is not the point. The point is Due Process – Clause 39 of the Magna Carta! Wasn't it your namesake William Watson who proclaimed *Fiat justitia et ruant coeli* – "*Let justice be done though the heavens fall*"? No rough justice! We cannot be the arbiters, or ignore the law in the same way that Muller does. We must leave justice for the boy in the hands of the Cretan authorities. Come, my friend, it's time to go. By now, Muller will too far into the quarry to hear us. I expect that, even as we speak, he is levering away with his crow-bar in the chamber itself."

"Quite, Holmes," I croaked. "Absolutely!" I stood. "I'm with you! Home we go!"

I plunged my hands into my pockets. "Oh my heavens," I cried out. "My father's pocket-watch! It must have dropped out at the tunnel entrance. Wait for me. I shall hardly be a minute, and we can drop by the authorities and press them to take Muller into custody. Or you may start off and I shall catch up with you in no time."

Holmes chose to await my return. He was standing by the Anadolu Ponies, holding their reins, when I came hurrying back waving my heirloom. "Found it," I muttered, urging him to mount. "I untethered the donkey and sent it packing. Now we can return to London. On arrival, dinner at The Travellers on me? On Fridays, they do an excellent *soupe au riz* with lemon, and *kebabs a l'huile*."

I was coming to a description of the Horned Melon for dessert when a sound like the muffled roar of an immense bull belched from the inmost recesses of the mountain behind me.

"Great Scott!" Holmes exclaimed, passing a set of reins to me with a knowing look in his amused eyes. "So Theseus didn't kill the hideous Minotaur after all! Muller must have woken it up."

"Must have," I agreed. "Bad mistake," I added, fingering the box of wax vestas in my pocket, freshly depleted by the two it had taken to set the fuse alight.

Alas, Poor Will

by Mike Hogan

The overture begins with a soft, melodious air that swiftly darkens into a nervous, menacing tone, and then bursts with a wild and tempestuous assault on the senses.

The curtain rises for the prologue, disclosing a full-scale, storm-tossed Elizabethan sailing ship lying beam-on to the audience. The master and boatswain cling to the ship's wheel as rain lashes, lightning flashes, and thunder rumbles.

The main topmast cracks and the mizzen sways before both crash on deck. Dark waves heave between the drifting hulk and the threatening shore, the sky is riven with livid lightning, and rolling thunder smothers the cries of the terrified sailors.

"Good, speak to the mariners!" *cries the master.* "Fall to 't, yareley, or we run ourselves aground: Bestir, bestir. "

"Heigh, my hearts!" *the boatswain calls to the crew.* "Cheerly, cheerly, my hearts! Yare, yare! Take in the topsail. Tend to the master's whistle. " *He waves a brave fist at the heavens.* "Blow, till thou burst thy wind, if room enough!"

The ship's passengers appear on deck, clutching at ropes and each other, appalled by the raging crescendo of tumult. They are urged back to their cabins.

"Hence!" *the boatswain cries.* "What care these roarers for the name of king?"

The ship staggers, the ship's wheel is abandoned in a welter of seething foam, and fire erupts from the lightning-struck sails.

An ethereal figure appears on the poop, dimensioned in glimmers of starlight, its gossamer wings sparkling in the lightning flashes. The ship's wheel spins, turning the bark towards the fatal shore, and the curtain drops.

I leapt up with the other members of the audience, applauding wildly, as cheers and even whistles came from the cheaper seats in the upper galleries.

I dropped into my seat as the storm died away. "I say!" I murmured, blinking at my companion.

"Hmm?" Holmes replied. "Did you note the newsboys' placards outside the theatre? Younghusband's expedition has returned from Lhasa with a treaty. This Tibetan venture is an abominable little war – worse even than our plunder of Burma."

Our neighbours tut-tutted us to silence as the curtains opened again. Prospero was revealed seated and reading from a thick tome, and Miranda entered and confronted her father.

I sat mesmerised through three acts of *The Tempest* until Ariel appeared for the last time, singing the song of the bee. Taking flight at the words "*Merrily, merrily shall I live now*," the voice of the sprite rose higher and higher until it merged with the note of the lark – Ariel was now free as a bird.

Caliban lifted his haggard face to the sweet air, then turned in the direction of the departing ship. The curtain fell, and the play ended – but yet, the curtain rose again to a heart-rending tableau. Prospero's ship was on the horizon and Caliban stretched his arms towards it in mute despair. Night fell, and he was left on the lonely rock, king of his desolate island once more.

I followed Holmes into the lobby of His Majesty's Theatre, where we collected our overcoats, hats, and canes. I had an inkling that, despite the grandeur of the Mr. Beerbohm Tree's staging of the play, my friend had remained immune to the spectacle. I turned to Holmes and smiled a question.

"It was cleverly conceived," he said as we stepped onto the pavement, "but I have to agree with the reviewer who suggested the staging has the defect of not leaving enough room for the imagination without being absolutely realistic. Mr. Tree has offered us a rare spectacle, a marvellous box of tricks, but it's mechanic work. It is not Shakespeare."

He grabbed an early evening newspaper from a stand. "Ha! Younghusband's treaty was signed only by the lesser lamas and the Chinese. The Dalai Lama repudiates it with contempt."

The newspaper seller held out her ink-stained hand for payment.

"The expedition was thus a terrible waste of lives in what is essentially a commercial enterprise," Holmes continued. "Several officers involved in the campaign have referred to it as a *Christie's War*, alluding to the auction house that sells their ill-gotten statues and wall-hangings."

Holmes tossed me the paper and I smoothed it and returned it to the lady with an apology. He put on his hat and buttoned his gloves. "I hope the Dalai Lama was not incommoded. He is a charming young man who was most hospitable during my stay with him a few years ago."

I was about to expostulate with my friend on the staging of the play when a page appeared in front of us. "Mr. Sherlock Holmes?"

I indicated my companion.

"Mr. Beerbohm Tree requests the pleasure of the company of Mr. Sherlock Holmes and companion for dinner at the Pall Mall at a quarter-to-six this evening, if he is at leisure." The boy drew a breath. "Mr. Tree apologises for the short notice, praying for the gentlemen's indulgence."

"Well-remembered, young man." I frowned. "The Pall Mall?"

The boy pointed to a restaurant on the other side of the Haymarket. I turned to Holmes, but he was already halfway across the street, dodging between cabs and 'buses.

I gave the boy a thruppenny bit, which he acknowledged with a grin and a salute, and I followed Holmes through the rush-hour traffic to the restaurant.

"They do an excellent after-matinee dinner for three bob, not including wine," Holmes said as I joined him in the cloakroom. He rubbed his hands together and grinned. "Oysters."

I handed my coat, hat, and cane to the attendant and, on mentioning the name of our host, Holmes and I were ushered by an attendant to a private supper room.

"Mr. Tree played Caliban with an affecting sympathy," I suggested as we took our seats at a table set *à trois*. "His monster was not the unfeeling wretch I'd always assumed him to be."

Holmes sniffed. "Prospero could have managed the affair in a few moments with a wave of his magic wand. But no, we are subjected to two hours of persiflage in a *faux* jungle."

A pair of attentive waiters offered *aperitifs* and lit the table candles. In their light, I consulted the souvenir programme the audience had been given to commemorate the fiftieth performance of Mr. Tree's *The Tempest*.

"Sir Arthur Sullivan's music was up to his usual high standard," I suggested.

"If we must have modern productions of *The Tempest*, at least let Ariel be played by a boy," Holmes replied in a tart tone. "Next we'll have Puck portrayed by a portly matron like the heroine of a Wagnerian opera."

"Come now, Holmes. Miss Tree, who played Ariel with great finesse in my opinion, is not portly. She has an uncommonly fetching figure."

The door opened, and a waiter moved aside for Mr. Beerbohm Tree. Holmes and I stood to greet our host and thank him for our tickets to the play and his invitation.

We sat, wine was offered, and the first course – a pleasantly herbed potato soup – was served, followed by Holmes's oysters raw and grilled.

Our excellent dinner wound its course, and Holmes and I chatted amiably with Mr. Tree on trivial matters until the waiters brought a decanter of port and a cigar humidor with bowls of fruit and nuts, then retreated, leaving us alone.

"I received a communication yesterday, just before the evening performance," Mr. Tree said as we had helped ourselves to port and lit our cigars. He placed an envelope on the table.

"Plain, good-quality, foolscap envelope, tuppence-the-dozen," Holmes said. "Blue-black ink of indifferent opacity. No stamp."

"It was given to the page-boy at the theatre by a thin, elderly man in a Scotch bonnet with a threadbare scarf about his neck," Mr. Tree said. "He spoke in a reedy, asthmatic tone with a faint accent, possibly Yorkshire."

"Your page is a bright and observant boy, although I doubt the existence of a *faint* Yorkshire accent."

Mr. Tree smiled. "Before we go any further, I should acquaint you gentlemen a little background regarding a persistent rumour within the thespian community of the existence, or perhaps non-existence, of a certain Shakespearean artefact – a rumour I had discounted, until a week ago."

Mr. Tree related that a visitor had come backstage after attending a performance of *The Tempest* the previous week. He had introduced himself as Professor Doctor Ulrich von Hardinger, Professor of Philology at Heidelberg University and a Director of the *Deutsche Shakespeare-Gesellschaft* (German Shakespeare Society). He informed Mr. Tree that the Society had been founded in Weimar in 1864, well before anything official had been set up in England, that they held an annual Shakespeare conference, and that the Society had recently erected a statue of the Bard to stand beside those of Wieland, Goethe, and Schiller.

Mr. Tree considered the end of his cigar for a moment before he continued. "I congratulated the professor upon his and his society's artistic discrimination and I asked him, out of mere politeness, whether he had enjoyed the play."

He pursed his lips. "Germans of the Hardinger type consider the staging of Shakespeare's plays a vulgarity. They have their notion of Shakespeare as a kind of *Sturm und Drang* Romantic poet, and our hearty English Shakespeare, full of life and energy, irritates their bourgeois sensibilities. The Germans think Shakespeare is too good for us, as if the dim-witted next-door neighbour of a violin virtuoso inherited a Stradivarius and used it as a banjo. The musician would be vexed. He could extract sounds and sweet airs from the instrument, but an ignorant brute is in possession, and it is a pearl before swine."

Mr. Tree took a long puff on his cigar. "The Germans have an obsessive and unhealthy fascination with the Bard. Schlegel called him '*ganz unser*'. They believe Shakespeare is *spiritually* of their race. They have all but naturalised him as a Teuton."

"Ignorant brute? Swine?" I said. "I reject such a characterisation of Shakespeare's countrymen."

"*Ganz unser*. 'All ours'," Holmes said. "Schlegel promotes a type of intellectual colonisation. We and the French have grabbed most of the worthwhile bits of land around the world, leaving Germany with a few plague spots in Africa and some insignificant Pacific atolls. Our avarice is sated, while that of the newly unified Germans is still sharp-set."

Mr. Tree tapped the envelope on the table. "A few days after the events I have just described, I received this." He slipped the contents of the envelope onto the table.

"A single sheet of cream, small-foolscap paper, and a photograph." Holmes glanced at the photograph and passed it to me while he closely examined the letter.

"An image of a human skull with a chipped cranium." I said. "Could it be a threat?"

Holmes looked up. "The artefact you mentioned?"

"As you may imagine," Mr. Tree answered, "I considered the German professor's visit impertinent, and certain words were exchanged before I bid him and his fellows good night. I was astonished when, despite my dismissal, Professor von Hardinger demanded a private interview. When my dressing-room door closed on his companions, Hardinger made an extraordinary and impudent proposal. He offered me a thousand pounds for information that would lead him to the location of the skull of William Shakespeare."

I blinked at the skull in the photograph.

"You may recall some nonsense in a magazine years ago suggesting Shakespeare's skull had been stolen from his grave in the Holy Trinity Church in Stratford-upon-Avon," Mr. Tree continued, "and a pamphlet five years ago reporting the rediscovery of the skull in the crypt under Beoley Church in Worcestershire. The story was Gothic nonsense, of course, and I thought nothing more of the matter until the professor's visit. But when this letter arrived yesterday, I had second thoughts. On the advice of a certain personage, I made up my mind to put the matter before you, Mr. Holmes. I sent you the tickets, and here we are."

Holmes passed me the letter. "Two inches have been cut from the top of the page with a dull blade, probably removing a header. The text is type-written." He narrowed his eyes. "On a Daugherty Visible I would say, although I reserve judgement until I have a chance to analyse the type under a microscope."

373

"The writer offers the skull of William Shakespeare for sale at three-hundred-and-twenty pounds, cash on delivery," I said. "The letter is signed, *Ariel*."

"Three-hundred-and-twenty pounds," Holmes mused. "An oddly exact sum." He turned to Mr. Tree and indicated the envelope and photograph. "If I might retain these for a day or two in order to conduct some tests?"

"Keep them, if you will," Mr. Tree replied. "Here is a copy of the *Argosy* of 1879 with the account of the theft of Shakespeare's skull, written as a horror story, and this is the pamphlet on the skull's rediscovery, published five years ago in a similarly sensational style."

Mr. Tree passed Holmes a dog-eared magazine and a pamphlet with a lurid red cover. He glanced at his watch and stood. "I must away. Today was the fiftieth performance of our *Tempest*, and the cast have insisted on a *soiree* to mark the occasion. Perhaps you could let me know what fees, *etcetera* – "

Holmes waved Mr. Tree's request away. "I consider myself amply paid by our excellent dinner."

We stood. "But I have one more favour to ask," Holmes added. "Perhaps I might speak with your page?"

"Certainly. Do take your time, gentlemen. The room is booked for another hour." Mr. Tree bowed and turned to the door.

"Did you tell anyone else about the letter?" Holmes asked him.

Mr. Tree turned back, his hand on the door handle. "At first, I thought the note was a comical reference to the Germans' visit, which I had mentioned to several of my employees. I charged members of the cast with the jape, and then I spoke with some rival theatre managers, but they all protested innocence."

He frowned. "I received a most exalted visitor to my dressing room this afternoon who expressed a keen interest in the matter and suggested a reward might be appropriate for the person who ensured the security of Shakespeare's remains. He advised I should contact you, Mr. Holmes, rather than the regular police, as the matter is delicate."

Mr. Tree opened the door, hesitated and looked back. "What did you think of the play, gentlemen?"

"I wonder whether it is wise for we moderns to attempt the staging of Shakespeare in our currently popular, naturalistic style," Holmes answered, "rather than contenting ourselves with reading his plays."

Mr. Tree flushed. "We must agree to disagree, sir."

"I thought it a masterpiece," I said. "Caliban in particular was portrayed with deep understanding."

Mr. Tree bowed and left us.

374

Holmes and I returned to our seats at the dining table, and I drew two candelabra together and examined the letter in their light. "The writer hints that other parties, including foreign persons, are interested in the object. He suggests that if Mr. Tree agrees to the transaction, he should place an advertisement in *The Times*' agony columns, signing himself '*Prospero*'. He will receive documents attesting to the provenance of the skull."

Holmes passed the port decanter. "If someone turned up at your home with Shakespeare's skull, what would be your reaction?"

"Scepticism, augmented by outright disbelief. First, I should require proof that Shakespeare's skull is missing from his grave. Then I'd demand corroboration from the thief, and from whoever received the skull and kept it all these years."

I filled my glass from the decanter. "In fact, as I come to examine the question, even if I wanted the skull, which I do not, no mere assertions of provenance would satisfy me. I should send the fellow about his business with a flea in his ear."

"The thespian community is a tight one, prone to rumour," said Holmes. "That letter will have been a topic of discussion in every bar and public house in the theatre district. With royal interest in the matter, its contents will be known farther afield."

"Three-hundred-and-twenty-pounds, Holmes. *Pounds*, not *guineas*. The seller of the skull is no gentleman."

Holmes gave me an odd look. "Is that a joke?"

A knock came at the door, and a waiter ushered in the pageboy we had spoken to earlier.

"Your name?" Holmes asked.

"Kip, sir. Short for Kipper."

I frowned.

"My real name's Jack, sir," the boy explained.

"Jack the Ripper. Kipper," Holmes said, smiling at me. He turned back to the boy. "You strike me as an intelligent lad. Close your eyes, take deep breaths, and concentrate on the gentleman who gave you the letter."

The boy complied with Holmes's instructions.

"Ready? He accosted you at the stage door."

"He was among the johnnies, sir, the Romeos waiting for Miss Tree with chocs and flowers."

"They tip well?"

Kip grinned. "I do all right."

"And the gentleman who gave you the letter?"

"A tanner. A righteous tip."

"What else do you see? Look around you."

"The johnnies, and a line of cabs, sir, as per usual." The boy frowned and seemed to hesitate.

Holmes smiled. "What more?"

"The gentleman was wearing a wig, sir, and his whiskers were false. The lines on his face were greasepaint, poorly applied. He would not do well at Mr. Tree's Academy of Dramatic Art."

Holmes bade the boy open his eyes, held up a half-crown, murmured instructions, and sent him on his way.

"Perhaps the old gentleman in the wig is a figment of Kip's imagination," I said as Holmes and I retrieved our coats, hats, and canes from the restaurant cloakroom. "The letter may be an attempt to extort money from Mr. Tree."

"Why, my dear fellow, what a cynic you are. Kip is a charming young man, doubtless destined for thespian greatness." Holmes smiled at my expression. "But you are right. That is a remote possibility."

We stepped out into the Haymarket. "I had hoped for something with a little more spice," Holmes remarked, "but this is straightforward detective work."

I frowned. "Did you say *royal* interest, Holmes?"

"The King was in the Royal Box. His snoring was one of the 'strange airs' referred to by Caliban." Holmes smiled. "And I thought I glimpsed Madame Sarah Bernhardt tucked behind the ample proportions of His Majesty. Perhaps she encouraged his interest in the fate of the Bard."

"The Germans can't have Shakespeare!" I exclaimed. "We will never allow them to kidnap a major English literary figure, even a deceased one."

"It's our own fault," Holmes mused as we strolled together towards Piccadilly. "We have harped on about Shakespeare being 'of the world'. We can hardly complain if the world takes us seriously."

Holmes took my arm. "Let's have a convivial glass at the Coal Hole, then head to our separate homes for an early night."

"I have surgery in the morning," I admitted, "but a pint or two of bitter beer can't hurt."

"It's me water again, Doctor," moaned Mrs. Rudge.

I stifled a yawn and struggled to stay awake. My evening in the Coal Hole with Holmes had been convivial, and Friday morning surgery was more than usually trying. Mrs. Rudge was an old campaigner, much put upon by life with her docker husband and riven with (mostly) imaginary agues.

"That salve you give me just spread the itch – "

My surgery door swung open, and a face peeked through. "Doctor Watson, we have an emergency," the intruder said.

I stood and faced Mrs. Rudge. "I'm terribly sorry – "

"But what about me water?" Mrs. Rudge cried.

"Doctor Watson," the intruder said urgently, "It is a matter of life and death!"

I reached behind me, took down a jar of pink sugar pastilles, shook out a couple of handfuls and twisted them into a paper cone. "Three times a day after meals, Mrs. Rudge. Come and see me if symptoms, ah – "

I darted for the door, leaving my bemused patient holding the packet and gaping at me from her chair. I gestured for my receptionist to attend to her.

"*How beauteous mankind is!*" Holmes said, grinning as he ushered me to a hansom. "*O brave new world, That has such people in't!*"

I climbed aboard the cab and my companion settled beside me. "Holmes," I said, "you must not interrupt a consultation – "

"Why not? It worked. I wanted you by my side, and here you are. And the matter is, if not quite of life or death, of national significance. Remember, His Majesty is taking an interest in the case."

I chuckled. "Has he ever read Shakespeare, or attended a performance before?"

"Not voluntarily, I would guess, although his education was draconian, directed by his father, Prince Albert."

I knitted my brows.

"Yes, Watson, another German."

We dropped down at Marylebone Station, the least crowded, quietest, and, in my opinion, most civilised of the London termini.

"I set young Kip on the case," Holmes said as we crossed the concourse. "The boy has the making of a first-class snoop. He found the cabby who took Mr. Scotch Bonnet to Benson's Private Hotel. The mark paid the fare up front, and no doubt discarded most of his disguise during the journey, not wanting to alert the staff at his hotel to his double identity. He emerged from the cab as Charles Frederick Copley, Acting Curate at the Holy Trinity Church, Stratford-upon-Avon."

I frowned a question.

"Kip spoke to the door boy at Benson's. Only the Reverend Copley arrived in a cab at about the time indicated by the cabby, and he stuffed something very like a Scotch bonnet into his pocket as he got down. He left the hotel this morning in a cab bound for this station, the terminus for Stratford-Upon-Avon."

Holmes led me to a train huffing and puffing at a platform.

"Tickets?" I asked.

He held them up and preceded me into a First-Class compartment. I closed the door behind us, and Holmes lounged across the seat, yawning.

377

"I am going through the motions as thanks for our splendid dinner. The case offers no interesting features. It is almost identical to a theft that occurred in Nantes Cathedral in '83 – "

The compartment door opened and a smooth-faced, dark-tanned young man in a black suit stood in the doorway. His almond eyes flicked from Holmes to me, then settled on Holmes. He clasped his hands together in a praying style and bowed deeply.

"*God dag, Herr Sigerson,*" he said in an Oriental tone before he stuck out his tongue!

Holmes stood and bowed in the same fashion. "*Heb-bar kaa-su-shu,*" he replied.

"*Hyggelig å treffe deg,*" the young man returned.

"*Kayrang kusu debo yimbay?*" Holmes said, smiling. "And that exchange of pleasantries depletes my knowledge of your language to its very depths."

The man handed Holmes a crimson-and-gold-lacquered tube. I leaned over to admire the chaste-work, and when I looked up the man had gone, and the compartment door was closed.

The train jerked into motion and chuffed out of the station.

Holmes slipped a gold-embossed parchment from the tube. "From the Dalai Lama, written in what I take to be Norwegian." He looked up and smiled. "Let us put this aside for the moment."

I blinked at my companion. "Holmes – "

"Tibetans greet each other by putting out their tongues to show they are not demons. Demonic tongues are black – or perhaps green, I do not recall."

"Norwegian?"

Holmes pursed his lips. "As you know, after our tussle with Moriarty in Switzerland years ago, I was obliged to make myself scarce. His hellhounds were on my heels, but I shook them off, first with a change of identity, and then by putting distance between us. I mentioned to you on our first meeting after my return to England that I became Herr Sigerson, the Norwegian explorer. It was in that guise that I visited Tibet and met the Dalai Lama in Lhasa."

"Portraying a Norwegian must have been difficult without a command of the language."

"I relied on the probability that few, if any, of the people I might meet on my travels would *be* Norwegian," Holmes said with a wry smile.

He looked idly out of the window as we passed through north London suburbs. "I had an awkward moment in Shanghai when a Norwegian *danseuse* was offered to me in payment for a small favour I had done a local warlord. However, in the privacy of my lodgings she admitted she

378

was a barmaid from Swansea who had adopted Norwegian nationality to enhance her exotic flavour, and therefore price. We shared a convivial bottle of gin (with a plate of pickled herring for authenticity), wished each other well, and parted with mutual expressions of good feeling."

I thought it best not to inquire further into Holmes's activities in the Far East, and changed the subject.

"Who would want the skull of William Shakespeare, and why?"

Holmes shrugged. "Mozart, Haydn, and Jonathan Swift all had their skulls stolen from their graves. In more recent times, thieves attempted to purloin President Lincoln's remains in '76."

"Again, I ask: To what purpose?"

"If obsessed collectors will pay for the autographs, death masks, and possessions of the great, why not their skulls?"

Holmes borrowed my tobacco pouch, packed his pipe, and continued. "There is a powerful potency to objects of veneration, particularly human remains – a truth the world's religions understand and exploit. Through these totems, devotees experience an empathy with the worthy or saint whose personal effects or body parts they handle. Add to that the thrill of possession, having that which no other has, and you have an intoxicating mix of desire."

A young man looking identical to the one who had presented Holmes with the scroll case at Marylebone Station waited for us at the Stratford-Upon-Avon ticket gate. He stuck out his tongue in greeting before he ushered Holmes and me to a corner table in the station restaurant, at which four similarly tanned young men sat.

The men stood and bowed, before three moved away and the remaining man indicated their seats and bade us sit.

"I am pleased to meet you again, Herr Sigerson," he said in excellent, strongly Indian-accented English.

He turned to me. "I am Lobzang Gyeltsen, the Eighty-Sixth *Ganden Tripa* and Regent of Tibet. In mufti, as it were, to avoid the attentions of your Special Branch detectives who make valiant attempts to dog me. We are a couple-of-dozen in our party, and we all look alike to the English eye, so I am usually able to outfox them with doubles.

"Your detectives trail one of me taking the waters in Bath, another on the Flying Scotsman to Edinburgh, and the third, poor fellow, attending a small theological college in rural mid-Wales."

"The *Ganden Tripa* and I met at the abode of the Dalai Lama in Potala Palace in Lhasa," Holmes explained to me before he formally addressed our host.

"May I present my friend, Doctor John Watson?"

379

Mr. Gyeltsen bowed again, but he did not stick out his tongue. I returned his greeting as well as I could.

I studied the Regent as he made small talk with Holmes about their earlier meeting. I thought him extremely young to be a high functionary of Tibet – he looked to be in his late twenties – but I knew Orientals often appear much more youthful than their age would warrant, and I supposed that in a religiously organised society, theological enthusiasm might be more revered than age and sagacity.

"May I invite you to tea, gentlemen?" Mr. Gyeltsen said, calling for a waitress. "I am informed that Warwickshire oatcakes are a particular delicacy of the town, though at first glance they do not appear so."

Pots of tea arrived, with a plate of oatcakes that did look rather unappetising, reminding me of small brown napkins or face flannels.

"Your country's recent intervention into our affairs puzzled us," Mr. Gyeltsen said after tea was served. "We are a religious, meditative nation offering no threat to any of our neighbours, and we wondered why you attacked us."

He smiled. "Of course, the Viceroy of India, Lord Curzon, who instigated the 'expedition', chose to blame Tibet for refusing to attend British representatives at our border with India to negotiate a peace treaty – one protecting Tibet from baneful Russian influence and, incidentally, forcing us to open markets for Indian goods we neither want nor need." He gave the oatcakes a wry look.

"In his enthusiasm for peace, the leader of the expedition, Colonel Younghusband, massacred seven-hundred monks who barred his way into my country."

"According to reports I have read in the newspapers," I said, "your monks were armed, and one of your lamas fired the first shot in the engagement."

"Your reporters did not interview the Tibetan dead."

I sniffed and made no reply.

Mr. Gyeltsen smiled again and continued. "Last year, we learned that, contrary to our bloodthirsty characterisation of him, Colonel Younghusband had certain sacred texts by him at all times. In camp, the books lay on a bamboo table at his bedside, and on the march, they were in his saddlebags. He did not allow his servant to pack them in his trunks."

He laid two well-thumbed volumes on the table – a Bible and a complete Shakespeare.

"The colonel's servant is your creature," I said. "You bought him."

"Hardly bought, Doctor. We rented him for a time and then returned him in good condition to his owner." Mr. Gyeltsen gestured to the table. "As we intend to do with the colonel's books."

380

Holmes picked up the Shakespeare volume and flicked through it. "Heavily annotated in a military hand."

"You refrained from killing Younghusband," I said. "I imagine if you had access to his tent, you could have done so."

"We *are* warrior monks, Doctor, but we are Buddhists and we hesitate to kill without reason. All life is sacred to us, including the tiniest micro-organisms, venomous reptiles, rampaging bears, belligerent English colonels, and even conniving, avaricious viceroys."

Mr. Gyeltsen sipped his tea. "Over the last several months," he continued, "our scholars have studied your New Testament to better understand English thinking. We swiftly concluded that the teachings of your Galilean prophet on humility, charity, and turning the other cheek are not central to the foreign policy of Great Britain, or to the morality of Colonel Younghusband, and still less of his master in Calcutta. We have therefore discounted the Bible as a key to your moral code."

He tapped the Shakespeare book. "These plays and poems made a great impression on the few scholars with the linguistic skills to understand them. Shakespeare opens a vivid mirror into the Western mind for us. I rather think Colonel Younghusband fancies himself another Henry the Fifth, although we in Tibet see him more in the role of Titus Andronicus."

I constrained a chuckle, covering it with a cough.

"The Dalai Lama's scribes are translating the works of Shakespeare, but it is a laborious process as most know no English. Imported Chinese scholars translate English into their own language, and then our scribes render their product into Tibetan. The results are less than satisfactory," Mr. Gyeltsen admitted, "but we persevere."

"You are in Stratford to visit Shakespeare's birthplace," I suggested.

"Not quite."

Mr. Gyeltsen explained that the Dalai Lama, while meditating on the Bard, had experienced a series of prophetic waking-dreams that emphasised the need to establish a manifest link between Shakespeare and the fortunes of Tibet. His Holiness consulted the famous treasure revealer, Terton Sogyel, regarding his recurring visions. Sogyel endorsed the Dalai Lama's interpretation, a view that was further confirmed by the Nechung Oracle – the Tibetan Delphic Sybil.

Mr. Gyeltsen smiled at my doubting expression. "We take dreams and portends more seriously than you do, Doctor. Perhaps our greater elevation allows us to pick up heavenly signals more effectively."

I blinked at the young man and turned to Holmes for his reaction, but my companion's face was as impassive as that of a sleeping Buddha.

Mr. Gyeltsen addressed Holmes. "My master, the Dalai Lama, requests your help in settling a question for him, sir, but first I am instructed to inquire who exactly I have the honour of addressing."

I knitted my brows.

"For some time," Mr. Gyeltsen continued, "We laboured under the misapprehension that Herr Sigerson had assumed the name of Sherlock Holmes as his literary *nom-de-plume*. We were clearly mistaken."

He smiled. "And I must apologise to you, Doctor Watson, for we also assumed that you too were a literary fiction, and that your admirable stories were written by another doctor, a Doctor Conan Doyle."

I bowed.

"What is the Dalai Lama's request?" Holmes asked, speaking at last.

"He wishes to know the location of the corpse of Mr. William Shakespeare, or at least the location of his skull."

I gaped at Mr. Gyeltsen in astonishment.

"We had assumed Westminster Abbey," he continued, "but my inquiries there were rebuffed, and I was informed that the gentleman's remains are interred in a church here in his birthplace."

Mr. Gyeltsen laid on the table a copy of the red-covered pamphlet that Mr. Tree had given Holmes. "My researches led me to a bookshop on the Charing Cross Road in London where I purchased this. The author summarises the story of the theft of Shakespeare's skull from his burial place in the Holy Trinity Church, its loss, and how it was rediscovered in the crypt of another church, in Beoley. (Is that the pronunciation?) The true skull may be known by a crack or chip in the bone suffered during the original theft."

Mr. Gyeltsen turned to me. "As Mr. Holmes saw on his travels through my country, we embalm our gurus and exhibit them for the faithful to venerate, as conduits, as it were, between us and the divine."

"Saints," I suggested.

"The analogy is not without merit." Mr. Gyeltsen answered. "We would be proud to do the same for your William Shakespeare, if his remains are in a condition that allows the process. We understand that important persons are buried in lead coffins, and his corpse might be well-preserved, but we are naturally concerned that, without a skull – "

He shrugged. "To us, not knowing enough of the ways of your country, the mystery of the location and condition of the body, if it has been removed from the church, is impenetrable."

"You cannot ask Holmes to find the skull of William Shakespeare so you may purloin it!" I looked to my friend for support, but he was busy doodling on his shirt cuff with a pencil.

382

"Why not?" Mr. Gyeltsen asked in a stiff tone. "We mean no harm to Mr. Shakespeare, nor to your country. Despite the no-doubt lurid warnings emanating from the viceroy, we are not here on a mission of destruction. We do not intend to poison your reservoirs or put a hex on the Archbishop of Canterbury, and we offer no threat to His Majesty. Mr. Holmes has spent time in our country, and he knows we mean no harm to anyone. Like every organism on the earth, we wish to continue to exist, but unlike most, we do not require the death of others to do so."

Mr. Gyeltsen glared at me for a moment, then he seemed to calm. He sipped his tea and continued. "Our aim is to conserve peace by creating a bond between our nations. We undertake to treat Mr. Shakespeare's body with the greatest reverence. We would be happy to swap one of our most revered lamas for your poet or pay a reasonable fee for his remains."

He nibbled a corner of an oatcake, and grimaced. "You focus on life, on this veil of tears, and we on death. Surely common sense would suggest that Tibet would be a fitting resting place for a poet whose works offer a window to a higher plane of existence? If I am wrong in construing the works of Shakespeare thus, kindly correct me, Doctor."

Again, I looked to Holmes for support, but he was still doodling. "I – I would not characterise his works in exactly such a way – although a reading of Hamlet in particular does offer an exaltation – " I frowned at my companion. "Perhaps Mr. Holmes can explain the matter more, ah – "

Holmes waved my suggestion away and continued with his scribbles.

I pursed my lips. "Warrior monks, sir?" I focussed on a flaw in Mr. Gyetsin's protestations of peaceful intentions. "Isn't that a contradiction if your faith professes to be non-violent?"

The young man considered for a moment before he replied. "We Tibetans accept this world of sorrows as it is, Doctor, and sometimes prayer wheels and coloured flags must be supported by more forceful practices to protect one's people's lives, land, liberty, and religion. If your monasteries had been defended by warrior monks, you might have given the Vikings second thoughts, to say nothing of Henry the Eighth. And if our monks had wielded Maxim machine guns and quick-firing artillery like the troops in Colonel Younghusband's peaceful 'expedition' into my country, instead of matchlocks and swords, we might have deterred his avaricious master, Viceroy Lord Curzon, from invading us and looting our monasteries."

He waved his hand over the plate of oatcakes. "And all this would be unnecessary."

He shrugged. "Every cloud has a gilt lining. The monks who died defending their homeland are free of their travails in this existence, and they will reincarnate to a higher sphere."

Mr. Gyeltsen stood, and Holmes and I followed suit. He and I shook the Regent's hand in the manly, English fashion before his entourage formed around the young man and they slipped out of the restaurant.

"Necromancy, Holmes! Portends and dreams! Stuff and nonsense."

Holmes smiled. "'*We are such stuff as dreams are made on; and our little life is rounded with a sleep.*' Necromancy? No, you are thinking of Doctor Dee, the Elizabethan mage. For Mr. Gyeltsen, there would be no point in resurrecting the Bard of Avon, as he has long been incarnated into another form."

We fetched our hats and coats from the stand.

"I would like to say Shakespeare has reached *nirvana*," Holmes continued, "but we must factor in the bad karma from his will: The matter of the second-best bed, which was all he bequeathed to his wife."

An anxious face peered around the door of the restaurant, and a carriage driver inquired the whereabouts of a Mr. 'Olmes and party for The White Swan in a rich Warwickshire accent.

The cab made its way into town, passing along well-kept roads lined with pleasant properties, many of great antiquity. We settled at The White Swan Inn, and after a wash and brush up, I joined Holmes in the bar for a pint of local ale and a pipe.

"An early luncheon, I think." Holmes rubbed his hands together. "This case has taken on an unexpected hue and '*Yet ere supper-time must I perform much business appertaining*'."

After an excellent luncheon, Holmes and I walked through the ancient streets and I marvelled at the number of Elizabethan buildings that had survived the ravages of time. After receiving directions from a lounger, we made our way along a towpath beside the River Avon the short distance to the Holy Trinity Church, the burial place of William Shakespeare.

The church was set back from the street and reached by a wide pathway lined with young elms. The building was surprisingly large, and dated, according to the guidebook I had purchased at the hotel, from the early thirteenth century.

Holmes paused at the parish notice board in the porch. He chuckled and as I leant forward to see what had amused him, a voice came from behind me.

"May I help you gentlemen?" A thin, pale young cleric had come from the graveyard. He did not seem pleased to see visitors to the church.

"You are the vicar?" I asked.

"I am not. He and the curate are both unwell. The trials and tribulations of keeping up this ancient building have had a deleterious

384

effect on their health. I am acting curate, *in loco*." He frowned. "Are you journalists? I'm afraid I have nothing more to say on the question of Shakespeare's burial."

"No, no," said Holmes. "We are simple pilgrims, no more. Might we view – "

"Very well." The curate opened a wicket in the Gothic-arched door to the church and ushered us inside. The interior of the building was as spacious as its ample outside dimensions suggested. Holmes and I crossed the north aisle, stood in the nave, and looked through the chancel to the superb stained-glass windows above the altar, seventy or more yards from us.

"We received almost fifteen-thousand visitors last year, numbers that would stretch the patience of a saint," Reverend Copley – for surely it was he – informed us in a cold tone. He yawned. "The crossing under the tower and spire dates from 1210, and the misericord choir stalls were installed about two-hundred years later – "

"Shakespeare's tomb?" Holmes asked.

"Follow me." Reverend Copley led Holmes and me under the tower, between the transepts, and into the chancel. He indicated a line of flagstones set into the floor before the high altar. "It is customary for visitors to make a small donation for the upkeep of the building."

We stood at a low railing looking down on the stone slabs. Shakespeare's was second from the left, between his daughter and Thomas Nash, who married his granddaughter. The famous curse was inscribed into Shakespeare's covering stone: *Good friend for Iesus sake forbeare, To digg the dvst enclosed here. Blese be ye man that spares these stones, And cvrsed be he that moves my bones.*

"May I?" Holmes pulled out his magnifying glass, dropped to his hands and knees, and glared at the slab covering Shakespeare's tomb.

"The blood of every Englishman is fired by Shakespeare's memory," I exclaimed, my heart pounding.

"More brightly for me, Doctor," Reverend Copley said with a smile. "I am not just an Englishman. I am a Warwickshire man."

Holmes stood and took the red pamphlet he had received from Mr. Tree from his pocket. "But not *the* Warwickshire man, the writer of this pamphlet."

Reverend Copley sniffed. "Hardly. He has revealed himself as the Vicar of Beoley, Reverend Langston, as is well known. I mentioned the donation, gentlemen. At least thruppence is usual."

"I believe I may be able to do better than that," Holmes said. "A few moments ago, I characterised myself as a pilgrim, a tourist. I feel I should admit that I am Sherlock Holmes, the consulting detective, and my companion – "

"Scotland Yard! Thank goodness!" Reverend Copley cried. "I thought of contacting you people a few days ago when I was first accosted."

Holmes and I sat on misericord seats in the choir stalls as Reverend Copley continued.

"A very vehement German gentleman visited the church. He spoke of Shakespeare in reverent – I might say *mystical* – terms, but then he asked whether the rumour was true that the Bard's skull was not under the gravestone in the nave. That it was in the keeping of the vicar."

"He offered you a thousand pounds for the skull of William Shakespeare," Holmes said.

"He did, sir. I see you are already on the case. We have lost Christ to convoluted, Teutonic excess. I will not be a party to giving Shakespeare to the Germans."

"Stout fellow," I exclaimed. I frowned. "*Jesus* Christ?"

"They have made war on Christ," Reverend Copley exclaimed. "German so-called theologians reject Trinitarian theology as a fantastic fable projected onto God. They argue that the supernatural elements in the New Testament are primitive myths that must be stripped away to reveal the Jesus of history – the simple teacher of righteousness." He gestured at the church around him. "There is no room in their theology for this."

I advised Reverend Copley to take deep breaths to calm himself.

"I sent the professor packing, but he insisted I take his card," Reverend Copley continued in a calmer tone, passing the card to Holmes. "He is staying at The White Swan until tomorrow."

"He set you thinking," Holmes said with a smile. "You are no stranger to greasepaint, Reverend Copley. You played Polonius in your local dramatic society's production of *Hamlet*."

The clergyman's glance flicked to the church entrance. "You saw the notices on the board."

"Type-written with a Daugherty on Vestry notepaper. You attempted a Yorkshireman in a Scotch bonnet at His Majesty's Theatre." Holmes looked up at the wooden ceiling. "I assume it is the roof."

"No, sir," Reverend Copley answered. "The roof is sound, but the floor of the nave is in a very poor condition. We have a quotation for repairs from a local firm for three-hundred-and-twenty pounds."

He shook his head. "The vicar *will* accede to representations from parishioners and the Town Council for the organ to be moved from hither to thither and back again. And donations of stained glass to replace our plain glass are well enough if sufficient funds accompany the gift to pay for the installation work."

"So, you reconsidered your position on the sale of the Bard's skull."

"Not at all," Reverend Copley replied. He opened a small cupboard under the pulpit and drew out two skulls, both missing their lower jaws and one chipped and battered.

"These skulls were left by the wicket gate, probably by a farmer who dug them up while he was planting or ploughing. It's not uncommon – we get a half-dozen a year. I would never take a skull from the cemetery, particularly not the sacred remains of our most famous resident!

"These skulls have no provenance. They might be pagans – Vikings perhaps – or Catholics. We cannot bury them in our consecrated ground." He smiled. "The idea came to me when I picked up this skull, and a chip fell off. You have read the '84 pamphlet?"

"I glanced through it," Holmes replied with a sniff. "The writer recognised the true skull of the Bard from damage it had incurred during its removal."

"These theatre types can afford the money," Reverend Copley said. "They make thousands from Shakespeare's plays, but they have no thought for the condition of the church in which his remains lie."

"*Mostly* lie," I interjected.

"There is no proof that Shakespeare's skull is not with the rest of his body, beneath that gravestone," Reverend Copley replied stiffly.

Holmes faced the curate. "I will offer you a proposition and if you agree, my companion and I will promise utter silence on the matter of your proposed sale to Mr. Tree and the presence or absence of the skull in question for, let us say, ten years."

Reverend Copley paled. "If not?"

Holmes maintained a neutral expression and said nothing.

The acting curate turned to me, wide-eyed. "The vicar would have a fit if he found out. I have no choice but to agree to your companion's terms."

Holmes rubbed his hands together. "I ask only that the stone covering the Bard's remains be lifted so we may ascertain whether or not the skull is where it should be. We undertake not to remove anything from the grave, and we will remain silent on the result of our endeavours – that includes publications, Watson – for the term agreed."

"There is the question of the curse, Holmes," I interjected.

"We need not invoke the curse. It specifically targets '*he that moves*', etcetera. The exhumation might be safely performed by matrons of the parish."

Reverend Copley sighed. "A quip grown stale with repetition, Mr. Holmes."

"And I must require that you leave the matter of the sale of the skull entirely in my hands." Holmes wrote on the back of the German professor's calling card, looked up, and smiled. "We three shall meet again, in thunder, lightning, or hopefully not in rain – at midnight, the witching hour."

He indicated the card. "I have invited Professor von Hardinger to join us at thirty minutes past."

Reverend Copley left us, and I looked up at the famous bust of William Shakespeare on the wall above the graves. "He is less imposing than I had expected," I suggested.

"Reminds me of the laughing sultan at the music hall," Holmes said, chuckling.

We dined exceeding well at The White Swan.

"The Shakespeare case has taken an interesting turn," Holmes said as we relaxed over brandy and cigars in the Smoking Room. "It eclipses the Nantes event in complexity, and in potential for violence."

I sipped my brandy. "The key point is that we cannot allow the Kaiser, nor yet the Dalai Lama, to kidnap William Shakespeare." I chuckled. "We have a new alliance with the French, but we continue to have an *entente discordiale* with the Germans. They offer a thousand pounds, Holmes – an absurd sum!"

"An index of monetary depreciation, Watson. Horace Walpole supposedly offered just three-hundred pounds for the skull of the Bard."

I gave Holmes a sly look. "Admit, my friend, that your ultimatum to Reverend Copley was inspired by nothing more than curiosity." I blew a stream of cigar smoke across the room. "You want to know the true location of the skull."

"Perhaps." Holmes slipped a telegram flimsy from his pocket and passed it to me. "From the Prime Minister, Mr. Balfour. The Viceroy of India wishes to engage me to track down the Dalai Lama, reputed to be have entered Europe via St. Petersburg and Berlin. He offers a high Indian order and a substantial sum in silver rupees."

I read the telegram. "Where next then, Holmes? Bath, Edinburgh, or a theological college in mid-Wales?" I smiled. "I must warn you that the rupee is not the stable currency it once was." I took another puff on my cigar and considered. "It's not that I am concerned where exactly our national literary lion is buried, although by rights he should be in Westminster Abbey. The point is that he is buried in *English* soil. Imagine

388

if the Tibetans take the skull and plant it on a mountain peak, or plate it with gold, and set it up as an idol."

Holmes was silent for a long moment. "I just attempted to imagine both those eventualities, and I my soul is unmoved. I'm surprised that you are taking the question of location so seriously. Does it matter where he is buried, and, if so, why?"

"You might as well ask why *Shakespeare* matters?"

Holmes glanced at the mantel clock. "A question we have to leave for the present."

I frowned. "You mentioned violence, Holmes. Should I have brought my service piece?"

Holmes and I walked through empty, dimly moon-lit streets, retracing our footsteps to the Holy Trinity.

We passed through the gates and into the churchyard. An owl hooted, a mournful sound, and something swift scuttled across the path before us. Holmes laid his hand on my arm, startling me, and intoned, "*Graves, at my command, Have waked their sleepers'.*"

"Shh," I hissed. "I wish, I *wish* you wouldn't do that. This venture is Gothic enough without you add more ghastly nonsense."

The church door was unlocked, and I followed Holmes inside, across the north aisle and into the shadowed nave, lit only by the moonbeams filtering through the stained-glass windows.

Holmes took my arm and pointed along the nave to the high altar. A glimmer of lamplight showed, and we groped our way towards the glow, stepping silently on the flagstones.

As we entered the chancel, two figures were discernible in the light of a bulldog lantern. One knelt, scraping at the floor with a tool and the other stood over him. The standing figure lit a second lantern and a pair of altar candles, and I recognised Reverend Copley's pale face.

Holmes and I joined him before the altar. A heavy-set man in a cloth cap picked at the mortar dividing the slab above Shakespeare's grave from his right-hand neighbour, Thomas Nash.

Reverend Copeland indicated the kneeling man. "Kemp, the gravedigger. Don't worry, he's – " He mimed drinking. "He'll have no memory of this in the morning."

As if to confirm his words, the gravedigger snorted, pulled a bottle from his coat, and gulped at it. The sickly-sweet smell of rum wafted up from him.

"He was a sailor in his previous life," Reverend Copley explained, "on a whaler."

Just visible in the spill of lamplight was the inscription of the famous curse, and on the altar two skulls. I shivered as the flames of the altar candles danced in a chill zephyr of wind. Fleeting shadows playing over the skulls produced an eerie sense of life and movement.

Kemp returned to his task with a will, and soon the mortar was removed. He jammed the flat end of a pickaxe into the join, and Copley, Holmes, and I helped him raise the stone slab from over the tomb and lower it onto the next grave, the nearest to the church wall, that of Shakespeare's daughter.

I picked up a lantern and shone it on the opening below me. "There is no vault," I exclaimed.

I had expected the stone slab covered the entrance to a mausoleum in which the coffins of Shakespeare, his family, and other worthies were placed. In fact, the grave was filled with dark earth crusted with greeny-brown mould.

I frowned. The top of a square, brick structure was visible, like an open box, two-feet in diameter, extending down into the grave. I could think of no purpose for the structure. It reminded me of a well, or a chimney, neither of which made any sense.

The gravedigger jammed his spade into the soil, scooping earth from inside and around the box onto the floor of the chancel. He dug down about three feet, and paused, grunting something unintelligible. A strong, humid smell rose from the grave, and I pulled out my handkerchief and held it over my nose.

Holmes pushed the gravedigger aside, knelt, and picked a white fragment from the exposed earth. He held it to the light.

"A finger bone," I said. "We are close to the burial, but I see no remains of a coffin, and that brick square is where I'd expect the skull to lie."

Kemp knelt again, rummaging his hands through the earth with professional insouciance and whistling softly to himself.

"Shh," I whispered, glancing apprehensively behind me into the shadowed chancel and dark nave.

Kemp delved into the earth up to his armpits but found nothing and withdrew. Again, Holmes pounced on something in the disturbed earth and held it up.

"A human cervical vertebra," I said. "A neck bone."

Reverend Copley turned away, sobbing quietly.

A noise in the nave behind us made me jump. A figure with a lantern stood in the aisle and the dim forms of others clustered behind him.

"Herr Professor Doctor von Hardinger, I presume," Holmes said, raising his lantern high.

"Whom do I have the honour of addressing?" A German-tinged voice replied.

"I am Sherlock Holmes, and this is my companion – "

"Doctor Watson! Of literary fame!" The professor cried.

"Why does the Kaiser want the skull of William Shakespeare?" Holmes asked.

A tall, thin gentleman, with a thick grey moustache and wearing a black overcoat, stepped into the circle of light from our lamps. "I cannot confirm that His Imperial Majesty has any knowledge of our enterprise."

Holmes laughed. "You have the good grace to look embarrassed."

"You English do not know your friends," Professor von Hardinger replied in a tart tone. "You flirt with the French, who will do you no good, as you should have learned from your frequent wars. Germany is your natural ally." He calmed and smiled. "We share Shakespeare – "

"We most certainly do not," I cried.

Professor von Hardinger ignored me. "I am prepared to offer one-thousand pounds for the skull of William Shakespeare, Mr. Holmes." He beckoned an assistant, who heaved a chest onto the pew beside me and opened it, revealing a sheet of lead foil on which a layer of gold sovereigns gleamed in the lamplight. "In gold."

"Done," Holmes replied.

"I say," I said, blinking at my friend.

"Actually, we have two Shakespeare skulls in stock." Holmes took them from the altar, stepped down to the chancel and held one skull in each hand, balancing them against each other. "I am certain that, of the two, this is the more likely skull of the Bard." Holmes held up the right-hand skull. "I would stake my kingdom, or at least my horse, on it."

"Holmes," I whispered urgently. I twitched my left eyebrow.

Holmes waved me away. "No, no, Watson. It is a matter of cubic capacity."

The professor smiled. "With your indulgence, Mr. Holmes, I will take the other skull."

"Herr Professor Doctor, I have just assured you that this skull is – "

The professor chuckled. "I am too old a bunny to be so distracted. You offer me the fake and keep the original. Oblige me, Mr. Holmes."

He reached up and snatched the chipped skull from Holmes. "I have read the pamphlet by Mr. Warwickshire, and I know of the damage to the real skull."

"Very well," Holmes said evenly, "but you must agree that our transaction is now complete. We offer no guarantees nor insurance against further loss or damage. Agreed, on your honour?"

"Agreed."

Holmes passed the professor a sheet of paper and held up our lantern while the professor read it. "Sign here." He slipped the signed sheet into his pocket and offered a second slip. "Here is a receipt for the gold."

Holmes handed me the rejected skull. "You might pop that back on the altar."

He drew me close and whispered, "Stay back and do not interfere, however much we are provoked."

Professor von Hardinger's eyes glittered in the lamplight as he contemplated his prize. He bowed a stiff bow, turned, and immediately started back as a figure reared up from behind a pew in a flash of orange, seized the skull from his hands and leapt away, seeming to melt into the shadows among the choir stalls and graves.

"Treachery!" Hardinger snarled, turning back to Holmes. He drew a heavy pistol. His companions lit matches and spread out searching the chancel.

Holmes stretched his hands in a placatory gesture. "Upon my honour, Professor von Hardinger, the gentleman who relieved you of the skull was not under my direction. He is a member of a sect of Tibetan warrior monks pledged to acquire the remains of William Shakespeare for the Dalai Lama. You will have noticed the gamboge robes that are a symbol of their faith."

"Orange," I translated.

Holmes ignored my interjection. "The Tibetans approached us with an offer to ensconce Shakespeare in a place of veneration in their country, a request with which we could not possibly comply. It seems they have taken matters into their own hands. But I say again, we bear no responsibility."

The professor growled, and Holmes waved a languid hand towards the altar. "There is always the other skull. Nobody need ever know."

"Do not insult me, sir. I am no mere pragmatist."

"Then our revels are ended, and our business done."

The professor glared at the chest of gold for a long moment before he abruptly turned and stalked down the aisle of the church, followed by his entourage, and the ancient door slammed shut behind them.

Holmes addressed the shadows. "Kindly give His Holiness my best wishes – "

A monk appeared out of the gloom. In the lamplight I recognised him as the young Regent, Mr. Gyeltsen.

Holmes smiled. "A most spectacular leap, sir."

"You saw me?" The young man frowned. "My amulet is guaranteed not only to protect against attack, but to render the wearer invisible." He slipped a knotted and braided silk string from his wrist onto the floor and grinned. "This one seems to be defective."

Orange-robed figures came from the shadows and heaved a second chest onto the pew beside the first.

"A thousand gold sovereigns," said Mr. Gyeltsen. "We traded them with the Afghans for silks and yaks. The Muslims have a surplus of gold from British regimental pay columns they captured during your various wars, and I believe Lord Curzon pays them a yearly stipend to keep them quiet."

Holmes bowed. I attempted to imitate him, and we both saw Mr. Gyeltsen and his followers to the side door of the church.

"I stopped off at St. Petersburg and Berlin on my way here," the Regent said as he shook our hands. "I was well received in both cities. Neither the Russians, nor particularly the Germans, have much good to say of the British, but words are easy, and, aside from wishing Tibet well in our altercation with England, neither of those two imperial kingdoms will lift a finger to aid us against you." He shrugged. "We must therefore be content."

He smiled. "But in a hundred years the world will be a very different place, Mr. Holmes. India and South Africa seethe under your benign yoke, as America once did. Empires come and go, gentlemen, and as your Bard says, *How poor are they that have not patience! What wound did ever heal but by degrees?*"

Mr. Gyeltsen shook Holmes's hand. "Who knows? Perhaps the English will tire of their material existence, eschew the accumulation of things, and embrace their spirituality."

"That would truly be a brave new world," Holmes said. "But in the meanwhile, we will cheerfully accept your contribution to the Holy Trinity floor fund."

Mr. Gyeltsen laughed and turned to me. "You need not be concerned, Doctor. The skull will be treated with all reverence."

His tone hardened. "However, should Colonel Younghusband or any other English gentleman conceive a looting expedition into my country, we will call upon the spirit of William Shakespeare for redress. With his intervention and our high arts, we will wreak a terrible vengeance."

He held out his hand. "I see you frown, Doctor, but if you will forgive an impertinence, we Tibetans not only occupy a physically higher position than you by virtue of our mountains – we exist on a higher metaphysical plane, with access to greater powers than exist in Lord Curzon's philosophy."

The young man shrugged. "Well, that's what we firmly believe."

His tone hardened again. "In any case, the wheel of life and death and life is inexorable, and I fear His Lordship and Colonel Younghusband have accumulated not just a heavy load of loot, but such a burden of bad karma that their perambulation on earth in their next incarnation may be on six legs, or none!"

"Take care," Holmes said, shaking his hand. "Von Hardinger will have surrounded the building."

Mr. Gyeltsen grinned and bared his arm. "A second amulet, just in case. And we have laid a false trail to the river."

"Ineffable nonsense," I murmured after the young man had led his entourage away, proudly bearing their skull.

I turned to a sound in the chancel, lifted my lantern, and saw that Reverend Copley stood astride Shakespeare's open grave holding a halberd at port-arms.

"Gentlemen," he cried in a grim tone that echoed through the church. "It is my firm belief that within a decade at the most, England and Germany will go to war and the world will be plunged into a chaos of flame and fury. If the Kaiser's forces prevail, Wilhelm will demand the formal surrender of Shakespeare to Germany and the transfer of his bones to his custody."

Reverend Copley raised his halberd high. "The first German grave robbers who seek to despoil this plot will swiftly feel the edge of Warwick steel."

Holmes and I left Reverend Copley guarding the grave and the gold chests and made our way back to our hotel.

"The young clergyman is vehement," I suggested. "I wonder from what source his Apocalyptic belief derives."

My companion raised a finger and pointed heavenwards.

"Holmes! You flirt with blasphemy!"

"Or perhaps the Dalai Lama's oracle," Holmes suggested.

We paced in silence until the yellow glow of welcoming lamps hung outside The White Swan became visible, beckoning us to our cosy beds.

I sighed. "Well, at least now we know."

"Do we?" Holmes pursed his lips. "We barely scraped the burial layer. I would not like to make a definitive statement on the location of the skull of the Bard."

We entered through a side door of the inn using a key hanging on a string. I lit a pair of candles in holders on a side table, and Holmes and I climbed the time-worn stairs to our bedrooms.

"What of the strange brick structure?" I asked.

"The grave has obviously been disturbed, and quite recently. The soil was loose, not hard packed as it should be after almost three centuries of repose. The brick column is to prevent subsidence."

"Perhaps something was removed," I suggested, "leaving loose earth and a space beneath the slab."

"Perhaps."

We bid each other good night.

"The Regent is an unusual young man," I said when I joined Holmes in the breakfast room the following morning, "and his English is remarkable."

Holmes offered the teapot. "Mr. Gyeltsen is very much more puissant than a mere regent. The *Ti Rinpoche* of *Gandon* is the highest rank to which a monk who is not an incarnation may rise. As you might expect, the current holder of the position is an elderly gentleman who resides in Lhasa. The man you met yesterday was born at dawn on the fifth month of the year of the Fire Mouse and enthroned at the age of three as Thubten Gyatso, the Thirteenth Dalai Lama."

I poured my tea. "I detected a regal quality in his manner."

Holmes slathered butter on his slice of toast and divided it into slices. "Lord Curzon offers a great deal of treasure and an exalted decoration for news his whereabouts. Without the Dalai Lama's seal and signature, the treaty Curzon forced on the Tibetans is worthless, and the bloodshed and expense of his war is rendered moot."

He dipped one of the toast slices into his soft-boiled egg. "I met His Holiness at the Potala Palace in Lhasa several years ago. A Russian Buddhist scholar had given him a Mauser pistol, and I instructed him in target practice. His bullets, made locally, were tipped with silver, not lead, and despite their vows of poverty, his shots occasioned unseemly scrambling in the butts by novices after the spent slugs. Marmalade?"

I passed the bowl.

"Incidentally, you may thank me for the Dalai Lama's fluency in our language. I found him in the thrall of Indian grammarians from whom he had assimilated an excellent grasp of the nuts and bolts of our language, but no notion of its use. I taught the young man the English language as an instrument of communication. Brevity and clarity were my watchwords.

"In our discussions yesterday, I noted several lapses in my pupil's diction – an inapposite metaphor and an error of vocabulary. An altercation, by definition, is non-violent – faults which I have communicated to His Holiness in a stern note."

"You were a *teacher*, Holmes!"

"The position of *guru* is highly regarded in Eastern societies."

A waiter placed an eggcup on the table before me and refilled the toast rack. I broke the shell of my boiled egg with my spoon.

"I am not of a metaphysical persuasion, Holmes. Yet, if the skull of William Shakespeare *could* do good in the world – "

"You do not mind its elevation to the cloud-capped towers, gorgeous palaces, and solemn temples of the Himalayas?"

"I find that I do not," I said. "Shakespeare's legacy does not depend, as the ancient pharaohs believed, on the survival of his corpse, or parts of it."

I looked about me and lowered my voice to a whisper. "And I am practically certain that both the damaged skull and its fellow were female. Their orbits were sharply defined, and their superciliary arches were unridged, characteristics of that gender."

I frowned. "I wonder what happened to the second skull?"

Holmes smiled. "Reverend Copley may have popped it into the vacant space in Shakespeare's tomb, giving future scholars something to puzzle over."

"Should we not inform the authorities? The King has taken an interest in the matter."

"No, no. We will let sleeping skulls lie. The case of the missing skull, if such a case there be, shall remain unsolved."

Holmes tapped the shell of his second egg. "However, the Dalai Lama, in a letter – now tendered in English rather than Norwegian – offers an astonishing reward for my efforts on his behalf that I am pleased to accept. With His Holiness' help, augmented by several thousand prayer wheels and hundreds of chanting monks in the Potala Palace, I am assured that, on my demise, I have every chance of being reincarnated as a fire-dragon."

The Case of the
Haunted Chateau
by Leslie Charteris and Denis Green

Sherlock Holmes and The Saint
An Introduction by Ian Dickerson

Everyone has a story to tell about how they first met Sherlock Holmes. For me it was a Penguin paperback reprint my brother introduced me to in my pre-teen years. I read it, and went on to read all the original stories, but it didn't appeal to me in the way it appealed to others. This is probably because I discovered the adventures of The Saint long before I discovered Sherlock Holmes.

The Saint, for those readers who may need a little more education, was also known as Simon Templar and was a modern day Robin Hood who first appeared in 1928. Not unlike Holmes, he has appeared in books, films, TV shows, and comics. He was created by Leslie Charteris, a young man born in Singapore to a Chinese father and an English mother, who was just twenty years old when he wrote that first Saint adventure. He'd always wanted to be a writer – his first piece was published when he was just nine years of age – and he followed that Saint story, his third novel, with two further books, neither of which featured Simon Templar.

However, there's a notable similarity between the heroes of his early novels, and Charteris, recognising this, and being somewhat fed up of creating variations on the same theme, returned to writing adventures for The Saint. Short stories for a weekly magazine, *The Thriller*, and a change of publisher to the mainstream Hodder & Stoughton, helped him on his way to becoming a best-seller and something of a pop culture sensation in Great Britain.

But he was ambitious. Always fond of the USA, he started to spend more time over there, and it was the 1935 novel – and fifteenth Saint book – *The Saint in New York*, that made him a transatlantic success. He spent some time in Hollywood, writing for the movies and keeping an eye on The Saint films that were then in production at RKO studios. Whilst there, he struck up what would become a lifelong friendship with Denis Green, a British actor and writer, and his new wife, Mary.

Fast forward a couple of years . . . . Leslie was on the west coast of the States, still writing Saint stories to pay the bills, writing the occasional non-Saint piece for magazines, and getting increasingly frustrated with RKO who, he felt, weren't doing him, or his creation, justice. Denis Green, meanwhile, had established himself as a stage actor, and had embarked on a promising radio career both in front of and behind the microphone.

Charteris was also interested in radio. He had a belief that his creation could be adapted for every medium and was determined to try and prove it. In 1940, he

397

commissioned a pilot programme to show how The Saint would work on radio, casting his friend Denis Green as Simon Templar. Unfortunately, it didn't sell, but just three years later, he tried again, commissioning a number of writers – including Green – to create or adapt Saint adventures for radio.

They also didn't sell, and after struggling to find a network or sponsor for The Saint on the radio, he handed the problem over to established radio show packager and producer, James L. Saphier. Charteris was able to solve one problem, however: At the behest of advertising agency Young & Rubicam, who represented the show's sponsors, Petri Wine, Denis Green had been sounded out about writing for *The New Adventures of Sherlock Holmes*, a weekly radio series that was then broadcasting on the Mutual Network.

Green confessed to his friend that, whilst he could write good radio dialogue, he simply hadn't a clue about plotting. He was, as his wife would later recall, a reluctant writer: "He didn't really like to write. He would wait until the last minute. He would put it off as long as possible by scrubbing the kitchen stove or wash the bathroom – anything before he sat down at the typewriter. I had a very clean house." Charteris offered a solution: They would go into partnership, with him creating the stories and Green writing the dialogue.

But there was another problem: *The New Adventures of Sherlock Holmes* aired on one of the radio networks that Leslie hoped might be interested in the adventures of The Saint, and it would not look good, he thought, for him to be involved with a rival production. Leslie adopted the pseudonym of *Bruce Taylor*, (as you will see at the end of the following script,) taking inspiration taking inspiration from the surname of the show's producer Glenhall Taylor and that of Rathbone's co-star, Nigel Bruce.

The Taylor/Green partnership was initiated with "The Strange Case of the Aluminum Crutch", which aired on July 24th, 1944, and would ultimately run until the following March, with *Bruce Taylor*'s final contribution to the Holmes Canon being "The Secret of Stonehenge", which aired on March 19th, 1945 – thirty-five episodes in all.

Bruce Taylor's short radio career came to an end in short because Charteris shifted his focus elsewhere. Thanks to Saphier, The Saint found a home on the NBC airwaves, and aside from the constant demand for literary Saint adventures, he was exploring the possibilities of launching a Saint magazine. He was replaced by noted writer and critic Anthony Boucher, who would establish a very successful writing partnership with Denis Green.

Fast forward quite a few more years – to 1988 to be precise: A young chap called Dickerson, a long standing member of *The Saint Club*, discovers a new TV series of The Saint is going in to production. Suitably inspired, he writes to the then secretary of the Club, suggesting that it was time the world was reminded of The Saint, and The Saint Club in particular. Unbeknownst to him, the secretary passes his letter on to Leslie Charteris himself. The teenaged Dickerson and the aging author struck up a friendship which involved, amongst other things, many fine lunches, followed by lazy chats over various libations. Some of those conversations featured the words "Sherlock" and "Holmes".

It was when Leslie died, in 1993, that I really got to know his widow, Audrey. We often spoke at length about many things, and from time to time discussed Leslie and the Holmes scripts, as well as her own career as an actress.

When she died in 2014, Leslie's family asked me to go through their flat in Dublin. Pretty much the first thing I found was a stack of radio scripts, many of which had been written by *Bruce Taylor* and Denis Green.

I was, needless to say, rather delighted. More so when his family gave me permission to get them into print. Back in the 1940's, no one foresaw an afterlife for shows such as this, and no recordings exist of this particular Sherlock Holmes adventure. So here you have the only documentation around of Charteris and Green's "The Case of the Haunted Chateau" . . . .

Ian Dickerson

The Case of the Haunted Chateau

Originally Broadcast on October 30th, 1944

<u>CHARACTERS</u>

- Sherlock Holmes
- Dr. John H. Watson
- Station Master
- Mrs. Gibson
- Gason
- Susie Gibson
- Vicomte de Verlon
- Announcer: Bill Forman

FORMAN: Petri Wine brings you . . .

<u>MUSIC: THEME . . . FADE IN</u>

FORMAN: Basil Rathbone and Nigel Bruce in *The New Adventures of Sherlock Holmes.*

<u>MUSIC: FULL FINISH</u>

FORMAN: The Petri family – the family that took time to bring you good wine – invites you to listen to Doctor Watson tell us about another exciting adventure he shared with the greatest detective of all time – Sherlock Holmes. Looking at my watch, I can see that you've probably had your dinner by now – and I hope it was a good one. I'm sure it was if, along with your dinner, you had a glass of Petri California Sauterne. Because that Petri Sauterne sure can make good food taste better. You'll know exactly what I mean if you've ever had roast chicken and Petri Sauterne. Mm . . . mm – a bite of tender golden-brown roast chicken and a sip of that clear golden Petri Sauterne is a flavor combination that's out of this world. You'd need a whole dictionary. full of adjectives to really describe it. That Petri Sauterne has a really wonderful flavor . . . a flavor that's subtle and intriguing . . . a flavor that reminds you of luscious sun-ripened grapes – picked when they're still covered with early-morning dew. And say – the flavor of that Petri Sauterne is great with fish, too. Or with any kind of seafood for that matter. Try Petri Sauterne – and serve it well-chilled . . . really cold. You can serve it proudly because it bears the name "Petri" – the proudest name in the history of American Wines.

MUSIC: "SCOTCH POEM"

FORMAN: And now for our weekly visit with the genial Doctor Watson. Let's join him in the study of his California ranch house. Good evening, Doctor.

WATSON: Evenin', Mr. Forman. Sit down and make yourself comfortable.

FORMAN: Thank you, Doctor, I always enjoy your Monday night stories, but after the hint you gave us last week – well, I can hardly wait.

WATSON: (CHUCKLING) You mean the –

FORMAN: I mean the French Chateau and the pistol packing mamma. When did the story begin, Doctor?

WATSON: In the spring of nineteen-hundred-and-five. Holmes and I were in Paris, when he received a telegram. I find that I still have it filed away with my records of the case.

SOUND EFFECT: CRACKLE OF PAPER

WATSON: Listen to this: (READING) *If you are half as good a detective as they say you are, you should have no difficulty in earning an old lady's thanks. In return, all you have to do is to catch a ghost.* And it's signed (READING) *Mrs. Harrison Gibson, Chateau Verlon -sur-Rhone, near Lyons.*

FORMAN: An intriguing telegram, Doctor. By the way, Mrs. Harrison Gibson wasn't your pistol packing mama, was she?

WATSON: Yes. (LAUGHING) It was probably the politest message she ever sent in her life.

FORMAN: And Holmes accepted the invitation, of course?

WATSON: Yes, Mr. Forman. The case sounded interesting, the fee was unusually large, and Verlon-sur-Rhone was right in the heart of the wine-growing country. Holmes was something of a connoisseur of wines, you know, and he'd often expressed a desire to go through those particular vineyards.

FORMAN: I imagine if he were staying out here with you now, Doctor, he'd like to . . . .

WATSON: (LAUGHING) Yes, Mr. Forman, I'm sure he'd be interested in your Petri vineyards, too. But if you want me to tell my story, you'd better leave him in Verlon-sur-Rhone, for that's where we found ourselves twenty-four hours after receiving this telegram. We'd spent most of the afternoon gazing out of the train window, as the incomparable French countryside sped past us. Finally, just as dusk was merging into night, the wheezy querulous train drew to a stop (FADING) at our destination . . . .

SOUND EFFECT: TRAIN DRAWING TO STOP. TOOTING OF HIGH-PITCHED TRAIN WHISTLE

HOLM ES: Wake up, old chap, we're there.

WATSON: (DROWSILY) What? No need to shake me. Holmes. I wasn't asleep.

HOLMES: Nonsense. You've been snoring for the last ten minutes.

SOUND EFFECT: TRAIN STOPPING. HISSING OF STEAM. TOOTING OF WHISTLE.

WATSON: (OFF A LITTLE) I'll get the bags down . . . . Oh, they are down . . . .

SOUND EFFECT: CARRIAGE DOOR OPEN. BACKGROUND NOISES (UP)

HOLMES: Mind the step . . . that's it.

SOUND EFFECT: FOOTSEPS ON STONE

WATSON: We seem to be the only passengers getting off here.

402

PORTER: *En voiture! En voiture!*

SOUND EFFECT: THREE SHRILL TOOTS ON WHISTLE. SOUND OF TRAIN RE-STARTING AND FADING OFF

HOLMES: (AFTER A MOMENT) And there goes our train. Next stop – Lyons.

WATSON: What a gloomy little station. Not a soul in sight.

HOLMES: Gloomy it may be. But it has some claim to distinction. Don't you remember the Lyons train robbery a few months ago? This station of Verlon figured quite prominently in the case.

WATSON: By Jove . . . Yes, I do. Something about a train wreck.

HOLMES: That's right.

SOUND EFFECT: FOOTSTEPS STOP

HOLMES: Well, here we are at the ticket office, Watson. And there's still no sign of a living soul. The ticket window isn't even open.

SOUND EFFECT: RAPPING OF KNUCKLES ON WOOD

WATSON: (AFTER A MOMENT CALLING) Anyone here?

HOLMES: Knock again, old fellow.

WATSON: This place gives me the creeps.

SOUND EFFECT: MORE RAPPING ON WOOD. AFTER A MOMENT, PANEL SLIDES OPEN

STATION-MASTER: (OFF A LITTLE. FRENCH ACCENT. MIDDLE-AGED, SINISTER) *Que voulez vous?*

HOLMES: *Vous perlez Anglais?*

STATION-MASTER: *Oui.*

HOLMES: We want to go to the Chateau Verlon. Can we get a carriage?

STATION-MASTER: No carriage . . . and if there were, no one would drive you there. Strange things happen at the chateau. If you are clever men you will not stay here. Wait for the next train and go back to where you came from.

SOUND EFFECT: PANEL SHUTS. KNOCKING. PAUSE. PANEL OPENS

WATSON: Now look here, my good man, I don't know what your game is, but you can't frighten us. Just tell us where we can get a carriage, and stop talking nonsense.

STATION-MASTER: You can get no carriage to drive you to the chateau.

HOLMES: Hmm. The ghost seems to have made a great impression.

STATION-MASTER: Do not try to go there! People that go there (FADING) do not come back alive!

SOUND EFFECT: PANEL CLOSED VIOLENTLY

WATSON: That man's mad, if you ask me.

SOUND EFFECT: FOOTSTEPS. DOOR OPENS. WIND UP. DOOR CLOSES

WATSON: I can't say I'm very impressed with Mrs. Gibson's hospitality. It seems to me that . . . .

SOUND EFFECT: HORSE CARRIAGE APPROACHING AT FULL GALLOP

HOLMES: There's our hostess now, unless I'm much mistaken, driving that coach-and-pair. Seems to have changed places with her coachman.

SOUND EFFECT: CARRIAGE PULLING TO VIOLENT STOP ON GRAVEL ROAD

GIBSON: (YELLING, OFF. ABOUT FIFTY, RAUCOUS AMERICAN PIONEER TYPE) Whoa, Nellie! Whoa Bess! . . . Goldarn it! Whoa, can't you!

SOUND EFFECT: SNORTING OF HORSES, RATTLE OF CARRIAGE STOPPING. (FADING IN)

WATSON: Good Lord, Holmes. D'you think she can handle those horses?

HOLMES: I shouldn't worry about that. She's doing an expert job.

SOUND EFFECT: CARRIAGE STOPPING. NEIGH OF HORSES

GIBSON: (OFF A LITTLE) You must be Sherlock Holmes?

HOLMES: Yes, madam. And this is my friend and colleague, Doctor Watson.

GIBSON: Well, jump' in, boys. Gaston, go get their suitcases.

GASTON: (FRENCH ACCENT, ELDERLY, SPOOKY, FADING IN) Very well, Madame. Your bags, *messieurs* . . . .

SOUND EFFECT: CARRIAGE DOOR OPENING

GIBSON: (OFF A LITTLE) Settle yourself in the back there, boys. Sorry I wasn't here to meet you, but I was cookin' up a pot roast for dinner. Nothing like a good pot roast after some of these fancified French dishes. Hope you're hungry?

WATSON: Yes, Madam, I've quite an appetite.

GIBSON: Let's quit this "Madam" stuff right in the beginning. I come from Cheyenne, Wyoming where they call me "Two-Gun Gibson", on account of I can shoot the skin off a rice pudding at two-hundred yards. (YELLING) Hop up there, Gaston. I guess I'll have to let you drive so that I can talk to the boys.

GASTON: (OFF) *Oui*, Madame.

GIBSON: (FADING IN) What handle do you boys use?

405

WATSON: Handle? I don't quite understand you, madam.

GIBSON: What's your moniker? Your name?

WATSON: Oh. His name is Holmes . . . . Sherlock Holmes.

GIBSON: I know that. What's yours?

WATSON: Watson. Doctor Watson.

GIBSON: Didn't they give you a first name?

WATSON: (BEWILDERED) First name?

HOLMES: Really, Watson, you're being very obtuse. His first name is John. John H. Watson.

GIBSON: Then I'll call you Johnny and Sherlock. Never could get along with this fancy "mister" and "madame" stuff. (YELLING) What are you waiting for, Gaston? For Pete's sake get going! I've got a pot roast waiting.

GASTON: (OFF) Very good, Madame . . . .

SOUND EFFECT: CRACK OF WHIP. CARRIAGE STARTING. ESTABLISH HOOFBEATS THEN DOWN AND UNDER ENSUING

GIBSON: (MUTTERING) Madame. Well, boys, you probably wonder what I brought you here for an' why I plan to give you five grand?

HOLMES: Your telegram was . . . .

GIBSON: (INTERRUPTING GUSTILY) Forget the telegram. My daughter sent that because she figured the one I wrote hadn't any class. Here's the whole thing in a nutshell. When my better half died, three years ago, he left me two-million in cash, and as much again on the hoof.

WATSON: On the hoof?

GIBSON: Beeves, Johnnie. Beeves! But I've always had a yen to get the stink of cattle out of my nostrils. My daughter Susie – you'll meet her in a few minutes – had been educated in France an' was crazy about the place, And so, a year ago we came here and I bought this hunk of old masonry they call the Chateau Verlon for three times what it's worth, just to make my gal happy, an' to get away from the smell of them beeves, (YELLING) Gaston, if you can't go any faster we'll get out and push.

SOUND EFFECT: CRACK OF CARRIAGE NOISES INCREASE IN PACE

GIBSON: That's better. Now listen, boys, here's the trouble. This chateau of mine's haunted.

WATSON: Haunted? Good Lord.

GIBSON: Now don't get me wrong. I'm not frightened. There's nothing can scare me that a six-shooter couldn't take care of. But I can't get any servants, except that old buzzard you see sitting up on the box there. He's been with the chateau since it was built, I guess.

HOLMES: You say the chateau is haunted. What exactly has taken place that frightens the servants away?

GIBSON: Oh, nothing to get het up about. We've heard some funny sounding noises in the night, and there's a piece of furniture keeps movin' around. My gal Susie's frightened to death. And now we've got her count, or vicomte, or whatever he calls himself, staying with us. The kids are engaged.

WATSON: Really? Your daughter is engaged to a vicomte?

GIBSON: You're darned tootin' she is! Anything wrong with that?

WATSON: No, no. Oh certainly not.

GIBSON: He's got the blue blood and the handle, an' ten cents to his name. Susie's got a nice figure, blue eyes, an' a bank roll you could choke a horse with. That's a fair exchange. (SUDDENLY) There you are! There's the Chateau Verlon now.

407

WATSON: (ENTHUSIASTICALLY) What a beautiful place. Perched on the edge of the hillside and looking right out over the valley below.

HOLMES: Magnificent architecture. Must be fifteenth or sixteenth century.

GIBSON: Yep. An when you try the plumbing you'll believe it, Sherlock. And the whole house is built backwards. The hall's on the ground floor. You go downstairs to the parlor, an' down some more stairs to the bedrooms. (YELLING) Whoa! Nellie! Whoa, Bess! What are you trying to do, Gaston? Drive us right into the hallway?

SOUND EFFECT: CARRIAGE DRAWING TO STOP ON GRAVEL

GIBSON: Now skip out, boys, and I'll take you in to meet Susie ant her boyfriend. I always cell him "Butch", an' it makes him madder'n fifteen scalded wildcats. Open up the door there, Johnnie.

SOUND EFFECT: CARRIAGE DOOR OPENED

GIBSON: That's it. Jump out, (FADING A LITTLE) Gaston . . . you leave the bags in the hallway, and then take the carriage to the stable.

GASTON: (OFF) Very good, Madame.

GIBSON: (FADING IN) Straight ahead, boys. The door's open.

SOUND EFFECT: FOOTSTEPS

WATSON: After you, madam.

GIBSON: Quite a one with the ladies, aren't you, Johnnie?

SOUND EFFECT: HEAVY DOOR BEING OPENED

WATSON: (MUMBLING) Only natural that I should . . . .

GIBSON: Don't mumble, Johnnie. I can't understand a word you say.

SOUND EFFECT: DOOR CLOSE. FOOTSTEPS ON WOOD. SLIGHT ECHO

GIBSON: Leave your coats and hats there . . . That's right . . . and now down these stairs

SOUND EFFECT: FOOTSTEPS ON STAIRS

GIBSON: I'll just introduce you to the lovebirds and then beat it. Gotta keep my eye on that pot roast. (YELLING) Susie! Butch! Where are you?

SUSIE: (AMERICAN, YOUNG, CULTURED AND CHARMING) Here we are, Mother.

GIBSON: Come here, lovey. I want you to meet Sherlock Holmes, and his friend, Johnny Watson.

AD LIB: HOW DO YOU DO'S

GIBSON: Where's Butch? Oh, there you are . . . Come here, Butch.

SUSIE: (SOTTO VOCE) Mother, don't. You know how it embarrasses him. (LOUDER) Gentlemen, allow me to introduce my fiancée, Vicomte de Verlon.

FURTHER HOW DO YOU DO'S

VERLON: (THIRTY, EXCESSIVELY SUAVE, ALMOST DANDIFIED, STRONG FRENCH ACCENT) *Enchanté, messieurs.* I am so 'appy that Madame has brought you 'ere.

GIBSON: He's got a smooth line, hasn't he boys? Well, I must go and take a peek at that pot roast. (FADING) Butch, you show the boys to their room.

SUSIE: You mustn't mind Mother, gentlemen. She's on awfully nice person when you get to know her.

VERLON: *Mais oui.* Her . . . 'ow you say . . . Her bite is worse than her bark.

SUSIE: No, darling. It's the other way around, but never mind. Why not show the gentlemen to their room? (FADING) I'll see you all at dinner. I must help Mother . . . .

409

SOUND EFFECT: DOOR CLOSES

HOLMES: Amazing view from this room, Vicomte. Just look at the valley spreading out there below in the moonlight.

VERLON: You think that is beautiful. Let me open the French windows . . . . so . . . .

SOUND EFFECT: FRENCH WINDOWS BEING OPENED. WIND UP IN BACKGORUND

VERLON: And now step on the terrace 'ere.

WATSON: (AFTER A MOMENT) Magnificent! That sheer drop below. Gives one the feeling of being suspended in space.

HOLMES: Quite an architectural feat, building the chateau on the side of a mountain.

VERLON: *Oui*, and when you consider the castle was built 'ere in 1734, it makes it even more remarkable. And now, *messieurs*, I will show you to your room.

SOUND EFFECT: FRENCH WINDOWS BEING CLOSED. WIND OUT. FOOTSTEPS ON WOOD

HOLMES: I notice, Vicomte, that your name is the same as that of the chateau.

WATSON: Just going to comment on that myself. I imagine it's not coincidence, sir?

VERLON: Oh no, it is not a coincidence.

GASTON: (FADING IN) Hero are the bags, *messieurs*.

WATSON: Put them down, my good man, We'll carry them.

GASTON: Merci, *messieurs*. (FADING) I am not as strong as I was.

VERLON: Poor Garston . . . he's so old and decrepit . . . but he is the only servant who will stay. I hope you don't mind carrying your own bags, *messieurs*?

HOLMES: Of course we don't.

VERLON: I would 'elp you . . but as you see, 'ere on my hand, I have a bad burn. I did it trying to cook my breakfast this morning.

WATSON: That's a nasty burn, my boy. Better let me dress it for you. I'm a Doctor y'know.

VERLON: It is nothing. This way, *messieurs*. Down these stairs . . . .

SOUND EFFECT: FOOTSTEPS OF STAIRS. (SLIGHT ECHO)

VERLON: You mentioned just now that my name is the same as that of the chateau. *Messieurs* . . . this was my family's chateau. *Mais non*. Madame 'as ben very good to me. When she bought it, she insisted that I stay on here. But of course it is not the same. We Verlons have great pride in the chateau. Someday, maybe, I make money and buy it back again.

SOUND EFFECT: HEAVY DOOR OPEN. FOOTSTEPS STOP

VERLON: 'Ere is the room, *messieurs*. I gope you will be very comfortable.

HOLMES: I'm sure we shall. It's palatial.

VERLON: (WISTFULLY) It *was* palatial, but I'm afraid it's a little faded now . . . like the Verlon fortunes.

WATSON: Vicomte, what do you think of this story that the Chateau is haunted?

VERLON: (SIMPLY) *Oui*, it is haunted. It has always been so . . . 'ow shall I say . . . *sympathetique*. But we Verlons do not mind. No one has been turt. Guests have been frightened because they have not been . . . how shall I say . . . *sympathetique*. But, *messieurs*, I leave you now. I 'ave talk too much. Dinner will be –

GIBSON: (OFF YELLING) Boys! Boys! Where are you?:

VERLON: (CALLNG) Down 'ere, Madame.

GIBSON: (YELLING) The pot roast's ready! (CHANTING) Come and get it!

MUSIC: BRIDGE

WATSON: That was certainly a most delicious dinner you cooked, Mrs. Gibson.

GIBSON: Give me a piece of Wyoming beef an' I could really show you something.

HOLMES: Mrs. Gibson, before we retire for the night, there are one, or two questions I'd like, to ask you.

GIBSON: Sure, while the lovebirds are still out on the balcony, I might as well tell you exactly what's been going on here. Besides those rumblings and clankings late at night, there's been a peculiar smoky smell in this room, even when we've had no fire.

HOLMES: I see. You mentioned a piece of furniture being moved?

GIBSON: Yep. You see that armchair by the bookcase there? Three times now, I've come up here in the morning and found that chair moved from where it's been left the night before.

WATSON: Couldn't the servant Gaston have moved it when he cleaned out the fireplace in the mornings?

GIBSON: Yeah, Johnnie, but he didn't, because I'm always up first – that's a hangover from my Cheyenne days.

HOLMES: I see. When was the last occasion this happened?

GIBSON: Three nights ago. The next morning, I sent you that telegram.

SOUND EFFECT: FRENCH WINDOWS OPEN AND CLOSE (OFF). APRROACHING FOOTSTEPS

GIBSON: Here come the lovebirds now. How was the moon tonight, kids, or (MEANINGLY) mebbe you weren't looking at it? (SHE ROARS WITH LAUGHTER)

SUSIE: Mother, don't.

GIBSON: Rubbish. Don't be so touchy. Go along down to bed now, Susie.

SUSIE: All right, Mother. (FADING) I am rather tired.

VERLON: I'll walk to your room with you, darling, so you won't be frightened.

GIBSON: Yes, Butch, and you'll come right back and lock up.

SUSIE: (OFF) Good night, everybody.

AD LIB: GOOD NIGHTS

GIBSON: (CONFIDENTIALLY) They're plannin' to get married in three weeks, you know. Well, I think I'll hit the hay, too. (FADING) Good night, boys. See you in the morning.

HOLMES AND WATSON AD LIB GOOD NIGHTS

WATSON: What d'you make of it, Holmes?

HOLMES: A very interesting case, old fellow. Very interesting. Come on.

WATSON: But where are: we going?

HOLMES: To bed.

SOUND EFFECT: FOOTSTEPS

WATSON: I'm not tired.

HOLMES: Nor am I, old chap.

WATSON: Then why . . . .

413

HOLMES: I merely suggest that we go downstairs to our bedroom and wait.

WATSON: Wait? What for?

HOLMES: Remember the old Scotch saying? *"For ghoulies and beasties – and long legged ghosties – and things that go bomp in the night . . . ."*

MUSIC: BRIDGE

WATSON: (SLEEPILY) Holmes, it's nearly one o'clock. When are we going to turn in?

HOLMES: How can we catch a ghost if we don't wait up for him?

WATSON: What's that paper you're reading?

HOLMES: An old newspaper I found in the chest of drawers. Oddly enough, it has a front page story about that train robbery I mentioned earlier on. A special train carrying carloads of gold passed this station safely, but arrived in Lyons half-an-hour late, crashing into the buffers, with the crew shot and the gold missing. Too bad that in these reports more stress is laid on the platitudes of the magistrate than upon the details of the case.

SOUND EFFECT: SCUFFLE OF MUFFLED FOOTSTEPS OFF, THUD. CRY

WATSON: What's that?

HOLMES: Come on, Watson! That came from the living room above us.

SOUND EFFECT: DOOR WRENCHED OPEN. RUNNING ON STAIRS. (AFTER FOOTSTEPS ARE ESTABLISHED, A HORRIBLE MOANING FADING IN)

WATSON: Great Scott! Listen to that!

SOUND EFFECT: DOOR WRENCHED OPEN. FOOTSTEPS STOP. MOANING UP STRONG

WATSON: Look, Holmes! Over there . . . There's someone moving!

HOLMES: (VIOLENTLY) Watson!

WATSON: Great Scott, Holmes! The chandelier! If you hadn't pushed me out of the way, it would have killed me!

HOLM ES: Yes. I fancy it was intended for both of us. Here, I'll strike a match.

WATSON: I'll light the gas. That's better . . . . (AFTER A MOMENT) Holmes . . look! Under that fallen chandelier!

HOLMES: The body of the stationmaster we met earlier on this evening.

WATSON: Killed by the chandelier falling on him . . a death intended for us!

HOLMES: Oh no. He was already dead, Watson. If you'll look closely, you'll observe there's a dagger through his chest. D'you notice anything else?

WATSON: No. What?

HOLMES: The armchair – by the bookcase. It's been moved again – just as Mrs. Gibson told us.

WATSON: And the room's empty. Yet I swear I saw a figure in the moonlight as we came in. Holmes, I don't believe in the supernatural . . . but . . . .

HOLMES: Nonsense. Somewhere in this house there's a flesh-and-blood murderer . . . and it's our job to find him!

415

FORMAN: "The Case of the Haunted Chateau" will continue in just a few seconds – which is all the time I need to remind you that no matter how good a cook you are, when it comes to cooking a roast or broiling a steak, that roast and that steak will taste infinitely better if served with a Petri California Burgundy. Petri Burgundy is a he-man wine – rich red in color . . . hearty and full in flavor. One sip tells you that the flavor of Petri burgundy comes right from the very heart of the grape. And say, you just haven't been around until you've had an old-fashioned spaghetti dinner . . . served with thick slices of French bread and big glasses of colorful Petri Burgundy! Mister – that's eating! Or tell you what – try that Petri burgundy together with a juicy hamburger steak or with any meat or meat dish. If you like good things to eat – you should certainly find out immediately about Petri Burgundy . . . it terrific!

MUSIC: "SCOTCH POEM"

FORMAN: And now, back to tonight's new Sherlock Holmes adventure. In answer to a telegram from Mrs. Gibson, Holmes and Doctor Watson have come to an old chateau in the south of France – a chateau reputed to be haunted. On the night of their arrival, a man has been murdered, and Holmes and his colleague have narrowly escaped death from a falling chandelier. As we rejoin our story, it is after dinner the next day, and bitter argument is (FADING) going on amongst the family . . . .

GIBSON: A fine thing . . . the local stationmaster smeared all over my best carpet with a knife through him – and no one even knows how he got here. An expensive chandelier smashed to pieces. The cops here all day an' they can't figure the thing out. A fancy detective snoopin' around and he's no smarter. I'll pay you your five grand, Sherlock, because I'm a woman of my word, but I don't think you've earned it.

HOLMES: Madam, I shouldn't dream of accepting your fee without solving the case . . . and that I propose to do before the night is out.

GIBSON: You mean you've got an idea who's back of all this?

HOLMES: Madam, my day has not an idle one.

416

GIBSON: Well, I can tell you, my *night's* not going to be an idle one. Sherlock. Personally, I'm going to sit up with a six-shooter in that armchair that moves itself around. This chateau's no more haunted than my Uncle Elmer, an' I'm going to prove it, too!

VERLON: Perhaps you should not have bought the chateau, Madame. There has never been trouble 'ere until you came. If you want to sell, for not too big a price. I will raise the money to buy it back.

GIBSON: Sure you will, you slinky two-timer! You probably organized the whole thing so that you could get your chateau back for a song, trying to frighten me off my property. Wall, I don't scare easy, see, an' if you . . . .

VERLON: (ANGRILY) Madame! You have insulted me! If you were a man, my seconds would call on you in the morning. I shall (FADING) leave Verlon by the next train.

GIBSON: Good riddance of bad rubbish!

SUSIE: Mother! You don't mean that. Say you're sorry.

GIBSON: You're darned tootin' I mean it. I never did like him anyway. I only put up with him because of you, Susie.

SUSIE: (HYSTERICALLY) Well, going to marry him . . whether you like it or not! And if he goes on the next train (FADING) I'm going with him . . . .

SOUND EFFECT: DOOR SLAM

GIBSON: Gol-ding it! Now I've upset Susie. Sherlock, stop dropping your cigar ashes on my stylish carpet.

WATSON: (VERY SLEEPILY) Just what I was going to say. I've been watching you, Holmes. You've been knocking your cigar ash all over the place.

GIBSON: Thought you were asleep, Johnnie. You haven't opened your trap for quarter-of-an-hour.

WATSON: I do feel . . . very sleepy, I must say.

417

HOLMES: Better wake up, old fellow. We have work to do.

GIBSON: You and me both, Sherlock. Though from what I've seen of you in action, so far, I'll back my shooter (FADING) against your brains. See you later . . . .

SOUND EFFECT: DOOR CLOSE (OFF)

HOLMES: (URGENTLY) Watson! Did you drink that coffee tonight?

WATSON: Course I did . . . Love coffee . . . .

HOLMES: You fool! You blithering idiot. I told you not to.

WATSON: (HAZILY) Why are both of you . . . droppin' cigar ash?

HOLMES: Both of me? Why didn't you listen to me? Watson! (URGENTLY) Watson!

MUSIC: BRIDGE

HOLMES: Watson, drink this.

WATSON: (WOOZILY) Whatizzit . . .? Why are we in our bedroom?

HOLMES: Never mind that. Drink this.

WATSON: All right. (AFTER A MOMENT) Ohh . . . .

HOLMES: Feel better?

WATSON: Yes. What happened, Holmes?

HOLMES: The coffee at dinner was drugged. I told you not to drink it, I poured mine into a nearby vase. One sip told me the story.

WATSON: Drugged . . . But why?

HOLMES: To keep us out of the way, of course.

WATSON: Who did it?

HOLMES: I'm not certain – but I have very strong suspicions.

WATSON: You know, Holmes, I think . . . that Verlon boy's behind this.

HOLMES: Possibly.

WATSON: I'm sure he is. He wants the chateau back and he . . . .

SOUND EFFECT: THUMPING SOUND OFF. CRY. MUFFLED THUD OF FALLING BODY

HOLMES: Come on, Watson! Up the stairs!

SOUND EFFECT: RUNNING FOOTSTEPS. AFTER A MOMENT, STRANGULATED GURGLE FADING IN. DOOR WRENCHED OPEN. GURLGE (UP)

WATSON: Great Heavens! Young Verlon! With a sword through his heart!

HOLMES: Yes. And Mrs. Gibson. She's blue in the face. Better look at her, Watson.

WATSON: (AFTER A MOMENT) She's been half-strangled! Look at these finger marks on her throat.

HOLMES: Can we leave her safely for a few minutes?

WATSON: Yes. She's just in a faint. She'll be all right.

HOLMES: Good, because our murderer can't be far away.

WATSON: I was convinced young Verlon was the murderer, and there he is dead. D'you suppose Mrs. Gibson stabbed him?

HOLMES: Use your intelligence, old fellow. She has a six-shooter in her hand – why would she use a sword? And do you suppose she tried to cover her tracks by partially strangling herself afterwards?

WATSON: I suppose not. Then why . . . ? (SUDDENLY) What are you doing, Holmes?

HOLMES: (OFF A LITTLE) You commented on my dropping cigar ash earlier on. There was a reason for it. Cigar ash forms an excellent medium for recording footprints . . . Yes . . . These footprints lead to the bookcase here. Obviously, there is a secret door.

WATSON: By Jove, Holmes, there's the answer to the moving armchair! It usually stands directly in front of the bookcase.

HOLMES: Precisely. Anyone entering the secret door would have to move the chair to enter, Watson.

WATSON: Yes, and once inside, he would be unable to move the chair back into position again.

HOLMES: You will observe the chair is out of position now. Therefore, we may assume the murderer is waiting for us somewhere behind this bookcase. You noticed how the chateau is built on the side of a hill. Three sides project into space. The only place where there could be a secret room is on the closed side . . . and unless I'm much mistaken, this will be the entrance to it. The question is . . . Ah, here we are . . . Behind this well-thumbed book we find a button. We press it . . . so . . . .

SOUND EFFECT: HEAVY CREAKING PANEL OPENING

HOLMES: And "Open Sesame"! The bookcase swings back –

WATSON: And discloses a tunnel.

HOLMES: Exactly. Come on, Watson!

SOUND EFFECT: RUNNING FOOTSTEPS, ON ECHO, FOR A MOMENT, THEN STOP (NOTE: IN ENSUING SCENE, ALL VOICES ON ECHO)

WATSON: Good Lord, Holmes . . . a great cave. And look at those gold bars and machinery there . . . it looks like the mint.

HOLMES: Exactly. Here's the answer to two stories. The haunted chateau and the Lyons Train Robbery. (CALLING) Gaston, you have visitors!

WATSON: Gaston!

GASTON: *Bon Soir, messieurs.*

HOLMES: Gaston, will you tell the story, or shall I?

GASTON: There is no story.

HOLMES: Very loyal of you, Gaston, but not true. Here are the facts, Watson. Young Verlon staged the train robbery to pay off the mortgage on the chateau. I'm sure it wasn't hard to persuade Gaston, loyal servant that he is, to help him. But gold ingots aren't easy to sell, and so they installed the machinery that you see here, to convert the gold bars into coins.

WATSON: That would account for the strange noises and the burning smell that Mrs. Gibson mentioned .

HOLMES: And also the burn on Verlon's hand that prevented him from helping us carry our suitcases yesterday. Am I right, Gaston?

GAS TON: *Oui, Monsieur.*

HOLMES: The stationmaster that was murdered last night – he helped you with the train robbery, didn't he?

GASTON: *Oui, Monsieur.* He was my cousin.

HOLMES: And I suppose when he saw us arrive yesterday, he became frightened?

GASTON: *Oui*, he recognised you, Mr. Holmes. Last night he came up hero and demanded his share in the robbery . . . and my master killed him.

WATSON: But who killed your master?

HOLMES: That's obvious. Gaston did.

WATSON: Gaston? But why?

HOLMES: Tell him Gaston.

GASTON: It is simple. I loved my master, just as I loved his father before him.

HOLMES: But the honour of the Verlons means more to you than anything else.

GASTON: *Oui, Monsieur.* When he killed my cousin, the stationmaster, I kept his secret. Perhaps I could have kept quiet if he had killed you both last night –

HOLMES: – as he tried to when he cut the chandelier?

GASTON: But tonight, when I caught him trying to strangle Madame Gibson, I knew that the good blood of the Verlons was getting impoverished. He seemed to have no conscience about killing – he was a bad Verlon – and he would have disgraced the family name. And so, I killed him with his own sword. It is better so.

HOLMES: I understand your motives, Gaston, but you realise you'll have to pay for this, don't you? Probably with your life?

GASTON: (SCORNFULLY) My life? What is that worth compared the good name of the Verlons? I am an old man and I am ready to die. But no human judge will sentence me! (QUICK FADE) *Au revoir, messieurs*!

SOUND EFFECT: RUNNING FOOTSTEPS (ECHOING)

WATSON: Look out! He's trying to get away!

HOLMES: After him, Watson! Come on!

SOUND EFFECT: FOOTSTEPS CONTINUE, (OFF ECHO)

WATSON: Gaston . . . Come away from that balcony!

GASTON: (VIOLENTLY) There is only one judge . . . and his court is kinder than this world's . . . . (FADING) I go to him . . . . *Le Bon Dieu*!

SOUND EFFECT: CRASH OF BROKEN GLASS

WATSON: (YELLING) Holmes, he's gone through the windows and over the balcony, poor devil!

HOLMES: Yes, Watson . . . poor devil. But I think *Le Bon Dieu* will understand. Gaston was a faithful servant.

MUSIC: UP STRONG TO FINISH

FORMAN: Well, Doctor, that was an interesting story. So the old Chateau wasn't haunted after all.

WATSON: No . . . but I don't mind admitting that I certainly was scared when we first opened that secret door into the cave.

FORMAN: I don't blame you. Although you know, I wish I had a cave like that in my house.

WATSON: Now wait a minute – you're not thinking of doing a little haunting, are you? (LAUGH)

FORMAN: (LAUGHS) Without a license? Oh no. I'd like to have a cave like that full of Petri Wine. Oh brother! Then I'd be set for life . . . because believe me, that Petri wine is good wine. It ought to be . . . the Petri family has been making wine for generations. As you know, ever since they started the Petri business, way back in the eighteen-hundreds – that business has always been family-owned and operated. So just think of all the experience the Petri family has gained. They've been able to hand on down from father to son, from father to son, all they've ever learned about the art of turning luscious California grapes into fragrant, delicious wine. So whenever you're choosing a wine – a wine to serve before dinner, with dinner . . . or at any time . . . you can't go wrong with a Petri wine. Because Petri took time to bring you good wine. And now, Doctor. how about a hint of next week's story?

WATSON: Next week, Mr. Forman, I'm going to tell you a strange adventure that took place in a circus. It starts in a lion's cage . . . and ends . . on the gallows!

FORMAN: Tonight's Sherlock Holmes adventure is written by Dennis Green and Bruce Taylor and is based on an incident in the Sir Arthur Conan Doyle story "A Case of Identity". Mr. Rathbone appears through the courtesy of Metro-Goldwyn-Mayer, and Mr. Bruce through the courtesy of Universal Pictures, where they are now starring in the Sherlock Holmes series.

MUSIC: THEME UP AND DOWN UNDER

FORMAN: The Petri Wine Company of San Francisco, California invites you to tune in again next week, same time, same station.

MUSIC: HIT JINGLE

SINGERS: *The Petri family took the time, To bring you such good wine, So when you eat and when you cook, Remember Petri Wine*!

FORMAN: Yes, Petri Wine made by the Petri Wine Company, San Francisco, California.

SINGERS: *Pet – Pet – Petri Wine*!

FORMAN: This is Bill Forman saying goodnight for the Petri family. Sherlock Holmes comes to you from the Don Lee studios in Hollywood. This is the Mutual Broadcasting Network.

The Adventure of the
Weeping Stone
by Nick Cardillo

"It's the abominable noise, Watson," said Sherlock Holmes. "It's been upsetting the bees."

Holmes lifted his gaze from the honeycomb which he held in hand and addressed me from across the yard. He slipped the comb back in the apiary, then took up the can of smoke, and proceeded to pan it across the writhing bodies of the insects within.

I had expected some of Holmes's attention to be focused on his bees as I visited him that summer day in 1911, but I had not anticipated such myopia from my friend. Frankly, it was frustrating. I had seen very little of him of late, and I had been looking forward to my visit – one which I had coordinated to the minute detail so that I might not be away from my practice for too long, and which happened to coincide with my wife taking a trip into the country of her own. But now, as I stood in the yard of Holmes's cottage on the Sussex Downs, I found that the detective seemed to have little interest in my presence. He hadn't even greeted me at the door when I arrived. Instead, I found myself alighting from the trap which had conveyed me thence from the train station on my own, being welcomed to the cottage by the housekeeper. My bags were taken up to my guest room and I was told that Holmes was busy with his bees. As I stepped outside to warmly embrace my friend, I found him barely looking up before he exclaimed that the recent nearby commotion was offensive to his honey-producing acquaintances.

"And it is good to see you too," I grumbled. "I trust that your bees have been keeping you busy?"

"Exceedingly," Holmes said, as he crossed the yard, removing his thick gloves one finger at a time. He had divested himself of his net hat, which he cast onto a wooden rocking chair by his side. I looked at my friend's familiar countenance and could not help but feel that time was melting away. Save for a few lines to his gaunt aquiline features and touches of grey to his temples, Sherlock Holmes looked ever the same. He smiled a knowing grin as though he were able to divine my thoughts – a feat which he had done on more than one occasion – and then gestured for me to sit in the vacant chair opposite his.

"Time has been good to you, my friend," I said as I sat. Holmes waved away the notion with his hand. He reached into the inner pocket of his

425

tweed coat and withdrew his old cigarette case. Passing it across, I lit a cigarette and settled back in my seat, feeling for an instant that we two were once more seated around the fire of 221b Baker Street in London.

"Your practice has been a successful one," Holmes said. "Though I fear that your wife's attention to detail is beginning to wane."

"Whatever do you mean?"

Holmes indicated with a bony finger. "There is a spot of iodine on your right forefinger," he said. "Surely it has resided there since yesterday when you last attended your surgery. Mrs. Watson must have failed to notice it, for no wife would allow her husband to go out for so long with such a stain upon his person."

I chuckled. "Your powers have not faltered, my friend. However, my wife has gone on her own trip. She left yesterday afternoon. I saw her off during luncheon."

The housekeeper came with a tray and two glasses of claret. Holmes and I clinked our glasses together. The tableau could not have been a more familiar one.

"Do you miss it much," I asked. "Baker Street, I mean. Working as London's only *unofficial consulting detective?*"

Holmes parted his lips, preparing to speak, when we were arrested once more by the presence of the housekeeper.

"Beg your pardon, Mr. Holmes," she said, "but there is a gentleman to see you in your parlor."

"Are you expecting anyone?" I asked.

"No," Holmes replied. "Did he give you his name?"

The housekeeper handed him a card. Holmes studied it for a moment before passing it across to me. It read: *Dr. David Laramie.*

"His name is a familiar one," I said.

"Yes," Holmes replied. "Dr. Laramie is foreman of the excavation project on the beach below. It is his project which is causing such a commotion and upsetting my bees. Let us see what Dr. Laramie wants from us, Watson, and if nothing else I may complain about the noise."

We found Dr. David Laramie pacing the sitting room as we drew into it. He was a tall, fair-haired man in his early fifties, but was possessed of a youthful expression and physique that I could have easily mistook him for a much younger man. As soon as his eyes fell upon Holmes, he all but rushed across the room to meet him.

"Thank God you were in, Mr. Holmes!" he cried. "You are the only man who could possibly help us."

"Please, Dr. Laramie," Holmes said coolly. "Compose yourself. I am prepared to hear through whatever it is that you have to say." Holmes gestured for the man to sit on the settee. Laramie did so.

"This is my friend and colleague, Dr. John Watson," Holmes continued. "Dr. Watson, as you are doubtlessly aware, has been at my side for nearly all of my cases and has drawn up public records of them. I owe something of my celebrity to him."

Laramie flashed me a glance and a quick "How do you do?" but he returned his gaze to Holmes. The detective took a seat in his old, familiar velvet-lined armchair which had been a fixture of our sitting room in London for so long and pressed his hands together in his habitual, contemplative gesture.

"Now then, Dr. Laramie," Holmes said calmly, "what is it that you brings you to me this morning, and who are the *us* of whom you speak?"

I knew full well that Holmes knew already the answer to that question. Indeed, there were few households in England that were unaware of Laramie's work in the area. It had been a little over three months since a large rock had been found on the stretch of beach near Holmes's cottage. This unique discovery attracted the attention of one of the larger universities in the country who promptly dispatched a team – led by Laramie – to investigate.

In the time since, Laramie and his team had discovered that the large rock appeared to have come from South America. How this rock could have made it onto English shores was a mystery which they had yet to solve, and there were few corners of English academia which hadn't attempted to put forth a solution. On occasion, the papers would carry the latest bit of theorizing – the latest postulation suggested that the rock had been embedded in the cliff face overlooking the beach and had been exposed during a recent collapse, a notion which presented nearly as many questions as it did answers – but it seemed that Laramie and his team of archaeologists were no closer to answering the most tantalizing of questions so often on the lips of interested parties.

When the discovery of the rocks had first been made, I made sure to question Holmes about it during our irregular correspondence. He confessed to not being overly interested in the matter. *"That is one mystery, my dear Watson,"* he had written, *"which I feel is best left to the others."*

How ironic, then, I considered that Holmes should find himself drawn into the business after all.

"My entire team is being questioned by police this morning," Laramie said. "My assistant, Mr. Macaulay, was found dead this morning."

Holmes leaned forward in his seat. "Pray, Dr. Laramie, lay all the facts before me." I could see it in Holmes's cold, grey eyes the thrill of the chase. Like a bloodhound, he was once more on the scent.

"Macaulay was discovered on the beach this morning," Laramie reiterated. "He was found not far from the site of the dig. We have been studying the rock day and night, the area entirely cordoned off. There was no sign of any disturbance to the scene, save Macaulay's footprints, which were visible in the sand. And yet he is dead, Mr. Holmes. There are no marks of violence upon his body, but on his face . . . he looks as if he were frightened to death."

Laramie grasped the knees of his trousers to stop his hands from shaking. "I am not ordinarily an anxious man, Mr. Holmes, but this has unnerved all of the men. There's something devilish in all this."

"Surely there must be some rational explanation," I said, too afraid to admit that I found this man of science's belief in something otherworldly just a little disquieting.

"Ordinarily I would think so too, Dr. Watson," Laramie said, "but our investigation of the rock has born worrying results. There are inscriptions made upon it – hieroglyphs whose meaning we cannot divine. However, in comparing notes with a colleague who has made an intensive study of the ancient Inca civilization, we are currently of the belief that this stone may have been a part of ancient, ritualistic sacrifice. And . . . it would explain the blood."

"Blood?" said Holmes. "I thought you said that Macaulay's body showed no signs of violence."

"That is true," Laramie replied. "However, the stone itself has been known to . . . weep blood, Mr. Holmes. A number of the men are rightfully afraid. I have ensured that they have never touched the stone, you understand, but even being in such close proximity has felled a few of them on occasion. Men have become quite ill because of that stone. I'm sure of it. There's something unnatural about it, and poor Macaulay's death only proves that fact even further."

Sherlock Holmes considered, tapping a finger to his pursed lips. "When was Macaulay last seen?"

"He was in the company of my daughter, Rebecca, and Mr. Anderson, another researcher, at the Tiger Inn in the village. Macaulay left just before ten o'clock, I am told, and was not seen for the rest of the night. His body was discovered this morning. As soon as I was made aware, I contacted the police, and they have been speaking to all of the men since. I broached the subject of speaking to you with the investigating officer, and he begrudgingly allowed me to visit you."

Laramie drew in a deep breath. "Mr. Holmes, you would do much to ease my mind if you were involved in this investigation. Please, please say that you will accompany me back to the dig."

"I shall be happy to help, Dr. Laramie," said Holmes, rising from his seat. A rush of relief crossed the man's face. Turning to me, Holmes said, "You would not be averse to joining me, would you, Watson?"

I said that I should be happy to help in any manner I could.

A few moments later, we were seated together in the rear of Laramie's automobile, bouncing across the dirt road towards the excavation site.

It was a beautiful summer morning. The sun hung high in the sky, and a gentle breeze blew inland from the ocean which stretched out endlessly before us. If we weren't on our way to visit the scene of a man's death, I should have taken in the striking vista all the more. However, I was forced to temper my outlook and remind myself that we were currently engaged in solemn business.

Laramie's driver deposited us on the cliff above the beach. A number of wary-looking workman were standing and conversing in small groups, and at the far end of the beach I could plainly see the mysterious stone – each at least five feet in height and standing like a noble sentry upon the sand. Try as I might, I couldn't make out the form of the late Mr. Macaulay upon the beach, and in short order I realized why as an official-looking person advanced towards us.

"Welcome back, Dr. Laramie," he called. Then, catching sight of Holmes, he added, "How nice of you to join us, Mr. Holmes. I confess that I was rather reluctant to bring you in, but this sort of thing seems right up your street."

"My thanks to you, Inspector Mackenzie," Holmes airily replied, toying with the head of his stick as he spoke. "I see that you have already removed the body."

"Yes, Mr. Holmes," the representative of the law responded. "Tide was coming in and I knew it would do no good to have the corpse submerged in seawater." A smile crossed Inspector Mackenzie's boyish features. "Mr. Macaulay has already been conveyed to the mortuary and a *post mortem* will be conducted. We should have the results by this afternoon. All quite forward-thinking of me, eh, Mr. Holmes?"

"Oh, most forward-thinking, Inspector," Holmes acerbically answered, pointing with his cane. "However, in doing so, you have trod back-and-forth through the scene enough times to obliterate any traces of a second party's footprints."

"I can assure you, Mr. Holmes," Mackenzie said, "that there were no other footprints. Mr. Macaulay's were the only ones to be seen in the sand. I checked the outline with his boots myself."

"My felicitations, Mackenzie," Holmes said. "Might I be allowed to inspect the scene for myself?"

Inspector Mackenzie made a broad gesture with his arms. Holmes and I pressed on, Laramie shrinking back, perhaps still unnerved by the devilish nature of the area.

"Inspector Mackenzie is one of a new breed," Holmes said as we crossed the beach. His eyes were on the ground, darting this way and that, looking for a clue of any kind. "His self-assurance is his greatest weakness as a criminal investigator."

"I think it would be inaccurate to suggest that you were never self-assured, Holmes," I replied.

"Ah, your pawky humor has not deserted you, Watson," Holmes said. "However, there is one major difference between Inspector Mackenzie and me. I am Sherlock Holmes. He is not."

I couldn't help but suppress a guffaw at my friend's quip, and I caught once again a glimpse of his fast-moving brain, waiting for mental stimulation. Though I am sure he would never have admitted it, I knew my friend well enough to know that this: Searching for clues at the scene of an impossible murder brought him much greater fulfillment than his colony of bees ever could.

We approached the large stone, and as we drew nearer to the strange object, I could make out the bizarre symbols which Laramie had mentioned. A series of concentric circles, undulating lines, and curious depictions of things which are beyond my powers as a writer. I could easily see how this odd and ancient form of writing could have unnerved the men so. There was almost nothing – to the layman, at least – which suggested its meaning to us. Could these strange symbols be an auspicious omen, or were they a harbinger of doom?

Holmes cast his eyes over the symbols for an instant only before he had approached the stone and ran a hand over its rough surface. He drew this hand away, and then reached into his pocket, withdrawing his familiar magnifying lens. He peered at the stone once more beneath the lens and murmured to himself all the while.

"Anything?" I said at length.

"It is curious," Holmes muttered more to himself than to me. "Curious indeed."

He then turned on his heel and strode away, his examination seemingly complete.

"Dr. Laramie," Holmes called out to our client, who stood quietly conversing with the representative of the law. "You said something about this stone weeping blood. Can you be more specific?"

Laramie drew in a deep breath. "I don't know what I can possibly tell you, Mr. Holmes. I am at a loss. We all are. The stone has been known to

430

weep blood from time to time. Never much, mind you, but blood trickles out from the stone."

"Is it genuine?" Holmes asked.

"I'd like to think that I know blood when I see it," Laramie rebuked.

Holmes pressed on. "And this strange stone," he said. "It is your opinion that it comes from South America?"

"It has all the hallmarks of having come from that corner of the world," Laramie said. "The quality of the stone is similar to other rock deposits found there, and the markings – verified by one of my colleagues – do seem to be Incan. How it arrived here in England is a mystery to me."

No sooner had Holmes processed this staggering assessment than he was turning his attention wholly to Inspector Mackenzie once more. "You say that the body has been taken to the mortuary?"

"Yes, Mr. Holmes. An autopsy was to be scheduled immediately."

"I should have liked to search the body *in situ*, but under the circumstances . . . ." Holmes's voiced trailed off. "You would not be averse to Dr. Watson making an examination of Mr. Macaulay's mortal remains, Inspector?"

"Not at all, Mr. Holmes," the cocksure young fellow replied. "I should welcome any opinion that you may have."

"Then it is the morgue that we shall visit next," Holmes declared.

Laramie said that he was going to oversee the site once more and offered us the use of his automobile and driver. Gratefully accepting, we made our way back to where the vehicle was parked on the promontory overlooking the beach. Once seated inside, Holmes instructed the driver to take us to the police station. As we sat, I heard Holmes sigh satisfactorily and I realized quite suddenly that he and I were no longer the young men we once were. I am sure that leaping again into the fray as he was, Holmes still fancied himself the energetic investigator, ready to throw himself face-first onto the ground in order to examine the scene for clues. But to do so now was almost an impossibility. Holmes and I were both pushing sixty years of age. I suddenly felt my years – memories of my many years at Holmes's side suddenly played out before me, and I recalled that in my time I had lived twice as much as most men. A dry chuckle escaped my lips.

"You find this all amusing, Watson?" Holmes said turning to me.

"Hardly," I remarked. "I was simply reminiscing. This feels like the old days, does it not?"

Holmes laughed. "Indeed, it does. You asked me before we were interrupted by Dr. Laramie if I miss it: Being London's only 'unofficial consulting detective'. Our little adventure today seems to suggest that I have nothing to miss. And, but a few years ago I was engaged on another little matter which resolved itself in the queerest of ways. Really, Watson, one of these days I must tell you about the Lion's Mane. It is a story which, if ever written, I should think that no reader would believe."

"I feel quite similarly about this business," I said. "A stone which weeps blood. It's fantastic. Do you have any idea what caused Macaulay's death?"

"I have my suspicions," Holmes replied. "It is still too early for me to speak them aloud, lest I bias not only your judgment but my own. But, if my supposition is correct, then Dr. Laramie may have wished that he had never taken it upon himself to study that strange weeping stone."

The coroner – a big, bearded man called Mitchell – showed us into the mortuary. It had, thankfully, been some years since I had been surrounded by death, and the unpleasant smell of the morgue was one which assailed my nostrils as soon as we entered that pristine, tiled room.

"Devon Macaulay," Dr. Mitchell said, as he strode into the room. "Aged six-and-twenty. By my estimation, he was dead for nearly six hours before he was discovered on the beach this morning."

Approaching the slab on which the body had been laid out, Mitchell withdrew the white shroud which covered Macaulay's mortal remains. Holmes and I glanced down at the body of the young man, and I felt a twinge of sadness for a life which was extinguished so soon. I then recoiled in surprise, for Dr. Laramie's words had been apt. It looked as if Macaulay had been frightened to death. His eyes, wide in alarm and his mouth agape as if he were still screaming from beyond the grave, are sights I shall never forget.

Holmes knelt close to the body, passing his critical all-seeing eyes over the dead man.

"Are there signs of heart failure?" I asked. "The rictus is indicative of such."

"None that I could detect, Doctor," Mitchell replied. "And by all accounts, Macaulay was a hearty, healthy young man. It would be very unlikely that he had a weak heart."

"Then how do you account for the look of utter terror on his face?"

"I don't know," Mitchell replied. "His body shows no signs of violence at all. Poor man must have *seen* something in his last moments of life, though."

Sherlock Holmes indicated with a finger that I should draw closer to the body.

"His left leg, Watson," he said. "Feel it."

I did as I was instructed. "The muscle, it's stiff as a board. Far exceeding *rigor mortis*," I declared.

"Suggesting what?"

"A powerful poison of some kind," I replied.

"*Poison*?" Mitchell cried. "Surely not!"

"Surely it is so, Doctor," Holmes retorted sardonically. "It would do you and Inspector Mackenzie good to begin treating Mr. Macaulay's death as a violent one."

No sooner had Holmes made such a declaration than Inspector Mackenzie strode into the room, a prideful grin on his face.

"Speak of the devil and he shall appear," Holmes murmured.

"I could not help but overhear, Mr. Holmes," Mackenzie said. "And it looks as if I have beaten you at your own game. What do you like to say: 'This is a case of murder. Cold, calculating, deliberate murder'? Well, I am happy to announce that I have a suspect in custody at this very moment."

"Bravo, Inspector," Holmes blandly rebuked. "And just who is this unfortunate person?"

"Mr. Malcolm Anderson," Mackenzie answered. "Dr. Laramie's fellow researcher, and Macaulay's rival for the affections of Laramie's daughter, Rebecca. But the morgue is no place for a conversation like this. Let us decamp to my office and we can talk the thing through there."

A moment later, we were in Mackenzie's small corner office, a room overcrowded with papers. I sat across from the boyish inspector, who seemed to be engulfed by the large chair in which he sat, while Holmes stood by the open window, pulling contentedly on a newly-lit cigarette.

"It was really quite obvious," Mackenzie was saying. "It merely took a little creative thinking. Mr. Anderson was one of the last people to see Macaulay alive. According to Miss Laramie, Anderson and Macaulay had an argument before Macaulay's death. Obviously wishing to see the score settled, Anderson followed Macaulay out of the inn, trailed him to the beach, and poisoned him."

"Excellent, Inspector," Holmes said turning away from the window. "Excellent work."

A smug looked crossed Inspector Mackenzie's face.

"You have only failed to provide Mr. Anderson with a proper motive, a method of murder, and an explanation as to how he managed to follow Macaulay onto the beach without leaving any footprints in the sand."

Mackenzie's face fell. "Well," he began, "that can all be explained away. Anderson and Macaulay were obviously quarreling about something. Raised tempers led to the violence between men. He must have had some quantity of poison on his person and, forcing Macaulay to take it, he left the same way he had come, being sure to tread only in Macaulay's own footprints."

Holmes crushed his cigarette into an ashtray. "Your theory answers some of my questions, Inspector, but it presents plenty of others on its own. Frankly, you have fallen into the same habit as my former friends at Scotland Yard of concocting theories before one is in full possession of the facts. You have begun to twist your facts to pin the blame on Mr. Anderson alone. Think of it, Inspector: What earthly reason should Mr. Anderson have for keeping a quantity of some deadly poison on his person? And if he had managed to force it upon Mr. Macaulay, why should the dead man have a look of utter terror upon his face, and not pain from the attack?"

Mackenzie considered the detective's words for a moment and then remained silent. Obviously he had no rebuttal.

"Might Dr. Watson and I have a word with Mr. Anderson?" Holmes asked at length.

Mackenzie nodded, clearing his throat as he stood. "He has been detained for further questioning. If you gentleman would follow me this way."

Mackenzie led us out of his office and down a corridor towards what I soon discovered amounted to the constabulary's jail. Passing a uniformed officer, Mackenzie gestured for us to enter the small, cramped, barred room in which sat an unfortunate-looking young man, clasping and unclasping his hands, a look of equal parts irritation and dejection writ heavily upon his brow.

"Mr. Malcolm Anderson," Holmes intoned as we stepped into the cell. The young man looked up and nodded. "My name is Sherlock Holmes, and this is my friend and colleague, Dr. John Watson. We understand that you are currently being held in connection with the death of Mr. Devon Macaulay. I would like to put a few questions to you."

Anderson's tense shoulders lowered. What a relief it must have been for someone to speak to him so calmly, when I'm sure that the vainglorious Inspector Mackenzie had only belittled the young man in an effort to crush his spirit and elicit a confession.

"I didn't kill Devon," Anderson said. "I had an almighty row with him, that I will admit, but I did not kill him."

"This row," Holmes said. "What was it about?"

"Rebecca," Anderson replied after a moment. "Miss Laramie. Both Devon and I were rather keen on her."

"You were rivals for her affections?" I said.

Anderson nodded. "We would both go to the ends of the earth for her, and neither of us was willing to let the other have her. We had sparred over it on a number of occasions in the past, and last night Rebecca – er, Miss Laramie – and I were alone. We were seated, quietly talking in the lounge

434

of the nearby Tiger Inn, when Macaulay came in and sat himself down at the table. I tried to get him to go, but he wouldn't leave. I lost my head, Mr. Holmes. I started yelling the foulest things at him. I admit it and I regret it."

"What did you do next?"

"Macaulay sat and took it," Anderson said. "He weathered every insult, every name under the sun that I could conjure, and then at last he stood and strode off with his head high." Anderson chuckled in spite of himself. "The blackguard was a bigger man than me, it seemed.

"But that just caused my temper to flare up all the more. I stormed out after him, yelling at him even as he strode away from me. He didn't turn to face me once. Once he had disappeared from my view, I turned to rejoin Miss Laramie, but she had gone. I do not blame her."

"These insults," Holmes said. "What did you say? What precisely were your choicest words?"

Again Anderson chuckle – a dry, sardonic laugh totally devoid of mirth. "Honest to God, Mr. Holmes, I don't remember. I lost my head completely. I remember speaking, but the words themselves . . . they're gone."

"That is most unfortunate," Holmes replied. "But believe me when I tell you that I do believe you. I don't think for one moment that you murdered Mr. Macaulay. I shall do my utmost to clear your name as soon as possible."

"My thanks, Mr. Holmes. I have had some time to think on what I have done and I could not be more ashamed. Even if you absolve me of this crime, can you take away my own guilt?"

Holmes seemed to be in an even more contemplative mood than usual as we emerged from the station. It was early afternoon now, the sun slowly beginning to hang lower in the sky. The breeze over the ocean had strengthened, and I felt a chill pass up my spine as we stepped outside.

"And our next port-of-call is . . .?" I asked.

"I rather think that we shan't have to leave this very spot," Holmes replied.

I looked in the direction of my friend's gaze and saw a handsome young woman disembark from an automobile. As she approached, Holmes called to her. "Miss Laramie, I presume?"

"You know me?" the woman asked, tentatively drawing closer to us, a pair of older strangers.

"The resemblance to your father is a marked one," Holmes replied. "My name is Sherlock Holmes."

"The *detective*?" she countered. A smile crossed Holmes's mouth.

"The same. Quite by chance, I was called in to investigate the matter of Mr. Devon Macaulay's unfortunate death. Might my friend and colleague, Dr. Watson, and I have a word with you? It could go a great way towards bringing this matter to a satisfactory conclusion."

"I shall help in any way that I can to clear up Devon's death," the young woman replied.

"Excellent," Holmes said. "Allow us to step just inside, for I observed Dr. Watson take some offense to the decided chill in the afternoon air."

We stepped back into the lobby of the police station, Holmes and I doffing our hats as we did so. I elected to take a seat and Miss Laramie followed suit. Only Holmes remained standing, pacing back and forth as he addressed the young lady.

"You were doubtlessly on your way to speak with Mr. Anderson?"

"That is correct, Mr. Holmes. When I last saw Malcolm, he was in quite an unpleasant frame of mind. My father has just informed me that he is suspected of murdering Devon and was duly arrested. That cannot be true, can it?"

"I am quite confident in Mr. Anderson's innocence," Holmes answered. "But it is Mr. Anderson's *unpleasant frame of mind* which I wished to address. The young man has freely admitted that he spoke quite coarsely with Macaulay last night just before his death. What exactly did Mr. Anderson say?"

Faint traces of red rose in Miss Laramie's cheeks. "I should not wish to repeat everything that Malcolm said word-for-word, you understand. However, he was insulting Devon's bravery. His confidence. His manhood, Mr. Holmes."

"Was Mr. Macaulay not by nature a confident man?"

"Sadly, no," Miss Laramie said. "Devon was rather weak-willed, I'm afraid. He would frequently dine with my father and me and Devon could barely stomach some of the stories about ancient practices. One evening we discussed Incan sacrificial rituals over drinks and Devon sat, white as a sheet, throughout it all. Malcolm called Devon a child – a child who was wholly terrified of that queer weeping stone.

"Malcolm told Devon that a real man would be able to face that rock. That he could even approach one and stand on it if need be. Malcolm teased him endlessly, saying that Devon could never do it. And then Devon stood quite suddenly, wished me good evening, and strode out of the room. Malcolm followed him out and kept yelling at him, but I had had quite enough. I went up to my room and refused to speak to anyone for the rest of the night."

Holmes considered. "Miss Laramie, you have been of invaluable assistance to me. And if you may permit an old man to speak for another moment: Please do not begrudge Mr. Anderson. He feels responsible for Mr. Macaulay's death, and he resents his temper for getting the better of him. Mr. Anderson is quite keen on you. He told me himself. Go to him, Miss Laramie. If my suspicions prove correct, he may look to you for strength in the coming days."

Holmes turned to go but was arrested by the sound of Miss Laramie's voice. "Is he somehow responsible for this, Mr. Holmes? You said you believe him to be innocent, but . . . ."

"We shall know in time, Miss Laramie."

Then without a further word, Holmes had left the room. I caught up to him outside. "Now what?" I asked.

"We wait," Holmes replied. "I should like to conduct a little experiment, but it will be best if we carry it out by moonlight. In the meantime, let us enjoy an early supper. We shall want our strength about us tonight. I predict something of an ordeal is in our future."

We dined at Holmes's home that evening. As usual, my friend refused to speak of the case, and instead pressed me for details about life in London. For the first time that day, I felt as if my reunion with Holmes was going as planned, and it was wonderful to reminiscence about days of old with the man at whose side I had spent so many years. Truth be told, I thought I detected a rueful glint in Holmes's grey eyes as I spoke of London and my occasional run-ins with Inspector Lestrade or Stanley Hopkins of Scotland Yard – acquaintances whose presence on our doorstep was not out of ordinary at all. I spoke too of my practice, which now occupied my days when, years ago, I might have accompanied Holmes into some den of criminality in order to bring to book some cunning rogue. How the times had changed.

The sun had completely sunk below the horizon and the moon was ever-so-slowly taking its place in the sky when we set out. Holmes had equipped himself with a silver-headed walking stick (and had demonstrated its weighted head to me in his gloved hand before we had struck out) and an electric torch. We were on foot, headed back towards the site of Devon Macaulay's death and the weeping stone. Holmes was silent about his intentions as we descended the rocky crag towards the beach and, once we had arrived at the abandoned site, I couldn't help but pull up the collar of my coat as the breeze blew off the ocean and whipped around us. The rhythmic lapping of the ocean on the shoreline seemed miles away as Holmes and I slowly advanced across the sand, the detective's gaze fixed squarely on the strange stone.

We were just short of the weird edifice when Holmes clapped a hand to my shoulder. "Stay back, Watson! For God's sake be careful!"

"Of what?" I incredulously responded.

Holmes put a finger to his lips and then carefully stepped towards the stone. He then stopped, lifted the stick high over his head and brought it down upon the stone with a loud *thwack*. I stared at my friend in utter uncomprehending disbelief. Had I been asked on the spot to elucidate Holmes's actions, I could not have done it for the world. And yet he seemed entirely confident in what he did, repeatedly hitting the stone with his stick once more – then again, and again, and again. At last we stepped back and reached out an arm as though protecting me from something.

That was when the weeping stone bore its terrible secrets.

I watched first in fascination then horror as the stone began to weep blood. Slowly, the thick, viscus substance crawled down its side. We watched as blood oozed out of the rock and, only seconds later, the stone yielded another impossibility. Seemingly from the rock's very bowels, the largest spider I had ever seen in my life crawled into view. The creature was surely no smaller than the dinner plates on which we had just eaten that evening, and to see the thing move slowly across the blood-stained surface of the rock made my skin crawl and the hairs on the back of my neck stand on end. This monstrous apparition was followed by another and another until at least five hideously large arachnids were scurrying across the surface of the stone. Now I knew why Holmes had insisted on such precautions.

"They are nothing less than monsters, Watson," Holmes murmured. "Creatures from the deepest pit of the South American jungle. Spiders large enough to hunt birds and endowed with poison powerful enough to kill animals many times their size. Poor Devon Macaulay hadn't a chance when he ventured down here last evening."

One of the spiders crawled its way towards us and instinctively I stepped back, fearful that the beast might lunge at us from the rock, putting its eight long legs to use. Holmes reached out with his stick and brought the weighted end down upon the creature's thorax. I looked away as stick met animal and the spider quickly died. I felt no remorse whatsoever for its passing.

Holmes repeated the act with the several other spiders which soon crawled towards what remained of their kind. He dispatched all of them and, having done so, I caught a glimpse of my friend reaching a hand into his inner pocket and producing a handkerchief. First he passed the fabric across his brow and then clapped it to his mouth. To have destroyed so many hideous creatures so rapidly was, indeed, a nauseating act.

"They are all dead?" I said.

"We can only hope," Holmes replied. "But let us be on our guard nonetheless. You may not think it prudent, my dear fellow, but I wish to inspect the rock more closely."

I followed Holmes close behind as we cautiously drew nearer the stone. Holmes switched on the torch and rounded the back of the rock – a side of the strange monolith we hadn't yet seen. He cast the beam of light around the rock and then, kneeling, Holmes let out an exclamation of satisfaction and gestured for me to join him on the sand below. As I did so, I could plainly see what appeared to be a hollow crevice which extended up into the depths of the strange stone.

"Just as I suspected from the fore," Holmes said. "The rock is hollow. While we were so concerned with the odd markings on the opposite side, we never seemed to pay any heed to any other part of the stone. It is from here that those hideous creatures sprang. But let us be away from here, Watson. We do not know how many more reside within still, and I do not wish to know the answer."

Forty-five minutes later, we were ensconced in the warm environs of Holmes's parlor once more. We nursed glasses of brandy, while the familiar figures of Dr. Laramie, his daughter, and Inspector Mackenzie sat opposite us on Holmes's settee.

"From the beginning," Holmes was saying as he settled in his seat, "my curiosity was aroused by the blood which was purported to weep from the stone. I knew from that point on that the stone must not be what it seemed. The blood must come from somewhere within, so I realized that the stone was, at least partially hollow. My supposition was confirmed when I noted that the stone had barely made any impression in the sand. A rock that size would surely have showed signs from where it fell upon the beach if it had been displaced from the cliff face, as has been suggested, during a collapse. Since there were none, I knew that the rock couldn't have been heavy as it was and had not been lodged in the side of the cliff. The strange, weeping stone was indeed from South America, Its lightness making it buoyant enough to have floated all this way.

"Figuring, then, that the rock was hollow led me to wonder what else could be recessed within. My mind raced with possibilities, but it didn't take me long to settle on some kind of venomous creature which could have easily done the unfortunate Devon Macaulay to death. The horrified expression on his face suggested that whatever creature it was is a particularly nasty one, so I postulated spiders. That could be my own bias coming out, however. All of these suspicions were confirmed when I examined Macaulay's body and discovered that his limbs had gone entirely stiff – evidence of some powerful poison in his bloodstream. Additionally, I perceived several small pricks just above Macaulay's ankle where he was bitten by the spiders' poisonous fangs. Dr. Mitchell would certainly never have noticed it or given it much heed, but I was looking for it. What is more, this accounts for the mysterious illnesses of some of the men. Without even knowing it, they disturbed the resting place of the spiders as they worked. One single spider bite may not have been enough to kill a man, but merely to put him down for a few days.

"The spiders, too, explain away what you perceived to be blood weeping from the stone, Dr. Laramie. You told me that you hadn't studied it, and the viscous substance – some by-product of the creatures within, no doubt – surely looked – to the untrained eye, at least – like blood. You would surely be the first to confess, Doctor, that you are no entomologist. To you, the substance was blood, and you had little reason to suspect anything else.

"The circumstances, then, of Devon Macaulay's death were of the most unfortunate kind. Goaded on by Mr. Anderson's taunts last evening, Macaulay left with the intent of facing his fear and going down to the rock. I'm sure that this was done in some bid to win your affections, Miss Laramie. Macaulay did just as Anderson had told him: To face the rock and – if need be – to stand on it. Macaulay approached a rock alone, clambered up onto it, and waited. The act of doing so, however, disturbed the spiders resting just inches below his feet beneath the porous membrane of the rock's outer surface. So disturbing them, they crawled out to investigate. Macaulay was caught unawares, and surely scared half to death. He managed to jump down from the rock, but not before he was stuck by several of the spiders and fell dead upon the spot – the poison killing him almost instantaneously."

Holmes paused to take a sip of his drink.

"As I said earlier, Miss Laramie, we would soon see whether Mr. Anderson could be implicated in Mr. Macaulay's death. I argue that he remains guiltless. Macaulay's death was entirely an accident. He had no reason to suspect that the weeping stone harbored a secret so strange . . . or so deadly."

"Malcolm shall never forgive himself," Miss Laramie murmured.

"In time he must," Holmes said. "I urge you to help him as best you can."

A rueful smile played upon Miss Laramie's lips.

"And as for you, Dr. Laramie," Holmes continued, "I suggest that you take even further precautions should you wish to examine the mysterious stone further. It may not yet have given up all its secrets. Were I in your place, Doctor, I should return the stone to the ocean where it once was."

"But I cannot!" Laramie cried. "It is an archaeological discovery unparalleled in this century. The stone has only begun to tell us about our ancient world. Surely if we study it further, a whole host of questions can finally be answered."

"Perhaps," Holmes said, "those questions deserve to go unanswered."

I saw Laramie suppress a groan as the telephone rang in the next room. Holmes rose and excused himself, instructing me to show our guests out, insisting that the inspector free Anderson at once.

I returned to the room as Holmes hung up the telephone. Across his habitually cruel mouth he wore a wry smile. "That was my brother on the line," he announced settling into his seat. "He has been contacted by the Home Secretary. Storm clouds are gathering over Europe, Watson, and Mycroft wishes for me to play a small part in preventing it. He has asked me to come up to London on the next train. I shouldn't wish to end our weekend prematurely, so would you care to accompany me?"

As I sat across from Holmes, I suddenly had the impression that time was ticking backwards. We were no longer in the twentieth century – two men entering our dotage regarding each other from our seats in a parlor on the Sussex Downs. Once more it was 1895. Holmes and I were young again, and we were back in 221b Baker Street. A fire crackled in the grate, taking the chill out of the damp air. A fog swirled outside the window. A hansom cab rattled over the ancient cobbles, and somewhere in the distance Big Ben chimed the hour. The tableau was one which I had experienced so many times in my life: A comfortable, familiar scene which was forever etched in my memory. And it was playing out again now.

"I should happy to, Holmes," I replied. "I wouldn't miss it for the world."

Sherlock Holmes – young or old, it mattered not – jumped up from his seat. Reaching for his Inverness and deerstalker, he exclaimed: "The come along, my dear Watson. *The game is afoot!*"

The Adventure of the
Three Telegrams
by Darryl Webber

*"Good old Watson! You are the one fixed point in a changing age.
There's an east wind coming all the same, such a wind as never blew on
England yet. It will be cold and bitter, Watson, and a good many of
us may wither before its blast. But it's God's own wind none the less and
a cleaner, better, stronger land will be in the sunshine when the storm
has cleared...."*

Sherlock Holmes – "His Last Bow"

It was on a frosty morning early in January 1917 that I embarked on an
adventure with my old friend, Sherlock Holmes, which was to have global
repercussions. The delicate nature of the case and the national security
implications inherent in it were such that I was unable to share it with
readers at the time, but so vital was my friend's intervention in this matter
I felt it should be recorded.

I was temporarily in London, after a busy few months with my
regiment. Holmes had long since relocated to the South Downs where,
when not involved with the war effort, he kept bees, wrote monographs
about the creatures, and no doubt conducted the strange experiments that
drove Mrs. Hudson to despair when we shared rooms at 221b Baker Street.

It had been a quiet morning at my practice, a slow procession of
coughs, colds, and minor ailments, and I was glad to be interrupted by the
arrival of a boy from the telegram office just after eleven a.m.. I had no
further appointments, so I closed the door and eagerly opened the
envelope, hoping for adventure. I was not disappointed.

The telegram was from Holmes, requesting a meeting as "a matter of
urgency" that lunchtime. He suggested we rendezvous at Gordon's, the
well-known wine bar in Villiers Street by Charing Cross Station, a part of
London very familiar to us both. Holmes didn't give any clue as to the
nature of the urgent business he wished to talk to me about, but as we had
both been quite busy since that occasion three years earlier when we foiled
a German plot against Britain on the eve of the Great War, I surmised that
something of equal importance was at stake.

I asked my colleague at the practice to cover any appointments that
might come in, gathered my ulster and stick, and hastened to find a cab to
take me to the Strand. As the driver took us through the busy streets of the

capital, I reflected on the momentous events in Europe that would shape our lives for years to come. The Great War was showing no signs of ending, and the huge loss of life had taken its toll on the nation's morale. There was something sombre about the way people were going about their business. The British trait of resilience was intact, but there was also a sense of anxiety and melancholy in the air.

I extracted myself from the cab outside Charing Cross Station and walked across to Villiers Street, heading down the slope to the Embankment. I had always found the hustle and bustle of that street cheered my spirits and so it was that morning as I stepped down into Gordon's Wine Bar, which lies adjacent to Victoria Embankment Gardens. Holmes hadn't specified a spot to meet in this underground establishment, so I found a corner table and ensconced myself with a copy of *The Times*. A few moments later, a waiter with a shock of dark, curly hair and an extravagant moustache approached.

"*Señor*, welcome to Gordon's. You have been here before, I think?"

The chap was evidently Spanish and I was rather irritated by his blethering on and fussing around the table. He offered me a menu and I ordered a small port. He tried to engage me in a conversation about how Spanish wine was far superior to that from Portugal, but I must admit I barely listened, as my thoughts were preoccupied with whatever Holmes wanted to talk to me about.

Sensing my disinterest, the waiter disappeared and returned a few moments later with the port and the bill, then bowed extravagantly before taking his leave. After a few sips of what was a very fine port, I unfolded the bill and saw it was a scribbled note from Holmes:

Meet me at The Coal Hole, the Strand, in fifteen minutes. Find a quiet spot.

SH

I almost spluttered my port out. I looked around the bar for the Spanish waiter to ask him who had given him the slip of paper but there was no sign of him. A quick scan of the room yielded no sighting of Holmes, so I set out once again, headed up Villiers Street and onto the Strand. I headed east towards the Savoy, which I knew was next to The Coal Hole, a public house Holmes and I had visited before.

Ten minutes later, puffing somewhat I must admit, I was in The Coal Hole, nursing a bottle of ale while I waited for Holmes again. My mood of excitement had turned to one of irritation at being given the run-around, and my humour was not much helped when I saw the Spanish waiter from Gordon's approach me from a side entrance.

"What the blazes," I thundered. "This really won't do!"

"I'm sorry, *Señor*. You are upset, I see . . . ."

"I most assuredly am. I am meant to be meeting a colleague about an important matter and you keep bamboozling our plans," I cried.

"Come now, Watson, you're being a little harsh, surely?"

I looked at the waiter and saw he was removing that distinctive hair and moustache as he sat down next to me. From underneath the disguise, my friend Sherlock Holmes emerged smiling and with a glint in his eye.

"Forgive me, Watson, but my Spanish persona was entirely necessary. I have been working undercover as Manuel, and it is vital that my identity is not compromised. I had to double-back around the Embankment Gardens and various side streets to get here without detection. I haven't much time, but I know I'm under surveillance and I was rather hoping you might be able to help me." Holmes's eyes had the same old spark in them, even if there were a few more lines round them these days.

"I've been enlisted by Mycroft to help him break a German spy ring operating in London. The need becomes ever more urgent by the day as this terrible war rumbles on. Manuel has helped me infiltrate circles I couldn't have broached as myself, and I think I'm making some decent progress, which brings its own problems. I have good reason to believe that I am being followed as I go about my business as Manuel, which really won't do. Will you help me, Watson, by following the person who is following me?"

"But of course, Holmes. Whatever you need me to do, I will do gladly." In truth, was still struggling to take it all in.

"Excellent! I knew I could rely on my Boswell. I must return to Gordon's presently and resume my shift as Manuel. When it's over, I shall lead my shadow on a merry old dance through Soho until we can corner him. I would be obliged if you would wait on the corner of Villiers Street and the Strand after we leave here and look out for Manuel and whomever is following him."

A few minutes later, I was standing in the spot Holmes had specified, staring blankly at *The Times* while trying to discretely keep an eye out for his alter-ego. Sure enough, the shock-haired Spaniard appeared after a time, hurrying up Villiers Street towards where I stood. I stayed my ground and, as Manuel passed me and turned to go east along the Strand, I spied a slim figure in a long coat tracing my friend's footsteps from a few yards back.

Holmes was hurrying along at a fair pace along the busy pavement on the south side of the Strand, as was the Thin Man. As I started after them, I noticed another man who seemed to be following both Holmes and the Thin Man. This character was of a far larger set than the first pursuer, a broad man wearing a bowler hat and a substantial moustache. What a rum affair this was, I thought to myself, I was now following two men who were following Holmes.

This unlikely procession of four progressed along the Strand for a few hundred yards then Holmes crossed over towards Covent Garden and led us through a labyrinth of side streets before darting into Stanfords, the renowned map sellers in Long Acre, one of the few shops in which Holmes had ever showed an interest. The Thin Man followed Holmes inside while the Moustachioed Man took up a position just outside the shop and lit a cigar. Across the street I took up my paper again, glad to have a rest with my right leg causing me some discomfort. I couldn't make out Holmes or the Thin Man in the shop, and it was a few minutes before my friend emerged again with a package wrapped in brown paper and string, dashing northwest towards Charing Cross Road. Within seconds, the Thin Man reappeared too and resumed the chase, as did the Moustachioed Man, tossing away his cigar as he strode after them.

Holmes walked briskly through Soho, across Oxford Street, and into Rathbone Place. After a short while, he sidestepped into a street on the right, followed by the Thin Man, the Moustachioed Man, and finally myself, feeling a little breathless by now.

As I turned into this side street, I was confronted with a surprising sight. Holmes, minus his disguise, was smiling at the Thin Man who was holding aloft a sword stick while the Moustachioed Man was bearing down on both of them with gun drawn.

"My God, Holmes, look out!" I cried and pulled out my revolver and prepared to shoot.

"So glad you could join us, Watson!" Holmes cried. "You can put your revolver away. I think Mr. Barker has the situation covered." He gestured towards the Moustachioed Man who nodded towards me.

"You remember our friend from the Lewisham poisoning case? I believe you called it "The Retired Colourman" in your colourful account of those events. Knowing how dangerous our opponents are, I thought a little extra help might be advisable."

Rather put out, I grunted acknowledgement at Barker.

"Then who is this, Holmes?" I asked gesturing towards the Thin Man.

"Good question. A German agent, I'll wager, but we'll find out more at Baker Street. Wave down a cab back in Oxford Street, will you, Watson?"

In the short cab ride, Holmes explained that Mycroft had retained our old rooms at 221b and that he had been working from there these past few weeks.

"It's been just like the old days, Watson, but not quite the same without you at my side."

Barker kept his pistol trained on the prisoner throughout the journey and led him up the stairs to our old apartment. There was no Mrs. Hudson, but Mycroft Holmes waited at the top of the stairs in a state of curious excitement.

"Well, well, what have we here?" asked Mycroft, his corpulent figure looming over us and the merest hint of a smile at the corners of his mouth.

I must admit to a frisson of pleasure as I entered our rooms, which were little changed from the last time I'd seen them. But there was no time for nostalgia as Barker searched the Thin Man and emptied the contents of his pockets on the table in the centre of the room.

Holmes gestured to the Thin Man to be seated and examined his possessions as he questioned him, paying particular attention to a black, leather-bound notepad.

"What is your name, man?" demanded Holmes, peering over the pages of the notepad.

The Thin Man remained stony-faced. His small eyes, high cheekbones, and sneering mouth gave away nothing.

"The silent type, eh, *Herr* Muller?" Holmes offered. The prisoner started at the sound of his name, but then reverted back to his previous inscrutable expression.

"Well, your notebook makes for very interesting reading. It seems you have been busy these last few weeks."

Muller bristled. "You won't be so cheerful in a few days' time, *Herr* Holmes," he said witheringly.

"So you *can* talk, Muller. I think I can glean a great deal from your notebook about your activities and plans. Mr. Barker, perhaps you would be kind enough to escort our guest to the nearest police cell, where he can gather his thoughts a while."

"I'll go with you, Barker, to smooth things over with the local sergeant," said Mycroft.

As they shuffled out of our rooms and down the stairs, Holmes closed the door and sat in the chair by the window that he had always favoured, looking again at Muller's notebook.

"This is quite the find, Watson," said Holmes as he flicked through the pages. "There are details of meetings here in London and in Paris, Brussels and Berlin. Notes on German supplies and movements . . . . Hallo! What's this? My God, Watson, we've struck gold!"

446

Folded in a pocket at the back of the notebook was a piece of paper which Holmes unfolded to reveal a grid of letters, numbers, and symbols.

"What the devil is going on, Holmes?" I exclaimed. "I've been trying to catch up with you since Gordon's and still don't know what the deuce this is about!"

Holmes looked up from the notebook, surprised at the force of my statement, but quickly realising the strength of my feelings.

"My dear fellow, of course! How remiss of me. Let me explain things as best I can – but it will have to be an abridged version of events, as time is not on our side."

Holmes recounted how Mycroft had summoned him from the South Downs a month previously and briefed him on a German spy ring operating in London, compromised of a number of British agents with damaging and sometimes deadly results. Strategic advantages had been lost in various parts of Europe, and British intelligence services were struggling to track the activities of the German spy network across the Continent.

"I've been able to make reasonable progress in just a few weeks," Holmes confided, "and have tracked the epicentre of German espionage to a few individuals here in our capital. They are clever, resourceful, and utterly ruthless. They are difficult to locate because they take great care to remain hidden. Capturing Muller is a breakthrough that may be of the greatest import, Watson. Thank you for your part in apprehending him."

I nodded my appreciation.

"It has been useful to have Barker around too," said Holmes. "He is energetic, determined, and a perfectly decent detective. But he is no Watson."

Holmes had obviously sensed my sense of puzzlement over Barker's presence earlier, though I had to confess his muscular presence had been crucial in capturing Muller.

"What now?" I asked.

The great detective sighed and cradled Muller's notebook. "A long day and night working through this, Watson, hoping it will give us the clues we need to find the ringleaders. Hopefully, Barker can extract some useful information from Muller too. He can be quite persuasive when he needs to be."

"How can I help?" I asked, aware that there was little I could do to aid him unravel the mysteries of Miller's notebook.

"How are your culinary skills, Watson? Brother Mycroft did not think to send Mrs. Hudson when he rented these rooms, so I haven't eaten a proper meal in weeks. I really am quite famished."

"My cooking is rudimentary, as you know, but I'm sure that I can fix us something adequate. What food is there here?" I inquired.

"None that I know of," said Holmes after a minute or so, already distracted from our conversation by the notebook. A quick survey of the kitchen downstairs revealed little save a few condiments and an ancient-looking garlic bulb. I told Holmes I was going out to get supplies, but my declaration barely registered on him, and I left him peering through a magnifying glass at the pages of the notebook.

It was now late afternoon as I made my way down Baker Street. The warmth of the sun was fading and the air was chill once again. There would be a hard frost again tonight. I walked some time before I found a grocer's where I bought potatoes, eggs, a loaf of bread, butter, and a block of cheddar. A little further along I found a butcher's where I added sausages, bacon, and lamb chops to the haul.

Ever since I'd left 221b, I had been aware of a bespectacled man in my wake. This morning's excitement had made me vigilant. I patted the service revolver in my pocket as I left the butcher's and watched out for him. Sure enough, I spotted him looking at an evening paper at a kiosk opposite where I had paused. I walked straight over to where he stood and bought a copy of *The Standard*. I wanted to see his reaction to me being wise to him, but he didn't acknowledge my presence.

"It will be another cold evening," I said, looking at him. He was dressed smartly with a navy scarf, his long black overcoat and Homburg insulating him from the cool air.

"Even colder days are coming, Doctor. Winter is not over yet," he replied.

"How do you know I'm a doctor, sir?" I demanded.

The man folded the paper and smiled. "The name's Duckworth," he said. "I work with Mycroft Holmes. There are a few of us keeping an eye on his brother, Sherlock. It's a dangerous time and we must ensure he can go about his business. Having been an admirer of your gripping accounts of Holmes's investigations, Doctor Watson, it was straightforward to deduce you would be working with him once again. But it is best that we are not seen together, you understand, so if you'll excuse me . . . ."

"Of course," I nodded and watched as Duckworth melted into the multitudes in Baker Street. I hurried back to 221b, not quite sure what to make of this encounter.

Back in our old rooms, Holmes was still poring over Muller's notebook and barely noticed my return. I prepared two plates of food in the kitchen and found a dusty bottle of Bordeaux in the pantry. As I brought the most basic of meals into the sitting room, Holmes stood up in state of agitation.

"Watson, we're onto something. The code remains unbroken, but my German is at a tolerable enough standard to translate a note in Muller's book that mentions a meeting tonight. It's at the Alpha Inn in Great Russell Street at eight p.m.. By Jove, this could be crucial! It's a meeting of the Progressive European Society – this could be the spy ring, Watson. What time is it now?"

"Almost half-past five, "I replied.

"In which case, we just have time to take some refreshment before we prepare for the next instalment of this murky business."

After eating, Holmes disappeared into his old bedroom while I cleared away the dinner things and poured us a brandy against the cold. I stood at the window that overlooked Baker Street, like I had so many times over the years, and watched a mist rise in swirls around the gas lamps. I recalled the many adventures which Holmes and I had enjoyed, the great and the good that we had encountered, the wronged and the wretched we had helped. I was lost in this rather wistful reverie when I heard Holmes return – and yet it was not he who was before me as I turned around, but a rather sorry looking fellow with flushed cheeks, crumpled clothes, and ruffled hair.

"What do you think?" Holmes's sharp, authoritative voice was the only recognisable thing about him. "Will I pass muster as a drunk at the bar?"

"If I hadn't known it was going to be you emerging from that room," I replied, "I would have thought a drunk had invaded our old rooms. The transformation once again is remarkable."

"Quite so, Watson. Thank you. Now I think I'll adopt the mannerisms and accent of a wastrel who's fallen on hard times and make my way to the Alpha Inn to find solace. You remember the place, of course? Where the wild goose chase for the Blue Carbuncle once led us? My word, how long ago was that festive adventure? I wonder how different that establishment is all these years later."

I did remember visiting the Alpha Inn, as we tried to track down a goose that had something rather valuable stuffed down its crop.

I felt uneasy at letting Holmes go into a potentially dangerous situation alone and said so, but he would not be deterred, and I could see the logic for his argument. He could travel more quickly and discretely alone. My bad leg had become something of an impediment in recent years.

"If I sniff danger, my dear Watson, I will send word via an Irregular – they are primed and ready, and considerably quicker than any telegram over short distances."

With that, he shifted his gait to that of a down-at-heel drunkard and shuffled down the stairs. I watched him from the window of our old rooms as he headed south down Baker Street. I looked out for any more Holmes's followers, but could discern none in the gloom of the city.

While Holmes was gone, I busied myself by flicking through the day's newspapers. The chronicle of events in the war made for grim reading, with little glimmer of hope for an end soon. It seemed like a very different war to the one I had fought in Afghanistan. Elsewhere, I scanned stories of petty crime and society weddings before dozing in front of the fire. A sharp rap at the door roused me from my slumber. I looked at my pocket watch. It was gone nine. I hurried down to the front door where a young fellow, no more than ten years old, handed me a note. I unfolded it and read the note from Holmes.

> *Very interesting attendee at meeting. Have kept my cover and will follow him to see where he settles. Have a brandy ready to warm your old friend's bones.*

I read it and re-read it in a state of agitation. Then I noticed the young lad was still waiting by the doorway. I raised an eyebrow at him.

"Gentleman said you would give me some coin on delivery."

I pulled one coin from my pocket, but before the little ruffian could take it, I asked him a question. "Before you disappear, lad, can you tell me where you were when my friend gave you this, and towards where he was heading?"

"That's easy, mister. He was in Great Russell Street, not far from the Museum. Then he went on into Bloomsbury Square where all the toffs go. He didn't smell too fresh, neither," the boy said.

"All right, all right, off you go then. You might get another shilling if you see anything else of note around there."

I went back to the rooms and contemplated the situation while stoking the fire, my thoughts lost among the glowing coals. I could hardly wander around Bloomsbury looking for Holmes and not arouse suspicion if there were spies in the area. But I felt so useless here, unable to help him at such an important juncture. I resorted to pacing around the room like a caged tiger until I heard the key turn in the front door downstairs just after ten.

"Is the brandy poured, Watson?" I felt a great sense of relief at hearing Holmes's clear, concise tones. I was decanting two glasses as he came into the room pulling off his cap, mutton chops, and rather dirty scarf.

"Well, the game is certainly afoot now," he said as he took the glass and gulped down a generous measure. "Ah, that's better. It's cold out there when you've no shelter from the elements."

"Your note mentioned an interesting attendee at the meeting. Who the devil was it?" I asked excitedly.

"I'm glad the note reached you. The Irregulars really are a formidable resource. Even now, I've left a few of them stationed in Bloomsbury Square. But I see you are understandably impatient to learn of my adventures tonight. Let us be seated and I shall talk you through it."

Holmes sat cradling his brandy and stared at the fire as he recounted the evening's events.

"I arrived at the Alpha Inn just after half-past-seven and stationed myself at the saloon bar. Do you remember it from our visit all those years ago? It has barely changed, though the landlord is different – a rather gruff fellow it must be said. It wasn't very busy, but I kept a low profile leaning over my beer, watching the comings and goings.

"Just before eight, two serious looking men walked in and exchanged brief words with the landlord, who pointed them upstairs. On the stroke of eight, three more sombre gentlemen arrived and also went upstairs. One, a tall fellow with a dark, heavy beard, seemed familiar to me, and after he had disappeared into the meeting his name came to me: Von Bork!"

"Good heavens, Holmes, are you sure?" I spluttered, barely able to believe the German master spy we had captured three years ago was on the loose and causing mischief again.

"Quite sure, I'm afraid. Remember, I was under his employ as Altamont for many months and got to know his manner and habits very well. His gait, the way he holds himself, his intonation are all unmistakable."

"What on earth did you do next?"

"I waited and I waited. I could see no great advantage in crashing into the meeting where I would be outnumbered and had no concrete reason to apprehend Von Bork or any of his confederates. Instead, I bided my time at the bar and, when the party eventually came back down and dispersed, followed Von Bork and one of his men to a townhouse in Bloomsbury Square, where I despatched Arthur, one of the brightest of the Irregulars, with a message to you.

"The night grew clearer and colder as I waited in the Square near the house in question, watching for any further developments. From my vantage point behind a laurel bush, where I feigned a drunken stupor, I could see Von Bork and confederates deep in conversation for some time.

When the lights in the house were dimmed, I decided to end my vigil and come back here to continue the deciphering of Muller's notebook and to tell Mycroft that the ante has been upped considerably by the involvement of Von Bork in this increasingly tangled affair."

The thought that Von Bork was once again at large at such a grave time in our country's history sent a wave of revulsion through me. He had gotten the better of many British agents before the outbreak of war, and it was only Holmes's brilliance that had stopped his dastardly schemes back then.

"What now? What can we do?"

"First of all, my old friend, can you beckon over the young lad in the doorway opposite. It's our friend, Arthur. Give him this note and tell him to go the address on the front in Whitehall. He'll find Mycroft there, and other top brass no doubt."

Holmes scribbled the note, folded the paper, and I took it down to the lad, who hurried off, once I had sweetened him with another coin. I looked around. The streets were emptying now, though I could hear singing and carousing from an inn nearby.

When I returned upstairs, Holmes was lighting a pipe, his thin frame bent over Muller's notebook.

"My next task, Watson, is to decipher the code that Von Bork, Muller, and their cronies have been using. I've a feeling it may be a little more sophisticated than the goings-on we investigated in "The Dancing Men", eh? My plan is that if I can discern meaning in these symbols and letters, then I can communicate with Von Bork as Muller, now that I know where he is based. He must be concerned that Muller didn't make an appearance at the Alpha Inn. If I can crack this code, then I can pretend to be Muller and come up with some plausible reason for his disappearance. I can also lure Von Bork into a meeting where we can trap him once more and curtail his activities once and for all.

"But now, Watson, forgive me, I must immerse myself . . . ."

Even before he had finished speaking, his attention was once again on the notebook, and I watched him scribbling ideas down as he emitted great plumes of smoke from his favourite briar.

Sometime after midnight, I must have dropped off as the fire faded. I was awakened some hours later by Holmes gently shaking my shoulders. His face was drawn and sallow, but his eyes were bright and I could see he was excited.

"I think I have it, Watson!" he said holding the notebook aloft. "I think I have it! Von Bork is a sly devil, but we have the advantage over him now. We must get this to Mycroft immediately."

After a short walk down Baker Street, we found a cab, and Holmes told our driver to take us to Whitehall at full pelt and he'd be well rewarded. It was still dark, though there was a lightening of the sky in the east which suggested dawn wasn't far off. How quiet the streets were as we thundered through them with information that might be so vitally important to this great country's future.

As we entered the broad, grand expanse of Whitehall, our driver steered us to an unassuming doorway which looked as if it might be the base of a modest law firm. Holmes hurried to the door while I paid the cab, and within minutes we were in the company of Mycroft Holmes and three other very dignified looking gentlemen, two of whom wore military uniforms.

"Gentleman, I won't waste time with details because we are at the sharp end of events now," Holmes intoned. "I believe you had my note from last night, and will have some grasp of the situation and the return of our old adversary, Von Bork."

"Yes, an astonishing revelation, Sherlock," said Mycroft. "But the more one thinks about what's been happening these last few months, the more it bears his mark. My colleagues from Naval Intelligence Department are fascinated to hear your theories on Von Bork's codes."

Holmes put the notebook on a desk in the middle of the room while Mycroft and his esteemed guests gathered around. He then took them through it, and I must confess I couldn't make out the detail of what he was saying, but he draw nods of solemn approval through his short discourse until Mycroft proclaimed that they were satisfied that he had indeed unlocked the keys to Von Bork's communication lines.

"Remarkable work, Sherlock," Mycroft declared.

"Quite so," said one of the other men. "We could offer you a role at Room 40 with that kind of reasoning."

"Thank you, gentleman," Holmes smiled. "Are you satisfied that you have what you need? Good. Then Mycroft, may I suggest that our next step is to lure Von Bork out of his eyrie in Bloomsbury by feigning a note from Muller, using the code we have just unravelled? He will be suspicious if he doesn't hear anything from one of his top men, and we can use his code against him. Looking at the notebook, I'm sure that I can render a faithful imitation of Muller's style and have a telegram delivered to Bloomsbury Square."

Mycroft nodded. "Very good, Sherlock, I can summon some discreet force to help in his apprehension, but where will you goad him?"

"A scan of Muller's notebook reveals a number of meetings at the British Museum, which is conveniently close to Von Bork's base, so he will not feel too exposed. I will draft a note now which you can check

453

against Muller's scribblings before we send the telegram. I suggest a meeting later today, say four p.m., at the museum. Let us appeal to Von Bork's vanity and forward the idea of a rendezvous by the Rosetta Stone, that great key to understanding the Egyptian's hieroglyphs."

Mycroft nodded with a wry smile.

"That sounds a fitting place for a denouement to this affair. Gentlemen, I'm sure you will want to take that notebook back to Room 40 once we have composed our note. It will be of tremendous value in the war effort."

After close consultation, Holmes and Mycroft were satisfied with their message to Von Bork and sent a telegram to his address in Bloomsbury Square. The trap was set.

"Now Watson, after a long night, I suggest we return to Baker Street to recuperate and gather ourselves for one final adventure later today."

Back at our old rooms, I tried to sleep, but only did so fitfully – such was the state of apprehension and excitement that I was in. I'm not sure if Holmes slept at all but at three p.m., he suggested we take some air and make our way toward the British Museum.

The sun was getting low on that frost-bitten day and we could see the mist of our breath as we boarded the cab. I felt a great pang of nostalgia for our old days of charging around our great capital on adventures and felt that this might be our last hurrah. I tried to savour every moment of that journey. The cool air, the smell of wood smoke, the bump of the cobbles, the cries of market traders and newspaper sellers. And, of course, the company of Holmes, who looked as wistful as I felt as we neared Bloomsbury.

"One last bit of fun, old friend," he said quietly as climbed down from the cab and strode into the main hall of the British Museum. Holmes wanted us to be 'settled in' there long before our appointment with Von Bork, so we made our way around the rooms and studied exhibits of great treasures from around the world and reflected on the technologies of civilizations long gone. The numbers were thinning out as the clock neared four, and we approached the room where the Rosetta Stone was housed.

"Watson, would you kindly position yourself by the far doorway? If I can keep to this side of Von Bork, I believe that we have him cornered in this room."

Holmes assumed a deep interest in a collection of Ancient Egyptian tablets while I scanned a glass case containing Sumerian artefacts near one doorway. There were perhaps three other people in the room. At four, surely enough, a tall, well-dressed, bearded man walked by me and into the room. I kept my head down but tracked his every movement as he strode over to the central area where the Rosetta Stone was on display. He

454

seems to be reading rather intently the information about the stone when I saw Holmes approach from the far side of the room, slowly as if he was surveying the other exhibits. I moved a little closer myself, so I was within earshot of them. As Holmes reached the Rosetta Stone, he cleared his throat.

"Fascinating, isn't it? The key to understanding the secrets of a great civilization."

Von Bork wheeled around and I saw his eyes widen with astonishment when he saw it was Holmes.

"You!" He exclaimed.

"The game's up, Von Bork," Holmes cried.

"I don't think so, *Herr* Holmes," the agent said, composing himself. "There are plans afoot of which you know nothing. They are beyond your knowledge, let alone your control."

"Perhaps so, but I'm sure *Herr* Muller's notebook, with its very interesting key to deciphering your codes, will provide my colleagues with some very interesting material about your recent activities."

Von Bork started at the mention of the notebook.

"You think so?" Von Bork bundled past Holmes, drawing a revolver and levelling it at him as he went. He ran into the next room, a maze-like display of weaponry and other militaristic relics. We followed as best we could through the exhibits, now falling into long, dramatic shadows as the sun set. As I turned a corner, a report from the revolver whistled by me. Then I saw Von Bork running towards a doorway some fifty yards away.

"Holmes, he's getting away!" I shouted, having lost sight of my friend some minutes before. Von Bork looked back as he ran, not observing as a foot eased out in his path, tripping him and sending the revolver skidding across the floor. Holmes stepped out from behind a suit of armour with a rapier that he had purloined from the exhibit and held it to Von Bork's throat.

The gun shot had drawn Mycroft Holmes and various police officials into the room, as well as Barker, who was strong-arming another man that I guessed must be one of Von Bork's agents.

"Well, here's a pretty sight," said Mycroft looking at the helpless figure of the Baron. He glared at Mycroft, but saw that he was beaten.

"I seem to remember you besmirching the character and temperament of my fellow countrymen during our last encounter," said Holmes. "You'll have plenty of time to contemplate those words, and your actions, at His Majesty's pleasure."

Two officers handcuffed Von Bork and led him off, a disconsolate figure now he had been exposed.

"Your intervention couldn't have been more timely," Mycroft said to Holmes as we watched Von Bork trudge away. "The codes in Muller's notebook have helped alert us to a telegram being sent by the German foreign minister Zimmerman to their ambassador in Mexico. Its content, to say the very least, is explosive, and may yet provoke our American friends into this terrible conflict."

It was only later on that I learned just how vital the interception of the Zimmerman Telegram was, leading to the entry of the United States of America into the war which, of course, proved to be a turning point.

Holmes's crucial part in this affair has never been revealed, let alone recognised, but this is how he would have wanted it. I've lost count of the number of times he has borne the responsibility for our country's national security against enemy agents and malign influences. Yet he would never seek any recompense for his efforts, save the satisfaction of the work itself. That night, I pondered the strange chain of three telegrams that had led to Von Bork's capture – from the first, where Holmes requested my assistance, to the second, luring Von Bork to a supposed meeting with Muller at the British Museum, and finally, the third, a secret diplomatic communication from the German Foreign Office that arguably turned out to be the most significant intelligence triumph for Britain during the entire war – and only because of Sherlock Holmes's perspicacious capture of Muller and his notebook.

The next day, after a rather extravagant lunch at Simpson's, I accompanied Holmes to Victoria Station, where he was to enter a train to Sussex and his beloved bees. I had a tremendous feeling of sadness as we entered the station's concourse where the multitudes made conversation difficult. As we neared the platform, we turned to face each other and shook each other's hands. And then Holmes, quite uncharacteristically, embraced me.

"My dear Watson, you really have been the best friend that a man could ask for."

He then handed me a small parcel wrapped in brown paper. "It's not too far, you know. You must come to visit some time. Take care of yourself, Watson," he said, and then he strode off along the platform without looking back.

And so I said goodbye for a time to the finest man I have ever met, who had always put the pursuit of truth and righteousness ahead of any other consideration, caring not for title, rank or wealth. As I watched him join the crowd of people on the platform, I considered how they had no idea that the man in their midst had given our country such great service countless times, and may have once again turned the tide of history in our favour. I must admit to a great surge of emotion as I watched my dear old friend disappear among the soot, smoke, and hubbub of the station.

About the Contributors

The following contributions appear in this volume:
The MX Book of New Sherlock Holmes Stories
Part XV– 2019 Annual (1898-1918)

Maurice Barkley lives with his wife Marie in a suburb of Rochester, New York. Retired from a career as a commercial artist and builder of tree houses, he is writing and busy reinforcing the stereotype of a pesky househusband. His other Sherlock Holmes stories can be found on Amazon. *https://www.amazon.com/author/mauricebarkleys*

Brian Belanger is a publisher and editor, but is best known for his freelance illustration and cover design work. His distinctive style can be seen on several MX Publishing covers, including *Silent Meridian* by Elizabeth Crowen, *Sherlock Holmes and the Menacing Melbournian* by Allan Mitchell, *Sherlock Holmes and A Quantity of Debt* by David Marcum, *Welcome to Undershaw* by Luke Benjamen Kuhns, and many more. Brian is the co-founder of Belanger Books LLC, where he illustrates the popular *MacDougall Twins with Sherlock Holmes* young reader series (#1 bestsellers on Amazon.com UK). A prolific creator, he also designs t-shirts, mugs, stickers, and other merchandise on his personal art site: *www.redbubble.com/people/zhahadun*.

Nick Cardillo has been a devotee of Sherlock Holmes since the age of six. His first published short story, "The Adventure of the Traveling Corpse" appeared in *The MX Book of New Sherlock Holmes Stories – Part VI: 2017 Annual*, and he has written subsequent stories for both MX Publishing and Belanger Books. In 2018, Nick completed his first anthology of new Sherlock Holmes adventures entitled *The Feats of Sherlock Holmes*. Nick is a fan of The Golden Age of Detective Fiction, Hammer Horror, and Doctor Who. He writes film reviews and analyses at *Sacred-Celluloid.blogspot.com*. He is a student at Susquehanna University in Selinsgrove, PA.

Leslie Charteris was born in Singapore on May 12th, 1907. With his mother and brother, he moved to England in 1919 and attended Rossall School in Lancashire before moving on to Cambridge University to study law. His studies there came to a halt when a publisher accepted his first novel. His third one, entitled *Meet the Tiger*, was written when he was twenty years old and published in September 1928. It introduced the world to Simon Templar, *aka* The Saint. He continued to write about The Saint until 1983 when the last book, *Salvage for The Saint*, was published. The books, which have been translated into over thirty languages, number nearly a hundred and have sold over forty-million copies around the world. They've inspired, to date, fifteen feature films, three television series, ten radio series, and a comic strip that was written by Charteris and syndicated around the world for over a decade. He enjoyed travelling, but settled for long periods in Hollywood, Florida, and finally in Surrey, England. He was awarded the Cartier Diamond Dagger by the *Crime Writers' Association* in 1992, in recognition of a lifetime of achievement. He died the following year.

Ian Dickerson was just nine years old when he discovered The Saint. Shortly after that, he discovered Sherlock Holmes. The Saint won, for a while anyway. He struck up a friendship with The Saint's creator, Leslie Charteris, and his family. With their permission, he spent six weeks studying the Leslie Charteris collection at Boston University and went on to write, direct, and produce documentaries on the making of *The Saint* and *Return of The Saint*, which have been released on DVD. He oversaw the recent reprints of almost fifty of the original Saint books in both the US and UK, and was a co-producer on the 2017 TV movie of *The Saint*. When he discovered that Charteris had written Sherlock Holmes stories as well – well, there was the excuse he needed to revisit The Canon. He's consequently written and edited three books on Holmes' radio adventures. For the sake of what little sanity he has, Ian has also written about a wide range of subjects, none of which come with a halo, including talking mashed potatoes, Lord Grade, and satellite links. Ian lives in Hampshire with his wife and two children. And an awful lot of books by Leslie Charteris. Not quite so many by Conan Doyle, though.

Sir Arthur Conan Doyle (1859-1930) *Holmes Chronicler Emeritus.* If not for him, this anthology would not exist. Author, physician, patriot, sportsman, spiritualist, husband and father, and advocate for the oppressed. He is remembered and honored for the purposes of this collection by being the man who introduced Sherlock Holmes to the world. Through fifty-six Holmes short stories, four novels, and additional Apocryphal entries, Doyle revolutionized mystery stories and also greatly influenced and improved police forensic methods and techniques for the betterment of all. *Steel True Blade Straight.*

Steve Emecz's main field is technology, in which he has been working for about twenty years. Following multiple senior roles at Xerox, where he grew their European eCommerce from $6m to $200m, Steve joined platform provider Venda, and moved across to Powa in 2010. Today, Steve is Chief Revenue Officer at CloudTrade, a company that digitises large companies' accounts payables. Steve is a regular trade show speaker on the subject of eCommerce, and his tech career has taken him to more than fifty countries – so he's no stranger to planes and airports. He wrote two novels (one a bestseller) in the 1990's, and a screenplay in 2001. Shortly after, he set up MX Publishing, specialising in NLP books. In 2008, MX published its first Sherlock Holmes book, and MX has gone on to become the largest specialist Holmes publisher in the world. MX is a social enterprise and supports three main causes. The first is Happy Life, a children's rescue project in Nairobi, Kenya, where he and his wife, Sharon, spend every Christmas at the rescue centre in Kasarani. In 2014, they wrote a short book about the project, *The Happy Life Story*. The second is the Stepping Stones School, of which Steve is a patron. Stepping Stones is located at Undershaw, Sir Arthur Conan Doyle's former home. Steve has been a mentor for the World Food Programme for the last two years, supporting their innovation bootcamps and giving 1-2-1 mentoring to several projects.

Edwin A. Enstrom is a budding pasticheurs and an Army veteran who spent one year in Vietnam. Now retired, he worked for forty-plus years for one company in various capacities, mostly within Information Technology. He is an avid reader, especially of fair-play detective mysteries. He is a puzzle lover, especially cryptic crosswords. Additionally, he's an internet junkie, spending several hours daily surfing the web, but with no smart phone, no television, and no Facebook or social media.

Thomas Fortenberry is an American author, editor, and reviewer. Founder of Mind Fire Press and a Pushcart Prize-nominated writer, he has also judged many literary contests, including the Georgia Author of the Year Awards and the Robert Penn Warren Prize for Fiction. His Sherlock Holmes stories have appeared in such works as *An Improbable Truth* and various volumes of *The MX Book of New Sherlock Holmes Stories*.

Mark A. Gagen BSI is co-founder of Wessex Press, sponsor of the popular *From Gillette to Brett* conferences, and publisher of *The Sherlock Holmes Reference Library* and many other fine Sherlockian titles. A life-long Holmes enthusiast, he is a member of *The Baker Street Irregulars* and *The Illustrious Clients of Indianapolis*. A graphic artist by profession, his work is often seen on the covers of *The Baker Street Journal* and various BSI books.

Dick Gillman is an English writer and acrylic artist living in Brittany, France with his wife Alex, Truffle, their Black Labrador, and Jean-Claude, their Breton cat. During his retirement from teaching, he has written over twenty Sherlock Holmes short stories which are published as both e-books and paperbacks. His contribution to the superb MX Sherlock Holmes collection, published in October 2015, was entitled "The Man on Westminster Bridge" and had the privilege of being chosen as the anchor story in *The MX Book of New Sherlock Holmes Stories – Part II (1890-1895)*.

Denis Green was born in London, England in April 1905. He grew up mostly in London's Savoy Theatre where his father, Richard Green, was a principal in many Gilbert and Sullivan productions. A Flying Officer with RAF until 1924, he then spent four years managing a tea estate in North India before making his stage debut in *Hamlet* with Leslie Howard in 1928. He made his first visit to America in 1931 and established a respectable stage career before appearing in films – including minor roles in the first two Rathbone and Bruce Holmes films – and developing a career in front of and behind the microphone during the Golden Age of radio. Green and Leslie Charteris met in 1938 and struck up a lifelong friendship. Always busy, be it on stage, radio, film or television, Green passed away at the age of fifty in New York.

Melissa Grigsby, Executive Head Teacher of Stepping Stones School, is driven by a passion to open the doors to learners with complex and layered special needs that just make society feel two steps too far away. Based on the Surrey/Hampshire border in England, her time is spent between relocating a great school into the prestigious home of Conan Doyle, and her two children, dogs, and horses, so there never a dull moment.

John Atkinson Grimshaw (1836-1893) was born in Leeds, England. His amazing paintings, usually featuring twilight or night scenes illuminated by gas-lamps or moonlight, are easily recognizable, and are often used on the covers of books about The Great Detective to set the mood, as shadowy figures move in the distance through misty mysterious settings and over rain-slicked streets.

Jack Grochot is a retired investigative newspaper journalist and a former federal law enforcement agent specializing in mail fraud cases. He has written three books of Sherlock Holmes pastiches and a fourth nonfiction book, *Saga of a Latter-Day Saddle Tramp*, a memoir of his five-year horseback journey across twelve states. Grochot lives on a small farm in southwestern Pennsylvania, where he writes and oversees a horse-boarding stable.

Arthur Hall was born in Aston, Birmingham, UK, in 1944. He discovered his interest in writing during his schooldays, along with a love of fictional adventure and suspense. His first novel, *Sole Contact*, was an espionage story about an ultra-secret government department known as "Sector Three", and was followed, to date, by three sequels. Other works include four Sherlock Holmes novels, *The Demon of the Dusk*, *The One Hundred Percent Society*, *The Secret Assassin*, and *The Phantom Killer*, as well as a collection of short stories, and a modern detective novel. He lives in the West Midlands, United Kingdom.

Mike Hogan writes mostly historical novels and short stories, many set in Victorian London and featuring Sherlock Holmes and Doctor Watson. He read the Conan Doyle stories at school with great enjoyment, but hadn't thought much about Sherlock Holmes until, having missed the Granada/Jeremy Brett TV series when it was originally shown in the eighties, he came across a box set of videos in a street market and was hooked on Holmes again. He started writing Sherlock Holmes pastiches several years ago, having great fun re-imagining situations for the Conan Doyle characters to act in. The relationship between Holmes and Watson fascinates him as one of the great literary friendships. (He's also a huge admirer of Patrick O'Brian's Aubrey-Maturin novels). Like Captain Aubrey and Doctor Maturin, Holmes and Watson are an odd couple, differing in almost every facet of their characters, but sharing a common sense of decency and a common humanity. Living with Sherlock Holmes can't have been easy, and Mike enjoys adding a stronger vein of "pawky humour" into the Conan Doyle mix, even letting Watson have the second-to-last word on occasions. His books include *Sherlock Holmes and the Scottish Question*, the forthcoming *The Gory Season – Sherlock Holmes, Jack the Ripper and the Thames Torso Murders*, and the Sherlock Holmes & Young Winston 1887 Trilogy (*The Deadwood Stage, The Jubilee Plot*, and *The Giant Moles*), He has also written the following short story collections: *Sherlock Holmes: Murder at the Savoy and Other Stories, Sherlock Holmes: The Skull of Kohada Koheiji and Other Stories*, and *Sherlock Holmes: Murder on the Brighton Line and Other Stories. www.mikehoganbooks.com*

Christopher James was born in 1975 in Paisley, Scotland. Educated at Newcastle and UEA, he was a winner of the UK's National Poetry Competition in 2008. He has written two full length Sherlock Holmes novels, *The Adventure of the Ruby Elephant* and *The Jeweller of Florence*, both published by MX, and is working on a third.

Roger Johnson BSI, ASH is a retired librarian, now working as a volunteer assistant at the Essex Police Museum. In his spare time, he is commissioning editor of *The Sherlock Holmes Journal*, an occasional lecturer, and a frequent contributor to The Writings About the Writings. His sole work of Holmesian pastiche was published in 1997 in Mike Ashley's anthology *The Mammoth Book of New Sherlock Holmes Adventures*, and he has the greatest respect for the many authors who have contributed new tales to the present mighty trilogy. Like his wife, Jean Upton, he is a member of both *The Baker Street Irregulars* and *The Adventuresses of Sherlock Holmes.*

Kelvin I. Jones is the author of six books about Sherlock Holmes and the definitive biography of Conan Doyle as a spiritualist, *Conan Doyle and The Spirits*. A member of *The Sherlock Holmes Society of London*, he has published numerous short occult and ghost stories in British anthologies over the last thirty years. His work has appeared on BBC Radio, and in 1984 he won the Mason Hall Literary Award for his poem cycle about the survivors of Hiroshima and Nagasaki, recently reprinted as "Omega". (Oakmagic Publications) A one-time teacher of creative writing at the University of East Anglia, he is also the author of four crime novels featuring his ex-Met sleuth John Bottrell, who first appeared in *Stone Dead.* He has over fifty titles on Kindle, and is also the author of several novellas and short story collections featuring a Norwich-based detective, DCI Ketch, an intrepid sleuth who investigates East Anglian murder cases. He also published a series of short stories about an Edwardian psychic detective, Dr. John Carter (*Carter's Occult Casebook*). Ramsey Campbell, the British horror writer, and Francis King, the renowned novelist, have both compared his supernatural stories to those of M. R. James. He has also published children's fiction, namely *Odin's Eye*, and, in collaboration with his wife

Debbie, *The Dark Entry*. Since 1995, he has been the proprietor of Oakmagic Publications, publishers of British folklore and of his fiction titles. He lives in Norfolk. (See *www.oakmagicpublications.co.uk*)

David Marcum plays *The Game* with deadly seriousness. He first discovered Sherlock Holmes in 1975, at the age of ten, when he received an abridged version of *The Adventures* during a trade. Since that time, David has collected literally thousands of traditional Holmes pastiches in the form of novels, short stories, radio and television episodes, movies and scripts, comics, fan-fiction, and unpublished manuscripts. He is the author of *The Papers of Sherlock Holmes Vol.'s I* and *II* (2011, 2013), *Sherlock Holmes and A Quantity of Debt* (2013), *Sherlock Holmes – Tangled Skeins* (2015), and *The Papers of Solar Pons* (2017). He is the editor of *Sherlock Holmes in Montague Street* (2014) *Holmes Away From Home* (2016), *Sherlock Holmes: Before Baker Street* (2017), *Imagination Theatre's Sherlock Holmes* (2017), *Sherlock Holmes: Adventures Beyond the Canon*, (2018) and *The New Adventures of Solar Pons* (2018). He edited the authorized reissues of the *Solar Pons* stories, and is currently editing *The Complete Dr. Thorndyke*. Additionally, he is the creator and editor of the ongoing collection, *The MX Book of New Sherlock Holmes Stories* (2015-Present), now at fifteen volumes, with more in preparation as of this writing. He has contributed stories, essays, and scripts to a variety of Sherlockian anthologies, *The Baker Street Journal, The Strand Magazine, The Watsonian, Beyond Watson, Sherlock Holmes Mystery Magazine, About Sixty, About Being a Sherlockian, Sherlock Holmes is Like*, *The Solar Pons Gazette, Imagination Theater, The Art of Sherlock Holmes*, The *Proceedings of the Pondicherry Lodge*, and *The Gazette*, the journal of the Nero Wolfe *Wolfe Pack*. He began his adult work life as a Federal Investigator for an obscure U.S. Government agency. When the organization was eliminated, he returned to school for a second degree and is now a licensed Civil Engineer, living in Tennessee with his wife and son. He is a member of *The Sherlock Holmes Society of London, The Nashville Scholars of the Three Pipe Problem* ("The Engineer's Thumb"), *The Occupants of the Full House, The Diogenes Club of Washington, D.C.*, *The Tankerville Club* (all Scions of *The Baker Street Irregulars*), *The Sherlock Holmes Society of India* (as a Patron), *The John H. Watson Society* ("Marker"), *The Praed Street Irregulars* ("The Obrisset Snuff Box"), *The Solar Pons Society of London*, and *The Diogenes Club West (East Tennessee Annex)*, a curious and unofficial Scion of one. Since the age of nineteen, he has worn a deerstalker as his regular-and-only hat. In 2013, he and his deerstalker were finally able make his first trip-of-a-lifetime Holmes Pilgrimage to England, with return Pilgrimages in 2015 and 2016, where you may have spotted him. If you ever run into him and his deerstalker out and about, feel free to say hello!

Mark Mower is a member of the *Crime Writers' Association, The Sherlock Holmes Society of London*, and *The Solar Pons Society of London*. He writes true crime stories and fictional mysteries. His first two volumes of Holmes pastiches were entitled *A Farewell to Baker Street* and *Sherlock Holmes: The Baker Street Case-Files* (both with MX Publishing) and, to date, he has contributed chapters to six parts of the ongoing *The MX Book of New Sherlock Holmes Stories*. He has also had stories in two anthologies by Belanger Books: *Holmes Away From Home: Adventures from the Great Hiatus – Volume II – 1893-1894* (2016) and *Sherlock Holmes: Before Baker Street* (2017). More are bound to follow. Mark's non-fiction works include *Bloody British History: Norwich* (The History Press, 2014), *Suffolk Murders* (The History Press, 2011) and *Zeppelin Over Suffolk* (Pen & Sword Books, 2008).

Will Murray is the author of over seventy novels, including forty *Destroyer* novels and seven posthumous *Doc Savage* collaborations with Lester Dent, under the name Kenneth Robeson, for Bantam Books in the 1990's. Since 2011, he has written fourteen additional Doc Savage adventures for Altus Press, two of which co-starred The Shadow, as well as a solo Pat Savage novel. His 2015 Tarzan novel, *Return to Pal-Ul-Don*, was followed by *King Kong vs. Tarzan* in 2016. Murray has written short stories featuring such classic characters as Batman, Superman, Wonder Woman, Spider-Man, Ant-Man, the Hulk, Honey West, the Spider, the Avenger, the Green Hornet, the Phantom, and Cthulhu. A previous Murray Sherlock Holmes story appeared in Moonstone's *Sherlock Holmes: The Crossovers Casebook*, and another is forthcoming in *Sherlock Holmes and Doctor Was Not*, involving H. P. Lovecraft's Dr. Herbert West. Additionally, his "The Adventure of the Glassy Ghost" appeared in *The MX Book of New Sherlock Holmes Stories Part VIII – Eliminate the Impossible: 1892-1905*.

Sidney Paget (1860-1908), a few of whose illustrations are used within this anthology, was born in London, and like his two older brothers, became a famed illustrator and painter. He completed over three-hundred-and-fifty drawings for the Sherlock Holmes stories that were first published in *The Strand* magazine, defining Holmes's image forever after in the public mind.

Robert Perret is a writer, librarian, and devout Sherlockian living on the Palouse. His Sherlockian publications include "The Canaries of Clee Hills Mine" in *An Improbable Truth: The Paranormal Adventures of Sherlock Holmes*, "For King and Country" in *The Science of Deduction*, and "How Hope Learned the Trick" in *NonBinary Review*. He considers himself to be a pan-Sherlockian and a one-man Scion out on the lonely moors of Idaho. Robert has recently authored a yet-unpublished scholarly article tentatively entitled "A Study in Scholarship: The Case of the *Baker Street Journal*'. More information is available at *www.robertperret.com*

Tracy J. Revels, a Sherlockian from the age of eleven, is a professor of history at Wofford College in Spartanburg, South Carolina. She is a member of *The Survivors of the Gloria Scott* and *The Studious Scarlets Society*, and is a past recipient of the Beacon Society Award. Almost every semester, she teaches a class that covers The Canon, either to college students or to senior citizens. She is also the author of three supernatural Sherlockian pastiches with MX (*Shadowfall*, *Shadowblood*, and *Shadowwraith*), and a regular contributor to her scion's newsletter. She also has some notoriety as an author of very silly skits: For proof, see "The Adventure of the Adversarial Adventuress" and "Occupy Baker Street" on YouTube. When not studying Sherlock, she can be found researching the history of her native state, and has written books on Florida in the Civil War and on the development of Florida's tourism industry.

Roger Riccard of Los Angeles, California, U.S.A., is a descendant of the Roses of Kilravock in Highland Scotland. He is the author of two previous Sherlock Holmes novels, *The Case of the Poisoned Lilly* and *The Case of the Twain Papers*, a series of short stories in two volumes, *Sherlock Holmes: Adventures for the Twelve Days of Christmas* and *Further Adventures for the Twelve Days of Christmas*, and the new series *A Sherlock Holmes Alphabet of Cases,* all of which are published by Baker Street Studios. He has another novel and a non-fiction Holmes reference work in various stages of completion. He became a Sherlock Holmes enthusiast as a teenager (many, many years ago), and, like all fans of The Great Detective, yearned for more stories after reading The Canon over and over. It was the Granada Television performances of Jeremy Brett and Edward Hardwicke, and the encouragement of his wife, Rosilyn, that at last inspired him to write his own Holmes adventures, using the Granada actor portrayals as his guide. He has been called "The best pastiche writer since Val Andrews" by the *Sherlockian E-Times.*

Robert V. Stapleton was born and brought up in Leeds, Yorkshire, England, and studied at Durham University. After working in various parts of the country as an Anglican parish priest, he is now retired and lives with his wife in North Yorkshire. As a member of his local writing group, he now has time to develop his other life as a writer of adventure stories. He has recently had a number of short stories published, and he is hoping to have a couple of completed novels published at some time in the future.

Tim Symonds was born in London. He grew up in Somerset, Dorset, and Guernsey. After several years in East and Central Africa, he settled in California and graduated Phi Beta Kappa in Political Science from UCLA. He is a Fellow of the *Royal Geographical Society.* He writes his novels in the woods and hidden valleys surrounding his home in the High Weald of East Sussex. Dr. Watson knew the untamed region well. In "The Adventure of Black Peter", Watson wrote, *"the Weald was once part of that great forest which for so long held the Saxon invaders at bay."* Tim's novels are published by MX Publishing. His latest is titled *Sherlock Holmes and the Nine Dragon Sigil.* Previous novels include *Sherlock Holmes and The Sword of Osman, Sherlock Holmes and the Mystery of Einstein's Daughter, Sherlock Holmes and the Dead Boer at Scotney Castle*, and *Sherlock Holmes and the Case of The Bulgarian Codex.*

Will Thomas is the author of ten books in the Barker and Llewelyn Victorian mystery series, including *Some Danger Involved, Fatal Enquiry*, and most recently *Blood is Blood.* He was nominated for a *Barry* and a *Shamus.* He lives in Oklahoma, where he studies Victorian martial arts and models British railways.

William Todd has been a Holmes fan his entire life, and credits *The Hound of the Baskervilles* as the impetus for his love of both reading and writing. He began to delve into fan fiction a few years ago when he decided to take a break from writing his usual Victorian/Gothic horror stories. He was surprised how well-received they were, and has tried to put out a couple of Holmes stories a year since then. When not writing, Mr. Todd is a pathology supervisor at a local hospital in Northwestern Pennsylvania. He is the husband of a terrific lady and father to two great kids, one with special needs, so the benefactor of these anthologies is close to his heart.

Peter Coe Verbica grew up on a commercial cattle ranch in Northern California, where he learned the value of a strong work ethic. He works for the Wealth Management Group of a global investment bank, and is an Adjunct Professor in the Economics Department at SJSU. He is the author of numerous books, including *Left at the Gate and Other Poems, Hard-Won Cowboy Wisdom (Not Necessarily in Order of Importance), A Key to the Grove and Other Poems,* and *The Missing Tales of Sherlock Holmes (as Compiled by Peter Coe Verbica, JD).* Mr. Verbica obtained a JD from Santa Clara University School of Law, an MS from Massachusetts Institute of Technology, and a BA in English from Santa Clara University. He is the co-inventor on a number of patents, has served as a Managing Member of three venture capital firms, and the CFO of one of the portfolio companies. He is an unabashed advocate of cowboy culture and enjoys creative writing, hiking, and tennis. He is married with four daughters. For more information, or to contact the author, please go to *www.hardwoncowboywisdom.com.*

Darryl Webber is a journalist and author who lives in Essex, England. As well as penning stories under the banner of *The Secret Adventures of Sherlock Holmes* with fellow writer Duncan Wood, he also works for a number of newspapers and runs a film blog called *Chillidog Movies*. Darryl was born in Romford, Essex in 1968 and studied art and design at college before becoming a compositor at his local newspaper. After taking a career break to do a psychology degree at the University of East London, he retrained as a journalist and has held various senior editorial positions in newspapers in the southeast of England, specialising in culture and the arts, as well as working on the sports section of *The Sunday Times*. In 2016, Darryl co-authored a book called *The Man Who Fell To Earth* about the Nicolas Roeg film of the same name starring David Bowie. In this year, he became a part of the team that runs the Chelmsford Film Festival. Darryl's favourite stories from the Conan Doyle Canon are "The Bruce Partington Plans", "Silver Blaze", and "The Blue Carbuncle", and he firmly believes that the game is always afoot.

The following have also contributed to the companion volumes
Part XIII – 2019 Annual (1881-1890)
and
Part XIV – 2019 Annual (1891-1897)

Marino C. Alvarez, Ed.D., BSI, is professor *emeritus* at Tennessee State University. His book, *A Professor Reflects on Sherlock Holmes*, and other Sherlockian articles appear in the *Baker Street Journal*, *Canadian Holmes*, and *Saturday Review of Literature*, among others.

Hugh Ashton was born in the U.K., and moved to Japan in 1988, where he remained until 2016, living with his wife Yoshiko in the historic city of Kamakura, a little to the south of Yokohama. He and Yoshiko have now moved to Lichfield, a small cathedral city in the Midlands of the U.K., the birthplace of Samuel Johnson, and one-time home of Erasmus Darwin. In the past, he has worked in the technology and financial services industries, which have provided him with material for some of his books set in the 21st century. He currently works as a writer: Novelist, freelance editor, and copywriter, (his work for large Japanese corporations has appeared in international business journals), and journalist, as well as producing industry reports on various aspects of the financial services industry. Recently, however, his lifelong interest in Sherlock Holmes has developed into an acclaimed series of adventures featuring the world's most famous detective, written in the style of the originals. In addition to these, he has also published historical and alternate historical novels, short stories, and thrillers. Together with artist Andy Boerger, he has produced the *Sherlock Ferret* series of stories for children, featuring the world's cutest detective.

Derrick Belanger is an educator and also the author of the #1 bestselling book in its category, *Sherlock Holmes: The Adventure of the Peculiar Provenance*, which was in the top 200 bestselling books on Amazon. He also is the author of *The MacDougall Twins with Sherlock Holmes* books, and he edited the Sir Arthur Conan Doyle horror anthology *A Study in Terror: Sir Arthur Conan Doyle's Revolutionary Stories of Fear and the Supernatural*. Mr. Belanger co-owns the publishing company Belanger Books, which released the Sherlock Holmes anthologies *Beyond Watson, Holmes Away From Home: Adventures from the Great Hiatus* Volumes 1 and 2, *Sherlock Holmes: Before Baker Street*, and *Sherlock Holmes: Adventures in the Realms of H.G. Wells* Volumes I and 2. Derrick resides in Colorado and continues compiling unpublished works by Dr. John H. Watson.

S.F. Bennett was born and raised in London, studying History at Queen Mary and Westfield College, and Journalism at City University at the Postgraduate level, before moving to Devon in 2013. The author lectures on Conan Doyle, Sherlock Holmes, and 19th century detective fiction, and has had articles on various aspects from The Canon published in *The Journal of the Sherlock Holmes Society of London* and *The Torr*, the journal of *The Poor Folk Upon The Moors*, the Sherlock Holmes Society of the South West of England. Her first published novel is *The Secret Diary of Mycroft Holmes: The Thoughts and Reminiscences of Sherlock Holmes's Elder Brother, 1880-1888* (2017).

Matthew Booth is the author of *Sherlock Holmes and the Giant's Hand*, published by Breese Books and the co-author of *The Further Exploits of Sherlock Holmes*, a collection of new stories, commissioned by Sparkling Books in 2016. He contributed two original Holmes stories to *The Game is Afoot*, a collection of Sherlock Holmes short stories published in 2008 by Wordsworth Editions and contributed a story to Wordsworth Editions' collection of original crime tales, *Crime Scenes*. He is the creator of Anthony Rathe, a disgraced former barrister seeking redemption by solving those crimes which come his way. The character first appeared in a series of radio plays produced and syndicated by *Imagination Theatre* in America. Rathe now appears in Matthew's latest book, *When Anthony Rathe Investigates* published by Sparkling Books. A lifelong devotee of crime and supernatural fiction, Matthew has provided a number of academic talks on such subjects as Sherlock Holmes, the works of Agatha Christie, crime fiction, Count Dracula, and the facts and theories concerning the crimes of Jack the Ripper. He is also a member of the *Crime Writers Association* and a contributor to their monthly newsletter, *Red Herrings*.

Andrew Bryant was born in Bridgend, Wales, and now lives in Burlington, Ontario. His previous publications include *Prism International*, *On Spec*, *The Dalhousie Review*, and second place in the 2015 *Toronto Star* short story contest. "The Shackled Man" is his first Sherlock Holmes story, written after visiting 221b Baker Street.

Thomas A. Burns, Jr. is the author of the *Natalie McMasters Mysteries*. He was born and grew up in New Jersey, attended Xavier High School in Manhattan, earned B.S degrees in Zoology and Microbiology at Michigan State University, and a M.S. in Microbiology at North Carolina State University. He currently resides in Wendell, North Carolina. As a kid, Tom started reading mysteries with The Hardy Boys, Ken Holt and Rick Brant, and graduated to the classic stories by authors such as A. Conan Doyle, Dorothy Sayers, John Dickson Carr, Erle Stanley Gardner, and Rex Stout, to name a few. Tom has written fiction as a hobby all of his life, starting with The Man from U.N.C.L.E. stories in marble-backed copybooks in grade school. He built a career as technical, science, and medical writer and editor for nearly thirty years in industry and government. Now that he's truly on his own as a novelist, he's excited to publish his own mystery series, as well as to contribute stories about his second-most-favorite detective, Sherlock Holmes, to *The MX anthology of New Sherlock Holmes Stories*.

Harry DeMaio is a *nom de plume* of Harry B. DeMaio, successful author of several books on Information Security and Business Networks, as well as the ten-volume *Casebooks of Octavius Bear – Alternative Universe Mysteries for Adult Animal Lovers*. Octavius Bear is loosely based on Sherlock Holmes and Nero Wolfe in a world in which *homo sapiens* died out long ago in a global disaster, but most animals have advanced to a twenty-first century anthropomorphic state. "It's Time" is Harry's first offering treating Holmes and Watson in their original human condition. A retired business executive, consultant, information security specialist, former pilot, and graduate school adjunct professor, he whiles away his time traveling and writing preposterous articles and stories. He has appeared on many radio and TV shows and is an accomplished, frequent public speaker. Former New York City natives, he and his extremely patient and helpful wife, Virginia, and their Bichon Frisé, Woof, live in Cincinnati (and several other parallel universes.) They have two sons living in Scottsdale, Arizona and Cortlandt Manor, New York, both of whom are quite successful and quite normal – thus putting the lie to the theory that insanity is hereditary.

C.H. Dye first discovered Sherlock Holmes when she was eleven, in a collection that ended at the Reichenbach Falls. It was another six months before she discovered *The Hound of the Baskervilles*, and two weeks after that before a librarian handed her *The Return*. She has loved the stories ever since. She has written fan-fiction, and her first published pastiche, "The Tale of the Forty Thieves", was included in *The MX Book of New Sherlock Holmes Stories – Part I: 1881-1889*. Her story "A Christmas Goose" was in *The MX Book of New Sherlock Holmes Stories – Part V: Christmas Adventures*, and "The Mysterious Mourner" in *The MX Book of New Sherlock Holmes Stories – Part VIII – Eliminate the Impossible: 1892-1905*

Anna Elliott is an author of historical fiction and fantasy. Her first series, *The Twilight of Avalon* trilogy, is a retelling of the Trystan and Isolde legend. She wrote her second series, *The Pride and Prejudice Chronicles*, chiefly to satisfy her own curiosity about what might have happened to Elizabeth Bennet, Mr. Darcy, and all the other wonderful cast of characters after the official end of Jane Austen's classic work. She enjoys stories about strong women, and loves exploring the multitude of ways women can find their unique strengths. She was delighted to lend a hand with the "Sherlock and Lucy" series, and this story, firstly because she loves Sherlock Holmes as much as her father, co-author Charles Veley, does, and second because it almost never happens that someone with a dilemma shouts, "Quick, we need an author of historical fiction!" Anna lives in the Washington, D.C .area with her husband and three children.

Edwin A. Enstrom – *In addition to a story in this volume, Ed also has stories in Parts XIII and XIV of this set.*

James R. "Jim" French became a morning Disc Jockey on KIRO (AM) in Seattle in 1959. He later founded *Imagination Theatre*, a syndicated program that broadcast to over one-hundred-and-twenty stations in the U.S. and Canada, and also on the XM Satellite Radio system all over North America. Actors in French's dramas included John Patrick Lowrie, Larry Albert, Patty Duke, Russell Johnson, Tom Smothers, Keenan Wynn, Roddy MacDowall, Ruta Lee, John Astin, Cynthia Lauren Tewes, and Richard Sanders. Mr. French stated, "To me, the characters of Sherlock Holmes and Doctor Watson always seemed to be figures Doyle created as a challenge to lesser writers. He gave us two interesting characters – different from each other in their histories, talents, and experience, but complimentary as a team – who have been applied to a variety of situations and plots far beyond the times and places in The Canon. In the hands of different writers, Holmes and Watson have lent their identities to different times, ages, and even genders. But I wanted to break no new ground. I feel Sir Arthur provided us with enough references to locations, landmarks, and the social conditions of his time, to give a pretty large canvas on which to paint our own images and actions to animate Holmes and Watson." Mr. French passed away at the age of eighty-nine on December 20th, 2017.

David Friend lives in Wales, Great Britain, where he divides his time between watching old detective films and thinking about old detective films. Now thirty, he's been scribbling out stories for twenty years and hopes, some day, to write something half-decent. Most of what he pens is set in an old-timey world of non-stop adventure with debonair sleuths, kick-ass damsels, criminal masterminds, and narrow escapes, and he wishes he could live there.

Tim Gambrell lives in Exeter, Devon with his wife, two young sons, two cats, and seven chickens. He has had short stories published in *Lethbridge-Stewart: The HAVOC Files 3* and *The Lethbridge-Stewart Quiz Book* (both Candy Jar books, 2017), *Bernice Summerfield: True Stories* (Big Finish, 2017) and *Relics . . . An Anthology* (Red Ted Books, 2018). Tim has written a novella, *The Way of The Bry'hunee*, for the Erimem Range from Thebes Publishing (due 2019), and his first full novel, *Lucy Wilson and The Bledoe Cadets*, will be published by Candy Jar Books in 2019 as part of the *Lethbridge-Stewart: The Laughing Gnome* series. Tim has contributed to a number of charity publications, including *A Time Lord For Change* (2016) and *Whoblique Strategies* (2017) from Chinbeard Books, and *You and 42 & Blake's Legacy: 40 Years of Rebellion* from Who Dares Publishing (both 2018).

Jayantika Ganguly BSI is the General Secretary and Editor of the *Sherlock Holmes Society of India*, a member of the *Sherlock Holmes Society of London*, and the *Czech Sherlock Holmes Society*. She is the author of *The Holmes Sutra* (MX 2014). She is a corporate lawyer working with one of the Big Six law firms.

Arthur Hall – *In addition to a story in this volume, Arthur also has a story in Parts XIII and XIV of this set.*

Liz Hedgecock grew up in London, England, did an English degree, and then took forever to start writing. Now Liz travels between the nineteenth and twenty-first centuries, murdering people. To be fair, she does usually clean up after herself. Liz's reimaginings of Sherlock Holmes, her Pippa Parker cozy mystery series, and the Caster & Fleet mystery series (written with Paula Harmon) are available in ebook and paperback. Liz lives in Cheshire with her husband and two sons, and when she's not writing or child-wrangling, you can usually find her reading, messing about on Twitter, or cooing over stuff in museums and art galleries. That's her story, anyway, and she's sticking to it.

Carl L. Heifetz Over thirty years of inquiry as a research microbiologist have prepared Carl Heifetz to explore new horizons in science. As an author, he has published numerous articles and short stories for fan magazines and other publications. In 2013, he published a book entitled *Voyage of the Blue Carbuncle* that is based on the works of Sir Arthur Conan Doyle and Gene Roddenberry. *Voyage of the Blue Carbuncle* is a fun and exciting spoof, sure to please science fiction fans as well as those who love the stories of Sherlock Holmes and *Star Trek*. Carl and his wife have two grown children and live in Trinity, Florida.

Stephen Herczeg is an IT Geek, writer, actor, and film-maker based in Canberra Australia. He has been writing for over twenty years and has completed a couple of dodgy novels, sixteen feature-length screenplays, and numerous short stories and scripts. Stephen was very successful in 2017's International Horror Hotel screenplay competition, with his scripts *TITAN* winning the Sci-Fi category and *Dark are the Woods* placing second in the horror category. His work has featured in *Sproutlings – A Compendium of Little Fictions* from Hunter Anthologies, the *Hells Bells* Christmas horror anthology published by the

Australasian Horror Writers Association, and the *Below the Stairs, Trickster's Treats, Shades of Santa, Behind the Mask,* and *Beyond the Infinite* anthologies from *OzHorror.Con, The Body Horror Book, Anemone Enemy,* and *Petrified Punks* from Oscillate Wildly Press, and *Sherlock Holmes In the Realms of H.G. Wells* and *Sherlock Holmes: Adventures Beyond the Canon* from Belanger Books.

Paul Hiscock is an author of crime, fantasy, and science fiction tales. His short stories have appeared in several anthologies and include a seventeenth century whodunnit, a science fiction western, and a steampunk Sherlock Holmes story. Paul lives with his family in Kent, England, and spends his days chasing a toddler with more energy than the Duracell Bunny. He mainly does his writing in coffee shops with members of the local NaNoWriMo group, or in the middle of the night when his family has gone to sleep. Consequently, his stories tend to be fuelled by large amounts of black coffee. You can find out more about his writing at *www.detectivesanddragons.uk.*

David Marcum – *In addition to a story in this volume, David also has stories in Parts XIII and XIV of this set.*

Jacquelynn Morris, ASH, BSI, JHWS, is a member of several Sherlock Holmes societies in the Mid-Atlantic area of the U.S.A., but her home group is Watson's Tin Box in Maryland. She is the founder of *A Scintillation of Scions*, an annual Sherlock Holmes symposium. She has been published in the BSI Manuscript Series, *The Wrong Passage*, as well as in *About Sixty* and *About Being a Sherlockian* (Wildside Press). Jacquelynn was the U.S. liaison for the Undershaw Preservation Trust for several years, until Undershaw was purchased to become part of Stepping Stones School.

Mark Mower – *In addition to a story in this volume, Mark also has a story in Part XIII of this set.*

Gayle Lange Puhl has been a Sherlockian since Christmas of 1965. She has had articles published in *The Devon County Chronicle*, *The Baker Street Journal*, and *The Serpentine Muse*, plus her local newspaper. She has created Sherlockian jewelry, a 2006 calendar entitled "If Watson Wrote For TV", and has painted a limited series of Holmes-related nesting dolls. She co-founded the scion *Friends of the Great Grimpen Mire* and the Janesville, Wisconsin-based *The Original Tree Worshipers*. In January 2016, she was awarded the "Outstanding Creative Writer" award by the Janesville Art Alliance for her first book *Sherlock Holmes and the Folk Tale Mysteries*. She is semi-retired and lives in Evansville, Wisconsin. Ms. Puhl has one daughter, Gayla, and four grandchildren.

Tracy J. Revels – *In addition to a story in this volume, Tracy also has stories in Parts XIII and XIV of this set.*

Roger Riccard – *In addition to a story in this volume, Roger also has a story in Part XIV of this set.*

GC Rosenquist was born in Chicago, Illinois and has been writing since he was ten years old. His interests are very eclectic. His eleven previously published books include literary fiction, horror, poetry, a comedic memoir, and lots of science fiction. His latest published work for MX Books is *Sherlock Holmes: The Pearl of Death and Other Stories* (April 2015). He has had his work published in *Sherlock Holmes Mystery Magazine*. He works professionally as a graphic artist. He has studied writing and poetry at the College of Lake

County in Grayslake, Illinois, and currently resides in Lindenhurst, Illinois. For more information on GC Rosenquist, you can go to his website at *www.gcrosenquist.com*

Geri Schear is a novelist and short story writer. Her work has been published in literary journals in the U.S. and Ireland. Her first novel, *A Biased Judgement: The Diaries of Sherlock Holmes 1897* was released to critical acclaim in 2014. The sequel, *Sherlock Holmes and the Other Woman* was published in 2015, and *Return to Reichenbach* in 2016. She lives in Kells, Ireland.

Brenda Seabrooke's stories have been published in sixteen reviews, journals, and anthologies. She has received grants from the National Endowment for the Arts and Emerson College's Robbie Macauley Award. She is the author of twenty-three books for young readers including *Scones and Bones on Baker Street: Sherlock's (maybe!) Dog and the Dirt Dilemma*, and *The Rascal in the Castle: Sherlock's (possible!) Dog and the Queen's Revenge*. Brenda states: "It was fun to write from Dr. Watson's point of view and not have to worry about fleas, smelly pits, ralphing, or scratching at inopportune times."

Stephen Seitz has reported for newspapers as politically diverse as the *Brattleboro Reformer* and the *New Hampshire Union Leader.* He has covered everything from natural disasters to presidential campaigns, and has interviewed an original cast member from every *Star Trek* television series. Other notables include James Earl Jones, Jodi Picoult, Jerry Lewis, James Whitmore, Senator George McGovern, and many others. He is also the host of cable TV's *Book Talk.* Sherlock Holmes has been a part of Steve's life since the age of twelve, when, while putting homework off, he discovered *The Hound of the Baskervilles* in the stacks at Brooks Memorial Library in Brattleboro, Vt. More than forty years later, he is still an avid Sherlockian and speaks to scion societies on occasion. Naturally, more of his Sherlock Holmes stories are on the way.

Matthew Simmonds hails from Bedford, in the South East of England, and has been a confirmed devotee of Sir Arthur Conan Doyle's most famous creation since first watching Jeremy Brett's incomparable portrayal of the world's first consulting detective, on a Tuesday evening in April, 1984, while curled up on the sofa with his father. He has written numerous short stories, and his first novel, *Sherlock Holmes: The Adventure of The Pigtail Twist*, was published in 2018. A sequel is nearly complete, which he hopes to publish in the near future. Matthew currently co-owns Harrison & Simmonds, the fifth-generation family business, a renowned County tobacconist, pipe, and gift shop on Bedford High Street.

Shane Simmons is a multi-award-winning screenwriter and graphic novelist whose work has appeared in international film festivals, museums, and lectures about design and structure. His best-known piece of fiction, *The Long and Unlearned Life of Roland Gethers*, has been discussed in multiple books and academic journals about sequential art, and his short stories have been printed in critically praised anthologies of history, crime, and horror. He lives in Montreal with his wife and too many cats. Follow him at *eyestrainproductions.com* and *@Shane_Eyestrain*

Mark Sohn was born in Brighton, England in 1967. After a hectic life and many dubious and varied careers, he settled down in Sussex with his wife, Angie. His first novel, *Sherlock Holmes and the Whitechapel Murders* was published in 2017. His second, *The Absentee Detective* is out now. Both are available from Amazon.com. *https://sherlockholmesof221b.blogspot.co.uk/*

Robert V. Stapleton – *In addition to a story in this volume, Robert also has a story in Part XIII of this set.*

S. Subramanian is a retired professor of Economics from Chennai, India. Apart from a small book titled *Economic Offences: A Compendium of Crimes in Prose and Verse* (Oxford University Press Delhi, 2012), his Holmes pastiches are the only serious things he has written. His other work runs largely to whimsical stuff on fuzzy logic and social measurement, on which he writes with much precision and little understanding, being an economist. He is otherwise mainly harmless, as his wife and daughter might concede with a little persuasion.

Kevin P. Thornton has experienced a Taliban rocket attack in Kabul and a terrorist bombing in Johannesburg. He lives in Fort McMurray, Alberta, the town that burnt down in 2016. He has been shortlisted for the *Crime Writers of Canada* Unhanged writing award six times. He's never won. He was also a finalist for best short story in 2014 – the year Margaret Atwood entered. We're not saying he has luck issues, but don't bet on his stock tips. Born in Kenya, Kevin was a child in New Zealand, a student and soldier in Africa, a military contractor in Afghanistan, a forklift driver in Ontario, and an oilfield worker in North Western Canada. He writes poems that start out just fine, but turn ruder and cruder over time. From limerick to doggerel, they earn less than bugger-all, even though they all manage to rhyme. He also likes writing about Sherlock Holmes and dislikes writing about himself in the third person.

Charles Veley has loved Sherlock Holmes since boyhood. As a father, he read the entire Canon to his then-ten-year-old daughter at evening story time. Now, this very same daughter, grown up to become acclaimed historical novelist Anna Elliott, has worked with him to develop new adventures in the *Sherlock Holmes and Lucy James Mystery Series*. Charles is also a fan of Gilbert & Sullivan, and wrote *The Pirates of Finance*, a new musical in the G&S tradition that won an award at the New York Musical Theatre Festival in 2013. Other than the Sherlock and Lucy series, all of the books on his Amazon Author Page were written when he was a full-time author during the late Seventies and early Eighties. He currently works for United Technologies Corporation, where his main focus is on creating sustainability and value for the company's large real estate development projects.

Peter Coe Verbica – *In addition to a story in this volume, Peter also a story in Part XIII of this set.*

Mark Wardecker is an instructional technologist at Colby College. He is the editor and annotator of *The Dragnet Solar Pons et al.* (Battered Silicon Dispatch Box, 2011) and has contributed Sherlockian pastiches to *Sherlock Holmes Mystery Magazine*, Solar Pons pastiches to *The New Adventures of Solar Pons*, and an article to *The Baker Street Journal*, as well as having published other fiction and nonfiction.

I.A. Watson is a novelist and jobbing writer from Yorkshire who cut his teeth on writing Sherlock Holmes stories and has even won an award for one. His works include *Holmes and Houdini, Labours of Hercules, St. George and the Dragon* Volumes 1 and 2, and *Women of Myth*, and the non-fiction essay book *Where Stories Dwell*. He pens short detective stories as a means of avoiding writing things that pay better. A full list of his sixty-plus published works appears at:

Marcia Wilson is a freelance researcher and illustrator who likes to work in a style compatible for the color blind and visually impaired. She is Canon-centric, and her first MX offering, *You Buy Bones*, uses the point-of-view of Scotland Yard to show the unique talents of Dr. Watson. This continued with the publication of *Test of the Professionals: The Adventure of the Flying Blue Pidgeon* and *The Peaceful Night Poisonings.* She can be contacted at: *gravelgirty.deviantart.com*

Sean Wright BSI makes his home in Santa Clarita, a charming city at the entrance of the high desert in Southern California. For sixteen years, features and articles under his byline appeared in *The Tidings* – now *The Angelus News* – publications of the Roman Catholic Archdiocese of Los Angeles. Continuing his education in 2007, Mr. Wright graduated *summa cum laude* from Grand Canyon University, attaining a Bachelor of Arts degree in Christian Studies. He then attained a Master of Arts degree, also in Christian Studies. Once active in the entertainment industry, in an abortive attempt to revive dramatic radio in 1976 with his beloved mentor the late Daws Butler directing, Mr. Wright co-produced and wrote the syndicated *New Radio Adventures of Sherlock Holmes* starring the late Edward Mulhare as the Great Detective. Mr. Wright has written for several television quiz shows and remains proud of his work for *The Quiz Kid's Challenge* and the popular TV quiz show *Jeopardy!* for which The Academy of Television Arts and Sciences honored him in 1985 with an Emmy nomination in the field of writing. Honored with membership in *The Baker Street Irregulars* as "The Manor House Case" after founding *The Non-Canonical Calabashes, The Sherlock Holmes Society of Los Angeles* in 1970, Mr. Wright has written for *The Baker Street Journal* and *Mystery Magazine*. Since 1971, he has conducted lectures on Sherlock Holmes's influence on literature and cinema for libraries, colleges, and private organizations, including MENSA. Mr. Wright's whimsical *Sherlock Holmes Cookbook* (Drake) created with John Farrell BSI, was published in 1976 and a mystery novel, *Enter the Lion: a Posthumous Memoir of Mycroft Holmes* (Hawthorne), "edited" with Michael Hodel BSI, followed in 1979. As director general of The Plot Thickens Mystery Company, Mr. Wright originated hosting "mystery parties" in homes, restaurants, and offices, as well as producing and directing the very first "Mystery Train" tours on Amtrak beginning in 1982.

The MX Book of New Sherlock Holmes Stories

"This is the finest volume of Sherlockian fiction I have ever read, and I have read, literally, thousands." – Philip K. Jones

"Beyond Impressive . . . This is a splendid venture for a great cause! – Roger Johnson, Editor, *The Sherlock Holmes Journal,* The Sherlock Holmes Society of London

Part I: 1881-1889
Part II: 1890-1895
Part III: 1896-1929
Part IV: 2016 Annual
Part V: Christmas Adventures
Part VI: 2017 Annual
Part VII: Eliminate the Impossible (1880-1891)
Part VIII – Eliminate the Impossible (1892-1905)
Part IX – 2018 Annual (1879-1895)
Part X – 2018 Annual (1896-1916)
Part XI – Some Untold Cases (1880-1891)
Part XII – Some Untold Cases (1894-1902)
Part XIII – 2019 Annual (1881-1890)
Part XIV – 2019 Annual (1891-1897)
Part XV – 2019 Annual (1898-1917)

In Preparation

Part XVI – Whatever Remains . . . Must be the Truth
Part XVII – 2020 Annual

. . . and more to come!

Publishers Weekly says:
Part VI: *The traditional pastiche is alive and well . . . .*

Part VII: *Sherlockians eager for faithful-to-the-canon plots and characters will be delighted.*

Part VIII: *The imagination of the contributors in coming up with variations on the volume's theme is matched by their ingenious resolutions.*

Part IX: *The 18 stories . . . will satisfy fans of Conan Doyle's originals. Sherlockians will rejoice that more volumes are on the way.*

Part X: *. . . new Sherlock Holmes adventures of consistently high quality.*

Part XI: *. . . an essential volume for Sherlock Holmes fans.*

Part XII: *. . . continues to amaze with the number of high-quality pastiches . . .*

The MX Book of New Sherlock Holmes Stories
Edited by David Marcum
(MX Publishing, 2015-   )

MX Publishing

MX Publishing is the world's largest specialist Sherlock Holmes publisher, with several hundred titles and over a hundred authors creating the latest in Sherlock Holmes fiction and non-fiction.

From traditional short stories and novels to travel guides and quiz books, MX Publishing caters to all Holmes fans.

The collection includes leading titles such as *Benedict Cumberbatch In Transition* and *The Norwood Author*, which won the 2011 *Tony Howlett Award* (Sherlock Holmes Book of the Year).

MX Publishing also has one of the largest communities of Holmes fans on *Facebook*, with regular contributions from dozens of authors.

www.mxpublishing.co.uk (UK) and *www.mxpublishing.com* (USA)